BAPTISM

BAPTISM

Max Kinnings

Quercus

Quercus

New York • London

© 2012 by Max Kinnings
First published in the United States by Quercus in 2014

ISBN 978-1-62365-102-2

Library of Congress Control Number: 2013937738

Distributed in the United States and Canada by
Random House Publisher Services
c/o Random House, 1745 Broadway
New York, NY 10019

Manufactured in the United States

2 4 6 8 10 9 7 5 3 1

www.quercus.com

For Ange and Mabel

10:02 AM

Tunnel between Leicester Square and Tottenham Court Road stations

From the train, Glen could just make out the faint sound of voices, passengers talking most probably. Sweat dribbled down his face and his heart thumped against his sternum. *Remember the training.* It was a mantra that had been drilled into him. If he remembered the training, everything would be all right. As a member of CO19, he was at the sharp end of one of the world's most elite police special operations groups. They had earned a bad reputation in the past due to a couple of high-profile mistakes. The media had made a lot of those while playing down the successes. But Glen felt proud to be a member of CO19, proud that he had passed the psychological tests and been invited to attend the eight-week training course at the Metropolitan Police Specialist Training center to learn about firearms, methods of entry, fast rope skills, scenario intervention, rescue techniques, and potential terrorist attacks. His colleague, Rob, was one of the top specialist firearms officers in the country, and by being chosen to be on operation alongside him, Glen knew that he too must be held in high regard by the powers that be.

The voice was relayed into his headset: "Can you see anything?"

"Nothing," said Rob.

"Okay then, move in closer and keep talking to me."

Rob stood up first and moved past Glen, who followed him, aiming his 9mm Glock 17 pistol at the train. This was not the most dangerous part of the mission but it was close to it; they were in the open, approaching a static target, with no cover. But they had darkness and the enclosed space of the tunnel on their side. It was unlikely that a night scope would pick them up at this distance. A few feet further on, Rob crouched down on one side of the tunnel and Glen did the same a few feet behind him, careful not to touch the live rail.

"Okay, we're about twenty feet away from it now," said Rob into his mouthpiece. "There's nothing moving and all is quiet." But just as he said these words, something did move. There was a flash from the cab and a soft popping sound. Glen felt a spray of warm liquid and grit on his face. He glanced at Rob but there was something wrong with him. The upper right-hand quadrant of his head was completely missing, leaving a jagged fringe of shattered bone fragments and ruptured brain in its place from which blood sluiced freely as his legs gave way and he collapsed to the ground.

"Rob?" Glen didn't know why he said it. It wasn't as though Rob could hear anything.

"What is it?" came the voice over the headset.

"Shit." It wasn't an exclamation. Glen spoke the word softly. He looked at the train and suddenly felt very lonely. The rules of engagement seemed so far away now. He knew what he had to do but he also knew what would happen when he did it. He raised his pistol and took aim at the rear cab of the train, from where there was another flash followed by a pop. Before he could fire off a shot, the entire top of his head, from the bridge of his nose upward was sheered off and he fell backward onto the sleepers between the rails.

"Someone talk to me." The calm, flat voice came from the bloody remains of two radio headsets. But no one was listening.

12:04 AM (TEN HOURS EARLIER)

Inside Madoc Farm, Snowdonia

It sounded like laughter. It came from along the corridor. Varick looked up from his book and squinted into the darkness beyond the bubble of light thrown by the candle on his desk. Why would someone be laughing so loudly after midnight? The Church of Cruor Christi didn't forbid such things, didn't trouble its flock with rules and regulations. They weren't needed. The brothers and sisters at Madoc Farm were there because they wanted to be there, they wanted to live the life. They had chosen it, just as they themselves had been chosen by God. But laughter, so loud and unrestrained at this time of night, was odd.

When Varick realized that what he was hearing wasn't laughter, he picked up the candle from his desk and made for the door, shielding the flame from the onrush of air as he made his way down the corridor toward the source of the sound.

All the doors to the bedrooms were shut, apart from the one next to the bathroom, Father Owen's room. The sound wasn't coming from there but the bathroom itself. Brother Alistair was on his knees by the side of the bath. He had succumbed to some sort of hysteria, tears streaming and his mouth stretched wide, emitting the sound that Varick had mistaken for laughter.

Varick was about to drag Alistair to his feet and slap him to his senses when he saw what was in the bath. Trembling, naked, his gnarled hands gripped around the sides of the bath as though trying to prolong his life through sheer force of will alone was Father Owen. Sticking out of his throat was the handle of a carving knife. The bath water was the color of rosé wine.

The candle dropped from Varick's hand and went out. The only light came from the candles burning in Owen's room next door. Varick reached down to the old man, this kind old man who had taken him in and saved him when he was lost, and he half-lifted, half-dragged him from the bath and laid him down on the stone floor in the hallway.

"Who did this to you?" asked Varick. There was more light in the hallway and Varick could see the old man's face as he tried to speak. The only sound that Owen could make, however, was a faint whistling from the wound in his neck as his tongue churned blood in his mouth. Owen made another attempt to speak before his body went limp and his head cracked back against the floor as the blood bubbles around the blade in his neck popped their last.

"Who could have done such a thing?"

Alistair managed to find a gap long enough between his sobs to provide Varick with a response. "It was Tommy."

As Varick took in the implications of Alistair's statement, the growing sense of unease that had plagued him all day came into needle-sharp focus. Of course it was Tommy. It could only be Tommy. The day before Father Owen had come to find Varick in the vegetable garden, where he was digging, to tell him that he had found something "most distressing," as he had described it. Worried about Tommy's recent behavior, Owen had done something that Varick disapproved of and searched the young ex-soldier's room. There he had found a notebook in which Tommy had written about his mounting frustration relating to his faith and the state of the world in general. Nothing unusual in that, particularly among the younger members of the church of Cruor Christi, but Owen had read something in the notebook that had alarmed him, something that he felt compelled to impart to Varick. Hot from the sun and tired of digging, Varick had been angry with the old man and told him it was wrong to go into Tommy's room and read his diary.

"Do you know where Tommy is now?"

"I heard him run," said Alistair, sniffing. "There were others too."

This was the final confirmation that Varick needed. With Father Owen dead, responsibility for the church's future had devolved to him. He knew where Tommy was going. The details of what he wanted to do were all laid out in his notebook. If Tommy was serious about carrying out his mission—and Owen's murder could only suggest that he was—this was more than just an attack on the church of Cruor Christi, it was an attack on everyone who failed to share the insanity of Tommy's grand designs. Varick knew what was happening. God was testing him.

12:07 AM

Outside Madoc Farm, Snowdonia

They were on their way. The moment she had been waiting for for so long had arrived. Her flesh tingled. She felt strangely intoxicated but also completely in control. It was a spiritual feeling. Never once had she doubted her brother, never once had she found cause to concern herself regarding the legitimacy or morality of what they were embarking on. Tommy was a prophet. She was a prophet too. Tommy had told her she was.

She hadn't liked watching what Tommy had done to the old man. It reminded her of her mother and father. It wasn't nice. But if she was honest—and she always was because God knew when she lied—she was pleased with herself that she had been strong enough to witness it. It made her realize that she would be able to do what had to be done later in the day. This was something that she had given great thought to in the past few weeks. She didn't want to let Tommy down.

While Tommy put his bag in the trunk of the car he had stolen earlier, Simeon said, "What's happening? Why now?"

"Just practicing," she said. She didn't like lying to Simeon but he would find out the truth for himself soon enough. Of course they weren't "just practicing." Why kill the old man if they were practicing? Not that Simeon knew that Father Owen was dead. Tommy had made sure that Simeon was in his room when they dealt with Father Owen. But there was no more time for Simeon to ask further questions; Tommy climbed into the car, started the engine and they set off.

It reminded Belle of when she was little, when their parents were still alive and they went out in the car for the day. She didn't care where they were going; it was the journey she loved, sitting there in the backseat looking out of the window at the scenery going past. She felt the same excitement now, sitting next to Tommy as he steered them along the mountain roads. Their destination was still a few hours away and she could enjoy the journey, safe and secure in the car with the two men she loved most in all the world: Tommy and Simeon.

Tommy had kept telling her to expel all doubt from her mind and sometimes she found it hard. Many people—most people probably—would find it almost impossible to understand what they were going to do, but that didn't mean that it wasn't right. Jesus had been misunderstood, had been persecuted for his beliefs. Suffering was all part of the process but, now that they were on their way to London and the waiting was over, she felt sure that her suffering was nearly at an end.

12:09 AM

Inside Madoc Farm, Snowdonia

Varick hurried back to his room, the familiarity of his surroundings allowing him to navigate in almost total darkness. He went to the desk in the office next to his bedroom, opened the drawer, and took out a large metal flashlight and a Smith & Wesson revolver. Never had the gun's checkered stock felt so reassuring in his hand. It always supplied him with strength of purpose. Clicking on the flashlight, he headed toward Tommy's room at the other end of the corridor. The door was open and he could see before he even stepped inside that the room was empty.

Varick went to the shelves above the bed and dragged down the shoeboxes in which Tommy kept his personal possessions. The boxes' contents spilled open on the bed. There were letters, postcards, sports trophies, diaries, notebooks, computer disks, and a pack of playing cards. Varick didn't know what he was looking for but, as he looked through Tommy Denning's possessions, he realized how little he had really known him.

Cruor Christi was an evangelical Christian order that welcomed troubled souls. Varick was a troubled soul himself. His own personal experience gave him vision and understanding. Tommy had been something of a special project for him. Fiercely intelligent yet damaged, when Tommy had first come to Madoc Farm he had been like a coiled spring. Varick thought he could save him; he thought that Cruor Christi could succeed where other institutions had clearly failed. It was a struggle but he had known that it would be. Tommy's childhood traumas and his time fighting in Afghanistan had left him in a dangerous state of mind, one in which he would surely have ended up in prison if Varick hadn't taken him in. Owen, however, was convinced that Tommy and his sister Belle, who had joined the church before Tommy and had encouraged him to join too, would be disruptive influences at Madoc Farm. Owen and Varick had clashed over this a number of times. Now it looked as though the old man had been right all along.

Feelings of dread and fear came to Varick just as they had done in the old days, the days before he was born again. He looked at himself in the mirror on the wall. He looked old. He would be fifty next birthday. But he was still big and strong, still resolute. He would do what had to be done.

With the door to Brother Thomas's room closed behind him, Brother Varick walked back along the corridor. There was no point knocking on Brother Simeon's door; he knew the room was empty before the beam of the torch on the empty bed confirmed it. He closed the door and continued to Sister Belle's room. Empty. Tommy had his two foot soldiers with him.

Varick could hear other brothers and sisters stirring in their rooms, awoken by the disturbance, no doubt, and reaching for candles and matches. At the end of the corridor, kneeling next to Father Owen's body, Brother Alistair continued to sob, but more gently now. Looking up as Varick approached, he said, "Tommy's gone hasn't he?"

"Yes," said Varick. "He's gone. All three of them have gone."

"What are we going to do?"

"We're going to London." This was enough to stop Alistair crying. He looked afraid as Varick continued. "We're going to give Father Owen the last rites and then we're going to London."

"Me too?" Alistair shook his head as he asked the question, as though willing a negative response.

"Yes, you too. We've got to find Tommy and the others and we've got to make them stop."

6:45 AM

Inside 14 Highfield Road, South Wimbledon

George Wakeham's radio alarm clock clicked on and the voice of the travel-news reporter filled the room. It was the Scottish one with the singsong tone who spoke cheerfully of job action by baggage handlers and security staff at Stansted, which had affected outbound flights. The 43 bus route was diverted in Muswell Hill; a truck had shed its load on the A40 in Acton causing eastbound delays; the Strand Underpass was closed and the Hangar Lane traffic circle was "snarled up through sheer weight of traffic."

"And now to the tube . . ." George listened more intently. Of the two hundred and seventy-five stations on the network, one was closed due to construction work—Southfields on the District Line—and one—East Acton on the Central Line—was shut due to staff shortages. Aside from these flies in the collective ointment, all remaining stations were open for business as usual.

"London Underground has issued a travel warning, following predicted daytime temperatures in excess of ninety-five degrees Fahrenheit. Travelers are advised to take a bottle of water with them on their journeys and people who are susceptible to heat-related disorders are advised to stay at home."

There he was, the Scottish bloke, sitting in some air-conditioned office explaining that it was going to be the hottest day of the year. George could have done without that. He had been awake since four. His insomnia had no specific cause. It was just the standard issue middle-aged paranoia that gives you a shove in the middle of the night and sits with you, prodding you until any thought of sleep is futile.

The sun was already beating down on the roof of George's small terraced house in South Wimbledon. He could feel it coming through the ceiling and the walls, ceiling and walls in need of paintwork, his paintwork, work that he kept meaning to get around to but never seemed to manage.

They would issue a warning for just about anything nowadays. Like people were too dumb to realize it was hot and they should behave accordingly. They needed someone to warn them, patronize them. Like the posters cautioning against reckless drinking, paid for by the liquor companies. Treat people like morons and they'll behave like them.

The electric fan at the foot of the bed blew gusts of warm air across George's body, a body pretty much unchanged from his days at school when he played on the wing in the first eleven. His arms and legs were still muscular but around his middle was proof of his sedentary lifestyle, proof that was beginning to creep over the edge of his belt.

His hair needed a trim too. The spiky cut he had gone for in the spring was long grown out and his sideburns were bushy and accentuated—or so he feared—his full cheeks, depriving him of a face that had led a former girlfriend to comment that he looked like a young Albert Finney, an observation he had proudly mentioned a number of times since, long after said girlfriend had become someone else's. He sometimes wondered if his Albert Finney similarity might have continued with age so that he now looked like Albert Finney at forty, after a few too many pies.

George enjoyed the breeze from the fan but the time on the radio alarm kept niggling at him. It was always the same. As soon as he felt like sleeping, it was time to get up. Maggie didn't have that problem. She was asleep as soon as her head touched the pillow and she only woke if Sophie or Ben stirred in the night. It was like she had a sixth sense as far as the children were concerned. But neither of them had woken and Maggie slept on with her back to him, the sheet pulled tight around her shoulders.

When he and Maggie had first met and started seeing each other, he had struggled to believe that a woman so good looking could find him attractive. She seemed to like the fact that, unlike her friends from college who studied business and marketing and wanted to go out and do well for themselves, he wanted to lead a more—he hated the expression—alternative lifestyle. The fact he had no money—he was the bass player in a band called Crawlspace at the time—was not a problem. Maggie had a good job in the West End working for a theater-marketing agency and she could afford to indulge his artistic ambitions.

What had kept him going as a young man while he trawled from one low-paying job to another was a supreme confidence that there was some great creative achievement awaiting him just around the corner. At varying times, he had planned on being a pop star, a writer, a comedian, and an actor, but every time he tried to establish himself within his chosen field he gave up at the first taste of rejection. If he had concentrated on one specific vocation he might have made it; perhaps he spread himself too thinly—an expression he had overheard his parents use about him when he was a boy.

Ten years before he had seen a notice in the *Evening Standard* for staff at Morden tube station, the most southerly station on the Northern Line and not far from where he lived. He applied for a job and he was successful. It was a stopgap, he told himself, until something else came along. But after a few weeks, he saw an advertisement in the weekly *Traffic Circular* and applied for a position as a train operator. Again, he got the job, and after a short training course, he was "on the handle"—a London Underground train driver.

It was a novelty at first; it made him feel like he was breaking away from his middle-class roots to work with "the people." It appealed to the left-wing principles he had developed at college, where he had briefly studied psychology before dropping out. He joined the union, ASLEF, and went along to a few meetings with the intention of trying his hand at politics but found that he was too shy to assert himself among the shop stewards. What was that Smiths song about shyness stopping you from doing things in life that you'd like to do?

All that music he had listened to over the years. All those records—he still had them in boxes, all those bands with integrity and passion and fire in their soul, all those manifestos for a different life he had believed in as a young man, all now pushed to the back of the closet on the landing. What use rebellion when you've got storage requirements for jumbo packs of Pampers? It was funny how life sanded down the corners of your idealism. One minute you're a spiky young guy in black clothes with a dedication to the pursuance of cool that is as serious as your haircut, and the next you're an overweight dad with a receding hairline and a scary mortgage.

He still harbored dreams of artistic endeavor. He still wanted to be the guy who wrote that book—it's really good—did you know he was a tube driver? Or the bloke who played guitar for that band—he used to drive a tube train, you know? Anything so long as he wasn't just George Wakeham, tube driver.

When Maggie worked for the agency in Soho, he sometimes accompanied her to the first nights of shows. There were all the comedians, the television personalities and the celebrities of the day—the ones only too eager to accept free tickets to the opening of another bloody musical—and he convinced himself that deep down he had more talent than they had. He just needed to find some outlet for it. This yearning for artistic success was motivated by vanity, pure vanity, he knew, and this self-knowledge helped fuel the creeping anxiety that he was wasting his life, wasting his potential driving a tube train all day.

If only he could accept his lot like the other drivers and station staff. That would make life a whole lot easier. But he couldn't. Maybe they couldn't either. How depressing was that? He envied people who enjoyed their work, people for whom the job was enough, people who were happy. There was a time when driving a tube train was just a day job, something to pay the bills while he tried to pursue a creative career. But now he was a tube driver—that alone—and nothing more.

The red diodes on the clock radio were taunting him: it was time to wake the children. He pulled at the clammy sheet that had become twisted around his waist but he was lying on it and it stuck fast. For a moment he felt a twinge of claustrophobia before he managed to release himself.

Sometimes he could go for days without feeling anything, but then he would be held at a red light in the middle of a tunnel for a couple of minutes and the sweating would start. If he was stationary for anything longer than a few minutes he knew he would be in trouble.

All was well when he was moving. The fact that he was locked in one of the deepest and narrowest railway lines in the world meant nothing. When he was motionless in a tunnel, on the other hand, that was something entirely different. Every two or three months there would be a lengthy delay. Perhaps five or six minutes. He could deal with that. He would feel wretched but he could cope. Only once had he nearly come unstuck. A passenger had run amok with a knife at Elephant and Castle and the station was closed down. George's train was stuck in the tunnel for nearly an hour.

The discomfort had come in waves, each wave peaking that little bit higher, sustaining itself that little bit longer, until it broke. Each time the claustrophobia had struck, he knew that the only way to deal with it was to move even if the train itself was stationary. There were only two ways to go, either through the J door, as it was known, between the cab and the passenger area, or out of the M door at the front of the train leading out onto the track itself. To make a run for it in either direction would have meant the end of his career as a tube train driver but during the final few minutes of his ordeal it seemed like an increasingly small price to pay. Finally, the all clear was given and he was saved. Never had he been so relieved to see a green light and he set off once more, sweating, hyperventilating, but safe.

He knew it was ridiculous, comical even. Did you hear the one about the tube train driver who suffered from claustrophobia? But George didn't find it funny, not today, the hottest day of the year.

6:58 AM

Highfield Road, South Wimbledon

Simeon sat in the backseat of the car outside the train driver's house and ruminated—as he had for the past few hours—on why they were proceeding with the plan a week early. If it was a rehearsal for the real thing then why bother waiting for the driver? He might not even be on the same shift rotation this week. But whatever the truth, Tommy wasn't saying. He was in one of his moods where it was almost impossible to get any sense out of him, fielding all questions with his usual enigmatic bullshit.

When Tommy had come to fetch him just after midnight, he was wiping blood from his arm. Simeon asked him whose blood it was. What the hell was going on? But Tommy had told him, whispering, that they were on their way to London and they had to leave immediately with Belle. When Tommy had said that he would explain everything later, Simeon immediately had a bad feeling about the whole thing, which was compounded when he heard what must have been Brother Alistair sobbing. He didn't have a chance to make further inquiries, just collected his things and left with Tommy and Belle.

It was Belle who led him to believe that it might just be a dry run. As they waited in the car outside Madoc Farm while Tommy loaded his things into the trunk, Simeon had asked her what was going on.

"Just practicing," Belle had said, and before he could question her further Tommy was in the driver's seat, and they set off down through the mountains in silence. From where he sat in the back, Simeon could see Tommy's face reflected in the rearview mirror. Tommy stared ahead at the narrow winding roads lit up in the flare of the headlights but his thoughts were clearly elsewhere.

As they made their way along the M4, Tommy said that he and Belle should try and get some sleep. Simeon didn't want to push the questioning but he tried again: "So we're going early? Or is this some kind of rehearsal?" His and Tommy's eyes met in the rearview mirror. Even though Simeon couldn't see Tommy's mouth, he could tell that Tommy was smiling. He could see from the wrinkles in the corners of his eyes. The bastard was enjoying this. Tommy didn't even answer his question, just went right on smiling.

As they sat in the car outside the train driver's house, Simeon could sense Tommy's and Belle's nerves. They weren't behaving as though it was a dry run. Tommy was alert, acutely focused. Belle watched her brother intently and waited. Simeon felt compelled to speak.

"So we're going to go this morning?" He tried to sound hopeful, like this was something that he had dreamed of. He never was much of an actor, always avoided drama classes at school.

"Surrender," said Tommy, turning around in his seat and smiling right at him.

"What do you mean?"

"Surrender to God's will."

As soon as he heard Tommy say this and saw the mobile phone and headset in his hand, Simeon knew that today was no rehearsal.

7:06 AM

Inside 14 Highfield Road, South Wimbledon

George made his way through to the bathroom. Maggie was still asleep. Being the first one up, he could avoid the rush. He looked at himself in the mirror. He was forty years old. His parents used to say of the passing years, "Where does it all go?" and he didn't know what they meant. Not until now. The name of a Charles Bukowski poem summed it all up, although he had never actually read the poem itself. He was reading a Charles Bukowski book, *Post Office*, and one of Bukowski's other works listed at the back was called *The Days Run Away Like Wild Horses Over the Hills*. And it was true, they did. Bukowski was right on the money.

As he had grown older, he had found himself becoming more emotional, more likely to tear up at a sad moment in a film or a tragic incident on the news. It might have had something to do with his recent "one under"—his first suicide on the job. For a while, he had been appalled but also strangely intrigued by the prospect of seeing someone jump. It wasn't as though he was chasing a perverse thrill, far from it, but if he had to come to terms with its likelihood then what better way to do so than with an air of mild curiosity? Some of his colleagues were traumatized by the experience while others didn't seem to give a damn. George often wondered how he would react when his time came. It would come eventually—there were over a hundred incidents every year. He wondered how it would feel to watch someone die. It happened to most tube drivers if they drove for long enough. Then, one day, sure enough, it happened to him.

He was pulling into Warren Street station six months previously. It was about five o'clock. The platform was full of the usual late-afternoon crowd, people trying to beat the rush—and failing. He was about halfway into the station when one of the faceless hordes, a smartly dressed woman in her early fifties, launched herself off the platform edge straight in front of the train. As an exercise in efficient life termination, it was spot on. She timed it perfectly. Her body slammed into the front of the cab and dropped down under the wheels. She was killed instantly. George was lucky in that respect. He guessed the woman was too if she was serious about her desire to die, and he could only presume from her very definite leap that she was.

Colleagues of George had told him about instances where people had jumped and were only injured, trapped under the train. That could be harrowing for all concerned. So he was thankful that his one under, when it came, was mercifully quick for both himself and the jumper.

Giving evidence at the inquest was more difficult than he had anticipated, especially seeing the woman's grieving relatives. After the verdict of suicide was returned, the woman's husband had approached him outside the coroner's court and apologized for his wife's actions. George had found the experience extremely moving.

He took the leave he was entitled to and accepted an offer of counseling, not because he felt he really needed it but because he had never had any counseling before and wondered if it might help him with his anxiety and corresponding insomnia. It didn't.

As George showered, he enjoyed rinsing away the sticky glaze of sweat coating his skin. It was close half past by now, had to be. Time to wake the family. He pulled a towel around his waist, squeezed some toothpaste onto his toothbrush, and started on his teeth as he made his way back toward the bedroom.

"I thought you were going to wake me," said Maggie as he appeared in the doorway.

"I am waking you," he said with a mouth full of white foam. "That's what I'm doing now."

"Well there's no need because I'm already awake."

"So why are you chewing me out for not waking you?"

"I'm just teasing." That tone of voice. She was in a good mood. He liked it when she was happy.

"What time is it?"

"About twenty past seven."

She yawned and stretched out her arms. George smiled at her and she smiled back. He was just about to say something affectionate, something about how she looked nice with her new hair—and she did, the short bob suited her—when she said, "God, you look rough."

"Thanks."

"Don't mention it."

George turned back toward the door.

Maggie said, "Can you wake Sophie and Benji?"

He grunted yes as he headed back toward the landing.

Sophie was fast asleep. George watched her for a moment, hoping that the sound of him brushing his teeth would bring her around, but she didn't stir. She was lying on her side sucking her thumb, her dark brown hair—the same color as her mother's—lay across her tiny pixie face. She looked so helpless. Her future lay in his hands, and as much as he wanted the best for her in all things, the best wasn't always possible on the salary of a London Underground train driver. He reached down and rubbed her back. Her eyes opened and she frowned at him for a moment, squinting into the light. "Hello, little one. Have you had a nice sleep?" The question was phrased in that tone of voice that he reserved for his children only. It was a high-pitched version of his normal voice and it made him cringe when he heard himself talking like that on family videos. Seeing himself on them was bad enough.

"It's hot, Daddy," she said.

"It is, darling, it's very hot." He lowered the tone so it was more like his normal voice, his Maggie voice, as opposed to the more macho, guttural one he used with colleagues at work. Lifting Sophie out of bed, he gave her a squeeze before setting her down on the carpet, where she tottered a little sleepily and yawned.

Ben was already awake, playing with his Action Man as George entered his room and said, "Morning, fella."

After a series of energetic vocal simulations of gunfire and explosions, Ben said, "Morning," and proceeded to question George about the pros and cons of machine guns as though they were already mid-conversation on that very topic.

"Is it my birthday today?" Ben asked as George tried to steer him from the battlefield into the bathroom.

"It's tomorrow," said George. "And where are we going, fella?"

"Mr. Pieces!" He shouted it and Sophie joined in, the two of them running and jumping as they cheered and sang out, "Mr. Pieces! Mr. Pieces!"

Mr. Pieces was in reality a restaurant called Mr. Pizza, but Ben had mispronounced it when he was little and forever more it was known as Mr. Pieces in the Wakeham household. Mr. Pieces was a family favorite.

Having corralled his two children in the bathroom, George supervised Ben's morning wash—"Dad? If you shot a man a hundred times, would he die?"—and helped Sophie sponge her face and clean her teeth. While Ben pulled on his jeans and a Spiderman T-shirt, George brushed Sophie's hair and dressed her in the clothes Maggie had left out on the chest of drawers outside the bathroom: a pair of pink jeans with a flower patch on the knee and a stripy top. To save time, he carried Sophie down the stairs behind Ben, whose stream of consciousness had re-routed from machine guns to breakfast cereal. When George arrived in the kitchen doorway, however, Sophie still in his arms, Maggie's face collapsed into an expression of annoyance.

"George, it's about a thousand degrees out there and you've put her in long sleeves."

"Well that's what was on the chest of drawers."

"Leave it to me." She said it with that long-suffering tone as though he was forever dressing his children in inappropriately warm clothes on hot days. George looked at Sophie and Ben and rolled his eyes as Maggie made her way back upstairs.

"Silly Daddy, eh?"

"Silly Daddy," mimicked Sophie, grinning.

George watched Ben and Sophie sitting at the kitchen table and even though he had kissed them both earlier, felt compelled to bury his nose and lips in their hair and kiss them again, relishing the smell of them, a smell somewhere between honey and freshly baked biscuits with just a hint of shampoo. God, he loved that smell.

Sitting on the work surface next to the microwave oven was Sophie's favorite doll, Poppy.

"Look! Here's Poppy Doll. Look, Poppy's saying hello. 'Hello Sophie!' she says. 'Hello Sophie!'" He was back to the high-pitched voice again. Sophie took the doll and gave it a squeeze as Maggie returned and George beat a hasty retreat, grabbing his bag from the banister rail and making for the front door. Turning back to the kitchen, he waved to Ben and Sophie, said, "Bye bye!"— high-pitched—and then back to his normal voice for Maggie: "See you later."

He blew her a kiss and she kissed the air and smiled. George closed the door and hurried off along the pavement. As he climbed into the car, put his bag on the passenger seat and was about to put the key in the ignition, he heard an unfamiliar ringtone nearby. He reached into his pocket for his phone. Perhaps Sophie had accidentally reprogrammed the ringtone from the opening bars of "Train in Vain" by the Clash that he had uploaded to it a couple of weeks before. He had always loved that track. When he took his phone out of his pocket, however, the screen was dark. Then he realized that the ringtone was coming from the glove compartment. He snatched it open and there was a cell phone—a much higher specification model than his—along with a wireless headset. As he picked up the phone, he looked at the name of the caller on the screen: Maggie. His Maggie? What did it mean? His wife was calling this phone—a phone that wasn't his.

And then it occurred to him: Maggie must be having an affair and her secret lover had left his phone in the car and now she thought she was calling him. It had to be that. She had been caught red-handed and he wanted her to know it. He pressed the Call Answer button and held the phone to his ear.

"Maggie?"

"Look at the window, George . . . of the house . . . look at the window." Her voice sounded weird, like she'd been crying. Maybe she'd realized her mistake, a mistake of marriage-wrecking proportions. He looked at the window. Perhaps he was wrong about the affair. Maybe she was going to wave to him? Or maybe Sophie and Ben were. But why? They didn't normally, and why the strange phone in the glove compartment?

Suddenly a man stepped into view in the living room window, a slim man dressed all in black, wearing a balaclava. With one hand, he held Sophie, crying and struggling, and with the other, he held a gun to her head.

7:45 AM

Inside 14 Highfield Road, South Wimbledon

Any lingering doubts that perhaps today was a practice run had been dispelled when Tommy had opened the back door of the house and they had made their way inside. Tommy behaved as though he had done this a thousand times before. He didn't even seem to be nervous. Simeon, on the other hand, felt sick as he pressed his gun into the woman's back as Tommy explained what she was to say into the phone.

"Please don't hurt them," the woman had shouted when Tommy approached the children.

"Keep quiet and everything will be fine." Simeon felt as though he was reciting lines from a script. He had no idea whether anything would ever be fine again. There were times in the past few weeks when it felt as though Tommy and Belle's plans were fantasy. That wasn't to say that the two of them weren't serious and meticulous about everything but, as with the po-faced religious observance at Madoc Farm, it felt as though they were all involved in something that wasn't real, something make-believe. Obsessing over every minor detail was something that Tommy and Belle clearly relished. But Simeon had suspected that when all the strategizing was at an end, they might then start preparing for another hypothetical attack. As though that was how they liked to amuse themselves during the long boring nights. The events of that morning, however, had proved him spectacularly wrong.

Tommy scooped up the little girl with one arm and pointed his gun at her head. Simeon pushed the gun into the woman's back, her cue to tell her husband on the phone to look at the window where Tommy stood. It was an audacious way of ensuring the train driver's compliance. What if someone had been driving or walking past the house and had seen what was going on? But they didn't. If Tommy could do this and get away with it so easily, Simeon was in no doubt that he could do everything else that he had planned.

7:46 AM

It felt like a vent had opened up in the quiet suburban facade, allowing George Wakeham a glimpse of hell. But just as soon as the image was branded on his memory, the man holding Sophie stepped away from the window.

"Maggie! What the fuck is going on?" On the phone, he could hear Sophie and Ben crying.

"Don't get out of the car!" Maggie screamed so hard it hurt his eardrum. George had the door halfway open already. He slammed it shut. "If you get out of the car they'll kill us."

"What do they want?"

No reply.

He heard Maggie talking to Sophie. She said, "You're all right now. You're all right, Mummy's got you."

"Maggie!"

"George, I've got to read something to you." Her voice was trembling. "You have to listen to it very carefully, okay?"

"Okay."

"Unless you do exactly as instructed, the three of us will be killed. Any attempt to raise the alarm will result in us being killed.

Any attempt to deviate from the implicit nature of any instructions given to you, however minor, will result in us being killed. Do you understand?"

He couldn't speak. His mouth was devoid of saliva and he felt sick.

"Do you understand? George!"

"Yes, yes."

"You must take the headset that is with the mobile phone. Can you see it?"

"Yes."

"It has an on/off switch on the side. Put on the headset and turn it on. Do it now."

George picked up the headset. With shaking fingers he found the switch, flicked it on, and hooked the earpiece around his ear.

"Can you hear me?" asked Maggie.

"Yes, I can hear you."

"You must keep the headset on at all times and keep this line open until you are instructed to do otherwise. Have you got that?"

"Yes."

Norman, a bespectacled oddball of a man who lived with his mother at the Bates Motel, as George and Maggie called the house, stepped out from behind his brown front door and made his way along the street. Maybe George could communicate with Norman and have him raise the alarm? Maybe he could write something on a piece of paper and hold it up? Norman saw him in the car and waved.

George looked away as though he hadn't seen. Trying to raise the alarm was a stupid idea. It would never work.

But Norman had stopped almost level with the front window of George and Maggie's house. George gestured to the mobile phone to show Norman he was on a call.

"George? You're not trying to do anything are you?" Maggie sounded desperate. "You're not trying to signal to anyone are you?"

"No."

Still Norman stood there. George looked away.

"Then why can they see a man on the pavement looking at you?"

"He's just going." But he wasn't. Norman was watching him.

"George! For God's sake! They've got a gun against Ben's head!"

In the background, he could hear Ben shout, "Mummy!" George had to do something, anything. So he held up two fingers to Norman, flicked a "V" at him and mouthed, "Fuck off," as unmistakably as he could muster. Norman frowned and blinked a few times, bemused. He went to say something but thought better of it and walked away.

"Tell them he's going away," said George.

"Christ, George, okay, okay."

"Maggie, I want to speak to them."

Pause.

"They won't allow it, all communication must come through me. Now you must continue with your day, exactly as normal. You must go to work and you must keep the headset on with the line open until instructed otherwise."

"Maggie, ask them what they want."

"They can hear you. They're listening."

"So? So what is it? What's this all about?"

Dead air for a moment and then: "They say that you'll find out everything in due course but now you should do as you are told."

"In that case I want them to know that I will do whatever they want, on the condition that they don't harm you or the children in any way."

"They can hear you, they want you to know that they agree but you must now proceed as you would on any other day and they want you to know that they will be watching you and listening to you at all times. If you do anything . . ."

"I know, I know, you'll be . . . I know."

"George, you'd better get going."

He started the car and set off, his foot trembling against the accelerator pedal. As he drove past his house, he looked into the living room. There was no one there but he could just make out Sophie's doll, Poppy, on the arm of the sofa.

As he pulled out into the traffic on the main road, his eyes filled with tears and he listened intently to the faint hiss from the headset during the ten-minute journey to the depot. When he pulled up at traffic lights and pedestrian crossings, he watched people as they went about their business, oblivious to the horror in which he was cocooned. Could he signal to one of them? Could any one of them become his family's savior? The answers to these and every question he might ask of himself regarding possible solutions to his predicament went unanswered. Any attempt to raise the alarm, to alert the world to his situation was a potential reason for his family to be harmed. Such was his fear and dread that turning the car into the parking lot at Morden, he retched.

"Maggie?"

"Yes?"

"Is everything all right?"

"George . . ." She was cut short and he could hear a man muttering something. He couldn't make out what he was saying. George felt the need to keep speaking, to say anything.

"I'm at the depot."

"George, listen to me." There was an intimacy to the way she spoke that George hadn't heard in a long time. "You've got to keep quiet. Please. Don't speak unless you really need to."

"Okay, I just want you to know that I love you." He needed to say it. It made him feel better.

No reply, just the hum of the open line. How long did they intend to utilize this communication channel? It was all well and good above ground but if they wanted to talk to him once he was in the tube tunnel then they would need to use some other method. They had to have thought of that, hadn't they?

Parked up in the station lot, he took his bag from the passenger seat. Holding the mobile phone in his hand, he climbed out, locked the car, and walked toward the depot building with his head down.

"Hi, George!" Panic stabbed him. He looked up. It was Louisa. She worked in the cafeteria. They had developed a friendship over the past couple of years. George found her attractive, and sometimes he couldn't help but fantasize about how things might be if he was about ten years younger and unmarried. Louisa smiled at him, the sort of smile that, until today, had the ability to make him blush. Now, he felt nothing.

"Hi, Louisa. How are you?"

"Fine, thanks," she replied. "You?"

"Yeah, I'm good." My wife and children are being held hostage by an armed gang was what he wanted to say. He didn't; he couldn't.

It was still early but already the heat was in the high seventies. Louisa looked as cool and fragrant as ever but George could feel the perspiration forming on his upper body.

Louisa fell in beside him as they climbed up the steps and in through the front door of the depot. His conversations with Louisa usually followed a certain pattern. He would tell her some anecdote, try and make her laugh. Impossible now but he knew he had to say something.

"Another hot one." It was all he could think of.

But she didn't get to reply as Neville, a fellow driver, a big ungainly Scot who prided himself on his irreverent humor, came bounding down the corridor with a big grin on his face. He and George were friends. They sometimes went for a beer together after work.

"Georgie-boy! Finally embraced the new technology, I see!" He pointed at the headset George was wearing. Neville had only recently joked about George's phone being not just last year's model but last century's.

"Yeah, I thought it was time I took the plunge."

"Give us a look then." Neville held out his hand.

"Neville, I'm speaking to someone."

As soon as he said it, he realized how ridiculous it would sound to Louisa, who was smiling, preparing herself to enjoy Neville's good-humored ribbing of "George the technophobe." She looked confused. They had just walked across the parking lot and George had made no indication that he was on a call.

"Come on," said Neville. "You can still talk, I just want to have a look at the handset." He made another grab for the phone.

"Just fucking leave it!"

The ferocity of George's response was glaringly inappropriate to those who didn't understand his unique predicament. Louisa was taken aback. She muttered, "I'll see you later," and hurried off.

Neville froze, eyebrows raised in surprise.

"I'm sorry, Nev, but I'm on the phone, all right?" George pushed past him.

When George went to sign on with the duty manager, a round pink man who was sweating through his shirt, he was told that the city branch of the Northern Line had just been closed due to a "security incident." This would normally have been enough to prick George's curiosity. A security incident was fabulously vague. It was the sort of thing announcers said to customers over the public-address system in a station, not the sort of explanation given by a duty manager to a driver. But George had more important things on his mind.

He made his way to his train, number 037, in Bay 12 of the shed. The mobile phone had become slippery with sweat and he slid it into the top pocket of his shirt slowly, being careful not to knock any buttons or keys and making sure he could still hear the open line humming in his ear from the headset.

"They want to know what time you leave from Morden," said Maggie as he approached the train.

"Eight seventeen."

"Okay."

George hung up his bag and his jacket in the cab. The temperature being what it was, he made sure the heating was turned off. Then he checked the lights and changed the destination blind to MILL HILL EAST VIA CHARING CROSS. He was so used to the procedure he could sleepwalk through it. He checked that the PA handset was working, and the interior lights were on, and he tripped out the motor alternators and overloads and reset them. Turning on the radio, he heard the bronchial wheeze of the depot shunter as he called other trains out of the depot.

George checked the wipers and whistle, the air-pressure gauge and the brakes. Satisfied there were no faults with the train monitoring system, he carried out a lamp test followed by a traction test, and checked the heat and vent system, the doors, and the passenger alarm. It was a few minutes before he was due to be called so he wandered through the six cars of the train checking that everything was as it should be.

A group of maintenance engineers were working on a section of track in the shed. They were laughing at something. George had never felt so alone in all his life. He returned to the cab, slamming the J door—the door between the passenger area and the cab—after him. Usually he just sat and did the crossword in the *Metro* newspaper that he picked up on his way to the shed until the depot shunter called him down to leave the depot. Sometimes, as he waited to be called down, he played a game on his mobile phone called Snake. But as he thought of his own mobile phone, all thoughts of the game were forgotten. Why hadn't he thought of it before? Reaching into the side pocket of his jacket, he took out the phone and looked at it. He couldn't call anyone for fear of being overheard but he could send a text. Who could he send it to? Was it possible to text 999? Could he text a friend—Dougie perhaps? My family are being held hostage—call the police but tell them not to do anything for fear of alerting the hostage takers. Dougie would think he was joking, putting him on. Even if he did believe him and raised the alarm, his actions might inadvertently cost the lives of George's family.

George slid his phone back into his jacket pocket and sat with his legs bouncing up and down on his toes, his nerves jangling out of control. He felt like a condemned man. It was a struggle to keep the panic at bay. After years of mundanity and routine, something so frightening and profound was happening to him that he felt as though if he allowed himself to think about it with any clarity his brain would run away with itself. Because in whichever direction he looked, it was too much to take in. The people who had taken his family were armed and, more frightening than that, they were clever. There was no point trying to raise the alarm because he knew for a cold certainty, from that one-second image in the front window of his house that kept replaying over and over in his head, that if he did and they found out, they would kill his family without compunction.

On the radio, the depot shunter called him forward to the outlet signal. George took hold of the dead man's handle, pushed the lever into drive and the train moved off out of the shed. When the signal cleared, the train headed down the track to Morden station and he heard the radio switch across from the depot channel to the line channel.

He pulled up to the signal in the station and opened the doors. Usually he would lean out and watch the commuters climb aboard. He enjoyed people-watching and often, to try and dispel a crushing sense of boredom, he would weave little stories about his passengers and where they were going. Sometimes it might be nothing more than trying to work out someone's name from his or her appearance. With some people it was tricky but for others—a total Jeremy, for example—he liked to feel he could spot one a mile off. But today he didn't indulge this interest; he stood in the cab and looked at the two tunnel entrances at the end of the deep man-made gorge up ahead, where the train would enter London Underground's longest network of tunnels.

George wasn't a geek like some of his colleagues but he did know that from Morden to East Finchley on the Northern Line was—at over seventeen miles—one of the longest and deepest railway tunnels in the world. And once inside it, all phone signals would die. So, in approximately two minutes, he would be left all alone with only the radio channel linking him to the line controller. The people who had kidnapped Maggie and Sophie couldn't listen in to him on that, could they? Would this present him with an opportunity to raise the alarm—if he felt it was safe enough to do so? Would he ever feel it was safe enough to do so?

When the signal changed, George pressed the buttons to close the passenger doors, checked the pilot light was out, and turned the dead man's handle. The train moved forward out of the station into the shadow thrown by the high sides of the gorge leading to the tunnels. George slid the mobile phone out of his top pocket and watched the reception bars down the side of the screen collapse to nothing as the train was swallowed by the darkness. As the line went dead, he took off the headset and put it in his pocket with the handset.

It was a strange feeling being suddenly released from the surveillance that he had been subject to. It afforded no relief from his all-pervading sense of dread, however, and now he felt himself consumed by indecision. Was now the time to attempt to communicate his unique predicament to the authorities? Turning off the main light in the cab as he always did, in order to see more clearly in the tunnel, he reached for the radio handset on the console. But as his fingers touched the molded plastic, he heard an unexpected sound. Someone was opening the door into the cab.

8:17 AM

He loved the rain in the Welsh mountains. It wasn't like the rain in Louisiana, which was cleansing and ferocious, sometimes even biblical as it had been with Hurricane Katrina. Snowdonian rain could be powerful too but what he loved was the gentle patter that often went on all day.

As Brother Varick of the church of Cruor Christi stood on the northbound Northern Line platform at Leicester Square tube station, he wondered whether he would ever feel the Welsh rain on his face again. He wished it would rain today—it might cool things down. But there was little chance of that. When he and Brother Alistair had entered the station, the sun was high in the sky and there wasn't a cloud in sight.

After they had bought their tickets and made their way down onto the Northern Line platforms, Alistair had caught the first southbound train on his quest to find the children. Both men had a mission. When they had set out from Madoc Farm that morning in the Land Rover, Varick had anticipated that Alistair would join him in his efforts to stop Brother Thomas and the others from completing their vile deeds, but after their discussion on their way into London, it was clear that one of them would need to save the train driver's children. Alistair was hardly a man to whom heroics would come naturally but, on this occasion, he wouldn't necessarily need to be. He just had to find them. It was imperative that amid all the other potential loss of life, the lives of two of the youngest and most innocent potential victims weren't forgotten.

Travelers sweated as they rushed around Varick, climbing on and off trains, while he stood still on the platform peering over the top of the free *Metro* that he had picked up in the ticket hall earlier. He pretended to read it as he watched the front cab of each of the trains that rattled into the station.

Varick knew that in one of them would be Brother Thomas; he also knew that his unmoving presence on the platform, watching the trains—it was at least an hour he had been standing there now— might arouse suspicion.

Another train entered the station with a solitary driver in the cab. Varick knew that it had to be this line and it had to be this station. That was the plan that Owen had found in Brother Thomas's notebook, the information that had cost him his life. So Varick stood and waited. His patience would be rewarded. He didn't know exactly when but Tommy Denning would be there soon enough.

8:19 AM

Northern Line Train 037, driver's cab

London Underground procedure states that all staff entries into a cab should be made while the train is in a station but whoever was entering the cab had the standard issue London Underground J door key—so named on account of its J shape. The intruder alarm went off—beeping away—until the door was shut again, deactivating it, as George turned to see a slim, muscular man dressed all in black and carrying a large canvas bag. Although clearly not wearing London Underground livery, his bomber jacket was of a sort a nightclub bouncer might wear, and lent him an official air. George thought he might be a member of staff, after all, even though he had not been informed of anyone scheduled to be joining him in the cab. The man was in his mid-twenties, his head shaved to the length of the thick dark stubble on his face. The eyes that stared into George's were a light blue, almost aquamarine, with pupils the size of a teenager's on ecstasy.

"Hello, George," he said as he put his bag in the corner of the cab. The voice was British, almost accentless, with just a hint of London and the southeast—what's known as "Estuary." It had a soft, almost intimate tone.

"Maggie and Sophie are fine." George felt the relief flood through his innards. The guy was special forces, SAS possibly. They had taken out the bad guys and he was here to tell him that all was well and George was now free to sell his story to the papers, maybe even appear on a reality TV show. But the words that followed were like torpedoes that sank George's hope: "And rest assured, they will continue to be fine so long as you do exactly as I tell you."

"What's this all about?" asked George.

"Just keep quiet, carry on with your job and we'll get along famously."

George looked him up and down. He was only a kid. Maybe he could take him in a fight. George was taller than him by a good three inches after all. But the kid had that supple wiry physique that hid unexpected strength. That, and he was about fifteen years younger.

"I need to know what this is all about," said George attempting to convey an air of authority.

"Why?" It was said with a smile.

"Because this train and all its passengers are my responsibility."

"Good." The smile remained. "Then I suggest that you carry on being responsible for them."

"What do you want?" George allowed a hint of desperation to enter his tone, which he regretted.

The smile was gone. "I want you to allow your wife and children the opportunity to survive this situation and I want you to know that if you try to stop me from doing what I've come here to do then they won't. You have to trust me on that one, George. If you try to do anything to stop me, they *will* die. Have you got that?"

"Yes. But . . ."

"Sssshhhhh . . ." It was a soothing sound, the sound a parent might use to calm a baby with troubled sleep.

"The next station is South Wimbledon." The voice came from CELIA, the Complete Electronic Line Information Announcer, and was relayed throughout the carriages as the train entered the station. At the far end of the platform, gathered together in a tight group in the midst of the commuters was a party of schoolgirls aged no more than seven or eight, George guessed, all dressed identically in blue blazers, pink dresses, and straw hats. As the train came to a halt, George opened the doors and the sound of excited little girls' voices could be heard as their harried teachers ushered them on board the train.

"This train terminates at Mill Hill East via Charing Cross," said CELIA.

There followed a station announcement on the platform: "Please be aware that there are currently no Northern Line trains running via the Bank. Customers are advised to take the first available train and change where necessary." This sent some more of the passengers who would normally have waited for a "via Bank" train hurrying on board, leaving the rest of the platform empty. George closed the doors, checked the pilot light and turning the dead man's handle sent the train rattling into the tunnel.

George's need to establish what was happening was irrepressible, his compulsion to speak impossible to resist.

"Can I ask you something?"

"Looks like you just did."

"Why me?"

"Go on."

"I'm asking you, why me?"

"And I'm asking you to get all the questions out of the way now before this goes any further. Come on, you can do better than 'Why me?', can't you?"

"Okay, so how did you know who I am, where I live, who I live with, what time I go to work, what car I drive—how do you know so much about me?"

George's sense of unease felt like an abscess, throbbing, poisonous, agony. And when the kid spoke he felt it erupt.

"It's you, George, because you were the one who responded. You were the one who told me everything that I needed to know."

For a frustrated dreamer like George, the Internet provided a release. It allowed him to connect with people the world over. He enjoyed the immediacy and anonymity of chat rooms but he also liked the sense of community provided by message boards and those in particular that were hosted on the site that had been established by one "Piccadilly Pete" some ten years previously. The message boards on Piccadilly Pete's site had become the central community forum on the Internet for London Underground staff and anyone interested in discussing the mechanics, society, and culture of the tube. Many of the discussion threads were overtly technical and George didn't bother with them but often there were discussions of day-to-day procedure and working conditions that he found of interest. Sometimes a writer or journalist would post a message eliciting information for their research; sometimes prospective LU employees would ask for advice about finding work or request details of various aspects of the job.

It was via Piccadilly Pete's message boards that George had started an ongoing e-mail correspondence with a member of the community who posted under the name of "Pilgrim." Here was a young man who clearly had a burning interest in becoming a train driver. When George had replied to his initial question regarding the best way of getting a job "on the handle," George offered him the benefit of his own experience and a sort of Internet friendship had developed. George had found himself strangely flattered by Pilgrim's attention and the reverence with which he treated him. George had opened up to him probably more than he should have done, more than was strictly safe. But George was a big boy; what possible harm could come of it? He hadn't even stopped to consider when Pilgrim had gradually made his inquiries more personal. Now, however, George could see that he had been the subject of an ongoing grooming process.

"You're Pilgrim aren't you?"

The question received a smile.

"I thought you might have figured that out before now."

George felt the bile rise in his throat, hot and stinging. It was a strange form of betrayal that he felt. Pilgrim's smile faded as he said, "We can talk more later, but now I need you to concentrate on the job in hand, so let's keep quiet. Okay?"

The threat was implicit and George nodded, trembling, returning his gaze to the darkness of the tunnel up ahead.

The stations passed by, each one announced by CELIA's automated monotone. At Stockwell, about a third of the passengers left the train to change to the Victoria Line. But others climbed aboard George Wakeham's train, train 037, and sat down or stood holding the yellow handrails and read newspapers, books, tablet computers, listened to music or played games, nursed hangovers, sipped coffee, cast surreptitious glances at someone attractive, or just stared into space.

"Okay, zero three seven," said the line controller as George waited for the signal to clear. "There's a trainee driver at Kennington going up to East Finchley, wants to watch how it's done. All right?"

It was common enough, trainee drivers riding in the cab or "riding on the cushions" as it was known by LU staff. There was no way George could decline the request without arousing suspicion. Pilgrim clearly knew this because, when George glanced nervously at him, he nodded his assent.

"Fine," said George into the radio handset. Once clear of Oval, George saw the tiny point of light at the end of the tunnel grow larger and he felt his panic intensify as he worried about how to explain away his existing passenger to the trainee driver.

As the train pulled into Kennington, George could see him in his uniform standing at the end of the platform. He was about thirty, of medium height, slightly overweight with a ponytail. He waved to George as the cab pulled past and George waved back. Stationary at the signal, George opened the offside door to the cab and the trainee driver stepped aboard.

"All right, mate," he said, seemingly unfazed by the extra passenger in the cab.

"All right," said George, closing the offside door.

The trainee nodded at Pilgrim, who nodded back, expressionless. The signal cleared and they moved off into the tunnel, all three of them in a line, George in his seat and the other two standing.

It sounded like a pool cue striking a pillow. George looked around to see the trainee driver's legs crumple beneath him as he fell sideways and a jet of blood pumped from a hole in the side of his head. As he landed on the floor of the cab, his legs kicked out in the death throes. Pilgrim looked down at him impassively, holding an automatic pistol with a silencer attachment from which there curled a wisp of smoke.

"Oh Jesus!" George gasped, breathless and numb with shock.

"Keep your hand on the handle, George." Pilgrim's voice betrayed some urgency for the first time before it resumed its confident purr. "Nice and steady, that's it."

The trainee's legs spasmed a couple more times and then he lay still, the blood from his head wound squirting across the cab floor, the trajectory of its arc decreasing with each dying pulse.

George glanced down at the body; blood was lapping from side to side in the little gullies on the floor beneath the poor bastard's head. He looked away. This was the second dead body he had been in close proximity to in the past two months. The one under and now this. But they could not have been more different. The one under was something he had been not exactly anticipating but something for which he was at least prepared. This wasn't.

His limbs felt as though they were made of rubber and it took all his strength to hold the dead man's handle. He stared ahead through the glass into the tunnel. Colorful kaleidoscopic patterns danced in his peripheral vision; his head felt like it was way too big for his neck, which felt reedy and unsteady. As the train passed a green signal, CELIA's now echoing voice announced: "The next station is Waterloo." George's head began to tip forward. The thought came to him that maybe he had been shot too. Perhaps these were his dying moments. Someone was holding his hand.

Pilgrim stood beside him with his hand on top of his own, maintaining the pressure on the dead man's handle. With his other hand, he slapped George on the cheek repeatedly while cradling his head in the crook of his arm.

"I'm okay," said George, his face stinging as the fog started to clear.

"Don't go passing out on me, George."

"I'm sorry." An apology for his tormentor.

The train pulled into Waterloo station and a crowded platform. George pulled the train up to the signal and opened the cab door to look back along the cars. The air that he sucked up was warm and metallic and offered little oxygen. As he stood there watching people embark and disembark, he thought it might be possible to step out of the cab and make a run for it. But the thought never made it past the planning stage. His legs were too shaky. He knew he would never make it.

"This is Waterloo station, change here for the Jubilee Line, the Bakerloo Line and national rail services."

The platform was busy with tourists pulling suitcases on trolleys, commuters, day-trippers and backpackers, businessmen, schoolchildren and students, pensioners, women with babies.

"Please stand clear of the doors, this train is ready to depart."

The signal cleared, and as George propelled the train into the tunnel once more, moving beneath the Thames toward Embankment station, he chanced a couple of glances at the man he knew as Pilgrim. There he stood still and stiff-backed—the pistol was nowhere to be seen—and he stared out of the front window, deep in thought, the corpse of the man he had so recently murdered at his feet.

8:46 AM

Varick knew that in a little room somewhere he might be framed on a CCTV security monitor. If Tommy Denning didn't come soon, someone would come for him. Impatience joined his other strained emotions. But the waiting had also given him time to think, and when he wasn't contemplating Tommy's arrival, he thought about his journey from New Orleans to the mountains of Snowdonia. It had been a trial, a test that Varick had finally passed. God had given him a task and he had carried it out. During those lawless days back in September 2005 after the levees had broken, it was as though the world had been turned upside down. He had done some things—firing on looters being one of them—which troubled him deeply. He had tried to justify it: society had broken down. What else were he and his colleagues in the New Orleans Police Department—those who hadn't already deserted—expected to do? But however he tried to explain away his actions, they had continued to prey on his mind. After Katrina, his drug consumption had increased as though he were attempting to blot out what he had done and what he had seen.

It was not long after he had last been here, in the West End of London, that Jesus had spoken to him and shown him the one true path. He had made the London trip with a girlfriend. Frieda, her name was. She was half-German. She loved to party. It was the first vacation he had been on since Katrina. It was meant to be a week's sightseeing, although the only sights they really got to see were the inside of the hotel room, where they fornicated energetically, and the inside of numerous nightclub toilets in which they snorted lines of cocaine from the bag he had smuggled through customs up his ass.

The devil had stalked him, waited for him in the shadows. Varick could see that now. But at the time it had felt as though it was how life was meant to be. A couple of months after he had returned from his trip to London with Frieda, Jesus had steered him toward Father Owen at Madoc Farm. There was no other explanation as to why he had found himself on the website of a sect of British evangelical Christians by the name of Cruor Christi. Despite thinking of himself as a Christian since birth, other than funerals and weddings he hadn't been to church since he was a teenager. Yet there he was, late at night, sitting at his computer with a head full of cocaine, searching for something, searching for meaning and it was the simple reassuring words of Father Owen that had struck a chord in his heart. Owen was a man who genuinely wanted to help those less fortunate than himself. Here truly was a Good Samaritan and Varick felt that altruism that had made him want to serve his fellow man in the NOPD, that selflessness that had laid dormant for so long, stir once more beneath the corrosive effects of his debauchery.

Initial e-mails to Father Owen had led to a series of phone calls and, within a couple of months, Varick had turned his back on drugs and alcohol, resigned his position with the New Orleans Police Department, and been on his way to Wales and Madoc Farm in Snowdonia. The rest was history, preordained just as surely as his immediate future was now as he set out on his mission to find Brother Thomas. Some things were meant to be.

The first few months in Snowdonia had been tough. It was winter and the farm was in a terrible condition. He had set about rebuilding part of the roof himself and fixing the plumbing. Gradually, as God decreed, he and his fellow brothers had rebuilt Madoc Farm and Varick had allowed himself a little pride in his achievements.

Madoc Farm in Snowdonia was now his true home. It was a home where he could go about the work that Jesus had seen fit to bless him with, the saving of troubled young men and women, prising them from the clutches of the devil and returning them to the path of righteousness. Many of those who made up Cruor Christi's flock were from military backgrounds, like brothers Thomas and Simeon. Others were ex-drug addicts like Alistair. The world was full of casualties from the wars on drugs and terror. Cruor Christi, however, was there for them and would be forever. Those poor spiritual refugees were not alone—he would make sure of that— and he would do all in his power to stop Brother Thomas from destroying the special bond that united the brothers and sisters at Madoc Farm. Responsibility lay with him now and him alone. The authorities would have no cause to trouble the good people of Madoc Farm if the members of the church of Cruor Christi could be seen to have averted this potential cataclysm themselves. Father Owen's death would not be in vain. Varick would ensure that his good work continued.

He had had a bad feeling about Tommy right from the start. Tommy's hotheaded, almost sociopathic charisma was something he had seen in other young men during his years working for the NOPD. The police often attracted that sort of person. But there was something different about Tommy. It was as though he was just watching and waiting, biding his time. He only really came alive when he was talking about personal sacrifice.

Tommy was fascinated by radical Islam and jihad. He believed that the promise of virgins in heaven supposedly given to would-be suicide bombers was all just propaganda by Western media, a way of trying to discredit their steadfast purpose and strength of will. These people knew what they were doing. Their vision should be admired. They were dying for what they believed in. Christianity did not have that strength. Christ had displayed it but his followers had failed him. Christians had always fallen far short of the example that Christ had set them. It needed someone to come along and show the way. To make a statement. To stand side by side with his Muslim brothers.

Tommy often spoke about the values and commitment of the suicide bomber. Sometimes Varick decided to draw him out on the subject, but when he did the ex-soldier was reluctant to open up, and gradually Varick's concerns faded as other more pressing day-to-day matters arose from everyday life on Madoc Farm. Then came Owen's discovery of Tommy's notebook. Much of what it contained was indecipherable, just rambling notes and ideas and quotations from the Bible. But alongside his plans for the train driver's family and the occupants of the train, there was much mention of the river, which played such a part in his sick idea. One biblical quotation that appeared to refer to it had stuck in Varick's mind. It was Revelation 22:1. "And he shewed me a pure river of water of life, clear as crystal, proceeding out of the throne of God and of the Lamb." This was written out a number of times as though mention of the "pure river" in the scriptures seemed to offer Tommy some sort of divine confirmation that what he was doing was right.

Another train pulled into the station. Varick watched it over the top of his newspaper, dreading a solitary driver. But this one was different. The driver was a large man with a serious, worried expression. Standing next to him was a younger man, wiry and muscular, leaning forward and peering out onto the platform. Even before the light caught his face and confirmed it, Varick knew that it was Tommy Denning. He didn't like to think of him as Brother Thomas any more. He was no brother of his.

The train stopped and the automated voice started up once more: "Please allow the passengers to leave the train first. This is a Northern Line train to Mill Hill East." Varick had positioned himself in the middle of the platform so as to join the train well away from either end, which he knew from the plan would be occupied by Tommy and his team.

As Varick entered the carriage, he felt a strange sensation of destiny unfolding. This was how it was meant to be. He might have become a man of God but he still knew how to use a revolver. Especially the one he had tucked in his belt beneath his shirt. He had used it thousands of times during target practice and he knew all its little nuances. It pulled to the right slightly and he knew exactly how much he would need to aim left to compensate. The Smith & Wesson was the only possession that he had kept from the old days back in Louisiana, from before he was born again. Smuggling it into the UK was easy; he had dismantled it and hidden its individual components throughout his possessions in the packing crate in which they were shipped. He wasn't the only one who loved guns. Almost all the members of Cruor Christi had weapons. Some of them were more than just handguns. In the armory at Madoc Farm—where Father Owen insisted that all weapons were kept— there were semi-automatic assault rifles, most of which were now in Tommy's possession. There was even a small quantity of plastic explosive. One of Cruor Christi's members, "Big Bob" Wilcox, had been involved with ordnance and explosives in the army and had managed to "liberate" it—as he put it—from a depot where he worked. It did trouble Varick, all that firepower. But he concluded that among the members of his unique flock, paranoia often came with the territory, and if they felt safer with their weapons—and didn't use them irresponsibly—then so be it. He was hardly in a position to preach on the subject what with his own background and firm belief in the right to bear arms.

After finding Owen dead the night before, Varick had checked the armory and it was all but empty. What guns had not been taken had been rendered inoperable by having their firing pins removed. Tommy had obviously expected Varick to come after him. But Varick had his Smith & Wesson with him and it was all he would need. He knew that he could finish this when the time came. Just so long as he could get within range, Tommy Denning would be—as he might have described it in his former life when he wore the powder blue shirt of the New Orleans Police Department—a dead man walking.

8:54 AM

Northern Line Train 037, driver's cab

George had to do something, not just for his family and the hundreds of people on the train, but for himself. If he died and did nothing then his life was a waste. It wasn't as though he was a religious man. If pushed, he would have claimed agnosticism as his faith. Some people called that a cop-out. If you're going to deny God then at least have the guts to be an atheist; agnosticism is spineless, nothing more than sitting on the fence. It was usually the religious types that came out with stuff like that. Like a taunt. To George, agnosticism was the only rational reaction to religion: I don't know. I don't know because no one can know. Some things are unknowable. But it wasn't something that he had ever given much thought to. He and Maggie had been married in a church; the children were christened. If there was a God then they were covered. It was insurance. George thought it was like that for most people. What he did feel, however, was a sense of destiny, regardless of whether there was or wasn't a God, and he could feel that destiny now compelling him to act. He would have to try and stop these people. Never before had he felt so protective toward others, but never before had he felt so afraid that his own emotional frailty would let him down.

"Oh Jesus." He said it so softly under his breath it was inaudible. Blasphemy was a constant in his life. George was a hardened blasphemer. Bang his toe: Jesus Christ. Slam his finger in a door: fucking Jesus. And far lesser sources of grievance, everything from the sub-standard driving of his fellow road-users to the poor state of the weather he greeted with blasphemous profanity. Today was no exception. But today, during those moments when the emotion and fear became too much for him and he needed some form of release, he found his muttered blasphemies were altogether more pleading, as though attempting a dialogue with a God whose existence he doubted.

George was no stranger to panic. He was one of life's worriers. And often that worry manifested itself as panic. Usually it was late at night, when he woke up consumed with the fear that he was wasting his life. All his great heroes, all the writers and musicians who informed his outlook, were people who had a handle on existence, who knew who they wanted to be—or seemed to. He had considered therapy, but felt squeamish at the thought of opening up to a stranger. Besides, there were more important things to be spending his money on. More benefit might be derived from a few drinks and the odd joint here and there. At least then he could look at life and laugh at the absurdity of it all. At least then the panic would lift, or be reduced to a vague sense of unease. But even on those rare occasions when he did manage to attain a state approaching contentment, his mind would conjure up some image for him, some bold and incontrovertible fact about the state of humanity and the nature of the world that would cast him back into the gloom. Somewhere a child was being abused; somewhere an unspeakable act of cruelty was being committed and there was nothing anyone could do about it. The horror never went away.

A song was playing in George's mind, continually repeating on his psycho-jukebox. It was "London Calling" by the Clash. The band's front man, Joe Strummer, was one of his heroes, and when he was a boy he had been lucky enough to see him play live. Strummer was passionate and uncompromising, everything that George aspired to be and feared he wasn't.

George and his best friend, Dougie, another lifelong Clash fan, had a private expression between the two of them for when a situation appeared desperate: "What would Joe Strummer do?" It came to him now as "London Calling" repeated once again in his mind.

When Joe Strummer died, George and Dougie had met for a drink, and every so often during the evening they would break off their conversation to raise a glass to Joe. By closing time, they both had tears in their eyes.

What would Joe Strummer do? What would he do now? Driving a busy tube train into a tunnel with an armed hijacker in the cab with him. What would he do?

The only comfort that George could manage to derive from the situation was that this man he knew only as Pilgrim didn't look like an Islamic fundamentalist. He was white Caucasian for a start. That had to mean something. Didn't it? But any hope this shoddy racial profile might have offered was immediately snuffed out by his awareness of the dead body on the floor of the cab. Whatever else this man was, he was also a killer.

As he sat in the train cab moving through the warm air in the tunnel, George wavered between déjà vu and *jamais vu*—everything was strangely familiar one moment and terrifyingly new and hyper real the next. When he had pressed the buttons at Leicester Square to open the doors, it was as though he had never seen them before. He once dropped some acid when he was at college. Objects that he had looked at and handled a million times in his life felt new and vibrant. As now. But when he looked at the hijacker it was as though that face had loomed in his subconscious all of his life. It was like an ugly spirit made flesh.

When George had shut the doors at Leicester Square, checked the pilot light, and driven into the tunnel, the train was carrying a little over half its passenger capacity. Not far out of the station, George was told to "Slow down now." George did so. Now was not the time for heroics. He needed to choose his moment.

"Slower . . . slower . . ."

The train moved to walking speed. The man was alert, his turquoise eyes darting around as he looked into the tunnel up ahead. It was as though he was searching for something.

"Okay, now really slow. That's it, George, that's lovely. Now . . . stop."

George stopped the train but he kept the dead man's handle in the "coast" position out of habit.

George was told to, "Take your hand off the handle now."

"But it'll set off the alarm," said George.

"That's fine."

George let go of the handle and they both stared into the tunnel as the motor idled. The line controller came through on the radio: "Zero three seven, is there a problem? You appear to have stopped. Zero three seven? Hello? Is everything all right?"

What would Joe Strummer do?

Pilgrim looked at him and smiled. "Okay, George," he said, "this is the end of the line. This train terminates here."

8:56 AM

As soon as the train came to a halt in the tunnel between Leicester Square and Tottenham Court Road stations, Simeon knew that the first part of Tommy Denning's plan had been concluded successfully. It may have been a week early but everything else was to the letter. It was four minutes to nine by his watch. Tommy had said it would be nine when they reached the target—give or take a few minutes. In the passenger area on the other side of the rear cab door was the train driver's wife. The three of them—Tommy, Belle, and Simeon—had debated long and hard about whether to take her on the train or not. Belle had said she thought the woman might be a liability, but Tommy had said it was worth having her along in case the driver needed some mental support or further emotional arm-twisting and they could put her on the walkie-talkie and have her talk to him. Simeon had said that he would keep an eye on her, make sure that she didn't cause any trouble. He had already scared the hell out of her—if she did anything to raise the alarm, her kids would die. As far as the children themselves were concerned, they were all in agreement that they shouldn't be brought onto the train. It was rough on the train driver's wife but the trauma and fear engendered by her separation from them would mean that she would be thoroughly compliant. You only had to take one look at her to see that she was going to do whatever it took to see them again. You had to hand it to Tommy, it was a hell of a plan, twisted but brilliant. There was only one flaw in it and that was him, Simeon. If it wasn't for him, Tommy and Belle might have been able to get away with all this. But he was there to make sure they didn't. The children would be okay. He would have them out of there soon enough. First he had to let Tommy make his intentions known to the wider world. Once that was done, he could proceed as planned and all the hard work would be over. But despite all that he had had to endure in the past few weeks, there was one good thing to come out of it, and that was getting to meet Belle.

There she was sitting next to him in the rear cab of the train, so cute, so damaged. Despite the extreme, almost insane beliefs that Belle shared with her brother Tommy, Simeon couldn't help but feel attracted to her. Her lithe, supple body had a vibrant energy to it that was palpable. Even sitting here in the rear cab of the train, having come here to do what they had come here to do, he couldn't help but find her intensely arousing. This made his emotions all the more conflicted when he considered that, before the day was finished, he would have to kill her.

8:58 AM

Flat 21, Hyde Park Mansions, Pimlico

He clicked up his speed another kilometre per hour. This was the time that he liked most on the treadmill, about fifteen minutes in, when he was all warmed up and the blood was pumping; it felt as though the serotonin was being released. That sense of disappointment that he often felt on waking could only really be lifted by a run. He ran miles every day, here in the corner of his bedroom. It stimulated him on so many levels. It kept him fit, kept his weight down, provided him with "flow"—allowed him to think with more clarity than at any other time of the day. Some mornings were harder than others. It depended on what time he had gone to bed the night before, whether he'd had a glass of wine. Some mornings it just felt right and this morning it felt as good as ever. In a couple of hours, it would be too hot to run. Now, he could really fly.

When he had lived in Muswell Hill back in the old days, he used to run through Alexandra Park. His favorite section was along the front of Alexandra Palace with its views over London. He imagined himself back there now as his sneakers thumped out their mesmeric rhythm. And for a moment, it was as though he had achieved some sort of transcendence and could forget the truth. The sun was shining down on him from the north London sky. To his left was the huge, round stained glass window of Alexandra Palace; to his right London stretching away to the horizon.

Ed reached for the remote control for the stereo and clicked on the radio. It was tuned to a classical station. He used to fool himself that it was soothing. An admission that he needed to be soothed, however, didn't help and besides, he wasn't angry any more. Anger had given way to resignation just as all the psychologists said that it would. Acceptance would be next. He hadn't got there yet. Not by a long way.

The nine o'clock news. "This is Marsha Wilson." Ed often wondered what Marsha Wilson looked like. He listened to her every morning. He liked her voice; he liked the way she could switch from a serious tone, something she employed when telling you about an earthquake or a pedophile, to sounding smiley and upbeat at the end of the bulletin, when she was reporting a giant squash or someone building their own space rocket in their garage. There was nothing in the news. Nothing interesting. They used to call it the silly season. Everyone was on holiday. The news was canceled for a few weeks. Ed didn't wish ill on his fellow man but sometimes he yearned for a major incident somewhere, a story in which he could immerse himself. Not today though. All that was on offer today was the weather. It was going to be hot, possibly the hottest day of the year. And next up the first movement from Bach's Brandenburg Concerto no. 3 in G Major. Not one of his favorites so he brutalized it with the rhythm from his sneakers on the treadmill.

He wasn't exactly dressed for running—boxer shorts and sneakers—but no one could see him and it was hot. Twenty minutes previously he had thrown some cold water on his face in the bathroom and stepped straight onto the treadmill to warm up with a brisk walk that had developed into a jog and then this, not exactly a sprint but not far off. Running was an effective distraction. Waking up was always a reminder of what had happened just over thirteen and a half years ago. The events of that day might be receding into the past, but they were still as painful as if they had taken place yesterday.

Due to a media blackout, the Hanway Street siege never made the news. But the fact that what happened went unreported did nothing to lessen the torture of its memory.

Conor Joyce was spoken of as something of a legend among Ed Mallory's Special Branch colleagues. An explosives expert, he was thought to have constructed and deployed a number of devices as part of the IRA bombing campaign. During the late nineties, however, he had found that his services were no longer in demand. What's more, he had met and fallen in love with a Protestant woman and renounced his fierce Catholicism and accompanying republicanism in order to be with her and subsequently marry her. This fundamental change in his life had meant that when the British secret service came knocking, he turned. MI5 was interested in his knowledge of potential arms caches as they tried to ensure that the IRA complied with the decommissioning terms of the Good Friday Agreement. Yet despite Conor Joyce's apparent readiness to provide certain limited pieces of information, he was considered slippery and his service handlers were never convinced that his cooperation was not a meticulously constructed false front and that they were the ones being handled rather than the other way around. Nonetheless, some of his intelligence had proved valuable and he was shrewd enough to drip-feed it gradually, thus prolonging his time on the payroll.

As part of the deal that Joyce struck with the service, he was provided with a flat in Kensal Rise in northwest London complete with a panic alarm, in case his cover was blown and a former colleague from the Provisionals came looking for him.

It was Boxing Day morning when the panic alarm was activated. A Special Branch counterterrorism unit was dispatched to Hanway Street but when they approached the address and tried to enter the building, shots were fired at them and they were forced to withdraw. The entire street was evacuated and sealed off.

It was only Ed's second official assignment as a hostage negotiator. The first assignment had involved an elderly husband armed with a cricket bat barricading himself and his much younger wife in their home. The man was convinced that his wife was having an affair with a neighbor, but Ed soon realized that he was dealing with someone suffering from mental health problems when it became apparent that the neighbor in question had been dead for a good ten years. After a few minutes of gentle coaxing, the old man put down the cricket bat and the crisis was resolved. Hardly a tough gig, so as soon as he heard the details of the incident in Hanway Street that Boxing Day morning, Ed knew that his training and aptitude would be tested for the first time.

Due to the sensitive nature of the situation, Ed was only one of a larger team made up of Scotland Yard negotiators and MI5 counterterrorist personnel. But he arrived on site first and quickly took up position in the hastily established command center in a flat above a row of shops directly opposite Conor Joyce's no-longer-safe safe house. It was apparent that Joyce's cover had indeed been blown and he was being held hostage by an IRA hit man who had come to kill him.

Whether or not the hit man had succumbed to an attack of conscience when he found the target of his hit with a heavily pregnant wife was never established, but the subject—as he had now become in the language of crisis intervention—was using his hostages as bargaining collateral. If he was granted safe passage with them, he would allow them to go free once he was at his chosen destination. If not, they would both die. He had a hand grenade from which he had removed the pin and he made it known that if a marksman were to try and take him out then everyone would wind up dead.

There was no way the British government would allow the escape of a known IRA hit man from the scene of a hostage-taking, so Ed settled in for a long negotiation. The subject, however, wanted to play things differently. He was impatient to talk. Ed was nervous but also excited. He would play it by the book, maintain an ongoing dialogue, calm the subject, establish trust, and gather information through active listening, all skills he had acquired through his extensive training.

But the subject was like no other hostage taker that Ed had ever come across in the case studies. He was a hardened Provo who would stop at nothing for what he believed in, and what he believed in, caged in that small flat in northwest London, was his need to escape.

"My name is Ed Mallory, I'm a negotiator and I would like to help." Name, role, and intention—a standard opening gambit once telephone contact has been established with a subject.

The heavily Irish-accented voice on the other end of the line came through loud and clear.

"Fuck off, you stuck-up cocksucker, don't give me any of your psychology shit."

And from that moment on Ed knew it would be a tough negotiation, one that would require all his guile and ingenuity to resolve. It was unlikely this subject would respond to the standard crisis-intervention techniques. The man was working from a totally different set of moral values to those subjects Ed had studied up until then. But Ed was young—not yet thirty—and he was confident that he could get through to him. He was ambitious and he wanted to show his colleagues and superiors that he had what it took.

Ed tried to find out the subject's name but got nothing but obscenities. He tried to calm the subject down by telling him that he felt uncomfortable with his use of profanity. Bollocks, fuck you— more profanity. Whatever he said, he could not get through to him. The guy was completely unreadable and his behavior followed no accepted pattern. He went from anger and frustration to a calm psychological detachment with no apparent transition. Ed had never come across anything like it. He was one of those rare subjects that an FBI crisis-intervention trainer had told him and his fellow students about in a seminar once: someone completely impervious to all negotiation methods. Freud had said of the Irish, "This is one race of people for whom psychoanalysis is of no use whatsoever." Maybe the same applied to them in hostage negotiation.

The subject issued a demand and a deadline. Unless he had a call from Ed by four o'clock to say there was a car to take him and his hostages to a light aircraft, which would deliver them to an unspecified location in the Irish Republic, he would let off the hand grenade.

Ed knew all about deadlines. They held a central place within the study of hostage negotiation. He also knew that there was no way the subject was going to be allowed to go free. Ed was sure the subject knew it too. So he decided it was a choice between two distinct paths of conduct: he could either stall him, tell him that four o'clock was unrealistic and he would need more time, or he could try and gain the subject's respect by acknowledging that his demand was never going to be met and try to resolve the situation in a spirit of brutal honesty. He opted for the latter, told the subject straight. There was no way the authorities would let him go free.

"You've got until four," came back the reply and the line went dead. Ed told his superiors and the other members of the team who were now in situ that he thought the best thing to do would be to call back the subject a little before four to negotiate a new deadline just as the existing deadline was expiring. An effective tactic that he had learned in his training. Everyone agreed.

Ed was nervous as he picked up the receiver at five to four and dialed the number. He looked across to the first-floor window of Conor Joyce's flat only thirty feet away. The narrow street was deserted. All the properties were empty, apart from the snipers staring through telescopic sights at the same single window as Ed.

He could just make out the sound of the telephone ringing in the flat across the street. The call was answered and Ed started talking.

"What you're asking for is proving very difficult. I'm doing my best but you're going to have to give me more time." Ed had prepared himself for objections but the response from the subject was surprising: "Okay, mate, that's fine. At least we know where we stand." He sounded calm, almost cheerful. For a moment Ed felt a surge of confidence before he realized he was being reassured by the subject for no tangible reason, a characteristic often displayed by potential suicides when they have finally decided to kill themselves. Ed knew he had to act fast, had to establish a new line of negotiation. But he didn't get the chance. It was discovered subsequently that the subject had spent fifteen years in the Maze Prison. He wasn't going back. The sound of the explosion relayed into Ed's ear through the telephone headset gave him tinnitus for two weeks.

It wasn't his ears, however, that were the problem. He hadn't even considered the potential force of the blast. All that separated him from the exploding hand grenade were two panes of glass and one of those panes was only inches from his face. His face would be scarred for life, but as with his ears, that was a small price to pay compared to the blast's primary damage: glass fragments were embedded in the orbital tissue of both eyes. His left eye had a prolapsed iris; both eyes suffered multiple perforations of the cornea. The facial lacerations healed. People told him that the scarring wasn't too bad, which meant that it probably was. He would never know. According to the doctors who ran the tests, his left eye retained about thirty percent light sensitivity. He could see shadows but little else. The trauma his right eye suffered was such that for a couple of days after the injury, it was felt that it would have to undergo enucleation— complete removal. As it turned out, it ended up staying where it was, although it was totally redundant.

The grenade explosion killed the subject and Conor Joyce's wife and unborn child. Conor Joyce survived the blast but with multiple injuries. He was conscious—in great pain but still lucid—when they brought him out of the building.

Conor Joyce kept shouting, "You fucking let her die!" over and over again as he was loaded into the ambulance next to the one in which the paramedics worked on Ed. And in a way, he was right. Maybe Ed had let her die. For a long time afterward he blamed himself for what happened. Joyce's wife was the first person he would ever lose during a negotiation. There were others after her, both hostages and subjects. During his career, he had been involved in over forty-five crisis situations throughout the world, from the United States to the Middle East. Forty-three of those had been as a blind man. By the law of averages, he was bound to lose a few and he had learned to accept that sometimes, ultimately, you cannot take responsibility for someone else's behavior. People do what they want to do and even if you are armed with an acutely intuitive understanding of how individuals react to crises, sometimes you are unable to stop them.

For the most part, when subjects and hostages had died on his watch, Ed had dealt with it in his own way. Even when he had spent hours and sometimes even days in intense negotiation and really felt that he was getting somewhere with a subject and they had gone on to kill themselves or others, even then he had been able to assimilate it. But not so Conor Joyce's wife, and it was to her that his thoughts always turned, her death coinciding with the exact moment when he lost his sight. She was the only one he felt he had let down, just as he had let himself down in the process. He had been too cocky and self-assured, too keen to impress his superiors. If he had intervened with the subject earlier, if he had stalled more effectively, if he had encouraged the subject to open up more. If if if. Conor Joyce's wife haunted him every day of his life. It was as though he had been imprisoned on the day she died. Over and over, he was told he would finally come to terms with his sightless existence. Thirteen years now and he was nowhere nearer to accepting it. Maybe if he could then he could get on with his life.

After an initial desire to pension him off, the force had been good to him, realizing that his ability to listen and intuit potential behavior patterns in hostage takers' voices was enhanced by his blindness. His stock as a hostage negotiator had certainly risen after he was blinded, although at his most cynical and self-loathing he suspected he was only there to ensure that Scotland Yard achieved its disability quota. That was unfair, although he knew he wasn't being paranoid when he detected a sense among his colleagues that he was in some way to blame for what had happened to him. During the negotiation, his active listening was not what it should have been. He should have discerned more in the subject's voice, should have encouraged more dialogue. So, despite his injuries, it was not as a hero that he returned to work and he couldn't help but feel as though he had been kicked upstairs. His rank sounded fairly grand—detective chief inspector—but most of the time, it was nothing-work. Government liaison. Bullshit. His hostage-negotiation work had developed into something of an obsession but it was an obsession that found little release. There were only so many situations with oil company executives being kidnapped and held for ransom in Nigeria that he could advise on; only so many distraught Fathers 4 Justice to be talked down from on high. To save the lives of innocent people caught up in impossible situations was what he lived for. But as more and more people took the training and became involved in the world of hostage and crisis negotiation, he felt as though he was being squeezed out, marginalized. His special talents, his ability to listen and hear things that others might miss, didn't seem to count for as much any more. Months could go by and his only involvement in negotiation would be some lecturing and the odd seminar. Perhaps now it was time for a career change? Although job prospects probably weren't that great for a forty something blind policeman.

Ed clicked up his speed another kilometer per hour on the treadmill and sprinted through the park. The sun shone down on him from a clear blue sky. It felt good. London looked so beautiful today.

8:59 AM

Northern Line Train 037, driver's cab

George glanced at Pilgrim, who stood and stared into the tunnel, deep in thought. The Line Controller's voice came through on the intercom once again: "Zero three seven, please confirm your situation."

"Can you turn him off?" asked Pilgrim.

George was thankful for something to do even if it was something as basic as turning down the volume button on the intercom console.

"That's better, couldn't hear myself think. Oh, and you can turn on the light too."

George flicked off the radio and clicked on the light in the cab. There was no way of reading this guy. He spoke with the generosity of a genial host who wants to make sure that his guest is happy and at ease. But George was very far from at ease. As the seconds ticked by, he felt his claustrophobia intensify.

George knew exactly where it came from. For many claustrophobics, the phobia's trigger is a traumatic experience relating to a confined space, like being trapped in a lift perhaps. For him, on the other hand, it was reading a short story when he was eleven years old. It was in a book he had borrowed from the school library, a collection of short stories by Edgar Allan Poe. To his young mind the stories seemed very old-fashioned, with a dense, almost impenetrable prose style that had to be deciphered rather than read. He was just about to give up on the book and exchange it for something else when he came across a story called "The Premature Burial." As he waded into the arcane narrative, he felt an acute discomfort. To be buried alive and to know with every desperate futile scrape at the wooden coffin lid that there was no escape was a concept that haunted him. He couldn't get it out of his head. The more he tried not to think about it, the more it invaded his mind. And it was from this that his claustrophobia sprang. But, like all phobias, his didn't follow a pattern. He would be fine in an enclosed space so long as he was moving—hence his ability to drive a tube train—but as soon as he was rendered stationary, the sick feelings, the dry mouth, the sweating, and the breathlessness would descend on him. Only renewed movement or escape from the enclosed space would save him from a panic attack, the strength of which he had no way of gauging, having always managed to avoid prolonged exposure to the requisite stimuli in the past.

When trawling for possible cures for his condition on the Internet, he had found a website that suggested that one of the best ways of counteracting the effects of claustrophobia was nothing more than a type of positive mental thought. It stated that the claustrophobic does not fear the situation itself but the negative consequences of being in that situation. It suggested that a form of self-hypnosis that would infuse the consciousness with comforting "neutral" imagery might be of benefit, along with a repetitive mental refrain that "Everything will be okay." And when he had tried this method, when held at a particularly long red light in a tunnel, it had worked. To a degree. But this potential cure was not available to George now. At his feet—although he had managed to avoid looking—he knew there was a man with his brains leaking out all over the floor of the cab. He could smell the blood. Everything was most definitely not going to be okay. Not today.

Such was the heat, it was difficult to work out whether he was sweating more than usual, but he could feel his heart pounding in his chest and his mouth felt leathery and dry. Worse still, was the breathlessness. This was what always brought on the worst feelings.

"I'm a claustrophobic." He said it without thinking. And as he said it, he knew that it was probably the first time that he had ever articulated the truth so bluntly. Maggie knew that his working environment sometimes made him feel uncomfortable but they hadn't spoken about it for some time because he knew that, under normal circumstances, he could control it. But these were not normal circumstances and something in his subconscious had forced him to speak.

Pilgrim turned to look at him and smiled. "You're joking."

"No, I wish I was."

"You never told me that on the message boards."

"I never told you a lot of things."

"Plenty of things you did tell me though, George."

George winced at the thought of the incontinence of information that Pilgrim had managed to elicit from him. This intense young man had flattered him, massaged his ego, and he had responded. George could remember almost word for word what he had said about how he would do anything for his kids. Pilgrim had intimated that he had had a troubled upbringing. This had made the e-mail exchange become all the more personal. George had enjoyed the role of the comforting older brother. And now this. George had been played.

"So, you're a tube driver who suffers from claustrophobia?"

"Yeah, I'm fine so long as the train's moving." The words came out quickly, breathlessly. "I can cope for a few minutes but anything more and I . . ." And just as suddenly as the words had flowed, they dried up again. The fact was he didn't know what would happen after a few minutes. He was in unknown territory.

"The thing is we're not going anywhere." Pilgrim said it as though he felt genuinely sorry about it.

"Oh God."

"That's just the way it is, I'm afraid."

There was no point trying to act normally. It was impossible. George could feel his heart rate rise; the sweat was pouring off him now and he felt various parts of his lower body, his thighs and his buttocks, succumb to a chill tremble. But it was his breathing that was the biggest problem. There wasn't enough oxygen to sustain his hungry lungs.

"Deep breaths," said Pilgrim and, stepping over the body of the trainee driver, he took hold of George's hands and held them in his. His hands felt rough. The complexion of the palms belonged to a man who was no stranger to manual labor. He stared into George's eyes, unblinking.

"In," and he took a deep breath and indicated for George to do likewise. "And out," and he blew out the air and George tried to copy him. For the first few breaths, George felt no better but, as he surrendered to the slow deliberate rhythm, he felt himself calm down. The fear remained but the panic subsided. There was something about the man's demeanor, as though he genuinely had George's best interests at heart. More than that, it felt as though there was some sort of affection in his actions. It gave George hope and this helped calm him even further. This man genuinely wanted to help him, to ensure that he was okay. That he did so because he had a purpose for George was a good sign because if he had a purpose for him then he was not expendable. He would stay alive. And that was all that mattered, that and the fact that his family stayed alive too.

They breathed together for a couple of minutes.

"You're going to be all right, George. Everything's going to be fine. I'm not going to do anything horrible to you. Quite the opposite in fact. So don't despair, don't be afraid. All you've got to do is keep breathing slowly and deliberately and keep happy. This is going to be a big day. Not just for you and me and everybody on this train but for the peoples of the world, who will see it as a sign. Just put your faith in Christ and all will be well."

George shrugged and exhaled, shaking his head.

"Don't tell me you don't believe."

"Believe in what?"

"Who. Believe in who."

"I don't know what you mean."

"Jesus Christ. Who else?"

"No, I don't believe. Is that what this is all about, religion?" George turned and looked the man in the eyes. They didn't look like the eyes of a terrorist. Not that George had ever looked a terrorist in the eyes to know. But there was something kindly and benevolent about the way Pilgrim looked at him. It was as though he felt pity for George—and more so now that he knew that George was a non-believer.

"You must believe in something, George."

"I believe in nature, evolution, science. I don't believe in the supernatural."

The man was nodding at him; the smile had given way to a thoughtful expression.

In the past, George's lack of belief had provided him with comfort. No cosmic disappointments for him. No self-delusion. There was no God. He knew it; he had always known it. So what was that part of his psyche, that part of his human makeup that now made him reach out to a God in which he did not believe? Where did the compulsion come from? Was it born of desperation? Some sort of psychological clutching-at-straws? Whatever the reason, he couldn't help himself from pleading for someone, for something, anything, to save him.

"You don't feel claustrophobic any more, do you?"

The question caught him off guard.

"Not as much, no."

"You might not believe in God, you might never have believed in him, but hear me when I say that, before today is over, you will."

George wanted to say, "Never." He nearly did. But something stopped him. He knew it would sound childish, petulant. There was no point in antagonizing this man.

"The thing is, George," Pilgrim continued, "we're going to start a revolution today. Just you wait and see. And when you see the beauty and the truth of what we're going to do—you and I—then you'll be a sinner no more and God's love will fill your heart, now and for always."

9:16 AM

Northern Line Train 037, sixth carriage

Seated at the end of the carriage, up against the door to the bulkhead separating the passenger area from the rear cab, Maggie Wakeham sat on her hands and stared at the floor. The sick feeling wouldn't lift. It was like a constantly peaking wave. Maggie felt as though part of her had been amputated with no anesthetic and no concern for her well-being and ultimate survival. Her children were gone, her little ones taken. It was more than an amputation, it was as though the very core of her being had been ripped out and burned in front of her. She hadn't eaten anything before they came. So there was nothing to throw up, not that she felt she could have retched even if she had wanted to; her teeth were clamped together so tightly, it made her jaw ache.

They were going to Mr. Pieces the night after. It was Ben's birthday treat. He'd be six. Six years before, she had been in labor. She was in labor for a day and a half. It was horrendous. That's what she told people when asked to describe the experience. But it had all been worth it. Ben was a beautiful baby boy, and life for her and George was never the same again. Neither was their relationship. It wasn't necessarily worse—if a marriage can ever be judged on a scale with good at one end and bad at the other—but it was different. More fraught. Less affectionate somehow. She wished that sometimes he'd just take control, just take her in his arms and let passion take over. But maybe he didn't feel any passion. Maybe it had gone. She hoped not. She still loved him.

They had gone to Mr. Pieces the year before for Ben's fifth birthday. It was just an ordinary Italian restaurant but it was nice, it was cozy, run by a family. When the waiters—four Italian brothers—wanted to commence the ceremonial singing of "Happy Birthday," they threw their metal serving trays on the floor, which made a noise like a cartoon thunder clap. Crayons were provided in a little tin bucket in the middle of each table and diners were encouraged to scribble and doodle on the paper tablecloths. The best tablecloth was chosen at the end of each week by the waiters, scraped clean of any surplus food and mounted on the wall.

There was a group of schoolgirls further down the car. They were about seven years old—a little older than Ben—and wore pink dresses and straw hats. Their teachers were doing their best to be reassuring. Seated in their midst was a blind man in a linen suit. A couple of the girls stroked his guide dog. Opposite Maggie was a woman with black hair and black sunglasses. Her casual attire was expensive, fashionable—and all black. Her skin was pale and the only color on her was a slash of red lipstick. She was nervous, kept taking deep breaths and exhaling very precisely through her lips as though it was some sort of breathing exercise. Maggie knew she was a New Yorker. When the train had started out above ground at Morden station, she had spoken into her phone to tell someone that she was running late for a meeting. For a moment, Maggie had considered wrenching the phone from her and telling whoever was on the other end of the line that she was hijacked on a tube train on its way into central London. She didn't do it of course. All she could think about was her children. She wouldn't do anything that might expose them to harm.

Next to the slim New Yorker was a man of fifty or so in slacks and a sports jacket. Although contriving to make it look as though he might have been on his way to the golf club, the briefcase and trade magazine spread out on his lap gave away his office destination. Clearly troubled by the long delay in the tunnel, he dabbed at the sweat that trickled down his forehead with a white handkerchief. He looked around at the other people in the carriage. It was as though he was trying to catch someone's eye. The passengers had remained silent up until now but, as the delay lengthened, people's nerves got the better of them and the man in the sports jacket was the first to speak.

"How long's it been?"

The question hung in the intense heat of the carriage. Next to Maggie was a large West Indian man wearing a business suit, his short dreads immaculately disheveled. He looked up at the man in the sports jacket and said, "About fifteen minutes."

"Oh Jesus," came the reply. Maggie could tell that his anxiety was clearly being exacerbated by some underlying condition—claustrophobia perhaps. Now that he'd spoken, he needed to speak some more.

"Maybe we should do something."

"Like what?" said the New Yorker.

"Oh, I don't fucking know." His angst made him raise his voice more than he had intended. "I'm sorry." He looked around nervously as social embarrassment was now added to his anxiety. The New Yorker returned to her breathing exercise and the sports jacket closed his eyes and rested his head back against the window behind him. But he misjudged the distance and the back of his head thumped against the glass. He didn't acknowledge the pain. When he reopened his eyes a few moments later, he looked at Maggie and she looked away.

The children loved Mr. Pieces. When they'd been there last year on Ben's fifth birthday, everything had conspired to make it happy and memorable. The children were excited and she had watched their little faces and enjoyed their attempts to order their food from the waiter. Even George, who had become less talkative of late, especially when called upon to shell out for a meal for the four of them that they could ill afford, had opened up and been at his most amusing and charming, playing games with the children and making them laugh. She had watched him and been reminded of the time they went out to dinner together on their first date. That was an Italian restaurant too. They were both nervous and had drunk far too much. Two bottles of wine and a couple of Irish whiskeys each. But George had been a gentleman and put Maggie in a cab back to her flat in West Kensington, where she was living with some old friends from university. He had called the next morning to ask how she was and ask her if she'd like to meet up again in a few days' time. She was relieved, having spent an agonizing morning, worrying about having drunk too much the night before and whether she had made a fool of herself. Of course she wanted to meet up again. When you know, you know. And after that first night out with George, she knew.

She laughed at his jokes. She liked the way that he didn't take himself too seriously. He wasn't one of those pushy types that poison London with their ambition and their avarice. He wanted to do something artistic—make a success of his band or maybe write a book—and she respected him for that.

However much their relationship might have changed in the past few years, she still loved him. She just wished she could love him more, wished that they could both love each other more. George's problem was that he didn't much like himself at the moment. He felt guilty for not bringing in enough money. He felt as though life was passing him by and his dreams of artistic expression had come to nothing. It was during the aftermath of their last row, one of those moments when the truth comes tumbling out, that he had told her about his lack of fulfillment and unhappiness. His day job on the tube—while presenting him with plenty of time for dreaming his dreams—also gave him plenty of time to examine what it was that he was doing with his life. She wished he could feel more self-respect. That would make everyone's life in the Wakeham household that much easier.

Though he'd been nervous and frightened, the man in the sports jacket had broken the ice and social barriers started to come down. Conversations started up and down the carriage interspersed with the hollow clatter of forced laughter. Maggie kept her head down. She didn't want any form of social contact. She feared that if she so much as caught someone's eye her facade would crack and she would tell them everything, starting with the fact that on the other side of the door to the rear cab of the train were two terrorists, hijackers, kidnappers, whatever they were, and they were armed and dangerous. But she couldn't risk it. Whoever these people were—whatever they wanted—their plan with regard to her and George was brilliantly simple, based as it was on their natural parental obsession that nothing bad should befall their children. George, as a tube train driver, was obviously integral to the project's success. They needed him alive and willing to take orders and it was therefore imperative that it appeared as though Sophie and Ben were cowering somewhere with guns against their heads.

Not knowing her children's whereabouts was the cruelest torture she had ever known. Sitting there on the train, surrounded by people who might be able to help save her children, but also, in the worst-case scenario, unwittingly cause their deaths, was just an extra little horror. She glanced up at the peephole in the door to the cab. It looked like it had some sort of fisheye lens in it like those in the front doors of houses or apartments, so that even though she was sitting below it and to one side she would still be visible. For all she knew, she was being watched at that very moment.

Before they had boarded the train, she had been told by the younger of the two men, the one with the shaven head, that Sophie and Ben—he had even known their names—would be fine just so long as she did nothing to communicate to other passengers.

Her mind scrambled around trying to find something solid, something safe and reassuring to cling to. She closed her eyes. She was sitting with George, Sophie, and Ben in the corner of Mr. Pieces almost exactly a year before and the jolly waiters were throwing their metal trays on the floor. It was time. She watched Ben. He had been looking forward to his birthday for months and he could barely contain his excitement. Sophie giggled, a string of mozzarella hanging from the corner of her mouth that Maggie pinched away. As the clanging of the metal trays against the stone floor receded, they began to sing:

Happy birthday to you . . .

Sophie and Ben could barely articulate the words, their grins were so wide. Other diners in the restaurant joined in . . .

Happy birthday to you . . .

Maggie looked up into George's face and he was staring back at her, smiling, affectionate, his eyes sparkling. He reached across the table and took her hand in his. This was happiness. This was safety.

Happy birthday dear Be-en . . .

They were in there, behind that door, they'd taken her children, they'd defiled her family. Her hands on which she sat were sweating into the seat. She wanted to scream. She wanted to claw at her face with her nails, slam bloody hands against the door, she wanted to lose control.

Happy birthday to you!

Sophie and Ben were shrieking with delight as one of the smiling waiters approached their table with a birthday cake. The lights were dimmed and Ben blew out the candles.

"Make a wish!" Ben screwed his eyes up and thought hard.

George squeezed Maggie's hand and smiled.

Make a wish.

When George made an announcement over the PA once again, as he had a few times over the past hour, to reassure the passengers that everything possible was being done to move the train either forward or backward and "we'll have you out of here as soon as possible," she could hear the emotion in his voice.

His claustrophobia would be really bad by now. He would be close to cracking up and then what would happen? If the man with the shaven head was in the cab with him alone there might be a struggle. George was a little out of shape, probably didn't get enough exercise, but he was strong. If it was just the two of them in the cab together and no further accomplices had joined them, then he might be able to overpower the kidnapper. It was a possibility. It was something.

George's voice cracked when he said, "I'll keep you up to date with any information as and when I receive it."

Could the other passengers not hear that he was being forced to lie? She tore her gaze away from the floor of the carriage and looked around at the people. She was shocked by their expressions of willing acceptance. They were buying it. All except the man in the sports jacket. Why couldn't more of them be like him? People wanted to believe they were held in a tunnel because of a security incident at Tottenham Court Road station, as George kept telling them. To them it was the truth; to her it was a sick joke.

She wiped away a tear that made its way down her cheek but no one noticed. All eyes were on the man in the sports jacket as his panic got the better of him.

"It just doesn't make any sense at all. There's something wrong."

"Calm down," said the black man in the sharp suit sitting next to her. "I'm sure they're doing all they can."

"Don't tell me to calm down." It was loud enough that even the little girls stroking the guide dog were distracted.

The man in the sports jacket looked around at the faces turned toward him. He took a deep breath and retook his seat. "It's just so bloody hot," he said. "And there's no reason for keeping us locked up like this. They could just turn off the power to the track, open the doors at the back or the front and let us walk between the rails to the next station. That's what they should be doing. It's just appalling customer service, as always."

"There's nothing we can do about it," said the woman from New York, taking time out from her breathing exercises. "I'm sure we can all write letters of complaint as soon as we get out of here."

The sports jacket looked around at her, went to say something, but thought better of it and shook his head as he emitted a series of exaggerated sighs.

From the other side of the door against which she sat, came the faint sound of static from a walkie-talkie radio. Maggie could hear muttered voices but nothing she could actually decipher. She was the only one remaining in the carriage who had actually seen them enter the cab at Morden station. Before they went in, the male one had leaned toward her to whisper in her ear, close enough that she could feel the stubble on his chin scrape against her cheek. To someone who was watching—and no one was—it might have seemed like he was telling her a joke or even sharing an intimacy. But there was nothing loving about what he said.

"I'm just going through that door there. If you do anything to draw attention to me or try to raise the alarm in any way, you will never see your children again. Got it?"

She wanted to be in Mr. Pieces with her family. She wanted to hear the laughter as Ben blew out the candles on his birthday cake. She wanted George to be squeezing her hand and smiling—just as he had squeezed her hand and smiled at her on that first date.

They had come in through the back door just as George was walking out of the front. They must have had the house under surveillance. It was the young female one who frightened her the most. With her pretty gamine looks and pixie bob haircut, she looked so normal, in every way except the eyes. They looked as though they were emotionally switched off and she contemplated Maggie with all the humanity of a wolf.

The man with the crew cut was quiet, calm even. It was like he had done this before and he was clearly the one in charge.

When they first appeared through the back door she almost soiled herself. The door was open in a moment and there they were, guns pointed, telling her that so long as she cooperated with them in every detail they would let her live. It was something George used to say—I nearly shat myself—he would say. He was joking, talking about some horror film he had seen perhaps. But she really did think she might do so—or urinate at least. It was as though all her muscles had relaxed, slipped into a catatonia born of fear.

She used all her powers of persuasion to try and reassure Sophie and Ben that everything would be all right. But she could see it in their eyes. Their mum was telling them everything was okay but something else, something instinctive, was telling them it wasn't.

George had told her he loved her when he was on his way to the depot earlier. Her kidnappers had heard it on the speakerphone. The female one had smiled when he said it. A smile of derision. The man with the crew cut had told her to tell George to be quiet and continue with his normal routine.

Never in all the years that she had been with George had she wanted to see him as much as she did now. She wanted to see him and she wanted to tell him that she loved him too.

9:18 AM

Flat 21, Hyde Park Mansions, Pimlico

It wasn't only his sense of hearing that had improved after he lost his sight. His sense of smell was, if anything, even keener than his enhanced auditory perception. He'd never been a big one for aftershave, either on him or on others—the same went for perfume. The soap he used and the deodorant he wore were both unscented. The moisturizing cream that he applied to his face every morning to prevent the scar tissue from becoming dry and flaky was only very slightly perfumed—jojoba, aloe vera, or some such—and he liked the smell. He might have been known as "the blind guy with the fucked-up face"—a description of himself that he had overheard once—but he insisted on his personal grooming being the match of any sighted colleague. He always wore black; color no longer played a part in his life. A woman who he had almost become romantically involved with a couple of years before had asked whether he wore black out of mourning for his sight. He could tell from the tone of her voice and the way she said it that she had given this question much thought, believed that she was providing some psychological insight by asking it. Their nascent relationship ended soon afterward.

Romance didn't play much part in his life. There had been a couple of women since he was blinded; the one who had made the comment about his black clothes was one of them. A drawback to being more sensitive to people's tones of voice was that he could tune in more clearly to latent emotion, like sympathy. There were some women—men too—who were drawn to people who had disabilities, who were damaged in some way. The last thing he wanted was that someone should be attracted to him, even partially, because he was the blind guy with the fucked-up face. He was overly sensitive to it, possibly unfairly so at times, but he couldn't help himself; as soon as he felt, or even suspected, that someone was with him because they felt sorry for him, any potential there might be for an ongoing relationship was shot down in flames. That oversensitivity meant that he was probably doomed to being single. But, on balance, he could live with that. It was probably something to do with his lifelong bloody-mindedness but he liked to prove his independence, liked proving that the loss of his sight had not compromised the quality of his life, liked proving to himself and others that he could cope.

Ed planned on spending the next half hour answering e-mails via his speech reading and recognition software on his PC. He sometimes got more done in a half hour at home than during an entire morning at work. His car was booked for ten. Not for him, the white stick or the guide dog, the awkward accident-prone navigation of pavements and steps; not for him the reliance on the kindness of strangers to take his arm and help him across the road. It was stubbornness and pride that prevented him from doing what other blind people did—and it curtailed his personal freedom, no doubt about it—but that was how he wanted it to be and because of his job a car was provided for him on all official business.

As Ed finished applying the moisturizer cream to his face at the bathroom sink, his phone let out a soft beep, denoting an incoming call. He walked through to the bedroom and answered it.

"Ed Mallory."

"Ed, this is Serina Boise."

As soon as he heard the name and heard that unmistakably posh voice, with the hint of West Midlands accent so often imitated by his Special Branch colleagues, he knew there was work to be done. If it was an admin issue then an assistant would have called him. The fact that Commander Boise was calling him direct meant that, whatever was going on, things were moving fast.

"Hi, what can I do for you?"

"We've got a situation in the Underground; we don't really know anything at this stage—it might be nothing—but there's a train in a tunnel and it won't respond to any radio contact. I'm putting together a team just in case. I'd like you down at the incident desk at the LU Network Control center in St. James's."

She spoke quickly—she was nervous—and the "it might be nothing" was a clear tell. She didn't for one moment think that it might be nothing. As far as she was concerned—according to the intelligence she had—it was very definitely something.

"Okay, no problem," said Ed.

"There's a car on its way to you with Mark Hooper in it from G Branch at MI5. We're going to be collaborating on this."

There was the faintest hint of derision in her voice when she mentioned G Branch at MI5. It was not uncommon—he had come across it before, particularly in Special Branch. There was bound to be friction between two agencies so closely linked in terms of their common goals in counterterrorism, and yet so far apart in their approach.

"Hooper is heading up any potential negotiation at this stage, but I want you very closely involved."

"Okay."

"DI Calvert and DS White are also on the team. They'll meet you at St. James's."

Serina Boise told Ed that they would "speak soon" and rang off. Ed pushed the phone into the top pocket of his shirt and, realizing that he still had some stray spots of moisturizer between his fingers, rubbed his hands as he went across to the dresser, opened a drawer, and took out a pair of his favorite Ray-Bans. Sunglasses were his one concession to vanity. He kept his eyes closed most of the time—not much point in opening them—but when he did, he didn't want the sightless lumps of jelly in his eye sockets to be on display to the world.

When the intercom buzzed, Ed answered it and heard the voice of an ex–public schoolboy who introduced himself as Mark Hooper. Ed went down in the lift and came face to face with the man who would be his partner in any potential hostage negotiation.

"Hi, Ed, good to meet you."

"And you."

They shook hands. Ed thought Hooper was probably about thirty-five. His hand was manicured and smooth and his handshake was firm enough to suggest that he was somewhat physically insecure. Ed was just under six feet and it didn't sound as though Hooper was speaking from a lower trajectory so maybe it wasn't his height that he felt sensitive about. It could be anything, from facial appearance to an undersize penis but Ed was certain there was something. And he wore too much aftershave. It smelled soapy and alcoholic.

Hooper cupped Ed's elbow in his hand and led him across the street to the waiting car, which mercifully was chilled enough to dry up the perspiration that he could feel forming on his body after the short walk from the door of his apartment block. Once seated in the back of the car, a Jaguar judging by the smell of it and the sound of the engine, Ed said, "So, Mark, what's the latest on this train?"

"Well, it might be nothing."

"That's what Commander Boise said."

"What we've got is a tube train on the Northern Line between Leicester Square and Tottenham Court Road. It's stationary in the tunnel. London Underground is spooked because not only is the driver refusing to communicate but it would appear that he has tampered with the onboard computer so they can't even check from the control room if there are any technical faults with the train."

Ed couldn't resist needling Hooper with his next question: "So how come MI5 appears to have operational control of what appears on the surface to be a fairly minor incident?"

"There's been some chatter for a while about a possible attack on the tube. We've been monitoring it closely after last time." Hooper paused, tongue-tied by indecision about how much he should divulge.

Ed couldn't pinpoint why it was that he felt a certain amount of animosity toward Hooper. No doubt it had something to do with his perception that Hooper was a new breed of MI5 personnel, a product of human resource management, behavioral profiling, knowledge flow, mission statements, and performance appraisals. Gone were the days when young men and women at Oxford or Cambridge universities were approached by some old bloke in a tweed suit who asked if they would like to do some secret work for the government. For the likes of Hooper, the secret service was as viable a career choice as any other.

"So maybe the driver's passed out," offered Ed. "Or suffered some sort of seizure."

"Well, that's just it. They say he must be conscious because he's deliberately blocking radio signals."

"They?"

"The Northern Line Control center. You see, there's a safety feature on the 1995 train stock that they use on the Northern Line. It's called a one-person operator alarm and it alerts the control center if the dead man's handle is not activated for ninety seconds. Well, the alarm has gone off and, as would normally happen, the control center has tried to make contact with the train. Usually they would make a request over the PA in the carriages for someone to use the emergency handle and go into the cab to check the driver is okay. But the radio has been tampered with and they can't get a message through."

"So what would they normally do if the driver had passed out or died?"

"They would evacuate all the trains behind and pull them up end to end, open all the doors in the cabs, and evacuate the passengers through the trains to the nearest station—in this case, Leicester Square."

"And they don't want to do that."

"Not until they know exactly what's going on and what the driver's playing at."

"Presumably the Northern Line has been closed down."

"They're in the process of doing just that. The City branch of the line was closed down earlier on because of a bomb warning."

"I heard the line was closed on the travel news. I didn't realize it was a bomb warning. Was it coded?"

"No, just the threat of a bomb on a train at Bank but it was taken seriously enough to close down that section of the line."

"How many passengers are on this train?"

"It's a rush hour train, so maybe three, possibly even four hundred at that stage of the line."

The numbers jolted Ed out of his comfort zone. "We've potentially got four hundred people sitting in a tunnel in this heat? How long have they been down there?"

"About three-quarters of an hour so far."

"Jesus," said Ed, enjoying the cool breeze of the car's air conditioning, "I hope they've got plenty of water."

At the LU Network Control center in St. James's, Hooper once again took Ed's arm as he steered him through the labyrinthine corridors. Ed could feel his hand trembling. This coupled with something that Ed could hear in his voice—a certain breathy nervousness—made him suspect that Hooper knew considerably more about what was going on than he was prepared to divulge.

"So," asked Ed, fishing a little as they walked along, "who do you answer to on your side of things?"

"Howard Berriman." Hooper said it with a certain amount of pride in his voice. Howard Berriman was the recently appointed director general of MI5 and someone whose meteoric rise to the head of Britain's security services Ed had followed with interest.

When they arrived at what Hooper described as the gold control desk, which had been established as the operational hub of any potential negotiation, they were met by DI Calvert and DS White from Special Branch. Hands were shaken, Nick Calvert's big and muscular as befitted a six foot four inch, 238-pound bear, and Des White's, smooth and smelling of the alcohol handwash that he insisted on smothering his hands with, which had gained him the reputation of being something of a hypochondriac. Shaking hands between colleagues in the force wasn't something that Ed had been much aware of before he lost his sight but, robbed of his powers of visual recognition, it had become his way of saying hello. Those who worked with him on a regular basis always knew to shake his hand when they met.

It felt good to be working with White and Calvert. Ed knew that there were plenty on the force who had wanted to see him pensioned off after the Conor Joyce siege and even now there were those who felt that a special case had been made of him—and they were right, it had. But he had earned his place and it was people like Calvert and White who accepted that and let him get on with what he was good at. They weren't necessarily the best front men in a negotiation but they were solid, reliable, and also inventive and thoughtful. Calvert was one of the most tenacious, dedicated, and intuitive cops he had ever come across and White's technical abilities had almost condemned him to the sidelines as a technician until his abilities as a listener during a negotiation had been spotted by Ed, who had championed him as an asset to any negotiation team. The respect between the three men was mutual but it was clear, however, that this was not purely a police operation—Mark Hooper was calling the shots—and the mood in the room was awkward.

"Ed," said Hooper, "this is Paul Hinton, the network operations manager for London Underground. He's got a full breakdown of the train's movements up the Northern Line since it left Morden this morning."

Ed shook Hinton's hand—sweaty—and, taking the seat that was offered him in a cluster of chairs at which they all sat, he listened while the man described how train number 037 had proceeded up the Northern Line from Morden that morning with an operator by the name of George Wakeham on the handle. Hinton spoke with a strong, almost cartoonish, London accent, and his breath smelled of coffee and cigarettes.

"Anything unusual about Wakeham?" asked Ed.

"We've looked at his files and there's nothing I can think of." *Nuffink arcan fink uv.* "He's a good driver. No disciplinaries. Anyway, when the train got to Oval station, the controller had a request from the training department to let a trainee driver ride on the cushions—"

"Ride on the cushions?" asked Ed.

"Sorry, it means that another driver was getting a lift in the cab—up to the East Finchley depot, as it happens."

"And he definitely entered the cab?" asked Hooper.

"Yeah, he was seen going in by another member of station staff."

"Is that normal procedure?" asked Ed.

"Yeah, nothing out of the ordinary. And we've checked him out too."

"We're already digging deeper, running both drivers through the database," said White.

The incoming call alert went off on Ed's phone. It was the call alert he had dedicated to Serina Boise earlier.

"Serina, hi."

"Hi, Ed. I take it you're now at St. James's?"

"Yes, I'm with the team."

"Good, all communication links with the train are being patched through to you there. Just to say that we've approved the plan to send the two CO19 officers into the tunnel."

"What CO19 officers?"

"I thought Mark Hooper would have briefed you about it. It's just a standard approach to see if we can make physical contact with the train in the tunnel."

It sounded crazy to Ed but he tried to mask the tone of exasperation in his voice as he said, "Why don't we send the train behind number 037 into the tunnel to connect up with it and have the CO19 officers enter the train via the connecting doors in the cabs? That would provide them with much more cover."

"We've taken the view that it would also destroy the element of surprise. Our thinking is that if we can get our men on the train without alerting anyone to their presence and have them mingle with the passengers then we have a much stronger advantage."

"The chain of command here seems . . ." Ed pretended to be fishing for the word, inviting Boise to offer one, which she did.

"Weird, I know. It is but we're going to have to go with it for the time being. I want you to talk the officers into and out of the tunnel, okay?"

"I don't have a problem with that, but I just want to ask whether this is the best course of action at this stage before we even know what sort of threat we're dealing with."

"It's a decision that's been made in consultation."

"With who? MI5?"

"Yes."

Ed had hoped when he took the call that the others in the room might have continued speaking so he could question Commander Boise without an audience but it was clear that he was center-stage.

"Okay, I'll talk them in and out but I'd like this on record that I'm not convinced that this is the safest course of action at the present time."

"Noted, Ed."

Despite his misgivings, Ed knew when he had been given an order. He and Commander Boise agreed to speak later and she hung up. Ed turned to Hooper and asked, "How do we know that a bomb hasn't gone off down there?"

It was clearly something that Hooper had given some thought to and his answer came out fully formed. "There'd be survivors on the track. We'd have picked up something on the radio. There'd be smoke in the tunnel. We've had none of those things."

There was a moment's silence as the team gathered their thoughts in preparation for further talk of strategy and potential solutions. Before the chatter began again, however, Ed could feel something in the vibrations given off by the men in the room. There was no mistaking it; the fear came off them in waves.

9:52 AM

Leicester Square

They were told it might be nothing, a tube train in a Northern Line tunnel between Leicester Square and Tottenham Court Road. It might be that the driver had lost his marbles. That's how Rob had put it. Glen was glad it was Rob. Glen was the youngest member of CO19, the Specialist Firearm Command; Rob was the oldest. Not that Rob was that old. Forty-two to his twenty-eight. But there was something father-like about Rob and, if Glen could have chosen anyone to buddy up with on his first official assignment, it would have been him.

Rob drove them over to Leicester Square in the armed response vehicle. He could tell that Rob was deliberately trying to keep the atmosphere calm and Glen was thankful for it. Even though it might be nothing, Glen was nervous. But nerves were important; they kept you on your toes. It felt wrong, he knew, to be thinking like this but he kind of hoped it wasn't nothing. He felt like losing his cherry. He wanted to prove to himself he was up to the job. All the training and theory in the world can only teach you so much. He wanted to face a real-life situation and deal with it, do whatever needed to be done.

The streets around Leicester Square had been hastily evacuated. They looked odd being empty, the pavements that were normally so busy, offices, shops, restaurants, coffee bars, theater-ticket agencies, their doors usually flapping continually and now standing still.

When they came to the cordon around the tube station, Rob showed his ID to a couple of uniforms and they drove through and parked up. From the trunk of the car, they took the flak jackets and Rob took the silver flight case containing the two identical 9mm Glock 17 pistols.

As they went down a flight of steps into the ticket hall, Glen tried to match Rob's nonchalance even though his heart was racing.

"You would," said Glen.

Rob frowned for a moment before he saw a large illuminated advertisement on the wall opposite showing an attractive young woman in a bikini. It was advertising sun cream.

"And you would," said Rob.

Glen had passed through the circular ticket hall only the week before with his nephew on their way to the latest Pixar movie in Leicester Square. But it was busy then, there were people everywhere.

At the control room, they were met by a Special Branch techie who wired them up with walkie-talkies and headsets through which they could keep in contact with each other and, via a three-way link, with DI Ed Mallory at the Network Control center at St. James's. They checked the equipment and everything was working fine. Mallory came through on the radio to run through the details of the operation.

"You're to go into the northbound Northern Line tunnel and approach the train, taking care not to touch the two live rails. We're going to leave the power on so as not to alarm the passengers by throwing the train into darkness. Once at the train you must try and gain entry to the rear cab using the appropriate key, which will be provided. Having holstered your weapons so as to reduce passenger anxiety and also to give the appearance of being passengers yourselves, you should make your way through the train. If there appears to be nothing untoward, you should proceed to the front cab and try to establish contact with the driver."

"Why don't we approach the front of the train from Tottenham Court Road?" asked Rob, his words being relayed with a tiny delay into Glen's headset as he said them.

"From a psychological point of view," said Ed Mallory, "it would be better if you approached the driver from within the train itself rather than from outside. If the driver is in a state of mental trauma, he might be alarmed by the sight of figures in the tunnel. Now, once you've made contact with the driver, you should evaluate whether he is in a state whereby he might potentially cause harm to himself or to others, and if he is, then restrain him and call for paramedics. His name—and I want you to use it if you can—is George Wakeham."

"George Wakeham—got it," said Rob. "Are we under standard ACPO rules of engagement?"

"ACPO rules, that's right," said Ed. "But remember the bit about 'unless this risks serious harm,' all right?"

Ed Mallory knew his stuff and he was clearly trying to prise away the sticky fingers of the state firearms legislation to give them some more autonomy, should they need it. The Association of Chief Police Officers rules of engagement stated that they "must identify themselves and declare intent to fire, unless," as Mallory had pointed out, "this risks serious harm." Secondly, they "should aim for the biggest target (the torso) to incapacitate and for greater accuracy." And finally, they "should reassess the situation after each shot." It was made to sound so bloody simple.

"Hopefully, you won't need the guns," said Ed. "The best-case scenario is that the driver's had some sort of breakdown and when he sees you guys walk into the cab with him, he'll probably crumble. But we can't be too careful."

"Okay, you're the boss," said Rob and rolled his eyes at Glen, who smiled, thankful for any excuse to escape his nerves.

"If you see anything, however, that leads you to believe you may be in imminent danger—anything at all—then I want you out of there straight away. This is no time for heroics. What you're doing is purely fact finding, got it?"

"Okay, sure."

Rob opened up the flight case, took out one of the two pistols and passed it to Glen along with a clip of ammunition. Glen loaded the gun and slid it into the holster mounted under the left armpit on the side of his flak jacket. Rob holstered his gun and they walked down the stationary escalators and made their way through the deserted corridors, digital advertising panels on all sides vying for the attention of the 250,000 people who passed through the station every day, ads for theater shows and magazines, films, books, and music, all of them now redundant, seen by no one, ignored by the two men walking past.

They made their way down a second bank of escalators and followed the signs onto the northbound Northern Line platform. There they were met by a group of uniformed officers and an overenthusiastic London Underground engineer who was clearly excited to be involved in the operation. He shook Rob's hand and then Glen's before he reached into the side pocket of his jacket and took out two metal objects that looked like oversize Allen wrenches.

"This," he said, taking hold of a T-shaped key, "will let you open the door into the cab. And this"—he held up a J-shaped key—"will get you through the J door between the cab and the passenger area."

Rob took the two keys and slid them into his pocket. Then the engineer gestured for them to follow him down a metal ramp that had been placed between the platform edge and the middle of the track, between the two sets of rails.

"These little buggers here," he said, pointing at two rails mounted on white porcelain insulators, "are the live rails. Keep away from these and you'll be fine. Now, you got a flashlight, ain't you?" Rob took out his flashlight and switched it on, briefly blinding the engineer. "Ah, right you are then. Well, good luck to you, boys." The man's cheeriness would have been funny if Glen had not been so tense. As the engineer made his way back up the ramp onto the platform, Glen and Rob walked into the mouth of the tunnel, light from Rob's light flashing around the dark cable-lined interior.

They moved slowly between the lines, their sneakers crunching against the grit on the narrow ties. About fifty feet from its mouth, the tunnel went into a slight bend and descended through a shallow gradient for another fifty feet or so before it leveled out. With any residual light from the station now left far behind, they trudged through the cone of white halogen thrown by the flashlight. Mice scurried about, playing tricks with their peripheral vision, and hinted at the movement of something much larger and more sinister.

They made their way toward the red light of a signal up ahead and as they passed it, they could just make out the two lights on the rear cab of a train about a hundred yards further up the tunnel.

"I've got a visual on the train," said Rob. Silence. Static on the headset. Then Ed Mallory's voice: "Okay. Are the lights on or off in the rear cab?"

"Off."

"Approach the target with care and keep me updated."

Glen drew his pistol from the holster and, holding it in a double grip, he raised it up and pointed it at the train as they moved forward, Rob shining the torch. The air was hot and smelled rubbery, like bumper cars at the fair.

Closer still and they could see well enough from the lights on the train that Rob no longer needed the torch.

"We've got movement on the train," said Rob.

Glen squinted and could just make out the window in the door in the middle of the cab as it was lowered. He felt Rob's hand on his shoulder, a signal for them both to crouch down.

"What is it?" asked Mallory.

"The window in the cab door is being opened," said Rob.

"Wait and observe," came the reply.

They waited.

10:04 AM

"Maybe the radio link has gone down," said Hooper. To Ed, it sounded as though he was in need of reassurance, desperate for anything to contradict the reality of what they had all just heard. Maybe that was how they did things at MI5 nowadays, it was acceptable for operatives to give a loose rein to their emotions. Or maybe Mark Hooper genuinely felt scared and couldn't conceal it.

"No," said Ed. "The line's still open, I can hear it."

White's fingers clicked a computer mouse and keyboard nearby. "Yeah, the line's still open," he said and Ed heard Calvert sigh. Had it really come to this so soon, that people were dying?

"It's too early to speculate on what's happened to them," said Hooper, sounding to Ed as though he was masking his nerves with bluster.

"Is it?" said Calvert. Ed could detect some of his own feelings toward Hooper reflected in Calvert's voice and he was glad that it wasn't just him who found the man's manner irksome. Ed was also aware, however, of the morale within the team and how imperative it was to safeguard it, especially if this situation was as potentially complex and exacting as it was shaping up to be.

He couldn't get it out of his head, the thudding sound that he heard on the radio and the strange way that the CO19 officer had said, "Shit." It kept replaying over and over. His guess was that the two men were indeed lying dead in the tunnel. There was no point considering whether he should have suggested a different strategy. It had been agreed that sending two armed officers into the tunnel to make contact with the train was the right course of action. That he had had reservations meant nothing now. It served no purpose analyzing what they might have done differently. The inevitable inquiry that would take place afterward could look into all that. From now on it was essential that he kept a clear head, unclouded by emotion. The two CO19 officers were out of the equation; his years of training and experience would have to take over as he pursued potential resolutions.

The balance of power in the room had shifted. Whatever MI5's involvement in this—whatever they might have been doing up to this point—this was now a police operation. Hooper was clearly feeling emotionally bruised by the outcome of this first collective initiative. Ed wasn't. Someone needed to take control while the negotiating cell was being put together and all the corresponding roles assigned.

Ed could feel the nervous expectancy in the room as the others waited for him to speak. All the bureaucracy and the seminars and meetings and lectures, all the incessant talking, all the bullshit, all of it was in preparation for this moment. It was no time for petty vendettas or posturing, so when he addressed Hooper, he used his first name.

"Okay, Mark, I'll leave you to brief your people but, as far as our side of things is concerned, we'll report back that we've got what looks like a terrorist hijack situation on a Northern Line tube train."

10:05 AM

It was over an hour since the train had stopped in the tunnel between Tottenham Court Road and Leicester Square. All soft drinks and bottles of water had been drunk. Heart rates had increased. Claustrophobia—whether apparent and articulated or suppressed and internalized—was rife. Panic stalked the carriages.

As the voice came over the train's public address system, people stopped talking; those listening to music turned off their audio devices or pulled out hissing earpieces; eyes flicked up from books, newspapers, and magazines.

"This is George, the driver, back with another progress report. Apparently we're still here because they can't evacuate us down the tunnel in either direction on account of security incidents at Tottenham Court Road station and now Leicester Square station as well. They're telling me that everything possible is being done to resolve the situation but, in the meantime, rest assured that you're perfectly safe down here and everyone should relax and await further news. Sorry, folks, I know it's been a horribly long time but that's where we are at the moment. As soon as I hear anything else, you'll be the first to know. Oh, and if anyone toward the front or rear of the train can hear voices and movement, it's just some maintenance engineers who are down here with us and can't get evacuated either. But don't worry, they're perfectly harmless and getting on with some work."

Maggie listened to her husband as he lied to the passengers. It was the sort of reassuring banter that everyone wanted to hear. But although it was unconvincing to her—she could hear the terror in his voice—it seemed as though most people were buying it. But not all. The man in the sports jacket on the opposite row of seats muttered, "Bollocks," under his breath. Another panic attack was just below the surface and it didn't look as though his fragile psyche could contain it. Maggie watched the faces of the other passengers as he said, "Either this dick of a driver is lying or he's being lied to by people further up the chain of command. There's no way there are two separate security incidents at consecutive stations at the same time. No way." His stream of consciousness was delivered in a hissed monotone. "There's something going on."

This was too much for the black man in the sharp suit sitting next to Maggie. The lack of oxygen in the air and the withering heat had crippled his morale. "Listen, mate, keep your opinions to yourself. You heard the driver." He gestured up the train. "They're doing what they can to get us out of here."

"That's what the people on the planes that went into the Twin Towers were made to believe."

"It's not like that."

Mention of 9/11 had the woman from New York rolling her eyes and tutting.

"Look, can we just keep the histrionics to a minimum here?" she said. Maggie could see from her demeanor that she felt as though she had said too much and now she needed to explain her outburst.

"I was in Soho when it happened, saw the whole thing. So let's not even suggest . . ." She looked down at the floor. As she looked up again, she caught Maggie's eye. "I'm Daniella," she said, holding out her hand. Her spontaneous introduction was a way of coping, a way of distracting herself from the tension of the situation. Both their hands were clammy and trembled as they touched.

"Maggie."

"Adam," said the black man in the suit, holding his hand up in greeting.

The three of them looked at the fourth member of their group. It was a group now. Because of their close proximity, these four people were a unit of sorts—all adults over the age of thirty—just one of a myriad of pockets of humanity thrown together at random by the London transport system.

"I'm Hugh." Confessing his name appeared to calm him a little but Maggie thought he still looked unhinged. If only this creep had stayed at home, or been delayed by a few moments, enough to mean that he had missed this train, or even just ended up in another carriage. She wanted everyone to know the truth about their predicament but this guy was not the right conduit for the information. He looked as though he might succumb to full-blown hysteria at any moment.

"I remember 9/11 really well," said Hugh. "I guess everyone does. I was due in the hospital on September 12th to have a lump removed from my testicles. They thought it might be cancer—it turned out it wasn't—but before the operation I'd convinced myself that it was. So I had a kind of end-of-the-world feeling already, which perfectly complemented what I was seeing on the television. All those people trapped in the towers." Hugh looked up from his hands in his lap. "Maybe we're trapped down here. What's that expression? Just because you're paranoid, it doesn't mean they're not after you."

It was the first time that Maggie had actually thought about the fate of the other passengers on the train. Her own personal circumstances were so horrific and her thoughts so tightly focused on Ben and Sophie that she hadn't considered that everyone else on the train was someone's son or daughter, mother or father. Her predicament was only different from theirs because she had knowledge. She knew they were all victims—of what exactly she couldn't be sure—but they were victims all the same.

"The atmosphere's getting worse," said Hugh.

"It's so bloody hot," said Adam.

"No, I don't mean the temperature, I mean the mood." Hugh's voice sounded petulant and whiny. "At first, everyone accepted the situation. It was just a delay. This is London Underground, for God's sake. There are always delays. But it's too long now. People can feel it. As for the driver, well, he's saying just what you'd expect a driver to say under the circumstances. But there's something about the way that he's saying it. Can't you hear it?"

Hugh asked the question of Maggie, looked straight at her. Maggie nodded. He was right. More right than he might ever imagine.

"He sounds afraid, as though he knows something more than he's telling. Whatever's going on up there is serious, you mark my words. Look . . ." He gestured along the carriage. "You can see it in their faces."

"That's enough now, mate," said Adam, failing to hide the anger in his voice.

"I know you don't want to hear it but I'm telling you, we're in serious shit." Hugh leaned forward and buried his head in his hands.

"Mind your language," said Adam. "There are kids present."

"Yeah," said Hugh, "and they're not going to make it to adulthood at this rate."

"Look, just take it easy."

"And just accept it like a fucking sheep?"

"Look, we're all feeling anxious—just calm down."

"Yeah, just cool it for Chrissakes." This from Daniella, her New York inflection sounding stronger than before, enriched by emotion. Her outburst silenced Hugh for a moment and Adam took his chance for further placatory words.

"Come on, mate, it's going to be fine. Trust me."

Hugh's voice had gone up an octave when he said, "Oh Christ!" and pulled himself to his feet. Conversations halted as people turned to watch him. If she had had the emotional strength, Maggie would have tried to intervene herself, but all she could do was hope that the arrival of Hugh's panic attack could be delayed in some way. Hugh cracking up would do none of them any good. Maggie felt too close to cracking up herself.

Adam stood up opposite Hugh and put his hand on his shoulder. "Come on, mate."

Hugh seemed to deflate. "I hate the tube. Always have. I have nightmares about something like this happening."

Maggie thought of George and how he might be coping with his own demons.

"It's going to be all right," said Adam, gesturing for Hugh to retake his seat. But Hugh had other ideas and as his emotion took hold he flung his arms around Adam, who clearly decided that the best way to respond was to reciprocate and the two men stood embracing each other in the middle of the carriage.

On the opposite row to Maggie three seats down was a mother with a little girl on her lap, about Sophie's age. She had covered the little girl's ears with her hands when Hugh had started to swear. Maggie saw the concentration on the little girl's face as she tried to decode the meaning of what she was witness to.

"It's all right, darling, those two men are happy to see each other," said her mother by way of explanation.

"Happy?" asked the little girl.

"Happy," came the reply.

Through the door to the rear cab came the sound of laughter. No one else seemed to hear it. It came from the woman who was part of the reason for all this. To Maggie it sounded like the coldest laughter she had ever heard.

10:06 AM

Northern Line Train 037, driver's cab

"They're not going to believe me for much longer," said George.

"Don't put yourself down," said Pilgrim. "I think your acting abilities are commendable. If it wasn't for the fact that I know what you're telling them is a lie, I'd probably believe you myself. You can be very convincing, George, especially when you consider that it wasn't so long ago that you were hyperventilating rather spectacularly."

There was that smile again and George couldn't help but reciprocate.

"Look, you're even smiling at me. We're going to get along just fine."

"Maybe I'm suffering from Stockholm Syndrome." Pilgrim said nothing, just stared at him. "In the early seventies some hostages in a Stockholm bank began to feel sympathy and even loyalty for the two men who held them hostage."

"I know what Stockholm Syndrome is. I read papers. I went to school."

"I'm sorry," said George, "I didn't mean to—"

"Some victims of abuse maintain loyalty to their abuser. They think that it has something to do with the way that newborn babies form an emotional attachment to an adult figure in close proximity because that adult figure is their best shot at survival. It's like baby animals forming an almost unbreakable bond with the first creature they see when they are born, regardless of the species."

"Looks like you know more about it than I do."

"Maybe I do. Then, again, maybe you're being compliant so that you can choose your moment and try to escape."

"Do I need to try to escape?"

The smile on Pilgrim's face was well and truly gone now. He put his head on one side and narrowed his eyes as he scrutinized George.

"I hope you'll come to realize that what we're doing here—the situation that we're creating—is not something that you should want to escape from."

"What's your real name?" It was a question George had considered asking a number of times over the past hour. Knowing the man's name might help. He was convinced, however, that the question would go unanswered, so the response surprised him.

"My name's Tommy Denning."

Tommy Denning extended his hand and George shook it instinctively. The irony of the situation was not lost on him, that he should be shaking hands with the man who presented an enormous threat to him and his family. But now that this introduction had been made, George thought he might try and capitalize on it. George remembered from a film he had once seen on television the importance of a hostage continually confirming his character and humanity in order to make himself into a person rather than just an object with which to be bargained. If he could arouse some empathy in Tommy Denning then he was less likely to wind up dead.

"So what is this situation that *we're* creating?"

"You'll find out, I promise you that. You will find out."

"And what about my family?"

"As I told you before, they're fine, they're absolutely fine. You do what you're told and you'll see them again soon enough. You have my word."

There was a long pause while George thought about how to phrase his next question but then he gave up on his verbal deliberations and just said it as it came to him.

"So, are you some sort of terrorist?"

"To be a terrorist, you've got to terrorize someone, haven't you? And before you say that this bloke here on the floor might see things differently, I'd just point out that he was dead before he got to feel any terror. Why are you so inquisitive?"

"I think you'd be inquisitive if you'd had the morning I've had."

"Fair enough." Tommy Denning pulled down the window in the M door set into the front of the cab. He peered out into the tunnel that climbed away from the train at a slight gradient toward Tottenham Court Road station. The pistol hung from his fingers. It was less than five feet away from George's hand. If he was quick, he could lean across and grab it.

"So where did you get the J key from to get into the cab?"

"Why do you want to know that?"

"Well, it's not something that you can just buy in a shop."

"If you must know, my dad did some work on the Underground. He had a couple and I sort of inherited them."

Denning dangled the gun by the trigger guard from his forefinger. Five feet. If George leaned forward in his seat it was only four feet. Was the safety catch on? Did it even have a safety catch? He looked along the black metal body of the gun. Nothing. Not that he knew what he was looking for but nothing all the same. One lunge and he was there, he could pull the gun from Denning's finger. The handle was pointed toward him at the perfect angle.

"So why here, why now?" asked George, his eyes fixed on the gun.

Denning sighed as he stared out of the window. "That's a big question. It needs—deserves—a big answer, and if I thought I could do it justice for you right now then I'd have a go. But I'm saving myself. Be assured, you'll get your answer soon enough and, believe me, when you do it'll all make perfect sense. This whole thing hasn't been easy. It's taken a lot of time and effort." He said it like he'd organized a day at the seaside. "But it will be worth it. For all of us." He said the words with conviction and still the gun hung from his forefinger. Four feet away. Four feet.

"Do you have any idea," said Denning, "what it feels like to wake up in the morning and know that of all the thousands of days that you've spent on this earth, that today of all days you will make a difference, that today is the day that you will truly come alive?"

George stared at the gun. He'd grab it and kill him if he could. There was no point even trying to take him hostage. He was too athletic, there might be a fight and George didn't fancy his chances. So he would have to be quick. Grab the gun, point it at his head and pull the trigger, hope to God there was no safety catch and, if there was, that it was off. But what if he failed? What if Denning was offering the gun to him as some sort of test?

As Denning turned to look at him, George tore his attention from the gun and met his stare.

"You ever done anything remarkable, George?"

"Depends on what you mean by remarkable. If you mean, have I ever climbed Mount Everest or swum the English Channel then no, but I've had my moments."

"I'm sure you have."

"We had children. Me and Maggie. Ben and Sophie. You met them."

"And very cute they are too."

As Denning turned back to the darkness in the tunnel, George wanted to kill him now more than ever. The satisfaction of pumping a bullet into this bastard's head would be almost sexual in its intensity.

The gun dangled from the finger. It might not be there for much longer. He had to take the chance.

"You're right, bringing life into the world is remarkable." Denning's voice was softer now, little more than a whisper, as though he was speaking to himself.

George leaned forward and the gap between his hand and the gun closed even further.

Do it now, George, do it now.

He lunged forward, arm outstretched but, as his fingers approached the checkered grip of the stock, Denning stepped back and spun around. Before George could register the lack of anything solid within his hungry grasp, the end of the silencer was pressed against his forehead. All the nervous anxiety of the past five minutes was spontaneously evacuated from his lungs in a gasp.

"Ssssshhhhh, George, keep it down," said Denning, his voice steady and measured and betraying no sign of his sudden exertion. "We don't want to alarm the passengers, do we? Now, on your knees."

George stood his ground. If he was going to get a bullet in the head there was no way that he was going to kneel for it. Denning pressed the gun harder against his skin.

"Kneel, or I'll shoot you where you stand." There was no anger in his voice. It was calm and measured and George knew that if he allowed his natural cussedness and rebellious nature to get the better of him then he was a dead man. As he knelt, he felt the trainee driver's still lukewarm blood soak into his standard-issue navy London Underground trousers. The end of the gun barrel remained pressed against his forehead.

"You've got a nerve." Denning's tone of voice had changed. Though still hushed, it was more high-pitched, angry, as he forced the end of the silencer against George's skin.

"Did you read the scriptures when you were at school?"

"Yes."

"Remember any?"

"None in particular. I've never had much time for religion."

"Come on, you must remember something."

"The Lord's Prayer, I suppose."

"Everyone knows the Lord's Prayer. How about the psalms?"

"I don't know, I don't think so."

Terror made George's voice high-pitched too. It was a child's voice. He was a boy again, frightened and alone in the playground as the bully approached. But whatever might happen to him in these next few moments, he was determined that he wouldn't give this creep any satisfaction in seeing his fear.

"Come on, everyone remembers Psalm 23." Denning's voice hissed with fury, although its volume level was still low enough that anyone on the other side of the door to the carriage would hear nothing more than a whisper. "Everyone knows it. Come on."

"The Lord is my shepherd? That one?"

"The Lord is my shepherd, that's right. Now say it."

"I don't know it all the way through."

"Then say as much as you can remember."

"The Lord is my shepherd; I shall not want . . ."

"Excellent, the King James version. That's good, now keep going."

"He maketh me to lie down in green pastures; he leadeth me beside the still waters . . . uh . . ."

"Come on, George."

"I can't remember any more."

"Try!" Denning's breath blasted into George's face. It smelled sour and earthy.

"He saveth my soul?" It was something to do with soul. But Denning remained silent. So maybe this was it. He had got it wrong so now he must die. He thought of the trainee driver, how the life had gone out of him and the muscles in his body had relaxed as the first jet of blood pumped from his head and he dropped to the floor.

"He *restoreth* my soul." Denning had the voice of a petulant schoolmaster now.

"He restoreth my soul . . ."

"He leadeth me in the paths of righteousness for his name's sake. Now you must remember the next bit, George, you must."

"Something to do with the valley of the shadow of death."

"Got it in one. How apt. Yea, though I walk through the valley of the shadow of death, I will fear no evil: for thou art with me; thy rod and thy staff they comfort me." He was into his stride now. His voice was back to its soft purring best. "Thou preparest a table before me in the presence of mine enemies: thou anointest my head with oil;

my cup runneth over. Now George, I want you to say the next bit with me. Okay?"

George was going to die. These would be the last moments of his life; his last glimpse would be the blood-caked interior of a 1995 stock Northern Line tube train. When it came, he wouldn't even know he'd been shot; he'd be dead by the time his body hit the floor. Just like the trainee driver, blood spraying around the cab.

"If you're going to kill me, do it. Don't make me recite all this shit."

"Shit, is it? Some of the most beautiful and poignant words ever committed to paper. You're such a disappointment. Aren't you going to beg me for your life?"

"No."

"Right, well let's finish the psalm."

"Not if you're going to kill me at the end of it."

"I'll definitely kill you if you don't. So repeat after me: surely goodness and mercy shall follow me all the days of my life. Say it."

"Surely goodness and mercy shall follow me all the days of my life."

"And I will dwell in the house of the Lord forever."

"Just kill me if you're going to."

"Say the words, George."

The end of the silencer broke the skin on George's forehead and he felt warm blood mingle with sweat.

"And I will dwell in the house of the Lord for ever." Every nerve in his body was jangling, waiting for the bullet. For the first time all day, he felt cold. A ball of ice in his abdomen radiated a feverish chill through his body.

"Do it," said George. "Just fucking do it."

"You almost sound as though you want me to. Things not going well at home?" Denning took the end of the silencer from against George's forehead. "The fact is I'm not going to kill you. You're my accomplice, my man on the inside, my confidant." His voice gave no hint of the violence that was to follow. Denning grabbed a handful of George's hair and forced his head downward, crushing it cheek to cheek against the trainee driver's bloody face. The skin was cold meat against George's sweating face. He could smell the blood.

"That's what'll happen to you if you try to stop me doing what I need to do. Take a long, hard look. I didn't do this lightly. You think I can just drill a hole in a man's head without batting an eyelid? It's hard, George. I'm not a murderer. Have you ever considered the strength of will it takes to do this? Have you?" George's cheekbone was grinding against the corpse's beneath it. "Have you?"

"No."

"Have you ever stopped to think that perhaps the jihadis are the greatest embodiment of human endeavor and they are right to do what they do? Maybe America *is* the devil. Think about it. Shopping malls, happy meals, fat people, TV evangelists, Mickey Mouse with extra fries to go. The banality of evil in glorious Technicolor."

Tommy let go of George's hair and George pulled himself into a kneeling position once again, clawing at the blood smeared on his cheek.

"Now I want you to get back on the radio and speak to the passengers. They are still your responsibility, I believe. Are they not?"

"Yes they are." George stood up and looked down at his blood-soaked clothes. "What do you want me to say?"

Denning opened up the M door set into the front of the train and maneuvered the trainee driver's body through, letting it drop onto the track outside. As he slammed the door shut again, he said, "Let's give them a lift. They've been very good, very patient. Let's tell them you've had the all-clear to proceed to Tottenham Court Road station from where they will be able to make alternative travel arrangements. And on behalf of London Underground, you're sorry for any inconvenience caused."

"Even though it's not true?"

"Even though it's not true."

"What if they don't believe me?"

"Oh, come on. You know as well as I do that people will believe anything if they want to badly enough. Now hurry up and put them out of their misery. For the time being at least."

George picked up the handset and held it to his mouth. Denning watched him, smiling.

10:10 AM

There was no turning back after Belle had killed the two men in the tunnel. The thud of the shots and the crimson mist that hung in the air for a few seconds after the two bodies had fallen felt like a demarcation line. Simeon watched her as she sat back down in the driver's seat of the rear cab after her expedition to retrieve the two Glock pistols from the bodies.

"Seventeen 9mm rounds in the handle," she said, admiring the guns.

"I know."

He did know. He liked guns. Not as much as Belle did, of course. Although it was more than like with Belle. It was love. She was obsessed.

"A brace of Glocks," she said and smiled. "Like a brace of pheasant and brand new by the looks of them."

She didn't look disturbed. She didn't look as though she could kill two men as easily as that and then sit there and smile about it. Her dark hair was tied back. Earlier on, when they took the driver's wife and children, she had worn a black woolen skullcap but she had taken it off as they entered the rear cab of the train at

Morden. She was pretty, almost elf-like. He liked petite women. They accentuated his masculinity, made him feel more in control. He had suspected that all her gung-ho assurances that she was ready for this mission were just false bravado and, when it came time, she would bottle it. But he was wrong. She had maintained her composure throughout and had shot the two men in the tunnel and then gone to fetch their guns with all the excitement of a child on a shopping trip for a new toy.

It had been a tough few months. Looking back now with the benefit of hindsight, prison would have been preferable to his time at Madoc Farm with the brothers and sisters of Cruor Christi. But it was a deal that he had struck. He was working for British Intelligence now. It sounded grand. He had even told his mother—told her to keep her mouth shut about it—and she had been impressed. She thought it was like James Bond, poor mad cow. It was the beginnings of Alzheimer's. Maybe if it went well today, her final few coherent memories might be of him as a hero. But it was a fragile hope. He had a bad feeling about all this.

Say what you like about Tommy Denning. Extremist nut job maybe, but he was clever. The kid was forever reading. There was the Internet as well during the hours when the generator was up and running. There was an unspoken rule that Tommy would get priority when using the single desktop PC that catered to Madoc Farm's IT needs. It was as though the others realized that it was a form of release for him and without it he would become even more high strung and opinionated than usual. That ramshackle old farmhouse on the side of a mountain was bad enough without Tommy Denning being upset.

Some of the brothers seemed to enjoy the spartan existence. It was all in the name of God and therefore all part of the deal. What do you need nice food for when you've got God? Why bother with hot water to wash in when you've got God? What use home comforts when you've got bone-chilling drafts, fluttering candles, and God? God lived among the brothers and sisters of Cruor Christi as surely as the rats did. Sometimes he was everlasting and almighty, sometimes gentle and all-knowing, but he was always there.

When she had raised up the Heckler & Koch PSG1 sniper's rifle she had fitted with a homemade silencer, he hoped she was just using the telescopic sight to see who was approaching. She had a name for the gun. She called it the Pulverizer because of what the high-velocity dum-dum bullets—which she customized herself by filing a cross into the end of each lead cap—could do to the pumpkins that she used for target practice around the farm. And the men she shot might as well have been vegetables for all the remorse she showed for having shot them.

When she opened fire, it sent Simeon's rising sense of panic off the scale. He was frozen to the spot as she calmly muttered, "Bingo!" and then resighted on the only remaining shadow in the tunnel and fired the second shot, congratulating herself on her marksmanship with a whispered, "Gotcha!" It would all be worth it—he had to keep telling himself that—it would all be worth it in the end. Besides, what choice did he have?

"So go on," she said with a Glock in each hand. "Tell me about Helmand."

"I've told you loads of times."

"Tell me again. I need to hear it again today."

There was no point denying her. If he did, she would become agitated and it was essential that she remained calm. Until the time came. Maybe telling the story might help him stay calm too. He looked down at the floor, at the bloody footprints that Belle had left there after she had collected the guns from the tunnel, and he cast his mind back to Afghanistan.

"What you've got to bear in mind is that our softly-softly approach with the locals had all been forgotten—there was none of that hearts-and-minds bollocks."

"Bollocks, yeah," said Belle, like she knew.

"We were on a routine patrol. One minute there we are, two Land Rovers, a few kids playing on a dirt track, everything nice and calm. I'm in the second vehicle, sitting in the back, and I'm miles away, thinking about my little boy, Josh—he was just two then—and thinking about what I'm going to get him for Christmas. Something from Hamleys—you know, the big toy shop in London."

There was no hint of recognition on Belle's face and she looked as though she found this diversion from the narrative annoying.

"Anyway, suddenly there's a bang up ahead. The first Land Rover had taken an RPG . . ."

"Oh yeah, er, erm, a prop . . . a, prop . . ."

"A rocket-propelled grenade."

"Oh yeah, I've read about them."

Maybe she had; he had seen her reading some old military hardware magazines that her brother had given her. She had coveted them as though they were religious texts.

"Two of the guys were dead. One of them was a bloke called Jakey from Tyneside. We were quite close. Another guy lost an arm and the rest of them had blast injuries, burns and stuff."

"You could smell it, yeah?" asked Belle.

Once when he was telling the story, he had mentioned the smell of cordite and burning flesh after the explosion, and ever since then she liked to have this detail included and would remind him if need be.

"That's right, you could smell it," he said. "It was disgusting."

"Yeah, disgusting," she confirmed. "Horrible."

"It was obvious where the RPG had come from. There were some houses off to one side. Someone said they could still see the smoke from the launcher. So we went for it—we could have called in an air strike and flattened the place—but we were so fired up we thought we'd just go straight in."

"You'd never seen action before, had you?" She was keen to prevent any attempts he might make to abridge the story.

"That's right, and I was scared. I was the first through the door into the house. Everyone was shouting—we were going to kill the bastards—and there was this old woman standing in the doorway to one of the rooms. She was shouting something. I didn't know what it was. I shot her in the chest. She dropped to the floor and didn't move. Then we were in the front room and I just stuck her on automatic . . ."

"You were using an SA80, right?" The type of gun was important to Belle.

"Yeah, that's right."

"Did 'em up good and proper, yeah?"

She watched him, relishing the story.

"There were about six of them in the room. An old man, a couple of women, and some kids. So I'm standing there, firing."

"Took out the lot of them," said Belle with satisfaction.

He took a deep breath. The cathartic effect he had hoped for by telling the story had not materialized. If anything, the telling of it had made him feel worse.

"Belle, you know what happens from here on in." It was a lame attempt to bring the story to a close. Of course she knew what happened and that was why she wanted him to tell her. It was her favorite story.

"Come on, Sim, I want to hear it today. It's important."

The way she spoke, he could tell that if he refused, she'd become upset. So he continued with the story and told her how he couldn't cope with what he had done, about the investigation that was launched into what was now being described as a massacre; and he told her about the patrol they went on the following day and how he had managed to separate himself from the other men in a street market and had spoken to a local man, a community leader who he had met a few days previously, and how he had pleaded with the man to help him escape.

"Obviously I didn't tell him I was involved in killing that family. I just told him I was sickened by it and couldn't go on. He said he would help me. It wasn't as though I was turning against my country, I was just turning against my country's government. I had seen with my own eyes that what we were doing there was wrong. I had been part of the problem and now I wanted to be part of the solution."

Simeon didn't expect her to understand—and didn't care whether she did or not. It was just that whenever he told the story he needed to reassure himself that what he had done by deserting was somehow noble and not the behavior of a man who felt guilt for an atrocity of which he was the primary architect.

As he had told Belle so many times before, his Middle Eastern appearance, inherited from his mother who was Egyptian, made it possible for him to pass himself off as an Afghan and join a group of refugees who were fleeing the country. Once in Pakistan, he managed to make his way through the Middle East, Europe, and finally back to the UK.

"I needed to get home. I needed to see my boy. That was all that mattered to me. I didn't really care if they arrested me and put me in prison for what I'd done. I just needed to see my boy first."

As Simeon looked through the window into the tunnel, he questioned his own motives in prolonging this situation. Why didn't he just shoot Belle and get it over and done with? Perhaps it was because, despite thinking she was a psychopath, there was no getting away from the fact that he found her attractive and it was an attraction that he knew was mutual. There had been a few opportunities in the past to consummate the lust they felt for each other but each time fear had made him draw back. If they had started sleeping together at Madoc Farm, she would have found it impossible to keep it secret and that might have opened him up to reprisals from Tommy. It was much easier to enjoy the flirtation and bide his time. But today was the last day they would ever spend together. He knew what he was meant to do—and he would do it— but the sight of her watching him made him realize that before he killed her he wanted to have her, and if it had to be on a tube train with only a thin door between him and the hundreds of hostages for whom he would soon be a hero, then so be it.

10:17 AM

Howard Berriman shifted in his chair but the movement only intensified the shooting pain down his left leg. So he opened the bottom drawer, reached inside and with practiced efficiency popped two more Nurofen from their foil dispenser and tossed them into his mouth, chasing them down his gullet with a mouthful of water from the glass on his desk.

"Headache?" inquired Yates, his assistant.

Berriman had noticed he was making a habit of this, breaking off from whatever it was they were talking about to inquire about medical trivia.

"Bad back, actually. It'll be fine."

"Trapped nerve?"

"Sciatica."

"You should see an osteopath," said Yates. "A friend of mine could barely walk with back pain and he went to see this chap in Harley Street and he's as right as rain now. I'll find out his details for you, if you like."

He wished he had a pound for every time someone had recommended an osteopath to him. He had seen plenty of osteopaths and plenty of osteopaths had seen him. Didn't do any good.

"That would be great. Thanks. Now what time am I due at Westminster?"

"One o'clock."

"Okay, well I'll catch up with that report from the Met and give you a shout when I'm ready."

"Right you are," said Yates, turning to go.

Despite his sometimes irritating little foibles, one thing for which Yates could not be faulted was his intuitive understanding of the tone in his boss's voice that meant that he wanted to be alone. It was a good quality for an assistant to possess. Commendable. Berriman watched him leave the room. Yates was tall, slim, and athletic, and moved with a physical grace that never ceased to make Berriman feel inadequate in comparison, waddling about, overweight, and hunched on account of his back. What the hell. It said nothing in the rules about the director general of MI5 having to be a fabulous physical specimen. Good job too.

What he had omitted to tell Yates was that it was highly unlikely he would be going over to Westminster at one o'clock. Not after the news that Mark Hooper had given him earlier, news that had sent his anxiety levels off the scale.

Why didn't Hooper ring back and update him? He had his direct line, a secure line, and he had asked him to call him back in half an hour. That was forty minutes ago. There he was, a fifty-five-year-old man behaving like a teenager waiting for a girlfriend to call.

Come on, ring.

Twenty-eight years in the security service, working his way up through the ranks, respected by colleagues and politicians alike and it had come to this.

Ring, you bastard.

The only voices of dissent that had greeted Howard Berriman's appointment to the top job had come from left-wing elements in the media. Nothing he couldn't handle. That bloke at the *Guardian* had insinuated that he was a government stooge. But what the smart-ass didn't realize was that he was locked in an ongoing battle to ensure that government funding for the service was sufficient to enable it to protect the nation. It was a time of war, and if people appreciated what lengths the service had to go to to keep them safe, they would not spout off quite so much with their liberal, touchy-feely bollocks. But he could take it. Someone in his position was never going to be universally liked. It was an impossibility.

He couldn't wait any longer. Picking up the telephone, he pressed the speed dial button for Hooper's mobile.

Hooper answered, said, "Hi, bear with me a second." Berriman could hear voices in the background that faded as Hooper clearly moved somewhere more private. "Sorry about that," he said in a low voice.

"You said you'd call back in half an hour," said Berriman, unable to hide his frustration.

"I know, I'm sorry. It was difficult."

"So is it him?"

"Possibly."

"What do you mean 'possibly'? You must know by now whether it's him or not."

"Not exactly."

"Have there been any demands?"

"Nothing, we've had nothing at all through from the train."

"So it might still be something else?"

"It might be but, let's face it, it's unlikely."

"Why?"

"We lost radio contact with the two CO19 officers who went into the tunnel."

Berriman felt a sharp stab of sciatica in his left buttock. Only the weekend before he had congratulated himself on the fact that he had been in the job for all of four months and not once had he lost his "legendary" temper, as that bastard in the *Guardian* had described it. But that was about to change.

"For Christ's sake, Mark. Are you telling me that he's killing people down there?"

"It's possible."

"How did this happen? How did we get to this point? What was it you said the other day? 'It's as tight as a drum.' Well, it doesn't feel that way now, does it?"

"Everything will be fine."

Berriman could tell from Hooper's tone that he didn't believe what he was saying. He sounded increasingly like a creepy schoolboy whose cunning plan to ingratiate himself with the headmaster had been found wanting.

"Listen, Howard, we don't know anything at the moment. We don't even know if he's on the train."

Howard? He was pretty sure that Hooper had never called him by his first name before and he wasn't sure that he liked it. It hinted at a certain level of disrespect.

Hooper continued, "I'm sure that all Denning wants is his moment in the spotlight and once he's had that then he'll come quietly. He'll spout off with all his delusional shit, then we'll lock him up and no one gets hurt."

"No one gets hurt?" Berriman gasped the words in a shouted whisper imagining his sciatic nerve as a vicious, blood-red snake writhing and snapping within his vertebrae. "I'd say it was a bit late for that by the sound of things."

"But there's no way we can let Mallory and the others know what we know, right?"

Berriman's confidence in Hooper who, up until about two hours ago, he had thought of as a possible future director general, was beginning to take a severe pounding and he allowed his temper to get the better of him.

"No, of course we fucking can't. This is between you and me. And it'll stay that way. The last thing we need is someone like Mallory screwing everything up."

"Look, I'm going to have to go," said Hooper in a strained voice. "We might have something coming through from the train."

"Listen, Mark, make sure you keep me up to speed with everything, okay?"

Berriman didn't bother saying good-bye, just hung up and reached into the desk drawer for another Nurofen.

10:19 AM

Belle loved the way he spoke. It was so measured and thoughtful. Of all the times he had told her the story, this was the best telling of all. As of course it had to be. Today of all days. The way he had to whisper too. It sounded intimate. For no one else's ears but hers. He looked so good. So tall and handsome. They would be together for ever. He might not know it yet but she did.

She watched his mouth moving, his soft almost feminine lips and his straight teeth, so white and clean against his skin. She imagined her lips on his, their flesh moving together.

Simeon told her of his time in London. She knew this part of the story by heart, and she wasn't listening to it so much as admiring its delivery. He lived on the streets after his ex-wife had refused to allow him to see his son. Then he had an epiphany and remembered the name of a place he had once heard about that helped people like him.

"And the rest you know," he told her and she was back there—was it only four months ago?—meeting him for the first time at Madoc Farm and him looking at her with that selfsame expression he wore now. At that moment she knew there was something between them, some sort of psychic bond.

The walkie-talkie crackled into life and there was her brother's voice from the front cab of the train: "Belle, can you hear me?"

She put down one of the Glocks, picked up the radio and pressed the "talk" button.

"Yeah, Tom. We're just talking, me and Sim."

"Quietly, I hope."

"Yeah."

"Everything all right?"

"Good as gold."

"No one else tried to reach the train?"

"Nope, not since those two earlier."

"It won't be long now."

"Absolution, right?"

"That's right, all our sins will be gone forever."

"So even if we do bad things today, well, that's all right, isn't it?"

"Whatever we have to do today is what has to be done. Remember that. And our reward will be in heaven."

"I love you, Tommy."

"I love you too. Now let's keep it nice and quiet, and nice and calm. We're nearly there."

"Okay, Tommy."

Belle put down the walkie-talkie and the other pistol on the top of her bag. Smiling at Simeon, she stood up and moved toward him.

Surely she could allow herself a moment's sin? Tommy would never know.

He had hoped this moment would come. As she put her hand on the back of his neck and pulled him toward her, her head slightly to one side, he should have said to her, "Belle, we mustn't." Better still, he should have taken out his gun and shot her there and then. But two men had died for this. He could have shot her at any time since they had boarded the train. Instead, he had chosen to wait. He hadn't reckoned on her complete moral ambivalence about killing the two men. She seemed to thrive on the violence and, as hard as he tried, he couldn't help but find that attractive. It was so hot down there. As hot as Helmand in the summer. He craved a release from it but, if he was being completely honest with himself, he also craved her. So what if the authorities found out? He would say that it was all part of his covert mission, he could tell them that she had pulled a gun on him or something. It might even enhance his heroism in their eyes.

"Belle, what are you doing? Think of Tommy. Think of the Lord."

"You heard Tommy on the radio." She pulled his head closer and he let her. "He said that whatever we have to do today is what has to be done, and that our rewards will be in heaven."

Their lips brushed together. "You know this is not what he meant," said Simeon. "If we sin so badly now, we may never make it to heaven."

Her grip wavered, loosened; immediately Simeon felt regret. His mouth was saying one thing but his body was screaming another. He needn't have worried; whatever thought process had made her doubt the wisdom of her actions, lust had overpowered it, and she pressed her lips against his. He would kill her straight afterward. Maybe he'd snap her neck as he came—or when she did. She'd die happy and he could get on with the task of being a hero. In a few minutes it would all be over. The dark world that he had entered when he walked into Madoc Farm would become a distant memory. But first he needed to do this.

She had imagined this moment so many times. She used to watch him during evening prayers. He was so good-looking. She knew that his praying was a fake but it didn't bother her. Cruor Christi attracted all sorts. She had imagined what it would be like to undress him, run her hands over his muscular body, take him inside her.

When Tommy told her that Simeon was part of End Time, she knew that this was the fulfillment of her destiny, a marriage of sorts. Simeon was different from the rest. He saw something in her—he told her he did—and she loved him with all her heart. And now they would be together in eternity.

10:23 AM

Network Control center, St. James's

"This is George Wakeham, driver of train number zero three seven out of Morden to Mill Hill East via Charing Cross."

The voice from the speaker commanded instant silence in the control room. Ed Mallory spun around in his swivel chair.

"Can someone let me have the handset?" asked Ed, his voice maintaining its even tone. Calvert pressed it into his hand and, depressing the "talk" button, Ed held it up to his mouth.

"This is Ed Mallory in the Network Control center in St. James's."

A short pause before the response came back: "What's your position?"

"Please repeat the question. My position in terms of?"

"Your job, what's your job?"

There was no point attempting to lie. Ed knew that he needed to initiate a mood of honesty and openness. An untruth at this stage might prove awkward down the line. He wanted the subject to trust him right from the start.

"I'm a detective inspector at Scotland Yard. I'm also a crisis negotiator."

Ed could just make out a whisper in the background, proving what he suspected, that Wakeham was being told what to say.

"Are you in charge?"

"Am I in charge of what?"

A pause as further instructions were relayed to George Wakeham. "Are you in charge of dealing with this situation?"

Ed knew there was no point painting himself as merely a single cog in a much larger machine. It was clear that whoever was speaking through George Wakeham wanted to feel that they were communicating with someone at the top.

"At this present moment in time, yes. But can you please clarify exactly what your understanding of this situation is?"

There was a longer pause than before.

"What's your position within the hierarchy of the negotiating team?"

It was not the sort of question one would expect from a train driver who was experiencing technical difficulties with his train.

"There is no negotiating team, George. Should there be?"

A pause, then: "Yes."

Ed felt the muscles in his abdomen tighten. He knew the answer to the question before he asked it but asked it anyway: "Can I ask, are you being told what to say by someone else?"

"The two men you sent down here to retake the train are dead."

Ed's stomach muscles were wound tighter still. Calvert muttered, "Oh Jesus," under his breath.

Ed knew that pushing his line of questioning might be dangerous but he decided to try one more question as to the authorship of the words he was hearing.

"Okay, George, would it be possible to speak to the person who's telling you what to say?" A long pause this time. "George?"

"Be aware that any further attempt to make physical contact with the train will result in dire consequences for the passengers. The carriages have been rigged with high explosives which will be detonated if anyone is seen in the tunnel or any physical contact is made with the train."

"George, please ask the person you're with to speak to me directly."

As the seconds ticked away, Ed knew he was not going to get a response.

"George?" he said but he was talking to himself.

10:28 AM

Northern Line Train 037

The temperature in central London was ninety-two degrees Fahrenheit, making it the hottest day of the year so far. This information would feature in many morning news bulletins but only as a secondary item after the lead story that the entire London Underground network was closed due to a security alert and a section of the West End had been evacuated.

News crews and mobile broadcast units were scrambled to points in front of the police lines on the outer perimeter of the evacuation area. No statement had been issued by police, which aroused much speculation in the media, fueled by the presence of biochemical units at the evacuation sites, that London was under threat from a "dirty bomb." Other news sources reported that the Underground network closure and evacuation in the West End were due to a tube train being hijacked.

With so few hard facts to report, news crews were forced to interview members of the public who had witnessed the massive police deployment. A no-fly zone was put in place over central London, the only aircraft allowed over the West End being police helicopters hovering low over Charing Cross Road and providing a mechanical thrum to the soundtracks of the outside broadcasts from the scene.

On the MI5 website the security threat level had been raised to critical, a fact that did not go unnoticed by the media, although no accompanying explanation was given. Everything pointed to the government and security services being caught unawares by a threat about which they had no foreknowledge. They were being forced to react as swiftly as possible to events as they unfolded on the ground.

On the train, the temperature was a little over a hundred and four degrees. Eleven passengers had succumbed to heat exhaustion and dehydration and were receiving treatment from other passengers with medical training. The apparent mood among many passengers was one of anger—many spoke of London Underground's lack of regard for the health and safety of its customers—but all were afraid. For over an hour and a half they had been stationary in the tunnel. Whatever was going on, it was serious.

In the sixth carriage consumer affairs columnist Hugh Taylor was convinced he could hear voices from the rear cab of the train. But for the time being he decided to stay quiet about it. He had managed to keep a lid on his panic now for over twenty minutes. An attempt to meditate for the first time since he had gone backpacking around Asia over thirty years before had seemed to do some good. The voices he heard could be his paranoia playing tricks on him, and even if he could hear voices they probably belonged to the engineers that the driver had said were in the tunnel.

In the second carriage, a man in his mid-thirties with no history of heart problems was complaining of shooting pains in his chest and was being made comfortable on the floor of the carriage by a porter from Guy's Hospital.

Empty water bottles and lunchboxes were used to urinate in. People stood in the corners of carriages and shielded one another.

Two adults and four children on the train had by now soiled themselves.

In the first carriage a Greek woman who ran a restaurant in Brighton and was visiting London to meet an old friend from school decided that she wanted to speak to the driver. It was at least fifteen minutes since his last announcement that they would be evacuated from the train imminently and she wanted to find out what was going on. She banged on the door to the front cab.

"Driver!" she shouted. "Open the door! Driver!"

George Wakeham was heartened by the sounds of potential insurrection from the other side of the bulkhead. Denning told him to make another announcement.

"This time, George, sound a bit more convincing, will you? Sound heartfelt. Tell them you're doing all that you can. Don't worry, they'll believe you. They still have no reason not to. And get the woman on the other side of the door to shut her mouth while you're at it."

George picked up the handset.

"This is George, the driver, again. I'm really sorry about this extended delay. I've spoken to the controller and I've been assured that we will have you out of here soon."

If he were a hero, he would tell them the truth; he would quickly tell them that the train had been hijacked and they should try and escape. Some of them would manage it. Their sheer weight of numbers would make it a mathematical certainty. But George was not a hero, not in his own mind. All he wanted was to see his wife and children again and he would do nothing to jeopardize that.

"I'm really, really sorry about this, everyone, I've been assured that we're being kept here for safety reasons. I realize that it's incredibly hot and stuffy but I'm being advised that we have to stay put. So please just sit tight and I'll keep you posted. Oh and to the lady who keeps banging on the door here and shouting: can you please stop because it's giving me a headache?"

"I like it," said Denning as George replaced the handset. "You're getting better at this." Denning's amused little smile, the wry curl of his top lip, was really beginning to bug George. He had never thought of himself as a violent man but how he longed to banish Denning's smile by driving his fist into it.

"Can I ask you a question?" said George.

"Looks like you just did."

"Why are you drawing this out? Why not just do whatever it is that you've come here to do?"

At least the question put a stop to the smile.

"Don't you know anything about theater? Performers don't just walk on stage as soon as the audience arrives. That's not how it works. You have to build up the audience's expectation; you have to let them get high on the anticipation of your performance. You have to make them wait. It's all about show business. Before Adolf Hitler arrived at his rallies, he kept the crowds waiting and then finally he would arrive by helicopter. He literally came down from the sky. That's powerful symbolism. Don't get me wrong, I'm not a fan or anything, but the man knew a thing or two about how to make an entrance. And, anyway, I'm waiting for the media to 'set up' as the expression goes. I don't want anybody to miss anything and it's barely even breakfast time in New York."

George felt like asking him, if Hitler's symbolism was that he came from the sky, what was Denning's? Emerging from underground—was his symbolism that he came from the sewers?

It seemed to George as though Denning was becoming more confident as time went by, as though he was feeding off the power that the situation had given him and drawing strength from it.

"Now I want you to get on the line to that Ed Mallory bloke and tell him that you've got the first of your demands."

"*My* demands?"

"You know what I mean."

"And what is my first demand?"

"You can tell him that I want a wireless router installed in the mouth of the tunnel at Leicester Square station so that the entire train will have access to the Internet. There must be no passwords required, nothing. It must be Internet for all. I want everyone on this train connected to their loved ones. I'll give them until eleven-thirty to put it in place and then I'll start killing the passengers, one for every minute I'm kept waiting over the deadline, in the accepted Hollywood manner."

10:41 AM

"George, you need to ask the person you're with to speak to me directly otherwise we're not going to be able to sort this out."

"That's not possible. You need to put the router in place by exactly eleven-thirty, at the latest, otherwise the passengers start to die."

"I can't promise that I can do that. I have to speak to the powers that be. I'm not sure if it's even feasible, technically speaking."

"It is and it needs to be open access. Any attempt to limit the signal in any way will be taken as a failure to comply and the passengers will start to die at a rate of one a minute."

"George." Ed lowered his voice to make it sound as conspiratorial as possible, knowing full well that whoever was with him would be listening in. "You need to tell the person you're with that it's extremely unlikely that I'm going to be able to fulfill their request. Getting a makeshift Wi-Fi signal along the tunnel to the train is going to be difficult. If I can speak to this person directly then it's more likely that I can find out exactly what it is that they want and I can set about trying to do what I can to help."

It was all bluster, anything to get the subject on the line. Ed knew that his confidence would be boosted immeasurably if he could hear a voice, hear the words and their delivery. Without them, there was no way that he could build up a profile, no way to deconstruct the perpetrator's personality and start working on him.

"You've got until eleven-thirty and then someone dies."

"George?"

It was too late. Ed was talking to a dead line. He took off the headset and put it down on the desk. He rubbed his hand across his face, his fingers sliding across the ridges of scar tissue.

"Ed, this is Laura Massey," said Calvert. "She's going to be the negotiating cell's coordinator."

Ed was pleased it was Laura. They had worked together once before on a siege in the East End. Four days they had spent together, locked up with the rest of the negotiating team in a council high-rise, trying to talk down a crack-addled father of seven who had taken his wife hostage after finding out that she had been having an affair with his brother for the past five years. It was a grueling negotiation but he had found Laura to be fiercely professional and also human. In addition to her skills at running a successful negotiating command center, she was also an excellent negotiator in her own right.

Ed held out his hand and Laura shook it. Her hand felt soft and dry. She didn't wear perfume; her aroma came from a combination of deodorant and moisturizer. Ed liked it.

"Hi, Laura. Are we going for a standard cell?"

"Yes, Ed, you're the number one, Calvert and White here are numbers two and three respectively."

"I understand we're staying here for the time being," said Ed.

"That's right, we can set up the console and plug it straight into the London Underground system so we can have direct access to the radio in the driver's cab on the train. We'll look at moving to the command center later on if we need to."

"Presumably Serina Boise is incident commander."

"That's right. She wanted me to reiterate to you that MI5 must be kept in the loop on everything."

"Yeah, right." Ed didn't care if his displeasure at this was apparent to Mark Hooper, who was standing nearby, or to anyone for that matter. There was no point wasting time thinking about it but conversely there was no getting away from the fact that the constant affirmation of MI5's involvement was just plain odd.

"Any news on the Wi-Fi?" asked Ed.

"They'll have to employ some heavy-duty hardware to get the signal far enough into the tunnel to reach the train. But it should be possible."

"Good," said Ed. "We'll turn it on just after the deadline has passed. I realize we've got hundreds of people down there in extreme conditions but we must still play for time. The normal rules apply. We slow this thing down. There's no rush. We've got all the time in the world."

"And what happens when they've got Internet access down there?" asked Hooper.

"Well, unless we can restrict it in some way, then they go live to the world. With just a shop-bought laptop, they can broadcast sound and vision anywhere they like. They've got their very own reality TV program."

"That can't be a good thing," said Hooper. He said it in such a way that it felt to Ed as though he was taking this situation personally, as though it made him resentful in some way.

"What's the alternative?" asked Ed.

"Well, we have no control over the Internet. Signals can be made; messages sent to accomplices."

"It's a risk we're going to have to take for the time being. It could even work in our favor. They'll have a communication link but so will we. We should find out the identity of as many passengers as possible. You never know, we might find there is a person—or persons—who has the knowledge and expertise to launch a counterattack from within the train. Failing that, we should still be able to harvest valuable intelligence. The passengers can act as our eyes and ears. Just as much as the hijackers want to use the Internet to broadcast their message, we can use it against them. We need to have GCHQ analyzing all communications, every single word that is spoken in a conversation, every e-mail. We must be constantly updated on everything going into and out of that train."

"I'm still not sure." Hooper again.

"We have no alternative," said Ed. "If what we are being told is true, they've already killed two men. And anyway, the Wi-Fi also provides us with bargaining collateral. We give them that then ask for something in return. What do people think?"

"Children out?" Hooper suggested.

"We'll try if we get the chance but I have a feeling we won't succeed."

"Why not?" asked White.

"If they want to freak us out, which is what I think is going on here, then keeping the kids in there is going to do just that."

Over the years, Ed had tried to condition himself to think that the number of hostages in any given situation was immaterial. But it was difficult. A big number was always scary. Like the RAF Brize Norton hijack of 2003 in which a soldier on his way to Iraq for Operation Iraqi Freedom kept sixty-four fellow troops and crew hostage for a day and a half, threatening to blow himself and the plane up with a couple of hand grenades. It never made the news. The authorities wanted it that way but it didn't make it any less stressful. When Ed had managed to talk down the squaddie—a nineteen-year-old with mental health problems—it was an achievement for which he felt some pride. Although that pride had soon turned to frustration when the gold commander on the incident had suggested that it was his blindness that had provided him with his abilities, as though anyone who was blind would be able to resolve an extremely complex hostage situation.

He'd always been good at listening to people. It was instinctive. Even as a young child, he seemed to have a natural understanding of people's moods and feelings. He had an aunt, his father's sister, and it was clear to Ed that she was troubled. Others didn't seem to see it. He didn't mention anything to his parents. How could he?

He was a child. But his suspicions were confirmed when she had a nervous breakdown and was admitted to a psychiatric hospital from which she never returned to normal society. But whenever he visited her—and sadly it wasn't often—the nurses would tell him that it was in his company that she was at her most calm and contented. It was this natural ability to communicate with people and make them feel comfortable that had proved a crucial asset in his professional life. And it wasn't just with hostages on the other end of a phone line. It didn't matter who it was: he had the ability to put people at their ease. It was as though he didn't have an agenda. And maybe that was because he didn't, not at the moment that he was speaking to someone. He could focus on another person's point of view; he could empathize. Other hostage negotiators he had come across—most of them—never allowed the purpose of the hostage negotiation to slip into the background. It was always there, like the elephant in the room. But Ed could create a relationship with a subject and even if only momentarily, the subject could forget about their often desperate, life-or-death situation. With one subject in a crisis situation in Nigeria, he had discussed Manchester United's UEFA Cup chances. "Keeping the channels open," he had heard it called by psychologists. This skill, whatever it might be called, could not be taught. Ed had it—had always had it—and it helped.

But everything that had gone before in his career now paled into insignificance. He was faced with a gang of terrorists of an indeterminate number with hundreds of hostages and no apparent motive other than a desire to achieve communication with the outside world. It was this desire for communication, however, that gave Ed some hope. If they wanted to harm the passengers, they would have done so already. It appeared that what they really wanted was media exposure and once they had that, it was possible they would let the passengers go. He could exert control over them by threatening to cut off the communication. The apparent enormity of the hijack and the potential loss of life might just be a smokescreen for something else; and if he allowed his optimism to have free rein then maybe the two CO19 guys were not dead either. Perhaps they were being held hostage and their demise being reported only as a means to give the impression that the hijack was a deadly serious venture. The thought that this might just be some sort of crazy publicity stunt allowed Ed comfort. Misguided theatrics he could deal with. It was terrorism that made him nervous.

11:02 AM

Northern Line Train 037, sixth carriage

Despite the intense heat, Hugh still had his sports jacket on. Maggie couldn't decide whether she wanted him to suffer another panic attack or not. Part of her wanted something—anything—to happen, a situation to develop that would force the truth on her fellow hostages, make them realize that they *were* hostages. Another part of her, however, wanted nothing, least of all some loose cannon jeopardising whatever chance she still had of seeing her family again.

Why them? The question came to her once more. Of all the train drivers who worked for London Underground, what twisted confluence in the random streams of chance had led these people to their door?

Whatever thoughts she could muster that were not concerned with Sophie and Ben, and where they might be and what might be happening to them, were a welcome relief from the crushing despair. When they had told her that she was to be separated from the children, she had tried to scream and shout out to passersby—they were in the street at the time—but the Asian man had put his hand over her mouth and told her that if she continued to shout he would personally kill the children himself. She hadn't seen the other man—the white man with the shaven head—or Sophie or Ben after that. She fired questions at the man and woman who accompanied her into the tube station but all she was told was that the more questions she asked and the more protestations that she came out with the worse it would be for her.

"If you don't shut up, we'll kill them." The woman had said it a couple of times. By the time they were on the train and the two hijackers had gone into the rear cab, Maggie knew she had to keep quiet, play dead, until such time as she could work out if there was anything she could do.

Hugh was on his feet again. He looked across at Adam opposite, as though willing him to calm him down like he had done the previous time.

"There are people in there having sex." Hugh gestured at the door to the rear cab. "They're in there screwing. Can't you hear them?"

Maggie had heard them; Adam must have heard them too. They weren't loud, but it was unmistakable, the meaty rhythm, the breathing and the muted gasps.

Adam stood up. "It's okay, mate. It's all right." He placed his hand on Hugh's shoulder but before his attempts to soothe could take effect, Hugh had broken free of his grasp and taken a run at the door to the rear cab, charging at it with his briefcase held up in front of him like a battering ram. The case crashed against the rear door and as it did so, he started to shout, "I can hear you. Stop it! Open the fucking door!"

His leg was pressed against Maggie's and she could feel him trembling through his trousers. Adam was close behind him: "It's all right, mate, calm down." But Hugh managed to take another swing at the door with his briefcase before Adam could restrain him.

11:07 AM

Northern Line Train 037, rear cab

On the other side of the door, Simeon and Belle heard the commotion but as they were both reaching orgasm at that moment, it was all they could do to refrain from crying out. Sweat came off them as though they were in a sauna. Belle relished the feeling of their bodily juices comingling. It felt as though they were both made of liquid. It might have been the forbidden nature of the situation, it might have been because it was today of all days but Belle was certain that she had never experienced an orgasm as intense as that before. She leaned up and pressed her lips against Simeon's, her tongue writhing against his. She wanted to savor this feeling. He placed his hands around her neck. His thumbs dug into the flesh; she loved his strength. He was still hard and he pushed himself into her one final time before their hungry grinding came to an end.

"I knew this would happen," she said. Simeon still had his hands around her neck. He stared into her eyes. She said, "I love you Simeon." There was a strange intensity to his gaze. His fingers dug into her flesh. She adored his physical strength. It felt as though he could crush the life out of her in a moment. She placed her hands on his and whispered, "We can do it again before, you know . . . But maybe now we should make ourselves known to the people on the train." He let her pull his hands from her throat and she placed them on her breasts as she told him again, "I love you Simeon."

Dressing was difficult, the slick on their bodies made their clothes stick to them. She kissed him again before she picked up the walkie-talkie, raised it to her mouth and pressed the "speak" button: "Tommy? Can you hear me?"

The walkie-talkie crackled into life: "Hi, Belle, what's happening?"

"The passengers are getting uppity. Shall I give them a scare?"

"Hold on for the time being," said Tommy. "I'll get the driver to make the announcement."

Should he kill her now? Now would be as good a time as any, before anyone actually got hurt, before she could "give them a scare." He would give her a double tap—two from the Browning 9mm—into that pretty face. She wouldn't be giving anyone a scare after that. Then he would release the passengers and prepare for his debriefing. But the fear kept nagging away at him. Why had they gone a week early? Who was to blame for this? Or, more importantly, whom would they choose to blame for this? He should shoot her straight away, get it over and done with. He had had his fun. It was one of the most intense sexual experiences he had ever had. That was part of the problem he now faced. He knew he must kill her and put a stop to the madness but he also wanted to repeat the pleasure of lifting her up, pulling her legs around him, and relishing that sweet, runny feeling of having her slide down upon him. Could he not do both?

"It's going to get good now." Raising the two Glocks, she aimed them at him. "Pow! Pow!" she said and giggled.

There was a faint hum from the public address system before the driver said: "Right, I've got some good news and I've got some bad news. The bad news is that the power to the train has slumped so we can't proceed to Tottenham Court Road under our own steam, but the good news is that I've just had word that we're going to be towed out of the tunnel by another train, which is going to be with us in a moment. Now, as a safety procedure, I'm afraid I need all those passengers in the first and last carriages to move down toward the center of the train because we need to evacuate them. I repeat, passengers need to evacuate the first and the sixth carriages and move toward the middle of the train."

On the other side of the door Simeon could hear movement. People were doing as they were told. But the man continued to shout despite the voices attempting to placate him. "Open the fucking door," he kept shouting. There was a scuffle. It sounded like he was being restrained. Simeon watched Belle. She was excited, like a child waiting to go on a scary fairground ride. The thought of killing her didn't bother him. He could live with it. Any pangs he might feel as he shot her would be as nothing to what he felt after he had killed the family in Helmand. Having sex with her again before he dispatched her was greedy, lustful. There would be other women, other times, other places. He had to do what he had come here to do. She might fuck like a porn star but she was also a murderer. Scum. He reached into his pocket and his fingers closed around the grip of the Browning. He clicked off the safety catch and watched her as she said, "I'm going to enjoy this." She was intoxicated with the thought of shooting more people. Aside maybe from her brother, she was the sickest person he had ever met. Whatever childhood she might have had to endure, however much her mind might have been screwed up by religion, there was no excuse for this. She had to die. There was no alternative. Now was the time to bring all this to an end. He had the Browning out of his pocket in one fluid motion and placed the barrel only inches from her face.

"I'm sorry, Belle." He waited perhaps half a second while she turned to look at him, not enough time to allow her to raise up one of the Glocks, but enough time for him to see the flash of realization on her face that she was about to die. But it never came. She just stared back at the gun impassively. What the hell.

He pulled the trigger. Two squeezes one after the other—a double tap—two clicks, metallic, inert, dead. Instead of the slurry of brain matter on the wall of the cab and the slumping body with that facial expression—that strange gasping expression that people wear as they die—there was silence as Belle continued to study him. He squeezed the trigger again, twice. But there were two more mute clicks.

"I don't know, Simeon. We have beautiful sex together and then you go and try and shoot me in the face. You really don't know how to treat a lady."

Simeon frantically pulled the trigger over and over but Belle had a Glock in her right hand and pointed it at him. "I knew you'd feel the weight difference if I just left it empty so I disarmed the bullets myself."

When MI5 had come knocking after his return to the UK, he had had a bad feeling about the mission that he'd been assigned. But he couldn't turn them down, not a man in his position.

"Come on, Belle, I'm just messing with you." It sounded pathetic and he knew it wouldn't work. He knew she knew, and as though to confirm it, she said, "You're a terrible actor, Sim. Me and Tommy knew about you all along."

She was glad she didn't have to use the Pulverizer—the Heckler & Koch PSG1 sniper's rifle with the dum-dum bullets. She didn't want to make a mess. Not that she would ever have shot him in the face. She needed his face. So she shot him in the heart. Twice. Double tap, just as Tommy had told her. Simeon slumped back against the driver's console and then down onto the floor of the cab, staring into her eyes all the while just as she had hoped he would.

"It's all right, Sim, I know you can't talk right now,"—the air was leaving his lungs in a long sigh—"but we'll be together again soon enough. Wait for me and before you know it, I'll be there with you."

When he stopped blinking and his final breath petered out into a gurgle, she bent down to him and kissed him on the lips. They were still warm, still sensual and alive, at least for a few moments more. She forced her tongue into his mouth and tasted him as he died.

Today kept getting better and better, just as Tommy had promised. Today was the day she could do whatever she wanted. She put down the Glocks, picked up the Pulverizer and checked it over before she opened the door to the carriage.

11:11 AM

The flow of passengers from the sixth carriage into the fifth was stemmed by a group of men coming in the opposite direction. Hugh Taylor was not the only passenger at the rear of the train who thought that the information they were being given by the driver was suspect. Coming through the door from the fifth carriage was a group of five men who'd got talking. They'd had nothing else to do for the last two hours. Potential interpretations of the information they were getting from the driver had been analyzed and processed. Their suspicions had been aroused. They saw no reason for evacuating the sixth carriage. Why, if the train was going to be towed to Tottenham Court Road station, would they need to evacuate the first and last carriages of the train? It made no sense. They were coming to sort things out. No one was going to stop them. They were professionals. Two were in IT, one was a metals trader. One was on sabbatical from an insurance broker's prior to joining another one. One was studying for a MBA at a private American college in London.

The driver was clearly deluded or incompetent. He should be telling the authorities to get the passengers off the train before someone was taken ill. It was time to take matters into their own hands. There was no point fighting their way through the train to the driver's cab. They would just go to the sixth carriage, open the door and make their way into the rear cab and from there down onto the track and off down the tunnel, making sure to avoid the live rails as they went. They had missed meetings; their schedules were all messed up. But problem-solving was a key component of their busy lives. They found it challenging. They were born to it. There were five of them. Five men varying in age between twenty-seven—the MBA student—to fifty—the insurance broker. Their collective endeavor had provided them with an official air. Some of the passengers they asked to stand aside to make way for them found this reassuring. These men were here to help.

At the other end of the carriage Adam was trying to pull Hugh away from the door when there were two loud bangs from behind the door to the rear cab. They didn't register with Hugh and Adam, so absorbed were they in their difference of opinion.

"I'm going to carry you, if you don't move now," said Adam.

"Don't fucking touch me," shouted Hugh. "They're lying to us. Can't you see that? It's all bullshit."

Adam had decided to try and carry Hugh in a fireman's lift into the fifth carriage. If he tackled him hard enough—jabbed his shoulder into his solar plexus as he did so—he might leave him winded enough to prevent him struggling until they were safely there.

As Adam bent down to carry out this maneuver, two things happened, one closely followed by the other. Firstly, the five men from the fourth carriage arrived at the door to the rear cab. Pumped up by the zeal and fervor of their mission, they were about to explain their intentions when the second event unfolded.

The door to the rear cab was opened and in the doorway stood a pretty young woman holding a gun, an automatic rifle. To Hugh, this was unequivocal proof of his worst fears and suspicions. The five men were momentarily paralyzed by the sight of the armed woman. It looked so incongruous, almost as though she were an actress in an alternative theater production, in which the players mingled with the audience. The men were expecting London Underground bureaucracy; they were ready to puncture the petty laws of health and safety in order to get on with their busy lives. They were not expecting an attractive woman with a gun.

Even as she turned the muzzle of the rifle toward them, it felt as though it was some sort of elaborate hoax, playacting, make-believe. A smile began to form on her lips. Two of the men in the group of five found themselves smiling back. She really was good-looking, after all. She looked great in her tight vest and black combat pants.

Shooting from the hip, she opened fire.

The sound the gun made was like a series of muffled thuds, as if the entire carriage was being squeezed in the tunnel. It was as though a piledriver was hammering chunks of flesh from bodies. Blood sprayed from gaping wounds. The five men on their mission were cut apart by the exploding lead, which tore through one body and into another. By the time the shooting stopped, of the seven men who had been crowded around the door, six of them were on the floor of the carriage. Five of them were dead or dying and one of them, Adam, was beginning to scream. His left leg was severed at the knee. His lower leg—what remained of it—had skidded in its own bloody lubricant along the floor of the carriage.

"Now move," shouted the woman in the doorway. She looked straight at Hugh and for a moment, as colors danced across his field of vision, he thought he might pass out. She raised the gun, pointed it at him, and with Adam's screams reverberating around the carriage, he turned around. As he did so, he reached down—it was an instinctive action—and he grabbed hold of Adam's arm and started to drag him along the carriage through his own blood and over what remained of his lower leg toward the door to the next carriage.

11:13 AM

Network Control center, St. James's

Who was he? What did he want? Presuming that it was a he. The few whispered words that Ed had heard over the radio from the train sounded as though they were spoken by a man. His motivation had to be terrorism. He was employing terror as a tactic in a negotiation. By anyone's definition he was a terrorist. He hadn't put a foot wrong so far. His planning and reconnaissance were meticulous. He had accomplices, which hinted at a common cause. At this moment in time he had the upper hand.

Ed listened to the setting up of the makeshift negotiating cell all around him. The voice of Laura, the cell's coordinator, was a constant as she ensured that everyone in the room had what they needed. Ed had asked for fans and air conditioning. The heat was intense and, due to his heightened heart rate, he was feeling it more than he might otherwise have done. Excessive sweat had a tendency to irritate the scar tissue on his face.

"Ed, I've got Howard Berriman for you," said Mark Hooper. His voice was devoid of its earlier surfeit of emotion; it was subdued as though attempting a sort of intimacy. Ed had managed to compartmentalize his concerns regarding the involvement of MI5 in the negotiation but this development dragged it into his conscious thoughts once more. What did Howard Berriman want with him? It would have been understandable if he had wanted to speak with the incident commander, Serina Boise, but why would he want to speak to the number one negotiator? Ed didn't have the time to ponder on this before a BlackBerry was pressed into his hand.

"This is Ed Mallory."

"Hi, Ed. This is Howard Berriman."

"Hi. What can I do for you?"

"You're no doubt aware that we're involved in this?"

"Everyone seems to want me to know that."

"I'm sorry if it's creating any problems, it's just we've had some recent intelligence."

"Anything that you want to share with us?"

"It's nothing that's going to help you with any ongoing negotiation so it's probably not worth discussing at this stage."

"You're sure about that?" Ed didn't care if he sounded difficult. There was no reason for this heavy-handedness from MI5 and he didn't like the way that Scotland Yard and his superiors appeared to be groveling. If he was going to attempt to talk to the perpetrators of this scenario and try to find a solution then he could do without the politics.

"It's nothing that's going to help you in any way, but I wanted to get an update from you personally as I know you've been speaking to the driver of the train. What's the current situation?"

Standard negotiation protocol was being bulldozed on all sides. This was a bizarre situation by anyone's estimation but this added layer of weirdness compounded it.

"The driver's just been on the radio issuing statements from an unknown party. He says the two CO19 officers we sent into the tunnel are dead and if anyone else approaches the train, explosives will be detonated. A demand has also been made for Wi-Fi access to the train with an accompanying threat to kill passengers if it's not in place by 11:30 a.m. But I'm guessing you know all this."

"And still no demands other than the wireless connection?"

There was no reason why Berriman would need to get this information from Ed but he played along with the charade. "No, no demands as yet other than we keep away from the train."

"And you think that allowing them Wi-Fi is a good idea?"

"It works in our favor as much as theirs. We can gather intel from the passengers and possibly initiate their mobilization if required."

"Do you think it might be al-Qaeda?"

"It's not exactly their MO."

"Home-grown crazies like 7/7?"

"Could be—it's too early to say."

"Listen, Ed," said Berriman. "I realize that the last thing you need at this stage is further pressure but I want to ask that, either directly or through Mark Hooper, you keep me informed of what is occurring at all times. We cannot allow anything to happen to the people on the train. Whoever it is who is holding them, we cannot allow them to threaten our freedoms." Berriman sounded like he was rehearsing a sound bite.

"Right you are, Howard," said Ed.

"I'm told you're the best negotiator we've got."

"I couldn't possibly comment on that," said Ed with enough mock seriousness to make Berriman chuckle.

"Bye, Ed."

Ed's day was getting stranger. Now he had the head of MI5 phoning him up and treating him as though he was going to be on his Christmas card list. There was no apparent reason for it. Berriman's and Hooper's motives were difficult to read but they both clearly had an agenda. Of that there was no doubt. But Ed had more important things to think about. As a blind man, he couldn't be provided with relevant research and intel in written form and it would take too long to have the material transcribed into Braille. So all he could do was ask questions. A lot of questions.

"What sort of exclusion zone have we got around the command center?"

It was Nick Calvert, now Ed's operational number two, who answered. "We've got two inner perimeters containing Tottenham

Court Road and Leicester Square tube stations and then the outer perimeter takes in an area that extends approximately one hundred yards either side of Charing Cross Road and an area of the same distance radius around each respective station. The evacuation is now complete and there is an SAS unit on standby at each station."

"Is Laura here?"

"Yes, Ed."

"What's the situation with communications from the command center?"

"We're trying to get visual and audio from the tunnel but everyone's jumpy after what happened with CO19 earlier."

"Do we have a rapid intervention plan in place?"

"They're working on it," she replied. "You know they like to work on a simulation first before attempting anything real world so it might take some time. Boise will be speaking to the relevant coordinator."

Whereas at other times and in other places, special forces backup might have made Ed feel reassured, now it gave him little comfort.

11:15 AM

Northern Line Train 037, first carriage

Terror follows no rules. It is anarchy, pure and simple. No one knows how they will react to it. Aside from a small number of specialist military personnel—a minute fraction of the population—no one is trained to deal with it. Scientific studies—other than those that deal with purely physiological manifestations of terror such as the secretion of pheromones—are pointless. Terror is impossible to simulate, roleplay is ineffective. Nothing can re-create terror other than terror itself. The passengers on train 037 out of Morden—the adults at least—felt terror. It passed along the length of the four carriages in which they were now gathered like an electrical charge.

This was news transmission in its most basic human form—word of mouth—and all the more horrific for its immediacy. There had been shooting in the rear carriage of the train. Men had been killed. The train had been taken by terrorists. They were hostages, victims of a hijack.

Some prayed to their gods; others cursed them. Some became silent, withdrawn; others talked, ranted, pleaded, wept.

By the time the news swept through the train to the second carriage, which now contained the evacuees from the first carriage, a collective escape impulse was activated in the passengers. But before this could become a coherent surge back along the empty first carriage, the door to the cab was thrown open and a slim man in his twenties, Tommy Denning—Brother Thomas of Cruor Christi—stepped through it and walked purposefully between the empty seats to the adjoining doors to the second carriage. In his hand was an automatic pistol with a silencer attachment.

A markets analyst, newly married—a really decent man—as the newspapers would subsequently describe him, was not alone in thinking that Tommy Denning was someone official, a member of special forces perhaps who had stormed the train and would now set about securing the passengers' release.

As the one nearest to Denning, he took it upon himself to speak to him, asking, "What the hell's going on?" Denning raised the Browning automatic and shot him straight through the forehead, leaving a small perfectly round entrance wound in the middle of his well-moisturized skin, a neat wound in comparison to the gaping butchery of the exit wound, which distributed skull and brain matter across a wide radius of passengers. The screaming started as the man slumped to the floor and a tide of bodies recoiled from the horror.

Denning slammed the two doors shut between the carriages and, taking a chain from his pocket, looped it around both handles and pulled it tight before securing it with a padlock just as he knew that Belle had done on the doors between the fifth and sixth carriages at the other end of the train. George was in the cab. He could make a run for it. He could open the door in the front of the train and set off down the track. Denning knew that, but he also knew that George wouldn't try it.

"Remember, George," he had said to him before he left the cab, "if I don't achieve what I've come here to do, then you'll never see your family again. So it's up to you." It wasn't necessary to say any more than that. Denning knew he would behave himself, and if he didn't then Denning would shoot him. It wasn't as though he was important any more. Although Tommy had to admit that he rather liked having someone speak for him, issue his demands. He liked the power.

"George," he shouted along the carriage, but the hubbub of voices—the shouts and screams—made it inaudible. "George!" he shouted louder this time and got a response.

"Yes."

"Make the announcement to the passengers, just like I told you."

Tommy Denning turned back to the adjoining doors between the carriages. The man he had shot lay in an expanding pool of blood. Other passengers cowered further along the carriage. For a moment, Tommy thought he might shoot another one. Just for effect. But the moment passed. This wasn't about senseless murder.

The PA hummed and there was George's voice. Good old George. He was glad it was George, someone spiritually empty. It made it easier somehow.

"This is George, the driver. As some of you may have realized by now, I've been lying to you. The train has been hijacked by an armed gang and wired with explosives. But so long as everyone remains calm and makes no attempt to interfere with the hijackers then no one will be harmed. I've been told to tell you that anybody—including women and children—who attempts to escape will be killed. In the event of a sustained escape attempt, explosives will be detonated."

"Okay, that's enough," said Denning. He didn't need to shout, the people on the train were quiet as George switched off the PA. He knew that the passengers wouldn't remain quiet for long. But for the time being they were cowed by the knowledge that their lives were in danger. Their self-survival instincts were being activated as they processed the unsettling news.

Denning walked back along the first carriage toward the cab.

"Come on, George," he said as he stepped into the cab and slammed the door behind him. "We need to take a walk."

George watched Denning, whose excitement was almost childlike. But he didn't seem to be mad, or psychopathic, or suffering from anything that would compel him to hijack a tube train for no apparent reason. And now he wanted to go for a walk in the tunnel. What could that mean? Was Denning going to kill him? If so, why not kill him here? Denning pulled a package from his canvas bag, opened the door in the front of the cab and gestured for George to go first.

George climbed down from the cab, making sure not to stand on the trainee driver, who was lying where Denning had let him fall, his lifeless eyes staring up at the roof of the tunnel. George had never been in a tube tunnel outside a train before. Only scant light was thrown from the cab and, as he stared into the darkness up ahead, he wondered if there was anyone there, watching them, lining up their rifle scopes. Denning must have been thinking the same because he made George walk in front. They didn't go far, ten yards at the most. Denning flashed on a torch and shone it at the wall. He found what he was looking for, a set of flimsy metal steps up the side of the curved wall, which disappeared inside a hole in the ceiling about two feet in diameter.

"You stay here. I'll hear you if you try and make a run for it. We're friends now, so don't make me kill you."

Denning looked at him and smiled, like a boy who has watched some violent gangster movie that he shouldn't have and wants to act out the dialogue for the benefit of a friend. But behind the juvenile posturing there was a violent unpredictable energy.

"Okay?"

George returned Denning's stare and nodded.

With the agility and precision of a gymnast, Denning was up the ladder and swallowed by the narrow hole. His ascent was accompanied by the creaking of the old metal struts. George looked up the tunnel and then back at the train. Whatever escape plan he could conjure up, he knew he wouldn't put it into practice. He had to believe that what Denning had told him was true, that if he did exactly as he was told then he would see his family again. He had to cling to that. Without it, he knew he would go to pieces. Just like it sounded some passengers on the train were doing. There were loud voices, most of them male. One man was shouting something that sounded like a biblical incantation, a prayer perhaps, and another man was shrieking a string of obscenities. A baby was crying. A woman screamed, then a man.

The ladder started creaking as Denning descended.

"All done, George," he said. "It's out of our hands now." As he jumped down onto the track, George noticed that he was unraveling a reel of red wire that led up into the bolt hole. They walked the few yards to the train with the wire trailing behind them. As they climbed up into the cab, Denning passed the reel through the window in the cab door, before closing the door behind him and pulling up the window, leaving an inch gap at the top for the wire.

"You might want to cover your ears and open your mouth," he said as he fiddled with a large powerpack battery. George looked confused. "It'll protect your ears." George felt a sense of rising panic and as Denning said, "Don't say I didn't warn you," he covered his ears and opened his mouth. Denning touched the wires against the electrodes on the battery and there was an explosion in the tunnel that cracked the glass in the cab windows. Even with his hands over his ears, George could feel the air displacement punch his eardrums as the sound of eviscerated brickwork and masonry raged in the confined space. As a gritty wind blew down the tunnel followed by wafts of dust, the passengers remained silent for a moment as a pulse of fear was transmitted through the carriages. Then the shouting— more urgent and frantic than ever—started up once again. But as George took his hands away from his ears, he heard something else, something wholly unexpected. It was the sound of running water.

11:16 AM

"All messages and web activity can be directed into a cache which we can analyze," said Laura. "But what concerns me is if the hijackers realize that we're tampering with their web access."

"I doubt they will," said Ed. "They'll have more important things on their minds, like staying alive long enough to get out their message."

"But if they do realize, Ed, they might start killing hostages."

"We should only revise our negotiation if we have intel that proves conclusively they're killing people. Without that, we keep negotiating. How long have we got until the deadline?"

"Twelve minutes," said White.

"And the router is in place in the tunnel?"

"Yes. Just needs turning on."

"Okay, well I guess we're going to have to let them speak. Without any communication whatsoever, there's no way of resolving this. We give them this. We get them talking and we take it from there."

"How long after the deadline do we leave it?" asked White.

"Let's leave it forty-five seconds."

"You're sure about that, Ed?" asked Laura.

"Absolutely," replied Ed. "We have to use every opportunity we can to claw back some control, however minute. When they see the time go to exactly eleven-thirty and there's no wireless, they're going to be afraid. Yes, they can kill a hostage but they're not going to straight away. Like everyone else on the planet who has ever used a personal computer, they're going to think that there's something wrong with their connection. They're also going to have a niggling doubt in the back of their minds that we're not going to be as compliant as they want us to be. We inject a little drip of fear into their brains. We unsettle them."

"Okay, okay . . ."

Ed could hear the indecision in Laura's voice. "Laura, this is the only way we can play it. We have to start chipping away at them from the start. We have to make out that everything they want is a problem and it's going to take time. We own time, they don't."

"All right, Ed, I don't need a lesson in hostage negotiation. I'll see what can be done."

Ed turned to Laura, attempting a fix on her exact location and directing the lenses of his Ray-Bans at it. "You mean to tell me that we haven't actually got clearance to switch on the wireless connection yet?"

"No, I need to phone it through to Commander Boise. Only she can sign off on this."

"Laura, you'd better do that fast. We've got—how long have we got?"

"Nine minutes thirty seconds," said White.

"Okay, let me make the call."

Ed balked at the old negotiating maxim that "the negotiators negotiate and the deciders decide." He wanted to be closer to the sharp end of the decision-making process. He knew standard procedure dictated that in a negotiating cell everyone had one specific job and there should be little overlap but, while he could see the reasoning behind this, he also found it frustrating.

When Laura returned, she said, "They're calling back." Ed could tell that she shared his frustration about this from the way that she said it and he couldn't prevent himself from feeling a flash of anger.

"This is fucking ridiculous." Ed didn't raise his voice, didn't give any indication that he was angry aside from his choice of words. "We should have more autonomy to make strategic decisions related to the negotiation. If they don't give us the go-ahead, we might as well pack up and go home. What was the point of getting all the Wi-Fi equipment down there in the first place?"

"Ed, there are enormous implications here. We've got an armed gang with hundreds of hostages and they want a media link to the world. Politically, this is extremely sensitive."

"So we wait."

"Everyone knows the time frame."

They sat and waited. Ed thought about throwing out some deflective chatter in an attempt to diffuse the tension but his mind kept racing elsewhere. They had to allow the connection. It would be madness to deny it, although nothing would surprise him now, as the usual rules of the game seemed to no longer apply. On the positive side, however, the setting up of the negotiating cell was complete. All the equipment was in place. They all had their headsets, their coffee, and water. A fan had been set up on the desk in front of Ed and cool air was blowing across his scarred face.

At three minutes to the deadline, Ed heard the door open and a whispered conversation between Laura and one of the support staff.

"Okay, Ed," said Laura. "We've got the go-ahead."

"Good, so when we get to deadline plus forty-five seconds, we switch on the juice. Not a second before."

11:17 AM

Northern Line Train 037, driver's cab

"What's that sound?" asked George.

Denning smiled. He pulled down the window in the M door in the front of the cab and cupped his ear theatrically. "That, my friend, is holy water."

"What do you mean, holy water?"

"Have you ever been baptized?"

George's mind flashed to the framed photograph that his parents had on the table in their hallway, a picture that despite his protestations, remained there to this day. It showed a one-year-old George wearing what looked like some sort of white silk shroud. It was taken at his christening and his mother always said he looked like a little angel in it. But George had never shared his mother's religion, much preferring his father's strong religious skepticism. This didn't, however, stop him getting confirmed when he was fifteen. All his friends were doing it and there were presents, so he was told, although all he received was a book called *Words for Worship*, which ended up in the back of a closet somewhere. It wasn't really the sort of present that he'd had in mind.

"Yeah, I was christened," he said.

"Good," said Denning but his mind was elsewhere, focused on the sound of footsteps in the tunnel. Pulling down the window in the N door in the side of the cab, he leaned out. He saw something further up the train and, drawing his gun and grabbing his bag, he said, "Come on, follow me." Denning opened the door and George followed him into the first carriage, where a man in his forties, red faced and sweating, was trying to make his way down the outside of the train. As soon as he saw Denning move toward him, he pitched forward to try and get below the level of the window but a 9mm bullet was already on its way toward him and, having punched a hole in the window, it struck him in the left ear, exiting in a crimson flower-like wound on the right side of his neck. As the man slumped dead against the side of the train, Denning was on the move again, walking toward the end of the carriage.

"There goes another one," he shouted. He stood at the door and looked through the window at the terrified passengers. "I've got a lot of bullets. I've got enough for every one of you if need be. So if you want to die like this, then keep on coming." He turned away from the door and walked back along the carriage opening up his canvas bag and taking out a laptop computer. Then he took out extra batteries wrapped in clear plastic. In the middle of the carriage, between the two handrails set into the ceiling of the train, he stretched a piece of doubled-over bed sheet and pulled it tight, using a staple gun to secure it. In the middle of the sheet, he placed the laptop and opened it up.

George watched Denning as he worked. He could tell this was something he had rehearsed many times. Once the laptop was up and running on the makeshift hammock, he connected a webcam to it and after tapping on the keyboard for a few moments, a window appeared on the screen in which there was a real-time image of him. He smiled when he saw himself.

"Isn't technology miraculous, George?"

11:30 AM

Northern Line Train 037

At exactly forty-five seconds past the deadline, a miniature symphony of pings, chimes and other electronic alerts greeted the switching on of the wireless signal. The compulsion to communicate would not be denied. The tension and fear had to be relayed above ground to friends, family, and loved ones. Social networking, e-mails, web-based phone and video calls, the communication stream began to flow from Train Number 037 and soon the flow became a torrent and doubled back on itself in a swirling parabola of news. This was media of the masses, naked expressions of human emotion, unedited, uncensored, the raw material over which the media industry could now scavenge for highlights, moments of drama and narrative continuity. This was an unfolding tragedy brought to the people of the world in the international language of the day's top story.

There were journalists on the train, two freelancers and a features editor for the *London Evening Standard*, but their professional status meant little; there were amateur journalists all along the train, reporting from the front line of their own experience. The images and film footage radiated from the stricken train, to be consumed by a hungry global audience eager for an opinion to take.

Militants seize London tube train.
Terrorists attack London.
Tube hijack: terrorists take commuter train.
Hundreds of hostages on the London Underground.
Londoners' courage on day of terror.
Stacey's makeover: pictures.

11:31 AM

As the train driver came through on the radio once more, Ed Mallory thought he could detect a greater degree of fear in his voice.

"This is George Wakeham, the driver of—well, you know who I am."

"George, this is Ed Mallory."

"You were late switching on the wireless connection. Any further delays in carrying out demands will result in passengers dying."

"George, I need to speak to the person who is telling you what to say."

"That's not possible. You need to write down this web address."

"Okay, but can you tell me why we need this address?"

The frequency of the hiss relayed into Ed's headphones changed as the radio connection cut out momentarily and then George's voice came on the line once again. "You need to shut up, write it down and then connect to it."

Ed knew that George was merely relaying the words of one of the hostage takers but he noted the element of anger and impatience in his delivery.

"Okay, let's have the address, George."

"It's denning23.co.uk. Have you got that?"

"Denning23.co.uk," repeated Ed and he heard White tapping on a keyboard nearby.

Calvert squeezed Ed's arm. This was the sign they had decided on for when Ed should enable the mute facility on his microphone.

"We've got a visual on a white male in his mid-twenties," whispered Calvert. "He's standing in front of a webcam in the middle of a deserted tube-train carriage. He's got short cropped hair and he's wearing black. He's of medium build—"

Calvert was interrupted by a voice coming out of the computer speakers, clearly the voice of the man on the train speaking into his webcam and microphone: "Check they can see and hear me, George." It was the voice of a young white male, a Londoner or longtime resident of southeast England. The voice was calm, measured, confident.

George's voice came through Ed's earphones: "Can you see and hear him?"

Ed clicked the mic back on and replied: "Yes we've got visual and audio. Tell the guy you're with that he's coming through loud and clear."

"That's a yes," said George, shouting to the man.

Calvert squeezed Ed's arm and Ed clicked off the mic again to hear him say, "The perp's looking straight into the camera like he's about to read the news."

Ed slipped his earphones forward on his head and listened to the voice as it came through the speakers.

"This web link has been sent to all major news organizations," said the man in a tone that made no attempt to hide an underlying sense of excitement. "A group mailing has gone to everyone from Al Jazeera to CNN. It'll probably take a short while for the e-mails to filter through and for the journalists to realize what's going on, so in the meantime, I need to lay down some ground rules. High-explosive charges have been rigged throughout all six carriages and any attempt to make physical contact with the train will result in me detonating them. Now I reckon there's about—what?—three hundred and fifty people on this train and with a series of explosions in such a confined space, everyone will die. That's a lot of bodies, so let's not have any heroics."

If the guy was lying, he was a good liar. Often Ed could pick up something in a hostage situation even when those around him could see the subject on a visual link and detect nothing in their body language or behavior. But this guy gave off no "tell" in his vocal inflexion.

"My name is Tommy Denning and I am leading a team of heavily armed hijackers who are positioned throughout the train."

As soon as the perp had said his name, Ed could hear the activity in the negotiating cell as it was typed into keyboards and the process to construct a full character profile of him was set in motion.

"I have a message for the world," said Tommy Denning.

It sounded to Ed as though he was enjoying himself. It was as though he had rehearsed this moment in the bathroom mirror a thousand times.

"At exactly twelve noon, I will broadcast my message. If any attempt is made to prevent me from doing so, I will detonate the explosives on the train. Please do not be under any illusions: we are all fully prepared to die and to take everyone on the train with us."

The ensuing silence was unbearable for Ed while the rest of the team watched the video link to the train.

"What's he doing?" he whispered.

Calvert said, "He's walking away from the camera back toward the driver's cab."

Ed could just make out the sound of distant shouts and screams on the train. He felt his tactile watch. It was 11:35 a.m. Twenty-five minutes until Denning's message. Plenty of time for the world's media to focus on this solitary webcam deep beneath the streets of London.

All of the crisis negotiations that Ed had been involved with over the years had involved one-on-one communications with the subject. Conversations were invariably taped and covert audio and visual connections were always attempted. This situation, however, was totally different on account of the subject's ability, thus far, to control the flow and direction of the communication. What the hell was it that this Tommy Denning had to say? Did he have some great secret to impart? Or was his message going to be the typical ramblings of some delusional paranoid? The three types of psychological profile assessment—either mad or bad or mad and bad—were difficult to apply in this case. From the way Denning presented himself to the world he didn't easily fit into any category.

The more Ed thought about Tommy Denning's announcement, the more he thought that they hadn't fully evaluated the implications of allowing him a voice and one that all the news media would be only too happy to trumpet from every rooftop. But that was an intangible and now he had to focus on those aspects of the situation that he could control.

"Try and raise the driver on the radio," said Ed. "Denning might be so pumped up by the fact this whole thing is going better than in his wildest dreams that he might let us through."

A moment later, White said, "Ed, you're on."

Ed slipped on his headset. "George? Are you there? This is Ed Mallory from the Network Control center. Can you hear me?" There was nothing for a few moments, just radio static before George's voice came through the speaker.

"Hi, it's George."

"Can I speak to Tommy Denning?"

There was a muffled conversation in the background before George came back on the line.

"No, he will only communicate via the webcam. You must wait until twelve noon."

"Please tell him that it's essential that I speak to him because we've got a problem fulfilling his request."

Another pause. There was a crackle on the radio connection before another voice—Tommy Denning's this time—came on the line.

"Listen, Mr. Mallory, I know you'd like to get into a conversation with me and try to talk me down but you've got to realize that I'm not up for a chat, okay?"

Hearing his voice again, Ed guessed that he was definitely a Londoner but the accent wasn't strong enough to allow him to hazard a more specific origin.

"Mr. Denning—can I call you Tommy?"

"You can call me what the hell you like, it's not going to do you any good. Although I have to say that I rather like the fact that we're calling each other 'Mr. Denning' and 'Mr. Mallory,' it sounds very refined. Now don't take offense from this—it's nothing personal—but I'm not going to be talking to you, okay? All you need to know is that if anybody tries to stop me making my announcement at twelve o'clock then I'll kill all the passengers on the train."

"The problem I have is that the wireless access is very unstable. Our technical people are struggling to keep it going. It may pack up before twelve noon."

"You're lying, Mr. Mallory. You know it and I know it. If the connection is so unstable then you'll get some backup. What's that compared to the deaths of hundreds of people?"

Ed could hear something in the background. He had heard it on the computer, on the link to the webcam, but on the radio it was louder. It was a rushing sound, like wind blowing through trees.

"Tommy, if we're going to resolve this situation, we're going to have to create some trust here. We're giving you the Internet connection so we're going to need something in return."

"You are getting something in return—you're getting the lives of the passengers on the train."

"We're going to need something more tangible than that, Tommy. I'm thinking that it would reflect really well on you if you were to release the children."

Denning chuckled. It was unforced. It sounded like a genuine expression of goodwill, as though he was enjoying their conversation and felt confident he was in complete control of it. He sounded like no other hostage taker Ed had ever come across. He was calm, collected, and thinking clearly, behaving as though this was something he was born to do.

Denning clearly wasn't going to respond to his line about the children so Ed thought he would try another tack. "What exactly is it that you want, Tommy?"

"You'll find out," said Tommy and the line went dead.

"He's enjoying this," said Ed to the occupants of the negotiating cell. "He's having a ball."

11:36 AM

Through the cracked window, George could see that the puddles in the tunnel were merging, lapping at the rails. Soon there would be a continuous expanse of water in front of the train. How long the power supply through the rails would continue was difficult to say but, once it had gone, the battery on the train would continue to provide electricity for a while until it ran down and the entire train would be thrown into darkness.

The negotiator, Ed Mallory, was trying to keep Denning talking. But it was never going to happen. There was no way that Denning was going to respond to any sort of conversational psychology. It sounded like Mallory was probably aware of that. George chewed his gum as he listened to the attempted negotiations. It was Juicy Fruit. Denning hadn't wanted any when George had offered him a piece.

"All you need to know," said Denning into the radio handset, "is that if anybody tries to stop me making my announcement at twelve o'clock then I'll kill all the passengers on the train."

Why the water? Why flood the tunnel? By asking the questions, George hoped he might be able to find an answer other than the one that kept offering itself to him and made his claustrophobia flare up and steal the breath from his lungs. There was no avoiding it; there was only one answer—the water was a threat. And as the driver of the train, George knew that he should try to do something about it. The passengers were technically still his responsibility. There had to be something that he could do. Something that would not jeopardize his family.

He had been trying to avoid looking down at the floor of the cab—he was never very good with blood—but as he glanced down, he saw that stuck to the drying blood was a plastic bottle of Diet Coke about half full. It had fallen out of the trainee driver's jacket pocket when he slumped to the floor. The fact that it was Diet Coke made its owner's death even worse somehow. It personalized it. The poor bugger had been a little overweight—like George—and maybe he had wanted to slim down, through health reasons or possibly vanity. Whichever it was, it didn't matter now.

Then it came to him. If he drank the Coke, in addition to quenching his thirst—it was so damned hot, the chewing gum felt like rubber in his mouth—he would have an empty plastic bottle in which he could place a letter, a message in a bottle.

Could he scribble a note on a piece of paper to the effect that Tommy Denning was flooding the tunnel? It was clear that Denning had no intention of telling the authorities the full details of the hostage scenario that he was engineering, otherwise he would have done so already. It obviously served his purposes not to. So if George could let it be known some other way, provide some forewarning of what was going on down there then the authorities might be able to put in place some evasive procedures. There was clearly a small amount of current in the water caused by the deluge cascading down from the bolt hole in the tunnel roof where Denning had set off the explosion. It might be just enough to carry the bottle past the train to where it might be found by someone. But no sooner had the idea come to him and he had embraced what scant hope it offered than he rejected it out of hand. It was a stupid idea. Quite apart from the fact that Tommy Denning would have been alerted to what he was up to when he started writing a letter, even if he could manage to put his message in the bottle and cast it into the water, the chances of it actually reaching anybody in time for them to do anything were infinitesimal; the risk far outweighed any possible benefits.

Despite the plan's failings, the idea of alerting the outside world to the exact nature of what Denning was up to was still sound.

The radio handset, there it was. There was his mouthpiece to the world. But it would take more than just speaking into it. This would take ingenuity.

"What exactly is it that you want, Tommy?" asked Ed Mallory through the speaker console.

"You'll find out," said Denning, taking his finger off the push-to-talk button on the side of the handset and passing it back to George. The chewing gum was already out of George's mouth and in his hand. He kept the talk button pressed down and packed the chewing gum around it tightly to hold it in position. The channel was still open.

But as soon as George had done this, all he could see was the piece of chewing gum. There it was on the mouthpiece hanging in its cradle on the radio console. It looked enormous. It might as well have been red and throbbing. What was he thinking? He wasn't a hero. His recent attempt to snatch the gun from Denning had very nearly got him killed. This was far more reckless. An open channel would sometimes—often—hiss and crackle. Denning would only need to hear this, look across at the handset and see the chewing gum on the talk button. He wouldn't think twice. It would be George's turn to be thrashing around the cab, blood pissing from a hole in his head. This time he really was going to die.

Talk, George. That's all he could do. He would have to try and mask any sounds from the handset. And for Christ's sake, George, stop looking at it.

Denning stared through the cracked window at the water in the tunnel. He looked confident, like whatever his sick plan was, it was all going smoothly.

Say something, George.

"So, what's with the water?"

Denning glanced at him—disaster—before returning his gaze to the tunnel.

"Think of it as an egg timer," he said, smiling, pleased with his explanation.

George glanced at the radio console. The gum around the button was beginning to stretch as the spring behind it forced it away from the main body of the handset. The channel would not stay open for long. He had to describe the situation more clearly, at any moment the radio might crackle and he would be found out.

"So you're trying to drown us by flooding the tunnel, is that it?"

Had he overdone it? Had he killed himself? Had he killed Maggie? Had he killed his children?

Denning looked at him. He would only have to glance a little to one side and he would see the handset and the gum on it. In his peripheral vision, George could see the talk button straining against the sticky tendrils.

"It's not a matter of drowning. This is much more important than drowning. This is a blessing."

The last of the gummy tethers was about to give way, allowing the press-to-talk button to snap back into place, closing down the channel and emitting as it nearly always did a crackle of static.

Say something. Anything.

"It's so damned hot."

When it came, it was more of a hiss than a crackle and it coincided with the "want" as George said, "Do you want a drink?"

George stooped down and picked up the bottle of Diet Coke, prying it away from the congealing blood. If he looked up and saw Denning pointing the pistol at him then he knew it would be the last thing he would ever see. He couldn't bear to look so he focused on the top of the bottle as he unscrewed it. There was no avoiding it now, he had to look at Denning. What would his expression be? Had he heard? The hiss from the radio might as well have been church bells to George. It was loud and unmistakable. But when he managed to look at Denning again, he was met with an expression of disgust. Was it disgust at his woeful attempt to communicate with the outside world? Was it disgust that could only be banished by pumping a bullet into his head? It was impossible to say. George's thirst felt terminal. If he was going to die, he wanted to have a drink first. He raised the bottle to his lips and took a sip. The fizzy liquid was warm and not as fizzy as it should have been. It probably contained a few milliliters of its former owner's saliva.

"How could you?"

George felt like sobbing with relief. He took another gulp and held out the bottle to Denning.

"Want some?"

"No."

Denning watched him as he took another gulp.

"Drinking a dead man's drink," said Denning with disgust.

"Well, you killed him."

George didn't know where it came from. Suddenly he was a comedian, joking about the darkest and sickest subject matter imaginable. And Denning was smiling at him, amused. But this wasn't the time for complacency. There was still a big sticky bolus of chewing gum on the radio handset and the implications of Denning's reply to his question regarding the running water had now filtered through his mind and made him feel sick.

"So what are you after, what are your demands?"

"Look, I don't want to spoil it for you. If I told you, it wouldn't be a surprise now would it?" The smile was gone as he took out the walkie-talkie and spoke into it: "Belle?"

The woman's voice on the other end crackled back: "Yeah, Tommy?"

"Everything's as it should be. I'm going to make my speech at twelve noon, so sit tight, not long now."

"Okay, Tommy. Oh and Tommy, Simeon's dead."

"You did what you had to do. Remember, today is the day. This is our time."

"I love you, Tommy."

"I love you, Belle."

As Denning pocketed the walkie-talkie, George caught his eye. "She your girlfriend?"

"Sister."

"She's at the other end of the train, right?"

"Got it in one."

"Who's Simeon?"

"He was a false friend."

"So he had to die?" Denning said nothing, just nodded while watching George, who decided to capitalize on this moment of openness to question him further: "So what now?"

"We wait."

"You haven't really wired the train with explosives, have you?"

Denning's expression changed.

"What is it with you? Doesn't it worry you now I've made myself known and established my link with the outside world that I might not need you any more? That maybe you could be surplus to requirements."

George knew it might sound desperate but he didn't care. "You promised that so long as I did as I was told you would spare me and my family. That's the truth, right?"

Denning nodded thoughtfully. "Of course it's the truth. Why would I lie to you? You're my friend. But now you're going to have to keep quiet because I've got a speech to rehearse." He took some sheets of legal-size paper from his canvas bag and flicked through them.

George returned his gaze to the water in the tunnel up ahead, avoiding the handset and the piece of chewing gum. With sideways glances, he watched Denning as he pored over the sheets of paper, reading the words written in blue ballpoint. The handwriting was small and neat and there were numerous crossings out and words underlined. Denning muttered to himself as he read, pacing in the confined space.

His guard was down. Both his hands were on the pieces of paper and the gun was in his pocket. If George hit him as hard as he could, smashed his fist into his face, he would be debilitated for at least a few seconds. Enough time perhaps to land some more punches and prevent him reaching for his gun. Enough time possibly for George to get his hands around his neck and squeeze the life out of him. As the thought came to him, he clenched his fists, his fingernails digging into his palms. His murderous thoughts kept his claustrophobia at bay. There he was, a man who had never thrown a fist in anger, not since he was a child, and yet he knew with a cold dispassionate certainty that if he got the chance, he would kill this man and feel nothing, no remorse, nothing. It would feel good. It would feel liberating.

11:39 AM

"So, what's with the water?"

As soon as Ed heard the train driver, George Wakeham, say the words—they were faint but clearly audible through his headphones—he knew it was significant. Wakeham had managed to keep the radio channel open.

Everyone in the negotiating cell—White, Calvert, Hooper, and Ed Mallory—listened to it and behind it there was that sound. It was unmistakable now. Flowing water. Falling water. "What's with the water?"

"Think of it as an egg timer," said Denning. His voice sounded different. The tone was more subdued, more conversational. This was how he spoke when he wasn't grandstanding and Ed could tell straight away that he had no idea that he was being listened to.

Ed willed George to ask another question, and he did. "So you're trying to drown us by flooding the tunnel, is that it?"

Ed winced. Was that too exclamatory? Would Denning realize that he was being steered?

"It's not a matter of drowning, George. This is much more important than drowning. This is a blessing."

A blessing? What the hell did that mean?

"It's so damned hot." George Wakeham sounded nervy, he was speaking too loudly. Was his ruse about to be discovered?

"Do you w—"

The radio cut out. It was the start of a question; what was George about to ask him?

"Can you play it back?" asked Ed. "The bit about flooding the tunnel."

White clicked away on a computer nearby and there were George's words again: "So you're trying to drown us by flooding the tunnel, is that it?"

"Again," said Ed.

"So you're trying to drown us by flooding the tunnel, is that it?"

"Laura?"

Laura spoke to him from the direction of the doorway. "Yes, Ed?"

"I've got a really bad feeling about this. We need to put a whole new strategy in operation. And we need to move fast."

11:43 AM

Northern Line Train 037, driver's cab

Father Owen had turned toward him as he had approached with the knife the night before. It had felt as though God's hands were guiding him as he pushed Owen back into the bath and pressed the tip of the blade against his throat.

"What . . . what are you doing?" Stripped from Owen's voice was the assured confidence that he employed for his interminable sermons, preachings that had become so tiresome of late. What did he know about washing away the sins of the world, about rebirth?

Like everyone whom God had seen fit to accompany him on this journey, Father Owen was a prophet. Tommy's was the task of beginning the End Time but others were to play their part in the great unfolding of the end of days. He felt a strange sense of love for them. It was God's love shining through him.

When he had sacrificed the old man, he had stood so close to him that he could smell the whiskey on his breath. As the arthritic old hands struggled with his in a vain attempt to prevent the inevitable, Tommy leaned forward against the knife. It burst through Owen's throat, squirting blood as the gristle crackled.

It was a line that Tommy had heard the old man use many times before, a line taken from the Book of Revelation, although Owen and all the other members of Cruor Christi had mistaken its significance and meaning. Their foreheads were touching, sweat mingling; they were so close that Tommy's words as he had spoken them were inhaled by the old man as he breathed his last: "And the waters shall rise."

And now was Tommy's final opportunity to get all those other precious words straight in his mind. There would be no notes when he went live. Christ didn't have notes. Great words, great speeches, came from the soul. God would guide him. Just as he had guided him here. Everything came from the Almighty Father and he had never felt so close to him as he did now. God had always been with him, even on that day all those years before. Especially on that day. Although it had not been possible to know it at the time. How was he to know that what he felt was God's presence in the room when his father picked up the bread knife off the chopping board and pushed it into his mother's stomach right up to the handle?

At first it had felt like a joke. Time stopped. Everyone in the room looked at the wooden handle of the knife sticking out of his mother's floral-patterned apron. It looked absurd. He was about to laugh. But before the laughter could reach his lips, his mother started gasping and slumped to the floor, where she whimpered and then lay still. He remembered when they used to play cowboys and Indians. His dad never joined in but his mother, who had been interested in amateur dramatics as a younger woman, had thrown herself into the childish roleplay with a vengeance. Tommy had killed her. He had drawn his gun, shot her, and she had rolled onto the carpet and pretended to die. Her dying when they played cowboys and Indians and her dying on the floor of the kitchen as her family watched—it felt the same. It always felt the same every time he thought of it, and he thought of it a lot.

The feeling was there then and it had never really gone away again since. The feeling was God and God had stayed with Tommy and Belle in the kitchen when their father walked calmly out of the room as their mother's blood pooled on the cracked linoleum by the breakfast table.

They could hear him banging about in the garage next door, then it went quiet. When Tommy went through after a few minutes—he wanted to know whether he should call an ambulance—he found his father hanging from a metal roof beam, the cord from the power drill around his neck. Remembering it now, God was there in everything, from the urine that dripped from his father's trouser leg into the puddle on the floor to the faint rubbery creak of the cord as the body slowly turned a quarter circle and then back again. Before they dialed 999, Tommy and Belle watched *The Terminator*, which their dad had taped a couple of nights before when it was on television but their mother had said they were too young to watch. The film gave Belle nightmares for weeks.

Tommy opened the door to the first carriage. At the other end of it there was movement on either side of the train. Despite the public executions he had carried out earlier and the threat of detonating explosives, people were trying to escape again. They wanted to take their chances. Tommy raised up his pistol and emptied the magazine in two bursts, the first at one side of the carriage and the second at the other. There were cries, screams, the splashing of bodies into water. That would give the others pause for thought and it would buy him some more time.

The laptop was in position on the makeshift hammock slung between the handrails. Another few minutes and he would stand in front of it and address the world.

With the pistol reloaded and holstered in his pocket, he closed the door to the cab and turned his attention to the speech once again while George, the driver, sat in the driver's seat and stared out into the tunnel. But however hard Tommy tried to concentrate, thoughts kept forcing themselves into his mind, memories from childhood, and one memory in particular, of his father telling him about the River Lime.

His dad might have been a hard bastard but he told a good story. He had worked on the London Underground in the early seventies before he met Tommy's mother. An engineer was what he said he was, but knowing how he exaggerated, he was probably involved in little more than track maintenance. He regaled Tommy with stories of secret tunnels and forgotten stations, and one of the stories that he told him was about London's underground rivers, tributaries of the Thames like the Walbrook, the Fleet, the Tyburn and the Lime, that had once flowed on the surface but had been boxed into culverts by the encroachment of the city. It was the story of the River Lime that particularly interested little Tommy. Rising from the same springs on Hampstead Heath as the Fleet River, it flowed down through Camden Town and under the easternmost section of the West End to rejoin the Fleet in Holborn and from there into the Thames at Blackfriars Bridge. When the Charing Cross, Euston, and Hampstead Railway—later to become the westerly branch of the Northern Line—was being built in the late 1890s and early 1900s, it was necessary to house the River Lime in a tunnel for a two-mile section from Goodge Street in the north to Covent Garden in the south to prevent flooding in the newly constructed underground railway line. It was a major feat of engineering. The flow of the river could not be described as fast but still constituted thousands of gallons per hour.

Following a major survey of the London Underground carried out in the early seventies, it was decided that the tunnel housing the River Lime should be shored up to prevent any danger of leakage. One area in particular was considered to be most at risk and that was the section beneath Charing Cross Road, where the Lime ran very close to a section of train tunnel, which was itself in a low-level area between the stations either side of it—Tottenham Court Road to the north and Leicester Square to the south. The survey report had said that in the event of the River Lime flooding in this section, the Northern Line tunnel would fill with water in a matter of hours.

Tommy's dad was part of the engineering team that reinforced the tunnel carrying the water, and he had told Tommy how he and his fellow workers had joked that if someone like the IRA— the main purveyors of terrorism to Londoners in the seventies— wanted to pull off a spectacular attack, they could flood the northbound Northern Line tunnel and any train that happened to be in it. And there it was, a seed in little Tommy Denning's mind. Almost exactly halfway between the two stations in the northbound tunnel—that's what his dad had told him. A flight of metal steps. A maintenance access shaft to all that remained of the River Lime, the forgotten river. Tommy never forgot.

After his father died and Tommy grew older, this random piece of information took on greater significance. It was secret knowledge. It was a gift. When he found Christ and was born again, the gift became more precious and significant as did other events in his life. Like the attacks on the Twin Towers.

He watched it all on television, right from the moment when United Airlines Flight 175 went into the South Tower. At the age of fourteen, suddenly his life had meaning. The lines were drawn. The army was his only option. He was going on a crusade. But then came Afghanistan and everything got confused. It wasn't the crusade he had hoped for. The Afghans weren't the enemy. For a time even his faith in Christ was shaken but he did what he had to do. Even when his friend, Jed, was blown up by a roadside bomb, he could not bring himself to hate, as so many of the men he fought alongside did. He bided his time and he got out when he could. During his time in Afghanistan, he managed to avoid killing anyone. That wasn't to say that he didn't see people get killed—he did, plenty— but God had decided that it wasn't right for him to kill. Not yet.

When he came home, Belle was living in Wales, in Snowdonia, in an old farm that was now the monastic headquarters of an evangelical sect called Cruor Christi. Typical Belle. She never did things by half. Bored and frustrated after years in foster homes around London, she had written to him to tell him she wanted to move to the country. But he never expected a farm converted into a monastery on the side of a mountain.

It was good at first. They seemed like decent people. But as Tommy's faith grew stronger, it also changed, and he found it difficult to share his new brothers' and sisters' convictions, grew tired of their blinkered attitudes, particularly those of Father Owen. To Owen, Christ was the only way, and all other religions—even those who interpreted Christ differently—were wrong, sinful. The strength of the old man's faith was admirable but it was misguided. The same went for Brother Varick. They were fighting the wrong battle. The lines were drawn but not where they thought. 9/11 was a call to arms but not for believers to fight one another as some deluded souls believed. It was a rallying cry.

The Muslim brothers and sisters were in pain but no one was listening to them. God allowed 9/11 to happen because he wanted to send a message to the world. But mankind, as always, and particularly in the West, misunderstood the symbolism and poured oil on the flames.

9/11 was like a diamond bullet. The strength of will that it required, its pure crystalline simplicity. The World Trade Center became an epic metaphor beamed into homes across the globe. So too the Pentagon and, as for United Airlines Flight 93 going down in that field in Pennsylvania, this offered humanity hope. Destiny can be changed. Man can make a difference.

And the more he thought about 9/11 and what it meant, particularly after the lunacy of Helmand, the more he thought about the River Lime and his secret knowledge. He knew it was no accident that he had been given this information. The hand of God was guiding him. It felt as though everything was coming to a head. The pressure was building. When Simeon Fisher arrived at Madoc Farm and his true identity became apparent, it was a sign to begin preparations.

Like Mohammed Atta before him, Tommy decided he would utilize existing hardware and infrastructure and turn it against the enemy. It was what God wanted, he could feel it, and the true gold of this psychic alchemy was the discovery that a great battle had once taken place on an ancient bridge over the River Lime between Boudicca and the Romans. Before the battle, the river was blessed by one of the first Christian missionaries to visit Britain, Matthew of Parnassus, an old man who when he was a child had met Jesus. All of which meant one thing. The River Lime flowed with holy water.

11:44 AM

Morden Tube Station parking lot

The heat was intense as Brother Alistair retraced his steps yet again between the rows of cars. It didn't feel like England. It felt tropical. When he closed his eyes, the sun beat down on him, coming through his eyelids in a reddish brown. Opening them slightly, he looked away from the sun into the blue sky streaked with the vapor trails of airliners. Then he looked at the cars all around him. What were the odds of him finding the children? If he was a betting man, which he supposed he probably was being a former junkie, then he might have thought it was about a ten-to-one shot. Those were good enough odds for him. And the likelihood of his finding them was in direct proportion to the amount of time that he spent looking. The trouble was the number of cars. After living in the countryside for so long, it was almost too much for his mind to compute that there could be so many people and so many cars all crammed together in one place.

But as time dragged on, he could feel the odds of finding the children safe and sound lengthen. He had been in the parking lot since just after nine o'clock, and apart from a short break when he had gone to the shop to buy a bottle of water, he had wandered between the cars, both in the parking lot and in the streets surrounding the station.

It bothered Alistair more than anything else, more than the hijack of the tube train, more than what Tommy Denning intended to do to the passengers. It was the unthinking cruelty of it that was so much more shocking than all the other aspects of his sick plan. In the car that morning, as they made their way along the motorway toward London in the milky early morning light, Varick had told him about the contents of the notebook Father Owen had found in Tommy's room. Varick had looked for the notebook before they left but he couldn't find it. Tommy must have taken it back before he had driven the carving knife through the old man's neck. But Varick could remember the contents and, as he had told Alistair what the plan entailed, he mentioned the children only in passing. Clearly, their part in the whole thing was just one atrocity out of many, but Alistair couldn't get the image out of his head, just as he couldn't banish the memory of how he had found Owen thrashing around in the bath with his neck impaled on the knife's blade.

"In order to make sure that the train driver does exactly as he says," Varick had said as he drove the car, "Tommy's going to tell him that he has taken his children hostage and any attempt to raise the alarm or release the passengers from the train will mean that they'll be killed. In his notebook, however, it says that the children will be locked in the trunk of the car they use to get to the tube station."

Varick had gone on to explain the other aspects of the planned atrocity but Alistair wasn't paying much attention. The thought of two children locked in the trunk of a car on a day as hot as this haunted him. As they had parked in a public lot just off Piccadilly Circus, Alistair could keep his thoughts to himself no longer.

"We should try and find the children," he had said as they walked through Soho.

"It's more important that we find Tommy."

"But we can't leave the children in the boot of a car. They'll die in this heat."

Varick frowned as he said, "Let me think about it."

By the time they reached Leicester Square tube station, Varick had reached a decision and he put his hand on Alistair's shoulder as he said, "We both have a mission here, Alistair. I'll find Tommy, you must find the children."

They had bought tickets and taken the escalators down to the Northern Line. But whereas Varick took up his position on the northbound platform to begin his wait for Tommy, Alistair had taken the first train southbound.

When he had arrived at Morden station a member of London Underground staff, a man in his fifties with grey hair and a belly grown from too many years seated at a desk was taking questions from members of the public who had arrived at the station expecting to be able to travel into central London. Brother Alistair joined the crowd of people and listened to what was said. There had been an incident on the Underground and the network was closed down. Tommy had clearly managed to put his plan into operation. Whether Brother Varick could stop him from taking it to its ghastly conclusion was something that was in God's hands now. He felt bad about leaving Varick to try and save the train passengers all by himself but he felt confident that he would succeed. Besides, Alistair now had far more pressing concerns. If he didn't hurry up, the children would be dead before he found them.

11:48 AM

About certain events in his life George had almost photographic recall and his first date with Maggie was one of them. She had worn a striped Breton top with jeans and a leather jacket. Her hair was much shorter than it was now. They both smiled a lot; both had lasagne and drank far too much wine because they were nervous. He had toyed with the idea of asking Maggie if she wanted to come back to his place but decided that if he really was serious about her—and the butterflies in his stomach were testament to the fact that he was—the best thing would be to show a bit of gallantry and make sure that she got home safely in a taxi. When she sat in the back of the cab, he leaned in to give her a goodnight kiss on the cheek and she had pulled him close and kissed him on the lips. He knew then that it was more than just drunken affection. It was obvious that she liked him as much as he liked her. He walked home that night, all the way to Muswell Hill from the West End; he just wanted to keep walking, enjoying the warm summer night and his thoughts of Maggie.

Ever since that night, Italian restaurants had held a special resonance for them because they were reminded of their first date.

Like all couples, he and Maggie had developed their own little conversational rituals and traditions. Whenever the bread rolls were delivered to the table in an Italian restaurant, George would often take two pieces of bread, pop one in each cheek and do his "Marlon Brando in *The Godfather*" impersonation: "You come into my house on the day my daughter is to be married and you ask me to do murder for money." She groaned every time he did it but she still laughed all the same.

They had passed their affection for Italian restaurants on to Ben and Sophie. Mr. Pizza, or Mr. Pieces rather, had become a family favorite. Would they ever go there again? Not if Tommy Denning saw the chewing gum on the handset or if the threat of flooding the train didn't force the authorities into succumbing to his demands.

"Okay, George, I want you to kneel with me and pray." Denning had that expression on his face—the little smile and the raised eyebrows—as though he was a child goading his friend into a dare.

"I er, I don't pray."

"I know you say you don't believe but try to open your mind for a moment. Didn't the psalm that you recited earlier mean anything to you?"

"It might have meant something to me when I said it."

"It might have meant something to you when you said it." Denning spoke like a barrister, repeating the words of a witness in an attempt to make them sound ridiculous.

"Yeah, I don't know."

"Well maybe another prayer might mean something to you now."

"Maybe."

"The thing is, I want to pray now and I don't want to pray alone. I think you're very important to this whole—" He looked around the cab trying to find the word. Please God don't look at the handset, don't see the chewing gum. George was praying already. Denning found the word: "—occasion, this moment in time. Do you understand what I'm saying?"

An idea was forming in George's mind. Praying would involve kneeling; it might even involve Tommy's eyes being closed. What better time to launch an attack on the bastard than when he was in congress with whichever imaginary being he had chosen to believe in? He would be vulnerable. This might be George's best chance to disarm him. All it would take would be a lucky punch. If he hit him as hard as he could then it might buy him a few seconds, might allow him to hit him again, kick him, grab the gun even. He wouldn't need to worry about the chewing gum on the radio mouthpiece then.

"Your faith means a lot to you, doesn't it?"

Tommy chuckled at the absurdity of the question. "Of course, it means everything. Can't you see that?"

"Yes, I can and ... I envy you. I've struggled to believe in the past. I've tried but something just always held me back. Until now."

"Until now?"

He shouldn't overplay his hand but he needed Denning to know that he was serious about his intention to pray. The more relaxed Denning was the better. In addition to being his motivation, religion was also his weak spot, his Achilles' heel.

"In a weird kind of way, I guess I respect you." Was that too much? He didn't have time to judge. Denning looked convinced—so far. "I've spent my whole life compromising my real feelings and beliefs. And look where it's got me? I'm forty, I'm messed up, I'm in a job that I can't stand, all my hopes and dreams have turned to dust. Today for the first time in years—and despite the fear that I feel for myself and my family—I actually feel alive." Denning was watching him, expressionless. Could he tell that he was lying? Was he lying? It didn't matter, he was engineering an opportunity for himself. A choice had been made—it might not be the right choice but it was a choice. He was going to keep coming at this freak; he was going to keep testing him. He was going to find a moment of weakness and he was going to stop him.

"You're serious, are you? You can really feel God's love?"

"I don't know what it is but I can feel something. I feel different."

"I thought it would be more difficult than this. I thought you would fight against it harder. You've made me so happy."

George had not anticipated Denning's next move. He reached out to George and put his arms around him, hugged him, their cheeks pressed together. Before George could decide whether this might prove a better moment to launch his attack than later on, Denning had released him, put the gun down on the driver's console and was kneeling.

"Come, George, let's pray together."

Tommy Denning raised his hands up to his mouth and closed his eyes. George knelt too and did the same—except he kept his eyes open, watching, waiting.

"Dear Lord, our heavenly father, this is your humble servant, Thomas . . ."

11:48 AM

Ed could hear the distant sound of helicopters as they hovered over the West End. The wailing of sirens on the streets below was a constant. For a moment, it felt as though the barrage of sound was taunting him. Ed was trained to deal with pressure—he trained others how to deal with it too—but this was something else. No one in the negotiating cell could fail to feel it. These people were experts in hostage negotiation. They were experts in establishing psychological profiles and doing so rapidly so that negotiation tactics could be tailored to those profiles. But none of them had been faced with such a meticulously planned and executed scenario involving so many hostages and with so little apparent motive; none of them had come across someone like Tommy Denning before. In every hostage negotiation that Ed had been a part of over the years, he had gone into the negotiation knowing with an unwavering certainty that he had the upper hand psychologically speaking, that he was the one in control. But in this situation Ed knew he wasn't. Tommy Denning was shrewd, resourceful, calm, confident, and seemingly possessed of an innate understanding of the negotiation process and an ongoing refusal to be drawn into it. What Denning had created here couldn't help but make all the other situations that Ed had worked on seem low-key, trivial almost, in comparison. The sheer scale of this situation and the numbers of people involved elevated it into a different realm.

Ed's negotiating team, Des White, Nick Calvert and Laura Massey, were feeling the pressure—he could hear it in their voices—but they were responding to that pressure as the professionals that they were. Hooper, on the other hand, was an unknown quantity. His responses to the psychological pressure of the crisis were inconsistent. Ed couldn't read him. To Ed, the pressure felt like vertigo. He used to suffer from it when he was sighted; when blind it seemed to go away. Now it was back. It felt as though the negotiating cell was perched at the very top of a skyscraper of security infrastructure.

The whole area around the hijack was locked down, the command center was secure. Special forces were on standby while the rapid intervention plan was being devised. The police, the military, and the government—not to mention the victims and their families—were looking to Ed and his team to make the right decisions. Storming the train was always an option but the risks were clear. Over three hundred passengers stood to die if it went wrong, not to mention the SAS soldiers themselves who would have to undertake the operation. One thing he knew for certain—even if he was uncertain of anything else—was that when Tommy Denning said that he would kill everyone on the train if anyone tried to stop him making his announcement, he meant it. The conviction in his voice when he made his threats—whether articulated through George the driver or from his own lips—was unequivocal.

Without an immediate intervention, Ed and his team were faced with a negotiation with a subject that was going to be about as difficult as they came. To add to that, there was now the issue of the water in the tunnel. "Think of it as an egg timer," Denning had said over the radio link. George had then said, "So you're trying to drown us by flooding the tunnel, is that it?" Even though the radio link had been broken for some reason before George could tease any more from his captor, Denning's intentions were clear. He was going to ensure that everything was stacked in his favor. He held all the cards. Whatever his demands were, he fully expected them to be met. He had set in motion a series of events that could not be reversed. Either the authorities complied or the passengers would end up dead. It was as simple as that. Denning knew enough about hostage negotiation to know that the negotiators' premium commodity, time, was the one thing that he could turn against them to make it play to his advantage.

So, what the hell were his demands going to be? What could this evangelical ex-soldier possibly want? As soon as Ed knew what it was, the psychological balance of power in the negotiation would shift. Knowledge of what those desires were would allow Ed to manage them and use them to manipulate Denning and begin the process of securing a positive outcome.

Laura entered the room—he could tell it was her from her footsteps—and she was pulling pieces of paper from an envelope.

"We've got an interim profile and background on Thomas Denning," she said.

"Thanks, Laura," said Ed. "Can you paraphrase as we've only got a few minutes until he's going to make his speech?"

"Yes, let's hear it," said Hooper. It was clear to Ed that he was trying to reassert himself as a key player within the negotiating cell. He didn't seem to care about the protocol; you didn't bark orders at the negotiating coordinator, particularly one with the experience of Laura Massey. She didn't say anything in response to his comment and nor would he but it was yet another sign that Hooper was working to a different agenda.

"He's twenty-five years old," started Laura. "One of a pair of fraternal twins. The sister's named Belle. When they were nine years old, they saw their father murder their mother with a bread knife before he hanged himself. After that, Tommy spent most of his childhood in various foster homes in London and the southeast. Lots of petty crime, shoplifting, antisocial behavior." Laura flicked over a sheet of paper then continued. "Did time in Feltham Young Offender Institution, where it appears he found God. He's got a high

IQ but was diagnosed with a borderline case of dissociative behavior although it was not considered bad enough to prevent him from joining the army. He ended up fighting in Afghanistan. Did two tours there, one in '08 and one in '10. And then it looks as though he dropped out and, still big on God, joined up with an evangelical Christian sect located in a remote part of Snowdonia in Wales. The sect is called Cruor Christi. It means the 'blood of Christ,' blood as in blood spilled in battle, bloodshed, rather than 'sanguinis' which is the Latin for blood which is used in the communion. They've been under investigation by the local constabulary following reports of gunfire."

Ed said, "I take it the place is being taken apart as we speak?"

"Welsh Special Branch are on their way there. It's very remote. What we do know is that in addition to the core members who number about fifteen or twenty brothers and sisters as they call themselves, there's an ex–New Orleans police officer called Varick Mageau who is under suspicion of having fired on looters after Hurricane Katrina. It seems that Cruor Christi specialize in taking in people who have personal problems, mainly drug or crime related."

Laura flicked onto another sheet of paper. "So among the flock we've got a guy who did eight years for armed robbery, another one who burned down the family home but got off because of diminished responsibility, and another one here, Brother Alistair Waller, who is a former heroin addict."

"Sound like a nice bunch," said Ed. "So are we assuming until we have further intel that this hijack is the work of Cruor Christi collectively or do we think that Tommy Denning is a rogue element?"

"In my opinion, he's a rogue element," said Hooper.

"You sound very sure," said Ed. "And we also have to bear in mind that he has accomplices. This isn't a lone-wolf operation."

Hooper didn't have an opportunity to respond before Laura Massey said, "Ed, I'd like to introduce Professor Frank Moorcroft."

Ed held out his hand and it was taken in the weak grip of a hand that was old and leathery. Ed breathed in the aroma of the man to whom he was being introduced. The main components that he managed to isolate were books, paper, and the still air of musty offices and classrooms. It was the smell of a man who has spent his life within the confines of academia. He had also failed to shower or bathe that morning.

"Hello, pleased to meet you." It was the voice of a man who felt nervous and awkward, guilty even, as though he had been caught in the act of doing something shameful.

"Professor Moorcroft," said Laura, "is an expert on the London Underground's architecture, construction, and rolling stock."

"Glad to meet you, Professor. I'll get straight to it. As you have no doubt been briefed, we've got a hostage situation on the London Underground. Terrorists have taken a train with over three hundred people on board. We also think that they're trying to flood the tunnel. For the purposes of our negotiation and our understanding of the perpetrators' psychological profiles, it's essential that we understand whether it's possible that they could genuinely flood the tunnel to such a degree that it would threaten the lives of the people on the train."

"Well, the thing is, you see, there are numerous water sources in and around the London Underground—water mains, underground rivers."

Professor Moorcroft was a man whose opinion counted for a lot in his world. But he was clearly feeling a degree of culture shock to find himself in a situation so raw and urgent. He masked his trepidation with a tone and manner which he might have employed with a student, one in which the respective roles of intellectual and sub-intellectual were accentuated. It was a common trait of academics, Ed had found, but he was happy to indulge it—play the "sub"—if it meant that Moorcroft would give him the information that he required as quickly and efficiently as possible.

"This particular incident is in the West End I believe?" asked Moorcroft.

"Between Leicester Square and Tottenham Court Road in the northbound tunnel."

"Ah, now you see that will be the River Lime. It's little more than a big water pipe at that section but if it was breached in any way then, of course, you're looking at quite substantial flooding."

He might have come across as something of a weird fish but Ed was grateful for Moorcroft's clarity and focus. What he said next was confirmation of Ed's fears that Tommy Denning was a fierce adversary.

"The trouble you've got at that specific location is that there's a section of tunnel at a particularly low elevation with respect to the stations on either side of it and, to make matters worse, the ground is very unporous. The tunnel will fill in no time. I'd say these people knew exactly what they were doing when they chose the location for their, er . . . attack."

"When you say it'll fill in no time, what are we talking?"

"Well, I'd have to put together some figures, which I'm happy to do if someone can let me have access to a computer."

"Absolutely, of course, but in the meantime, can you give me a ballpark? Will the tunnel fill in a day? Half a day? An hour?"

"Oh gosh, I really couldn't hypothesize to that sort of degree . . ."

"Nearer to which?"

Ed suspected that Moorcroft was shaking his head, not realizing that he was blind.

"I really need to press you on this," said Ed. "It really is very important." He couldn't hide the desperation and urgency in his voice.

"Well, one would have to say that in the worst-case scenario you're looking at maybe two hours from the start of the flooding. In the best case, I don't know, three or four?"

Ed felt strangely light-headed as Professor Moorcroft said this. It was as though the sheer enormity of what they faced had finally been confirmed. In a typical hostage negotiation, Ed was comforted by the knowledge that he could settle in and wait, allowing the minutes and hours to tick by, knowing that with every moment that passed, the perpetrator's resolve would be weakening and the balance of power inexorably tipped in the direction of the negotiators. He had felt that same comfort earlier in the day. It had been something to cling to when there was no other information coming through from the command center. But now it was gone, snatched away by the realization that they were faced with a situation that was going to worsen rapidly. When Denning had advised George, the driver, over the radio link to "think of it as an egg timer," he knew exactly what he was saying.

"Okay, we need to stay completely focused now," said Hooper stating the obvious. He sounded anything but focused. His voice was imbued with a shrill note that whispered fear to Ed.

"This guy's clever," said Calvert. "He certainly knows how to pile on the pressure. He's got over three hundred people down there with a train that's wired with explosives and a tunnel that's filling up with water. He sure as hell wants to ensure that we give him what he wants."

"Professor Moorcroft, how long do you think it might be until the power to the train goes down?" asked Ed.

"Again, it's a question that's almost impossible to answer with any degree of accuracy," said Moorcroft.

"Try," said Ed.

"Well, what you have to consider is that just because there's water on the track doesn't mean that the power won't continue to function for some time. And once the power does indeed fail, the trains that are used on the Northern Line also have a battery that may keep the lights on for anything up to an hour longer. It really depends in what state the battery's in."

"Ed," said Laura, "I'm going to have to butt in at this point. Commander Boise wants you to take part in a conference call with COBRA. As the only person who has spoken to the perpetrator of the hostage-taking at this time—and as lead negotiator—she wants you to discuss the situation with the committee."

Ed was about to express his immediate thoughts and say that it was crazy that he should have to be taken away from the front line of the negotiation with Denning so close to issuing his demands, even if it was only for a moment, but he decided against it and said,

"Sure." He stood up and Laura took him by the arm and led him from the room.

They walked along the corridor—the same corridor he'd walked along earlier that morning with Hooper when he had arrived at the Network Control center—and Laura said, "They don't know about the water in the tunnel."

"So I guess I'm the messenger? Let's hope they don't shoot me."

Laura emitted a humorless chuckle as she led Ed into another office and placed a telephone receiver in his hand.

"Hi, this is Ed Mallory, lead negotiator."

"Ed, this is Malcolm Walker. I'm chairing this meeting of the COBRA committee. Can you please give us an update of where we are with this situation? Our last piece of news was about the Internet broadcast."

There was no point considering that this was the highest level briefing that he had ever been party to; no point even considering the deeper significance of his inclusion in this discussion.

"We're obviously treating this as a major terrorist incident due to the sheer scale of the hostage-taking, the possible death of the two CO19 officers, and the claim that the train is wired with explosives. We've also had some alarming news in the past few minutes. The train driver managed to keep the radio channel open so we heard some extraneous conversation between him and the main hijacker, Tommy Denning. This has led us to believe that there is some sort of flooding taking place in the tunnel which might be coming from a water source, namely the River Lime, which is an underground river that was boxed in adjacent to the Northern Line tunnel during the construction of the Underground rail network. We're worried that the intention is to flood the tunnel, thereby placing the passengers in further jeopardy, by way of a bargaining tactic."

Ed felt relieved; he sounded like a man in control even if he didn't feel like one. The members of COBRA were clearly stunned by the audacity of Denning's attack and, for a moment, there was silence on the line as they all hid behind the faint hiss of the multiple connection on the conference call. When they had turned up for work that morning, they could never have imagined they would be faced with an attack from such an unlikely source, and one that would gain such overwhelming media attention. Because despite the scene of the hostage-taking being hundreds of feet underground, the grainy, almost ghostly, video feed from Denning's webcam was replete with all the iconography of the World Trade Center as it had billowed smoke in the sunshine of that September morning.

The voices that filled the silence were imbued with palpable tension. In the absence of any coherent plan to counter the threat, talk in newsrooms throughout the world had already turned to intelligence failings and the apportioning of blame.

Taking advantage of a break in the chatter, Ed said, "From what we have gleaned so far from intelligence relating to Denning and his sect, it would appear that we are faced with religious psychopathy here. Despite his accomplices, I'd say this is very much of Denning's own devising and, let's face it, he's not come all this way to go away again. I can hear it in his voice; he's going all the way. In that respect, he's very much like a classic spree killer and once a spree killer has started his killing spree it's almost impossible to talk him down, even if a dialogue can be established. In the space of a couple of hours Tommy Denning has gone from being a nobody to being the most talked-about person on the planet. He has created his own myth. Nothing I can say is going to compete with that."

"So where does that leave us?" Head of MI5 Howard Berriman's booming upper-crust voice on the conference call was unmistakable. It was less than an hour since Ed had last spoken to him, after all.

"As lead negotiator in the cell, it's not really my place to offer thoughts on that."

"I'm just asking your opinion as someone who has much experience in this area," said Berriman.

"Well, we have a few options open to us. We can send in special forces to storm the train. We can inject gas into the tunnel that will overcome the hijackers and hostages alike. We can send in special forces under cover of a simultaneous gas dispersal. We can even drive another train into the tunnel and possibly tow or push the train into a station where it can be stormed more easily. Lack of options is not the problem. Clearly the most efficient option in bringing this scenario to a close is also the most difficult."

"And that is?" asked Berriman.

"Killing the hijackers simultaneously before they can set off any explosives. We could put snipers in the tunnel at either end of the train but what we don't know is whether there are further accomplices along the body of the train who might have the capability to detonate the explosives."

"And you really think there are explosives?" asked Berriman.

"We have to believe that there are."

"How long until the tunnel fills?"

"It could be no more than two hours."

Another unmistakable voice Ed had heard numerous times on radio and television news programs, that of the home secretary, chipped in with, "Do you think there might be someone down there on the train, like a policeman or a member of the armed forces, who might be able to try and take action?"

"It would be great if there was," said Ed, "but it's unlikely."

"Are you sure that it's wise to allow the hijackers the publicity they want?"

Ed understood the protocol well enough to know that he would need to show deference to those higher up the chain of command, police being thought of as lower than spies and politicians.

"This is not really my call as lead negotiator and I know this is being discussed in detail between the incident commander and the relevant coordinators, but my thinking on it is that the Internet access provides us with valuable intelligence from the passengers on the train. It is possible that there is someone who could intervene, someone who we may be able to mobilize. Denning has ensured that it's the only way we can find out his demands, and we need to know what they are in order to tailor our negotiation accordingly."

There was silence on the line. He didn't have much firsthand experience of politics but he knew enough to know that the fear of doing the wrong thing was all-pervasive. He could feel that fear emanating down the wire. But it was three minutes to twelve by his tactile watch and he needed to be elsewhere.

"I'm afraid I need to get back to the negotiating cell because Denning is due to issue his demands at twelve." Ed didn't wait to hear confirmation from his superiors, just passed the phone back to Laura and said, "We'd better go."

11:54 AM

Northern Line Train 037, driver's cab

George watched him as he prayed. Denning's eyes were shut tight as he concentrated on the words—lots of Dear Lords and Our Heavenly Fathers, lots of requests for blessings for the "dangerous task ahead." They were facing each other, kneeling in the cab, knees tacky against the treacly blood on the floor. George didn't rate his chances. He had never been in a fight before. The only punch he had ever thrown was at a school bully when he was twelve years old. When the taunting had got too much, he had snapped. He'd broken the bastard's nose, which had got him into lots of trouble and nearly led to expulsion from the school. It had, however, made him feel a whole lot better. The difference between that moment and this one was that, when he punched the bully at school, he was driven by pure rage. He felt rage now but it was twisted and neutered by the ever-present fear that sapped his strength, leaving his muscles soft and trembling. Denning was young and athletic. A halfhearted attack could be fatal both for George and his family.

"And Dear Lord Our Father, bless my sister, your humble servant, Belle. Her heart is pure and her will is strong." It sounded as though the prayer was coming to an end. If George were going to hit him, it would have to be right now. Denning's eyes remained closed as George pulled his fist back and lashed out, punching him in the middle of the face. It wasn't a bad punch but it wasn't enough. Momentarily shocked and blinded by pain, Denning slumped backward. George was torn between hitting him again and making a grab for the gun. He decided on the former and took another swing but this time, he missed and his fist crashed into the side of the driver's seat. Denning was regaining his composure. George aimed another punch and managed to connect but it was a glancing blow against Denning's jaw and had little effect. In a last desperate attempt to land a knockout blow, George started to rain punches down on Denning but his mad flailings came to an abrupt end as Denning pulled his left knee hard up against his chest and kicked his foot out, his boot connecting with George's throat.

George felt as though he had been hung. He fell back against the train wall. It was as though something in his neck that had resided there quite happily for the past forty years had been permanently dislocated. Breathing was an impossibility as he clutched his throat and coughed and gagged. Denning was on his feet, picking up the gun, and spinning around. He aimed it at George's face and pulled the trigger. As the shot was fired, George's existence was reduced to pain and darkness and the metallic stench of smoke. If he was dying, however, he was oblivious to the wound that was about to kill him. The pain remained located solely in his throat and his senses were otherwise unimpaired. As he opened his eyes, he could see through the watery blur of his tears that Denning remained standing over him. Scrambling to his feet, George turned and looked at the bullet hole in the train wall, inches from where his head had been moments before.

Instead of the fury that he expected, Denning looked sad and troubled. The gun remained pointed at George but his anger of earlier was absent.

"You lied to me."

George tried to speak but his trampled voice box would make no sound.

"You lied to me. You said that you were ready. You made me think that you had accepted your destiny and you were happy to come with me. George, we were *praying* . . ."

George tried again and this time managed to get out a whispered groan: "I'm sorry."

"You're sorry? What do you mean, you're sorry?"

"I was confused." His throat was throbbing and every syllable ached but his voice was gaining in strength. "Maybe I'm not ready yet. But I'm trying. It's hard for me. I can't stop thinking about my family. I'm afraid. I want to do the right thing but I don't know what the right thing is."

Denning must have realized that he was lying. The gun was raised once again and this time the end of the still-hot barrel was pressed against his forehead. This really was the end.

"Dear Lord, bless George"—George didn't want to be blessed; this bastard could stuff his blessing—"a good man, confused by the journey on which he has embarked yet still worthy of your grace. This your humble servant Thomas commends his soul to your mercy."

George shut his eyes waiting for the bullet.

"Let me be strong during these difficult and testing times, let me be strong enough to carry out your will as you see fit. Amen."

George opened his eyes to see that Denning was staring straight at him with an expectant expression on his face. Was George meant to say something? And then it occurred to him and he said it: "Amen." Ironic if this was to be the last word he ever uttered that it should be a word born of religion, a form of salutation to a God in whom he did not believe.

But the bullet didn't come and George knew that he was going to live for a few more minutes at least when Denning lowered the gun. The look that he gave George was one of affection, warmth even.

"You've made a terrible mistake. I think you know that."

"I do. I'm sorry, Tommy."

"You're my disciple."

"I know."

"Promise me you won't betray me again."

"I won't, I promise. Thank you, Tommy."

Denning stepped back and George glanced across at the chewing gum still throbbing, singing, screaming out to be noticed on the radio handset. Should he attempt to ride the wave of Denning's forgiveness and own up to what he had done? Before he could come to a decision, Tommy folded up his dog-eared pieces of paper, turned to him, and said, "Come on, I've got a speech to make and I want you by my side."

He opened the door and George followed him, relieved to be out of the cab and on the move, even if it was only to enter the first carriage and sit, as instructed, on the row of seats by the laptop hanging in its hammock swung between the handrails. Denning approached it as though he was approaching a pulpit in church, about to read the lesson and, in his own mind at least, that's exactly what he was doing.

11:59 AM

Network Control center, St. James's

As he reentered the negotiating cell, Ed took advantage of the silence to ask: "Do we have a list of passengers yet?"

"It's not definitive," said White. "Those passengers whose identities we have been able to confirm appear to be drawn from a typical London cross-section. Professionals, clerical and admin staff, students, academics, tourists, schoolchildren unfortunately; no one who looks like they might be able to intervene."

"Here he comes," said Calvert as Tommy Denning emerged from the driver's cab on the video feed. Ed could only take a seat and listen as the other members of the negotiating cell watched the images from the train.

"That must be George Wakeham following him," said Calvert. "Do you think he might be involved? Like he might be on the inside?"

"No," said Ed. "You've only got to listen to his voice to know that he's shitting himself. He's doing whatever he can to stay alive."

"He also appears to have blood all over his clothes," said White.

"Tell me what's happening," said Ed, failing to disguise the impatience in his voice.

"Denning is gesturing for the driver to sit down," said Calvert. "He's sitting down and staring at the floor of the carriage. He looks pretty freaked out."

"Well, I think you would be," said White.

"Denning's looking into the webcam," continued Calvert. "He's looking at his watch."

"Okay, so it's one minute until noon," said Denning. "I'm just going to check that you haven't stuck me on some secure link and I'm not going global. We wouldn't want that now, would we?" The sound of Denning's fingers tapping on a keyboard came through the speakers.

"I knew he'd check that," muttered Calvert.

"That's fine," said Denning. "Good to see that you haven't tried to censor me or do anything stupid. By my watch it's noon, so I guess it's time for me to explain what we're all doing here." As he said this, there was a series of screams from a woman in an adjoining train carriage as she succumbed to a fit of hysteria.

"Another of London Underground's happy customers reacting to today's unfortunate disruption of the Northern Line service," said Denning, smiling. He was as calm and composed as ever. The circus he had created was nothing to do with two-way communication; it was a performance, a well-rehearsed and carefully scripted performance, and one that he had looked forward to for some time.

"For those of you who don't already know, my name is Thomas Robson Denning. Tommy. I'm a twenty-five-year-old ex-soldier. I'm also a British subject. My mother and father were British and their mothers and fathers before them. I don't make the point because I'm obsessed by racial purity, it's just to show you what I'm not. I'm not a Muslim fundamentalist from Africa, Asia, or the Middle East. I'm not the accepted archetype of a modern terrorist."

Denning's roundabout admission that he was indeed a terrorist served to twist the nerves yet further in Ed's stomach.

"I come from a country of supposed democracy, freedom, and peace, a country opposed to oppression and cruelty. But when I look around me, that's not what I see. What I see is a society that feels the need to lie and cheat and deceive. There is a war going on in the world, a war between good and evil played out in a series of ongoing battles for hearts and minds. Wherever you look, propaganda is at work. The news networks peddle lies and untruths in order to further the aims and goals of the people in charge. The only way that I can broadcast this message is by utilizing the Internet, for many lost souls a den of filth and yet also the last bastion of free speech. Propaganda serves not to make an objective study of the truth but to incite. So I want believers everywhere to see that what I am doing here today is an act of incitement. I say this as a Christian and not a Muslim but I say it, standing shoulder to shoulder with my Muslim friends. I call on all Muslims and Christians to see beyond the lies of their governments and rather than fighting between each other, unite and fight the one true enemy. This is a war between believers and nonbelievers and standing here today, in front of the peoples of the world, I am igniting the spark."

Denning's voice was rising. His London accent was becoming more pronounced. The image he had cultivated at the start of his speech, of a reasoned, well-balanced individual with a message to impart, was beginning to fade as the firebrand preacher took its place.

"Make no mistake about this, I am a global insurgent, and I stand alongside my brothers and sisters to fight for what I believe in, a spirituality based on Christian and Islamic values, the belief in one God, prayer, peace, quiet contemplation; and I fight against the enemy, the forces of hypocrisy, greed, corruption, and war.

"Our so-called freedom represents destruction and deceit in the name of commerce and business, while resistance to this insidious plague is painted as terrorism and intolerance. But every action has a reaction and the truth is that democracy and capitalism afford us no more freedom than the world's most repressive regimes.

"My authority comes from one place and one place only, the Bible. 'For the Lamb which is in the midst of the throne shall feed them and shall guide them into fountains of waters; and God shall wipe away all tears from their eyes.' Revelation chapter seven, verse seventeen. I, Tommy Denning, am that lamb. And here beneath the London streets, I am about to guide the world to the 'fountains of waters.' I stand alongside my fellow believers and say that it is time for an eye for an eye—or rather—a terror for a terror. Vengeance is a simple motivation but it is also pure and just. It is something that people can understand. Know this: I'm not some outsider, I'm just a normal guy who leads a good and spiritual life and wants to make a difference. And as long as there are people in the world who are downtrodden and exploited and feel no security then their oppressors will feel no security either. The longer the godless oppressors can keep us divided, the longer they will keep us downtrodden. The war starts today between believers and nonbelievers. All those who believe, have faith, all those who have God in their hearts, must rise up behind me and prepare for battle."

As Ed listened to Denning's words, just as millions around the world were doing, he felt fear creep through his innards. He had never felt it so acutely before. Not just for all the passengers on the train but for himself. He knew as he listened to Tommy Denning saying the words that, unlike every other subject he had come across in his years of crisis intervention and hostage negotiation, he was afraid of him.

12:06 PM

Northern Line Train 037, second carriage

Varick moved toward the doors between the second and first carriages. The passengers were now tightly packed together following the shooting by the hijacker and their nerves were shot to pieces. No one knew exactly how many people had been killed; numbers varied from between five and ten. Whatever the truth, Tommy had crossed the line and now it was up to Varick to stop him. He felt no fear, God was with him. There was no rush. It was important that Tommy made his intentions clear to the world before Varick finished him.

Although he was moving against the tide, people were only too pleased to let him through as his displacement meant that there would be just that little bit more space behind him. And as he approached the first carriage, there was a collective assumption that he was there to help them, save them even, and he did nothing to dispel it. He *was* there to save them.

"I wouldn't get any closer," said a heavyset man in his late thirties, who looked almost drunk with trembling nervous energy. "He's already killed lots of people."

"I'm here to help," said Varick.

The man stepped aside and muttered, "Thank God."

Varick kept his head down as he moved along the now deserted section of carriage. Up ahead, he could see Denning through the windows in the connecting doors.

There was a body by the door, a man in a suit with his head resting in a puddle of congealing blood. But Varick remained focused on Tommy in the first carriage, who stood in front of a piece of bed sheet slung between the handrails set into the ceiling of the train. On it was a laptop computer into which he spoke. Varick stepped over the body and crouched down behind the door to wait. It was essential that the authorities had a full understanding of what Tommy was going to do before he acted. Tommy wasn't the only one mindful of his own publicity.

Varick listened as Tommy reveled in his newfound celebrity. It was the rambling of a fantasist but he had to admit that it was more coherent and rehearsed than he had expected. He'd seen him around Madoc Farm for the past few weeks, brooding, deep in thought, scribbling in his notebook. What he said was more cogent than the ranting of your average religious fanatic—although he knew that religious fanatic was what both he and Tommy would be seen as by the vast majority of people. But if he could only stop Tommy carrying out his mission, turn the tide, and make the world see that Cruor Christi were saviors and not aggressors, then he might succeed in changing people's perceptions.

Whether Tommy had managed to achieve the global media saturation that he hoped for was immaterial. This was a big enough event in its own right to make the news across the world. Varick's mother and father, elderly as they now were, sitting in their home in New Orleans—what would they make of this? What would they make of their son if he managed to save the lives of hundreds of people? He would be a disappointment no more. At last his mother would be able to speak of him with pride.

Tommy spoke about freedom and democracy. What did he know about freedom and democracy? Twenty-five years old and thought he knew it all. Varick hoped that in his last sentient moments as the bullets tore into him from the Smith & Wesson that there might be some realization that he was wrong, that he had chosen the wrong path. And although he knew that he should also hope with all his heart that Tommy might offer himself up to God's mercy and be saved, there was another part of him—there was no denying it—that hoped that Tommy's pleas would be refused and God would turn his back on him and damn him for all eternity.

His geopolitical diatribe at an end, Denning talked about the underground river, the River Lime that he had redirected into the tunnel with his explosives. But as Varick listened to the words, it occurred to him that it was not Tommy Denning who was speaking them but the devil himself.

It was up to Varick to carry out an exorcism.

As he looked back down the carriage behind him, the people cowering at the end of it stared at him, mesmerized. He nodded once, a simple gesture that conveyed so much: they must be patient, he would act, all in good time. He chanced a quick glance through the window in the door. Tommy was less than twenty feet away. He couldn't miss.

12:13 PM

George watched him as he spoke into the webcam. Denning was nervous at first—almost fluffed his lines a couple of times—but now George could tell he was building up to the money shot. When he came to the part about the River Lime, and how the holy water would fill the tunnel in a few hours, George understood the twisted genius of the situation that Denning had engineered. It was indeed an egg timer. Unless the authorities did exactly what he wanted them to do, the passengers—however many hundreds of them there were—would drown. The authorities were clearly reluctant to storm the train on account of Denning's threats about explosives rigged in the carriages, threats which, just like the boast of there being multiple hijackers throughout the train, George suspected were untrue.

Denning was reflected in the little black eye of the webcam. How many people were watching him? How many more would watch the recording of this in the coming weeks, months, or years? George had to hand it to him, it was an audacious concept. George and his family were part of a historical moment, but one he would have traded his life to be excluded from. No, that wasn't true; he wouldn't have traded his life. Anything, even this, was better than losing his life. He didn't want to die; he had never wanted to die less than he did at that moment. All he could console himself with was that he would know soon enough whether this was a situation that could be resolved or not. It all came down to Denning's demands. Whatever they were. If he wanted something mundane and domestic, something like the release of a relative from prison or even something political that might be negotiated then there might be a possible resolution. But George had a sickening feeling that Denning was not a man who wanted to pursue anything straightforward or reasonable. This was not a straightforward or reasonable way of getting the world's attention. Whatever he wanted, it would be something complex and difficult. George hoped the authorities would give in to it—lie if they had to—tell Denning that they would do what he wanted, even if they reneged on the deal later. They would have to do whatever it took. That was their job.

Listening to Denning, he could tell that he was building up to a finale. There was a relaxed manner in his tone, an acknowledgment that he was almost finished.

"You're wondering why I'm doing this. You're asking yourselves: what can possibly be worth all this? You want to know what my demands are. There are always demands, aren't there? People don't just do something like this for the sake of doing it. Do they?" Denning smiled and stared into the camera. "Well, I'll tell you what my demands are. At present, there are thousands of gallons of water flowing into this tunnel, a tunnel that is beginning to fill up. So, it's very simple. I have just one demand and it is this: that the people of the world should see my sacrifice and watch while everyone on this train, myself included, drowns."

12:16 PM

Northern Line Train 037, second carriage

Through the windows in the adjoining doors, Varick could see Tommy standing in front of the hammock slung across the carriage on which there was a laptop computer. The hammock was fashioned from a bed sheet from Madoc Farm. The thick bluey-grey cotton was unmistakable. Varick had bought a job lot when they first moved in. They had money for more expensive sheets but he and Father Owen had agreed that a house of God was no place for fancy linen.

Tommy tapped away on the keys and the mouse pad, his head visible from the chin upward above the back of the laptop lid. The hammock and the computer concealed his upper body, Varick's preferred target. A bullet in his lower abdomen would be debilitating and excruciatingly painful but would not kill him. Not quickly enough anyway. It would have to be a head shot. The lower part of the face would be best, the site of the ideal entry wound being between the top lip and the nose so as to ensure that the exit wound destroyed the top of the spinal cord, leading to instant death.

All those years of target practice with this very gun, now they meant something, now they had value. And he knew that he mustn't forget to aim slightly to the left. Not that it was a matter of forgetting; it was second nature, automatic.

There it was through the adjoining doors, the bullet's ideal entry point, Tommy's moustache of thick stubble. As Tommy continued to tap away on the laptop, Varick glanced back at the people behind him, cowering. Nearest to him was the large man who had spoken to him when he had made his way through the carriage. Their eyes met and Varick nodded to him: now was the time.

Turning back to the carriage up ahead, Varick stepped back from the window and raised the gun up in front of him. With the sight just over Tommy's right cheek, when the gun kicked right, the .38 caliber bullet would strike him just below the nose punching a hole clean through his head, rendering him dead even before his body hit the floor of the carriage.

Heavenly Father, please steady the aim of this your humble servant as he consigns his fellow sinner, Tommy Denning, to your flock and begs forgiveness on his behalf, for he knows not what he does.

That would have to do. He didn't have long. Tommy might look up at any moment.

He pulled the trigger and his hands braced the explosive kick, which sent the bullet on its God-given flight. And as the smoke cleared, he knew that it had reached its target when Tommy fell heavily to the floor. Evidence of the head wound was provided by blood spattered throughout the carriage and what his former NOPD colleagues might have referred to as "facial debris" which included a tooth that slid down a crimson slick on a window and then dropped to the floor with a faint click.

12:16 PM

Network Control center, St. James's

The information that Denning was going to flood the tunnel had come as no surprise to Ed thanks to the driver's ability to keep the radio link open. To hear him voice it in such a reasoned and clearly thought out way, however, was chilling. Ed Mallory could feel the pressure mount in the negotiating cell. The helicopters overhead had grown louder, the thrum of their engines and the *thwok-thwok-thwok* of their rotor blades had become more insistent than before. The government and the security forces were naked in the glare of the media arc light. Whatever the outcome of the scenario down there in the tunnel between Leicester Square and Tottenham Court Road stations, blame would be apportioned and the appropriate necks would be on the block once the necessary excuses and buck-passing had been attempted. Ed was part of the process. His was one of the necks in waiting.

After Denning's diatribe had finished, Laura came into the room to say that the members of COBRA were watching the live feed and the consensus was beginning to swing behind the notion of closing down the Tommy Denning Show. Hooper felt the same.

"Serina Boise is getting a lot of pressure on this," said Laura.

"If you're asking me what I think," said Ed, "I think we keep the line open. You heard what Denning said, if the link is broken or compromised in any way, he will start killing passengers. There is every possibility that if he is denied the oxygen of publicity then he will set off further explosives. His instant celebrity appears to be as important to him as his desire to kill all the passengers on the train. So faced with the option of killing those passengers either slowly as a piece of sick television, or quickly at the push of a button, he might take the latter option if denied the former. So my opinion, if it's being sought, is that we take the option that buys us the most time and that is to let him keep talking."

"Ed, I have to say that I don't agree with you." Hooper sounded more argumentative than ever and Ed toyed with the idea of telling him that he didn't give a shit what he thought but decided that such an open demonstration of hostility would be bad for the morale of the team.

"Then we'll have to agree to differ," said Ed. "As far as I'm concerned, the line should stay open. It's the only way that we can communicate with the hostage takers and the hostages."

"Denning could be signaling to others above ground to set off further attacks."

"He could be but I don't think he is. Denning has his stage, this is all he's ever wanted. There's no way he wants anyone else to come along and steal the limelight from him. It's all about him and his twisted hunger for celebrity."

Hooper tried to butt in but Ed kept on talking: "As with the most cravenly ambitious reality star, Tommy Denning hungers for fame and recognition, and while he's set on getting that he's less dangerous. Take it away from him and he's going to flip."

Ed knew that as soon as he finished speaking, Hooper was going to come right back at him. When he did, the animosity in his voice was unmistakable.

"All we've done since he stopped the train in the tunnel is act like his facilitators. We're like a bunch of television producers. We're giving him everything that he wants."

"I'm not arguing with you, Mark. My vote is that we keep the line open. Until we know more, I don't think it's a good idea to antagonize him any further. We need to negotiate ourselves into a better position before we start taking away his toys."

When the sound of a gunshot came through the speakers and headphones, it made them all jump.

"What the hell was that?" said Calvert.

"Someone's shot him," said White in a tone of voice that he might have used to comment on a particularly spectacular run at goal in a football match.

"What are you seeing?" asked Ed.

Calvert responded: "Because of the angle of the webcam, it's impossible to see him but, before he disappeared from view, a speck of blood splashed onto the webcam lens."

Ed waited, sick with anticipation, listening intently just as countless others around the world did the same.

12:19 PM

Northern Line Train 037, second carriage

A man cheered behind him in the carriage but Varick didn't look back, didn't acknowledge the growing hubbub of hope. The lead hijacker was shot; it was a message that spread through the train. Varick pulled the window down as far as it would go in the two adjoining doors and dragged himself through the gap to drop down onto the floor of the first carriage. Hunkered down on his knees, he looked along the row of seats. He could see Tommy's legs on the floor but, due to his angle of vision, the remainder of his body was concealed behind the laptop and its supporting bed sheet. He aimed the Smith & Wesson at the computer and squeezed off a shot. The bullet ripped through the back of the screen and sent it crashing to the floor. Now he could see that Tommy's head was marooned in a puddle of blood. The driver was watching it, motionless.

"Friend," Varick called to him, "is he dead?" There was no reply, or none that he could make out. It was difficult to hear above the voices in the remainder of the train that were growing in volume and excitement. He shouted louder. "Friend, is he dead?" Still no reply. There were gurgling sounds but nothing specific that he could make out. Tommy's head was moving. It could be nerve activity. An armed robber he'd seen killed back when he was in the NOPD had trembled for minutes after he'd been shot. The human body often behaved in curious ways following massive trauma.

Varick pulled himself to a standing position and made his way down the carriage, pointing the gun in front of him according to the standard police procedure he had learned almost thirty years before.

His eyes flicked from the body on the floor of the carriage to the driver sitting in the row of seats. Perhaps the driver was catatonic with fear. Perhaps he had passed out with his eyes open. He kept the gun sight aimed at Tommy's chest. The slightest movement and he would squeeze off another shot. Should he squeeze one off anyway, just to make sure that Tommy was on his way to the Lord? It was a question that he didn't get to answer as his attention was drawn to a strange sound. It could be the hissing of pressure in the train's pipes. It was rhythmic, breath-like but inhuman. As he stood not ten feet from the body on the floor of the carriage, he realized where the hissing sound was coming from. It was Tommy's ruptured face; it was his breath whistling through the shredded tissue of his right cheek as he held a walkie-talkie radio to his mouth and muttered into it.

Movement in his peripheral vision made Varick look up. It was the driver. He was shaking his head. No, not shaking—there was less movement than that—it was more of a tremble. The man's eyes were wide and unblinking, imploring, as they bored into Varick's. His face conveyed the message as well as if he had shouted: *it's not safe*. Varick's eyes flicked back down to Tommy—who was watching him.

"Varick," he said. But the voice wasn't human. It was uttered from a shattered face, gurgling blood. Varick could see everything now with infinite clarity and as Tommy raised the gun in his hand and fired the shot that speared his thigh, shattering the bone and sending him sprawling to the floor, he couldn't help himself. Despite being faced with an immediate and urgent need to avoid death, he couldn't prevent the thought forming in his mind. In all the years he had fired the Smith & Wesson, this was the one and only time that it had not pulled to the right. That had to mean something. That had to have come from somewhere. That had to have come from God.

The pain was intense but the fact that it emanated from his leg was a source of hope. He was still alive and one shot away from achieving what he had set out to do when he hurried from Madoc Farm in the early hours of the morning.

Dragging himself onto his front, he pointed the Smith & Wesson. The bullet would have less than six feet to travel. It wouldn't matter whether the gun pulled to the left or to the right. But as his finger began to squeeze the trigger, a bullet from Denning's gun struck his wrist, severing all the tendons that wired his fingers around the revolver and sending it thudding to the floor of the carriage. The pain and trauma from his bullet wounds—his very own stigmata—rendered him mute. Was this how it had felt that day at Calvary?

A force composed of pure animal rage crashed into him and slammed him against the floor, knocking the air from his lungs. What remained of Tommy Denning loomed over him, gasping and slathering blood.

Varick had failed; he had tried to be a good man, tried to do the right thing at all times but he couldn't fight this. It was too much for him. It was God's will. He would surrender himself to it.

As the demon began to strangle him, he closed his eyes and shut it out.

"In sure and certain hope of the resurrection to eternal life through our Lord Jesus Christ, I commend my soul, the soul of your humble servant, Varick Mageau . . ." But the words in his head petered out as the electrical activity in his brain came to an end.

12:19 PM

The bullet had ripped off half of his right cheek, taking with it a large quantity of gum tissue. It was a vicious wound that had shattered all the teeth on the right-hand side of his upper jaw. George could see the place where the teeth should have been through the hole in Denning's cheek from which blood sluiced across his face. An expression came to mind: "That's got to hurt." He had used it a few weeks before when Maggie had stubbed her toe on the corner of the coffee table. "That's got to hurt," he had said and smiled. But it hurt too much for Maggie to find it funny. She scowled at him and hobbled off. But here it was again: "That's got to hurt." He wanted it to hurt. He wanted it to hurt so much; he wanted it to be the most debilitating physical pain that anyone had ever felt. A bullet in the face. That's got to hurt.

These bizarrely jovial feelings had a dark flipside of agonizing indecision and cold paralyzing fear. Denning lay still on the floor. There was so much blood on his head that it looked as though he had been dipped in crimson and it took a moment for George to realize that from out of this bloody mess, Tommy was staring straight at him.

From the end of the carriage came the sound of someone climbing through the window in the connecting doors. A quick glance confirmed it. A middle-aged man with a strong build was approaching with certainty and purpose. Here he was, the savior, the man who would make them all safe. Denning must have known this but all he did was stare into George's eyes with no hint of the extreme shock and pain that he must have been experiencing.

Shoot him again. George nearly said it. But the way Denning looked at him stopped him.

There was another shot—for a moment George felt certain that his subvocal request had been answered but the laptop computer crashed to the ground and Denning continued to stare at him. George had to do something; he had to act. Denning was on his way out. This was the end for him. There was no way that he could survive this.

"Friend, is he dead?" It was an American accent, Deep South if he wasn't mistaken. Answer him, George, tell him the truth. He isn't dead; he needs another bullet. Put one through his heart this time or right between his eyes; it wouldn't really matter which but whatever you do, shoot him again.

Denning fumbled in his pocket and pulled out the walkie-talkie radio. Holding it to his mouth, he said, "If I don't get back to you in five minutes, kill the train driver's kids."

George froze.

"Friend, is he dead?" Louder this time, more urgent. George had to answer him, had to say something, had to *do* something, had to shout, "No, get back," and rush from his seat. Denning was less than six feet away from him. If George threw himself on him there wouldn't be time for him to pull the pistol from his pocket. The distraction would allow the man to put another bullet into him. Denning couldn't shoot two people at the same time, could he?

But George couldn't move. His would-be savior had become his children's potential murderer. If George had had a gun, he would have shot the man himself.

"Varick."

Denning said it just before he took the gun from his pocket and shot the man in the leg. What did it mean? Was it some sort of twisted salutation or was it a name? It didn't matter. The man slumped to the floor but he wasn't going to give up without a fight. Even as his leg gave way he pointed the revolver in his hand. But Denning managed to squeeze off a shot first, a shot that struck the man's wrist and the revolver dropped from his hand.

Denning was in control once more and George felt relieved. He watched motionless, frozen, paralyzed, as Denning hurled himself at the man and closed his hands around his neck. Denning could have shot him, the gun was in his hand, he could have shot him in the stomach or the chest or the head but he had shot him in the leg. His intention was not to kill. Not yet.

Denning straddled him, knees pinning his arms to his side as he drove his thumbs into the man's throat. The gun was back in his pocket and he stared at the man—at this Varick—with the same blank expression with which he had stared at George only seconds before.

"This is meant to be," he said, spitting blood onto the man who struggled beneath him. "Can't you see it? No one can stop me. This is the will of God. Look, you tried and you failed. You did well, Varick, I'll give you that. You did your best and you got close. You are a prophet and you'll join me on the other side. But you have to know that this is meant to be. *I* am meant to be. And you can't stop me. No one can."

Varick. A man's name. Named by his proud parents all those years ago and now about to die. George thought that he still might be able to save him if he tried. If he rushed Denning now, hit him with as much force as he could muster, he might be able to knock him off balance. But it was a straight choice now between Varick's life and his children's. Which meant that Varick was a dead man.

There was a gristly tearing sound as Denning crushed Varick's throat. Varick's legs kicked out and his final breath was a sigh that sounded almost contented in its finality.

Denning pulled himself to his feet and looked at George.

"Do I look pretty?" His pained smile was one of two openings in his face through which his bloody teeth were visible. It was like he had two mouths, one on the front of his face and one on the side. George was unlocked from his paralysis.

"That's got to hurt," he said.

One of the mouths closed.

"You bet it hurts. It hurts like crazy. But only on the surface. On the inside, I don't feel a thing."

The laptop had been destroyed by the bullet that had struck it. It lay on the floor of the carriage. Putting his head to one side, Denning looked at it dispassionately.

"My kids . . ." George's voice trembled.

"In a minute."

Pulling the gun from the pocket of his jacket, he aimed it down the carriage through the adjoining doors and into the second carriage. George couldn't tell how many shots he fired, they came one after the other so quickly, the brass bullet casings clattering to the floor. He only took his finger off the trigger when there were no more bullets, at which point, he released the empty clip from the handle and let it drop to the floor before he stabbed in a full one and locked and loaded. There were shouts and screams from further up the train; people were shot. There were injuries, deaths.

"Never underestimate the power of indiscriminate killing to instill terror in people. It's a winner every time."

"My children," said George again, more urgently this time.

For the first time since he had received his wound, Denning raised his hand up to his face and ran the tips of his fingers around the rim of the crater that the bullet had created.

Denning raised the walkie-talkie to his mouth: "It's me. What I said about the kids—forget it. For the time being."

Movement in George's peripheral vision distracted him and he looked down to see water seeping from between the cracks in the doors and racing along the floor of the carriage in rivulets that rapidly merged with one another. As though in recognition of this invasive flow, the lights in the carriage flickered and dimmed.

12:20 PM

Network Control center, St. James's

"We've lost the feed," said White. "And there's no response on the radio."

"Someone must have taken him out," said Hooper. He sounded more hopeful than he had done all day but Ed wasn't ready to share his optimism.

"Let's hope someone has because, if they haven't, it could mean that he's set off the explosives."

"I'll get straight on to GCHQ," said Laura. "Let's see if it's just him we've lost or whether there's any other chatter from the train."

Despite his suggestion that the news might not be as rosy as they all hoped, Ed could feel the mood in the room change. Gone was the doom-laden tension and in its place was a buzz of nervous expectation. Could this really be the end? Had someone managed to get at Denning? If so, how would the other hijackers on the train react? Without their leader, their figurehead, there was every chance that they would throw in the towel. The train passengers could be out of the tunnel in under the hour. Maybe the biggest and potentially most difficult hostage negotiation that he had ever been involved in would also turn out to be the most quickly resolved.

Ed, however, couldn't share his colleagues' nervous optimism. Of course it was possible that someone might have got lucky and taken Denning out—all the evidence pointed that way—but Ed couldn't help but feel with every second that passed that Denning was still very much alive.

Just from the sound of Laura's footsteps on the floor as she entered the room, Ed could tell that the news wasn't good. If it had been, she would have been in more of a hurry. Her tone of voice as she started to speak was enough for Ed to know that the situation was very far from over.

"Messages and Internet calls from the train indicate that there have been further shots fired in the first carriage and people in the second carriage have been hit and injured, some of them fatally. It would appear that the person doing the shooting is a wounded Tommy Denning. Whoever it was that managed to attack him in the first instance has failed and been killed."

"Shit!" Hooper smashed his fist down on the desk. It was a golden rule of hostage negotiation that personnel within a negotiating cell should keep a check on their emotions. That Hooper was failing to do that was further testament to Ed that he was allowing personal feelings to trespass on his professional behavior. If he had been a cop and Ed his superior, Hooper would have been long gone.

"Okay, let's concentrate," said Ed. "Is this now the right time to send in the special forces to storm the train? Do we hope that Denning is hurt badly enough and so rattled that he can be taken out?"

"I'm not sure that sending in special forces at this moment in time is even a possibility," said Laura. "Boise tells me that they're working on potential scenarios at the moment but, with the water rising, they're having to send for specialist equipment. We do now have the train driver George Wakeham's mobile number but our technical coordinator tells me that with only wireless access we're not going to be able to get to him because his phone isn't Wi-Fi compliant."

"Can't we arrange for phone reception in the tunnels?"

"We had enough trouble getting the Wi-Fi sorted out," said Laura. "It's going to be impossible to get phone network reception down there in the time necessary for it to make any difference."

"What about the passengers? What are we telling them?"

"Generic e-mails are being sent to those we've managed to make contact with, reassuring them that we're doing all that we can to get them out of there."

"Maybe we should be telling them to do whatever it takes to try and escape."

That no one even deigned to respond was all the proof Ed needed that this was never going to be a viable plan. It felt as though the temperature in the room had jumped a few degrees. A portable air-conditioning unit had been wheeled in and was humming away in the corner but it was having little effect, and a couple of desk fans that churned up the air only accentuated the heat by providing the occasional waft of cooler air against which the hot air was contrasted. Ed took off his sunglasses and dabbed at his face with a handkerchief before covering his eyes once again.

"Well, of course, there may be a way to drain the water out of the tunnel."

Ed had forgotten about Professor Moorcroft, who was sitting at a nearby desk, and he suspected that everyone else in the room had as well. By rights, he shouldn't have been in the negotiating cell. But the situation with Denning's speech and his subsequent attack had rendered him invisible.

Ed turned toward him. "How?"

Moorcroft's can-do demeanor of a few moments previously took a knock from the sudden attention that it attracted. He cleared his throat nervously. "Well, I was looking at the plans and charts for that section of the Northern Line. I was hoping that the southbound tunnel might have been adjacent to the northbound tunnel, or at least close to it, but sadly it's not at that point, they're set quite well apart."

Ed fought the urge to tell the professor to get to the point.

"However," continued Moorcroft, "there is a tunnel that runs near to the location of the train. It's one of a number of service tunnels that were built in the 1930s. It runs just to one side and slightly below the Northern Line from Leicester Square station up to Tottenham Court Road."

Ed couldn't help the impatience in his voice. "Frank, just tell us what we can do."

Ed listened as Moorcroft stumbled over the words, this man who had spent his life in academia. Never spent a day in the real world—that's what people probably said about him. Ed wanted to shake him.

"Well, I suppose the thing is, er, well yes, from the outcome of my calculations—rough though they clearly are without concrete data—I should say that at its closest point, the absolute closest point, there is about three meters, let's say, ten feet, between the two tunnels."

"Ten feet of solid earth," said Ed.

"That's correct but it might well be that a controlled explosion that worked in conjunction with the weight of the water might open up a fissure—that is to say hole—which might facilitate substantial drainage."

"Enough to stop the Northern Line tunnel from filling up."

By the time the professor said, "Exactly," Ed's feelings for him had undergone a transformation. Now he felt like kissing him.

"The only problem, of course, is that the sort of blast that would be needed to breach the two tunnels might also bring down a large section of the surrounding infrastructure. It would be a tricky explosion to judge."

Here was hope. This eccentric man with his curious aroma had presented them with a possible solution, a dangerous one—a mad one even—but one that had to be worth exploring.

"Laura?"

"Yes, Ed."

"We must get back to Boise with this. She needs to speak to COBRA and get it sorted out. This might buy us some time. Denning specifically said that he would only detonate the explosives if we tried to make contact with the train. Well, we're not going to. We're just going to slow down the flood. If we can reestablish contact with Denning then I might be able to work on him, try and make him believe that it's a sign or an act of God."

"I'm on it," said Laura and he heard her walk back to her office along the corridor to talk to the powers that be, away from the negotiating cell and any chance of allowing the negotiators to become too closely involved in the decision-making process. That was against the rules.

Ed turned back to Professor Moorcroft. "So, Frank, you really think we could drain some of the water from around the train?"

"Well, of course, it's impossible to say with any degree of confidence without all the hard data to hand."

"You're not changing your mind, are you, Frank?"

"It's not that I'm changing my mind, I'm merely responding to the limited facts that are being presented—"

"You did say it was possible."

"No, let me be very clear. I said it may be possible. *May* be."

"I realize that what I'm asking you to do is completely unfair and compromises your professional ethics but for a moment I want you to try and forget if you can about the human life involved here. All I need to know from you, Frank, is whether, if this were just a purely hypothetical exercise, you think that blowing a hole in the tunnel would be able to prevent it from filling with water."

"Well, the point at which the two tunnels are at their closest and the point that marks the location of the train are far enough apart that if an explosion was judged well enough—neither too large to compromise the safety of the passengers nor too small to create enough of a breach—then with the limited information we have at our disposal at the current time, I would have to say that it *may* be possible. But I'm no explosives expert. It would require someone with knowledge and expertise in that field."

"Thanks, Frank." Ed turned toward Calvert and White and said, "Guys, we should arrange for the military explosives people to speak to Professor Moorcroft here and put together the fastest feasibility study they've ever done. If we get the go-ahead for this, we need to make sure that everything's in place. This is the best shot we've got."

12:34 PM

Northern Line Train 037, sixth carriage

Whatever it was that had struck Adam, the black man in the sharp suit who had tried to calm Hugh down—was it only a bullet or was it some sort of explosive?—it had taken his left leg off at the knee. Maggie didn't want to look at the wound, the stump, but she couldn't help herself as Hugh tied his belt around Adam's thigh to try and stem the flow of blood. Adam drifted in and out of consciousness. Maggie preferred it when he was unconscious because when he was conscious, he shouted, shrieked. His cries were high-pitched, incongruous with his demeanor which until a few minutes before had been so calm and controlled, so eager to maintain order and bolster morale.

The rear half of the carriage was deserted; passengers had tried to get as much distance as possible between themselves and the female hijacker. Some of the schoolgirls were crying but the younger of the two teachers with the group, who didn't look as though she would have the emotional strength to prevent herself from succumbing to the terror everyone felt, was the only voice in the carriage that did not betray the horror of the situation. She spoke to the little girls about the British Museum, their intended destination when they had set out that morning. To listen to her, you'd think that everything was fine. You would never suspect that she was a hostage of terrorist hijackers. Her steady narrative about Egyptian treasures gave the children something to focus on aside from the harrowing sounds of distress. Whatever terror the woman felt, she repressed it. Her tone of voice displayed no other emotion than a warm willingness to engage. It was some performance.

The desperate voices were like nothing that Maggie had ever heard before. All social restraint had gone from them and the sound of crying denoted an emotional incontinence that was unnerving. The lights flickered on and off. They weren't going to last much longer. Maggie was surprised they had lasted as long as they had. The water in the tunnel had already started to enter the carriage, seeping between the doors, and was now an inch deep on the floor.

In the last carriage, the female hijacker paced around and Maggie could hear her talking to herself as her boots splashed in the water. She might have been reciting some sort of prayer. Maggie could make out the occasional "Jesus" and "Christ" and they weren't used as expletives; she was talking to him—whatever her idea of him was.

The woman's footsteps came closer and there she was, framed in the open windows in the two adjoining doors. People cowered, crouched down, tried to find any form of cover, even if that cover was the bodies of other passengers. The hijacker stared through into the fifth carriage, her eyes surveying the terror she had created, and she smiled to herself as though happy that everything was absolutely as it should be. Whereas the people in the carriage who were closest to her tried to keep quiet, the young teacher kept on talking to the children and it appeared that the hijacker was listening to her words until Maggie had the sickening realization that she was looking around the carriage, searching for her. The woman didn't even seem to register the man whose leg she had spontaneously amputated with her gun and Maggie's fears were confirmed when the woman looked straight at her.

12:35 PM

"Ed," said Laura. "I've got Commander Boise on the line. I'll patch it through to your headset." Ed didn't have time to ponder on the significance of why he was allowed to take this call in the negotiating cell, just slid his headphones forward onto his ears and said, "This is Ed."

"Ed, it's Serina Boise. Laura's told me about the explosives option. I can see why you like the idea of buying some more time in which to negotiate with Tommy Denning but it's extremely unlikely that we would ever get clearance."

"But we've got to at least try."

"You know I'll discuss it at the highest level but an explosion on the Underground network goes against everything that the police and security services are employed to prevent. There are numerous issues that have to be taken into account, not least the possibility that with so little time in which to plan and devise such an explosion, we might actually be putting the passengers on the train in more danger than they are already."

"Listen, Serina, I've got an expert in the construction of the tube who's telling me that he thinks it's a possibility."

Serina Boise's tone suggested that she wanted to get off the line as fast as possible rather than waste her time with some outlandish scheme to let off explosives underground. "Ed, there's no way it's going to be even possible to run all the necessary computations that would be needed to work out where the explosive charge should be placed and the quantity required. It's just not going to be possible. I'm sorry."

"I still think we need to look at it."

"No, Ed."

"Why not?"

"Because even if we could suss out the feasibility in time, we'd never get the go-ahead. It's not as though this is a small controlled explosion we're talking about. We'd need something big enough to blast through ten feet of solid brick and earth. The whole tunnel could collapse."

"I appreciate that, Serina, but there are over three hundred people down there. We have to look at every eventuality, don't we?"

"Ed, you're a great negotiator. You need to do all that you can to make contact with Denning and talk him down."

"I'm doing that but he's a religious psychopath. I've heard it in his voice, there's no way we can stop this guy through psychology alone. Drastic situations require drastic measures."

"I'm going to have the conversation, Ed. You know I'll do whatever I can but you also have to understand that it's never going to happen."

So there it was. The authorities would rather present the image that the passengers on the train had died while they battled an evil and audacious enemy rather than risk having to take the blame for killing the passengers with a highly controversial preemptive measure. Ed could understand that but it didn't make it any easier for him to accept.

As Ed's conversation with Serina Boise came to an end and he passed the phone back to Laura, he turned to where White and Calvert were sitting at their computers. "Keep trying the radio on the train. We've got to try and keep talking to Tommy Denning."

12:36 PM

Tommy paced up and down between the two opposing rows of seats, his boots splashing in the water. He held up his hand to his face and the blood streaked down his arm and dripped into the rising water in the carriage. George considered speaking to him but Tommy was deep in thought, locked in some form of meditation or prayer. His muttered indecipherable words were interspersed with groans that George supposed were borne purely of pain. The steady flow of blood from the wound made George hope that perhaps it might be enough to make Tommy lose consciousness. The human body held eight pints of blood—Tommy had to have lost at least a pint or two already. But if that didn't finish him off then George knew that he would have to launch another attack. Unlike his previous attempts, this one would have to be successful. George had been lucky last time inasmuch as Tommy had forgiven him for what he'd done. Prior to his speech to the world and his subsequent wounding, Tommy had been in a benevolent mood. The adrenalin was pumping, everything was going according to plan. But now events had taken a turn for the worse. He resembled nothing more than a twitchy psychotic and if, as he had stated during his speech, he wanted everyone on the train—himself included—to die, then George supposed he was happy to suffer the excruciating pain in his face for a little while longer before the rising water snuffed them all out. Another failed attack from George would almost certainly be greeted with a bullet.

In Tommy's left hand he held his pistol. Every couple of minutes he would fire a shot in the direction of the second carriage, either at someone whose desperation had reached such a level that an attempt to escape and almost certain death was preferable to remaining on the train, or indiscriminately through the windows in the connecting doors. Both side pockets of his black combat trousers were bulging with spare clips of bullets that he clicked into place as required. Whatever brotherly affection he might have felt for George earlier on would be long gone; it would be so easy for him to do to George what he was only too happy to do to those trying to escape. So George remained silent until the radio in the cab crackled into life once more. Tommy had ignored it previously but now he stopped pacing and turned to look at him.

"Well, George, it looks as though they're not going to leave us alone. Do you think we should talk to them?"

George shrugged as though he couldn't care less but all he could think about was the chewing gum on the handset. If Tommy decided to go to the radio he would see it and know that he had been tampering with it to keep the radio link open. Would it matter? Would Tommy even care any more? Or, would he see it as yet another betrayal by George—the final straw perhaps—and retaliate accordingly?

"You'd better answer it," said Tommy, his tongue slurring against his shattered gum.

12:38 PM

Northern Line Train 037, fifth carriage

"Ah, there you are," said the female hijacker, her face framed in the window between the carriages.

Maggie tried to pull herself even closer around the bulkhead behind the row of seats in the center of the carriage but there were people crushed against her on all sides and short of trying to push someone in front of her, she was in the hijacker's direct line of sight.

"You were supposed to stay up here with me but what with all the commotion with them blokes I completely forgot." She didn't sound like a woman who had only so recently committed multiple murders. Maggie was torn between staying completely silent and trying to engage the woman in conversation. Perhaps if they could open some sort of dialogue, she might be able to find out more information about Sophie and Ben. But before she could ask what had happened to them, the woman preempted her train of thought. "Sorry about your kids."

"Where are they?"

Maggie was shocked by how angry she sounded. She didn't feel angry. Broken with fear but not angry.

"They'll be pretty hot by now." The woman said the words like she might have said, "They'll be having a lovely time."

"Please tell me where they are."

"They're not on the train if that's what you're thinking."

"Tell me what you've done with them." The voices in the carriage, even the formerly hysterical ones, were subdued as people listened, trying to glean some meaning from what they were saying, trying to wring some hope from it.

"They're in the trunk of the car at the tube station," said the hijacker.

Maggie couldn't speak. The woman's words gouged at the terrible burning wound that Maggie felt inside and, for a moment, she thought she might throw up. Of course they were in the boot of the car. It all made sense. As she had been marched across to the entrance of the tube station at Morden that morning, she had looked back to see if she could see the children. As she did so, the woman had pushed something hard, like a gun barrel, into her kidneys and told her that if she didn't keep moving, "The kids will die." Maggie carried on walking but as she did so, she had heard the boot lid being slammed.

"They'll die in this heat." Maggie's words were automatic, spoken with no conscious intent, and as she said them, fury radiated through her body like iced water. She had slapped George across the face once during an argument but aside from that, she had never felt violent toward another human being. Violence was something that she left to men. But when the bitch responded by saying, "Most probably," she felt like gouging her eyes out. For a moment, Maggie weighed up the logistics of launching an attack, of throwing herself at her, lunging through the open windows in the adjoining doors and trying to get her hands around her throat. The normal rules of humanity no longer applied. She would kill her if she could. For a moment, the violent urge was such that it managed to blot out Sophie and Ben and their horrific predicament. But then it passed and the vile truth emerged once more.

Was it a lie? Could it be? She knew it wasn't.

She had to move. She knew how George felt when he had to wait in tunnels at a signal and became claustrophobic. Now it was her turn.

"Please, I need to get through." She stood up and turned back toward the scrum of people in the second half of the carriage. She had to move and if she was shot then so be it.

"Please," she said with more urgency this time, as though she was hurrying for a closing door on a crowded train. Like she was late for work. Like all that was going on was normal.

If the bullet was going to come, it was going to come now.

"There's nowhere to go," said the hijacker behind her, but she was wrong.

Maggie made her way between the people, picked her way through the children sitting on the floor as the lights flickered once again and dimmed.

"Ain't gonna do you any good," the woman shouted after her. The schoolteacher was still talking to the children and keeping them calm—she was telling them something about the tombs of the pharaohs—and Maggie could see the open doors to the next carriage up ahead. She had to get through them. She had to try and raise the alarm. She couldn't just sit there and let her children die.

She was through the doors and she was still alive. She was moving. That was all that mattered.

"I need to get through," she said as she tried to insert her body into any gap that she could find in order to move forward up the train. She knew she had to get a message to the outside world. Maggie looked at all the people clutching their phones, computer tablets, and laptops as though they were sacred objects. The mood was one of emotional anarchy as people wept and shrieked and prayed whilst others tapped out messages or spoke to relatives. Their communication with the outside world had become a precious lifeline.

"Please," said Maggie to a woman about her age who was clutching her BlackBerry and staring at its screen as though it held some profound significance, "I need to get a message to my husband." The woman looked up at her with tears in her eyes.

"I'm almost out of battery."

"He's the driver of the train and they've taken our children and locked them in the boot of a car. They'll be dying in this heat."

"I managed to send an e-mail to my mother," said the woman with a faraway look in her eyes. "She'll be trying to contact me."

"My children might be dying," said Maggie.

"You can't make an ordinary phone call. It's just Wi-Fi."

"Please, let me send a message."

"Be quick," said the woman. "Try not to use too much battery."

She held out the BlackBerry to Maggie who took it and opened up the browser on the screen and stared at it. Who was she going to contact? Who could she send an e-mail to who might conceivably be able to get a message to George in time? She could send it to her sister but she couldn't remember her e-mail address. The police, that was it, she should contact the police.

"Please, have you finished yet?" The woman wanted her phone back.

"How do I call the police? Can I do that?"

"I don't know. I know others managed to make a call but I don't know how. I don't know, okay?" The woman was teetering on the edge of hysteria. Maggie returned the BlackBerry and muttered, "Thanks."

Maggie looked at the people crowded all around her. Messages were being typed and sent, people were making calls. There was a heavyset man standing next to her whose pink business shirt was stained with sweat. He was shouting into his phone, "Well they've got to fucking do something, they're trying to drown us down here." He was speaking to the outside world. Whoever he was speaking to could get word to the authorities about the children. Maggie put her hand on his arm to get his attention. As he looked at her she made her pitch.

"I need your help. I need to get a message to the police."

The man looked at her with blank staring eyes and said, "They can't leave us down here. Someone's got to come."

"Can you help me? Please."

This second attempt at getting through to him was greeted with an angry expression and the man turned away from Maggie and shrugged her hand off his arm. She turned around and looked to others. A middle-aged woman with a calm impassive expression was standing with her back against a yellow vertical pole. She had her eyes closed and was clutching a mobile phone to her chest. As Maggie said, "Please, you need to help me," the woman opened her eyes and she snapped, "No!"

Everyone was so possessive of their phones and computers—their lifelines to their families—that to try and borrow one was going to be almost impossible. Even if she could, she didn't know how to make a call using the Wi-Fi link; she didn't know who she was meant to be phoning, and even if she did manage to get a message out, there would be so many messages and calls from the train that it would take too long to filter through the system to save Ben and Sophie. A few hundred feet along the train was George. If he knew the truth about the children then he would be released from his enforced compliance and he might be able to do something. If she couldn't get through the train itself then she would go down the side. If she didn't make it—if she was shot or attacked by a hijacker—then so be it. At least she would have tried. The thought of Ben and Sophie locked in the boot of the car in the blazing heat of the hottest day of the year was too much for her. All the time she might spend trying to work out how to send a message from one of her fellow passengers' phones—a message that might not even be read—was time wasted. She needed to get to George, now.

She splashed through the water on the floor of the carriage. When she managed to squeeze her way through the people in the fourth carriage and made it into the third, she could see the water in the tunnel through one of the sliding doors that had been partially wedged open.

An American man in a polo shirt and slacks stood by the doors, his fear manifesting itself as a jittery excitement. When he saw Maggie contemplating the water, he told her that the track might still be live. The lights in the carriage were still on, dimmed considerably, providing only a yellowy almost sepia tint, but on nonetheless. If she went into the water in the tunnel, the electric current might kill her.

But there was no way that Maggie could proceed any farther within the train itself. The bodies in front of her were packed too tightly together, crushed together in the center of the train where people had fled to from the scenes of violence at either end. Maggie looked through the open door, at the dim flickering lights reflected in the dark water.

As she moved toward it, the man who had warned about possible electrocution said to her, "They're shooting at people if they try to go down the side of the train." He said it as though he expected it to dissuade her. But her trajectory didn't waver and she pushed her way through the gap in the doors and dropped into the water. It was cold enough to make her breathless but as soon as she had found her footing on the uneven floor of the tunnel, she started wading down the side of the carriage, a space narrow enough in places to force her to press herself against the side of the train. Inside the carriage she could hear crying and raised voices; there were faces contorted into masks of pain and a smell of excrement came through a broken window. Some faces were blank, as though in acute denial of the reality of the new world they found themselves in. Some faces reflected a weird sort of acceptance as though they knew this was meant to happen, as if they'd dreamed it, as if it was meant to be. But Maggie thought of nothing beyond her children, roasting in the boot of a car.

She lost track of the shouted warnings. "Don't go down there . . . They'll shoot you . . ." Over and over. Maybe they would shoot her. But she couldn't stop herself. She had to get to George.

There was a man in the tunnel up ahead. He was trying to climb onto the roof of the train but he couldn't get a steady footing from which to lever himself up. He turned to face Maggie as the lights in the carriage flickered and for a moment he flashed up as a green negative on her retina.

"It's all over," he said.

"What is?" said Maggie.

"It was only a matter of time. It was bound to happen again. We brought this on ourselves." He wore a suit and tie; the side parting in his hair was still in place. But his mind had gone.

"I need to get to my children," said Maggie, hoping that her heartfelt mission might resonate with him. He looked like a father.

"You can get in there," he said.

"Thank you," said Maggie and following his direction to the carriage door that had been pried open, she climbed back onto the train in the semidarkness, the lights fading fast. It was easier to move among the passengers here. She was going against the flow. At the end of the second carriage there were bodies, their blood coloring the water in which they lay. There were muttered warnings behind her but she paid no attention and moved forward toward the door at the end of the carriage, picking her way through the arms and legs.

She looked through the window into the first carriage and there was a man's body halfway down. The door to the cab beyond it was open. There was movement from inside and she could hear someone speaking. The doors between the first and second carriages were chained together. She toyed with the idea of squeezing through the open windows in the doors but she decided against it and crouched down.

"George, can you hear me? George, it's me."

Any worries that she might have had that she hadn't shouted loudly enough disappeared when she heard George's shaky voice: "Maggie?"

She had to speak fast. She might not have long. She couldn't even stop to think of what sort of extra danger she might be putting George in. She just knew that she had to tell him about the children.

"Sophie and Ben have been locked in the boot of a car at Morden station. We've got to do something otherwise they'll die. You've got to use the radio."

A shot was fired. She would have worried for George if it weren't for the metallic thud of the bullet striking a part of the train carriage near to her. It wasn't George that was being shot at. She ducked down below the level of the windows.

"Did you hear me, George?"

There was no reply.

"You've got to do something, George. You've got to do something or they're going to die." Another shot and the bullet struck the door behind which she sheltered. She could hear footsteps approaching. If she stayed where she was, she was dead. In a running crouch, she made her way back to the first set of double doors in the carriage and ducked down behind the row of seats. When she chanced a glance, she could see a figure framed in the window in the door. It was the man who had held the gun to Sophie's head that morning. But there was something wrong with him. He clutched his face and his entire arm was red and shiny with blood. When she saw him raise up the gun, she ducked down once again and a shot thudded into the seats inches away from her head.

12:42 PM

The radio connection to the driver's cab on the train was relayed through all the headsets in the negotiating cell. Ed listened intently. His breathing quickened as the radio was answered.

"Hello?"

"George, it's Ed Mallory. I need to speak to Tommy."

The radio link crackled with white noise for a moment and Ed could hear a whispered conversation in the background before George came back on the line and said, "Tommy wants to ask you a question."

"Tell Tommy that he can ask me the question himself. It's essential that I speak to him."

George's voice trembled as he said, "Tommy wants to know whether you'd like him to shoot me."

"Tell Tommy that we don't want him to harm anyone on the train. And tell him that I need to speak to him as a matter of urgency."

A pause and then, "He wants to know what you want to talk to him about."

"Tell him that I want to talk to him about how we're going to resolve this situation so that the innocent men, women, and children on the train can be released."

Another pause before George said, "No deal, it's God's will that they must all die."

"George, tell him that there's some information that I need to give him related to that and I can only do it if I speak to him."

Ed listened to the muffled conversation in the background.

"He says no."

As long as the line was open, Ed would keep going, keep pushing, keep thinking. There had to be something that would make Tommy speak to him. There was clearly a degree of playfulness, however perverse, in the way that Tommy was fielding his requests via George. Ed had to keep believing that there was a switch in Tommy's psychological makeup that once thrown would compel him to communicate. Ed knew he didn't have long. He needed to find that switch before the line went down or Tommy tired of the game.

"Tell Tommy that I have information regarding the flooding of the tunnel that he's going to want to hear."

Ed waited.

"He says that he knows what you're trying to do. You're going to tell him that something is going to prevent the tunnel from filling up."

Tommy had got it in one. Ed was going to tell him that he had spoken to an expert in the construction of the tube who had stated quite unequivocally that once the water had reached a certain level, it would start to drain away and rise no further. His intention was to try and make Tommy think that his mission was futile. Even if it was a lie.

"No, it's something that I need to tell him directly." Ed had no idea what it might be but that didn't matter. He needed to get Tommy on the line. Once he had managed that, he would worry about what he was going to say.

"No deal," said George.

Ed needed something that would jolt Tommy out of the game he clearly felt he was playing.

"Tell him I want to talk to him about his parents."

Ed waited for his words to be relayed to Tommy. Silence over the line. Had the connection been broken? Before he could ask the question, he heard a voice that he hadn't heard before coming through his headphones.

"Ed Mallory." The words were pained and seemingly spoken with great difficulty.

"Is that Tommy?"

When the voice said, "Yes," Ed clenched his fists. He was through.

"Tommy, we need to talk." To people with no experience of hostage negotiation, the "we need to talk" line might appear corny but Ed knew that many perpetrators of hostage crises— Tommy included—had spent their lives being marginalized and shut out by family and wider society. No one had ever solicited their opinion on anything. No one cared what they had to say. The situation that they found themselves in was sometimes the only time they had been the focus of any attention. Ed was convinced that Tommy was enjoying his newfound celebrity; he was enjoying being famous, even if the fame and notoriety were only ever going to be short-lived.

"You might need to talk, Mr. Mallory, but I don't."

"Please, call me Ed."

"Aren't you guys meant to find someone from my past who means something to me like an old teacher or a former girlfriend?"

"Who would you like to talk to, Tommy?"

"No one, least of all you."

"Why least of all me? Are you afraid that I might persuade you to stop what you're doing?"

"Come on, Ed, you can do better than that."

"Tommy, you're sounding different from before. What's happened?"

"I've been shot in the face."

Ed didn't think that Denning would back down now just because of an injury, even if it was excruciating, but Ed was heartened by his growing willingness to communicate. This represented something of a sea change in his behavior but whether it would make negotiation any easier remained to be seen. It was impossible to verify his injury but if he hadn't been shot in the face then he was doing a good impersonation of someone who had been.

"Who shot you, Tommy?"

"Varick."

"Who's Varick?"

"Cruor Christi. Varick's the main man." The words tailed off into a gasp.

"What's wrong, Tommy?"

"It hurts."

"We could have you out of there in a few minutes and get you some medical attention, painkillers."

"Why would I need painkillers?" The antagonism that Ed could hear in his voice made him realize that Denning's outlook had changed from earlier.

"Tommy, if you put a stop to this now, you're going to earn a lot of respect."

"Don't insult my intelligence. That sort of shit might work with some of the losers that you have to deal with but do you really think that it's going to work with me?"

The negotiation wasn't taking the course that Ed might have hoped but at least Denning was asking questions of him, seemingly keen to perpetuate their dialogue. Time for a different approach. Ed softened his tone in an attempt to remove any sense of a superior speaking to a subordinate. This was man to man.

"Why don't you give it up, Tommy?"

There was a thin chuckle. "Just like that?"

"Just like that."

Silence, then: "Don't be ridiculous, Ed. You don't seriously think that's going to work, do you?"

Tommy's questions were telling. However rhetorical they were, he was still asking Ed's opinion. He was looking for reassurance. Now was the time for the ego massage.

"You're on every single news report in the world. What you've achieved here is extraordinary. Everyone will respect you if you show compassion and release the passengers."

"We both know that's never going to happen."

"I don't know that, Tommy, and I don't think you do either. If you let the passengers go now you'll be a folk hero. People will respect you for it. You'll have bought yourself a platform. You can tell the world about your thoughts and beliefs and the world will listen."

Tommy sucked at his shattered teeth and gums. "They're listening now, aren't they?"

"They are, Tommy. Everyone's listening to you now. And they'll listen to you even more if you let the train passengers go." Tommy remained silent, so Ed pressed on. "Don't do this. Think of all the people. Think of the children. Think of their parents, think of the families of all the hostages and what they must be going through." It was a tack that Ed rarely took, the emotional angle. He found that being rational and dispassionate was usually the best option; listening was as important as talking but he could hear something in Denning's voice. He was at a low point. After all the time spent planning and anticipating this moment, the reality of what he was going to do was upon him and a vicious counterattack from this Varick person had clearly shaken him. He was feeling the pain that he had planned to bestow on others. He was the cocky young soldier no more. If there was any way of talking him down, now was the time. It was almost certainly the last chance that he would get. The power to the train would have died by now and what light remained would be coming from the battery. This, however, would last for only a few minutes more and then all communication with the train would cease apart from the occasional message from those passengers whose laptop computers and handheld devices were dry and still had power.

Perhaps that might mean something to Denning. Here was a man who had contrived to get his face on every television screen in the world—he had come close—but now he was about to go off air for good. Forever.

"Tommy, you owe it to all the people all over the world who are watching what is happening here now. You need to show them the sort of person you really are."

It was a sound that Ed did not expect to hear during a hostage negotiation. Laughter was a commodity in short supply in situations like this, especially emanating from someone who has been shot in the face. But it was coming through his headphones. It was pained and awkward but there it was, Tommy was laughing at him.

"Come on, Ed, let's not go through this charade," he said. "You know as well as I do that I'm not going to walk away from this. This is more than just a piece of terrorism. It's more than just an attack. This was prophesied: 'For the Lamb which is in the midst of the throne shall feed them, and shall lead them unto living fountains of waters: and God shall wipe away all tears from their eyes.' Revelation, chapter seven, verse seventeen."

"But they're only words, Tommy. They could mean anything to anyone. That's just your interpretation."

"This will probably be our last chance to talk."

It was almost the exact same line that Ed was planning on saying to Denning. He hadn't expected to hear it said to him.

"You've done your best, Ed, but you never really stood a chance."

"Why didn't I?"

"Because I'm an honest man. I tell the truth. People like you can have no effect on me. You deal with fuckups, weirdos, losers, desperate men who are backed into a corner. I'm not like that. I know what I'm doing and I know that what I'm doing is right."

Tommy Denning was a religious psychopath and, as such, he represented the most difficult psychological character type with which to negotiate. Ed decided that there was only one thing to do now and that was to revert back to what had made Tommy speak to him in the first place.

"I want to talk to you about your mum and dad, Tommy. I suspect they have quite a lot to do with this."

Ed frowned at the slurping, gurgling sound that came through his headphones before he realized that Tommy was laughing again. "Listen to you, Ed, you sound like a shrink. Give it up, okay? This has nothing to do with my father and what he did. I was chosen to do this. The fact that this is happening, the fact that you and me are here talking like this says it all. It was meant to be."

"Maybe it wasn't meant to be, Tommy, maybe you're just making it happen."

"It's happening because I'm being allowed to make it happen."

"Come on, you know as well as I do that the authorities can't let you drown everyone on the train. They'll send in special forces before they'll let that happen."

"In which case, I'll set off the explosives. It can be baptism by water or baptism by fire, it's all the same to me. We are all of us God's children and for me and my flock down here beneath the streets of London, this is our end of days."

"This is wrong, Tommy. You say that you're a Christian but this goes against all of Christ's teachings. Do the right thing, Tommy."

"I am doing the right thing."

"At least let the children go." Damage limitation. Standard negotiating procedure. If you can't get them all out then at least get some of them out.

"The children are coming with me, Ed. They've been chosen too."

"They haven't been chosen. They're innocent. Let them go."

"I'm in a lot of pain, Ed, so I'm going to say good-bye now."

He had to keep him on the line. Without that, they had nothing.

"I know all about pain, Tommy."

"Oh yeah?"

"I was blinded in a hostage negotiation a few years ago."

"You're blind?"

"Yes, there was an explosion and breaking glass cut my face and took my sight."

"Bless you, Bartimaeus, I shall pray for you."

"If you want to do something for me, Tommy, then let the passengers go."

"I can't do that, Ed. This is God's will."

"It isn't God's will." He said it with much more force than he had intended but his frustration could only be suppressed for so long.

Calvert was squeezing his leg. It was a prearranged signal that he was—in the terminology of hostage negotiation—"falling in," becoming too absorbed in the negotiation and beginning to lose perspective. Tommy picked up on it as well.

"Don't be bitter, Ed. I know the authorities have been made to look very silly by all this."

"Why, Tommy?"

"Two words: Simeon Fisher."

"Who's he?"

"He's one of yours, or he was. He's dead now. You're lucky that my webcam and laptop were broken otherwise I would have announced it to the world, told everyone how dumb you all are."

"Tommy, I don't know who Simeon Fisher is."

"Then perhaps you're not far enough up the food chain but I'm sure you can find out."

There was a crackling on the radio. The sound faded in and out.

"Tommy, the radio link's not going to hold out much longer. You've got to release the people on the train."

But instead of a reply, there was further crackling followed by the sound of a woman's voice in the background. She sounded desperate. She was shouting about "the boot of a car." There was more shouting followed by the sound of a gunshot.

Silence. The woman started up again but it was impossible to make out anything over the white noise that whined and spluttered as the radio lost power. Another shot was fired then nothing, just crackle and hiss.

There was a break in the squall from the speakers and there was a sound like movement in the train cab.

"Tommy? Tommy, can you hear me?" Ed's questions were greeted by a crescendo of radio static and then silence once more.

Ed could hear White turning switches and clicking away on a computer keyboard before he said, "He's gone."

After Ed had dropped his headphones onto the desk in front of him, he took off his sunglasses and squeezed the bridge of his nose between his thumb and forefinger. He'd read somewhere that it eased tension. It didn't seem to help much now. Tommy Denning was so whacked out on God and religion that he had actually come full circle and sounded more sane and reasoned than Ed did. He was never going to release the passengers. No one was coming to save them.

"Shall I try and get through again?" asked White.

Ed said yes but he knew that it wouldn't be possible and the continued silence from White was confirmation. The thought of what was going on all those hundreds of feet beneath the London streets tortured him. If the lights in the carriages were still working, they wouldn't be for very much longer. And then the people on the train would experience the same darkness that he had for all these years.

"Why did he call you that name?" asked Calvert.

"Bartimaeus?"

"Yeah."

"It's the name of the blind man that Jesus cures on the road to Jericho."

There was no point in asking Laura if she had heard anything back from Serina Boise about clearance for the use of explosives to drain the tunnel. That was never going to get the green light. Yet the plan possessed an appealing logic and his mind kept returning to it. There was a man who might be able to help. He was a man who Ed thought about every day—couldn't help it—and as the idea started to take shape, he worried for his sanity that he should even consider it. The fact was he had run out of alternatives. This had to be considered. Nothing was off the table. Not in his mind at least. The plan that he was about to put in motion would almost certainly mean the end of his career. But this was bigger than one man's job and it was probably the only conceivable hope he had to resolve the situation. But when he started to say the words, they sounded all wrong. He said them anyway, turning in the direction of Calvert and White as he did so.

"I need you to find someone. He was the IRA's leading explosives man back in the day. He subsequently did some work for the secret service."

"Okay, Ed," said Calvert. "Who is it?"

"His name's Conor Joyce."

12:53 PM

"Tommy, I don't know who Simeon Fisher is," said Ed Mallory on the radio.

"Then perhaps you're not far enough up the food chain but I'm sure you can find out," replied Tommy Denning.

As Mark Hooper watched Detective Sergeant White tapping away on his keyboard, running the name through the database, he had that feeling again around the back of his ears. It had a certain heat to it. He had felt it when he was a boy and he had got in trouble at school—and now he had felt it twice in one day, once when he spoke to Berriman earlier and now here with Ed Mallory. Was this the moment when he was meant to throw his hands up and admit that Simeon Fisher was his man on the inside and he had known about Denning all along? No, that moment would never come. He would never allow anyone the pleasure of knowing that he had fucked up and there was no way that Ed Mallory, the blind bastard, would be able to tell that his attitude was anything other than that of a man under pressure.

Was this the end of the line? His whole life had been leading up to his career in the service. He had made sure he did everything right. That he was unpopular with colleagues on account of his naked ambition didn't bother him. He wasn't in the job to be popular. If people didn't like him then that was their problem. What he wanted was to prove that he had what it took. During his time at a minor public school in Cheshire, he had always been made to feel second best. Never good enough at sports to make varsity and not quite bright enough to shine academically, he had been told by some crusty old career adviser that he should aim for business management. But what did he know? By the time Mark was the rising star in G Unit, he knew that he had found his vocation. Not for him the boring middle-of-the-road life mapped out for him by his upbringing. In the service, he was pulling down jihadis, disrupting the rise of Islamic terrorism in the wake of 9/11, honorable work, and work that suited him. There was no way that he was going to throw all that away.

If only things hadn't played out like this. A month from today he was due in Whistler in Canada with his girlfriend, Anna. It was all planned. If Denning had moved a week later when he was supposed to then it would have given him three weeks to soak up all the plaudits within the service for preventing a major terrorist atrocity and then two weeks of skiing and quiet nights in with Anna, maybe even popping the question. There would have been no better time to do so than when he was at the top of his game and flushed with the confidence that would give him. But Denning had spoiled all that.

If he could just make it through these next few hours, however, then everything might still be all right. This was a test, a big one. The people who made the difference were the ones who could not only adapt and strategize but also keep their heads when the unexpected happened and turn a situation to their advantage. This whole operation looked bad, very bad; it would be difficult to make it right but he knew that, so long as he dug deep enough and drew on all his reserves of courage and determination, he would be fine; he would prevail. It was all about self-belief.

1:01 PM

A few minutes earlier his priorities had been so different. He had wanted to stay alive, he had wanted to protect his family; he had hoped that Tommy wouldn't notice the sticky pieces of gum on the handset that he had attempted to pick away as he had answered the radio to Ed Mallory. Now that he had heard Maggie calling to him from the next carriage, everything had changed. As the water lapped at his ankles, George looked at Denning, who met his stare, blinking nervously.

"Is it true?"

"Is what true?"

"You know exactly what I fucking mean. You heard her. What have you done with my kids?"

"Is that the wife?"

"Tell me!"

"I'm sorry, we didn't know what to do with them." He said it as though he was a child himself, one who had been caught out, discovered committing the very deed he had denied for so long. He was cowed. He might be the one with the gun and the mission from God but he was also a guilty little boy. And now he wanted to explain: "They may have aroused suspicion. They'll be all right. Someone will find them. We thought: what the hell?"

"What the hell? What the hell! I thought you were supposed to be a Christian. What about suffer the little children, eh, Tommy? You're not the new Messiah, you're the fucking devil."

"Don't worry about your kids, worry about yourself. We come into this world alone and we leave alone. You're going to be part of something the likes of which humanity hasn't seen for two thousand years."

George's rage was all the more acute for having been kept in check for so long. It felt like every feeling of anger and frustration that he had repressed since his first sentient moment was summoned up and brought alive.

"Think of them as a sacrifice," Tommy went on. "Abraham was prepared to sacrifice his son; you should be prepared to do the same. You are a prophet too. I've seen you in my dreams, George. You're one of mine and you're coming with me."

If what he was about to do would cost him his life, then so be it. George Wakeham had spent a lifetime swallowing his pride, suppressing his true self. No more. He threw himself at Denning. Clutching his mangled cheek with one hand, Tommy was caught off guard. He tried to bat George away with the pistol, striking him across the temple but George was bigger and heavier than him and his coiled energy was not going to disperse at the first sign of a counterattack.

Perception is everything, and in that explosive moment George's perception of his tormentor had changed. No longer was he the hard young soldier whose brain was scrambled by war, a killing machine whose wiring had gone. Now he was a potential conquest. George's sudden impulse to fight came from somewhere primeval. He was doing what he should have done all along—all creatures are at their most dangerous when their children are put in peril—he was saving his children.

By the time Denning was pulling the gun back for a second swipe at him, one with some more spirit-crushing brutality to it, George had his hands around his throat. His momentum and weight pushed Denning backward and he slammed him down into the water on the carriage floor. He forced his thumbs into Denning's throat, grinding them together. But he knew what was coming. All he had was impulse. There was no strategy. He wanted to kill; left to his own devices, he would crush the life out of Denning. But he was never going to get a free run at this. The first of Denning's strikes with the gun felt as though someone had taken a hammer to his head. But he felt it; he felt the skin open up and the blood spray. The pain was real. It was excruciating, but he was still conscious, still strangling the man who thought it acceptable to lock children in the boot of a car on the hottest day of the year. He was still killing him. He didn't feel the second blow.

All the lights went out.

1:02 PM

Northern Line Train 037, fifth carriage

When the water came through the doors, they lifted Adam onto one of the seats. Someone had said something about trying to prop up what remained of his leg; the blood flow was still heavy despite the belt Hugh had managed to tie above the wound.

Hugh's panic had gone. For how long he didn't know. But while his thoughts remained lucid, he channeled them into exploring a possible escape plan. He couldn't remember which of those torturous offsite management seminars it was that his magazine publisher bosses had seen fit to send him on but one of the numerous pointless aphorisms he'd been subjected to had stuck in his head. The exact wording of it he had forgotten but the meaning remained. In order to solve a problem, you've got to keep making choices and decisions. The moment you stop, you're sunk. It was clear to Hugh what had to be done. No one was coming for them. If they did nothing, they would die. The driver had relayed the information from the terrorists that if there were a mass escape attempt then explosives would be detonated. So they could either be blown up trying to escape or do nothing and drown. It wasn't a difficult decision to make.

The lights were dim. They had cut out altogether a couple of times. As terrifying a prospect as it was that in a few moments they would be cast into pitch darkness, it was also a situation that presented them with opportunities. Just as they would be rendered blind so would their hijackers, making an attack more difficult to repel.

That these thoughts came to Hugh so soon after his earlier panic attack gave him pause to think. Was this sudden clear thinking just another manifestation of his panic and, as with all the other stages that it had gone through, it would pass and something else would take its place? It was a distinct possibility. But he knew with a clarity of which he would not have thought himself capable that there was only one solution to their situation. He felt the need to voice it, to articulate it and thereby make it real. Even if it was real for no one but him.

"We need to try and retake the train." The words were whispered; he didn't want the female hijacker in the next carriage to hear but, as he said them, it was clear that he was clothing in words ideas that others had been mulling over for some time. Daniella, the attractive woman from New York who had helped him tend to their wounded co-hostage, looked at him and nodded. The faces of others who peered at him from the yellowy sodium glow of the fading lights were in agreement.

"It's going to be dangerous," he went on. "But it's the only chance we've got. If they set off the explosives then so be it." It came out like a line from a film and for a moment the absurdity that he, Hugh Taylor, should be articulating it was not wasted on him. Here he was planning and coordinating an attempt to retake the train. It was insane. He had to keep on speaking, if for no other reason than to repel the doubt that was firing missiles at his resolve.

"Does anyone have a weapon of any sort?" A penknife was passed forward. He had a sudden impulse to laugh. Someone trapped in this metal tube with him felt that a penknife was a suitable weapon against a psychotic hijacker with some sort of mobile cannon. But he took it and said thanks.

"I got this." It was a man's voice with a heavy London accent. Its owner stepped forward. He was dressed in regulation street gear, white sneakers—now underwater—sweat-suit trousers and T-shirt. In his hand was a large hunting knife. No one took it from him.

Hugh asked, "You know how to use it?"

"Not really."

"Are you going to come with me?" There needed to be a group of them. They needed to play the numbers game. The hijacker could pick off a few of them but so long as enough of them ran at her, some would get through and they could kick, punch, strangle, stab— whatever it took to finish her off. All that stood between them and freedom was a slight woman with a big gun. Hugh looked down the carriage and could see her framed in the window in the adjoining doors. So, which way would his potential recruit go?

"No, man. You take it, though." As Hugh heard the words and he took the knife that was offered to him, all the lights went out. There were screams and shouts from further up the train but in the fifth carriage, people remained quiet. The darkness wasn't complete, however, as light shone from media players, mobile phones and computers, as further voices both male and female volunteered to join the attempt to retake the train.

"So what we need to do," whispered Hugh in the half-light, "is make our way down either side of the tunnel and try and find a way into the carriage. Whatever it takes, we just need to get in there as quickly as we can and try and kill her."

1:03 PM

"Ed, we're going to move you all down to the command center in Leicester Square," said Laura. "We've got a dedicated negotiating cell on the back of an articulated truck within the perimeter. We can get the radio signal from the train patched through there."

"We're not going to get to speak to Tommy Denning again." Ed didn't care how pessimistic he sounded. He didn't need to think of the morale within the cell. It didn't matter what anyone else thought, the negotiation with Tommy Denning was at an end. Of that he was certain. And if he was being brutally honest, he knew that there never had been a functional negotiation.

"You may be right, Ed," said Laura. "We may not get through to him again. But we need to keep the negotiating cell up and running just in case. I've taken this cell off-line while we all relocate to the command center. There's another team of negotiators manning the radio link until we're ready to get down there. Serina Boise is going to conduct a review of the situation then."

"Still no plan for special forces to go in?"

"A strategy is being drawn up but there are issues with the water and the explosives on the train."

"Is Frank Moorcroft still here?" Ed asked the question knowing full well that he was still there; he could detect his musty aroma from across the room.

"Yes, I'm still very much here, Ed," said Moorcroft.

"Where do you think we are with the water level at this stage?"

"Again, incredibly difficult to gauge with any degree of accuracy but my calculations would suggest it's up to people's knees, possibly, maybe higher."

"GCHQ intelligence from all the communications into and out of the train confirm that," said Laura.

"So, Frank," said Ed turning toward the old academic, "how long have we got until the carriage fills?"

"It's very difficult to be exact as there are so many variables—"

"Imagine I've got a gun to your head."

"I'm a professor, not a hostage." He sighed. "Very very approximately, I'd say we've got about an hour."

"Are they going to get special forces in by then, Laura?"

Ed could detect something in Laura's voice. As far as she was concerned, Ed had crossed the line between being a talented hostage negotiator whose often unconventional methods should be indulged due to his ability to talk down crazies, and become a loose cannon who might at some later stage need to be sidelined. "I can only go on what I'm getting from Commander Boise." Laura's use of Boise's rank in terms of the situation meant that the shutters were beginning to come down. "Any intervention faces unique problems. They're having to revise their plans as the situation progresses."

As much as Ed had respect for Laura's abilities as a negotiating coordinator, she was part of the infrastructure now and as the seconds ticked by, Ed realized that if this situation was going to be resolved with the minimum loss of life—if the passengers on the train had any chance of survival—it wasn't going to be the authorities who were going to bring about the resolution. But not all the options had been exhausted. There was still one person who might be able to cut through the bureaucracy and make a difference.

Once Laura had told the members of the negotiating cell to reconvene at the command center as soon as possible where they would be required to remain on standby, Ed turned to the epicenter of Mark Hooper's aftershave cloud and said, "I need to speak to Howard Berriman. Immediately."

1:05 PM

It was as though George could watch and appraise his efforts to regain consciousness from some other realm. It felt as though the core of his being was still there, still alive, but it had withdrawn to the furthest reaches of his mind. Silence, pain, the side of his head felt as though it had a heart of its own beating beneath the torn skin, each beat performing a sharp almost unbearable stabbing pain. Someone was groaning. When he realised that it was him, he didn't stop; somehow the process of emitting the sound helped him to deal with the pain. When he opened his eyes, someone was shining a torch into his face.

"I'm sorry, George, I think I may have cracked your skull there. I didn't want to shoot you. You're important to me."

It was a voice that he recognized. It was an old friend. It had to be. What was he saying? Something about not wanting to shoot him? What was all that about? George was sitting down in a row of seats in a carriage. Why wasn't he in the cab driving the train? The train was flooded with water. And where were the passengers? Why were the lights out? He couldn't move his leg. Or, rather, he could but only so far. It didn't hurt but it wouldn't move. Looking down at it, he could see there was a chain and padlock securing his ankle to one of the yellow upright poles. What did it mean? As his eyes got used to the light, he could see the face of the man who was holding the torch. He had a hideous wound on his right cheek and his neck was bruised. George knew him from somewhere.

"Are you with me? I really don't want you to miss this. You probably thought that I'd shot you, like you'd never wake up. That's probably what you thought when you passed out. Or maybe you thought nothing. Didn't have time. I'm sorry about that. And I'm sorry about your kids too."

Kids?

The download was complete and the program was running. It was all there, instantly, and George was out of his seat and diving straight at Denning once again, hands outstretched. As he did so, the chain snapped tight around his ankle and he fell, flailing around in the water.

"Are you totally insane?" George remained on all fours in the water as he stared at Denning. For a moment, his ankle bettered his head wound in terms of pain. "You can't lock children in the boot of a car when it's a million fucking degrees. What kind of animal are you? You can't kill people for no reason, murder people and say that you're doing it for God."

"I'm not doing it for God, I'm doing it for us. I'm doing it for you as much as anybody. We all have so much to learn."

"What are we learning here?" George maintained eye contact and registered a minute victory when Denning looked away. "It's all in your mind. It's a delusion. There is no God."

"Not even you believe that, George."

"Yes I do. So do you, if you're honest with yourself. You know there's nothing there. Everyone knows there's nothing there. Deep down, in those moments when you are alone in your head and you're forced to put a bet on your own existence, you know. You know!"

"I forgive you for your blasphemy."

"I don't want your forgiveness. This isn't blasphemy, this is truth."

"I forgive you."

"Let my wife go. Let her save our children."

"I can't do that."

The water was cold and for the first time all day, George shivered. "Tommy, it's not Christian to murder."

"Don't tell me what is and isn't Christian."

"But I'm right, aren't I?"

"It's Christian to baptize . . ."

"Please let my wife go free."

George pushed himself onto his haunches and sat back on the seat. Tommy watched him and George thought that he looked like a man who was genuinely sorry.

"Let her go. If you let her go she'll be able to release the children. That's the Christian thing to do, Tommy."

Denning stood and watched him. Deep welts on his throat were visible from where George had tried to strangle him but it was clearly the missing parts of his face that bothered him the most and he continued to press his hand against the channel of excavated flesh as blood dribbled and spat from the wound.

"I can see what you're trying to do and I respect you for it but you're wrong. This is about metaphor, it's about symbolism. If I let her go, then what am I saying? I'm saying that I'm not committed to this, that this is not an act of love."

"Let her go, Tommy."

"It might seem hateful and vile to you but I'm doing this out of love. You must accept that and you must be baptized with love in your heart."

"They're children, Tommy. Their names are Ben and Sophie. Ben's five and Sophie's two. Ben likes pirates, he has a little wooden pirate ship and it's the center of his world. And Sophie, she's obsessed with her dolls. She's got four of them and she talks to them and has tea parties with them. Does God want you to kill them? Does he? Does God want you to kill children? Is that the role that he's specially picked out for you?"

"I know you think that you can test my faith. But you can't. There are plenty of children on this train. If I was going to waver then I would have wavered already, wavered before I'd even made this journey. What you have to realize is that your children are part of this too. They've been chosen as well. Can't you see? Two thousand years after Christ, another man has arrived to show the world the way to go. I am baptizing my flock; I'm washing away their sins. This was meant to happen. Just as it was meant to happen that a man called Simeon Fisher would come to betray me. I could have disposed of him before but, no, I brought him with me. Now he is dead. But he is as much a part of this great journey as you and I. Can't you recognize me, George? You must have seen me in your dreams."

Tommy stared at him, smiling, and George felt a moment's déjà vu. For a flash, it felt as though Denning was right, that he had always been there in some dark corner of his subconscious.

"What about your parents, Tommy? What happened to them?"

He had heard Ed Mallory, the negotiator, on the radio to Denning earlier and he had mentioned something about Denning's childhood and his parents. It wasn't much but it was something.

"They abandoned me."

"How does that make you feel?"

"Don't bother. I've spent years talking to people who were only too keen to make me answer that question. The fact of the matter is God decided what should happen. It was all part of my journey. But this isn't about my family or my upbringing." He met George's stare and held it. "This is all about sacrifice, George, all about sacrifice."

1:06 PM

How could something that had felt so right suddenly feel so wrong? The ongoing COBRA conference calls were torture. He had never felt so guilty in his life. Hooper was toast for this. The little shit was putting Howard's entire career in jeopardy. This thing needed wrapping up as quickly as possible one way or the other. It was meant to be a triumph for the service and him as its director general. The media would have been all over it like a cheap suit. It would have been a badge of honor for the security service under the leadership of its dynamic new director general. The home secretary and by extension the government as a whole could have basked in reflected glory and known who it was who had kept the country safe. The knighthood might have come earlier than expected.

But then came Hooper's news. A tube train parked up in a tunnel exactly as he had told him it would be. Right place, right time of day, right everything, except for one detail. It was one week early.

Hooper told him it was impossible to say conclusively that it was the work of Tommy Denning because he had had no intel from Simeon Fisher—their man on the inside—and he wouldn't be able to confirm anything until demands were issued. There was a small chance it was all a coincidence, a possibility that the train driver had suffered a heart attack or been otherwise incapacitated. Berriman had hoped to God that that's what it was. Anything but Denning one week early.

But he knew it was a false hope even while he clung to it and, sure enough, there was Denning on the bloody Internet feed spouting his madness. At least he hadn't mentioned that the service had infiltrated his group. Maybe he didn't know? But Berriman knew that that was probably a false hope too. Why go a week early unless he realized they were on to him?

It wasn't as though the media could paint it as a black op or anything like that, although given half a chance they would no doubt try. All that he and Hooper had—all that could be proved they had—was a little foreknowledge. They were monitoring Denning but they didn't have any specific intelligence. They might just get away with that. He and Hooper had been careful. Nothing was in writing. And nothing existed to tie him to it apart from Hooper.

As he reached into his desk drawer for another couple of Nurofen to try and combat the sciatic ache down the backs of his legs, his phone rang. It was Hooper.

"Mark."

"I've got Ed Mallory for you. Wants to speak to you urgently."

"Okay, put him on."

Ed Mallory's reputation as one of the best negotiators in the country had been built on his ability to construct psychological profiles of subjects through active listening. His blindness had given him increased sensitivity to speech patterns and verbal expression. Would he be able to tell that he was lying? Had he already done so during their previous conversations?

"Hi, Ed."

"You need to know that our negotiation is effectively at an end. There's no way that anyone's going to be able to talk Tommy Denning out of that tunnel. The only hope we have of getting those passengers out now is a rapid intervention by special forces."

"Listen, Ed, I've spoken to Major Burroughs, the SAS squadron OC, and there's no way he's sending his men in under the current conditions. There's been a direct and specific threat that the train will be blown up if there's any attempt to storm it."

"If we can't put together a rapid intervention at this time, we have to consider using explosives to drain water from the tunnel."

The only way that Howard was going to survive this was to keep his head down, play everything by the book and in the event that anyone started making accusations that he had prior knowledge then he would deny everything.

"A controlled explosion is even less likely to happen, Ed."

"You've seen Tommy Denning on the Internet feed—he's got no demands. All he wants is to die and take hundreds of people with him. Even if we could get through to the train, we're not going to be able to talk him down. We need to blow a hole in that tunnel wall. I have a professor here who thinks it can be done."

"I know, Ed. I've spoken to Serina Boise. But we're never going to get clearance for that either."

"So what are we going to do? Are you telling me that we're going to allow upward of three hundred and fifty people to die on this train? Is that what you're saying?"

"I'm not saying anything, Ed. We need to keep thinking of alternative resolutions. You're asking me and I'm telling you that, at this moment in time, special forces with or without explosives are not a possibility." Howard didn't care whether Ed could detect the frustration in his voice. Maybe it would mask his deceit. "Look, Ed, I'll do what I can, okay? Leave it with me. There's another COBRA meeting scheduled for later. I'll discuss this with everyone then."

"Okay, you do that. Oh, and one more thing: who's Simeon Fisher?"

The question punched him in the guts. But he couldn't show it.

"Simon Fisher?"

"Simeon."

"Doesn't ring any bells. Why?"

"Denning mentioned him, said he was 'one of ours'—whatever that means."

"No, never heard of him. Ed, we'll speak later."

He finished the call before he could be drawn into further conversation. Taking Ed's call had prevented him from having a drink of water to wash down the Nurofen and now he could feel the tablets moving slowly—and painfully—down his gullet. There was a cup of coffee on his desk that Yates, his assistant, had made him earlier and he had left to go cold. Picking up the cup, he took a big gulp but it didn't manage to shift them. His day just kept getting worse.

1:11 PM

Ed passed the phone back to Mark Hooper. As he did so, his fingers touched Hooper's palm, which was moist. The smell of the young spook's aftershave was fading as a faint smell of sweat began to break through it. And his hand was shaking.

"Ed, we've found Conor Joyce," said Calvert. "He lives on a houseboat on the canal in Camden."

Part of him had hoped that they wouldn't be able to find Joyce. He could have been dead; he could have emigrated to Australia. But no, he was living not five miles away in Camden. Ed could either use this information and explore its potential or he could do the right thing and put his crazy idea out of his mind. More than three hundred people were facing death beneath the London streets. If he had found a way to save them—even if it was acutely hazardous—was it not right at least to investigate it? The situation was changing by the minute as the water rose in the tunnel. Howard Berriman's words were fresh in his mind. Neither storming the train nor blowing a hole in the tunnel was an option.

Ed didn't even know that Laura Massey was in the room. But when she spoke, he could tell she knew exactly what he was thinking.

"Ed, you need to switch off now. You need to try and relax and make your way down to the mobile command center. The cars are ready outside."

There was no point arguing with her. She was right. If he was still part of the negotiating team, if he was still honoring his oath to the force, then he would do what was expected of him and make the trip down to the command center and wait while the other negotiating cell tried to make contact with Tommy Denning and failed. But in the time it had taken for him to process the information that Conor Joyce was nearby, his priorities had changed and he knew that he couldn't do what was expected of him because he knew that, if he did, everyone on the train would die.

"Sure, Laura, we're on our way."

As he listened to the others gathering their things and making for the door, he put his hand on Nick Calvert's arm and it was enough of a sign for him to hang back. As Ed listened to the footsteps leaving the room, he turned to Calvert and said, "You need to do something for me."

"Oh Jesus, Ed, you can't be serious about this."

"All I want to do is meet him and talk to him."

"Why?"

"I just need to know that it can't be done, that's all. You need to get me to Camden now. We can say we got stuck in traffic or something on the way to the command center."

"Ed, you could cost me my job."

"Nick, under normal circumstances, I'd deem that enough to pull back but not today. There's too much at stake. If it's not possible— and let's face it, it probably isn't—then you can drive me to Leicester Square and we'll sit and wait for them all to drown."

"Ed . . ."

"You're going to do it, Nick. I know you are. I can hear it in your voice."

Calvert emitted a bitter chuckle. "Oh shit. Look, I'll get you there, you can talk to him. But that's it."

"I want Frank Moorcroft with us and no one else."

"Jesus, Ed. You don't want much, do you? How am I going to insist that it's just us three in the car?"

"I don't know, we'll think of something." But just as Ed said this, his mind was elsewhere, diverted by the mention of a car. Since he had heard the woman shouting on the train when he was trying to negotiate with Tommy, something had been niggling at his subconscious and the mention of the car was enough for it to suddenly make sense. She had said something about *the boot of a car*. The woman was Maggie Wakeham, the train driver's wife. Her children weren't accounted for. Tragically, in the scheme of things, they were low down the list of priorities.

As he took Calvert's arm and they made their way from the room, Ed said, "I think I know where the train driver's kids are."

1:27 PM

Northern Line Train 037, first carriage

"Listen to me, Tommy. What you've done here. Well, it's not your fault, right? You're ill, you need help. If you let us go now, the authorities can treat you. You'll go to hospital and, when you're better, they'll let you out. You can get on with your life. You can get yourself a wife and have some kids."

"Sounds nice."

"Come on, Tommy, just put down the gun and let us go."

Denning had hung the torch by a piece of string from a handrail set into the ceiling of the carriage. The light shone downward onto the surface of the water that was now above their knees. Watery reflections bounced and danced around the ceiling of the train. Tommy stood just outside the cone of light that shone down onto the water but there was enough peripheral light for George to see him raise up the pistol and fire more shots down the carriage, from where the desperate cries of the passengers were emanating. Bullets struck metal, pinged and clanged, and George thought of Maggie out there in the darkness in the next carriage.

"Listen to them, George. Just listen to them."

George wasn't having any trouble hearing the sounds; they were a constant torture, unavoidable. Sounds of desperation: shrieks, screams, bursts of manic shouting, sobbing, praying, children crying.

"Tommy, it doesn't have to be like this. Just let Maggie go. Let her save the children."

Denning was little more than a shadow in the darkness. As much as George tried to add whatever impact he could to his words, he couldn't make eye contact with him.

"I don't expect you to understand."

"But that's it, Tommy, I do understand. I know what it says in the Bible. I learned the Ten Commandments at school. I can't remember all of them but I can remember the most important one: 'Thou shalt not kill.' It's there in black and white in your holy book. 'Thou shalt not kill.' Doesn't that mean anything to you, Tommy?"

"It means everything to me. It's the word of the Lord."

"So let us go."

"You know I can't do that. This is God's work."

"But 'Thou shalt not kill,' Tommy. 'Thou shalt not fucking kill!'"

1:31 PM

Camden Town

Calvert was so tall that Ed could hear his shaved head scratching against the vinyl interior of the car as he steered them through the streets. Professor Moorcroft sat next to Ed in the backseat while Ed fired questions at him regarding the logistics of a controlled explosion in the service tunnel near to the location of the train. Knowing that what he had said to Ed regarding his hypothesis had set in motion a sequence of events that appeared to be rapidly running out of control, Moorcroft was modifying his original hypothesis with numerous caveats. When Ed asked him questions regarding the amount of explosives that might be required to open up a fissure between the tunnels, Moorcroft stonewalled him and refused to be forced into hazarding a guess.

"Really, you have to believe me when I say that it would be a dereliction of duty if I were to allow you to cajole me into even offering an estimate."

"Come on, Frank, when you told us about the possibility earlier on, you were sounding a lot more positive."

"It's really not a matter of being positive or negative per se. All I can do is respond to empirical evidence as it presents itself to me at any given stage. At this moment in time, I have to say that, having reflected on the logistics of the situation, I feel neither more nor less positive than I did before as to the feasibility of—"

"Okay, sure." Ed couldn't face further bluster from the professor. It was getting them nowhere. The plan might possibly work. That was the best he was going to get from him.

Nick Calvert had been silent since they had set off from the London Underground Network Control center earlier. He had insisted to the uniforms that it was an operational necessity that he commandeer a squad car for just himself, Ed, and the professor. Ed had been able to hear in Calvert's voice his hatred of the deceit implicit in doing so. Ed knew that he was pressuring Calvert and Moorcroft into taking part in something that they didn't feel happy with. But unless he was seriously deluding himself, he could also hear something in both their respective demeanors that meant that as crazy as they thought he was for even contemplating this course of events, they didn't think that a positive outcome was completely unfeasible. Ed concluded his questioning of the professor and settled back in his seat. He didn't want to use up all of his co-conspirators' goodwill just yet. If he was going to do what he was planning, he would need as much of it as he could get.

As for Conor Joyce, he had no idea what he was actually going to say to him when they met. What could he say to the man whose wife had died as a result of his negligence? No, it wasn't negligence. Ed was all for self-laceration regarding the events of that day but it wasn't entirely negligence that had made the Hanway Street siege turn out so badly. It was more like overconfidence. His failure to talk down the IRA hitman and his resultant death alongside Conor's wife, Mary, had—aside from the lifelong disability that it had caused Ed himself—made him more diligent and cautious in subsequent hostage situations, something that had perhaps saved many other lives. Or was that just a way of making himself feel better about the whole thing? Perhaps there was some sort of ironic symmetry to the fact that today of all days he was going to come face to face with the man who represented his single worst professional failure to date.

All Ed knew was that Conor Joyce might offer him a solution to the situation, a solution that was almost certainly illegal and most definitely went against all forms of relevant protocol.

"Here we are," said Calvert and Ed was snapped out of his thoughts as the car swerved to a halt.

"You stay here, Frank," Ed said to the professor. "We won't be long." Frank murmured in the affirmative and Ed opened the door and stepped out of the car onto the pavement, where Calvert offered him his arm. Ed took it and they made their way down the steps onto the canal towpath.

As the first smell of the oily water reached Ed's nostrils, Calvert said, "The uniform who's with him said he was pretty pissed off to be detained with no reason given."

"I can imagine."

"Apparently he's threatening all sorts of legal action."

"I can't blame him. Now listen, Nick, you just get me in to see him and then leave me to it. You don't need to be involved in this."

"I'm already involved, Ed."

"You can cut me loose any time you want, Nick, you know that."

"I know." It was a tone of voice that Nick Calvert probably employed with his children when they had disappointed him. It was not the tone of voice of a man who had reached the end of his tether and Ed was thankful for that. He was only moments away from meeting the man whose destiny had become so cruelly tangled with his own thirteen and a half years ago. It would have been so much easier if he had lived hundreds of miles away or had died some years previously. Ed would have known then that there was nothing that could be done. But with Joyce alive and living nearby, Ed's hand was forced. There was no way that he could allow a chance like this to pass him by.

They walked along the towpath and Calvert spoke to a police officer, before ushering Ed onto the deck of a canal boat.

"I'll be right out, Nick."

"Okay."

Ed listened as Calvert stepped back onto the towpath and struck up a conversation with the uniforms. The hatch into the cabin was open. Ed ran his hand along the wood and rapped his knuckles against it.

"You'd better come in." It was the same voice that had told him, "You fucking let her die," all those years before. Now it sounded calmer though still possessed of an acute antagonism born of mistrust. Ed had never seen Conor Joyce in the flesh but remembered seeing a photograph of him. He had a short muscular figure with a square jaw and short hair, already gray by his forties. He had to be in his fifties now.

"Hello, Conor."

Ed stepped forward into the cabin. Conor wasn't going to provide him with directions or take his arm. There was an aroma on the boat that was unmistakably male. This was the home of a single man who had let things slide. The air was stale and inert. Tobacco smoke competed with greasy cooking and the odor of a man who didn't pay as much attention to his personal hygiene as he might once have done.

"They fixed your face up pretty good, all things considered. You were in a right state when I last saw you."

"They did their best. I wish things had turned out differently that day."

"You're telling me."

"I'll get straight to the point."

"You do that."

Conor's tone was combative. He was conceding nothing. The police had invaded his home as they probably had done on a number of occasions over the years. He had constructed a wall around himself. Whether it could be broken down was something that Ed needed to establish. Fast.

"I take it you've seen the news?"

"Yeah, hottest day of the year. Might go sunbathing later."

"We've got a major terrorist hijack on the Underground. An armed gang has taken a tube train, they're holding the passengers hostage and threatening to drown them by flooding the tunnel."

"Ah, I saw something about that. Nasty business."

"The hijackers are religious psychopaths."

"Islamic?"

"No, Christian."

"Christian? Jesus."

"We think you might be able to help." We? There was no we, it was his crazy plan and his crazy plan alone, but maybe it would sound more convincing if there was an air of consensus to it.

"Really?"

"The tunnel's filling up with water. We've got less than an hour before the passengers drown. It appears that there's a service tunnel that runs close to the tunnel in which the train is situated. If we can let off an explosion that will break through the adjoining wall then we might be able to drain off some of the water and buy ourselves some time."

It sounded totally ridiculous but there it was, it was done. The pitch was made. He wasn't going to plead or beg; either Joyce would help him or he wouldn't.

Joyce chuckled to himself but it was a form of laughter entirely devoid of humor. Ed listened as he opened a packet of cigarettes, took one out, put it in his mouth, and lit it with a lighter that had to be a Zippo—the click the lid made when opened and the smell of the flame were unmistakable. He blew smoke around the cabin and Ed waited, knowing with every second that passed that the water would be getting higher in the tunnel and the passengers would be getting that bit closer to oblivion.

Would he help them? Was he even able to help them?

Ed battled his impatience, wrestled with an urge to prompt Conor for an answer. Fate had decreed that the paths of these two men should converge after all these years. But what outcome would fate decree for this furtive, desperate encounter? Joyce could so easily say no. Ed would be powerless as his final chance of saving the train sank beneath the water in the tunnel along with all those hundreds of people.

"There are children on the train. Chances are there'll be quite a few." The emotional blackmail was heavy-handed and Ed winced at his own unsubtlety.

"Children you say?"

"Yeah, we don't know how many but we've had reports there's an entire class of them on a school trip."

"Mary and I were going to have kids. She was pregnant when . . . You remember that?"

"There's not a day that goes by when I don't think about what happened."

"Me neither."

Joyce's voice was measured and devoid of emotion as he said: "I'd love to help you, Mr. Mallory, but the thing is this is your war, not mine."

"This is everyone's war." Ed's voice was weak, almost childlike. "This is just a group of isolated religious lunatics and we need to stop them from murdering hundreds of innocent people."

"The same was said about me and my lot once upon a time."

Silence. Ed felt sick, numb. This was his last chance; it was their last chance—and it was slipping away.

"If you're not going to help me, Conor, I need to know now so I can try and figure out some other solution."

"It was good of them to keep your job open after what happened to you."

"I don't think they wanted to. It hasn't been easy."

"What I don't understand," said Conor after a deep lungful of cigarette smoke, "is why me? You need an explosion but instead of calling on the might of the British army, you come and see—sorry—come and *find* me. Me! Are you fucking mad?"

"Maybe I am but the truth is I can't get the go-ahead for the explosion. The powers that be say no. They can't get the SAS into the tunnel in time. So if I don't try and do something, there are going to be hundreds of dead bodies down there. So, there it is, I thought of you."

"You need a big fucking explosion on the London Underground and you want me to do it? And it's unofficial. So even if we can save the people on the train and the explosion doesn't kill them, I still go to prison."

"We can worry about your defense later. You can tell them that I made you do it. All I know is that we've got less than an hour to try and save those people."

Conor Joyce rubbed his forehead with the flat of his hand whilst he thought. Ed waited, his innards feeling empty and tremulous.

"It was never me that set off the explosives. You do know that, don't you?"

Ed didn't and he suspected that Conor didn't either. He said it in such a way that Ed could hear a state of denial shrouding the words. But if that was his way of dealing with the past then so be it. It was unimportant now.

"I just got them for others. I know that none of you lot believed that but it's the truth. I was a sort of fixer, dealer if you like. I've got a vague knowledge of how to make the stuff go bang but that's it."

Ed felt sure that Conor had much more expertise than that but he dodged the issue, not wanting Conor to lose the train of thought.

"There's no one else I can turn to."

"You're not setting me up here, are you?" The antagonistic tone had returned. "I try and find you some explosives and you lock me up?"

"No, you have my word."

"And that's meant to count for something, is it?"

"Right at this moment, it's all that I've got."

Conor sighed. "Okay, well, let's give it a shot. It's not like I've got anything else to do today."

1:33 PM

Morden Tube Station parking lot

Thinking about the children made him feel suffocated. The thought of them roasting to death in the boot of a car was sickening, abhorrent. When he was a little boy, maybe five or six, his sister had locked him in a closet for what felt like hours but was probably no more than about twenty minutes. He never forgot it. The heat, the darkness, that sense of terror that he would never escape, never breathe fresh air again, never be free. He had shouted and screamed for the first few minutes of his incarceration but after that he had become silent, traumatized. If the train driver's kids behaved in the same way then he would never find them.

He walked along slowly, hands by his sides listening all the while, waiting to hear sounds from the cars. Children's voices, knocking, tapping. They would be thirsty after their ordeal. He would buy them cold drinks, he would pay, he was thirsty himself. His treat. They would be frightened. They would want to know what had happened to their parents. They would need comforting.

Up one row of cars and down the next. Up another row and around the corner. They were here somewhere. If the police had found them already then there would have been some evidence of that. But there were no police other than a couple of community policewomen he had seen by the tube, who were just standing there looking bored, watching the world go by.

Could the children have passed out already from the heat? Were they too traumatized to even make their presence known? Those poor children; Tommy Denning had so much to answer for.

Alistair walked between the rows of cars, listening, straining to hear anything, any movement that might betray the children's whereabouts. As he began yet another circuit of the parking lot, he became nervous that perhaps his continuing presence might alert the authorities. Varick had told him that London was under constant scrutiny via CCTV cameras. So Alistair decided to leave the parking lot and go to the corner shop he had been to earlier to buy another bottle of water. There was a small portable television on a shelf behind the counter. On the screen was a blurry image of Tommy Denning standing in a tube carriage. There he was, broadcasting to the world. The news anchor explained that due to a wireless Internet connection that had been installed in the tunnel to allow negotiation with the hijackers, people on the train were able to send e-mails and photographs; some could even make calls. But it was the image of Tommy staring into the camera that the TV channels kept returning to, like an itchy wound they couldn't help but scratch.

Time was ebbing away. If Alistair didn't find the children soon, they would be dead. He took a swig of water as he left the shop to carry on searching. It was while he was walking past a row of cars he had already passed a couple of times before that he heard faint crying and muffled knocking. He needed to establish exactly which car it was. Another couple of passes and it was obviously the dark blue Vauxhall. The car wasn't even locked. He pressed the button on the boot, the lid flipped up and there they were, hot and frightened but otherwise unharmed. They blinked in the harsh sunlight as they climbed out and stood looking at him. The little girl was crying and the boy took her hand as he turned to look at Alistair and said, "Where are my mummy and daddy?"

"They'll be back soon," he said. "They just had to take a trip. They asked me to look after you until they get back."

"What's your name?" asked the little girl between sobs.

"I'm Alistair, I'm your friend."

"I'm thirsty, Alistair," said the boy.

"Let's go and get a nice cold drink then."

Slamming the lid of the boot, he ushered the children in front of him. He didn't hear the cars pull up at the entrance to the parking lot; he didn't hear the footsteps. He was thinking about the children, he was thinking about the cold drink he would buy them and how he had saved their lives.

As soon as he heard a voice through a bullhorn, he knew the ensuing words would be directed at him.

"You, in the jeans and the gray T-shirt. Stay where you are." There was no one else in jeans and a gray T-shirt; there was no one in the parking lot besides him and the children. He turned around and there they were. They weren't the usual ones; this was all to do with Tommy Denning. They were crouched down behind a row of cars on the other side of the lot. They had guns; he couldn't see them but he knew they were there. It wasn't as if he'd done anything wrong. All he had done was rescue two children who otherwise might have died. But no one would ever see it that way. He was involved. He was implicated. They would look on their computers and they would see who he was.

"Alistair? What's going on?" asked the little boy, but he didn't get to answer before the bullhorn cut through the hot air once again.

"Sophie! Ben! Walk toward us, keep walking toward this voice."

"You'd better do as he says," said Alistair. The little girl was crying again. She was so young, so innocent, she didn't deserve this.

"Don't worry, Sophie," he said, "everything will be all right. Go on now, you'll be fine. Just go over there toward those cars." And she did, she started walking. So did her brother. Alistair was all alone now. He hadn't done anything wrong. But that didn't matter. Not any more.

They wouldn't understand, they never did. They would make it their business to misunderstand. They would twist his words, make it appear that he was trying to hurt the children. They would make out he was in league with Tommy Denning when, in fact, he was doing everything in his power to save two innocent children from Tommy's madness. They would want to know why he hadn't gone to the police in the first place. In his desire to help the children, they would see subversive desires at work. They would probably suggest that he was in the process of abducting them. He would never be able to make them understand. They would create their own phony confusion. Throughout his life he had spent so many hours in police stations, so many hours in cells, he couldn't face any more.

He knew what he had to do. It was playacting. When he was a little boy, he had been in all the school plays. Overacted terribly. But it didn't matter. Just as it didn't matter now. He started to shout as he ran, screamed, heading straight for the kids, putting his hand in his pocket as though he might be pulling a gun. Today of all days, it would be enough. They couldn't allow him to hurt those children.

The voice through the bullhorn was shouting at him but he couldn't hear the exact words above his screams. It took longer than he thought it would. He was almost upon Sophie as the first bullet hit him. It hit him low down, in the stomach. It might not be enough so he carried on running, hurling himself forward and the second one hit the mark. Middle of the chest. He wasn't going to hospital. He would be all right; he was flying straight into the arms of Jesus.

1:49 PM

Coopers Lane, Somers Town

"He's walking across the road and approaching some railway arches. He's knocking on a door set into the timber facade."

Ed sat in the back of the car with the professor while Calvert commentated on Conor Joyce's movements.

"The door's being opened by a white male in his forties, thick set, about five nine. They're talking to one another. Joyce has gone inside and the door's been closed."

Ed slid down on the upholstery. Conor Joyce's involvement was providing him with a whole new set of problems. While he had proved easier to persuade than Ed had feared, it was his seemingly compliant attitude that worried him. It didn't take much psychological intuition to realize that Conor had an ulterior motive and it wasn't difficult to conceive of what that motive might be. Ed knew all about frustration and how it could brew and fester. On that day over thirteen years ago Ed and Conor had both lost something dear to them. Wounds like those didn't heal. Now Ed had given Conor a shot at revenge and he had to accept that Conor might very well take it.

The air conditioning struggled to combat the hot air baking the car. He tried to empty his mind, knowing that even if he could do it for only a few seconds it would help. Ed's use of meditation had no spiritual angle to it, nothing more ritualistic than trying to cleanse his mind for a few minutes each day. It helped him think clearly. It was difficult to do knowing what he knew of the passengers on the train but he needed to try and get a perspective on what he was about to attempt. He knew that if he asked Calvert and Moorcroft their opinion, they would construct their answers based on their perceived professional obligations. Although they were very different, one a dedicated streetwise cop and the other a lifelong academic, they both had a strong sense of duty. But in this instance, it was misguided. Ed felt certain of it. What the situation needed was someone who didn't care about his career or his place in society, someone who sometimes found himself dangerously uninterested in his own personal safety.

"What's he doing in there?" asked Calvert.

"He's collecting something," replied Ed and just as Calvert was about to ask him—as he knew he would—exactly what it was that he was collecting, Ed asked him, "You got any children, Nick?"

It was two boys if Ed remembered correctly. Calvert had mentioned them one time during a coffee break at a counterterrorism seminar at which they had both been speaking. The voice of the big fearsome-looking Special Branch officer softened as the connections were made and he thought of his children.

"Jack and Felix. Jack's eight and Felix is five."

"Where are they today?"

"They're both at school. Ed, we need to get going—"

"I never had kids. It just never seemed to happen. Shame really. My younger brother's got three. They're beautiful." Ed could hear Calvert turn to look at him as he spoke about his brother's children and how, in the absence of children of his own, he had tried to be the best uncle to them that he could possibly be. He reminisced about Christmas the year before and how his brother's youngest, Jasmine, had staged her own song-and-dance routine—anything to avoid the subject of what they were doing there outside a railway arch in King's Cross. But he was interrupted when Calvert said, "He's on his way back. He's carrying an old cardboard box. Oh shit, he's putting it in the trunk." Ed listened as Conor slammed the trunk and climbed into the passenger seat. His story having served its purpose and, with Conor Joyce and his provisions now on board, Ed remained silent while Calvert started the engine, swung the car around and set off.

1:50 PM

Northern Line Train 037, first carriage

"If there is a God, you'll burn in hell for this."

"You don't know what you're saying, George."

"Stop talking to me like I'm your friend. Stop calling me George. You can kill me, but you can't befriend me."

"You've got spirit, I'll give you that."

The water was now over George's waist, higher on Tommy, who continued to fire his pistol down the carriage every few minutes as though compelled to do so by the distant sounds of desperation from the passengers.

"Why don't you just kill yourself?" asked George. "Why do we have to die with you? Just put the gun in your mouth and pull the trigger. It'll be over in a second."

"I wish you people would stop wishing me dead," said Tommy. "All my life people have been trying to keep me alive. In Afghanistan, blokes were getting shot at all the time. Me? Not once. But now everyone wants me to die. Am I not going to be dead soon enough?"

"Don't be a prick," said George. "Don't delude yourself. You're a murdering psychopathic scumbag. That's why people want you dead. You're no prophet. You're about as much of a prophet as that David Koresh or Jim Jones."

"Bless you, you're doing what you think is best."

George pulled against the chain that bound his leg to the pole even though it sent shooting barbs of pain up his shin. The pain was a distraction from his agonizing frustration.

"Maggie?" George shouted into the darkness.

"Yes, George, I'm here." She sounded distant, further away than the twenty feet or so that he knew it to be.

"You've got to get as many people together as you can, and you've got to come down here, and if there are enough of you and you're determined enough, you'll be able to overpower him and kill him."

"Yes please, Maggie," shouted Denning. "Bring them here. Once I've shot poor George here, I'll shoot them too."

"Do it, Maggie," said George. "Do it for Sophie and Ben."

George could just make out Denning watching him, shaking his head slightly, like a father might, disappointed at the behavior of a child.

"You know she won't do that. She's terrified. You're all she's got to cling to, and besides they're going to start coming for me soon anyway."

He left the statement hanging there; George didn't want to give him the satisfaction of asking him to qualify it but curiosity got the better of him.

"They?"

"The passengers. Back in the old days, it was possible to do something like this and they'd stay put, wait, hope that you were sincere when you told them that they would be all right so long as they did as you said. But United Airlines Flight 93 changed all that. They're going to come for me and I've got to be ready."

Denning reached into the duffel bag that he had slung around his neck so as to keep it above the water. His arm glistened in the light from the torch, varnished with blood from the wound in his face that he had been pressing his hand against. As he retracted his arm from the duffel, he was holding a semiautomatic rifle.

"I'm ready for them," he said. "I'm prepared for all eventualities. But what about you? All this shouting to your wife that she should bring some bigger boys to beat me up, well, it makes me think that perhaps you want to die."

"I'm going to die soon anyway, isn't that right?"

"You're going to die and you're going to be resurrected to eternal life. But maybe you don't want to wait."

George watched as Denning pointed the gun at him.

"If you'd rather, I can baptize you now and send you on your way. Would you like that? After all, you suffer from claustrophobia, right? Those two or three minutes in the water while your lungs give out, that might not be a very pleasurable experience. Particularly if you go into it with the wrong frame of mind. So, as a special concession to you and because I like you, I'm going to give you the option. If you'd rather go here and now then tell me."

What had George got to live for? Just another few minutes of horror knowing that he was going to die and being powerless to stop it, tortured with the knowledge that he might have been able to do something if only he had tried harder, made different choices. And then at the end of it, drowning—something that had terrified him all his life.

Why not go now? If he was a coward—and he felt like one—then why not die like one? Why not just make things easier for himself for once in his miserable life?

"Just say the word, George. I know you're thinking about it."

"No, he's not!" shouted Maggie from the next carriage.

"Don't listen to her, she'll try and dissuade you."

"George! If we have to die then we have to die together."

"See? I told you. Ignore her. I'm prepared to do you a favor."

"*George.*" It was a tone of voice he had heard Maggie use a thousand times. It said, "Don't you dare."

"What do you say, one little squeeze of the trigger and all that pain goes away, just like a sweet little pill, only quicker?"

"Go fuck yourself."

Denning lowered the gun, chuckling as he did so.

"What's so funny?"

"You are, George. You really crack me up. I wasn't going to shoot you. Even if you'd pleaded with me. How many times do I have to tell you? You're coming with me."

1:55 PM

Hugh Taylor, consumer affairs columnist, his sports jacket now long discarded, waded through the water toward the doors between the fourth and fifth carriages. His way was lit by the screens of phones, tablets, and laptops. For the first time in hours there was a sense of hope among the passengers at the rear of the train. They knew there was going to be an attempt to retake the train by a group of men. Hugh was one of those men. He was more than one of those men, he was their leader.

He didn't know where it came from. For all his life he had felt excluded, left out, a watcher, a spectator, a nerd, a joke, and now here he was captaining the team. It felt surreal although the fear itself was real enough. He was afraid, not so much that he would die—he had resigned himself to the fact that he probably would—but afraid that he would revert back to the man he had been for the sum total of his forty-seven years. He enjoyed this new version of himself. Hugh Mark 2. This was the man that he wanted to be, even if it was only for the last few moments of his life. He believed in destiny, perhaps this was his.

Recruitment choices had not been difficult. He took every person who volunteered. There weren't many but there was no question of shaming people into making the journey with him; he could hardly sit in judgment over others with regard to their potential bravery or cowardice. It wasn't that long since his last panic attack and, although he was no psychologist and didn't hold with all that analytical self-help bullshit, he knew with an unwavering certainty that his panic attacks were born of fear and more than a little cowardice. But the need to take a stand had forced him into action. It didn't feel like bravery. It didn't really feel like much of anything. It was just the right thing to do. The water was up to his middle. The schoolgirls had to stand on the seats. They were frightened. Everyone was frightened. The expressions on the children's faces, lit by the glow from electronic equipment, were what drove him on. He couldn't just stand by and let the children die.

First out of the door, he squeezed himself between the end of the fourth carriage and the fifth and down into the cold water, up to his shoulders, and along the side of the carriage toward the rear of the train. The plan that they had hatched in urgent whispers only minutes before was that they would divide themselves into two groups and make their way along the tunnel wall on either side of the train and up to the sixth carriage. There they would attempt to draw fire from the hijacker to allow opportunities to enter the train and, once inside, try and kill her. The plan was weak: he knew it, they all knew it. But what choice did they have? Hugh had never even been in a fight before but he knew, if he could reach the woman, she was dead.

The others followed him; he could hear them climbing down from the carriage and into the water. They didn't look like heroes. They looked like what they were, frightened desperate people doing whatever it took to try to stay alive. Of the four of them who had sat together at the end of the carriage and introduced themselves to each other that morning, Maggie had set off along the train—God alone knew why—and Adam had lost half his leg, which meant that he and the New Yorker, Daniella, who had insisted on joining the attempt to attack the hijacker, were the only two remaining.

As far as the others in the team were concerned, Hugh knew that he couldn't think about who these people actually were. They were all of them someone's son, father, mother, or daughter. A strictly adults-only policy was his only hard-and-fast rule but other than that anyone could take their chances with the crazy bitch.

When Daniella dropped down from between the carriages, the water came to just over her shoulders. She pulled herself along the side of the train but, after a couple of footsteps, she lost her footing on the uneven ground and as she steadied herself—one hand on the side of the train and the other on the cables mounted on the tunnel wall—she took a mouthful of water. It tasted sour and muddy and she spat it out, gasping.

There was more light the closer she came to the last carriage. The hijacker stood in the glow from a battery-powered lantern hanging from a handrail, its light reflected in ripples on the ceiling of the train. Standing with her legs apart, she had her rifle rested across her shoulders, her arms hanging over it in the classic James Dean pose. She looked as though she was acting.

The plan was simple: to draw fire from the hijacker and through the resulting shattered windows, gain entry to the carriage. Once inside, the idea was to choose a moment when she might need to reload—or even better run out of ammunition—and then attack her, kill her if need be. Daniella had been wrong about Hugh. He might have been an unworldly guy with a panicky demeanor but he had somehow discovered untapped reservoirs of courage under pressure. The plan to retake the train had been his and it was impossible to know why Daniella had said yes when he asked for volunteers. Wherever the impulse had come from, it had made her feel better than she had since this entire nightmare had begun. There were moments back there when she feared she was cracking up. It was the inertia, the helplessness. Now she had something to do, something to focus on over and above the crushing despair. The fear didn't get any less but at least this was something positive. Now she had hope.

Hugh was the first to try and draw fire from the hijacker. The others pulled back behind the end of the fifth carriage, leaving him standing by the window, banging on the glass, waiting for the woman to shoot at him. As she did so, he jumped back and the dum-dum bullet smashed into the window of the sliding door at the end of the carriage, creating a hole the circumference of a large dinner plate. The exploding glass fragments ricocheted in the tunnel stinging the back of Hugh's head and when he dabbed at the cuts with his hand, his fingers came away wet with blood.

As they had planned, a young Iranian man banged and shouted on the other side of the carriage, and the resulting shot from Belle slammed into the metal carriage wall blasting a ragged hole in the metal. Another shout from Hugh and this time he stood his ground as the woman raised the gun. For a moment, their eyes met along the barrel and he threw himself back as she pulled the trigger. Blinking away the muddy water, he saw a hole in the window in the door. It was big enough. He waited for more shouting from his co-conspirators and, glancing up over the lower edge of the window, he could see the woman taking aim at the opposite side of the train.

He had to move fast. Finding a foothold on the tunnel wall, he pulled himself up and threw himself against the hole in the window. The shredded glass snagged against his back and chest as he clambered into the carriage. Holding his breath, he curled up in a ball underwater behind the row of seats as the thump of a large caliber bullet struck metal nearby.

He was in.

Pushing his head above the surface of the water, he sucked up a lungful of air. He looked across at the young Iranian, who hammered on the side of the carriage to try and distract the hijacker. But he mistimed his evasive maneuver and as a gunshot thumped the air half his head came away.

Hugh managed to turn around in the water and crouching on his haunches, he leaned back against the end of the row of seats. With his eyes just above the level of the water, he could see another team member, a man in a black suit, as he squeezed between the side of the train and the tunnel wall. The man was about to beat on the side of the train but the hijacker had spotted him and fired off a shot which splintered the metal in the door and he was hit by something, some sort of shrapnel from her diabolical weapon. Slumping down in the water, Hugh could hear him gasp and cry out but he was still moving and clearly audible as he retreated, making his way back down the side of the train.

Daniella Langton knew that she was probably level with the hijacker now. She had to climb over the young Iranian's body. His limbs were solid and heavy in the water. If she gave herself away, a shot through the side of the train would mean the end. But the carriage was tight against the tunnel wall. She would have to force herself through the narrow space. There was nothing else she could do. Once again, she had overestimated her abilities. It was something that her mother—who never failed to miss an opportunity to put her down—had said to her often enough. It was even said to her in her work appraisals until she reached a position in the company where she didn't need to care what others thought of her. And now she was going to die for it.

There was another gunshot. This was her moment; this was her chance. She pushed herself through the gap, her clothes scraping against the side of the train, and threw herself forward into the water trying to go as deep as she could until her fingers dug into the gravel on the bottom of the tunnel. Explosive gunshots above her head were muffled by the water; their impact against the side of the train punching her eardrums. She dragged herself along, her lungs aching for air. As her fingers curled around the end of the carriage, she pushed her head above the surface, drew a deep breath, and plunged back into the water.

Further sounds of gunfire came from the train. Maybe the second wave of people had begun their attack. Perhaps they would succeed. She wouldn't get to find out; she couldn't stop herself even if she tried. The impulse was irresistible. She just had to put as much distance between herself and the train as was humanly possible.

As the train receded behind her, Daniella felt safe enough to take another breath and do the front crawl as she swam along the tunnel toward a faint light in the distance.

Hugh's strangely beatific mood of confidence of only a few moments before had taken a pounding. He felt his bravery ebb. It was essential that he maintain his momentum. But he couldn't help but feel that rather than gaining entry to the carriage through his own guile and ingenuity, the hijacker had allowed him to do so. The thought unnerved him. Perhaps throwing himself forward blindly was not the best strategy. He worried that perhaps this reasoning was the onset of a resurgent cowardice and the thought filled him with more fear than he had felt all day.

Someone else tried to make their way into the carriage on the other side of the train. Hugh couldn't see who it was. As a shot was fired, another man clambered through the window through which he had come before a shot threw him backward against the tunnel wall and he slumped forward into the water.

It was time for Hugh to move but just as the torture of his indecision began again, two men managed to gain entry to the carriage through newly broken windows but he wouldn't give odds on their chances. It was obvious they were being allowed entry—just as he had been—and the ensuing shots and the splashing of their bodies in the water were confirmation of this.

No one else was going to try their luck. It was all down to him now.

It was dark in the carriage—the only light came from the single bulb in the hijacker's lamp swinging from a handrail. The water was dark too. If he could move cleanly beneath it without breaking the surface, he might reach the end of the row of seats and hunker down once again by the first set of double sliding doors. Could he pull himself along between the seats without giving himself away? There was nothing to be gained from pondering on the logistics of his plan, so he took some deep breaths to oxygenate his blood and set off toward her. He remembered from when he was a little boy playing soldiers with his brother in the garden that they always used to say you'd never hear the bullet that killed you. It was something they must have read in a comic or seen in a film. And here he was all these years later about to find out whether it was true.

She was only about ten feet away from him now. With the hunting knife in his hand, he pulled himself along under the water toward her.

1:58 PM

MI5 Headquarters, Thames House

"We both own this, Howard, but I'm the one who's been left to make the big decisions. If it all falls apart because one of us loses our nerve then we'll both be held responsible."

"Is that some sort of threat?"

"We both agreed that this could work. You can't walk away."

"Mark, there are hundreds of people down there. Special forces think it's impossible to get in there without exposing their men to Denning's threat to let off more explosives. Number Ten, the home office, COBRA, the media—at the moment, they're paralyzed. But once this is resolved either way, they're going to be all over us. It'll be impossible to contain."

Berriman's sciatica felt like a burning wire being held against his buttock. How could something so tiny as a nerve cause so much pain?

"What you seem to have forgotten," said Mark Hooper with that whiny hiss to his voice that he seemed to have developed in the past few hours, "is that if Denning succeeds then it is contained."

"If Denning succeeds, hundreds of innocent people will die."

"That's not something that we have any control over now."

"What about Ed Mallory and his idea about draining the tunnel by deploying an explosive charge?"

"His judgment's completely gone. He's trying to find some old IRA bomber."

"Have we considered what happens if he does manage to find a way to drain the water out of the tunnel?"

"You know as well as I do, Howard, that he's never going to get clearance to let off explosives on the Underground."

"None of this alters the fact that we were handling someone on the inside. We had clear provable foreknowledge of a potential attack."

"No, Howard. That's not how it was. We had an ongoing intelligence timeline. We interpreted it as best we could."

"We could have stopped the attack but we didn't because we were too preoccupied by the media and how the project would play with them."

"No, we made an error of timing, that's all."

"Mark, if this is going to leak then we need to manage it."

"We can't manage it, Howard. We just bury it. There's no paper trail. Simeon Fisher went AWOL in Helmand, he returned to the UK, moved to Wales, and got involved with Cruor Christi. There was no intelligence. We're as shocked about what's happened as everyone."

"I'm not sure, Mark."

"You are sure, Howard. Believe me, you are."

Howard started to respond but he realized he was talking to a dead line.

2:03 PM

Northern Line Train 037, first carriage

George had often wondered what it would feel like to be famous. What was his constant yearning to find some talent in himself that he could nurture, if not a fascination with fame and its transformative effects? When reality shows had first started on television, he had often found himself wondering what it would be like to be suddenly catapulted into the public eye. He liked to feel that it was intellectual curiosity that fueled his interest; he hated the thought that he might actually be part of the target demographic for the increasingly vacuous shows. He would never have actually joined the queues of hopefuls trying to take part in the tawdry carnival. But it was snobbery that held him back—of course it was—and within a couple of years of the first *Big Brother*, he had added his voice to the chorus of derision, so much of it hypocrisy, hypocrisy he was equally guilty of, seeing that he still watched the shows avidly.

What did it say about him—that he had a secret longing for fame? Why wasn't being himself ever enough? Maybe it was loneliness. He had always felt lonely but it wasn't the sort of loneliness that could be cured by the company of family or friends. If anything, they accentuated it, enhanced its potency by making him realize that even they couldn't save him from it. But just as he knew that having a crush on fame was all part of his desire to cure his loneliness, he also knew with stone-cold certainty that if he ever—for whatever reason—achieved even a modicum of public recognition, he would still be lonely, if anything, more so. And he could see that same loneliness in so many others around him. Mostly in men, of course. Men are good at being lonely, despite their inevitable packs and tribes.

The irony was that he would be famous now, fleetingly, as the driver of the doomed train—but he would be famous for only one thing, and that was dying. George would be reduced to just a statistic in the ensuing news story.

In these last few minutes of his life, he didn't feel lonely. His sense of bereavement was all-consuming. His wife and children were dying and they had never felt more precious. He thought of his own parents; how they would cope with this. His mother, his poor mother—from this day on, any mention of his name and the tears would come to her eyes. His dad too. What a burden they would have to bear—their only son, their daughter-in-law, and their two grandchildren, dead. All killed on the same day. Facing such trauma and at their age, they might never recover. He couldn't think about it, it was too much, like thoughts of Sophie and Ben and what had been done to them—what was still being done. His family was being violated and he could do nothing to stop it. But they were still his family. Whatever sick horror was being visited upon them—and this felt about as sick and horrific as it could get—no one could take that away from him. As he thought of them, he could conjure up their aroma, the soft, nutty, almost honey-like smell of the children; Maggie's smell—feminine, reassuring, alluring. He could smell the house, that homely smell of carpets and clothes, humanity and food cooking in the kitchen.

He was turning the key in the lock now, returning from his shift and there was the smell. What he wouldn't give for that smell now. Sophie ran toward him and hugged him around the legs. Benji came thundering down the stairs and standing on the second step, flung his arms around his neck. There was Maggie, framed in the doorway to the living room, smiling as he shouted, "Group hug!" and they all came together on cue, as they had so many thousand times before, he and Maggie scooping up one rascal each and all of them grabbing hold of each other. Afterward, laughter and games, playtime, bathtime, bedtime stories, kisses, "Night night, I love you," sleeping children, then down for supper, glasses of wine, feet up, television, and talking, a night in the Wakeham house. No more frustration, no more loneliness. Nothing else mattered. This was *his* god. Denning could keep his.

The water was up to his chest now. George would be dead soon. There was nothing he could do about it, not physically at least; he couldn't reach Denning now, not with his leg chained to the pole. His jailer stood there in the middle of the carriage, looking around at the havoc he had created with a look of wonder and pride in his eyes. This was Tommy's proof—if proof were needed—that he was doing God's work.

George knew there was no God; and he knew too that in a very short time, unless he could figure out some way of saving himself, he would be returning to the unknowable primordial hum from which he had sprung. This was his last chance.

2:05 PM

Northern Line Train 037, sixth carriage

It was like playing a video game. Not that she had ever played more than one in her life. *Kill Fire* it was called. She loved it. It was a "first person shoot 'em up." Jason, a boy she had been fostered with, had let her play it in return for handjobs. They were a small price to pay. The graphics were amazing. That's what Jason said anyway. So that's what she said as well.

You walked down a street in some desert town shit-hole. Iraq or somewhere like that. And ragheads came at you, ran at you from buildings, tried to shoot you, and you had to take them out. Some of them didn't even have guns. They were just armed with knives, and the nearer you allowed them to get to you, the higher their score value when you drilled them. She played the game a lot, which meant plenty of handjobs for Jason.

It was a buzz when they came for her. In the space of just a few hours she had become hooked on killing. She had a need, a hunger. Tommy had said to her that she should only kill people if they tried to stop them carrying out the baptism. So that meant that what she was about to do was fine. It was okay, it was allowed. They were trying to make her smash the windows with gunshots so they could get into the carriage and try to rush her. It felt as though she was playing *Kill Fire* all over again and it was up to her to try for the highest score possible. So she allowed one of them into the carriage with her. She could have shot him easily as he clambered through the broken window but she wanted him to get closer.

Another one came down the opposite side of the train and she shot him in the head. It was almost too easy, like shooting fish in a barrel. That was an expression that Tommy came out with when he was playing video games. She only ever played *Kill Fire* with him once and even though she had played it hundreds of times more than he had, had practiced and improved, he beat her best score on his first attempt. And that's what he kept saying every time he killed someone: "Like shooting fish in a barrel." She loved Tommy. He had engineered all of this. He had the intelligence and understanding to realize that he had been chosen. A lot of people might have missed it, might have gone through their lives without realizing that they had a mission. She knew in her heart of hearts that, without Tommy, she would not have realized that she was special too, chosen to carry out God's work. She was lucky. She was blessed.

She and Tommy had spoken about this moment for so long and now here they were just as Tommy had said they would be. Tommy talked to God a lot and told her about their conversations.

"God loves you, Belle," Tommy told her. Of all the millions of people on earth that God had created, he was thinking of her. More than thinking, he loved her. She was special to him. And it was Tommy who had made her realize it. Tommy might have been at the other end of the train but she could feel him; he felt as close as if he was standing next to her.

"Not long now." He had said that to her so many times in the past few weeks. And it really wasn't long now. There was no death. Not for her. She would be resurrected to eternal life and she would sit alongside God and Tommy and Jesus. She would sit alongside the disciples.

Some more of them made their way down the side of the train and she shot at them. One of them ducked down beneath the window and she shot him through the carriage wall. Evidence of her inch-perfect aim was plain to see as part of the man's skull, complete with hair, slapped against the window. Another one she shot as he climbed through the broken window through which she had allowed the skinny bloke to climb a few moments before. She let the other two make their way into the carriage as well, let them think they were going to be able to reach her. She even pretended to reload the gun and swore as though she was having problems, enticing them ever closer. She thought she might try and take them both out with one shot. That was a triple bonus score. But she settled on shooting them one by one. The first one wasn't very satisfying. The shot hit him in the chest and he was thrown back against the seats, dead before he even hit them. But the second one was choice. Took his head clean off.

Where was he, the skinny one who she had allowed into the carriage first? She knew he was crouched down behind the end of the row of seats. He'd probably lost his nerve and who could blame him after what the Pulverizer had done to the others? He must have known he was going to die. Brave of him really. She could respect that.

She waited. When he made himself known—made a run at her or whatever he was going to do—she would let him get close. But where was he?

She took a step forward and there he was, rearing up out of the water straight in front of her. He was too close, way too close and he had a big hunting knife in his hand with which he slashed at her. She could feel the air displacement from the blade against her cheek. Another inch closer and he would have taken her face off. They struggled; he might have been skinny but desperation made him strong. Another swipe with the hunting knife which nearly caught her throat and she managed to push him backward and maneuvered the Pulverizer into position.

The bullet almost tore him in half. Only a short section of his midriff, just a few inches of flesh, remained after the dum-dum bullet had done its work. He dropped the knife into the water but with one final supreme effort, he managed to get his hands around her throat. His face looked up at hers as his intestines flopped into the water from his gaping abdomen. And then he did the strangest thing. As his fingers lost their strength and he began to collapse into the water, where he would drown in a soup of his own guts, he managed to fight against his impending death long enough to spit in her face. She wiped the spit away with the back of her hand and kicked him away from her. That had to be a triple score. If he was close enough to spit in her face, it had to be. But she didn't like it that he had got that close. It was too close. It unnerved her.

Belle reached into the side pocket of her jacket that was now below the level of the water in which she stood. She felt for a fresh magazine but there wasn't one. Not to worry, there were plenty more. She waded through the water back to the rear cab. By the light of her torch, she could see that Simeon had tipped forward from where he had slumped after she'd shot him. Blood hung from his wounds in big clouds in the water. She considered kissing him again but decided against it. Feeding the Pulverizer was more important. And besides, he would be cold by now.

Somewhere in the water was the bag that contained the ammunition. She tried feeling for objects with her feet. She felt something by the door, it wasn't a bag, it was something small and hard—it was one of the Glock pistols but as she reached down into the water, she knocked it out of the open doorway.

Never mind, there was another one around here somewhere and she had plenty more bullets—food—for the Pulverizer. She just had to find the bag. She stepped over Simeon's body and explored the other side of the cab with her feet. Nothing. There was only one place that it could be—under Simeon. Rolling him over, she reached underneath his body and felt the reassuring touch of the canvas bag against her hand. She pulled it out of the water and opened it up. It wouldn't matter that the bullets had got wet. She had applied wax sealant to them to ensure they were waterproof. She reached inside the bag. It was empty. Her fingers frantically scoured the bag's interior and finally she turned it inside out. No magazines, no bullets.

But Simeon had packed them . . .

And there it was—Simeon had packed them.

She felt sick. She held the torch between her teeth and went through his pockets. She knew they weren't there. Just as she had loaded his gun with dud bullets, so he had disposed of her ammunition. But as she straightened up, God saw fit to throw her some small consolation. There on the driver's console, now half in and half out of the water, was the other Glock. She stepped over Simeon and picked it up. A Glock would fire when wet; it would even fire under water. It held seventeen rounds. Being the one from which she had fired the two shots into Simeon, there would be fifteen rounds left. Hopefully that would be enough if there were any further attempts to attack her. There was also one bullet left in the Pulverizer. One of her holy bullets with the cross carved into the end. She wouldn't tell Tommy about losing the other bullets. He would think she had been sloppy in her preparation and he would be right. She wouldn't tell him but she needed to speak to him. The water was rising fast. She might not have another chance.

She took the walkie-talkie from her top pocket and pressed the switch. When he answered it, he sounded different, almost like it wasn't him.

"Tommy? What's the matter? You sound really weird."

"I've been shot. It hurts but I'm okay."

"How did it happen, Tommy?"

"It doesn't matter. It's not important. We must stand firm. They'll keep coming for us right up to the last moment. But once the baptism is complete then we will have accomplished God's work. Just remember that no one will ever forget the name of Belle Denning."

"I love you, Tommy. I'll see you on the other side."

"I love you too, Belle, always and for ever."

2:11 PM

Northern Line Train 037, first carriage

His sister's voice was so full of hope. It gave him strength when he heard her speak like that. The pain in his face had settled down into a series of stabbing jolts that kept time with his heartbeat. It felt as though someone was kicking him in the face with a sharp, pointed boot, a silver-capped cowboy boot perhaps. Over and over again, almost every second, and some kicks were worse than others. At times it felt as though the person doing the kicking had taken a running start. He needed the end to come quickly now to stop the pain. Sometimes the frequency changed. Instead of deep and thudding, it would be high-pitched and the cowboy boot would be replaced by a handful of needles jabbed mercilessly into his gums.

But he knew this for what it was and he could take it. It was a test. If he could pass the test and carry out the baptism then all the angels in heaven would sing his name. He hadn't come this far to fail. God was with him. God was with his sister too. Tommy could hear God in his sister's voice. Belle was a prophet.

"Bye, Tommy."

"It's not good-bye, Belle. This is not the end but the beginning."

"I know, Tommy."

"Be strong, Belle."

"I will, Tommy, I will."

He took his finger off the switch on the walkie-talkie and let it drop into the water. He didn't need it any more.

His bond with Belle was more than just spiritual. They had great sex. They fitted together perfectly. Maybe it was something to do with being brother and sister, twins. They could go for hours but they would always come at the same time. And in a funny sort of way, today would be the same.

2:19 PM

Unmarked Police Car, Leicester Square

Ed listened to Nick Calvert as he showed his ID to the police officers manning the perimeter of the evacuation zone on the edge of Leicester Square. As Calvert spoke, his voice was imbued with a frequency usually absent from it. In among the masculine low notes was a screech that betrayed his inner conflict. He and Ed hadn't spoken as the car had made its way through the West End traffic. They didn't need to. Ed knew that Calvert was torn about what they were doing. Nick Calvert was a career cop. He did everything by the book. You could never wish for a more reliable colleague in a negotiating cell. Ed was asking him to compromise his most cherished principles. If Ed could have carried out his mission without enlisting Calvert's assistance then he would have done so but they both knew that it wasn't possible. So here they were, entering one of the most heavily secured and policed locations on the planet, and doing it with an illegal cache of Semtex and a former IRA bomber in the car with them.

With their credentials confirmed, the uniformed officer said, "Okay, you can park up. The negotiating cell's on that artic over there."

"Thanks."

Calvert pressed the button to raise the window and it slid back into place with a faint hum. He drove on for a few yards before swinging the car around and cutting the engine.

"Ed, we're here. I'm presuming you're not coming to the negotiating cell so I need to know what to tell them in there."

Ed could hear the fear and confusion in Calvert's voice. Ed had no doubt that when he answered, his own voice would contain the same emotions. Calvert was the gatekeeper of his plan so he knew that he must maintain an air of self-confidence. It was crucial that Calvert felt that what he was doing was right and that Ed's plan was the product of serious tactical considerations and not a panicky act of desperation. In reality, it was somewhere between the two.

"Here's what I think we should do, Nick. I'm going to stay here in the car with Conor and the professor. I think you should go to the negotiating cell and collect as much information as you can. What's the intel from GCHQ on the communications going into and out of the train? That goes for passengers and terrorists. We need to know how high the water is; we need to know if there is any movement on the rapid intervention plan. And, finally, you need to get back here as fast as you can."

"What if I don't agree to this, Ed?"

It was a question that Ed was hoping Calvert wouldn't ask but he had his response ready nonetheless.

"If you don't agree to it, Nick—and you're perfectly entitled not to, all things considered—then there's nothing else we can do. We just sit and wait."

"For them to die, right?" Ed remained silent. Calvert had answered his own question. "Oh, what the hell am I doing?" He muttered the words and Ed couldn't read them. Was this Calvert backing out, throwing in the towel? He didn't get a chance to decide before Calvert was out of his seat and slamming the door.

Ed turned to Frank Moorcroft sitting next to him. "Frank, as briefly as possible, how long until the tunnel fills?"

"It'd have to be very approximate because there's no way of judging exactly how porous the masonry and earth around the site of the flooding is. But taking into account the flow of the River Lime, the level of the Thames, the water table, the amount of potential seepage . . ."

"Please, Frank, give it your best shot."

Robbed of his potential variables, Frank fell silent for a moment before he said, "About twenty minutes, half an hour? But of course—"

"Do you think it's possible it might be more than that?"

"It's possible but unlikely."

"It's more likely to be less?"

"More likely, yes."

"How high do you think the water might be now, Frank? I know it's painful that you can't be exact in your answers but just give it your best shot. Whereabouts would it be on a man of average height—midriff, chest, shoulders?"

"Chest? Possibly."

"And the explosives in the service tunnel, Frank, do you have any thoughts on the optimum location to place them in the event of an attempt to drain water from around the train?"

"I have to say that this is most improper inasmuch as I am being asked to provide opinions on incomplete data—"

"Frank, none of the responsibility for this is going to rest with you. You have my word on that. I want you to give me your opinion. That's all. What I do with that subsequent information is my responsibility. Ultimately all I'm trying to do is save the lives of some—if not all—of the passengers on that train."

Frank's reservations were eased a little by Ed's pep talk but his verbosity was uncowed as he explained that, based on the location of the train, the ideal location for the attempted breach was approximately twenty yards from the rear of the train.

Ed attempted clarification: "And that's not so close to the train that we're going to do the terrorists' job for them and blow up the passengers?"

"One would feel that it would be far enough away from them, taking into consideration that the main force of the blast would hopefully be taken by the stone and rock between the two tunnels. That would have to be the general idea anyway."

The driver's door was snatched open.

"There's nothing from the train," said Calvert as he climbed in and closed the door. "Serina Boise has been talking about ways of getting a line of communication to Denning. My guess is it's not going to happen. Word from GCHQ is that the level of chatter from the train has dropped considerably in the past hour as batteries on phones and laptops have given out. From what they can make out, the water's rising fast."

"Any talk of special forces going in?" asked Ed.

"Scuba equipment is being sent for but, even if it can be got there in time and we can get a consensus from COBRA, it's unlikely to make much difference. And, Ed, they're looking for you."

"Why?"

"You're the only one who's spoken to Denning. They think if they can get him back on the line, it should be you at the other end of it."

"It's not going to happen."

It needed saying again. It needed reinforcing within this cell that comprised Ed and his three conspirators, this post-negotiating cell, this unofficial covert intervention team. "If we don't try and do something, then there's nothing else that can be done. With that in mind, each of you needs to tell me now whether you're prepared to help me or not."

The interior of the car fell silent. The upholstery creaked as the men shifted in their seats. Conor spoke first.

"I'm in." There it was again—Conor's mysterious enthusiasm for the job at hand.

"Well, I suppose, all things considered, I am too," said the professor.

"Fuck you, Ed Mallory." Calvert's sudden venting of frustration was accompanied by his hand slamming down on the steering wheel with such ferocity that it sent a tremor through the car. "Let's do it."

2:33 PM

Northern Line Train 037, first carriage

"Don't you think that London has suffered enough, after last time?"

Denning watched him by the light of the torch hanging from the handrail in the ceiling of the carriage. George could see two of him; his head and shoulders and their reflection in the rising water. It was up to their shoulders now.

"London is the most important city in the world," said Denning. "It is a cultural and spiritual crossroads. It's the perfect place to start a war."

"It didn't happen before."

"It's different this time."

"Why?"

"Because it's me that's doing it."

"Do you have any conception of how delusional you sound?"

"I'm not the one who's deluded, George."

"There is no God," said George. "Religion was made by man. It was a primitive attempt to make sense of the world before science came along. It's a superstitious relic from the past."

Denning said nothing, just smiled. Whatever George said, he couldn't help but betray his animosity. If he had any chance of saving

the people on the train and his children, he had to think clearly; he
had to find a key to unlock Tommy's mind. Faced with imminent
death and physically immobilized—his leg ached within the chain
that bound it to the pole—all he had was his voice and his mind.

"So your parents abandoned you, did they?"

"Not this again."

"Go on, tell me."

"If you really want to know, my father knifed my mother over the
breakfast table and then he hung himself."

"So what did you do?"

"I carried on eating breakfast."

"I don't believe you."

"Believe what you like. It means nothing to me what you believe.
You can come out with as much heresy and blasphemy as you want.
Nothing will change the course of your destiny now."

George didn't know where he was going with this but he knew
that he needed to keep him talking. Denning's mood had changed.
Faced with imminent death, perhaps his resolve was weakening.

"If you could turn back the clock, would you try and stop your
dad from doing what he did?"

"Whatever for?"

"He killed your mother. Didn't you love your mother?"

"She was all right, I suppose."

"How can you say that about your own mother? Jesus loved his
mother. Jesus preached that everyone should love their mother."
George was winging it. He had no idea whether Jesus preached
any such thing—he had failed his religious studies exam—but his
comment made Denning think for a moment.

"Maybe I would."

"Maybe you would what?"

"Have stopped him doing what he did but it doesn't matter now.
Nothing matters."

"It matters now more than ever, seeing as in a short while you're
going to be meeting up with your mother and father again."

"I don't think so."

"Why not?"

"I just don't."

"But you're going to heaven, aren't you?"

"They won't be there."

"Your mum and dad will be in hell, will they?"

"Maybe."

"Have you thought that if you kill hundreds of innocent people, you'll probably meet them there?"

"I'm just doing what I was destined to do."

"Have you ever stopped to think for just one moment," said George, trying with all his might to sound measured and thoughtful when his natural instinct was to hurl obscenities, "that perhaps this is not what God wants, that perhaps you've misread the signs? Every nut job that carries out an atrocity like this thinks they've got God on their side."

"Why are you talking to me about God when you don't even believe?"

"Because I'm trying to show you that what you're doing is wrong. By every law of humanity or religion or whatever you want to believe in, this is wrong. This is cold-blooded mass murder."

"No, George, this was prophesied two thousand years ago." Suddenly alert, Denning stopped talking and listened. Someone was trying to make their way down the side of the train, trying to make their way between the side of the carriage and the tunnel wall. He raised his assault rifle, fired off a burst of rounds and the sound of movement outside the carriage stopped.

"Can't you see?" said George. "Can't you comprehend for even one moment that what you're doing is wrong? If there is a God, you're going to be judged and damned. Don't you see that?"

Denning turned and pointed the rifle at George.

"Stop."

"Am I getting to you?"

"I want you to be baptized, I want your sins to be absolved but if you have to die a sinner then so be it."

George held his stare and said nothing. Denning broke eye contact when he heard more movement but this time it wasn't coming from the side of the carriage as before but from above. Someone had climbed out of the doors between the carriages and managed to make it up onto the roof and was now crawling along it, trying to be as quiet as possible. Unfortunately, the sound of his or her clothes dragging along the metal was impossible to hide. Whoever it was—and George would never know—they were struggling to stay alive. When Denning looked up and George could see him calculating in his mind the exact angle and trajectory of the shots that he would fire into the ceiling of the train, he couldn't help the tears that came to his eyes. After a short burst of gunfire, the sound of crawling stopped.

"These people just don't want to learn. They are so close to salvation and yet they keep trying to throw it all away."

He turned to George and, holding the rifle in one hand, he pressed his other hand against his ruptured face and said, "I like you, George, please let me save you. Don't let me have to kill you, not after all that we've been through together. You'll thank me when you see what lies in store for you and your family. You'll be reunited on the other side. You are all prophets. I am leading you into the promised land. You'll see."

At the moment that he spoke, George didn't care whether Denning shot him or not. "Fuck you," he said, "and fuck your God too."

2:42 PM

Leicester Square

"Nick, do you think you can get Conor and I down into the ticket hall?"

"I don't know, Ed."

"Come on, we're cops. They're going to let us down there."

"It's what we're going down there with that worries me."

"You think there'll be dogs?"

"Yeah, bound to be. They're going to start howling when they get a load of what's in that cardboard box."

"Well, we just need to make sure that we keep away from them."

The four men made their way toward the Underground entrance on the west side of Charing Cross Road. Ed didn't dare think what they must look like to the massed ranks of police and special forces milling around the empty streets around the tube station—the blind man with the tall shaven-headed man holding his arm, the crusty academic, and the stocky Irishman carrying the cardboard box. They would look strange and incongruous under normal circumstances—what the hell would they look like now?

"There are two CO19 officers at the Charing Cross Road entrance to the tube," whispered Calvert.

"Dogs?"

"None that I can see. But what are we going to tell them we're doing?"

"Leave it to me. All you need to do is point me at them."

Calvert led on, while Ed held his arm and thought about what he was going to say.

"Hi," he heard Calvert say to the CO19 guys. "This is DI Ed Mallory from Special Branch."

Ed took his ID card from his pocket, showed it to them, and said, "We're going to need to get access to the tube station. This is Professor Frank Moorcroft and Dr. Conor Joyce from Imperial College London." Ed pocketed his ID. If they were going to challenge him, ask to see ID for Joyce and Moorcroft, then they would do it now and his plan would be foiled.

"Okay, gov," said one of the armed officers and as soon as Ed heard it, he knew they were in.

"We're going to need a member of London Underground staff with a passkey to allow us access to where we need to go."

"The station manager's down there in the ticket hall."

"Thanks."

Calvert steered him through the doorway and down the steps toward the ticket hall. Ed heard Joyce's and Moorcroft's footsteps as they followed them down.

Calvert called ahead to someone—the station manager—and while Professor Moorcroft explained where they needed to go, Ed listened to the stillness of the tube station. There were a couple of subdued voices far off to his left, uniformed police most probably, and he was certain that he heard the whine of a dog.

"Conor?"

"Yeah."

"Who's down here with us?"

"There are some paramilitary-looking fellas over there."

"Have they got a dog with them?"

"Jesus, yes, they have. Spaniel."

"We need to move. Nick, come on."

"Hold on a sec," said Calvert.

Ed tuned in to the conversation between the professor and the station manager. They were taking too much time.

"Frank? Frank, listen. Do you have the key and do you know where you're going?"

"Well, er—"

"Yes or no."

"Well, yes to the key and, I'm afraid, no to—"

"Let's go. Now. Down the escalators. Bring this guy with us."

The dog barked again. Its behavior could attract attention at any moment if it hadn't done so already. Ed took hold of Calvert's arm and almost pushed him forward, trying to set the pace. They made their way down the stalled escalator. Ed listened for footsteps behind them or the clicking of dog's claws on floor tiles. He heard neither but a distant bark set his nerves jangling.

"I think it's down toward the Northern Line," said the station manager.

"Show us where you think it is," said Ed.

"I know I've been there. We used to use it for storage."

"It's extremely important that we find it now."

All the supposed might of the British government, all the security forces, all the committees, all the counterterrorism strategies and the fate of the passengers on the train was in the hands of this unlikely group of men.

Ed struggled to contain his frustration as they all came to a standstill once again and the station manager said, "No, I just can't seem to . . . No." Ed was about to give free rein to his boiling impatience when the man said, "Oh, hold on. Here we go." They were moving again. Twenty feet further along a pedestrian tunnel and then they stopped. Keys jangled. A lock was turned. A door opened—heavy, metal, hinges creaking.

"Okay, Conor. It's just you and me now," said Ed.

"Great." Ed couldn't miss the Irishman's sarcasm.

"Nick, you need to go back and scope out the ticket hall, make sure that if anyone comes looking for us you delay them as long as you can. Frank, you just need to tell us how far we have to go into the tunnel."

"I'd be happy to come with you." For once, Frank had got straight to the point.

"No, Frank, I can't ask you to do that. Just tell us where you think we need to be."

"By my calculations, the best place is about two hundred and thirty-two yards from the mouth of the tunnel. Here, use this."

"What is it?" asked Ed.

"It's a laser measuring device—all the estate agents use them. You press the button on top and it tells you the distance between the device and whatever surface you place the laser dot on."

"Give it to Conor, it's no use to me."

"And I'll need a flashlight too," said Conor.

"Here, have this," said the station manager.

"Okay, let's go," said Ed, taking hold of Conor's arm as he made his way into the doorway and down the steps. Before the professor was out of earshot, Ed could no longer put off asking the question he had been so afraid to ask for the past few minutes.

"How long do you think we've got, Frank?"

"Impossible to say, I'm afraid. I'd just be as fast as you can."

As they reached the bottom of the steps, the air became cooler. Ed listened to Conor's labored breathing. He listened as he put the cardboard box down on the ground.

"You're not going to like this," said Conor.

"What's the matter?"

"We're never going to make it."

2:47 PM

Northern Line Train 037

Those children tall enough to keep their heads above the surface of the water stood on the seats; those too short to do so were held by adults and clung to the handrails in the ceiling of the carriages. Adam did the same, his arms aching as he struggled to remain conscious despite his increasing blood loss. The guide dog paddled around in a tight circle. Her owner, a man who knew all about perpetual darkness, kept pulling on the lead that was looped through a handrail as the water level rose, maintaining the tension to alleviate the strain on the dog's tiring legs.

In the second carriage of the train, Maggie Wakeham stood on the seats, clinging to the handrail, straining her head up into the apex of the ceiling, sucking at the air in the thin gully that remained, the only space that the water had not yet filled. All but the most water-resistant of the electronic devices that had provided some tiny points of light from the people further down the carriage were now extinguished; they had either run out of power or been doused in water. But if she could see nothing, she could still hear plenty and there were sounds that she would rather not have heard. The prayers, shouts, wails, cries, and pleas had gone and all that remained were the sounds of people desperately trying to stay alive, thrashing around in the water, fighting to find those last few inches of warm, oxygen-depleted air.

2:55 PM

Leicester Square Tube Station, service tunnel

"What is it, what's the matter?" Ed couldn't disguise the fear in his voice. Just when he felt as though they had a real shot at trying to save the passengers on the train, Conor's words had him rattled.

"The tunnel's blocked."

"What with?"

"Shelving units, filing cabinets, office shit."

"Well, we need to get them out of the way."

"You should see it."

"Wish I could."

"Yeah, right."

"Come on, give me the box, you start shifting it."

Ed held his hands out and Conor dumped the box into them. It was heavier than he had anticipated. Conor was muttering and swearing as he pulled at metal objects that scraped and screeched across the stone floor.

"How deep into the tunnel do you think they go?" asked Ed.

"There's no way of guessing."

"Conor, I can't tell you—"

"Don't you fucking dare. Jesus!" It sounded as though a metal shelving unit had slipped and fallen onto Conor. He swore and cursed but he continued pulling at the metal obstructions. Whatever they were, they had clearly been down there for some time because when moved, they threw up clouds of dust that caught in the back of Ed's throat and made him cough.

"Okay, stay with me."

Ed pushed the cardboard box against Conor's back as he forged a path. Conor threw himself forward, pushing his way between the metal obstructions. Ed's arms ached under the weight of the box. The air was warm and gritty. Ed's shirt began to stick to him as he fought his way through; his shins and ankles cracked against metal, making him wince and curse. A piece of shelving slid back from where Conor had pushed it away and caught him on the side of the forehead. The pain made him cry out and he could feel a lump form and start to throb. But at least it distracted him from the time they were wasting, time that might mean the difference between life and death for hundreds of people.

"Okay, we're going to have to climb over this," said Conor.

"What is it?"

"Just a load of—oh fuck it, you don't need to know. Give it to me."

Conor took the cardboard box from him and lifted it upward. Ed reached out to feel the obstruction. It felt like a wall of individual metal shelves stacked one on top of the other. He felt for the top one which was at chest level. Ed pulled himself up and started to crawl along the top of the shelving after Conor, who was doing the same, pushing the box of explosives in front of him, the cardboard scraping against the metal.

"Okay, we're getting down here, it looks like it's clear from here on in."

Ed heard Conor jump down to the floor ahead of him as he moved as fast as he could, his shirt snagging and tearing against the sharp corners of the metal objects over which he dragged himself.

"How far do you think we've come?" asked Ed as he jumped down onto the tunnel floor.

"I have no idea."

"Do you think you can use the measuring device that Frank gave us?"

"No, I don't."

"He said it was two hundred and thirty-two yards from the start of the tunnel. Let's say we've done the thirty-two, we need to go the other two hundred yards."

"If you say so."

"Come on, give me the box and you hold the torch. Watch out for me, if I'm heading for a wall."

Conor said nothing, just emitted a derisory snort as though the thought of Ed running full tilt into a tunnel wall rather appealed to him.

They ran. It was hard going with the box of explosives in his straining arms. But his thoughts weren't focused on his discomfort as he tried to guess the distance they had traveled and how much further they needed to go. At this rate, even if they did succeed to rupture the tunnel wall, they might very well be draining the water away from a train full of corpses.

When running on his treadmill at home, Ed always finished off his jogging with a short sprint. He reckoned it was roughly about two hundred meters. He imagined himself at home now, pushing himself to the limit as he forced himself onward. Occasionally, he could feel the tunnel wall snag against his shirt sleeve and he recalibrated his trajectory. Conor's heavy breathing and footsteps provided him with a sound source that he could focus on and plot his course by.

"How far do you think we've gone?" asked Ed.

"It's got to be about two hundred yards now. My vote is we go for it here."

They stopped running and Ed put the cardboard box on the ground.

Conor's knees emitted a faint cracking noise as he knelt down to the box and started opening up its cardboard flaps.

"I'm going to use all of this." It wasn't a question. Conor had made a decision.

"If that's what you think."

"Yeah, I do."

The insolence was still there in Conor's voice but it was tempered by urgency. Objects were being unwrapped from polyethylene. Conor muttered and cursed as he went about his work.

"What are you doing?" asked Ed.

"I'm baking a fucking cake, what do you think?" Conor sighed then muttered, "I'm molding the Semtex against the wall, then I'll use some electrodes to connect it to the detonator."

"Are you nearly done?" Ed made no attempt to conceal his impatience.

"Shut your mouth."

Ed stood and waited as Conor went about his work. It had to be ten minutes they'd been down there, possibly twelve. Their estimation of where the point of the blast should be was wholly inexact and Conor was clearly uncertain regarding the quantity of Semtex needed to get through the tunnel wall. But somewhere, just a few feet away from where they stood were thousands of gallons of water pressing against the brickwork.

3:07 PM

Northern Line Train 037, first carriage

Water had dribbled into his mouth through the wound in his face. Amid the earthy, oily flavors was a sweetness. It was something he had tasted before although he couldn't remember when. It was comforting; it made him know that this was how things were meant to be.

"When you got up this morning," he said in George's direction, "you were just a tube driver. A simple man, doing a simple job. And now you will die a prophet and rise again to sit with God."

"Don't," said George. "I don't want to hear it."

"Feel the water, it's cleansing you. It's making you pure and whole. This is holy water, George."

"No it isn't. It's just water. Cold, dirty water."

George was afraid; he was suffering. Tommy forgave him. The water was up to his neck and it felt good. The pain in his face had begun to subside and he was filled with the glory of God. He knew the end to his suffering, to all their suffering, was close at hand. He felt a oneness with himself and the world and when he looked at George, he knew that he was his brother. They were fellow travelers on the same journey. He and George, his sister Belle, and everyone on the train. They would all die together and rise again.

3:11 PM

Leicester Square Tube Station, service tunnel

"Come on, let's clear off." As soon as Ed heard Conor say the words, he started moving back along the tunnel. But Conor was slower than him as he unspooled the cable. Ed felt sicker with each passing second. Aware of what the people on the train might be going through, he felt as though he was succumbing to some sort of phantom suffocation all of his own. The air was thin and stale and it felt as though there just wasn't enough of it to fill his lungs.

"Can't we move any faster?"

"We mustn't pull the wire out of the Semtex. It's not like we've got time to go back and fix it all up again."

They carried on walking. Conor had managed to speed up but then he came to a standstill.

"What's the matter?" asked Ed.

"Oh no. Oh shit."

"Conor, what is it?"

"The wire's come to an end."

"What does that mean?"

"Well, we're only about fifty yards from the Semtex. If I rig up the detonator here and set it off, we might not survive."

"Just set it up, get it ready and give it to me. I'll do it."

Conor hesitated. He was clearly thinking about it. Ed held out his hand.

"No way," said Conor. "You'll only fuck it up, you blind bastard."

"Conor, I was responsible for your wife's death. Don't make me responsible for yours too."

"It's too late for all that now. It won't be the first time I've been blown up, will it?"

Ed listened while Conor busied himself with the detonator.

"I'd turn around, crouch down and cover your ears, if I were you. It probably won't save you but it's worth a go. Ready?"

"Do it."

Conor flicked the switch on the detonator. Nothing happened. He flicked the switch again.

Silence.

3:12 PM

Northern Line Train 037, first carriage

The surface of the water slapped gently against George's chin as he stood on the seat, the top of his head touching the ceiling of the carriage. The chain made his leg ache. He had managed to slide it up the pole; it was the only way that he could keep his head above the water. The pain fueled his anger and his anger was the last thing that kept him together, held back his final despair.

"You murdering scumbag. Come on! This is your last chance to do the right thing." George only had a few moments left before the water closed over his nose and mouth. He couldn't help but think about all the time he had wasted earlier in the day. All those opportunities that he might have taken to disarm Denning or kill him, but here he was, immobilized as much by his own inadequacy and failure as he was by the chain around his leg. He had failed himself, he had failed his family and he had failed all the people on the train.

He turned toward the few remaining inches of open window in the adjoining doors through which somewhere, his wife, the mother of his children, was clinging onto a handrail in the darkness and the filthy water.

"Maggie?"

Her voice came through clearly above the sounds of desperation in the distance. "Yes, George."

He had never heard her sound so afraid. It made him want to cry. What should he say to her? What could he say that would mean anything at a moment like this? There was only one thing, but just as he had decided to say it to her, she said it to him: "I love you."

"Oh Christ, I love you too, Maggie. And I'm sorry."

"Don't be sorry, George. This is not your fault."

"I'm just sorry for bringing this on us."

"We were in the wrong place at the wrong time."

"The right place at the right time," muttered Denning. Maggie's voice was stronger than before, more emotionally robust as she said, "Whatever delusion or madness is causing these people to do this, if there is a God, they'll rot in hell for what they've done."

"I baptize thee in the name of the father, the son and the holy ghost."

George had wondered when Denning would start in on the religious bullshit again. Even if a deity were to make itself known to George now, during the final few moments of his life, he would curse him. Damnation would be infinitely preferable to some sort of union with an entity that thought that Denning's pointless mass murder might in some way be a good thing.

"Dear Lord, Our Father, accept these humble souls into the kingdom of heaven."

George looked at what remained of Denning's face caked in semi-congealed blood, his head tilted to one side, sucking at the last few inches of warm fetid air through his nose, mouth, and the wound in his cheek, as he spoke to "the Almighty."

"There's no one there, you stupid bastard," said George. "No one's listening."

But Denning kept right on, talking about the "sure and certain resurrection to eternal life," and George put his head back in the water, so his ears were beneath the surface and he didn't have to listen. This was how a condemned man must feel, thought George, waiting for the moment of death and fearing the pain that precedes it.

Any hope that the authorities might be able to do something was fading fast and the sounds that were coming from along the train were the most gut-wrenching he had ever heard. Hundreds of people were about to die—and they knew it. George was about to die. His nose was pressed against the ceiling of the train. He had to time his breaths to coincide with those moments when the water dropped away from the ceiling before rising up to slap against it once more.

No one was coming.

George took a mouthful of water as he tried to suck up some air from the tiny pocket around his mouth. He choked, coughed, spluttered. More water entered his mouth. He choked again. He pressed his mouth against the ceiling and managed to suck up some air before the water closed over his mouth. It would be his last breath. The water he had swallowed made him choke once more but he fought the urge to spit out the air. He kept his mouth crushed against the ceiling preferring the sharp pain that it caused to the dull sickening ache in his oxygen-starved lungs.

No one was coming.

As though in recognition of his final breath, the torch that Denning had hung from the handrail which had flickered and fluttered underwater for the past couple of minutes, finally gave out, throwing the submerged carriage into total darkness. The words echoed in George's head as Joe Strummer sang "London Calling" for the final time.

3:19 PM

Northern Line Train 037

There was silence along the submerged train. Spots of light from mobile phones and handheld computer devices—those whose light had survived the water—illuminated desperate faces, cheeks bulging, as men, women, and children held their breath, in final seemingly futile attempts to delay the inevitable.

It is common knowledge that the person who panics uses more oxygen than the person who keeps calm. But who could keep calm when confronted with a single lungful of air and no apparent hope of another one? Panic reigned on the train and panic squandered all those lungfuls—all those hundreds of pockets of air—in those hundreds of bodies.

Every single living passenger felt the agony of oxygen starvation, knowing that it was merely a prelude to oblivion. Most of the passengers clung to the rapidly depleting lungful of air that they had sucked in before the water reached the ceiling of the carriages. But there were some, like those who had chosen to jump from the Twin Towers rather than face the flames, who roared the oxygen from their lungs, hoping to reduce the torture and die more quickly.

No one was coming.

3:20 PM

Leicester Square Tube Station, service tunnel

Conor pressed the switch a third time. Still nothing.

"What's the matter?" Ed sounded scared.

Conor didn't reply, just threw the detonator against the wall of the tunnel. Plastic splinters and pieces of circuit board clattered to the stone floor.

"Tell me what's happening, Conor."

"I'm sticking the wires straight onto the battery."

Ed listened to Conor's troubled breathing as he fiddled with the detonator's components. Then he exhaled, long and hard. Ed didn't have a chance to ask him what this meant. He felt the explosion before he heard it. The vibration in the ground traveled up through his feet and into his legs. Then came the sound, a deafening crack followed by a low rumbling thunder that swelled as it moved along the tunnel. The blast knocked both of them off their feet and sent them crashing to the floor turning over and over amid the smoke and billowing brick dust.

Ed lost consciousness for a moment and he came around, as though waking from a dream, unsure whether he was asleep or not.

His sunglasses had been knocked off in the blast. As he sat up, he started feeling for them. He did it automatically, without thinking.

"Conor?"

No reply. His hands scrambled around through the brick dust and pieces of rubble all around him.

"Conor?"

His fingers touched a warm liquid, which he raised to his nose. It was blood, either his or the Irishman's.

"Conor?"

He got lucky. His fingers closed around the sunglasses and he put them on. The lenses were cracked but still in place, still providing a barrier between his sightless eyes and the outside world.

"Conor?"

"Jesus, my feckin' head," muttered Conor in a pained voice. And then Ed heard something else. It was slapping against the walls of the tunnel as it picked up speed and momentum. Conor's words had allowed Ed to ascertain where he was. He moved toward him and managed to grab hold of his arm as both of them were engulfed in a tide of cold muddy water.

3:21 PM

Northern Line Train 037

In the band of air in the apex of the train carriage ceilings, mouths opened up like flowers. Gasps erupted from the surface of the water as it dropped from the ceiling of the train and the passengers on Train 037 coughed and spluttered the first breaths of their new lives. There were some ruptured eardrums caused by the shockwaves of the explosion in the water and many heads ached, but everyone who had gone under had come out alive and they brought back with them hope that somehow their collective nightmare might now begin to recede.

George sprayed out the stale air from his lungs and breathed in the new. Never had a breath tasted so good.

"Maggie?"

It was a struggle to keep his mouth above the water and his voice was tremulous and weak and unlikely to reach her in the next carriage. Fear made him desperate and the desperation made him shout louder.

"Maggie!" He heard a voice but he couldn't be sure if it was hers so he called again. This time when she responded he knew. She was alive.

And so was Denning, close by, somewhere in the darkness. George reached out and the fingers of his right hand touched Denning's face. He could hear him sucking air into his lungs, breathless from oxygen starvation.

"George?" He sounded confused, disorientated. This wasn't in the plan. George said nothing but as his hand brushed against the wound in Denning's cheek, he curled his fingers around the bottom edge of it as though it were a handle and gripped tightly. Denning emitted a scream of acute pain and rage but George was not going to let go and he pulled Denning's head toward him by his mangled cheek. With his other hand, he tried to find his eyes but Denning started flailing at him, lashing out at the source of the pain. A fist caught a glancing blow against George's forehead but it lacked power and precision and George brought his left hand around and approximating the target in relation to the position of his right hand, he started firing punches at Denning's head. The water dulled his fist's trajectory and there was another blow from Denning, this time more powerful and desperate but still not enough to stop him.

The chain around his leg, anchoring him to the vertical pole tore at the skin around his calf muscle but no amount of discomfort was going to stop him. Denning's next strike, however, was altogether more brutal and well equipped. The square barrel of the Browning automatic whipped across George's nose. He couldn't contain his reflexes, which made his hands retract and paw at his bleeding face.

Denning flailed around in the water swinging the gun at George, trying to hit him again. They struggled as a sound grew louder outside the train, a sound made incongruous by its location in the flooded tunnel. It was getting closer. It was the sound of a boat's outboard engine.

3:23 PM

Leicester Square Tube Station, Northern Line Tunnel

Andy spent a lot of time thinking about the types of operation that he might find himself involved with. Much of it was just daydreaming. There was plenty of waiting around in this job after all. But he had never envisaged this. A hijacked tube train was one of the scenarios they had discussed at a seminar only recently. No one joined the SAS to sit around in rooms listening to people talking and pointing to things on blackboards but he did enjoy devising resolutions to hypothetical crisis situations. And he felt that most of the potential situations had been covered during his ten years on the job. When the call came through that the terrorists were flooding the tunnel, he knew that this was something new, something that had never entered the collective mind of the security services and the powers that be. As with 9/11, the terrorists' imagination was one step ahead.

It had been decided that there would be two teams, one in Tottenham Court Road station and one in Leicester Square station at either end of the tunnel. When news of the flooding arrived, word came from on high that those with advanced diving skills were to make up two patrols of four. But by the time all the operational necessities had been seen to and all the equipment put in place, including one IRC, inflatable raiding craft, for each team, they were informed that the possibility of further explosions meant that an attempt to storm the train could not be sanctioned. Both teams were told to take up positions at a safe distance, far enough away to avoid any potential sniper fire. There they were told to wait while ongoing negotiations were made with the terrorists.

Andy was given operational control of Group A, the team to the south of the train operating out of Leicester Square station. He and his three men—Pat, Todd, and Smithy—waited in the water holding onto the inflatable as the level rose.

When Pat had said that he could see someone swimming toward them through his night scope, Andy had felt nervous. Was this some sort of ambush? He picked out the swimmer with his torch and shouted, "Make yourself known." The swimmer stopped and trod water while she explained that she had escaped from the train. Having checked that she was unarmed and free of explosives, Pat and Smithy escorted her back to Leicester Square and returned a few minutes later smiling about some private joke. Andy envied them their nonchalance. The flooded tunnel had him spooked.

But just when it looked as though the water would reach the top of the tunnel and they would be forced to use their newly supplied breathing apparatus, there was a huge explosion that sent waves slapping against the tunnel walls. Almost immediately, the water level began to drop and the radio crackled into life as Andy's operations officer gave them the green light to go in.

As they made their way toward the train in the inflatable, he felt that buzz of excitement and adrenalin that he always had when a mission was under way. The water was still high enough to force them to duck to avoid cracking their heads against the top of the tunnel. The scream of the outboard engine was almost deafening in the enclosed space but it was the thought of the explosives that bothered Andy the most. All he could hope was that, by now, all the pieces of detonation equipment would have been given a good soaking and might not be in the best shape to do their job.

Pat sat in the prow and shone a portable arc light to try and dazzle anyone intending to shoot at them. As he had expected, the shots started when they were about a hundred feet out from the train. There were a series of muzzle flashes from a handgun. Bullets ricocheted around the tunnel and one of them struck the arc light making it shatter in Pat's hands scattering debris throughout the boat.

"All right, Pat?" shouted Andy above the sound of the engine.

Pat shouted back a "Yeah!" but Andy could see by torchlight that he was bleeding from a minor head wound. If nothing else, the gunfire proved that they wouldn't be confronted by a train full of corpses. If one of the hijackers was still alive then the chances were that some of the passengers were too.

"Cut the engine!" he shouted and Todd killed the outboard motor but the IRC's forward momentum propelled it toward the train. If whoever was firing at them had a night-vision scope, they would be easy targets.

The men hunkered down in the boat as more rounds were fired, two of which struck the inflatable hull, pitching them forward into the water. Smithy tried to keep his Heckler & Koch G36 level as the flashlight attachment on the end of it lit up a figure with a handgun standing in the doorway set into the cab. Smithy positioned the red dot reflex sight on it and started shooting but the deflating IRC made it impossible to hold his line of fire and the bullets struck metal. Forced to swim as the IRC sank, Andy and his men were left facing an enemy that had seized the upper hand. They needed to regain the initiative—and fast.

3:25 PM

Belle saw the red dot just in time and stepped back into the cab out of the way of the burst of automatic fire. This wasn't the first time that she had been forced to deal with attackers and, while the men making their way toward her now were far more of a danger than the passengers on the train had been, she felt sure that she could repel them just as easily. Whatever it was that had happened, whatever it was that had caused the explosion that had made the water level drop, Tommy would think of something. Tommy always thought of something. All she had to do was to stand firm, maintain her position, and counter all attempts to enter the train. Tommy had told her that it wouldn't be easy, that the journey would be long and perilous. As always, he was right.

She could hear them in the water coming closer. If only she had more holy bullets in the Pulverizer then she could have truly shown them the wrath of God. But there were—how many?—about seven or eight bullets left in the Glock. She had lost count but there was no way that God would forsake her now. Not after she had come this far. Tommy had told her that despite the journey being long and difficult, the outcome of their crusade would never be in doubt.

The water from the holy river would never stop flowing. The tunnel would fill up with water once more and she would feel it close over her head just as it had done before.

Belle stepped back into the doorway and fired two shots into the water. Another burst of automatic gunfire was returned but once again she had already stepped back into the cab when it came. She felt invincible. She was doing God's work.

They came closer and she allowed them. The darkness made it impossible to aim with any degree of certainty but, just as it made things difficult for her, it did the same for them. Let them come closer, let them believe that they were going to kill her. It would do them no good. People had underestimated her all her life. So let them do so now. Let them see the truth of God's work; let them see how his wrath was channeled through his servant, Belle Denning.

They were close now; she could hear them. Despite the clamor of voices from the passengers on the train behind her, she could hear their every movement in the water. Stepping out into the doorway, she fired the Glock down into the darkness once more.

The first round that struck her shattered her thigh bone, the second bullet hit her just above the vagina, smashing her pubic bone; and the third entered through her navel, passed through her abdomen and severed her spinal cord. Belle slumped back into the cab, floundering in the water before she came to rest against Simeon.

It hurt. It hurt so much but it had happened, clearly it was meant to be. She had been baptized, born again. She would never die. Pointing the Glock into the doorway, she kept her finger on the trigger until it stopped bucking in her hand and she let it drop into the water. She reached for the Pulverizer and by the torchlight in the tunnel making its way toward her, she could just make out the silhouette of Simeon's face in the darkness. She leaned forward, kissed his cold dead lips then spun the Pulverizer around in her hands and put the end of the barrel in her mouth. It was there in the chamber, the last holy bullet. The cross had been carved into the lead by her own hand, steadied by the hand of God. That same hand of God was steadying hers now. This was how it was meant to be.

The pain from the bullet wounds was receding and being replaced by a warm feeling, a feeling of love and peace. This was God's glory; he was reaching out to her to pluck her from this dark place and take her in his arms.

The light was getting closer now. She could hear voices. One of the men in the tunnel said, "I think we got her." He was wrong. They would never get her. Never. She caressed the Pulverizer's trigger with her forefinger and as the light came closer still, she pulled the trigger and launched the last holy bullet, that blessed little lump of heavy metal with the cross carved into it that would send her on her way to heaven.

As the four SAS soldiers made their way on board the train, they were confronted by the sight of two corpses. One a man, and the other a decapitated woman. As they hurried through in the semidarkness toward the voices further along the train, none of them noticed the blood, brain and bone fragments that dripped down on them from the interior of the cab.

3:25 PM

Northern Line Train 037, first carriage

The engine was getting closer and with it, an increasingly powerful light which shone through the windows into the carriage. George could make out Denning's silhouette standing in the water nearby. He readied himself to dive under the water at the first sign of the gun being pointed. But he need not have worried; Denning took his Browning automatic and pressed it against the bottom of his own chin. He started muttering something, some sort of valediction, and anger propelled George forward once again. He had to try and stop him. As the chain snapped tight around his ankle, he swung a fist at the pistol, managing to knock the barrel away from Denning's face as he pulled the trigger. The shot clanged into the ceiling of the train. Denning tried to pull the pistol back into position but George had his hand around it now and they struggled with it, face to face.

"Let me die, George."

Legs waded through water in the cab. Torches flashed in the carriage. Denning looked George in the eyes. The vicious pain in his face had sapped his strength and he looked broken, like a frightened child.

"You have to let me die. This is God's will."

A gloved hand reached out and grabbed hold of the pistol, pulling it from their collective grasp.

"Where are the explosives?" said the soldier who took the gun. "Tell us now!" Denning was pulled to his feet. There were four of them in total and all pointed their automatic weapons at him.

"Where are the explosives?"

Denning suddenly became calm. He caught his breath and staring back into the eyes of each of the soldiers in turn, he said, "They're just about to blow."

3:28 PM

Frith Street, Soho

"Clearly, Simeon Fisher has failed to prevent the attack," said Berriman.

"Clearly," said Hooper into his phone as he walked along the pavement, not even bothering to mask his sarcasm.

Any respect that he might have felt for his boss had evaporated in the past few hours. In reality, he knew he was running the operation alone. That's the way that it had to be if it was going to succeed. And it still could. Choices, that's what it was all about. He had to keep making them. So long as he did that and those choices were good ones, based on the best intelligence he could gather, then he knew he was still in with a fighting chance.

"Mark, it sounds to me as though we should resume this conversation at another time. You're sounding rather agitated."

"I'm fine. This whole operation can still work."

"How can it work, Mark? You don't seem to understand. The cat's out of the bag. Or it soon will be."

"What do you mean?"

"I've just heard that the water level in the tunnel has dropped. It could be that Ed Mallory's plan that you told me about has been put into operation. It doesn't mean that we're out of the woods. But hopefully it means that the passengers won't drown."

Hooper felt the heat of guilt burning behind his ears again. This spelled trouble. He had never thought for one moment that Ed Mallory's idea of using some IRA dinosaur to blow a hole in the tunnel wall would actually work. But if he had succeeded, as Berriman suggested, then this changed everything. With potentially live witnesses and—even worse—live terrorists, the truth about the service's and most notably his, foreknowledge, would almost certainly be discovered.

"Well, we'll just have to make sure that some people don't make it out alive."

"You are joking."

Berriman's perpetually negative tone was infuriating but he knew that he had to keep a lid on his temper. If he lost control, he was more likely to make mistakes. He couldn't afford to do that. There was too much at stake.

"All it means is that anyone who knows the truth does not survive the evacuation."

"This is insane, Mark. The hijackers of the train know. The driver of the train probably knows. I know. You have to face it. This is impossible to contain."

"You're not going to tell anyone. The terrorists are going to die. And as for the driver—"

"Mark, you're not making any sense. You need to stop. You need to stand down."

"No, Howard, you're the one who's not thinking straight. I can still make this work. We do whatever it takes. This is a war."

"What are you talking about? These aren't Islamic fundamentalists. They're Christians, Mark, Christians."

"They're all the same," said Hooper as he walked across Charing Cross Road. "What's it matter where they come from? What's it matter which god they believe in? There is a growing tide of lunatics and extremists who are driven by a belief that they are doing the work of a supernatural figure. We have to fight them; we have to stop them." Hooper flipped his ID at the police line and made his way toward the steps down into Leicester Square station. "You've got to trust me, Howard, it's all going to be fine." He could hear Berriman call his name a couple of times as he took the phone from his ear and hung up.

It was true what he'd said. This was a war. This was about right and wrong, however simplistic that might sound. So what if operational procedure wasn't being followed? At a certain stage, pragmatism had to come into play. That was the nature of the job. So long as the good guys won, that was all that mattered.

Hooper knew that if he failed today, it would mean the end of his career. There would be shame, not only for him but for his family too. All those privileged jerks at school who had said he would amount to nothing would be proved right. They would have won. He couldn't let that happen. That's why before he had made his way down to the command center in Leicester Square, he had gone home and made sure that he had the right tools for the job.

3:29 PM

Northern Line Train 037, first carriage

"He's lying," said George. "There are no more explosives as far as I can see." He spoke to the soldier nearest to him, who was doing all the talking and appeared to be the one in charge.

"When he caused the explosion that started the flood he had wires and a detonator but I haven't seen anything to suggest that he's rigged up anything else."

George could feel Denning's eyes burning into him but he had more important things to consider. "Someone needs to find my children," he said as Maggie clambered through the window from the adjoining carriage and waded through the water toward them.

"Your children are safe," said the commanding officer. "They're at Leicester Square tube station, waiting to see you."

"You're sure?" asked Maggie, her voice trembling with emotion.

"Yes, I was told to tell you. They're fine."

Maggie fell against George and they threw their arms around each other. But their joy at being reunited was interrupted by Denning as he lunged forward and made a grab for one of the soldiers' automatic weapons. It wasn't a serious attempt to launch a counterattack; his actions were clearly nothing more than an attempt to incite one of the soldiers into shooting him.

"Do me a favor," said George. "Keep him alive, will you?"

The soldier fixed George with a nervous stare. "You're sure about the explosives?" he asked.

"As sure as I can be. The only wires I saw him use were for the first explosion."

The soldier nodded at one of his colleagues and muttered something. Denning was roughly spun around and his hands secured behind his back with a plastic tie.

A crackle of short-wave radio and the commanding officer received word from the SAS team at the other end of the train that all the carriages were now secured and they were going to begin the evacuation.

As the chain that Denning had used to shackle George's leg to the pole was severed with bolt croppers, Denning looked up at him and their eyes met.

"See you," said Denning blankly.

George hesitated for a moment before he said, "I don't think so."

Never usually the most demonstrative of couples, George and Maggie clung to one another as they were led through the train toward the rear carriage. The water they waded through was a soup of discarded clothing, bags, books, newspapers, cell phones, music players, notebook computers—all the accoutrements of the urban commuter—now discarded, rendered obsolete and lifeless by the water that had swallowed them.

As the water level dropped yet further, people climbed down from the rear of the train and waded along the tunnel toward Leicester Square station. But the mood was somber; the bodies of those cut down by the terrorists' bullets both on the train and in the tunnel were a brutal reminder of the carnage that had taken place.

George and Maggie with their special forces minder, a stocky bulldog of a man with a ginger crew cut, brought up the rear of the trail of refugees. When they arrived at the northbound Northern Line platform at Leicester Square, the soldier led them away from the others and up a flight of stone stairs to a low narrow corridor. George's and Maggie's shoes squelched as they walked along, their clothes dripping. They were shown into a room that had chairs and a table in the middle of it, at which a policewoman in uniform was seated playing a board game with Sophie and Ben.

The hallucinatory sheen through which George had watched the day's events unfold was at its most intense as Maggie scooped up Sophie and he picked up Ben and they fell into a group hug.

"Daddy, you're stinky," said Ben, and George and Maggie laughed through their tears.

3:31 PM

Leicester Square Tube Station, service tunnel

The return journey back through the filing cabinets and metal shelving frames was marginally less difficult than before—Ed and Conor's outward trip had cleared a path of sorts. The water slowed them down; it was up to the tops of their thighs but they weren't in a hurry anymore. Ed's ears were ringing from the explosion. The skin on his face, despite the fact that he had turned away from the blast, felt leathery and scorched, as though he had been lying in the sun for too long. Conor complained of a headache and concussion but his mood had been transformed. When Ed asked him whether he thought the blast might have secured the desired outcome of draining the Northern Line tunnel, there was no disguising his confidence. "I can feel it in my bones," he said.

"I hope you're right," said Ed.

"Well, I guess we'll find out soon enough. And at least we didn't blow the whole of Leicester Square off the map. Funny, 'cause thirty years ago, that's exactly what I would've wanted to do. That and to kill you. In fact, that's what I intended to do when you came knocking earlier on."

"What stopped you?"

"I guess I wanted to try and save the people on the train more."

Calvert met them at the top of the escalators. "We heard the blast. The special forces in the tunnel have reported that the water level has gone down. They've secured the train."

"Survivors?" asked Ed.

"We don't know numbers or details but yes, it looks like there are."

"What about further explosives?"

"Seems there weren't any."

"Weren't any?"

"Looks like Denning bluffed us."

"Jesus."

"Ed!" He could recognize the voice—it was Frank's—but it was the product of an altogether different disposition than before. The professor's footsteps approached. "Ed, well, what can I say? It looks like we got it right." Ed held out his hand but Frank ignored it and gave him a hug. He hadn't taken Frank as the hugging kind but he reciprocated and patted him on the back.

"Well done, Frank. We couldn't have done this without you."

"Sorry to break up your romantic moment," said Conor, "but I think I'll be getting on my way."

"Ed?" Calvert had lowered his voice to a conspiratorial whisper aimed at Ed's ear. Ed leaned toward him. "We're going to need to have a pretty serious debrief about all of this. We may need Conor."

Ed didn't care who overheard what he said, Conor included: "Nick, I need one more favor from you and then we're done. I need you to get Conor outside the cordon. And Frank. If it wasn't for what these two have done—and you—we'd have a train full of dead bodies on our hands. Whatever fallout there is from this, I'll deal with it."

"Sure." Conor's wasn't the only demeanor that had changed after the blast. The tension and reticence had gone from Nick Calvert's voice. He clearly knew that explaining the nature of what they had conspired to do—and the legality of it—would take some doing, but the mission had succeeded. That should be enough to swing official opinion their way.

"Good on you, Conor," said Ed.

"Don't get soppy on me, I don't think I could take it."

"What you did here today will probably never be known for obvious reasons but you've saved a lot of lives."

Ed felt Conor's hand slide into his and squeeze it.

"You'll need to get yourself a new pair of sunglasses. Those ones are fucked."

"I will," said Ed. "And thanks."

As Nick Calvert ushered Conor and Frank away, Ed heard footsteps making straight for him.

"DI Mallory?" It was a young woman's voice. "I'm PC Holland. I've got a call for you."

3:49 PM

Leicester Square Tube Station, ticket hall

The circular ticket hall was busy. Passengers from the hijacked train were being brought up the escalator from the Northern Line. Hooper watched a group of little girls, their pink dresses wet and muddy. The sight of them was like an emotional punch. Right there in front of him was evidence that what he was doing was right. He was saving children from the clutches of radical lunatics.

Near to where he stood, a group of paramedics administered first aid to those with gunshot wounds and other injuries. One man had lost his left leg at the knee. He was clearly in shock but was being stabilized. The place was hectic with police and special forces. It felt like a war zone. It *was* a war zone. And sometimes in times of war, it falls to one man to clean up the mess.

The logistics of what he was going to attempt made him feel sick with trepidation. How exactly was he going to clean up after his failed operation? How would he explain to the powers that be that his actions amounted to an operational necessity? It haunted him. He was stepping over the line. But he had no choice.

There were some junior service personnel loitering about outside the control room in the center of the ticket office. They were beneath him in the pecking order; he could pull rank. He sidled up to a guy called Johnstone. He was a low-grade wannabe. A nobody, in the scheme of things. They nodded a mutual greeting.

"Where's Denning?" asked Hooper.

"They've just put him in there." He gestured toward the control room in the ticket hall.

Hooper knew that if White or Calvert were there, he was in trouble. But if they weren't, if it was just some grunt who was watching over him then he would be able to do the job. He stepped inside.

He was in luck. There was just the one CO19 officer standing in the room. Hooper flashed his MI5 ID at him. Denning sat on a chair at a table pressing a large piece of bandage against his bloody face.

"I just need to ask him a few questions," said Hooper.

"You're going to have to be quick," said the grunt. "He's off to St. Mary's with Special Branch to get his face patched up before he goes to Paddington Green."

Hooper nodded. He *was* going to be quick.

"Who are you?" asked Denning looking up.

"MI5," said Hooper.

"Oh dear," said Denning. "Not one of your better days."

"Why's that?" Hooper tried to keep a flat measured tone to his voice. He pulled out the chair opposite Denning and sat down, listening for footsteps outside the door.

"I should think there'll be a few job cuts after this little lot leaks out."

"Why should you care, Tommy? I thought this was all about God and your need to wipe out hundreds of people in his name."

"This was prophesied in the Bible."

"Listen, Tommy, you need to tell me how many people know about Simeon Fisher."

"Who's he?"

"Don't play games, Tommy. How many knew?"

"You knew. I knew. My sister knew."

"Who else?"

"Why are you so interested all of a sudden?"

"Did the driver know?"

Denning turned and looked at the CO19 officer and then looked back at Hooper. "George was such a disappointment to me. I thought he was one of us."

"Tommy, I haven't got time for this. Does he know about Simeon Fisher and MI5's involvement?"

Denning looked Hooper in the eyes and said, "Yeah, he knows. George knows everything."

"No one else?"

"No one."

It was old school and he loved it for that. A Walther PPK with a silencer. Bond's gun. Iconic. He had bought it on the black market. It couldn't be traced back to him. It could just as well have been Tommy Denning's as his. And now it would be Tommy Denning's. For all time.

Beneath the table, he pulled on the surgical glove and drew the gun from the holster on his ankle.

"What are you waiting for?" said Denning.

Hooper raised the gun and shot over Denning's head. Two bullets, straight into the CO19 officer's face. He fell heavily but not loudly enough to arouse suspicion outside the door.

"Bless you," said Denning. He looked up and had just enough time to say, "Father, into your hands I commit my spirit," before Hooper forced the gun into his mouth and pulled the trigger. A bloody spray peppered the wall from the exit wound in the back of his head before he fell forward onto the desk.

He had to move fast. Taking off the holster from his ankle, he strapped it to Denning's. He wiped the surgical glove on Denning's right hand to provide the necessary firearm residue before he curled his fingers around the Walther PPK.

And there it was. Denning had managed to keep a concealed weapon about him and when the time had come he had killed his guard and shot himself in the mouth. Regrettable of course.

Hooper walked from the room and pulled the door closed after him. When interviewed, he would say that when he left the room, everything was fine. And it was. Absolutely fine.

But he would worry about that later. Now he would update Berriman, then he would find the train driver.

3:54 PM

Leicester Square Tube Station, station manager's office

PC Holland was struggling to keep a lid on her nerves during a scenario for which she was mentally ill-prepared. As Ed took her arm, he could feel a slight tremble through the starched cotton of her blouse. Once they were inside the station manager's office, she pressed a telephone receiver into Ed's hand and he raised it to his ear.

"DI Mallory."

"Ed, there you are. I'm so glad to have located you." Howard Berriman's tone was radically altered from their previous conversations. He sounded solemn, contrite and more than a little panicked.

"What can I do for you?" asked Ed. He was expecting some sort of congratulation or at least acknowledgment of what he had succeeded in doing to drain the water from around the train. He received neither.

"I need to talk to you about Mark Hooper. Have you spoken to him?"

"Not since we were at the Network Control center in St. James's."

"Do you know where he might be?"

"No idea."

"The thing is, Ed, I think today's events have conspired to make him suffer some sort of breakdown."

"He seemed okay earlier. He was very guarded about things but I figured that it had something to do with professional friction between our two departments."

"Well, since then, things haven't panned out as he'd envisaged and I think it's pushed him over the edge."

"What things, Howard?"

There was silence on the line and Ed had a curious feeling. His subconscious was stirring. Thoughts were forming, thoughts that he didn't even realize he had been having. And once they had started to form, his enlightenment was rapid. Everything tumbled into place and when he said the two words, he said them as a statement, not a question.

"You knew."

There was relief in Berriman's voice when he said, "Yes." Guilt was Howard Berriman's burden and he was only too pleased to offload it. But there were caveats—of course there were.

"We only knew the vaguest of details. All we knew was there was going to be a hijacking on the Underground. We thought it was going to be next week."

"And you only tell me now when they're evacuating the train?"

"It wouldn't have helped you to do your job."

"Shouldn't I have been the judge of that?"

"Look, I'm sorry, Ed. All we knew was that Tommy Denning was going to try and hijack a tube train. Hooper was handling someone on the inside who told him it was going to be this time next week."

"So why weren't we doing all we could to bring them in?"

"Look, Ed, I can't deny that it wasn't a politically motivated decision. I thought if I delivered a result on the day with maximum news and media coverage then everyone would come up smelling of roses—the government, the service, me . . ."

"And Hooper was your boy."

"He was the one who brought it to me but they moved early. Denning must have found out about our man on the inside—"

"He wasn't called Simeon Fisher was he, by any chance?"

"Yeah, how did you—"

"Denning."

"Right, well, it allowed him to catch us off guard. There was no point you knowing. It wouldn't have helped."

"And now you think that Hooper has lost his grip."

"Ed, I think he might try and kill Tommy Denning."

"What?"

"When we last spoke, he said he was going to try and take out anyone who knew about the operation."

"Jesus, Howard."

"He thinks he can clean up the mess and we can all walk away."

"I take it you've put a call out for him to be stopped on sight?"

"We're speaking to Commander Boise."

"Let's hope they can bring him in straight away."

"I'm sure they will."

"And what about me, Howard? How do you think what I did will go down with the grown-ups?"

"You got the passengers out, Ed. You'll be fine."

"That's easy for you to say. There are still going to be a lot of questions to answer about the methods I employed."

"I'll be in your corner, Ed, you know that."

Berriman's words offered little reassurance. Ed knew that Berriman would have too many problems of his own regarding his prior knowledge of the attack to spend time trying to save some cop's skin. Ed's feelings toward the director general of MI5 had gone through various twists and turns during the day but now they felt as though they had resolved themselves in his mind. It was straightforward enough, he just didn't like the guy.

"And Ed? What I've just told you about this operation remains between the two of us for the time being, is that clear?"

"Sure, Howard."

"We'll talk about this later."

"If that's what you want."

"I do, Ed. I really do."

The line went dead.

3:58 PM

MI5 Headquarters, Thames House

Howard had lied to Ed Mallory; he hadn't put the call in to Serina Boise. He wanted to find out whether Mallory knew where Hooper was first. As he put the phone down, he snatched it up again, his finger poised over the keypad. He would make the call now.

But what if Hooper did manage to make it all go away? If the train driver did know about the service's complicity and he didn't make it out alive then perhaps they would be in the clear. He could blame Hooper for what had gone on. He could blame it on his mental state. Tragic that a young man like that should crack under pressure but it happens. That's life. Who else was there? Only Ed. And what possible advantage or benefit could he have in raining on his own parade? What he had done was unconventional, foolhardy maybe, but because of the outcome for many he would be perceived as a hero. Maybe Hooper was right. Maybe the shitstorm could be averted. There was no harm in just leaving it a few minutes. Wait and see. If he got a call from Hooper to say that it had all been taken care of then what was the point in rocking the boat? He could still have him taken out of the game. And as for Ed's safety down there, well, if he didn't make it out alive either then that would be tragic too. He'd say nice things about him, make sure he got some sort of posthumous award.

Hooper had sounded disturbed when he'd phoned just before he spoke to Ed but that was only to be expected. Perhaps he sounded unbalanced because what he was proposing was, by anyone's estimation, insane. But that didn't mean that he might not be able to see it through. Howard needed to look at the big picture. As the director general of MI5, he needed to make the big decisions.

Howard Berriman took his finger away from the telephone keypad and drummed it against the top of the desk as he thought.

Wait and see. It was definitely the best course of action.

3:58 PM

Leicester Square Tube Station, ticket hall

Ed took PC Holland's arm as she walked him across the concourse in the ticket hall toward the offices where Denning was being held.

"What's your first name?" asked Ed.

"Jessica. Jess."

"Well, listen, Jess, you may not like what you're about to see."

"What am I about to see?"

"Two dead men."

The angle of her delivery changed as she spoke to someone up ahead. "This is DI Ed Mallory."

Ed held out his ID and said, "I'm here to see Tommy Denning."

The officer opened up the door and Ed and PC Holland went inside the room. The air smelled of blood and aftershave. Mark Hooper's recent presence there was confirmed when PC Holland lost her composure and muttered, "Oh my God."

Ed let go of her arm and putting his hands on the table top, made his way around it to Tommy Denning's corpse slumped in the chair. Ed ran his fingers over Denning's face, feeling the massive wound in his cheek and the shattered teeth and lacerated gum tissue within it. He touched the stubble on Denning's head that would grow for a few more hours at least. He felt the ridge of ruptured skull at the back of his head—the exit wound—then he reached down and felt for Denning's right hand. He lifted it up and held it between his own. It was still warm. Holding it to his nose, he took a deep breath. There was blood of course, oily water from the flooded tunnel, the smell of gunpowder residue from all the shooting he had done but beneath all of that was the smell of human skin, the smell of Tommy Denning.

Within seconds, PC Holland had raised the alarm and the room was full of police officers. But Ed didn't intend to hang around to explain the intricacies of the situation. Ed said to Holland, "You need to take me to the train driver and his family."

4:04 PM

Leicester Square Tube Station, admin office

"Everything's going to be all right now," said George, and Maggie smiled at him. It was a corny line but he didn't care. They had survived the storm. They were alive. Everything came into focus now. Every moment was precious.

There were footsteps in the corridor outside followed by a muttered conversation on the other side of the door. The door opened and a policewoman entered the room followed by a slim man dressed all in black. His face was scarred and he wore cracked sunglasses, clearly the prop of a blind man. The state of his filthy soaking clothes made it appear as though he had been on the train with them.

"George Wakeham?"

"Yeah, that's me."

"I'm Ed Mallory. We spoke earlier."

George recognized the voice. Mallory held out his hand and George shook it. But the mood was anything but convivial.

"Thanks for all your help," said George.

"Don't worry about that now. What happened to your security detail?"

"Well, there was someone with us earlier who brought us up from the train but—"

"George, I need you and your family to follow us."

"Is something the matter?" asked George. Ed Mallory's tone and demeanor had taken the shine off his celebratory mood.

"You need to come with us. Now."

George felt his fear return but he needed answers, he needed to know the nature of this new threat.

"What's going on?"

"You and your family are in danger."

George felt the moment wrap itself around him like plastic wrap. He sucked at the air but it was hot and devoid of oxygen.

"Please, we need to move fast." George and Maggie gathered the children together and they followed Ed Mallory and the policewoman out of the room toward the top of the escalators.

"What the hell is going on?" asked Maggie in a frantic whisper.

"I don't know," said George. "But we should trust this guy."

"How do you know?"

"I just do."

Ed held onto the arm of the policewoman, who looked around nervously as though searching for someone in among the crowds of paramedics, police, special forces, and evacuated train passengers. She gestured for George to follow them down an escalator. While Maggie held the children's hands, George caught up with Ed and said, "Do you want to tell me what this is all about?"

"Soon. Let's keep moving," said Ed.

They came to a red steel door that stood ajar set into the side of a pedestrian tunnel. Ed said to PC Holland, "Make contact with DI Calvert and tell him where we are." She hurried off, leaving him standing in the doorway.

"Inside quickly and close the door," said Ed, and George ushered Maggie and the children into the dark interior and pushed the steel door shut on its screeching oil-free hinges. "I'm sorry about this," whispered Ed in the pitch darkness behind the door. "The problem is we have a rogue MI5 agent who's had some sort of breakdown. He may be dangerous. Armed police officers are on their way but we're going to have to wait for them. Here's as safe a place as any for the time being."

"Okay," whispered George and pulled Ben, Sophie and Maggie close to him as they waited.

4:07 PM

Leicester Square Tube Station, ticket hall

It was the policewoman holding his arm that did it. If it hadn't been for that, Mark Hooper might not have recognized him. Ed Mallory was dripping wet and his formerly pristine black clothes were soaked in muddy water. After Mark had seen to Tommy Denning, he had gone to the office in the ticket hall where the train driver had been reunited with his family, but there was a special forces soldier on duty. He had been forced to wait. But clearly believing that the driver was no longer in danger, the soldier had obviously been instructed to stand down. Just as Hooper was about to move in, however, Mallory had arrived with a policewoman. Now, they were leaving, heading down the escalators with the train driver and his family. Where the hell were they going? It didn't matter. He had come too far to turn back now. With the train driver taken out of the equation, the intelligence leak was contained. It was a tough call. An innocent man who had already gone through so much was going to have to die. Possibly his family too. Possibly Ed Mallory. A cover story would be difficult but not impossible. Ed Mallory had already gone rogue. What was employing an ex-IRA bomber to blast a hole in the tunnel if not evidence of a mind gone awry? Mark would try and pin the train driver's death on him. So he was blind, that didn't mean that he couldn't go berserk with a gun. If only the blind bastard had just stuck to the script and accepted that his negotiation had failed then everyone on the train would have died and no one would have been any the wiser as to the service's foreknowledge. That was all that had needed to happen. But now Mark was exposed. All roads led back to him, and Berriman would be only too happy to hang him out to dry. Well, if he was going down, he was going down fighting.

At the bottom of the escalators, Ed Mallory and the others turned into one of the pedestrian tunnels leading to the train lines. Keeping them in a clear line of sight, he followed them and only hung back when he saw them turn into a doorway. Ed Mallory spoke to the policewoman. He couldn't make out what was being said but he knew that he had to take cover as she turned and made her way back toward him. Near to where he was standing were some stairs providing access to the two Piccadilly Line platforms. He descended the stairs taking two steps at a time and waited for the policewoman to go past. When he could hear her footsteps recede, he climbed up the steps and reached into his pocket, his fingers closing around the handle of the Glock. It wasn't his favorite handgun. That accolade went to the Walther PPK he had left in Tommy Denning's hand. But this would do its job well enough when the time came.

4:11 PM

Leicester Square Tube Station, service tunnel entrance

Ed could hear footsteps on the other side of the door. The person making them was walking on tiptoes, trying to be as quiet as possible. There was only one person who would see fit to try and keep their approach a secret. The footsteps stopped but Ed could smell Hooper's aftershave. They needed to move fast but he didn't want to alarm the children in case they cried out and gave away their position. He put his hand on George's shoulder and was about to steer him toward the steps down into the flooded service tunnel when the door was kicked open, the hinges screeching, the air displacement brushing against his face.

"No!" George's voice was charged with fear. The threat to which it referred was implicit. Ed threw himself forward, fists clenched. Hooper wasn't big; if Ed could reach him, he might be able to restrain him long enough for George and his family to escape into the service tunnel. But before his hands could find Hooper, his shoulder was speared with a pole of agony as a muted gunshot made a flat echo in the enclosed space and he was thrown backward, staggering into George and his family. He struggled to maintain his balance and realized that it was futile to do so when his foot reached out for the floor and found nothing. He was pitched backward; his shoulders, one of them shattered by the bullet that had, only moments before, passed through it, smashed against the stone steps as he fell. Ed's head made contact with a stone riser and just before he blacked out, he felt himself falling into water, sinking deeper and deeper.

4:12 PM

Leicester Square Tube Station, service tunnel

The man with the gun looked around the dark enclosed space. Ed Mallory wasn't his only target. He was searching for someone else. Looking at Maggie first, he raised his gun, finger on the trigger, then he looked at George. Their eyes met. The man was going to kill him. George had never been so sure of anything in his life. He threw a reflex punch that made contact with the man's abdomen and with his other hand, he made a grab for the gun, pushing it back, cracking it against the wall. Lunging forward, George's forehead connected with the man's nose. He battered the gun against the wall again and he heard a reassuring clatter as it fell to the floor. The man was dazed but there was plenty of fight left in him. He lashed out and his fist made contact with the side of George's head. It was a powerful blow and George knew that he was in trouble. This guy was in the secret service; he had probably been trained in unarmed combat.

"George!" Maggie was shouting at him. The children were crying. The two men struggled at the top of the steps. Another punch struck George's jaw. Before the man could draw his fist back once more, George pushed him backward, past Maggie and the children to the top of the steps and over, the two men falling, the stone edges providing far more painful blows than either of their fists ever could. The cold water into which they fell brought some clarity back to George's perception. He appeared to have survived the fall in better shape than his attacker and, seeing the man rise up out of the water in front of him, flailing around, George threw his head forward into the man's face for a second time. His forehead cracked against the man's nose and as he heard his gasping pained exhalation, George held him at arms' length, his hands closing around his neck as he forced him down into the water. George was bigger than him, his arms were longer; he had a whole lot more to lose.

The man lashed out with everything that he had, kicking and punching, but the impact of the blows was reduced by the water and George could cope with the pain as he drove his thumbs into the man's neck and forced him downward. George pulled his head back so the fingers that desperately scrambled around for something to hold onto fumbled across his face but could find no purchase.

George dragged the man toward the tunnel wall and cracked his head against the brickwork, once, twice, three times. The kicks and the flailing arms became more desperate but weaker now and George pressed even harder against his neck. The man's hands picked at his fingers, trying to pry them off, but they lacked the necessary strength and finally they dropped away. George felt the life go out of him and he flopped back into the water.

"George!" Maggie shouted from the top of the steps. "George, are you okay?"

"I'm fine, it's over."

But this wasn't enough for Maggie. She had been through too much that day to accept a vague reassurance.

"What happened? Where is he?"

"He's down here," said George. "But stay where you are." Sophie and Ben were still crying after their shock and fear of moments earlier but were consoled by the sound of George's voice.

It was a struggle to unclench his fingers. They were locked in a stone grip and he had to concentrate to relax them. He looked down at his victim. He didn't look like a bad man, just an office drone with his smart shirt and his tailored slacks, someone who wanted to get along; someone who had ambition. He had seen the type at school. You knew they were going places; but you also knew that whatever they did, it would never make them happy. But happiness didn't come into it now. This guy would never be happy again, would never be anything.

George turned to where Ed Mallory lay in the water, slumped against the side of the tunnel. A cloud of blood hung in the water around his neck. The bullet had entered through the top of his back by his shoulder blade breaking his collarbone. He was semiconscious, groaning and struggling to keep his head above the water. George dragged him to his feet.

"You're going to be all right," he said.

George had no idea whether this was true. But from the amount of bleeding, it looked as though the bullet had missed any arteries or major blood vessels and the wound was far enough away from the spinal cord and the heart so he would probably make it.

"You killed him," said Ed.

"I had to stop him," said George.

"It was self-defense," said Ed. "I can attest to that."

Blood seeped between Ed's fingers as he pressed down on his shoulder and George helped steady him as they climbed the steps to join Maggie and the children. As they made their way toward the escalators, Ed stumbled and George put his arm around him to hold him up.

"Do you want me to go and fetch someone?" George asked Ed as they started climbing up the stalled escalator with Maggie and the children following behind.

"No, it feels as though I'm losing blood so we'd better keep moving. But you need to remember this. Think of it as an insurance policy. Two names: Howard Berriman and Mark Hooper. Berriman is the head of MI5—you've probably heard of him—and Hooper is, was, the guy in the tunnel just now. They knew all about Denning's intended hijack, but they let it happen because they wanted the kudos of appearing to have stopped it right at the last minute. The trouble was that Denning got wise to what they were up to and he moved the attack to a week earlier. That's what all that was about down there. Mark Hooper thought that you knew the truth and he could save his skin if he took you out."

"But what about Tommy Denning?"

"Hooper killed him."

George didn't have time to explore his feelings about the death of the man who had engineered the horror that he and his family and so many others had been forced to endure. He had wanted him to live, had wanted him to suffer for what he had done but it was not to be.

"So what will happen to Howard Berriman?" asked George.

"His career's over," said Ed. "I'm going to take great pleasure in bringing him down."

They made their way into the ticket hall and seeing Ed Mallory limping, clutching his bleeding shoulder, a tall man with a shaven head rushed forward.

"Ed, I only just got the message, what happened?" he asked.

"It's all right, Nick, I'll explain later after I've got some medical attention," said Ed. "In the meantime, I need you to look after these people." Ed explained who George and his family were and introduced them to Detective Inspector Nick Calvert.

"I'll be in touch," said Ed to George. "Don't worry, it'll be fine." Ed held out his right hand that he had been holding against his bullet wound and George shook it, their palms both wet and sticky with blood.

As Ed was helped onto a stretcher by a paramedic, Nick Calvert ushered George and his family up the steps leading from the ticket hall to ground level. As they emerged into the daylight, George thought that the London air, so much maligned under normal circumstances, tasted cleaner and fresher than ever before.

George saw the reflection of a man in a shop window on the opposite side of Charing Cross Road. He was filthy, marinated in sludge and his face was swollen, bruised and bloody. It took a moment for him to realize that he was looking at a reflection of himself. He looked like a refugee from a nightmare. His outward appearance, however, belied his state of mind. His hands had stopped shaking; his breathing had steadied. Despite his recent ordeal on the train and his even more recent explosion of violence, he felt calm, strangely uplifted, somehow new and cleansed.

George heard someone call his name and then someone else did and then more voices were calling to him. He looked toward the perimeter of the evacuation zone to the news crews and photographers that had gathered behind the barriers.

"George! How are you feeling?"

"George! Over here."

They knew him; they had seen him on Denning's video feed from the train. The media had processed him and now he was part of their story. After all those years of craving recognition for something other than driving a tube train and now here it was, a direct response to doing exactly that and nothing he could do to prevent it.

News of who had just emerged from below ground had spread fast. Cameras and camera phones were pointed from the growing crowd as George held Maggie and the children close. People jostled to catch a glimpse of them as the shutters clicked and the sun shone down from the cloudless London sky.

A Winter Marriage

Poetry by Kerry Hardie

———•◆•———

A FURIOUS PLACE

CRY FOR THE HOT BELLY

A Winter Marriage

A Novel

— ⚬┃⚬ —

KERRY HARDIE

LITTLE, BROWN AND COMPANY
BOSTON   NEW YORK   LONDON

For Sean
Without whom there'd be no book

——— •◆• ———

Originally published in Great Britain by HarperCollins U.K.

Library of Congress Cataloging-in-Publication Data
Hardie, Kerry.
    A winter marriage : a novel / Kerry Hardie — 1st American ed.
      p.   cm.
    ISBN 0-316-07622-8
     1. Middle-aged women — Fiction. 2. Mothers and sons — Fiction. 3. Remarried people — Fiction. 4. Farmers' spouses — Fiction. 5. Farm life — Fiction.
    6. Ireland — Fiction. I. Title.
PR6058.A622 W56 2003
823'.914 — dc21
                                                2002020781

10 9 8 7 6 5 4 3 2 1

Q-FF

Designed by Alyssa Morris

Printed in the United States of America

Acknowledgments

MY GRATEFUL THANKS to all the following, who helped or read or advised:

Carmel Cummins, Olivia Goodwillie, Paddy and Dorothy Jolley, Barbara and Irene Kelly, Kieran Lineen, Val and Marian Lonergan, Pat Murphy, Helen Parry-Jones, Helen O'Brien, Paddy and Fintan Ryan, and all those at Butler House.

The author also wishes to thank the Tyrone Guthrie Centre at Annaghmakerrig.

Kerry Hardie studied English at York University, England, and worked in current affairs for the BBC in Belfast and for the Arts Council of Northern Ireland in Derry. She married writer and TV producer Sean Hardie in 1979 and lived in Glasgow for five years before moving to the Republic of Ireland.

The recipient of numerous prizes and commendations for poetry, including the Friends Provident National Poetry Prize, she has taught creative writing in adult education and adult literacy programs, and was a founder of the Kilkenny Prize for poetry.

— •◆• —

A Winter Marriage

Chapter One

SHE MET HIM AT A WEDDING she had gone to only because she needed a husband and a wedding wasn't a bad place to begin looking.

She didn't try to hide much from him, which was sound judgment because he didn't know much about women and he couldn't have talked to a woman who wasn't straight with him. But more than judgment, Hannie had luck. She met Ned when he was looking anyway, so most of the work was done for her. And he took to her, he liked her crooked straightness from the start.

She came from nowhere, had no family, no country and no background. None of that would have mattered only she had no money either so she needed somewhere to live, something to live on. She was fifty-two, she made no secret of it, nor of the fact that her need for a husband was overwhelmingly financial.

That didn't put Ned off. Nor did the fourteen-year-old son she'd left in Africa while she came prospecting for their futures.

Ned didn't know what he wanted when he met her, he'd only just admitted to himself that he wanted anything at all, so her directness eased things for him. He didn't know it, but he couldn't have coped with a woman of delicacy who left him to do the running, and he couldn't have coped with a woman who wasn't an outsider.

So the way of it was she decided Ned might do and she got around

Tom and Beth so they helped her, and Ned went along with it not because he was trapped by her as his friends thought, but because she was what he wanted all along.

———•◆•———

SOCIAL SITUATIONS were what she needed, and introductions to the right sort of men: men who didn't know her history or reputation, who might be charmed and cajoled into taking her on. By luck a widow this time not a divorcée, she still had a few respectable connections to exploit, so when she decided on taking this trip to England she phoned the Grenvilles from Kenya and asked Beth for a bed.

"For the wedding," she said. "Maybe a day or two after, I'm not sure of my movements. So much to be taken care of — Andrew's English estate — London — Andrew's solicitors . . ." She left it vague.

Strictly speaking, she hadn't asked, she'd just said her piece and then waited, knowing that Beth wouldn't be able to let the silence run on. Beth was soft, everyone knew that, most of all Hannie, who was anything but soft. There were other people she could have asked, but she didn't. If you were going to use someone, best choose someone trustworthy who assumed that you were the same until they were reminded that you weren't. It wasn't long before Beth was reminded, but by then it was too late.

The wedding invitation was more luck. The bride had been Andrew's goddaughter, the embossed invitation had come in the post a bare six weeks before he died. Andrew had answered at once: congratulations to his little Sophie (not so little anymore, it seemed); he and Hannie would most certainly be there to see her married. Between this acceptance and his death a few weeks later he had issued his ultimatum and Hannie had left.

But Sophie didn't know this and neither did Sophie's parents, who wrote their commiserations when the death notice appeared in the London *Times*. The letter was addressed to Andrew's widow, Hannie Bennet.

Hannie wrote back that she would be in England on business matters and she very much looked forward to this meeting with Andrew's old friends and his goddaughter at her wedding. Andrew had spoken of them so often, she felt it only right to be there as his representative.

She sealed the letter, trusting they wouldn't yet have heard the gossip. Even if they had, they'd hardly write and tell her so. Or make a scene when she turned up at the church.

———•◆•———

SHE WAS STILL AN ATTRACTIVE WOMAN, Beth thought, watching Hannie sitting at a table on the lawn. There was the usual wedding marquee but the day was fine and dry, the tables had all been moved outside.

Very attractive, whatever Tom might say. Tom liked more grooming: nice hair, a little makeup, something finished in the look. Yet he woke up when Hannie was around, he pretended he didn't, but he did.

Any fool could see she was trouble, Tom used to say; there were always nods and murmurs of agreement from his listeners. Beth thought men saw the trouble and they liked it, even Tom. They liked the aloofness, the lack of involvement, the way she walked by herself.

Hannie had kicked off her shoes under the table, her hair was sunbleached and she wore a not-new dress in faded gray. Beth pulled the floral frock she'd thought she liked so much down over her stomach. She wished she'd tried for elegance not prettiness. She wished she didn't care that her waist had broadened and her stomach bulged. She wished that, like Hannie, she didn't try to hide it.

Funny how it looked all right if you didn't care. Except it probably wouldn't on her. She resolved to eat less, walk more. She knew she wouldn't. She resolved to stop worrying so much about what she looked like, to "accept" herself (that curious language that her children spoke). Hannie had just done that thing she did when she stopped being interested by whoever it was she had been being interested by. Switched off the light and gone out. Beth had almost forgotten that trick, the way she could not-be-there, like an abandoned puppet, a rag doll left out in the rain. Men always fell for it, they suddenly got frantic that she wasn't listening anymore, wasn't interested when she had been, so intensely. Funny how easy it was for some people.

———— •◆• ————

IT DIDN'T FEEL easy to Hannie. It was all smooth and smart and understated, all grooming and opinions. She had to wrench herself up to the mark, make herself perform, not give up and go under. She felt blunt and shabby and old. And tired, really tired.

She met Ned through a young woman called Jessica who'd sought her out and introduced herself.

"My mother knew your husband. She said you might be here. I'm to offer you her sympathies."

Hannie hovered for a moment on the edge of paranoia. She dismissed it. This Jessica would neither know nor care about the marital gossip of another generation on another continent.

"She knew the family. Years ago in Oxfordshire. She had a thing about the oldest brother."

"Edward," Hannie said.

"Edward," Jessica agreed. "You must tell me how he is. She'll want to know in detail —"

"He's dead. Died before I ever met him."

"Really?" Jessica sounded quite interested. "My father will be relieved. Edward was her untraveled road. She does rather tend to let herself regret him out loud when she's cross."

Jessica was tall and slender with gray eyes and perfect skin and perfect self-possession. A woman, not a girl, nearer thirty-five than twenty, her voice was clear and well bred and she wore a loose green linen dress, which showed off her wavy, fair hair. She was like daylight, Hannie thought, not liking her.

She had a man with her, following a few paces after like a dragged anchor, so that he didn't seem to be with her though he was. He caught up with her and stood almost beside her and she introduced him. Ned Renvyle.

Hannie shook hands. He was very tall and bony, with a full head of fine gray hair. The hair was much younger than the face, which was tanned and folded into long broken creases like the wandering courses of wadis in the dry season. The eyes were withdrawn and almost invisible between deep lines and puckers.

Jessica had finished with Hannie, she had inquired about her mother's old flame and was ready to move on, but a sudden eddy of people pressed into them and the space for retreat closed. Resignedly the two women began again. Ned Renvyle stood and listened.

Jessica worked in broadcasting, a producer not a secretary, Hannie's assumptions smoothly corrected. She spoke briefly of a series she was executive-producing, throwing in a couple of observations that were meaningless to Hannie but made Ned Renvyle nod appreciatively. It was all gracefully done: self-aware, modest, informative. Hannie glanced at the hands. Jessica wore no rings.

"What do *you* do?" she asked Hannie. Her tone was pleasant, conversational. Your turn, it said, I've done my bit.

What you don't do, Hannie thought. Live off men. When I get the chance.

"Marry," she said starkly.

Jessica looked startled. Hannie was startled herself, she probably hadn't intended to say it aloud, she wasn't entirely sure. The bony old man twitched slightly, the wine jumped in his glass. He had been watching Hannie closely while seeming not to.

Jessica laughed. She lifted her glass as though to drink to Hannie but it was empty. Ned Renvyle automatically held out his hand for it. "Perrier water," Jessica said. He held out his hand for Hannie's glass. "Red," she said. He turned and bored his way through the crowd.

"So you're currently out of a job?" Jessica asked lightly.

Hannie nodded. "I am looking for a new position."

"Oh?" Jessica said. "That must be tedious. Wouldn't you rather a break?"

"Economic necessity," Hannie said.

Jessica looked at her curiously. It seemed to occur to her that Hannie was serious. Her interest was almost caught — it was the tastelessness of Hannie's remarks. She seemed about to speak but a tall, impeccably dressed man with a thatch of straight brown hair was shoving his way furiously through the crowd.

"That was Ned Renvyle," he accused as soon as he reached her. "I saw you talking to him, couldn't get near you . . . Honestly, Jessica, why didn't you hold on to him? You knew perfectly well I wanted to meet him."

This was not a boyfriend, Hannie realized, nor a lover awaiting divorce. This was a consort or a partner or whatever these things were called now; a husband she hadn't yet bothered to marry. Jessica introduced Hannie, but the man hardly glanced at her.

"He didn't want to meet anyone," Jessica continued calmly. "He wanted to hang on to someone so he didn't have to. I can't think what he's doing here. He's terribly shy —"

"Shy? You're talking about a man who marches up to headhunters and invites himself round for a year or two. He's not shy, Jessica, explorers aren't shy, for a halfway intelligent woman you do talk a load of crap."

"Shy in this sort of company. Stop making such a fuss and go and find him yourself. He's gone to get us drinks, but he's probably forgotten by now. Mine's Perrier water, Hannie's is red wine." She spoke like a mother ignoring a child's petulance.

He glared at her and headed off after Renvyle. Then he stopped, turned on his heel and came back. He addressed Hannie.

"Sorry," he said. "Very rude of me. Bit of an obsession."

He wheeled and stomped off again, ignoring Jessica.

"It's true," Jessica said. "The obsession bit. He read the books when he was a boy and just completely fell for them."

"What sort of books?"

"Travel. The Gentleman Adventurer. More Thesiger than Fleming, but slightly later and not so well connected. Quite obviously incredibly brave, only never ever written like that. Touching, really." She paused, her eyes on a woman who seemed anxious to shepherd them toward the lunch tables.

"Of course, they're hopelessly out-of-fashion and out-of-print and cluttering-up-the-secondhand-bookshelves. I shouldn't think Ned Renvyle's royalty checks are exactly keeping the mice from his door."

"Where is his door?"

"Oh, Ireland somewhere." Jessica spoke in a neutral voice. "Old family. You know the sort of thing. Nettles and decay."

———•◆•———

HANNIE DIDN'T, and it didn't sound very promising. Still, she wasn't exactly being bombarded with opportunities; she might follow it up for want of anything better.

She scanned the tables, found her name on a bit of card and picked up the one from the place setting next to it. Three tables up, she found Ned Renvyle's name card. People were beginning to take their seats but she ignored them, leaned over and changed his card for the one in her hand. She went back to her table, sat down, and put Ned's card on the setting beside her.

———•◆•———

JESSICA WAS RIGHT, Ned Renvyle lived in Ireland. Hannie had listened for an estate but heard only a house, a farm.

A family farm?

No, not a family farm but the next best thing. A farm near the places and people he'd known in his childhood. He'd bought it when he left off roaming around the place and came home.

Home? He was an Irishman?

His family had lived there for generations, he said, not answering her question.

But he wasn't a farmer?

He was now. Before that, he told her, he'd mostly traveled, written the odd book, given lectures, that sort of thing. There'd been some rooms in London where he'd lived when he wasn't away. Now he farmed a few acres. Nothing much, but it kept him occupied. He lived alone. Been married once, his wife had died. He was over for this wedding. And to see his publisher, visit friends.

THEY WERE SNARLED in a long line of traffic with no visible reason for the holdup. Hannie sat in the back of the car, staring absently out of the window while Tom and Beth bickered about Beth's choice of route.

Ireland. She hadn't thought of Ireland, had never been there. It might be the answer. He was on the lookout, she knew that, just from the things he'd said this afternoon. And he'd taken to her, she knew that too.

She'd have to find things out, she decided: how much land, if there was money to go with it, if there were any commitments.

You couldn't rely on family anymore, Andrew had said. Or schools. A chap could sound right and have nothing. These days, there was more likely to be money if he sounded wrong.

Ned Renvyle would definitely have sounded right in Andrew's book. Hannie didn't care what a chap sounded like as long as he wasn't flat broke.

She could probably hook him if she played him right, she thought, and he might be the start she needed. She could always leave him if she couldn't stand him, but he must be pushing seventy, he couldn't live forever, she might just stick it out until he died. With a bit of luck he'd leave her somewhere to live or enough to live on. With a lot of luck he'd leave her both.

If he turned out to have anything at all.

But she'd have to let him do the next bit. She wondered how fast he would move if he made up his mind to it. She wondered how fast she could move in her turn. If he did as he'd told her he planned to do and went up to London, she'd have to follow him, invite herself on someone. She couldn't afford a hotel, couldn't put all her eggs in one basket at this stage when nothing might come of it.

But he might not go to London, he might stay on. And if he did, she'd stay on too. She'd tell Beth the truth, or a version of it, ask for her help. Beth would understand. Not like that blond bitch at the wedding with her career and her salary and her future.

She would explain about the separation, which she hadn't so far mentioned. She would tell Beth there'd be no money coming, even after the will was settled, Andrew's children would inherit; she was broke and needed to marry again.

They'd hear it all anyway, and there was no predicting when. Africa gossip, it might take a while, but it would permeate through in the end. Tell Beth, but ask her not to pass it on to Tom. She would of course. So if they heard before she was ready, she'd be covered.

But she wouldn't tell her about Joss or the reasons for the separation.

The traffic began to move. Tom stopped telling Beth she'd chosen the wrong route and started complaining about the cold supper she was planning. All that fidgety food they pushed at you at weddings. You needed a decent dinner to settle you down, he said. He was quite drunk.

For once Beth stood her ground and stuck to her cold meats and salad. She was tired, they'd eaten a massive lunch, and the help had the evening off. It wasn't like Africa, she said over her shoulder at Hannie. Africa, where everyone had servants. There was nostalgia in her voice.

Hannie said nothing. Where everyone like *you* had servants, she thought, remembering days when she hadn't had enough to feed herself and Joss, much less a servant.

Ned Renvyle. Only if she was desperate. Maybe not even then. The next move was his, anyway.

—— • ◆ • ——

"Oh, the Woodburns," Beth said. "Minster Lovell, beautiful house, Jacobean, been in the family for generations. Jessica's the youngest. Nice, isn't she?"

Hannie said nothing.

"And terribly successful."

More silence from Hannie. Beth began to waver.

"It must be wonderful," she said, "to be like her."

Hannie looked at her.

"Oh, you know . . ." Beth flapped her hand around vaguely. "Not having to wait for the right moment. A job. Confidence. Beautiful clothes . . ."

"Career." Hannie corrected her.

"Career?"

"She has a *career,* not a job. She told me so."

The two women sat outside in the sunshine, helping the help. And Hannie was working on Beth, she was reestablishing herself and gathering information.

"I never liked stringing beans," Beth said. "I always slice my fingers as well as the beans. Shelling peas is different, I like shelling peas. The little bump-bump-bump noise in the bowl. Mummy made us volunteer but we never minded." She picked up the next runner bean from the pile on the table and looked at it balefully. "I bet Jessica Woodburn *never* strings beans."

"Are there many like her?" Hannie asked. Her voice was neutral.

Beth sighed and leaned back in her deck chair. "It's the way things are now," she said carefully. "Women like us . . ."

Hannie waited.

"Anyway, I like my life," Beth continued, "I don't really want to be like that. Except sometimes. Sometimes it's hard — feeling you haven't done anything. You have to *do* something, you know. Not just marry and have children and run a house. Sara says I'm a bad role model. That means an example for her to base herself on. She says it won't be her fault if she turns out just like me."

Hannie laughed. Then she remembered herself. "What does Tom say?" she asked tactfully.

Beth cheered up. She sat forward, waving a runner bean around as she talked. "Tom? He just wants things to go on as they've always done. His home the way he likes it, food the way he likes it, me here to look after him. To 'service him,' as Sara says. Even the boys talk like that since they went to Cambridge. And they're right, of course they're right, and I wish I was different, I'd so like them to be proud of me, especially Sara."

"These Jessica Woodburns," Hannie said, "do they have children?"

"Oh, yes. One or two. Late. It's all wonderful. Then they get a nanny and go back to work. Just like our mothers, my dear, only they went back to their social lives. Which is what work is to them anyway, as far as I can see. Still, it gives the lie to the men laying down the law about the sacrifice they make for us, slaving away in the office all their lives. These women simply can't wait to get back there."

Beth stopped suddenly. Hannie was looking across the lawn, that still, empty expression on her face. Beth heard herself and blushed to her hairline. So stupid, she'd forgotten for a moment about Hannie. She was always so poised, her English almost flawless, she had been so very much at home in Andrew's world where they had met her.

And it might not have been true, it could have been just spiteful gossip. She tried desperately to think of something to say but nothing came.

Hannie rescued her. "What do the men think?" she asked lightly.

"I don't know. They don't seem to have much choice. They're not really allowed to say anything, whatever they may think. Which is about time, really," she finished, brightening. "But *we're* not allowed to say anything either. Not even discuss. We've wasted our lives and we're jealous. But I'm not jealous, really I'm not, and I don't mind if that's what they want to do, I just don't want to have to start doing it myself. . . ."

Sara appeared in the doorway behind them.

"There was a man on the phone for Hannie. I said I'd get her but he got in a panic, said he'd ring back in an hour."

Beth swiveled around in the deck chair. She addressed her daughter. "What was his name, darling?"

"I don't know, Ren-something," the fifteen-year-old replied. "First he wanted her and then he didn't. Couldn't make up his mind."

Hannie couldn't, either.

Chapter Two

NED RENVYLE SAT ON A BENCH by the river in the late afternoon sunshine. He hadn't gone to London as he'd first planned. Instead he'd left his friends the Langtons and their hospitality for a timbered pub one village away from Hannie. He knew Jean and Alasdair Langton were perfectly aware of what he was about, knew this attempt at conceal-ment was both foolish and futile, but he felt, at least, less overlooked.

Courting was never a dignified business. Women might thrive on it, but it made men look like fools. A bit late to start worrying about that now, he decided. The river was narrow with dirty, thick-looking water and mown banks, the grass worn thin by picnickers and courting cou-ples. There were litter bins and benches and life belts on stands. Fish-ermen stood in line all day and threw back what they'd caught when they'd caught it. Hard to see what they got out of it. A travesty of a river. He should be grateful for the benches, he supposed; saved his piles.

He shut his eyes and a warm orange glow of sunny darkness closed over him. He dozed or dreamed, saw the small rushy meadows of home, the ragwort and the dampness, the cattle wandering about in them. He heard their quiet trampling and chomping and the harsh cry of a heron in the reed beds.

He felt miserable, weary and old. He wanted her all right, but al-most as badly he just wanted to get finished up here and go home. Suddenly he hardly cared about the outcome. With or without her, he'd go back to the farm and the fields and the river.

Yet at the same time he had wanted her badly enough to have sat it through this far, he had to remind himself of this in his dejection. Why he wanted her, he hardly knew. It wasn't for anything he could put into words and say aloud to someone else.

He had a picture that was really more of a vision at the edges of his mind. Sometimes he called it up deliberately, but more often it came when he wasn't thinking and floated in front of his eyes. He saw a hallway with dark wood, sun shafts, dust motes. And flowers leaning out of shadow into light.

With the picture came a jumble of sense-impressions: morning and a garden, dew and dewy grass in the early sun, the swish of skirts. Then a china jug pulled from a wooden press and water gushing in until it ran over.

The sense-impressions settled and stilled. The scent of flowers, the quiet drop of petals on old furniture.

Then a feeling of simplicity. Of his life inhabiting his body. Of his body sitting simply wherever he was when the picture came. Of this being enough.

He knew that this yearning vision of flowers was a yearning for home. Not the house he had now, but the home he had left fifty years ago to sit on the bare ground beneath unknown stars with strangers, with unfamiliar tongues and smells and sounds about him, and a peace in his blood more intense than fire or wine.

And nothing would do him then but to have those stars, that peace, and no price to be paid was too high. And nothing would persuade him that his life lived in Ireland wouldn't be narrow and diminished beyond endurance.

There'd been flowers too, in his wilderness places: carpets after rain, a white bloom clenched in a rock.

Only now he wanted what he'd left behind him all those years ago. Or the ghost of it. He was neither so old nor such a fool as to imagine that anything could be again as it once was.

He'd spent too many years in search of himself, confronting himself, until it was like living in a high altitude where the visibility is always intense and clear. Now, an old man, he found that he could not altogether bear this. Nor the losses time brought: that intense sweet peace only a memory now.

The truth was he was lonely, as simple as that, he told himself. Finally, after almost a lifetime away, he'd decided to come home. He had bought a house in the place he'd known in his childhood and now, five years later, he was still waiting for it to turn into his home.

Somehow he'd got it into his head that a woman might make the difference, and he couldn't get it out of his head, though he knew that acquiring one would solve nothing, the yearning would simply transfer itself to something else, he'd be led by the nose to follow another dream. That had been the way of it all his life. In the meantime he wanted a wife, so there was nothing to be done but to go and find one. But Hannie? The woman was a nomad, not a homemaker. Had he taken leave of his senses altogether?

The sun had left the bench where he sat and the coolness of the evening was upon him. It wouldn't be much longer now, he thought. He'd ask her. She might have him or she might refuse him. Either way, at sixty-nine, he'd look a bloody fool.

And he'd look a worse fool, bringing her back with him, than leaving her here and no one any the wiser. Fortunately his few close friends were scattered. If she said yes he would write to them, tell them his news by letter. Then they could let off steam, calm down, write him a civil note. No need to tell anyone at home, might as well just turn up with her. They'd know soon enough, probably before he knew himself.

Well, if he'd minded men's opinions he'd have lived a different life. Let them think him a fool, he supposed that he could bear it one more time.

And when he was with her, he didn't care. She had that effect on him. Caution left him. It was her attitude. *Why not?* she said, as others might say, *Why?*

She had a lopsided walk. He liked that, he didn't know why. He'd asked her about it and she'd laughed. No, no injury, she'd said. Just the way she was. Didn't seem offended.

He liked her, that was all he could say. Liked her untidy hair and the way she took her shoes off under the table and went fishing around for them when it was time to go. Liked the hearty way she ate and the way that she laughed with her head back and her mouth open. She got under his guard.

Oh, he knew she was untrustworthy, unsound, knew she was running, though he didn't know from what. If pushed he'd have said she was a selfish woman of loose morals and bad habits. But also courageous, strong-minded, energetic. She didn't try to cover or apologize. He recognized her as he would have recognized a man.

And he might have befriended such a man, but he'd never have let him come too close.

Then why was he letting *her?* Holding the door open, inviting her in?

He thought about this one for a long time and the answer he came up with confused him with its simplicity. He felt warmer in her company.

He'd cut his London plans. No point. He had no desire to sit in his club and talk to the other old fogies. The London part of his trip had only ever been an excuse to go looking for a woman. The whole thing was, if he was honest. But he'd taken her up for the day when he went to see his publishers.

Publishers. Hadn't published anything for years and then there was a letter out of the blue.

Backlists. Something might be done about backlists. Perhaps lunch? Next time he was in London?

As though he was in and out of London every second week. As though he lived that sort of life.

She'd worn her good dress, the same one she wore for the wedding. He'd liked that, that she'd thought enough of a day out with him to wear it. Not that he liked dressed-up women, he didn't. But he liked her in that dress, and he was flattered.

She impressed the publisher fellow, that was clear enough, though he'd been a bit put out when Ned first introduced her, had muttered something about business, and not knowing they'd have company. . . . Ned had ignored him, he'd reached the age when he didn't hear if he didn't want to.

Anyway, the petulance didn't last long. When the publisher fellow was doing his stuff she sat quietly and listened in and when he'd finished she joined easily in the small talk. He asked her about Africa and she told him. When he started asking her what she read, she said she read nothing, she used to read, but she hadn't for years. He started dropping names then — people he knew, people they published. She should read this, read that. He wrote the names down for her and she laughed and folded them into her handbag. She said she probably wouldn't read them, but she might. If she did she would write and let him know what she thought.

Ned liked it that she was honest, that she didn't need to seem to be what she wasn't. He hadn't any time for people who said with pride that they never read, but she didn't say it with pride, she just said that she had once, but she didn't now. She didn't explain why.

Ned smiled to himself. Publisher fellow wanting her to himself, trying to work out what it was about her, was she with him, what was going on? Chap half his age, too. Hannie with a good few years on him and not pretending that she hadn't.

He didn't think anything would come of this backlist business. Still, it was a decent place, she'd enjoyed it, and he'd enjoyed having somewhere to take her.

Afterward he couldn't keep it to himself. He fancied you, he'd said and, I know, she'd said, and laughed as though it was a good joke and made him buy her an ice cream to eat in the sun outside the National Gallery though she'd just eaten two puddings off the trolley.

She'd never been to the National before, knew nothing about pictures and never had. He said he'd write her a list to go in her handbag and she smiled. He had planned to take her to the English section, to the Turners and the portraits, show her the things he liked, but he couldn't remember the way and he couldn't get her to walk past anything that caught her eye. She spotted the Monet water lilies through the arch from the room before and once she was there he didn't want to move her away. She didn't say anything, just stood looking. He told himself he could see how she'd have looked when she was a girl, and it wasn't so different. He wondered why she'd never seen pictures when it was plain that she liked them.

She didn't bother to look at anything that didn't attract her right away. There was a Holbein she went for, a woman full-length in a black dress on a dark-green ground, a fine painting.

Christina of Denmark, he told her. Painted for Henry VIII to see if he liked the look of her. Lucky for her, he didn't.

But Hannie didn't know about Henry VIII and his six wives. He was taken aback. You didn't learn British history in Dutch schools, she said, especially when the schools were in obscure Dutch colonies.

She might not know much about history or pictures, but she didn't miss much.

When he asked her why she liked the picture she said because the woman owned herself. And then she said wasn't it funny she should go on owning herself even hundreds of years later when she was long dead. He knew what she meant if he didn't think about it.

When they came out and they hadn't looked at what he had wanted to show her, she said she was sorry but she'd been excited and had forgotten.

He didn't mind. He had enjoyed watching her excitement. She had taken his arm walking down the street. He was pleased. The expedition was a success.

He smiled to himself now, remembering. The picture of Hannie in London faded. He saw again the riverbank in the evening light. People strolling, a loiter of dogs and children. A little cloud of midges danced by his left ear. He scratched, reached down for his hat, got up and set off up the path to the village pub where he was staying.

"Been enjoying the sunshine?" The landlord was cheerful in his polished bar parlor. Ned thought of Keoghs, its wooden shelves and stacks of untipped Carrol's cigarettes and dusty bottles of Guinness. Mrs. Keogh coming through from the back, drying her hands on a dirty cloth. Serving him in silence, leaving when it was done.

He thought of the wide Blackwater, its wooded banks and hidden farms and windy skies.

He'd ask her, get it over with. Then he could go home.

Chapter Three

HANNIE HAD MADE HER MOVE as soon as it looked as though Ned Renvyle might come through. She'd told Beth she wanted to take her into her confidence, put all her cards on the table. Then she'd told her about the separation and the will.

She might get something in the end, she said, but then again, she might not. That was all in the future anyway. For now she was broke and she needed to remarry. She asked Beth for help.

Beth couldn't let a kitten drown, much less a scrawny old cat like Hannie, and anyway she knew the facts of life for women of their generation. Or rather she knew that she didn't. She had always lived in comfort, was terrified as to her future should Tom ever decide to abandon her, she had an acute imaginative sympathy for Hannie's dreadful position.

Tom didn't, but Tom let it run on because that was what Beth wanted and anyway he didn't mind having Hannie around for a bit, she livened things up, added spice to the daily fare, though that wasn't what he told his wife.

Tom was a dull man; he'd been dull in Kenya, and he was duller here. If she hadn't been at such a low ebb, Hannie thought, she couldn't have stood it for two hours, much less two weeks.

"Invite them," Andrew had said to Hannie years ago in Kenya. "He's a bore but he might be useful." Andrew had had an eye for useful men.

So she had. A little racing and a lot of booze — Tom and Beth, letting their hair come unpinned for a year or two, far from the Home Counties. Well, now they could pay for their fun.

"He's too old," Beth said. "They'll say you're marrying him for his money."

"Who'll say? I don't know anyone anymore. Besides, he hasn't got any money, or none that you'd notice. If he had, I wouldn't be dithering around like this, would I?"

"Oh, Hannie," Beth wailed, "I wish you wouldn't do that! You know how slow I am. I always think you're serious."

"I am. Totally." She got up, took out her cigarettes, remembered and put them back. She walked around the room to calm herself. Ned had been to the house for a drink. Now Beth was having second thoughts.

"He might die," Hannie said. "He's pushing seventy. At least then I'd have a house."

Beth shot her a swift look. She stabbed at the needlepoint she was working. "I do hate this cat," she said passionately. "All these marmalades and browns. I have such a lovely one waiting for when I've finished this." She gazed at Hannie, her eyes wistful and large.

"Roses and honeysuckle on a green ground," she went on. "Beautiful colors, all shading into each other. Andrew died, Hannie. It won't necessarily help —"

"True," Hannie said, ignoring the tapestry. "Andrew died. And no house. Not so slow, my dear Beth."

Beth flushed with pleasure.

"And it's not true that you don't know anyone, Hannie," she said, taking courage. "It's never true. One always knows someone, no matter where one goes. It's one of those laws."

Hannie said nothing. Beth retreated.

"Well, at least you wouldn't have to cope with sex." She had the air of one trying to look on the bright side.

Hannie stared. Then she roared: "Oh Beth, you great booby, how can you be such an innocent?"

It was Beth's turn to stare. "At his age?" she said weakly. "Oh no, Hannie, surely not?"

"At his age, either he can't or he'll rut like a baboon. At least till the novelty wears off. He won't be any good, though —" She stopped abruptly. She'd gone too far, had offended Beth's sensibilities.

But it seemed not. "Won't you mind?" Beth asked, concern in her voice.

"Why should I? That's not what I want him for."

"I don't mean that. I mean if he wants to do it all the time."

"I know that's what you mean. It won't make any difference either way. It's not what I want him for. Sex isn't the problem."

Her voice was indifferent. She glanced at Beth. Now she *had* gone too far. Too bad. She'd asked Beth for help, not counseling.

But Beth hadn't finished. "I couldn't bear it." She shuddered. "Someone one didn't know. At our age . . ."

Hannie looked at her. "How married you are, my dear Beth," she said lightly. "Only to have sex with someone one's known for twenty years . . ."

Beth blushed. She picked up her needlepoint. Hannie could be quite cruel.

"If you hate that cat so much, why are you sitting there martyring yourself over it? Why don't you just dump it, start a new one?"

"Sara," Beth said hopelessly. "Sara gave it to me for my birthday. Tom helped her choose. He said he thought I'd *like* cats with pansies in the border."

"Let me see."

Beth handed her the frame. Hannie carried it over to the window and studied it briefly. "Horrible," she said. "Why don't you have an accident?"

"Oh, Hannie, I couldn't."

"Why ever not? Spill something. So disappointing. But Sara would forgive you. You could console yourself with the other one. Would you like me to do it for you?"

"Oh no, Hannie, no. Please give it back. I don't mind it, really I don't."

Hannie shrugged. She handed it over.

Beth bundled the wools up together and pushed the whole lot out of sight.

In case I make a grab for them, Hannie thought.

Beth gathered herself. "Where is this house, anyway?" she asked, determinedly.

"Somewhere on a river called the Blackwater," Hannie said. "Near a town pronounced *Yawl* and spelled Y–o–u–g–h–a–l. It's where Sir Walter Raleigh planted his American potatoes. He seems to think that's important. But it's a farm, not a house. A farmhouse."

When Tom came in from the office looking for attention and a drink he found the two women on their hands and knees on the floor, poring over an atlas. Beth scrambled to her feet, talking about the time and how she hadn't noticed. Hannie stayed where she was, elbows on the rug, bottom sticking out, chin cupped in her hands, staring down at the opened book. When she'd finished staring she shifted her gaze up to Tom and regarded him balefully.

"We were just looking for somewhere," Beth was explaining vaguely. "The children had the atlas out — some argument they were trying to settle."

"We're trying to find where Ned Renvyle lives," Hannie said. She straightened up and sat back on her heels. "With a view to deciding whether or not I should marry him."

"Has he asked you?"

Hannie grinned. "Not yet," she said. "But he will, and I want to be ready with my answer. We're just adding up the pros and cons, working out his assets. If he's got any, that is. Or at least enough to make it worth my while. You couldn't help, could you, Tom? All your contacts? The Langtons? Somebody must know."

"No, I couldn't," Tom said. "And I'd stay well clear of the Langtons. They're fond of Renvyle by all accounts, won't want to see him taken advantage of. Any more than I do," he added pompously. "It's not decent, what you're doing, Hannie, you should lay off him. I've a good mind to ring him up and tell."

"But you won't," Hannie said, getting to her feet and giving Tom an affectionate pat on the arm on her way to the drinks tray. "You're much too English to go interfering. Besides, if you do that you'll never get rid of me." She handed him a drink. She poured herself a refill and fished out the glass that Beth had quietly pushed behind a vase out of Tom's sight. She poured a large gin into that, too, and held it out to Beth. Beth flushed and took it, not looking at Tom.

"I could throw you out."

Hannie shook her head. "You'd upset Beth. The house would be unsettled for at least a week. You'd hate that. Better marry me off to Ned."

Beth gaped at her when she said such things, but Hannie knew it earned her keep with Tom.

"Anyway," she went on, "I can't see what you're taking such a high moral tone about. Ascertaining assets is all I'm doing. Perfectly sensible and respectable and it's always gone on. I bet Beth's father wanted to know exactly what *you* proposed to keep her on. And if he didn't it was only because *her* mother had it all off your mother long before you even knew you liked her." Hannie sat herself down on a leather pouf. She looked intently up at Tom.

"Well, I haven't got a mother and I'm not thinking of marrying Ned for reasons of altruism. He'd understand. He'd probably show me his bank statements if I asked him. And he's quite medieval enough to believe in dowries and exchange of lands."

"Neither of which you happen to have."

"True, but if I had I wouldn't be thinking of marrying him at all, would I?" she said shrugging. "He's no catch, Tom. He's nearly twenty years older than I am and he wants a wife. He can't have it all ways, he'll have to deal."

"My God, Hannie, I'm glad I'm safely married to Beth. Is this what you did to poor old Andrew?"

"I didn't have to with Poor Old Andrew," she said. "Poor Old Andrew liked my terms. I married him in the nick of time to stop that Clayton woman he was screwing from leaving her husband and landing in on him. Remember her? Janine Clayton? Looked like Zelda Fitzgerald with a temperament to match? Poor Old Andrew was just begging to be saved from Janine. Anyway, it was a straight deal. A wife in his house and a mother for his children. Someone to tidy away his women. I needed a home for Joss."

"Andrew and Janine Clayton?" Tom was caught irresistibly. "But didn't she kill herself around . . . ?"

"Around that time? Two weeks after Andrew and I were married. Booze and pills. Got out of that one by the skin of his teeth, didn't he? And it nearly came out. Husband hysterical, wanting to tell the world, show Andrew up for what he was. Poor bastard loved her, you see. Under a lot of financial pressure, though. Got leaned on by the Powers-That-Be. Tell, and we won't lift a finger keeping off the vultures —"

"And did they?" Tom was unwilling to let the story go.

"Indeed they did. Helped him sell up, ship himself home." Hannie shrugged her shoulders, took a mouthful of gin. "Didn't you know all this? It wasn't so long after you left —"

"Who killed herself?" Sara stood in the doorway, her face young, blank, deceptively innocent. A strand of dark hair lay over her shoulder. She picked it up and chewed at it absently, her eyes intent.

Hannie swiveled lazily around on her stool. "A woman we knew once," she said.

"Because of your husband?"

"Partly. Partly because she was a mess." She swiveled lazily back, catching Beth's tightened mouth in the turn of her eye. The little bitch didn't like her. The little bitch was the apple of her mother's eye. Beth was shooing her out now, a good sheep dog, careful of its charge, firing darts of reproach at Hannie as she went.

Sod, Hannie thought. Now Beth would go all prim and proper on her again, remember she'd said she'd help Hannie find a husband but only if Tom didn't know. But she had to feed Tom the odd tidbit, keep him diverted, stop herself from dying of boredom. This way he'd forget to grouse at her living in his house and drinking his gin and leading his wife astray.

Chapter Four

NED TOOK HER FOR DINNER THAT NIGHT, to a place someone
had recommended. It offended him — the thick carpets, the starched
damask, the fancy words in the menu. And he didn't like the prices.

She watched him, his crotchety reaction. She saw his age, the setness
of his ways and opinions. She refrained from soothing him or playing
up to him. No sense in bringing him to the point, if she wasn't going to
be able to live with him.

He studied the menu while the waiter hovered. He looked up,
caught her eye, flushed.

"We could go somewhere else," she said neutrally.

"And have you think me a cheapskate?" He made an effort, smiled
self-consciously.

She raised an eyebrow, not returning the smile.

"What do you want, Hannie?" Ned asked her. The waiter was approaching.

She picked up the menu. "Whatever's most expensive."

"Is it a test?"

She nodded, not looking up. The waiter was standing there, silently
waiting. She ordered the lobster. Ned did the same. The waiter wrote
it down.

"Did I flinch?" Ned asked when he'd gone.

"Hardly at all," she said. "Call him back and we'll change it."

"No we won't."

"Yes we will. Try and hide your relief, Ned. The waiter will despise you."

"Do you?"

"Hardly at all. And I don't like lobster."

———•◆•———

THE FOOD WAS BETTER than the surroundings. Afterward, they sat on over the coffee. Ned had offered her information over the past days, not an account exactly, but a beginning: his family's ascendancy origin in Ireland, his childhood in his grandmother's house following his soldier-father's early death, the world war he had gone to fight in. Then his marriage, his travels, his books. An outline had begun to emerge.

Hannie had told him almost nothing and he hadn't asked. He had waited. Now she sat, folded arms resting on the table, telling him her story or the bones of it.

She had told it many times and many ways and it surprised her a little, how she was telling Ned now. She told him less than the whole but far more than she'd meant to, and she told it nearer the truth.

Perhaps it was her age, she thought. At fifty-two she had little appetite left for pretense, could not be bothered anymore with best behavior. Perhaps it was her desperation or the way he took it. He sat there quietly, looking at her as she talked, accepting what she told him without comment or apparent judgment. It eased her and it loosened her tongue. It made her think there might be more between them than she'd expected, that this plan of hers might be marginally less deranged than it seemed.

She didn't hide her origins, her past marriages or her need now for a new one. She didn't hide her financial situation. She spoke briefly of Joss, her son, whom she had left in Africa. She made it clear that she wanted him near to her when she settled, that she didn't care for smartness or reputation, just that the school was steady.

She had thought of looking for a job, she said, but she had no experience, references or qualifications.

"Do you have friends?" he asked, leaning back in his chair, his legs stretched out and his feet crossed under the table.

"Influential friends? No. I have acquaintances. A few people I can fall back on in a crisis. I had a friend once but she's dead." She didn't explain further. He nodded gravely. They both knew the sort of job she could get at her age and in these times.

"You'd better think about marrying me," he told her. "No great shakes. I'm sixty-nine. No money to speak of. Farm takes every penny and all my time. Quiet sort of a life, not much in the way of excitement, not very social." He paused. His eye swept the crowded restaurant, the muddle of smells and voices, the busy faces.

"But at least you can breathe there," he added passionately, "at least it's a life. Not like *this*."

Here Hannie held up her hand as though to stop him.

"We've had a week together, Ned, a pleasant week. It doesn't have to go any further, you don't have to solve my life for me. You could just get on your boat now and go back to Ireland. We could put all this down to experience, leave it at that."

He regarded her gravely. "Are you trying to save me the pain of rejection, Hannie?"

"I'm trying to make you think before you speak." She lit a cigarette, leaned back, inhaled. "I'm not in this for my ego, Ned, I'm not collecting skulls. If you ask me, I'll probably say yes."

"I'm asking you, Hannie."

"I'm not much of a catch," she said quietly, looking straight at him.

He liked that, that she wasn't doing the coy wistful thing and looking at the table as another woman might.

"You wouldn't be sitting here if you were."

He smiled suddenly, his face twisting. "Your loss, my luck," he added. "Whatever it was that you lost."

It wasn't a question. He knew there was something and he wasn't going to ask. Hannie sighed deeply. She rested her head heavily on her hand, the heel of her palm pushing up her cheekbone, and stared at him with a weary intentness.

"Can I have till tomorrow, Ned? I want to go through it one more time. I want to be sure."

He nodded. Her words didn't leave much room for illusion. He didn't quite know how it had come to this but still he didn't want to draw back.

———•◆•———

"Just the same," Tom was saying, "there must have been something. Hannie ran a tight ship and if that was the deal she had with Andrew, there must have been something big to break it."

"Someone else?" Beth's voice came softly. Hannie stood breath-still in the hallway.

Tom snorted. "It was an arrangement, you heard her. And Andrew liked things that way. Divorce too expensive, too disruptive, liked his women as mistresses and no fancy ideas about becoming wives."

Beth's voice, softly again. Hannie couldn't catch the words.

"Wrong tree there, old girl. He'd have turned a blind eye, part of the deal. He'd only have asked for a bit of discretion."

Beth, anxious now: "Tom, I'm sure I heard a car, I'm sure she's back. It's making me nervous, talking like this."

"Nonsense, we'd have heard her coming in. Anyway, she's living off us, isn't she — using us — what're you worrying about? Have you written to Kenya lately? Might be an idea. See what happened to make Andrew dump her. Drop Martia a line, or Dora Seaton. Don't say she's staying, just that we saw her at the wedding."

"Tom, I couldn't, I really couldn't. . . ."

"I don't see why not. I don't see why you always have to be so wet about things. She'd do it in your place without so much as stopping to catch her breath."

"Oh Tom, she wouldn't."

"She damn well would. And if you think otherwise you're a bigger fool than I took you for. Write tomorrow. Don't push for an answer but make it clear you'd like one."

"I can't, you shouldn't ask, it's not right, Tom, Hannie's my friend." Beth's mutiny ended on a low wail.

Very softly, very quietly, Hannie stepped back through the paneled hallway, back through the door through which she had come. Then she stood in the darkness, waiting. Noisily she remade her entrance.

———•♦•———

HANNIE POURED another gin and set herself to go through it all again. How easy he'd been to bring to the point, she thought. A word or two here, a sentence left hanging. Ned Renvyle had rushed into the breach.

Not so easy to work the same process on herself. Especially in the long insomniac nights when she paced about her room. Already she'd been over and over it, arguing it backward and forward, all the time knowing it was so much wasted effort because the truth was you couldn't ever know. Life with another human being — marriage, call it what you would — was always more than the sum of its parts, and it was always the small unknown, unnoticed things that made it unbearable or redeemed it. Beth, worrying about sex, had seized on the least of her problems. She didn't marry for sex, though fortunately most men did.

But she didn't think it was sex that had brought Ned Renvyle to the point. Clearly he could do without it, or he'd have lived a different life. And he wasn't queer, she was sure of that. So if it wasn't sex, what was it, and why her?

Companionship most likely. And to complete his picture of himself, his life. Return to his roots, a home, a wife in it. Romantic. That was his pattern.

He'd never lived with a woman, not really, but he thought he had. That brief marriage, all those years ago. Isobel, a distant cousin, who'd become an army nurse for the war that had overrun the world. He'd met her again in India afterward, and they'd come back on the same troop ship in 1947, happy to be thrown together, a childhood friendship renewed. They'd been married not long afterward in London. Six months later she was dead. It seemed she'd gone home for a visit, this Isobel, and fallen off a horse. A hunting accident. A grim look on Ned's face as he'd said it.

Idly she worked out how old he'd been, wondered what he'd been like then. Tongue-tied, she guessed, all suppressed feeling. Twenty-four, a melodramatic age. Astonished deep down inside himself that he'd survived at all.

Funny the way he talked about Ireland as home when he'd hardly ever lived there. She never spoke of Java as home, nor Africa either, she never spoke of anywhere. She would lay money he always had that look when he spoke of Isobel. Years of habit. A candle always burning before the shrine.

He had a portrait, he'd said; she could see it in her mind's eye. Some girl with dark cloudy hair, a pale, arrogant face. His class, one of his own.

He'd been lucky. What price his precious expeditions if she'd stayed on her horse?

And he'd never remarried. Had it all gone into his journeys? Perhaps. Perhaps he had a low sex drive, perhaps he'd just done without. . . .

But he liked women, you could tell that; for all his asceticism, he liked women. Well, nothing unusual in that. Men who loved hardship often loved softness between. They just liked it earned.

Prostitutes? Possibly. It went with his class. Maybe he'd bought sex the way he'd hired porters to carry his gear? Or maybe it was married white women, the wives of the men he stayed with in out-of-the-way places.

No. She shook her head to herself, the gesture underlining the mental negative. Not other men's wives, that wouldn't be done in Ned's book, not unless they threw themselves at him. No, not then either. He'd be pompous about that, would think them predatory, be ashamed for their husbands, for himself. . . .

Hannie stopped herself, this wasn't the point, she was getting sidetracked into stupid speculation. Sex wasn't difficult. He might have odd ideas, plenty of men did, but all she had to do was find them out and pander to them. And they'd have separate bedrooms. That, too, went with his class. For pleasure there were always other men.

She brought herself back to the problem. Marriage to Ned. Or not. She walked herself around the room as the thoughts walked around in her head. She stopped, lit another cigarette, poured more gin. The house was quiet beneath her.

She could marry again in Kenya, but she'd have to take a step down, perhaps quite a big step down. She moved in a small, tight caste and her history was becoming too well known. Correction: Joss's history was becoming too well known.

And it wasn't only Joss and his reputation that worried her. It was Africa, the demise of the glory days of white colonial Africa. Which she'd lived on like a tick on a sheep's back, sucking the rich blood.

Well, that was all changing now, even South Africa no longer a sure bastion of privilege and ease. Mandela was free, apartheid was crumbling, once the factions left off quarreling and pushed together they'd be hard to stop. Time to pack your bags, Hannie, time to move on. Survivors couldn't afford to hang around to see how things panned out.

Hence this trip. Getting started was the hard bit. She could marry Ned and as Ned's wife she'd be in. After that she could take her time, look around, see what else was on offer. . . .

She walked across to the mirror and stood squarely in front of it, meeting her own eyes. Who was she kidding? She was no Jessica, tending an immaculate CV. She grinned at herself, a painful, self-conscious grin. She was getting older, less employable, already there were too many job changes. And there was Joss.

Reality. She might as well start getting used to it because this was the way it was going to be from here on in.

And if no alternative offered itself, if she had to stay with Ned?

A farm again. Well, she wouldn't starve, it would be a home for Joss. And she was older now she might settle. Who knows what you can settle to if there isn't a choice? Certainly she, Hannie, did not.

And he might not be too bad. Beth said she didn't know anything about him, but Africa was full of men like Ned Renvyle, men who found the world noisy, suburban and overcrowded, with the wrong people running things. Romantics who couldn't accept the world as it was now.

But he was decent and straight and he wouldn't be cruel. And he had a hundred and thirty acres, some of it "marginal," whatever that meant. It didn't sound much, not when you were used to Africa, but there must be enough to live on or he wouldn't be asking her. She had made herself quite clear about Joss from the start and he'd accepted it: a reasonable, fee-paying boarding school until he was eighteen.

She couldn't leave Joss where he was much longer. The school was only letting him stay on over the summer because she had written and begged them, using Andrew as her excuse, his recent death, his empty place on the board of governors, promising that she was making other arrangements.

Other arrangements. She said the words aloud, her voice full of mockery and self-disparagement. Ned was her other arrangement, the best she could do for the moment, perhaps the best she could do at all. She went for the bottle, slopped more liquid into the glass. It was nearly four in the morning, the sky had lightened, sunrise was not far off. She no longer had any assets, only a liability, it all came down to that one thing. Joss, her fear for Joss, her need to build a life that would protect him.

And how would Ned react if Joss did something again? *When* Joss did something again.

He would stand by her. That's how he was, how Andrew wasn't, despite the schools, the lineage, the family history. Ned would stand by her because that was what he'd expect of himself. That was why she had come this far with Ned. None of the other reasons mattered a damn.

She crossed to the opened window and stood with the cool air of dawn flowing around her.

Or maybe she'd let him go, take a chance on another one. . . .

With the years closing in, the mirror giving her relentlessly back to herself?

Who was she kidding, she asked herself again. He was the best she could get, so she'd take him. Against the time when she would take what she could get.

She leaned her elbows on the sill and stared out at the thinning darkness. The security lights still burned, the swimming pool glowed blue by the shrubbery, pale rectangles of light lay over the shaved grass. And beyond the lawns and walls the orange glow of habitation and the low roar of traffic that had not ceased all night.

She felt her hopelessness, the fight gone out of her. In her mind, the soft thick darkness of another continent; the great, soft stars that bloomed through the turning night. Who knows, she thought bitterly, she might have more in common with Ned Renvyle than she thought. She longed for Africa, its endlessness and space.

———•◆•———

"So Beth thinks I'm too old for you," he said. "What does Tom think?"

"He thinks I'm taking advantage of you. He thinks you'll rue the day you met me. Or something like that." She spoke carelessly, her eyes on the rows of lichened graves lining the path they walked.

Ned turned to her. She wore a dark-blue blouse and a sand-colored skirt and her feet were tanned in her leather sandals. She looked well, strolling about in the dappled churchyard, he was proud of her.

"Do you?" he asked seriously.

"I wouldn't be surprised." She grinned up at him. "Would you?"

"No," he said thoughtfully, not grinning back. "I think I wouldn't be at all surprised. We may both rue the day. Do you want to back off?"

They'd stopped in their walk to stand by a sloping gravestone. She laid her hand on its mossy back. She looked at him, her dark eyes gone distant and unreadable.

"No. Do you?"

He didn't speak for a minute.

"Oddly enough," he said, "I don't."

He smiled then. He meant it. He thought, for all their mutual warnings, that it was straightforward. He didn't realize he would come to love her.

Chapter Five

"THE MONA VULLAGH MOUNTAINS," Ned said. He waved his hand at a long blue line of hills to the right. "And those are the Comeraghs beyond."

Hannie looked. She thought she was seeing foothills. She sat waiting for the mountains to appear.

"Irish mountains are small," Ned said. "Small and blue, small and brown. You'll get used to them, once your eye adjusts they'll seem quite high."

Ned was smiling all the time now as he drove. Hannie watched these mountains that weren't mountains and said nothing. They crested a rise and below was a bay with a town built around a harbor.

"Dungarvan," Ned said, as though they'd reached somewhere significant. They drove into the town and he parked on the quay under a battered notice offering boats for hire.

"Dungarvan's our nearest town," he said. "We'll get out, take a look around, you can see where it is you'll be living."

Hannie got out. The air was sharp with the stench of fish and seaweed. She stood looking down into the harbor.

"Tidal," Ned said. She nodded.

The harbor was deep and wide and empty of water. There were beached half-deckers under the wall and four small sailing craft lying about on the muddy sands. It was quiet, all but deserted. The tide must have turned, she could hear the trickle of the water running back into the harbor, seeping in around the beached boats. Wading birds dug in the silt, a few gulls rose and fell on the moist air, a single gray heron stood watch by a lone puddle.

Smallness, quietness, soft gray light. Whatever she had expected, it hadn't been this.

"King John's castle," Ned was saying, waving his hand to the right where abandoned warehouses and high walls of dark stone crumbled against the graying sky. "Important town in the fourteenth century."

The weather was breaking up, the day going cold. He walked her through side streets, past rain-stained, stone-built houses, often dilapidated or deserted, the slates off, the gutters full of weeds, saplings sprouting from the chimneys. Away from the harbor the town revived. The main square looked almost prosperous, the tall, elegant old houses painted up in pastel shades, the clear colors lending them a raffish, down-at-heel gaiety as they leaned in together, disdaining the street life below.

Hannie stood on the pavement surveying the shops and businesses. A bank or two, a heating supplier, a gents' shoe shop, a building society. The rest was pubs, take-aways, small plain grocers with not much in them.

Nowhere you'd want to linger, nothing you'd want to buy.

It had started well, she reminded herself. Setting off last night there'd been the expectation, the excitement and flurry of departure, standing in the darkness by the packed car she had felt her spirits soar.

It was movement, the release in movement, the scrunch of feet on the night gravel, the map and sandwiches and torch lying ready on her seat.

"Oh Hannie," Beth had wailed, "I feel as though you're going away for good, as though I'll never ever see you again."

And Hannie had laughed, free at last of this house, this friendship, free of herself as she had had to be here.

It continued well. She liked the night drive, the 3:00 A.M. boat, the snatched sleep on the cramped seats of the crowded lounge, the dawn light seeping in from the sea through the uncurtained windows. They had stood together on the deck as the land drew close; Ned, eager, showing her Ireland, pointing out the Wexford landmarks.

The ship had moved slowly in, long unbroken ripples fanning out across the sheened water with its passing. Hannie had stared at a herring gull perched on the railing, its unblinking yellow eye, the red stain marking its long hooked beak. It slid off as the ferry pulled in, dropped to the water, swept high again to join with a clamoring cloud. It was a perfect morning, the air vivid with salt, the empty harbor pearly and pale in the shining stillness.

They'd stopped when they got to Waterford. They bought breakfast, then walked along the quays inspecting the trawlers and tugs and the big cattle boats with their foreign names and foreign flags loading up with hay. She'd seen worse, she thought confidently. She liked the busy port, the wide river, the tugs and buoys and pilot boats. There was a world beyond this place.

A buoyant mood. Standing here in Dungarvan, it was hard to remember the feeling. She had fallen into the old trap, she told herself, the trap of thinking that once she got through the thing in front of her then all the rest would somehow be all right.

And she had got through. She had found Ned, she had married him, she'd embarked on another life in another world.

But had she thought enough about that world?

Ned touched her arm. She woke from her reverie and followed him back to the car.

A few minutes out of Dungarvan and the town, such as it was, might never have been. They headed north away from the coast, each time leaving the road they were on for one that was narrower, more winding and more potholed. The hedges closed in. They were high and dense and thickened with full-grown trees. Where the hedges broke there were old walls, long crumbling stretches breached like broken teeth in a rotting mouth, great ivy-burdened trees pressing up against them from behind.

Sometimes there were neither walls nor hedges, but little low-lying fields and boggy stretches of rock and rushes. Sometimes there were farms, the houses hidden, the outbuildings blank against the roadsides. Once or twice a bit of a field held a gaggle of unfinished bungalows. Then hedges and trees again for miles, their high wild branches cutting off the sky. Hannie sat very quietly in her seat, looking, saying nothing. She felt as if she were burrowing down, away from life as she knew it, back into some overgrown and forgotten past. Ned, sitting so close beside her, noticed nothing but his own emotions at returning.

"They'll want to know your maiden name and who your mother was," he said suddenly. "It's so that they can work out who you are."

She looked at him, but didn't speak.

"It isn't personal," he said, "don't take offense. They'll just want to find the connection."

"What connection?"

"That their mother's second cousin had a house off your great-aunt's brother-in-law in Kildare in 1926. Or better still, a horse." Ned laughed, pleased with himself, her bewilderment. "Ignore it, they'll lose interest once they find you're not from here at all."

Hannie watched his profile as he drove. She didn't know what he was talking about and she didn't care, but she noticed his anxiety and his excitement. At first she thought they were for her, were about arriving here and having her see the life he wanted her to share. Then she saw that it was something altogether simpler. He was nearly home, in the place he liked best, where he liked himself best.

She saw that she was the one being shown the bride.

A figure walking the road ahead called a sheep dog in to heel. Ned slowed and raised his hand in salute. The man saluted back.

"Best not mention the previous marriages," Ned said to her suddenly. "Catholic country, and all that." She looked at him sharply but he was edging the car around a deep bend and over a little bridge.

"This is it," he said, "this is home."

———◆———

THE HOUSE WAS BUILT of rough stone, rendered with plaster, and sat in a muddle of yards and sheds. It was long and narrow, with a newer wing built on at right angles, mature trees around it and a short shrubby drive to the road. The whole impression was not so much shabby as workmanlike and a bit down-at-heel. Probably mid-nineteenth century, Ned said, though he wasn't sure, he wasn't much interested in houses except for the big Georgian piles of his class and childhood. It was her domain, he said, she could explore it thoroughly herself and do what she liked within reason.

As soon as he'd done with the house Ned had taken her down to the river. It was tidal here, he explained. At low tide the pull of the sea all but emptied the river. A thick silt of pale mud called a slob lay wherever the water had been.

Step on to this slob, he said, and you went to your knees before you stopped sinking. Bring the boat in on an ebbed tide and you waded through mud like the Somme.

He had pointed to the middle of the water where it was flat and almost still, the current there curiously stationary. That was seawater pushing back up the river, meeting the river's flow, he said, the one briefly canceling out the other. Then the stronger sea-flow won and by high tide you'd think the river ran backward. There was six or eight feet of a drop between tides, and except at the lowest point of the ebb the water was brackish with salt.

It seemed he couldn't get enough of showing and explaining. There was his boat, called a "punt," on a very long mooring because of the tidal drop. Here was the "cut" where it lay, a little man-made creek sliced at right angles into the bank.

You had to know what you were doing at every moment on this river, he said. The ebb tide was worse than the flood, the rip of the current made fierce by the pull of the sea.

The near bank where they stood was rough grassland falling off into rushes, grazed by ambling sheep. At the river's edge a few saplings clung, ash and alder and willow, their roots knotting themselves frantically into the eroding soil. A path wandered between meadow and water.

She stood with her arms folded and her feet in the boggy ground. A light chill wind tugged at her skirt and hurried the sky. The weak sun shone in a vague glory, luminous behind the moving cloud. A squall of rain blew over, pocking the water, and was gone. The river went smooth and pewter-colored and white gulls dropped out of the sky and dipped to kiss other white gulls waiting under the water. Rings of black light spread out where they touched.

She looked across the sweep of the water. The far bank was bosomy with great, still trees, their deep green just bronzed with late summer. Downriver these trees thickened into dense woodland. Upriver the trees thinned and the riverbank lost itself in stretches of tall flagged reeds that moved with the wind.

You could see the house from where they stood. Its raggedy outline of roofs and buildings peered over the hummocky meadow like an old woman too anxious to see to be altogether discreet about not being seen.

The river flooded easily, Ned said. Heavy rain, big tides, the waters ran fast and furious over the banks and into the woods and the meadows. That's why the house was built up and back like that. He was proud of this strong dangerous river and its complexities, she heard it in his voice and in his words.

Hannie looked and listened but said little. She was tired now from the night journey and the stress of expectation. It was all smaller but oddly wilder than she had expected. She hadn't grasped what he'd been saying about seas and tides. How could she, what had such things to do with this place? It seemed so lost and inland — how could so short a journey bring her so far away from anywhere?

Chapter Six

NIAMH MOVED DOWN THE WASHING LINE, feeling the clothes as she passed, lifting a shirt here, the leg of a pair of jeans there, pressing the fabric to her cheek to test the stage of drying. She liked to iron straight from the line, liked the burning off of the last damp, the slight glaze, the smell of the fresh, folded clothes that she carried to the hot press. As a student she hadn't ironed, it was hardly done to be creaseless in art school, but left to herself she liked ironing and she liked shaking out pressed trousers in the morning and pushing her long arms into smoothed and folded T-shirts.

Nothing dry enough yet. The afternoon was damp and still, it smelled of grass and leaves and growing things. She ran her hands down her sides, down the narrowing-in of her waist, until they rested firm on her hips.

She stood so, liking the feel of her hips under her hands, absently inspecting the swelling apples on the mossed tree behind the line. Further back, on the straggle of lawn that was more like a field, Ned had planted six young apple trees, old-fashioned varieties local to the area, the strains carefully mixed for pollination.

"Worth the trouble," he'd said to her. "All this homogenization." He'd shaken his head in disapproval of the easy-grow, heavy-cropping varieties the garden centers sold.

It was like Ned to select carefully, to plant carefully leaving the right distance between each tree, to stake and to label. He was thorough in everything to do with the farm, never just settling for what was to hand. He'd get an idea, read up on it, ring someone who knew, then he'd write off and order exactly what it was that he'd decided on.

Often as not her father was the someone-who-knew whom Ned consulted. Her father liked Ned, he was considered capable of learning and forgiven his inexperience.

Her father would most likely have heard by now about this marriage, Niamh thought. Ned's latest acquisition, and one he certainly hadn't been consulted on. She'd maybe not phone home for a bit or she'd get the benefit of his opinion.

Niamh bent to pick fallen pegs out of the springy grass. A widow with a teenage son who'd been living in Kenya, Mrs. Coady had said. Not African but Dutch.

Afrikaans?

No, not Afrikaans and not Dutch from Holland, either. Some island that used to be Dutch but wasn't anymore. Part of Indonesia. God knows what she was, a mix-up like that. Never been to Ireland in her life before.

They'd said Hawaii in the post office. Niamh had been in buying stamps and they were all talking about it, the old people tut-tutting and the young ones enjoying it: Ned Renvyle had a woman half his age and he hadn't married her either.

A young lad with a lick of black hair falling over his eyes and a pale, clever face said he'd seen her. He was down by Haydn's cross, he said, bringing in an old cow, and she'd come around a bend in the road with nothing on her but a grass skirt and a big long loop of flowers around her neck.

Ned Renvyle had her from a newspaper ad, he said. And there were more where she came from.

The whole post office was sniggering but the postmistress had spotted Niamh out of the corner of her eye. She threw out a hard warning look, someone had jabbed the black-haired lad with an elbow and they'd all gone silent. Later when Niamh was coming out of Foley's with the paper, she'd seen the same boy and he'd started rolling his hips as if he'd a hula hoop on them. Niamh had grinned and he'd grinned back and then she'd remembered herself and looked away.

An old love, Niamh guessed. He'd probably known her for years, loved her for years, the husband's death Ned's opportunity. In her mind Niamh saw a letter in a wooden drawer in a woman's desk, a foreign stamp on the envelope and petals pressed into its fading pages.

Funny the way these clichéd images came up strong like that every time, she thought. Funny the way they kept their potency despite the tired and corny symbols. If you painted them you'd be laughed out, and yet they had something — a fragrance — all those women hoping and dreaming down all those years.

Maybe if you made it like a tiny installation you would get away with it. Drawers from an old desk, letters falling out of them, flowers and sealing wax and broad-nibbed handwriting. Everything real and old, the colors enhanced, a bit over the top.

But not by itself, by itself you'd never throw off the cliché.

A whole show of clichés, that's what you'd need, she thought. Women's dreams of love set in the narrow context of the lives they'd lived.

She could see the roof of the house and a slice of the gable-end wall from where she stood now, a column of smoke from each of the chimneys rising straight up into the still air.

The new wife, lighting fires to air the place. Mrs. Coady would be offended, she'd lit them all the day before, and anyway the place wasn't damp.

She was offended herself, she decided. This little romance-fantasy she'd been dreaming up was only a way of pretending to herself that she wasn't.

If only he hadn't gone and done this.

And if he had to do it, if only he'd married someone his own age. She made herself stop. She supposed you could be as lonely at seventy as at any other age.

It was no good, she was too angry. He was old, he had had his life, why did he have to be grabbing for more?

Niamh tucked back a loop of the dark straight hair that was working loose from the knot at the back of her head. Should she go over now, she wondered, or should she leave them alone a bit longer? The uncertainty was making her anxious, destroying her pleasure in the washing line and the tree. She didn't want anything to change now, just as she'd settled in, just as she'd fallen in love with her little house and its raggedy garden, just as she was doing what she wanted to do. These last weeks had been as close to perfection as she could have imagined.

She would go over this evening, she decided. She would take the fresh loaf but not the wildflowers, the bunch she'd picked before breakfast, now drooping in a jam jar on the table.

To hell with it, she'd go now and get it over with. She straightened up out of her indecision, lifted her arms and stretched, her back arched, her round breasts in the blue T-shirt pushing forward like the figurehead of a ship.

————•◆•————

"She's only just got here," Ned was protesting into the phone. "No, I'm not hiding her, of course I'll bring her over, but not yet." He was looking at Hannie. Hannie was shaking her head.

"No, she's not sick and she hasn't got three legs." He was laughing into the phone. "Perhaps in a day or two." He looked at Hannie again but he was still getting a negative. "When she's got used to the place, found her feet a little . . . No, you don't need to ring again, I'll ring back as soon as she's ready." He put the receiver down.

"It hasn't stopped since we got home," he told Niamh. "It's like Christmas, everyone ringing up, asking us over."

He sounded embarrassed and pleased at the same time. Niamh glanced at Hannie. She was smoking and drinking tea, a full ashtray on the table beside her.

"They want to get a look at the new wife," she said, addressing Niamh for the first time. Her voice was light, her eyes mocking.

"It's only natural," Ned said, a little defensively.

"Of course, it is," she agreed. "But it's for their benefit, not mine. They can wait till I'm ready."

"I doubt they'll do that," Ned said. "If we don't go there, they'll come over here, you'll see. Might as well do as they want, go and drink their whiskey, it's the same difference."

Niamh's loaf lay on the table beside Hannie's elbow. Its greaseproof wrapper was unopened. She wished she'd left it sitting on her own table, the flowers drooping beside it.

"It's a lovely house, isn't it?" She heard herself and cringed. It was a plain spare house with an ugly roof and not much grace to it. She sounded stupid and overeager to please.

Hannie reached across for the teapot. "It needs repainting."

Ned looked surprised. "Does it? I put a new roof on last year. Everything stripped right down, new beams, cement tiles, it's completely sound. Plaster's a bit stained, I suppose, but it'll do a few years yet."

"Inside," Hannie said.

"People go on about slate, can't understand why. Cement's tougher and cheaper."

Niamh opened her mouth to protest and closed it again. Ned was a funny mixture. In ways he was almost cool, and then he'd come out with stuff that would have shamed even her father.

"This kitchen's dark," Hannie said deliberately. "Another window would make a difference, don't you think? In the end wall, perhaps?" She was looking at Niamh, challenging her to agree. Niamh couldn't believe she was being hooked in so fast.

"It will all seem dark," she said stupidly. Now they both looked at her. "Ireland, I mean. After Africa. Mrs. Coady said you came from Africa."

"I was born in Java," Hannie said. "But it's many years since I lived there."

Niamh stared. She couldn't think what this woman was doing in Ned's kitchen, nor could she think of anything else to say to her. A few minutes more and she'd go. Leave them to argue about the house or his friends or whatever else they were into.

She'd draw those flowers, she thought. Try and get that half-alive, half-dead look wildflowers had when you picked them and put them in water. The I-can't-thrive look. And maybe she'd look up Java in the old school atlas that she'd brought from home.

———•◆•———

"You DIDN'T mention a cottage with a tenant."

"It was empty." Ned was surprised to feel that he was justifying himself. "It needed a tenant. Fires lit, windows opened, that sort of thing. No damp course, you see." He put down the paper and smiled patiently at Hannie. "Ireland's not like Africa."

"Niamh," Hannie said as though trying the word on her tongue. "Eve with an N. Who is she — this almost-Eve, and what's she doing here?"

"N-I-A-M-H." Ned spelled it out. "It's an Irish name, nothing to do with Eve, or not that I know of. Her father farms near here, he's by way of being a friend. And he's been a great help to me, so when he asked if I knew of anywhere to let . . ."

"You thought of the cottage and it suited everyone?"

"Exactly. Three birds with the one stone, so to speak. A favor for John, a tenant for me and a place for the girl till she finds her feet."

"It's a strange place for a good-looking girl to come to find her feet," Hannie said. Her voice was neutral. "Or is Ireland unlike Africa in that way, too?"

Ned smiled. "No, not in that way, but she wants to be an artist and she needs a quiet place to live and paint. John's against it, but he doesn't want to play the heavy-handed father. He thinks if she has a go she'll find for herself that it's no way to live."

"Enough rope to hang herself," Hannie said. "And you don't agree with him?"

"No, I suppose I don't. It's outside their ken, painting, she's stepping out of their world and he's afraid for her. He says she's an odd sort of girl, too soft for the farm, the sort who'll be on at you and on at you to save a calf then when it can't be saved she'll give you no peace till it's killed. Can't bear the waiting in watching it die. Well, the girl's by way of being John's calf, the youngest, the gentlest. They wanted a steady sort of life for her but when she wanted to go to the art school in Dublin they didn't stand against her. They thought she could train and then teach in a country school near home till she married. . . ." Ned trailed off, shrugging his shoulders.

"And she has other plans?"

"Exactly. John says he'll pay for a year while she has a go. When the year's up she can do teacher training. He says she's a good girl at heart and too responsible to be idling. All she needs is a little time and she'll see things his way."

"And you want to help her to be a painter?"

Ned nodded. "I'm looking out for commissions for her. People's houses, children, that sort of idea. Things that will help her to pay her way while she learns her trade. I want her at least to have the chance to try. She's a good tenant," he finished defensively. "She's turned that cottage inside out, everything's been stripped and aired and washed to an inch of its life. She's a worker all right."

"That is not quite the same as a painter."

"Perhaps not. Time will tell." Suddenly he didn't want to discuss it anymore. He picked up the paper. He liked Niamh, was charmed by her lovely, old-fashioned face and her quiet, serious ways. But more than that, he liked young people who dreamed of making their own lives in their own fashion. Suddenly he felt a little foolish and he wasn't quite sure why. He tried not to mind but his pleasure in Niamh's presence was diminished.

Chapter Seven

THE INCOMING TIDE WAS ALMOST FULL, the river ran wide and dark, its surface swollen with little eddies and currents that creased and dimpled the water. The great trees on the far bank leaned forward and dipped their green boughs in the river. They made with the living waters a closed circle of surrender and completeness. At night there were no lights here, no sounds but the river's flow, the night birds, the scufflings and death cries of small animals. The valley had an atmosphere that was dense and secret, knowing nothing but itself.

Human absence. But an absence altogether unlike that of Africa where men and beasts moved light as thought across the land. This absence was more like presence, it conspired with the centuries of human occupation, denying their passing. Everyone who had ever lived in this valley was still here, still moved in its light, still lived in its emanations of water and land. Standing here was like stepping back to meet them, Hannie thought, stepping back into a past that was also present and future. The place was thronged and dense with lives lived.

A little evening wind had got up. The river shone and shifted, flakes of white light seemed to float on the moving water. Standing beside it, Hannie remembered another place and another river, a greener, sunnier river where it merged into the sea.

It was the place, she decided, the lostness of it. The sense that fatally she must be taken in or rejected and no compromise offered, that the life here would close over her or push her out.

The fifth time a bride, she remembered the first time. Suddenly, and with no warning, in a country more remote from that Indonesian trading station than even the flatlands of Holland, she was beset by her memories.

Piet Boonjes stood before her. Piet Boonjes, solid, Dutch, an island trader; the age those years ago that she was now. Piet, his small blue eyes, his fatty freckled shoulders, his sagging dugs and sagging belly and legs gone skinny, handing her money to add to the store of cash she'd been skimming from his takings for the past two years.

His money, her cut. But mostly she hadn't bothered to justify it like that. She'd just stolen what she could, taking care it was never so much that he'd notice.

But he'd noticed every penny and when the time came for her to leave he'd known how much she had and given her more.

"Tell me where you want to go, Hannie." He'd held out a bundle of dirty notes. "I will speak to the captain and arrange your passage. Put this money with the rest, you'll have enough now for a decent start."

She had taken the money without looking up. She couldn't, it was too far beyond her comprehension. His acceptance of her, his acceptance of life. She couldn't believe he'd just open his hands and let go of her, letting his money go with her.

He'd laughed at her, but not unkindly. "I thought a year at most but you've stayed two, Hannie. A girl like you, less than half my age. Take it, it's not a gift, it's yours, I owe it to you. On this deal I can truly say I haven't lost."

She'd looked up then, meeting his eyes in his round clown's face with its comic-somber air of burden and sadness. The tufts of gray hair stuck out all around like a small boy just climbed from his bed.

"Go, since you must, but write to me from time to time. I will miss you, but only a little. I will have compensations. . . ."

He had always had compensations, though she hadn't at first noticed or understood this. Half-caste children ran around the tea gardens. Benign watchers followed her course, knowing she could not last. Everyone knew, even him. Only herself thinking it some secret she'd hatched and tended alone.

Piet was Indonesian-born Dutch, a hard, shrewd trader, with kindness only for women and natives and small children, shunning the fellow Europeans he despised. He had taught her books and storekeeping, who to cheat and who not to cheat, how to deal. Her mother had brokered the marriage and he had acceded to it; she saw now that she had merely played her cast part. Piet had married her without expectation, she saw that too. As he might have taken a bale of cloth against his judgment. Wanting it, knowing it would not sell.

Her passage was arranged and did not cost her. She hadn't written, though he'd sent money to a *poste restante* in Jo'burg those first years. She'd thought of him, but mostly only when she refused a man. In the end the letter she'd sent had asked for a divorce.

The letter back didn't come from Piet. She could marry whom she liked, it seemed, for Piet was dead.

She was astonished then; somehow it hadn't occurred to her that Piet could die. He'd been in a Japanese camp in the war and she knew he would not easily let life go.

"There's a time when it's nothing to die," he had said. "You're so weak and the door stands open and all around they're walking through that door. But if you come back to life after that, it's a different story. My God, you hold life so tight in your hand, you'll never loosen your grip."

His clenched fist had beaten softly on the flesh of his thigh as he spoke and his narrowed eyes had stared furiously ahead of him at nothing. Hannie recognized what she was seeing. Her mother had been in a Japanese camp for women. Her mother, too, had survived.

She was sorry then, for herself as much as for him. She had lost the last anchor mooring her to her first life. She had lived these months without it, never even knowing it had gone.

Sometimes in the early evenings, Piet had gone with her to the river to bathe. He would stand waist-deep in the sunny green waters, watching the shadows of fishes move over the sand. The fish floated above, bright and translucent, attached as by wavering threads to these more-real, darker, deeper selves. She would stand beside him, watching the shapes on the sunlit, sandy bottom. He would point and chuckle, he never tired of it. It was his indulgence, his gentlest time.

Would it come to that for her too? Could she ever be so satisfied?

She'd been nineteen then, her whole life ahead of her. Those shut-away years with Piet had been painful with impatience, but not with fear. Now here she was with Ned in just such a closed and forgotten place. Aging, with no money with which to escape, no place to escape to. And no hope for the future to make it easier to bear.

But also with Joss. They were seeing the school next week, she wanted that done before he arrived from Africa. Get him in on Ned's clout before they smelled a rat and asked for an interview.

Briefly she acknowledged to herself the mistake she had made in coming here. Then she set the knowledge aside. She turned from the river and walked back up to the house.

Chapter Eight

MRS. COADY THREW THE SHEET out from herself like a sail thrown to the wind. Hannie caught it with practiced ease. They settled it onto the bed, smoothing out the starched whiteness. The slanting sun laid a window of soft light across it. The window repeated itself on the blanket they threw over it, and onto the next and the next.

The same sun pulled rich gleams out of the polished furniture. The two women bent and stretched, lifted and spread, the house quiet and empty around them.

She knows what she's doing, Mrs. Coady thought, it's a pleasure to work with her. They'd been at it all day now and there was the rhythm of harmony between them.

Her son was expected, they were changing things around, preparing a room for him. They seemed to have done nothing but change things around since she arrived.

Move this, Mrs. Coady, move that. If she needs a dressing table, she must have one. Whatever she wants, Mrs. Coady, whatever it is that women need.

She'd shifted things here and shifted things there, his mother's dressing table from the house in Fermoy, the picture from the study that she'd taken a fancy to, the curtains with the knots of faded flowers folded away in the attic, now unfolded, washed, pressed, hung.

Mrs. Coady knew the signs. She'd see her walking around the house looking, and then she'd be walking around with him, pointing here and pointing there, planning. There was to be a new bay in the drawing room and a glass-covered porch by the back door and the kitchen was to be opened out to take in the two little end rooms with a window looking onto the garden. The new garden that Joe Casey's digger was maneuvering into being. And last week an automatic washing machine had arrived from Waterford.

Ambrose Power, builder and odd-job man, said as how he might as well move in. "Fair play to the women," he added hastily. "I never saw a bachelor change a house though he lived in it sixty year. If it wasn't for the women I'd hang up me hat and stay home."

There'd been no money before. Only for roofs. Always had a thing about good snug roofs, had Ned Renvyle. Anything else you could whistle for.

"Can't have what you can't pay for, Mrs. Coady," he'd say. Which was news to her. And there was no shifting him until this one turned up and persuaded the money out of him.

"It's not that he's mean, exactly, Mrs. Coady," she'd said, swishing the dregs of her coffee around in the mug and knocking it back.

"It's just he's got out of the habit of spending. It may even be it's a habit he never picked up in the first place." She stopped, looked thoughtful, and then spoke again in that voice that was not foreign like the Dutch and the Germans, but not English either and certainly not Irish. You wouldn't know, listening to her, where it was she came from at all.

"Still, it's never too late to teach an old dog new tricks, now is it?" she was saying. "And I wouldn't say he'd had much of an example, living around here?"

"No example at all," Mrs. Coady agreed. "Unless it's a horse they'd be wanting."

"They" meant his class, the Anglo-Irish, who lived in the great moldering houses scattered about the valley. This one never pretended to be one of them, she never pretended to be anything. No airs and graces to her, but a distance like a wall when she'd a mind to it. She'd sit you down and she'd be talking or you'd be talking and the next thing she was somewhere else altogether and you'd be left hanging there, the ladder pulled away, the sick feel of empty space under you. You never knew where you were with her.

Any more than his friends did when they came calling in their Wellington boots and their padded jackets and their old cars held together with bits of twine. It just depended how the mood took her. He didn't say anything. He was keeping his head down, ignoring the talk, pretending it wasn't happening.

But he was disappointed when she wasn't how he wanted her, you could see that. Well, he might as well get used to the feeling. She was like a wrong horse. One minute all pretty ways and gentle as you please and the next away off with herself and no holding her.

She was no one's, all right.

He looked a fool, standing there beside her, and he'd look a bigger fool before he was through with her. It was hard to watch — a decent straight sort of man as he was. He was proud of himself and proud of her still, for all she wouldn't behave for him.

They were finishing up the room now, she looking around, checking that everything was just so. It looked well. She'd had the broken sash on the window fixed and the chimney swept and she'd painted the walls and the ceiling herself. She'd sanded and restained the floor and waxed the boards until they shone. She wasn't afraid of dirtying her hands when she'd a mind to, you could say that for her, if you said nothing else.

It was funny she'd chosen this room though, away down the end of the corridor and looking out over the back field. And funny she wanted a school up there in the North, and no bringing him home at weekends and half-terms until he got a bit used to the way of things here. The empty room at the front of the house got the sun in the morning and longer into the day. There was to be a fire lit in here, for the boy was coming from Kenya and would have to adjust to the climate. Fine, settled weather they were having, and she always on about damp and cold. What would she say when winter came, what would she make of February?

Mrs. Coady had asked for a photo but she'd said she had none.

No photo, no stories, and no great rush bringing the lad home from Africa, either.

She was sorry she'd asked, she wouldn't do it again, she'd only opened her mouth out of kindness, pitying Hannie's strangeness in a strange place. Whoever heard of a woman with no picture of her own son?

Chapter Nine

HANNIE WATCHED THE NEW LIFE shaping up around her. She smoked more, said little. At least now she could smoke where she liked, when she liked. Sometimes it seemed the only compensation.

Ned also watched. He'd been pleased by her interest in the house until he realized she was serious in her talk of alterations. New windows here, walls knocked down there, floors torn up and replaced. Now. Not some time in the future when it suited. His pleasure quickly turned to apprehension.

At first he'd tried to warn her. It wasn't easy getting building done in Ireland, he said. Especially not fidgety bits of alterations, when the builder couldn't see what was wrong with the way it was to begin with. He'd start all right, but when a job came up on the farm he'd tack a bit of polythene over the hole in your wall and go off and attend to it. Priorities were priorities. When a better job came up he'd be gone for a month, calling now and again to say he'd be with you the next day for sure.

"I've dealt with natives all my life," she said.

His heart sank at the statement. He wondered how many fences he would have to mend, how many hard-won understandings he would have to renegotiate. He didn't look forward to the process. As he had learned not to look forward to introducing her to his friends and neighbors. Not that it always went wrong. Sometimes, for no reason he could see, she would decide she liked someone, or that they were worth an effort. And she'd leave them dazzled and amazed as she had him. But he never knew what to expect.

Ambrose Power seemed to like her. Joe Casey traded cigarettes with her and told her things that made her laugh. When they didn't come she didn't seem surprised. Watching her, it began to dawn on him that she didn't need to learn the ways of the country. She wasn't particularly sympathetic or patient. It was more that she was like that herself.

For Hannie the activity of the building work was enough. It kept her occupied, kept her from brooding too much on the place and on what she had done to her life and to Joss's. She refused to think about Ned, though she knew that she wasn't as he wanted her to be, she knew he was disappointed. Tough. He'd just have to get used to her the way she was. She had put so much effort into reassuring him, into appearing lighthearted when she didn't feel it. At least now they were married she could stop all that. Besides, she was doing up his house for him, he had nothing to complain about.

JOSS LOOKED TALLER, older; it was a shock. Somehow in her mind she must have lopped off a few inches, dropped a year or two. Babied him.

So he'd seem easier to manage, more amenable to her needs and wishes?

He hadn't seen her, or maybe he had and she just couldn't see him seeing her for the Ray-Ban wraparound look. He was wheeling his luggage trolley slowly out through Arrivals. Fair hair, gray cotton sweater, off-white trousers, and those black mirror-sunglasses, very appropriate for Cork airport. He looked cold and tense and tired underneath the tan.

Which meant he'd be angry and aggressive with her. She felt herself flooded with tenderness and dread in equal parts. Thank God she'd persuaded Ned to stay at home.

"Of course I'll drive you, you don't know the way."

"I'll find the way, Ned, it'll be good for me to begin to get to know my way around."

"You might break down. The Volkswagen's not reliable anymore, it needs handling."

"I'll learn that, too."

Ned had walked across the kitchen, stared out of the window, then walked back and stood over her.

"I ought to be there with you when he arrives, Hannie," he said. "Make sure he knows he's welcome."

"He hasn't seen me for two months and he's been traveling all night and half yesterday. You can make him welcome when he gets here." She had spoken carefully and reasonably, as though addressing an over-persistent child. Finally he had accepted her refusal.

And all the way here there'd been the tenderness and the dread that Joss inspired in her these days. An aching tenderness, a compound of cherishing and love and pity. The dread was simpler.

She had tried to think clearly while she still had the chance. What was she going to tell him if he pressed her? A firm line? That this was it, the future, whether he liked it or not, and he'd better start getting used to it?

But if he was vulnerable and frightened, if he pleaded with her, saying it was his life too? If he wanted her to reassure him, to promise not to make them stay here if he hated it? What would she say then?

Would she crack and comfort him and say it was the best that she could manage? That it was only to be going on with, that it might not be forever?

She'd anticipated it backward and forward, taut as a bowstring with the strain.

"Hallo, Mother." He took his glasses off, pecked her on the cheek, looked at her out of his light-blue eyes, put them on again. "What have you done with the geriatric?"

———•◆•———

THE FINE WEATHER PERSISTED — days of hazy gold sunlight and warm sweet air. The river moved against the great still trees and the fields swam in the dreamy light. To the north the blue mounds of the Comeraghs lay drowsy and heaped.

Everyone smiled like idiots and sighed and said over and over how lovely it was. Hannie thought they'd taken leave of their senses. Joss shivered in his cotton clothes, refusing the woolens that she'd bought for him. He walked the farm and the riverbanks without comment and spent long hours in his room. The mirror sunglasses he never left off.

Joss hardly spoke in Ned's company. He was well mannered and replied readily enough when directly questioned, but somehow the end of his answer was also the end of the conversation.

Ned let him be and did not press him. If Joss wanted to take his time and get to know him slowly, that was understandable. He approved of old-fashioned manners; he was almost relieved the boy wasn't a chatterer. He supposed Joss and his mother talked when they were alone together, and in time they would learn to accept him, too. Meanwhile the boy was only settling in and everything was strange to him. Ned set himself to patience.

He did very well, or he thought he did, interfering only when it came to the wearing of sunglasses at the table. He requested discreetly through Hannie that meals be eaten without them. She looked at him steadily, saying nothing. He felt her will against him. The next day Joss sat down to lunch, removed the glasses and laid them on the table to his right. Hannie looked at her plate. When the meal was over and the chairs pushed back, Joss picked up the dark glasses wordlessly and replaced them on the bridge of his nose.

After that Joss always removed them for meals with a careful ostentation. Ned stubbornly refused to think his request unreasonable, but he found himself disconcerted by the expressionlessness of his stepson's revealed blue eyes. He began to wish the glasses back in place.

Chapter Ten

"THEY'RE PROTECTED," Niamh said, looking up from her stance on her hunkers at Joss. "You can't just kill it and get it stuffed, it's illegal."

"So?" Joss sneered out the word.

Niamh flushed. If you said illegal someone always let on you were chicken. And if you said cruel, they let on you were soft.

Bad move either way with a weirdo like Joss: words like that only encouraged him.

The small owl in Joss's tight hands roused itself suddenly and struggled frantically in his grasp. It lunged at him with its beak but he held on, his knuckles showing white through his tanned skin, the blood springing up where the beak had struck home. It subsided. Joss didn't loosen his hold for a moment. Despite herself, Niamh was impressed.

"We'll have less of that," Joss said to the owl, his voice low and reassuring. "We don't want to be damaging ourselves, do we? Nor spoiling our pretty feathers?"

He stroked at it awkwardly with his forefinger, still keeping the vise-tight grip.

"There's a whole long future ahead to be thinking of. Posterity, presentation. All that shite. Think of a nice glass case on the wall in Joss's bedroom, eh? It's not going to look very good now, is it, owl? All this flaffing about, breaking things."

"Danno won't touch it if you kill it," Niamh said flatly. "He won't stuff an owl that hasn't died naturally."

"But maybe it *will* die naturally, Niamh," Joss replied. "Maybe it'll starve to death on account of its poor broken wing." He laughed softly, still stroking the bird with his finger, then looked up into Niamh's tight face.

"Of course it won't starve to death, stupid. What would be the point of that? A mangy poxy little owl that looks like it just flew out of Belsen? Squinting at you out of its glass case? Towit, towoo, a merry owl. I-am-the-ghost-of-a-Joss-starved-owl."

Joss made his eyebrows go round and raised and his small mouth pouted forward with his owl sounds. He looked so funny, Niamh laughed.

"Towoo, towoo, towoo, Niamh! What a merry way to scare yourself shitless in the small hours, eh . . . ?" Joss laughed, Niamh couldn't stop, their young fresh voices blithe and easy in the sunshine.

Hannie, flattened against the byre wall, ears stretched for every nuance of the conversation, sighed with relief and let her head fall back to rest on the warm stone. He wanted to talk to Niamh, that was it. That was what all the circling and inspecting had been about, the signs that she knew of old, the small details of obsession that she had to be constantly on the watch for. He had wanted to attract Niamh's attention.

And now it was done, and they were there together, Joss sitting on an old plank set across two drums, the bird in his hands, his back against the byre wall, Niamh squatting on her hunkers beside him.

Ned was wrong in supposing that Joss talked much to Hannie. Joss talked to no one, had talked to no one for years as far as his mother could see. But this not-talking didn't mean detachment or indifference. For stretches — sometimes long stretches — Joss was with her, as silent and close as her own shadow. Then suddenly he'd be off, his needs driving him, his attention totally elsewhere. The process was invisible, psychic not physical, but of an intensity that made her feel almost deranged. What she did know — instinctively, unmistakably — was the precise moment of his psychic arrival somewhere else.

Not half an hour earlier she had known it. She had stood in the yard in the empty sunshine and as surely as she knew the color of his hair she had known that it had happened, that Joss had stopped circling and had settled.

She didn't know where, she never knew where. He might have fallen down a well, he might have drowned himself in the river, he might have killed someone. She had stood there, quite motionless, a flat empty feeling of despair settling back inside her, a rat settling into its familiar nest. Then her ear had caught voices and she'd followed those voices around the side of the byre.

"Take it to Danno," Niamh was saying now. "He'll put a splint on its wing, he knows about owls, he'll save it if he can."

And then he'll release it back into the wild, she thought, keeping the thought to herself. Joss was weird all right, he might have other plans, but then again he might not. He knew about birds, you could tell that from the way he held the owl, the way he was liking looking at it, the same as she was. This talk of his might all be an act.

———— ◆ ————

"Who is this Danno that Niamh speaks of?" asked Hannie.

"Danno? Taxidermist. Poacher. Lives in a sort of shed by the river. Does a bit of this and a bit of that. Odd fish, Danno. Why?"

"Joss found an owl with a broken wing. Niamh says he must take it to Danno, that Danno will fix it."

"I expect he will. And if he doesn't fix it he can always stuff it. Badly. Danno stuffs everything badly, but he doesn't seem to notice. No more do his clients, they keep taking him things, James Beresford's pleased as punch with a pike Danno did for him, doesn't seem to notice how grotesque it looks."

"Pike are supposed to look grotesque, are they not?"

"Frightening-grotesque, not lumpy-grotesque. How do you know about pike, Hannie? Don't have them in Kenya, do they?"

"Andrew had one on the wall. A family heirloom from some Scottish river."

They were sitting outside on a bench by the wall, drinking coffee in the hazy Sunday morning sunlight. It was quiet and still, a day off from Ambrose Power and his sledges and drills. Joe Casey's digger had finished its work and beyond the little garden where they sat the new lawn lay raked and waiting to be sown. Joss was off visiting Niamh, or she hoped that was where he was.

"Didn't know Joss was interested in birds," Ned said. It was half a question. Hannie stretched up her hand to pull at a late rose on the wall.

"He is. Birds, and also insects." She turned the rose this way and that, inspecting the shaggy pink flower, the round black indentations on its smooth green leaves. "This rose needs spraying."

"It does, they all do, I just haven't got round to it. So you know about roses. Andrew had those too?"

"The English must have their roses, even in Africa. I looked after Andrew's roses, or rather the gardener did, and I instructed him. Would you like me to look after your roses, Ned?"

"Yes, please," said Ned. "The spray's in the shed, and I'm sorry there isn't a gardener to be instructed." He paused a moment. "I believe I am a little jealous of Andrew, Hannie," he said, surprising himself with the remark.

She smiled vaguely, letting go of the rose. It swung, a diminishing pendulum, on the still air.

———◆———

AFTER THAT Joss was around Niamh like a shadow.

Or a cat, Mrs. Coady thought, as she watched him prowl and stalk and sidle close. Very like a cat. So sleek and still. Not a hair out of place. The small mouth, the neat small tongue to lick cream.

A thief too, she wouldn't mind betting. Not the son you would think she would breed. But you never knew what would come out, you couldn't choose, and you always loved the bad ones best, for they'd no one else.

Niamh didn't seem to mind him. But Niamh liked cats. At least until they brought something in half alive and half dead and sat themselves down to torment it.

She slung the mat she was carrying over the line and beat at it with the back of the broom. Satisfying clouds of dust flew out of it. She wondered about the father.

Chapter Eleven

HANNIE TOOK JOSS TO CORK to buy clothes and kit for school. Not all of it, but the bulk of it. There were specifics she'd have to get in the school shop when they took him North.

She'd asked Ned for money and he'd taken out his checkbook and written a check out to cash. She could change it in Cork, he said, he didn't keep cash in the house.

She knew that already. And that he had no time for credit cards and didn't like banks, though he paid all his bills by check.

She could buy what she liked when she liked, he had told her. If she wanted anything she had only to ask and anyway all the local shops kept books under the counter, he would settle her bills when they were presented. There was to be no joint account.

She went first to the bank in Cork to cash the check and then to the school outfitters that Ned said everyone used. Methodically, she worked her way down through the list that the school had sent.

It seemed an enormous amount to amass, everything dark and heavy and thick. Joss was docile, almost cooperative, only occasionally attempting sabotage and never refusing outright. She was so surprised and relieved that she told him to choose something for himself when they'd finished. He gave her a long look and said there was nothing in the shop he'd wear unless he had to.

When she came to pay she found that Ned's cashed check wasn't enough to cover their purchases. She had no other money, no credit cards or checkbook to fall back on. The last of her own money had gone on Joss's fare from Kenya.

She picked up the list and began to edit. Joss drifted off to another part of the shop, leaving her to sort out the situation. She knew from the turn of his head that he was despising Ned for underproviding and despising her for landing them both with him.

Abruptly she stopped trying to work out what to keep and what to put back and instead she wrote out Ned's name and address and asked that their purchases and the bill be sent on. The assistant who was serving her disappeared to consult with a senior. Out of the corner of her eye she watched the two heads scanning the paper, the older one nodding assent. Ned's name was good for something, after all. When the young man came back she asked him to recommend a good restaurant.

They ate lunch off a starched white cloth with a good bottle from the list and waiters in attendance. Joss helped himself to the wine and she said nothing. He watched as she paid the large bill with cash from Ned's check. She felt defiant, placing the notes on the salver, she wanted to spend Ned's careful money wastefully, to dissipate it in ways he would certainly not approve. And she cared nothing for such surroundings, was indifferent to the manicured food, the snobbish, overpriced wine list. Joss liked it, but she wasn't doing it for Joss.

Why *was* she doing it? she asked herself. Why did she suddenly mind Ned's minding his wallet? He hadn't minded it when it mattered. When it came to paying the school fees, he hadn't hesitated. Why had her gratitude so quickly turned to vindictiveness?

Because now it was all settled.

Ned had arranged things and gone with her to the school and made it all possible. The school had taken Joss because of Ned: Ned's name and Ned's presence, they'd hardly bothered with her at all. She had sat in her good suit drinking tea and keeping her thoughts to herself while the headmaster and the housemaster and the matron all ignored her and basked instead in Ned and in Ned's modest, admirable reputation. They hadn't even queried the choice of a school so far from where they resided. Ned had served the Empire, it was natural that he should want his wife's son educated in its territory. Besides, he was a Protestant. There were Protestant schools in the South of course. Some would consider them dubious.

She had been so anxious on the drive up, so grateful for his willingness to help her and for his unspoken decision to accept what she asked for and leave her motives unquestioned. It was all she had thought of. She felt that if Joss was settled she might even be grateful to Ned forever. Or grateful enough to get by on for at least a bit longer.

Well, that had been then, she thought sourly. It seemed that her gratitude had worn thin before Joss was even dispatched.

———•◆•———

NED TRIED not to blame Hannie for her loyalty to Joss and he tried not to imagine pacts between them. He tried not to notice that the boy's politeness was often a form of rudeness and he told himself it was perfectly natural that Joss should resent a new authority, at least initially. He had known Joss would be a problem.

Nevertheless, he was disappointed. Gradually he became aware of the cause of his disappointment. Joss did not inspire affection, nor did he seem to wish to have affection extended to him.

Ned found himself blushing at this realization. What had he wanted? A son to love and be loved by? He got up and went out to the near meadow. The old mare he occasionally hacked around on came to the gate whinnying softly and blew into his hand. He liked the comfort of her. He grew calmer and tried to think more clearly. He didn't like this alliance of mother and son and he didn't like being shut out by them. And he didn't like this blank-faced boy in the mirror glasses, yet he wanted to like him and be liked by him. Most of all, he realized, he didn't like what he was learning about himself.

He knuckled the mare's bony face and she rubbed for more. Hannie had married him for a home for the boy, he knew that, she'd as good as said it, and he had accepted it. But already it seemed he'd begun to forget it.

Things were bound to be difficult at the beginning, he told himself; her loyalty was divided, that was where her coldness came from. The boy would be gone in a few days, he and Hannie would get used to each other, the school would settle Joss down.

It was a good school, straightforward and disciplined, with a sound reputation. He was relieved she hadn't wanted Joss nearer and home every other weekend, the way it seemed to be done now. He'd been surprised at the time but she seemed sure of what she was doing, and maybe it didn't seem far to her, being used to Africa. Then again maybe she was thinking of him and of their marriage, breaking him in gently, aware that Joss was difficult. Ned was pleased at this thought. He rubbed Connie's face again, dismissed her with a final pat. Yes, Joss would settle at school, make friends, get used to the climate. He'd be easier when he came home for the Christmas holidays.

Hannie, too, would be easier. He must be patient, he must give her time.

———•◆•———

HANNIE WAS AWARE that Joss was making things more difficult for her with Ned. With the boy standing watching and challenging, it was hard not to question her judgment in making this arrangement for their lives. She knew that this line of thought wasn't useful to her and she didn't want to be wasting her time in futile rebellion and resentment. She wanted to accept Ned as he was and thus be free of him: the chameleon's trick that had served her well in the past.

But when she was with Joss it was as though his wraparound glasses were clamped to her own nose. She criticized Ned with her actions and with her eyes. She allied herself with Joss against him.

It was partly because the stakes were so high for Joss. A new life, a new school, different influences. This was a chance for him and there might not ever again be such another. Her instinct told her to stay close to the boy, to support him sympathetically and emotionally and not let him be isolated through any intimacy of hers with Ned.

But it was also an emotional reaction against Ned and against the place she now found herself in. She hadn't anticipated so closed a life, nor that Ned's expectations would weigh so heavily upon her. At night she dreamed of blocked holes and locked rooms, of sealed and shuttered windows. She escaped from dream into consciousness and lay awake in her trap. She felt this life bearing down on her like a pillow pressed over her face and her panic and suffocation unbalanced her. Joss also unbalanced her. Try as she might she could not get through his refusal of her. She could not read him or reach him and his anger and avoidance of her enraged her and worried her sick by turns.

He escaped her to Niamh who accepted him without comment, like a cat that had wandered in and might perch on her sill or wind itself around her feet for a day or a week before disappearing.

He was there now. Hannie rose from her work of sorting and labeling and packing and crossed to the window. For a long time she stood scanning the deserted yard and the empty sheds as though they held some clue to Joss's heart that she might read if she looked hard enough.

Then she returned to the piled underwear, the marker pen and the labels. She was glad Joss was going in the morning, though she dreaded the pain and apprehension she knew she'd feel on his behalf once he'd left and her anger had subsided. Nonetheless she might be less emotionally swamped. She knew she would have to create some sort of a working relationship with Ned soon or the life here would rapidly become unbearable to them both. With Joss gone she might regain sufficient equilibrium to try.

Or to decide not to.

She knew Joss wouldn't write her letters or phone her. For a moment she wished she'd chosen a school that was nearer, that she could visit and be visited from. She refused the thought. The farther away the school, the easier the damage-limitation. That was the hard-learned fruit of experience. She mustn't start now on fantasies that Joss was other than he was.

At least he'd had Niamh to hang around while he was here, Hannie thought. At the same time she hated Niamh for the intimacy that Joss had bestowed on her. An unsought intimacy, probably also unwanted, she acknowledged bitterly to herself.

Niamh had a passion for moths and butterflies. Joss, too, liked insects, though ants and beetles were more in his line. It was a bond between them, this shared interest that wouldn't be most people's taste. Niamh had books that Joss consulted, they discussed species together, she could tell him what was rare, what common as mud.

But Niamh's interest was essentially more aesthetic than lepidopterous and she especially liked moths and butterflies in death. It was the way death inhabited them that fascinated her, the way it lived in them, invisible but for its stillness, yet intensely respectful of its own power. The small corpses she collected seemed to her to collude with some aspect of death's sense of itself: a sense altogether different from that which she'd seen displayed in its grosser occupation of human beings and farm animals. There was a propriety in its dealings with these insects. It was as though they'd been given notice and had served as their own undertakers. They had laid themselves out, wings spread, feet neatly crossed, bodies sleek in their furred coats now doubling up as shrouds. Then, having prepared themselves, the master had been invited in.

Niamh collected up their spent bodies wherever she found them. She perched them on windowsills and shelves as she passed, she laid them carefully on the flat surfaces of stones. Sometimes she retraced her steps, gathering in her harvest. Sometimes she just left them where they lay. Ned had noticed her preoccupation and begun to collect for her. A dusty saucer, full of his gleanings, sat on a scullery shelf.

Joss also joined in the game but instead of adding to Niamh's stores he raided them, creating tiny dramas that were parodies of the living forms. Meticulously Niamh's corpses were redistributed and resurrected. Furred brown moths clung by their stiff dead legs onto climbing roses, butterflies crawled the bright faces of late marigolds, small silvery moths hooked the porch geraniums. Niamh liked this, the way it made you look afresh at both corpse and flower, the way Joss sometimes changed things into art. But she wasn't so sure about all his insect activities. And she didn't share his fascination with fungi at all.

There were growths everywhere: it was the warm early September weather, the light night rains and heavy morning dews. He asked her endless questions but she didn't know the answers. She knew only the big horse mushrooms dotted about the fields. She liked picking these, easing them carefully out of the ground, breaking them open to check them for grubs. Not so Joss. These edible growths were too plain and serviceable for him, he only kicked and hacked at them, scattering soft shards of flesh across the bright grass. It was the stranger growths that he liked: their rich discoloredness, their spongy fluted branches, whiter than death.

Best of all he liked the big dense fungal clumps that grew in the rough grass on the edge of the potholed drive. These were not single forms but multiple manifestations, accretions of chestnut-colored platelets, layer on spiraling layer.

"Like cities," Niamh said, kneeling in the damp grass, peering into brown streets and alleyways. "Or those old walled towns in Italian paintings. You know the ones. Like snail shells. The houses all glued to those lumps of rock sticking out of the planes."

Joss didn't know, but he liked these impermanent cities. He lay on his belly for hours inserting ants and grasshoppers into their maze of alleys, prodding them into activity with long blades of meadow grass.

Niamh observed with a detached interest. She was getting used to Joss, making assumptions about him. His weirdness might just be loneliness, she decided. He might be an artist looking for a form.

Hannie also observed, but she did not disturb Niamh's assumptions. Niamh was a grown human being, old enough to be making mistakes and learning from them. Old enough to be acting her age.

Hannie slipped her hand into the last name-tagged sock, grasped its fellow and pulled the first one over it to make a pair. She tossed the bunched socks into the open suitcase. Then she rose and went downstairs, trailing her hand down the polished banister, feeling the lonely emptiness of the late-afternoon house. She wanted to go and fetch Joss

out of Niamh's, to harry him over this packing, to force him into sharing these last hours with her, but she made herself hold back.

What was the point? There'd be no confidences, nothing he'd say to
her now in intimacy, but wouldn't say tomorrow with Ned there. He
was punishing her, she was fairly sure of that, but whether for Ned or
for school or both she didn't know. And he seemed all right about tomorrow's journey. He'd be into crossing the border, he'd said, and seeing this famous North with its bombs and guns.

"Less boring than here, Mother. At least there'll be something going on."

But he didn't know how far it was, he didn't know how he'd feel
when he saw them turn the car and drive away.

Neither did she, she told herself. He might like it. On past form it
wasn't beginnings that were the problem, it was what happened after
he'd begun.

She crossed the hall and on an impulse went into the drawing room
and looked out over the front. They were there, both of them, standing
on the edge of the drive, Joss doing something, Niamh watching. Hannie moved closer to the window, careful not to be seen.

It was a ceremony. Joss had gathered together a pile of large round
stones and was meticulously bombing his cities, his face impassive as
the brown walls fell.

Hannie stood a few moments longer. Then she turned and went to
the kitchen to prepare the evening meal. Fried chicken, his favorite
dish. He'd be angry with her for doing it, angry if she didn't.

"Condemned man eats hearty last meal, eh, Mother?"

That's what he'd say when he'd finished.

Chapter Twelve

ON THE DAY FOLLOWING JOSS'S DEPARTURE the weather broke and it rained for three days. Hannie watched the water running down the clouded windows and gathering in puddles on the leaky sills. Drafts blew through the ill-fitting frames, bad-tempered winds plucked at the guttering, the tall Scots pines at the back of the house moaned and complained. Rain swept the valley in wavering curtains and the river lost itself in a hissing blur of gray.

Hannie walked from room to room, smoking too much and hating this dank sodden world she had come to. The kitchen was full of dust from the walls that Ambrose Power and his mate Liam were knocking down, the floor was mud from the wet that their boots had tramped in. For once she was narky and short with them.

The Change, their looks said, women are divils at the Change. They were disappointed in her, that was clear. Where had she gone and who was this harridan left behind in her place?

It was ever so, she thought. Women raged and men misunderstood. Then they felt injured and hard-done-by. She put on Wellingtons and a waterproof and went outside to tramp about in the drizzling rain.

She walked up the drive, away from the house, and came on the rain-blackened ruins of Joss's bombed cities. They were crushed and pulped now and smelled of excrement and decay. She stood over them, thinking of Joss in the rain in that gray Northern town on the wide gray lake. Despair settled upon her, the rain ran down her face and dripped off her hands.

Despair changed to rage and she kicked at the cities, scattering the ruins until all that was left was a blackened pulp in the long wet grass. She felt no satisfaction. The ugly feeling that had driven her was still in her. It was no use, nothing was any use, she could not protect him, nor keep him safe from himself. Strange growths came up out of the dark earth, they blossomed and decayed and you could not change that, no matter how you kicked and raged and trampled.

———•◆•———

FINALLY THE RAIN STOPPED. It was a different landscape: color-less, sodden, beaten down. Overnight a whole world had vanished. Hannie stood by the paddock fence and stared at the mud and the dy-ing vegetation. Nothing was as it had been. The tall ghost stands of wil-low herb were battered and flattened now, the fluffy seed heads that last week shone in the light like silk threads were all matted and draggled and done. The rain had stopped, but the sun had not returned. It was cold, the day was dark.

Hannie stood on, staring blankly at the rain's aftermath. She was awaiting a huge sun, floating up over the rim of the land, throbbing the life back into this cold, spent world.

It would not come, she realized. That sun lived in Africa, there was no such sun here, nor ever would be.

A gray Cortina drove up, battered and muddy. Hannie watched as a woman got out, opened the trunk, and stood looking down into it with an air of quiet satisfaction.

Alison Beresford. A small gray woman in her late fifties, deep-bosomed and slender, wearing trousers and clean Wellingtons and a plain, light-green headscarf. One of Ned's oldest friends, she lived with a husband called Vere in a crumbling gray house just a few miles away. Hannie watched her now as she straightened up and scanned the house-front with quiet, determined eyes.

The trunk of the Cortina bulged with muddy polythene bags that had leaves and bits of cut stem sticking out of them. Alison was rummaging about in there, opening bags and closing them, obedient to some order of things hidden in her mind. Hannie stood silently beside her.

"Oh yes," Alison was saying as she found the bag she was looking for and heaved it out of the trunk, "since we were children. Or rather, since I was a child — he must have been in his teens. They'd just come to live with Mrs. Valender at Oldcourt. His grandmother," she added, with the air of one making clear things clearer.

"Of course he seemed terribly grown up and glamorous. And tragic. His father had just died, you see, Oldcourt was his mother's home. About fifteen, I suppose he must have been. And I must have been about five." She hauled at another bag.

"Geraniums, cobalt blue. Masses of foliage, very fast spreaders. So useful in the right place, but you do have to be careful. Bullies, really, they'll take over the bed if you let them. Heavenly blue flowers, but only for about two weeks in June. Some people hate them, say they're not worth their keep."

On some of the bags Alison had scrawled clues as to content with a black felt-tip pen. She would look at the words, then open the bag anyway, and stare hard at the tangles of root and mud and leaf.

"He went to the war of course, but afterwards, after Isobel died, we thought he might come home. . . . But he didn't. He began on his journeys instead. This one's a little white saxifrage, so dainty, good on a wall or under a tree." She handed Hannie a bag and waited for her to open it and look inside.

"There's a small pink geranium in there with it. Quite dull, but makes neat little clumps and flowers for ages and ages." She dived back into the trunk.

"He always came backwards and forwards, all through the years. Then when Mrs. Valender died, Oldcourt was sold and his mother moved into Delaney's — which was only a step away, so it made no difference really, we saw as much of him as ever. Then she died too, but he still came when he could. He would go to West Cork for his cousins, but he'd always come here for a few days at the end and he always stayed with us."

Alison dumped the last of the bags with their fellows by the Cortina's back wheel. She straightened up, tightening the scarf under her chin in a gesture at once absent and automatic.

"There," she said with quiet satisfaction, "that should keep you busy. And don't be disappointed if the bearded irises don't flower straight away. They will when they get round to it — they simply hate being moved."

—◆•◆—

"ALISON CAME," Hannie said, setting the casserole down on the table. "She wants us to go there on Friday. 'Family-supper-in-the kitchen,' whatever that means. I said we were busy."

Ned frowned. He stabbed a potato, then reached for the butter. "Remind me," he said, not looking up. "I've forgotten."

Hannie said nothing. He looked at her.

"We're not busy," she said, "I just said we were. She wants me to help with church cleaning and flowers."

Ned lifted the lid off the casserole. "And will you?" he said neutrally, spooning lamb and mushrooms onto her plate.

"No," Hannie said, moving the lid out of the way, still not looking at him. "She'd been doing her border, splitting up her perennials. She brought us a trunkful of off-cuts for our new beds. A bit of everything — even things she doesn't much like, or thinks probably won't grow in our soil. She says it's so much nicer, having plants from someone else's garden. You think of where they came from and they give you extra pleasure."

"You don't like her," Ned said.

Hannie looked at him, a long straight look. She picked up her knife and fork and began to eat.

"She's a nice woman," Ned said. "It was kind of her to bring us plants, and she's absolutely right about associations." Hannie kept eating. "Besides, it would have cost a fortune, buying perennials from a garden center."

Ned reached for the salt in the silence. "You have to give people a chance, Hannie," he said reasonably. "You'll never make friends if you won't try."

"Why would I want to make friends?" she asked. "I have Joss, I have you, I am busy all day, why would I want friends?"

Ned sighed. "It will be easier if you make friends," he said carefully. "Easier to settle."

She put down her knife and fork and rose from the table. She picked up the phone.

"What're you doing?"

She didn't answer him. "Alison?" she said into the phone. "Alison, this is Hannie Renvyle. Change of plan. We can come on Friday after all. . . . About eight? That will be fine. Yes. I, too, am delighted."

She sat down and resumed eating.

———— •◆• ————

"I ASKED HER if she'd help with the church flowers," Alison said.

"And would she?" Vere was sitting at the long table, riffling through the new edition of the *Farmer's Journal*.

"She said she didn't qualify. She said she was an animist."

"A what?"

"An animist. She comes from Java. She said in Java animists are the norm."

He looked up, almost interested despite the fresh attractions in the journal.

"A Protestant animist or a Catholic animist?" He smiled, pleased with his little joke.

"A Lutheran animist." Alison put the boiled kettle and two mugs on the table and sat down.

"She won't get out of it that easily. Tell her Lutheran equals Protestant and as such she's expected to do her bit." He had lost interest, had already returned to the journal.

"She said her father was a Lutheran. The animism was on her mother's side." Alison was pouring hot water onto the instant coffee in each of their mugs. "What do you suppose she meant by that?"

Vere sat up, looking startled. "Was she serious?"

"Totally."

"I wouldn't know," Vere said slowly, reaching for his coffee and abandoning the journal altogether. "But if I was guessing, old girl, I'd say she meant a touch of the tar brush." He looked at his wife speculatively. "I wouldn't put it past old Ned, either. Would you?"

———— ◆◆◆ ————

THAT NIGHT Ned came to her room. Afterward, instead of going back to his own as was his habit, he stayed and slept beside her. Hannie dreamed, this time not of locked rooms and blocked corridors, but of Piet.

She woke in the darkness, Piet there in front of her eyes, Ned snoring gently beside her. The dream was a strong thick taste in her mouth. She lay finding her way back out of it, not wanting to return there when she slept again.

The dream was short. She was standing beside the river here, very early in the morning. It was like gray glass, and a mist crept up from the water in little trails and puffs. In the intense quiet a bird rose, its wings beating the still surface, breaking the smooth gray glass. She saw Piet standing, his feet astride, his hands clasped loosely together behind his back, his belly sagging. He lifted his head and glanced sideways at her. She wanted to ask what he was doing here, so far from home, but she couldn't speak. She saw that he was laughing at her. He rocked his weight from foot to foot, his belly jiggled. He would not tell her why he laughed, she had to guess. She could not. She looked down at her hands. They were greenish-gray and covered in small shiny scales like the skin of a fish. Then she knew she was waiting for something but she didn't know what. She knew that Piet knew, and she looked up from her hands to ask him, but he'd gone.

Chapter Thirteen

AUTUMN WAS FULLY UPON THEM. The river shone, a moving sheet of light. More and more she abandoned the house, Ambrose and the alterations. She would be outside and halfway down the avenue almost before she knew she'd gone. Above her the poplars, golden-green and thinning, streamed in the high blueness. A pheasant walked over the green meadow. The burnished oak trees stood against the thin, intense sky.

She learned to walk everywhere with her head tipped far back for the sky that was up there like grace, shining with light and swept empty and clean by the wind. She thought she could stand anything as long as there was this grace, this light. Only the wet gray days were too hard.

There were layers to the wind. Low down it was still and breathing, but throw your head back and you saw another world. Winds romped the sky, possessing the tall poplar trees, riding them, throwing them about like ships thrown about on the sea.

She would come home buoyant. She had been to the harbor: she might not yet sail on the ships, but she knew where those ships lay. It was like seeing the seagulls on the river. It promised that there was somewhere else.

Some days. On other days this illusion of escape eluded her. All illusions eluded her. What was the use of somewhere else if you were never in it? She would flee from the house and the yard and the half-planted garden and walk about for hours. Then she would trudge back across the fields, feeling the thinning grass, the dying light, the dense suck of the trampled mud where the cattle had clustered.

Every day the year's change came faster. The air thinned and the trees thinned and the colors sobered. The skies closed down. She felt bereft, shut in. She ranged farther, pushed beyond the meadows and into the stands of ancient woodland that clung, here and there, to the river. She liked these at first: their secretness and their neglect. But each day the light died a little sooner and somehow she began to fear them. The snapping of twigs, the frantic dusk alarms of the roosting birds, the patter of leaf-fall, the wet black smell of decay. They seemed full of small shiverings and dyings.

———◆———

THIRTY CALVES BAWLED and cried in the sheds by the house, re-fusing the meal that was brought to them. Ned spent hours in there, calming and coaxing, trying to wheedle them into feeding. It was no good, they wanted none of him: they were desperate for milk and their mothers.

"Try the treacly stuff, they love that . . . in the yellow bags . . . You know the one, the stuff that's got loads of molasses in it." Niamh hung around, throwing out vague suggestions, getting on his nerves.

Ned didn't know, but everyone else did, so every time he drove out through the gates he came back with a different sack that someone or other had recommended.

"Leave them alone," Hannie said. "They'll stop bawling when they're tired enough. They'll eat when they're hungry enough. Just let them be."

Ned said he knew that, but they'd lose condition fast when they were upset like this and anyway they were his calves and he didn't want them to suffer. Hannie heard the annoyance in his voice, so she folded her arms and shut her mouth and went back inside, banging the kitchen door to behind her.

Ambrose was sitting at the table with Liam, having their morning tea break.

"They do be missing their mothers," he said into his mug.

"Missing their food, more like. Bloody calves, bloody fuss, shouting their bloody heads off. Empty bellies is what's wrong with them, they'll forget their mothers the minute their bellies are full again."

"Ah no," Ambrose said gently, "it wouldn't be just milk, it's their mothers, too. 'Tis hard for them all, and some show it more than others." He was still staring into his mug, avoiding looking at Hannie.

"Sure I mind a calf the brother had," Liam said. "Weaned and grown and away from the cow for a year or more. And then didn't he put him into the same field as the mother and wasn't he trying to suck her right away? A big, lump of a bullock, as if he was only a calf again."

"Exactly," Hannie said furiously. "Bothering her long after he's grown up and well able to fend for himself."

Ambrose kicked Liam under the table, finished up his tea and rose to return to the job. Liam, looking surprised, did the same.

'Twould be noisy inside as well as out today, Ambrose told her. All the old stuck-down lino was to be chipped away, then the floor leveled up and the new skim of concrete poured.

"No point in laying new tiles on a bockety floor," he said. "We'll be all day getting that old stuff up. Sure we might as well get all the noise done with in the one go."

Hannie put on her boots and abandoned ship. On the edge of the woods she chose a path that was new to her. It ran through stands of old hardwoods, dense with tangled undergrowth and unthinned saplings, opening here and there onto patches of neglected planting. She followed this path until it petered out. Off to the left behind a tangle of laurel and rhododendron, she found another one. It was narrower and windier than the first, more an animal track than a path, but she followed it stubbornly. It ended abruptly in a thin screen of leaves. She burst through and stumbled into a once-cleared clearing, cluttered now with mossy piles of abandoned logs.

Near the center of this clearing rose a big old spruce, dead but still erect, the upper part of its trunk snapped abruptly off at twice her height. She walked around it, expecting the dark marks of a lightning strike but finding none. Instead she saw fungal growths like red-brown misshapen kidneys, near to the ground but climbing the trunk in tiers.

There was something shocking about them, indecent, she felt she should turn her eyes away. Like coming on a bad car accident unawares, she thought. People with bits of themselves on the outside instead of the inside, their private internal organs casually on display.

Growths everywhere. Perhaps it was the damp? She reached out her hand and made herself touch the flesh.

She had expected softness, a slimy dissolving, but the fungus was dry with the hollow hardness of old wood. She pressed harder into it with her fingers, but still it did not indent. Something at once frightened and violent rose up in her and she had to damage it, to break it or mark it, it didn't matter which. She tried to snap off a piece but it was like twisting thick old leather. She wrenched again. It gave abruptly and she staggered back, a piece of the leathery growth clutched in her hand.

She regained her balance without at once realizing that she still held it. When she did she started, then hurled her malignant trophy furiously away. It arced from her and smashed into the thinning brambles.

There was a short burst of silence, then a sudden wild crashing. A black dog rushed from somewhere behind her and threw himself at the undergrowth in pursuit. Two more Labradors appeared and danced and circled around her and the empty place was suddenly filled with noise. A man stepped from between the trees, calling the dogs. The first dog emerged from underneath the brambles, the half-moon clutched in his mouth, his tail thrashing in triumphant pride. He circled the man again and again, neck arched like a horse's to show off his trophy. He was fully grown, she saw, but still very giddy and young.

The man bent to the dog and removed the fungus. He turned it over and back, inspecting it, his face without expression. Hannie knew at once that he'd been watching her. Watching from a place of concealment and not intending to be revealed. It was like Africa, this place, eyes hidden everywhere. Only the missile and the young dog's exuberance had flushed him out.

"Root fomes," he said quietly, weighing the thing in his hand. "Always a killer. You think it's only external, but it rots right through to the heart." He shifted his eyes along the broken trunk, noting the other growths.

"That's why the tree died, d'you see? You didn't break it off, you couldn't have. The tree's so deeply rotted the wood crumbled when you pulled." He reached down and rubbed at the tree where the wound from the ripped-away fungus showed. The wood powdered off under his touch.

Surreptitiously, Hannie watched him. He was tallish and lean and not ill made, but curiously without presence. His features were regular, his hair dark and just touched with gray, his eyes gray and veiled behind heavy glasses. He wore Wellingtons and an old, torn waxproof and trousers made out of some brown stuff, long discolored and stained. He was camouflaged, she realized. Everything about him was somehow damped down, concealed, restrained. Only his thick dark eyebrows were energetic, even when he was saying nothing.

"The owl died," he said. "I thought she'd make it but she didn't. Boy settling all right, is he?"

For a moment Hannie thought she had misheard him, then light dawned. This was Danno, the man who stuffed birds.

"I haven't heard," she said bluntly, surprising herself with the flash of bitterness in her own voice.

He heard it too, she could feel his recoil. He didn't like emotion or contact with people, she realized. She could feel him wanting to get away but by effort of will making himself stay.

That he knew who she was did not surprise her. At first she had thought herself invisible here for no one stared or even seemed to register her presence, but she had soon learned the reality. Everyone knew her, it was as though her photo had been pasted up in the post office and passed through the houses and farms.

"The owl was doing well, or well enough, tell him. Something happened, I don't know what. She lost heart and I couldn't turn her round."

"Like the tree."

He looked puzzled.

"Heart rot," she said, gesturing toward the growth he still held in his hand. "You said it rotted right through to the heart." She stopped. She had a sudden strange impression that they were talking about Joss. She shook her head to dispel the illusion.

"*Heterobasidion annosum*," he agreed. "There's a fair bit of it in these woods. They need thinning and replanting, but no one gives a damn —" He broke off and involved himself with rounding up the dogs. His eyes, she noticed, had not once rested on her directly.

Ready to make his escape now, she thought. The instinct for flight. Like a lizard. A flick, and it was gone into its crack. No, not like a lizard, there was something overtly sexual about a lizard, there was a curious, damaged sexuality about this man.

She would hang on to him, she decided, make him show her the way back. She felt easy with him suddenly and faintly contemptuous but also hostile.

Chapter Fourteen

"'WHO WILL LEND A DIPPER OF WATER to save a fish in a carriage rut?' He quoted that to me. Then he paid my passage and let me go. He was a strange man, I didn't understand him, I still don't. He said he had dropped me into the rut, so it was only right he should lift me out."

Niamh was warming the teapot and gazing at Hannie with her big, shiny dark eyes as she sent the water swishing around in its base.

"Black tea or jasmine?"

"Black."

She was very self-possessed, Hannie thought, with her neat clean kitchen and her laid table and her choice of teas. Hannie took out her cigarettes and began to smoke.

"I dreamed my hands were covered in scales like a fish," Hannie said. "The dream wouldn't leave me alone, it kept coming back to me. I thought and thought but still I didn't connect it with that saying. Then I came walking here through the mud and the ruts and Piet's little fish dropped into my mind. He liked Confucian philosophers — their stories and homilies. He often quoted them, he didn't mind their neatness or their smugness. He liked that, he said, it helped ward off life's pain."

She was here for tea at the girl's repeated invitation. Young woman, she should say — that was how the girl referred to herself. Hannie ignored the proffered chair and mooched around the kitchen, talking and looking at things. Briefly, she wondered at this insistence on being a woman. Her own generation called themselves girls relentlessly until they died.

Niamh filled the teapot and settled the cozy down over it. She somehow couldn't quite grasp that this woman was Joss's mother, but she liked having her here, liked the funny jumps and disconnections in the way she talked. She felt a bit awkward with her but not shy in the way that she did with Joss or Ned, she was too interested. She didn't ask questions or interrupt in case Hannie noticed she was talking about her life and stopped. Niamh wanted to hear all about Piet and their marriage. She wanted to hear all of Hannie's crowded, exotic past.

"I hated these Confucians and their homilies. He used to say them to me all the time because he knew how much I hated them. I knew by looking at him when another one was coming. His mouth would go pouted and shiny as though he was sucking a boiled sweet. Then he'd laugh at me because I looked so sour. *Better a boiled sweet than a lemon,* he'd say. . . .

"There was one I liked, though. About a man on a white horse in a whirl of red dust. A young man, handsome and distinguished, and all the people coming out to watch. Lord Tung — that was his name — Lord Tung. He rode about the place looking for adventures and fine women. Piet knew he only had me till Lord Tung came riding by. I think perhaps he said it so often because he wanted me to know that he knew. And I never realized. I was too stupid and too young. . . ." Hannie's voice trailed off into silence.

Niamh waited, hoping for more, but nothing came. She called Hannie to the tea table. She talked as she poured tea, buttered bread and sliced the apple tart. She spoke of her pleasure in the cottage, and her appreciation. She spoke of her work, the back room she was sorting out, the paintings she would make from the drawings done in the fine weather. The rain ran down the windowpanes, the fire danced. It was like a painting on a plate, Hannie thought. So smooth and shiny and clean. She ate nothing. She smoked and drank tea.

Niamh was very attractive, Hannie decided. She had fine eyes, a wide mouth and smooth dark hair pulled into a knot at the nape of her neck. She was tall, her figure was slender but full, and she had slim, strong wrists and large graceful hands. There was something of the Madonna about her, an effect curiously accentuated by the jeans and sweaters she wore. Did she know this, Hannie wondered, did she deliberately cultivate the Madonna effect?

Probably not, she decided. Mostly because it wouldn't occur to her that she needed to. Niamh expected the kindness and indulgence with which she was treated, it had clearly never crossed her mind that the world might have been a harder place had she been plain and spotted, or buck-toothed with a cast in her eye. She was artless because she could afford to be.

Niamh's assumption that she was loved for herself alone offended Hannie, who had grown up without any currency other than that provided for her by her youth and her looks. She knew, very exactly, the value of this currency.

Niamh used this currency, but she used it unconsciously and her behavior produced in Hannie the same reaction that people who have had to scrape for every penny feel when they watch the next generation using unearned money thoughtlessly. To spend such currency idly was bad enough, but it was careless to the point of criminality to use it without ever being aware of what it was: a finite quality that won affection and privilege but would, with time, expire.

Watching Niamh now, Hannie came closer to understanding precisely how much indulgence she had been granted on that score in the past herself. It was a painful realization, for with it came the knowledge that the currency in which she had traded was all but spent.

So perhaps it was simply envy she was feeling? Well, so be it, she didn't care. She was happy to dislike Niamh, she enjoyed her own ill will.

———•◆•———

His blouse was the pale yellow of gosling down;
his face and figure were fine as a painting.
Always he rode a snow-footed horse,
whirling whirling up the red dust . . .

Tramping back through the rain, Hannie recalled a snatch of Piet's verse. Remembering it, she fell upon another painful little revelation. She was still waiting for Lord Tung.

"Because they are wasteful and stupid," Piet would say of his fellow Europeans if you asked him why he shunned them. "Because their greed is endless and they do not have the sense to be content with a full rice bowl."

Well, it seemed that neither did she.

She had a full rice bowl now, yet she wasn't content, she never had been. It was always the same. At first the marriage — the full rice bowl — was a big deal, but before very long the same deal looked smaller and when it did she found herself a lover.

You're a fool, Hannie, she told herself now. You can't just go on doing the same things over and over all your life. The same things now, when you're fifty, as when you were twenty, or thirty, or forty. Look around you, where is this lover, this dashing Lord Tung of yours?

I'll tell you where.

At home by the fire, smoking his pipe and scratching his belly and counting his snot-nosed grandchildren.

She pushed open the back door, kicked off her Wellingtons and flung them at a corner. But she could not kick off her thoughts so easily, no matter how she tried. They itched at her like flea bites.

———✦———

SHE'D BEGUN ON THE HOUSE because it was what he wanted, however he might resent the expense and complain of inconvenience. He'd said as much. He wanted a garden, flowers on the table, the place made into a home. A living life in the house that existed whether he entered it or not.

For her it was part of the deal, her way of earning the shelter provided. It meant she was not compromised.

But she saw now that deep in herself there was another reason. She was doing the house for the man who would come here and see her work and know this was what she could do. She was advertising, displaying her wares. So that the future might be different.

But no one was going to come, she saw that too. Her life here was a closed loop and would not change: Ned's friends, their modest, badly cooked dinners, their modest, penny-pinching lives. The same people, the same conversations: farm subsidies, the price of feed, what breed for the perfect cross, what had happened to what once-great house, the way things were now, the better way they'd once been.

And there was to be no salvation from outside, no wild card dealt into her hand, no young Lord Tung to take her up onto his horse and whirl her off. Lord Tung was grown elderly and married. She'd have to find her own alternative to Ned. Or walk away from him on her own two feet.

She stopped doing the house. She sent Ambrose off and told Ned she'd changed her mind about the shower and the new bay in the dining room. It was enough to be going on with, she said, she might think again in the spring. She wasn't short-changing him. She would still cook for him and clean and help him on the farm when needed. She'd run his house and go to bed with him and entertain his friends. But the things that were still unfinished, she left unfinished.

Ned made no comment. He couldn't help but see how she'd improved the place, and he liked to open the door and see that a woman lived there. But winter was coming on, he was glad to have the house private again, Ambrose gone, and no more expectation that he find the money to pay for what she wanted. He accepted that he should provide, but it was money he was convinced he did not have. Except for the farm.

Chapter Fifteen

You could get to Danno's by one of two ways. There was a path through the woods that followed the line of the river, or an old, narrow road, its thinly tarred surface broken by roots and rain and years. Hannie came by the path on her first visit.

Danno's house was built on a narrow strip of ground that dropped very steeply down to the edge of the river. It was small and old and single-storied, white-washed a long time ago and roofed in slate. The site was dank and awkward and everywhere there were steps and little runs and platforms, inexplicable except to the initiated. Cages and wire enclosures, some empty and some holding injured raptors, clung like mollusks to its walls. It was dark and damp, with a cluster of lean-to sheds huddling off to the left and the woods pressing in close, shutting out the light. Beyond it the river flowed, high and fast with the autumn rains, sinuous and muscled like a salmon.

Hannie banged on the door and then waited with her back to it. She had no explanation for her visit, had brought no excuse in the form of an injured bird or the ubiquitous pot of jam. She'd been walking over this way and thought she might call. Just curiosity. She thought she might take a look and then never come back again.

Nothing. She knocked again. A voice called something from inside but no one came. She knocked a third time. The door opened abruptly and Danno appeared, a scalpel in his right hand. He took in her presence without once looking at her directly.

"There's a knob on the door and it turns. Have you no hands?"

———•◆•———

AFTER THAT FIRST VISIT Hannie came often. She would open the door and let herself in and sit in his dusty, chaotic room that smelled of outdoors and feathers, smoking and talking as he worked.

He never once called her Mrs. Renvyle, it was Hannie right from the start. He never asked her questions or offered her anything to eat or drink, he never welcomed her, nor invited her back, but she came anyway, relieved of some burden by his privacy and his indifference.

Autumn and winter were his busiest times, he told her, the times for indoor projects and making the money to last him through the year. People brought him game birds to be stuffed, sometimes a frozen wild bird or the corpse of a pet, sometimes a big boastful fish from the river. He tied flies to sell to the fishermen, he carved the tops of the ash plants he'd cut and dried in the summer, he soaked the bundled sallies from last autumn and wove them into baskets.

He was busy. She could sit if she liked but he probably wouldn't talk to her and she wasn't to look at the hawk directly. If she wanted tea she could make it herself.

She sat. The room was untidy and plain and roughly finished. The walls had been painted a dark-cream color a long time ago but were discolored now and marked with big shambling patches of damp and dirt. Leather leashes and nameless tools hung from nails on the walls, photos of owls and hawks were pinned roughly about the place, there were grubby reference books on a long high shelf and piles of assorted things lay in heaps on the floor and the seats. A door gave off each end of the room and a single window, much larger and more recent than anything else in the house, ran most of the length of the back wall. This window was full of the river, of its moving mass of water. The river dominated the room and was its meaning.

At the left-hand end of the room there was a sink with a kettle and a wooden draining board. On the dirty tiled floor three dogs sprawled. At the right-hand end was his long wooden worktable and an old blue office chair, battered and torn but still revolving. Beside it, between desk and window, was an open-fronted box about two and a half feet high with a length of old blanket pinned across the window behind it. In the box an injured female sparrow hawk was recovering. Leather jesses loosely bound her feet but she could move around within the box and fly up on top of it to perch if she'd a mind to it. The blanket, Danno said, was to stop her flying straight at the window and knocking herself cold.

Hannie never saw beyond this room and the small one to the left of it. She presumed the one to the right was where he slept, but the door was always shut and she never saw him come out of it or go in. He might have slept in a cupboard for all she knew — on a bit of old mattress or a nest of rags, it would have been like him. There was a lavatory built on at the back, but no sign of a bathroom.

The small room at the left-hand end of the house was a sort of store where he kept unworked ash plants and big bundles of sallies and any sort of work-in-progress. On long shelves running all around the room were the birds and animals that were being stuffed, some all but finished, some with splints on legs and necks, some with clips and bits of wires sticking out of them. On the very highest shelves were the finished items awaiting collection. Also the ones that had never been collected. He told her this lightly, with a flick of his head at a pair of chub that swam in a painted box. She couldn't tell if he was angry at this omission. He was always secret and impenetrable. Like the river, its wide opaque surface, its unknown depths.

She didn't care, she didn't need to like him or know who he was; she sat talking about her life before she came here, aware that he couldn't see the pictures constantly forming and dissolving before her inner eye, but relieved nonetheless to be describing them. He worked silently on a bird or an ash plant as she talked, and when she got up to leave he barely nodded. She didn't know if he had listened but it didn't matter, his silence was not unaccepting. It helped her to emerge from the sense of nonexistence she so often had here, and it meant she could begin on the process of joining things up.

Chapter Sixteen

MRS. COADY WAS WASHING THE NEW TILED FLOOR in the kitchen. It looked well now, she thought, a big long room with the light coming in from both sides and the new window facing south for the afternoons. The curtains were new and the walls were a warm egg-yolk yellow. "Like the sun, Mrs. Coady," she'd said. She'd made the curtains and painted the room herself.

That was before. She'd no interest in the house anymore, she'd no interest in anything much anymore, she just walked around the place and wrote letters to the boy and sometimes she visited Danno or Niamh.

It was hard for her, he was a fine man but he wouldn't be everyone's cup of tea, and her so much younger. She never said anything or complained but sometimes she spoke of the light going and the shortness of the day. "I just can't get used to it," she said, "it feels like death."

She was always cold, she wore anything that came to hand, often his clothes, she didn't have enough warm ones of her own. Mrs. Beresford had hinted a bit but he didn't catch on, in the end she just said out straight it was time his wife had some new clothes. He'd looked surprised, and then the next thing they'd gone off to Cork and she'd come home with sweaters and a pair of trousers in a heavy cord. She should have had winter underwear, nothing like an extra layer to keep out this damp cold, but there was no sign of any around, no vests or leggings on the line. She wouldn't complain, and sometimes he didn't see the nose on his own face.

———•◆•———

A LETTER CAME, a queen's head on the stamp and a Northern postmark. Ned handed it to her, he watched her careful blank face and saw how her fingers trembled as she took out the single sheet and read.

"All well?"

"So it would seem." She lifted her coffee cup and drank. "But he needs more sports kit, he's sent a list, he's on a team."

"Which team?"

"He doesn't say, just that he needs it by next week." She put down her cup and began buttering a piece of toast. "If I send him the money he'll buy what he needs himself from the school stockists in the town."

Ned understood. She wanted a check. He went and got his checkbook and wrote one for the sum required. That was all she really wanted from him, he thought, not knowing why he minded so much; it had, after all, been the deal.

When he left the house she got out the writing pad. She wrote urgently, though there was no urgency, she knew that Joss would already have opened a charge account at the school suppliers, would already have acquired whatever he wanted and sold on what she'd bought only weeks before. When she had finished she sealed the envelope and addressed and stamped it. She had to stop herself going straight out to the post. It was pointless: the only post of the day left at four.

That evening she told Ned she thought she might try her hand at poultry. Ducks for the table and a few hens for eggs. He approved, it was traditional for the farm wife to rear poultry, it fell into his scheme of things.

"And we can give away what we don't eat."

Hannie nodded. She didn't intend that so much as an egg be given away or eaten without first being paid for, but she didn't say so.

When she thought of what she might earn she was discouraged. It seemed so little she was nearly ready to give up before she started but she had no choice. She needed no ready money so he gave her none. Even if this poultry scheme earned her nothing, at least it would give her access to Ned's checkbook and bank account as a matter of right. And she saw the time ahead when she might need money badly. Money she didn't have to explain or account for.

Chapter Seventeen

"A POOFTER? DANNO TUOMEY? Not bloody likely. More like old Brandy, I'd say: N.B.I. Not Bloody Interested. Happens sometimes — not a lot, but more than you might think." James Beresford stood in the crush of people by the parade ring at Clonmel races and bellowed his opinions down at Hannie. She gazed up at him, her gloved hand sharing his race card, her shoulder pressed comfortably against his chest.

It was as Ned had said; they all knew Danno, the taxidermist-fella-who-stuffed-things. They went to him with dead animals for their walls and mantelpieces. Sometimes they wanted to know what he thought of a dog.

Not a bad-looking woman, James was thinking. Tanned still, but been living out there for years, could take time to wear off. Or Vere's tar-brush theory might be true. . . . Could do with a visit to the hair-dressers, something decent to wear . . .

James's brother Vere stood on the other side of him, not speaking, absorbed in the horses as they appeared. Ned was across the ring with the rest of their party.

James had been explaining the going to her, translating the marks he had made on his race card about the runners and their past form. He had been enjoying himself — in full flight and oblivious of the carrying power of his voice in the quiet, soft-spoken crowd.

No one looked at him directly and you would not have known that the neutral faces around him listened at all. But from time to time a pencil hovered and a card or a folded newspaper was marked. Racing crowds were the same anywhere, Hannie thought. Suckers for a tip. Scouring the place for Someone-in-the-Know. Ready to ditch their most cherished fancies and bet all on a thrown word.

Hannie knew about racing — every colonial society had a race-course so she knew how to look at a horse in the parade ring and how to read form. She let James know she knew — at least enough to whet his interest in explaining the local situation to her. She was flirting with him in a low-key, idle sort of way. She knew he did not like her. For the moment it amused her mildly to wheedle her way around his dislike. And it pleased her to annoy his wife, Marjorie, who didn't much care for him but knew her rights.

"Don't know why it happens," James was banging on from above her, still on the subject of Danno's lack of sexual orientation. "There'll be theories, of course. Traumas and rot like that. All nonsense. Had Brandy since day one and never a flicker out of him. No mystery to it — born that way." Brandy was an ancient liver-and-white spaniel who dozed all day by the range in Marjorie's kitchen, living proof of Danno's situation.

She nodded now and laughed because she wanted to, which was an unfamiliar way of feeling these days. She saw Ned's eyes on her from across the ring. He was watching the circling runners with Alison, just as she was doing with James. Hannie grinned at Ned and waved. She watched his beaky contained face break open with sudden pleasure. She was surprised — embarrassed almost. She turned her eyes back to James.

James's gaze was on the ring and the led horses swinging their way moodily around the rails. "Danno Tuomey, a poofter . . ." he was saying, shaking his head and chuckling softly. "That's a good one."

A big bay was led in, the number 12 emblazoned in red on his gray stable blanket.

"I like him," Hannie said, referring to Danno, aware that James didn't. He looked at her with sudden strong approval.

"Good woman, yourself," he said warmly. "Red Kestrel. O'Shaughnessy trained. All heart. Fast, but carries a lot of weight." He lowered his voice. "Only his third time out. Another Arkle in the making, so I've heard. Keep it quiet. I'm off to see what the bookies are saying. . . ."

James pushed his hat firmly down on his head and plunged off through the crowd. Vere, who had been standing quietly on the other side of James, expanded slightly to fill up his space. Despite being twins, the two men were not physically much alike. Mentally they were even further apart, though this was not so immediately obvious, as Vere's voice was seldom heard above the noise James made wherever he went. Now Vere smiled vaguely at Hannie and returned his gaze to number 1 2, who was making a mutinous progress around the ring.

"All heart and no discipline," he said, quietly. "That's why they brought him out late. And hates this sort of going. So you like Danno Tuomey, do you? And why is that?"

Hannie shrugged. "He's easy to talk to. I tell him about my life in Kenya and he doesn't change the subject. Then I remember I existed before I came here." She smiled up at him, the slight foreignness in her voice and diction accented. "That can be a pleasant reminder."

Vere smiled back. Peculiar woman, he thought, where on Earth had old Ned found her?

"Are we really so parochial?" he asked.

"On the journey here," she said, "Ned told me you would all ask my maiden name. Then when you didn't know it you would ask me my mother's maiden name. When you found you didn't know that either, you wouldn't ask me anymore questions at all."

"What else did he say?" asked Vere, suddenly interested.

Hannie looked at him, unsmiling. Then, with a slight willful toss of her head, spoke with deliberate indiscretion.

"He said, 'Best not to tell them about the marriages. Catholic country, and all that.'"

Vere roared with laughter. From across the ring, his sister-in-law glared at him ferociously but he didn't notice.

———◦●◦———

THE LAST RACE WAS OVER, the crowd was dispersing, the darkness coming up out of the ground like smoke. A traveler woman thrust oranges at Alison. Giving them away, she said, dragging her emptying black pram across the rutted ground. Alison shook her head but James bought a Mars Bar apiece off her, though no one much wanted them. Red Kestrel had fallen at the last fence, but had got close enough for James to feel he'd had a race. He was resigned but not discouraged.

They tramped across the muddy parking field, looking for where they'd left the cars. Ned handed around a hip flask. Hannie had lost her high spirits, they'd slunk off like the daylight. Her wet feet burned with cold and her hands were numb through her leather gloves. This was not racing, this rite held in mud and bounded by darkness. She tramped along, her head bowed and her shoulders hunched against the cold.

Glancing across, Ned noticed her with sudden clarity, as he might have noticed a stranger. He saw that she was utterly discouraged and slowed his pace. Then he remembered her flirting with James and with Vere, ignoring him, ignoring their wives. She hadn't wanted him when she was full of herself, he decided, so why should he help her now? A stubborn self-righteousness possessed him. He stuck his chin out and pushed on over the freezing mud.

———◦●◦———

THEY THAWED OUT in Marjorie's kitchen with a couple of bottles of red wine, a reheated casserole and some dubiously labeled whiskey. Hannie got as drunk as she could manage. Now, she sat huddled in the corner of the car, not moving or speaking, just glad to be through with it all and going home.

Home? Was that what it was? Not home as others would mean it, but something all the same. A refuge. She closed her eyes and rested her head against the frozen window of the elderly Volkswagen. Her car. Or at least the car she drove unless Ned wanted it. Ned used the Land Rover, but only for short distances. It drank petrol.

Ned was looking straight ahead, his eyes intent on the unraveling ribbon of twisting road, which ran beside a once-great estate. The headlights discovered it out of the darkness: the bare, overarching trees, the crumbling demesne wall, the clusters of houses where pockets of land had been sold off. Beech and ash and lime. Old trees, sufficient and unstriving in the deepening night. Over and over the lights gathered them and let them go.

Hannie sank further into her own dazed state. The heater blasted out hot thick air, its warmth poured over her. Her kicked-off shoes, stiff and dry now from Marjorie's Aga, lay in the caked mud on the floor and her thawed-out feet throbbed and itched with vicious persistence. She'd have worn Wellingtons if she had known. She wasn't asleep, but somehow she was separated from herself, time and place dissolved into this unending tunnel of lit darkness. It was a sort of reverie of aloneness: a curious, stale aloneness, informed by night, discomfort, and hot, beating air.

She came to herself with a jerk. The car had stopped and Ned was getting out to open their gates, his movements careful so as not to awaken her. She went on pretending to sleep. He drove the car through, then got out quietly again to close the gates. She sat up. He appeared beside her, smiled at her, touched her hand.

Driving home through the night Ned had glanced across at her huddled form and thought her asleep. He had turned his gaze back to the unwinding road but with that small shift of attention something had changed in him. This was not just some fellow traveler behaving unreasonably, he realized, not some tracker or bearer deliberately making things difficult. This was Hannie, and she was his wife.

He had felt her there then vividly, the unlikeliness of it: her life curled up in the corner, her slack limbs, her body softened by sleep and age. If only they could pull together they could make some sort of a life for her and she could be happy or at least content. He had been flooded with a heightened, almost impersonal tenderness. His self-righteousness had dropped away.

He stood on the step now, fiddling the key in the door. The lock was stiff or the key needed filing down, it was always awkward. He was thinking he must see to it and at the same time he was trying in his mind to find some way of telling her his thoughts from the car. It had all seemed so obvious and simple when he was driving, but now he didn't know how to begin to speak.

He got the door open, groped for the light switch and felt her pushing past him. He called her name softly but she was already on the stairs and she didn't answer. He mustn't put it off and just let things drift, he decided. He'd get the whiskey and some glasses and take them to her room and they would talk.

But Hannie didn't go to her own room; she went to Joss's room and she locked the door. She pulled off her clothes, drew back the covers and got straight into bed. The sheets were icy and damp. There was a soft knock and she heard Ned's voice calling her name, but she didn't answer. She switched off the light. A few minutes later she heard his footsteps withdraw. She gathered the bedclothes tight around her neck and made herself small in the cave in the freezing bed.

It was no good, she would never sleep, it was too cold, she was too overwrought. She switched on the light again, got out of bed and pulled on her discarded jumper. Then she rooted in Joss's drawers for clothes and socks, glimpsing herself in the speckled mirror of the dressing table as she searched. She stopped rooting and stared at her dim reflection. She pulled her hair back from her face and held it like that with both her hands. Even in the poor light she could not avoid the truth of herself. Hair graying and losing its curl, throat sagging, skin gone spongy and white. Nothing bankable there anymore. She pulled on a pair of Joss's tracksuit bottoms, got back into bed and lay there with her eyes tight shut, too low for sleep.

There was an incident from the afternoon that she could not get out of her mind. A thickening, tallish man of about her own age had bumped against her in the crowded bar, jolting her arm and causing her whiskey to slop itself down his shirt. He had apologized promptly then disappeared, reappearing a few minutes later to put a double into her hand.

That done, he had stood back and stared at her. An open, arrogant gaze, a blatant assessment he did not bother to hide.

"Richard Thornton," he said, introducing himself. "You must be the new wife." He nodded his head toward the back of Ned's. "Welcome to sunny Ireland."

He was dressed in a thick sweater, worn jeans, leather boots and a torn, fringed suede coat. He had gray curling hair and a confident self-satisfaction. She knew at once she was being patronized and insulted. She knew he had come back with the drink to size up her sexual potential, knew that already she had been dismissed as too ramshackle, too close to his own age.

"Glad to see old Ned's got himself shacked up at last. Do him the world of good, a woman about the place. Hope you won't die of boredom, though. Not everyone's cup of tea." He grinned a big easy grin and jerked his head to where James and Alison stood with Ned. They looked glum and diminished in the warmth and life of the crowded bar-tent. They looked inbred and shabby and austere. None of the energy of power remained, only the habit. They looked what they were — the end of their line.

Hannie heard the note of easy contempt in Thornton's voice. They were old buffers. So was she, for the company she kept. Hannie hated him — his curls, his self-satisfaction, his fringed coat. She would rather have Ned, she thought furiously. At least he was honest and not cruel. She turned her back on Richard Thornton and walked away.

Now, in the cold bed, it was not so easy.

The music business, Vere had said. He had made a pile, could live where he liked, do what he liked. He had the old Cantelon house but he wasn't here much. America. A womanizer. Young women, half his age, one after the other. Seemed to have no trouble getting hold of them. He'd had a lot of work done on the house — everything as new. God knows what it had cost. The last word, or so they said. Locals very impressed.

Vere, clearly, was not. But he was wistful about the young women; the wistfulness of a life not fully lived. Then he had shrugged his thin shoulders slightly, letting it fall away. She saw that he settled for less without much struggle. Most likely had always done so. She felt his defeat.

Now, in the freezing night bedroom, she felt her own. She had met Lord Tung — not nodding by the fireside as she had fancied, but abroad still and roving. And he had seen her from up there on his fine white horse and had coldly passed her by.

Dust and ashes were in her mouth and she could not spit them out. In the arrogant eyes of Richard Thornton she had grasped what her life ahead must be. The future — whatever future she might have — lay where it had always lain, in marriage. But not, as she had imagined, in some marriage as yet unmade. It lay in the marriage she had now, with Ned.

Change of plan, she thought, grinning bitterly into the darkness.

She must knuckle down. She must stay married to him until he died and left her what he had. Then things would be different. She would be able to live for the rest of her life without being married to anyone at all.

Chapter Eighteen

THERE WAS ANOTHER LETTER FROM JOSS. Hannie read it, Ned watched. She finished the letter, replaced it in the envelope and held it in her hand as she talked.

"He wants to stay with a friend for half-term."

"He must be settling in then, making friends."

"Yes. A place called Omagh. He says it's not far from the school."

"About fifty miles." Ned pushed back his chair, aware that he wasn't being shown the letter. "It's a bit soon, don't you think? And we don't know this boy."

"Girl," Hannie said flatly.

Ned looked startled. He still hadn't really grasped the facts of coed boarding. There was a short, tight silence. "He can come home now and go to Omagh in the summer," he said finally. "He can't just go traipsing off to strangers —"

"Why not? They've invited him."

"It's too soon."

"So you just said." Hannie'd got to her feet and started vigorously clearing the table.

"He lives here now, Hannie. He can't just go gadding about the place, he has to come home."

"Why?" she challenged. "There's nothing for him to do here, no one his own age to talk to, why must he come? Because you say so?"

"Because *you* want to see him," Ned said quietly.

There was another silence. When Hannie spoke again she didn't look at him. A knife danced on a plate as she lifted it onto the tray.

"Yes, but I also want him to be happy. There are several of them going to Omagh. If it makes him happy to be with other young people then I want that for him too."

"It will do him good to be here, Hannie," Ned said reasonably. "He's not a child now, he can't just do what he wants, he'll have to learn —"

"He *will* learn. Life will teach him, it always does. And he's tired of traveling, tired of traipsing around."

"He'd have to travel to get to Omagh, too." Ned's voice was suddenly sharp with irritation. "He's only been in Ireland a couple of months, Hannie, it will disorientate him going to Omagh at this stage. He should come home, get to know the place, settle in."

"Listen to Ned Renvyle the famous explorer. I must settle, Joss must settle — all you ever think about is settling! Why must we settle? Because it suits you? Because you want it that way?" She banged a cup furiously down on the table. "He can go to Omagh for two days, then come here for the rest of the time. And don't worry, you won't have to pay for extra petrol, he can get a bus direct from Omagh."

"There may not be one."

"There *will* be one."

———◆◆———

"— CUTTER ANTS," Joss was saying. "Big dark ants with jaws like scissors. They eat vegetation. You'll see a line of them trailing through the grass, then a minute later you look again. . . . There's a line all right, but not an ant in sight, they've mown that grass right down to the roots, cleared a highway. Amazing!"

"Like locusts?" Niamh asked vaguely, not moving her eyes off the large dead moth that lay on its back on the windowsill.

"No, stupid, like veggie ants. What do you call this moth?"

"I don't know, I never saw one before." She pored over the moth. "It's huge, isn't it? And look at its horn-things."

"Huge?" Joss sounded derisive.

"Huge for here," Niamh said.

"Nothing here's huge. Everything's small and brown. Insects, birds, flowers. Small and brown . . ."

The smooth black eyes that stretched around Joss's face pointed in her direction. He's like a moth himself in those glasses, Niamh thought. The blank, expressionless eyes.

"The flowers aren't brown."

"Might as well be," Joss said. "You should go to Africa, see some real insects. Everything's bigger, stronger, more interesting."

"I like it here," Niamh said steadily.

"Lucky you," Joss sneered.

———•◆•———

HANNIE'S HAND MOVED of its own volition to wave, but she realized in time and lowered it. Joss didn't like waves, kisses, fuss, didn't even like her standing waiting for the bus to leave. She turned to go.

To hell with him, she thought suddenly, she needed it even if he didn't. She turned back and stood at a decent distance, stubbornly watching the back of his poised blond head behind the glass. Joss looked around once, saw her and turned resolutely away. He was wearing his dark glasses so she couldn't see what his face said. He didn't look around when the bus moved off.

It hadn't been an easy visit, it had started badly, and then got worse. She hadn't been very clever about it either. She'd dug a big hole over the Omagh trip, and then jumped into it in plain view of Ned. She had wanted to believe Joss, that was the problem, wanted the picture he offered her, everything healthy and normal, everyone young and blithe. At the same time she'd known perfectly well it was just a ploy. Joss wouldn't go to a happy teenage house party in some country town called Omagh. He'd go to a city, find himself company, stay away until things fell to bits. Then he'd come home.

And it wouldn't be the first time, either.

But Ned shouldn't have interfered; Joss was hers, for good or ill, the only thing she had that was wholly hers. No one was going to order him around but her.

So despite her defiant words she'd written at once to Joss saying he had to come home and he mustn't accept any invitations. Then she'd phoned the school and said she'd pick up the boy herself at the start of the half-term break.

So he wasn't to be sent to Belfast after all? they asked innocently.

No, he wasn't to be sent to Belfast. She'd collect him and bring him home. And she'd phone again if there was any change of plan.

She told Ned the Omagh girl's mother had rung and canceled. She'd broken her arm, she said, and just wasn't up to all those kids. Ned made no comment.

She had collected him herself from the school but he wouldn't speak to her at all on the journey. At home he'd produced only monosyllables and he'd spent all his time with Niamh. She'd been beside herself. When he was at Niamh's she'd ached to have him with her, but when he was with her and all she got were blank yeses and nos she'd fumed with helpless rage. Ned had said nothing. It was just as well, there was nothing he could have said that wouldn't have made it all worse.

She'd planned to drive Joss back, but the clutch had gone on the Volkswagen and Ned said he needed the Land Rover, he hadn't said why.

She wished they could have driven. On the long monotonous journey he might have tired of his silence and opened his heart.

Pigs might fly. Suddenly, all her anger evaporated and she saw him in her mind, not difficult and devious as she'd been thinking him, but a vulnerable, awkward boy, sitting alone in a crowded bus, a tinny trickle of music spilling from his headphones, the empty miles opening out before him. She would drive him the next time, no matter what, she told herself. And she'd fetch him as well.

A child ran across the empty tarmac. By the bus shelter his mother waited, her hand outstretched. The child took the hand and together they moved away. An old man in a shabby dark suit and a cloth cap also moved away.

The bus had gone, the other witnesses to its going had gone, there was nothing left for her to do but leave as well. Instead she crossed the street and pushed open a door and went into a bar. It was dark and quiet with only a couple of men on stools at the counter and another reading the paper at a table by the fire. They glanced up discreetly, looked away again. She crossed to the counter and stood waiting for the barman to appear. She looked around her. From the mirror behind the bar stared a whey-faced woman with a shock of grizzled hair. She stared back, not realizing at first that she was looking at herself. Then the barman came out of a door at the end, polishing a glass as he walked toward her. Suddenly she remembered she'd given all her cash to Joss.

Even a month ago, finding herself in a bar without cash wouldn't have bothered her. She'd have ordered a drink, waited to have it set up, opened her bag. No purse. What a surprise.

And some man would have offered to pay.

Not now. Suddenly she didn't blame Lord Tung or Richard Thornton, or whatever it was he called himself. She wouldn't have bothered with herself either.

Chapter Nineteen

SHE WAS LOSING HER LOOKS, Mrs. Coady thought, but she didn't seem to care. The warm-brown color had faded from her skin, it was going yellowy-looking and stained, and you'd notice the gray coming through in her hair where before it was bleached by the sun.

"The sky's fallen down, Mrs. Coady," she'd say, standing at the back door, staring out at the low damp day and the cling of moist air in the yard. Then you'd see her around the house, her hand moving to switch on lights she'd already switched on, wanting more brightness, unable to thrive in this squinting daylight.

"I miss the colors, Mrs. Coady," she'd say, her face all strained and pinched up with the cold. She was sorry for her then; there were many that found the short days hard, and them not used to the warm sun and the bright air the way she was.

Tom was on at her to pack in the job and stay home. They didn't need the money, he said, and he was tired of her coming in so dispirited and out of sorts. She was tired of it herself, and she wasn't working for the money, though she let on that she was, that she liked having money that was hers alone to spend or waste as she wanted.

She didn't tell him the truth, that she still couldn't face the house every day because it reminded and reminded of Joanna.

She'd get over it, the same as she'd got over the sleeplessness, but she had to take her time, to find her own way out of the dark maze. It was two years before she'd slept the night through after Joanna died, but she'd got there in the end. Tom thought she didn't talk about Joanna because she was protecting him; that she didn't want to be reminding him on account of him thinking the accident mightn't have happened if he'd thought ahead.

But it wasn't that, she wasn't protecting him, an accident was an accident, a mistake, no one's fault or intention, that was what the word meant. It was just that she needed to be private, even from him — especially from him — she needed to manage it in her own way. And you had to go on living.

People had said she was wonderful, she was so brave, but she knew that behind her back they had said she was hard and it wasn't natural and they'd have liked her better if she'd taken on like Tom. Well, the world hadn't stopped, though for a while there she'd thought it had, and it wasn't as if Joanna was their only child.

Still, she was the youngest, the afterthought, there'd been a special sweetness. It was five years now, the world had all but forgotten Joanna, but she hadn't, there wasn't a day when she didn't see Joanna in her mind and think of her.

Hannie'd cut back her hours, said there wasn't enough work for the two of them. Which was true enough, there wouldn't have been any need for help at all if she'd spent less time traipsing about the place and rolled up her sleeves. And she was able for it, she had proved that from the start, she was a worker all right when she'd a mind to it.

Hannie hadn't told Ned about the hours, Mrs. Coady was certain of it, she'd seen him leave out the money for wages on the table, the old amount, and Hannie had said nothing. Then, when he'd gone out, hadn't she subtracted the extra and taken it and hidden it away in a drawer?

She was saving it for Joss most likely, for the times when she would need it and she didn't want him knowing about it.

—— • ◆ • ——

HANNIE WAS WITHDRAWN and morose. It didn't worry Ned overly, he thought it was worry over Joss or the pain of adjustment and the season pressing in on her, the somberness of it.

Sometimes he hatched schemes and plans but he never really tried to realize them because he didn't know what she wanted or how to change things, and in the end it was easier to stay quiet and watch and wait and endure. He endured as he would have endured the hardships on one of his journeys: stubbornly and without surprise or complaint. Knowing that either it would pass, or it would not.

It should have been easier, once she'd realized her fate, Hannie thought, but it wasn't. Decisions were one thing, living with them was another.

The problem was that of a life which has been lived in action and movement and then finds itself abruptly arrested. Hannie felt like a victim of shipwreck or marooning. She had survived, but the price was this existence with Ned in a hidden valley from which there seemed no escape. Profoundly she didn't want this break in her life, this empty space that was like a mirror showing her back to herself. She was not reflective or used to reflection. She had no wish to confront herself or to understand herself or her life as far as she'd lived it.

More particularly she didn't want to be understood by Ned. She didn't even want to be seen. And she felt him constantly watching her and waiting, drawing conclusions, trying to fit those conclusions together. She felt her privacy violated by this meticulous, attentive observation.

Farm life threw you together, she knew that from her short-lived farm-marriage with Stan. But Stan had only wanted her sexually; apart from his frequent welcomed invasions of her body, Stan had been totally taken up with himself. Ned was different and that difference was more than a different landscape and different time of life. Ned not only wanted to understand her, he wanted intimacy and he wanted to incorporate her into his life. She hadn't expected this, and she hadn't expected to feel so pressurized and observed.

When she couldn't stand it or herself any longer she went to

Danno's and talked about Piet or Africa. Danno didn't take any notice of her. He just got on with carving the knob of an ash plant into a fox's head or putting the rand on a log basket or whatever it was that he happened to be doing when she landed in.

Besides he was growing used to her, her fiery energy, which burst out in anger and complaint and then suddenly left her and leaked away into nothing. He didn't try to reassure her or placate her. He didn't know what it was she was trying to figure out or think through and he didn't care. He just let her come in and walk around his room, talking and talking until it was enough for the time being and she could leave him and return to her life.

She talked about Piet a lot but she never once spoke of Ned. "My first husband," she called Piet, making it clear she'd had several. He liked to hear her talk of him, his trading station, his time in the Japanese camp, his little homilies and sayings. Sometimes he'd wondered that Piet should be so vividly there in the front of her mind after all these years, but he didn't ask.

"A fish in a carriage rut." That was what she said she felt like. It was an apt enough image, he thought, but he doubted Ned Renvyle would ever do as her Piet had done. He'd think she'd get used to the carriage rut, would grow to like it, wouldn't even realize she needed water not air. But she'd only herself to blame for it. She'd jumped into this rut of her own accord and she didn't seem to be about to find a way of jumping out of it.

Chapter Twenty

COLD WINDS BLEW FROM THE NORTH and winter came early. The river was burnished where the sun reached — a dull, matte gleaming, like hoarded silver paper smoothed with a child's wet finger. The trees were emptying. Ned loved the ash best — its slender naked-ness. A stripe of soft light followed each limb, each twig, where the weak sun shone. Here and there, in the copses of cherry, tattered red leaves hung on. There was a poignancy about them, a defeated courage — the pennants of lost armies trailing home, the winter press-ing. The oaks under the lee of the hill still clutched their old brown leaves. The rest were swept bare, the leaves gone.

Color leached from sky, woods, fields. Only the ivy kept its strong dark green, it glittered in the pale light, burdening up the hearts of the trees in great hanging masses that swung in the cold winds like gallows fruit. The ash were mauve-gray on the hill, the spindles had lost their leaves, their last berries stood in pinpoints of cerise against the gray. By the river the tall buff skeletons of charlock and thistle rattled in the bleak wind. On the paths, black sludges of fallen leaves.

Even the sounds thinned and grew monotonous: the hungry bleating of sheep, the wing-whir of pheasants in the mornings, the dry rattle of magpies all through the short, dark days.

Late one afternoon, the light dying, Ned decided to talk to Danno about shooting the vermin on his land. He had done it himself at the start, had liked walking the land with a gun in the early morning, but the farm took more of his time now and Danno wasn't above poaching across his bounds. Might as well legitimize the situation, make an arrangement, Ned thought. Danno could go on shooting the odd bird in return for a haul of dead crows and the occasional fox.

Danno was agreeable, the business was done and he should have gone but he hung on, trying the sentences this way and that in his head and liking none of them. Danno sat at his worktable fiddling with a half-stuffed pheasant and saying nothing. No matter what way Ned tried he couldn't slide over the fact that he wanted to ask his wife's friend what could be done to make her happier.

"You could get her a dog," Danno said, when he'd got the gist of what Ned was saying. He heard himself, and a twisty little smile worked his mouth. "Not a house dog or a pup," he went on. "A grown trained dog she has to work and exercise. One she can be proud of." He looped a fine wire under the wing-feathers and chose his words with care. "She can handle a gun, can't she? I've heard her speak of game-shooting in Africa? Well, she can go along with you when you shoot. As a gun or as a picker-up, it doesn't matter. So long as she's there in her own right, not just stuck in a corner with the wives." Danno paused; he was glad Hannie couldn't hear him.

"She might not take to it," Ned said, his hands deep in his pockets. The pause in the room lengthened. "There's no telling with her," he added, staring intently out of the window at the deepening gloom beyond.

"She rides, you know. Sits a horse as well as any woman. Marjorie Beresford offered her the use of those two mares of hers any time she wanted, said she could use a bit of help exercising them since her back went. As good as begged her." Ned waited, but Danno did not comment.

"No interest," he went on. "I told her if she doesn't want to go to Marjorie's there's always old Connie. I might as well be suggesting she go to mass. How do I know it would be different with a dog?"

"You don't," Danno said. He didn't say anything else but kept his eyes and his hands on the pheasant he was wiring. He was angry and embarrassed at this conversation. Ned should have known better than to ask him — did know better — but chose to ignore what he knew. Ned should have kept it to himself that his relations with his wife were not all they should be.

He knew, of course, and Ned knew that he knew. But Ned shouldn't have brought it out and set it there in the middle of the room for them both to look at, it was a gross intrusion. It hadn't been Danno's idea that Hannie come calling on him.

"It's a shot in the dark, but it might be worth a try," Ned said. He had cheered up, his voice had regained its confidence. It was the opposite for Danno. His hands shook as he worked and he knew he'd have to rewire the legs when Ned had gone. Who did these people think they were? he thought furiously. Those days were long over and done.

And if Ned believed a dog would solve Hannie's problems he must be either desperate or stupid.

———•◆•———

NED TURNED IT OVER in his mind as he drove back home. Odd fish, Danno, difficult childhood, there were stories. Mrs. Coady said he was an outside child. Some said he was a spoiled priest as well.

Somehow he gave the impression that he didn't much like Hannie. That she'd taken to visiting, though he didn't want to be visited.

It was typical of her, Ned thought. She wouldn't like the people who wanted to be her friends and she took up with someone who didn't. Maybe he shouldn't have gone there, shouldn't have asked. Danno certainly hadn't made it any easier.

Chapter Twenty-one

"WONDERFUL WOMAN, ALISON. Been the making of old Vere, don't know how he would have managed without her. How any of us would have managed, come to that." James stood at the fire, one arm resting on the high mantelshelf. He stared moodily into his half-drunk whiskey, swirled it around in the glass. Then he sighed, tipped back his head and threw in the remains. "I'll have a word," he said, as though that sorted the problem. "Get Alison on board. . . . Give Hannie someone to talk to. . . . Shouldn't be running around with oddballs like Tuomey and girls half her age . . ."

Ned said nothing. He avoided looking at James. He knew the avoidance was cowardly, but there was nothing he could say, certainly not that Hannie didn't seem to like Alison. He wished sincerely that he'd talked to Hannie himself when he'd meant to, and left his worries unshared. James was about as sensitive as a concrete bollard, but even James would have kept his mouth shut and his thoughts to himself if Ned hadn't started in on it. Wives were wives, in James's book, and you pretended it was all roses and sunshine even when you could feel the floodwater lapping around your ankles. Unless the husband raised the thing, declared the subject open.

James was pleased with his solution. He sincerely admired his sister-in-law and was confident of her tact and abilities, which had been exercised on her husband's family over the years and as the need arose. She was neither bossy nor managing and could be relied upon to gently insinuate herself into your affections and equally gently to nudge you in the right direction when you needed it. She was intelligent and self-deprecating and still reasonably presentable in late middle age. As a young woman she had been a beauty. She was, in James's view, the perfect wife.

The only thing that was quite beyond his understanding was why she had saddled herself with Vere and, in time, with his extended family. She must have "fallen for him," he would say to himself, or Marjorie, when he had cause, once more, to examine the puzzle. "Falling for people" was something women did. Marjorie said nothing. She was grateful for Alison's influence on James and her as yet undefeated ability to call him back from the bottle. She did not much care for Alison and she thought her dull company, but she knew a good thing when it came and sat down under her nose.

James strolled over to the drinks tray and helped himself to another whiskey. You could wait all night before old Ned would think to offer you one. Fellow was a natural ascetic. Tents and camp beds and deserts and all that. Made an ass of himself over this Hannie woman. A baggage, if ever there was one. A strap, as the country people would say. Must have got carried away with himself. Plenty of time to regret it now.

Ned watched James quietly and followed all his assumptions. He was neither surprised nor offended by them, but Hannie certainly would be. He was aware that talking to James — even to the limited extent that he had — had been both unwise and disloyal. But it was done now and couldn't be undone. He just hoped that Hannie wouldn't appear before he got rid of James.

They had been at the mart together, had run into Niamh's father, and somehow the result had been this misplaced confidence. With James at his elbow, Ned had steered his way out of the building and down through the pens for a last look at the calves he'd just let go. The cattle were anxious and unsettled and a steady reek of shit and fear was acrid in his nostrils. The mart was busy and he could hear the echoey boom of the auctioneer's voice on the Tannoy. The wintry sun had all but gone; its last rays lifted the wet concrete yard and the metal rails of the pens to a cold glory, it aureoled men and beasts with radiant light.

The air smelled frosty and keen above the cattle-reek. Ribbons of peat smoke from the chimneys of all the little houses around the mart ran straight up into its clear stillness. The sky to the west was lemon, the night was ready to fall. Something in Ned quickened. He felt the timelessness of this life, the ancient repetition of ceremony and act and season. He had spent so many years searching for myth in other lands and among other peoples, yet it was here all the time and could be lived from the inside.

John Comerford was standing over by the mart wall watching him with the quiet steady gaze of a man who has been doing it for some time and knows that his attention will be rewarded. When Ned saw him he nodded quietly and smiled. Ned made his way over to him.

"That's a fair price you're after getting," Comerford said.

"I've done worse," Ned said, his spirits rising at this approval.

The mart was always an ordeal for Ned. He knew that his inexperience showed, that he didn't yet know the nuances of pricing, of when to sell and when to hold back from selling, and he was afraid that he was mocked behind his back. He told himself that he didn't care what these farmers thought of him, but he was lying, he cared a great deal, and all his prickly pride was invested in the regard of one or two men.

"You were selling yourself?" he asked, though he'd seen Comerford's calves under the hammer just after his own. Asking was courtesy, it was part of the ritual dance of the conversation.

"I was," John Comerford said. "And I'm not sorry either." He looked up and then down at his feet. "There's a change or two in your life, or so I'm hearing?"

Ned agreed that there was. "Will you thank Mrs. Comerford for the jug? Hannie was very pleased with it, she said she'd be writing." He must remember to tell her to do so.

James appeared. He nodded at Comerford but he didn't join in. It was clear he was ready to leave and was waiting to extract Ned. James was a dogged companion, if you were with him you were with him, there was no getting rid of him.

"Kathleen would have me ask if Niamh is being a trouble to you?" John Comerford asked. "She was home there last week and she talked a lot about Mrs. Renvyle. Kathleen says you're to tell her straight if she's under your feet."

Ned assured him that Niamh was not being a trouble. On the contrary, he said, she was company for Hannie, who was lonely in this new country with her son away at school. It was good for her to have a young face around her, good for them all.

Comerford nodded and seemed satisfied. They shook hands and he thanked Ned again for his care of Niamh, and Ned said again that it was a pleasure and a small return.

James's old green station wagon was parked off a side street, the passenger door secured with a knotted length of rope. Ned had to get in on James's side and shift himself across under the steering wheel. The awkward movement caught at his hip and a sharp stab jarred through his body, making him suck in his breath with the pain. James heard the sound. He passed over the hip flask he'd been nursing in his gloved hands.

"Arthritis," he said cheerfully. "Goes with the climate — happens to us all. They'll saw you up when it gets bad enough — doctors all butchers at heart, no interest in a pill if there's a chance they can get to cut holes in you, fire out the bones, stuff you with plastic instead. Seems to work, though. Have to live with it till then, that's the problem. There's a healer fella over at Coolnabawn you could try. Lays you out on a table and pulls you about. Some Johnny out of nowhere, married the mistress after old Henry Nairn passed on. Englishman, or so he says. Definitely not an officer. Funny ideas about food. Not half bad with animals, though — Marjorie uses him on her ponies, believe that's how he wormed his way into the grieving widow's graces. Or there's a Seventh Son of a Seventh Son over Clonmel way. Bit too close to voodoo for my taste, but the country people swear by him. Peasants. Rag trees and water out of a holy well and a bit of clay from a saint's grave under your pillow when you sleep. Superstition."

James rattled on in a steady flow as he twiddled the choke and crashed the gears and negotiated his way awkwardly onto the road. Ned sat back and listened and nodded. It would probably have been all the same to James if he hadn't, but he was fond of James, despite Hannie's contempt for his company. Hannie couldn't seem to grow fond of those she disliked or was disappointed in. She couldn't put away her expectations and let them grow on her like that old coat of his she took down off the peg and wore about the farm.

"What was all that about Comerford's daughter?" James asked suddenly, changing tack. "Heard you'd let her a cottage. Marjorie said she painted houses. What's the sense of that, I said — a slip of a girl setting herself up to paint houses? — she'd never be able for it. Marjorie said I'd got the wrong end of the stick, as usual. Said the girl paints pictures, not rooms. Pictures of houses. I said well she'd better not go painting Ned's house till Hannie stops messing it around, better find her something else to paint. Houses the only thing she can do? What about animals? I've a dog she could turn her hand to, that black setter I have off O'Reilly. Wouldn't object to her having a go at Jacko if she'd a mind to it. Strange-looking creature. A Gordon setter, O'Reilly called him, but I'd say there's retriever in there and more besides. Looks like the wrath of God and hunts like an angel. Never had a dog like him, the softest mouth I ever saw. He'll lift a hen pheasant out of the nest and bring her home and lay her in my hand. 'Dead, Jacko,' I say, and he unhinges his jaws a fraction and out rolls the bird. Dead, my arse. Not a mark on her. Gets up and flies away once she's over the shock."

Ned had listened more than once to the wonders of Jacko. He allowed himself to distract James.

"She may do animals, I don't know, you could ask her. She'll say no if she doesn't want to — not shy about that sort of thing. It might depend on how much you were thinking of paying her."

James looked shocked. Ned could see that payment had never crossed his mind. James had volunteered Jacko as a favor, he was trying to be helpful.

Ned pressed on. "It's by way of an experiment, all this. She wants to see if she can earn a living at it."

James gathered himself. "And what's she living off in the meantime?" he asked. "What's she living off while she's experimenting? Comerford, I dare say. And Comerford's fobbed her off on you till she comes to her senses. Daughters! Worse than sons. Come on at you all eyes and tears. Yes Daddy and no Daddy and butter wouldn't melt in my mouth, Daddy. Before you know it you have them so spoiled they think it's your duty to keep them for life."

James spoke with feeling. He had two daughters of his own and their maintenance in the style that both they and their mother considered appropriate had long been a sore point. Handing them over to husbands had temporarily eased the situation, but hadn't solved it.

"So if she wants to keep on at this painting game," Ned was saying, "she has to start making it pay. I'll mention Jacko to her if you like, sound her out?"

But James was not to be pinned down so easily.

"Bloody stupid name," he said grumpily. "Don't know what's come over people. Bloody stupid fashion for Impossible Bloody Irish Names. Surprised at the man. Nothing Irish about Comerford. Good Norman name, papist or no. Next thing you know she'll be changing her surname, putting the whole damn lot into some sort of unpronounceable caterwaul, won't even know who she is, who her people are. Hannie like her, does she?"

It was Ned's turn to be discomfited.

"Not much," he admitted.

"Humph," James responded. "Thought Comerford said the girl couldn't stop talking about her?"

"Hannie's at a bit of a loose end, just now," Ned said quietly. "Niamh made friends with her boy when he was here. Hannie's taken to calling in with her from time to time. Bored, I'd say. And I'd rather she was there than spending her time with Danno Tuomey. At least the girl's educated, comes from a decent family."

"Heard about Danno," James said, for once not taking his eyes off the road as he talked. "Wondered how much there was in it?"

And that was how Ned had got himself into this mess, with James tramping around the study, helping himself to whiskey, immune to all attempts to get rid of him, and Hannie due to walk in at any moment.

Life was simpler before, Ned thought. He thought it without regret or recrimination. It was simply a statement of fact.

Chapter Twenty-two

ALISON HAD BEEN GOT "ON BOARD" and was quietly doing her best. "Hovering around like a bad smell," as Hannie, exasperated, had put it. "Persecuting me with invitations."

Hannie had said no to beagling in Tipperary, to an afternoon's pruning course in Kilkenny, to the selling of Armistice-day poppies to people-who-might-be-thought-to-be-sympathetic. She had refused invitations to inspect graveyards and once-great houses and poke around in ruined gardens. But she had agreed to a tree walk and to shopping in Cork. Of the two she had marginally preferred the tree walk.

"You can always tell ash," Alison said. "Those lovely smooth limbs, beige-gray, and the arms just raised in that gesture like wonder. Ash is the masculine tree and hazel the feminine since ancient times. You'll see them together at holy wells, the ash and the hazel, the masculine and the feminine. Odd really, ash is so graceful. Perhaps it's because hurleys are made from its wood. . . ."

Hannie was leaning against a crumbling wall, smoking a cigarette and staring at the blowing sky behind the empty branches of the small gray tree. From time to time Alison would pass her a twig or a bit of bark and she would glance at it absently, then drop it into the mud and resume her staring. She didn't know what hurleys were, or holy wells, and she didn't care. She was used to the foliage and blossom of Africa, she couldn't see what Alison saw, what stirred in her voice and lit her face.

"Beech," Alison said, moving on. "Isn't it lovely? So graceful and wide and all those lacy twigs like fine hair standing out from a head. They blow down in the gales. Big wide shallow roots, the winds rock the trees and they just keel over."

Alison was absorbed in her subject. She would reach up to catch hold of a branch, pulling it down to show twig structure and shape and buds already forming for the spring. She would rub the moss off bark to show its pattern, and suggest ways of remembering names by associations, which mostly depended on an intimate knowledge of nineteenth-century English literature and meant nothing to Hannie. Hannie mooched along behind her kicking at sludges of dead leaves, hearing Ned's voice in her mind.

She's a nice woman, she means well, couldn't you just go for a walk with her?

Well she had, and this was the result. She was disappointed in Ned over Alison. She had thought him more honorable, had thought that at least he wouldn't have discussed her, would have left her to work out her own fate. She cursed herself now for letting him persuade her into this.

———•◆•———

ALISON STOOD AT THE SINK, scrubbing and disinfecting flower-pots to put away for the spring. They needed doing and she always cleaned something when she was worried or upset, it meant you could think things over without getting too overwhelmed by them and even if your conclusions were completely depressing at least you'd done something useful while you were reaching them.

Vere appeared in the doorway in his stockinged feet, rubbing his hands and blowing on them to get some warmth into them. He took off his damp coat and arranged it on the rail in front of the Aga.

"Good walk?" he asked. "Interested in trees, was she?"

"Not much," Alison admitted without looking around. "But it got her out of the house."

"Hmph. Wasting your time, old girl. Ned married her. Let him look after her."

Alison scrubbed hard. "The Jeyes fluid's finished. I must put it on the list."

"Getting on, are they? No, well I expect he's regretting it now."

"I don't think so. She's an unusual woman. And think how Ned's spent his life. He's always been fascinated by nomads."

"Nomads? You're an incurable romantic, Ali. The woman's not a nomad, she's a tramp."

———◆———

HANNIE WOKE the next day and stood back from herself. Something had nudged at her introversion and suddenly she was critical of the habit of drift she'd slipped into. She felt she'd done nothing for weeks but exist in a torpor of walking and staring. She must act, she decided, if only to defend herself from Ned and Alison. Joss was blessedly quiet but the silence couldn't last forever, already it felt ominous. She'd have to get started on something sooner or later, be it hens or theft or prostitution. She went to the library in Dungarvan for a book.

She asked at the desk and the librarian waved her to a shelf marked DIY. Obediently she went through its contents. There were books on geese and on bees, there was nothing on hens. She went through the shelf again then crossed to the desk, annoyed, for she'd set her mind to action.

"It is odd, is it not, this omission?" she asked, her voice at its most foreign. "And in a country library?"

"Dungarvan isn't country," the librarian said haughtily. She stood looking at Hannie, daring her to contradict. Hannie glared back. There was a moment's impasse, then the librarian relented.

"Sure, why would we keep books on hens?" she asked. "Doesn't everyone know how to rear them?"

Hannie picked up the book on bees and opened it. "I don't," she said, looking at a diagram of a beehive and not at the librarian. "That's why I wanted a book."

In the end she got out the volumes on bees and geese on Ned's ticket, reasoning that their presence in the library must mean a wider ignorance than there was over hens, and a wider ignorance might signify a hungrier market. And she took out a book on herbs as well. It was sitting on the counter looking at her, Ned wanted to diversify, he'd been talking about lavender and scented herbs, she might as well show willing.

———•◆•———

NED CAME HOME with a pup, a little Springer bitch straight out of the litter. He put it into Hannie's arms and said it was hers. Hannie looked at it and smelled Alison. She put the pup down on the floor and it peed with fright. She prodded the pup with her foot. The little creature caught hold of her shoe and chewed at the leather. She lifted her foot and the pup fell over onto its back.

A baby will settle her. That's what was always said of a new wife. This would be Alison's version: a pup for a woman past childbearing. She picked up the empty washing basket, put on her boots, and went out in the dusk to the line. She hauled at the wet clothes that had hung all day in the damp air. Well, Ned had bought it, he could look after it, she would not.

Later she watched as the pup played into his hands and would not eat.

"What shall I do?" he asked her, trying to involve her.

"Whatever you like," she said sourly. But she went to the fridge and took out an egg and some milk and broke bread into the beaten-up mixture. She gave it to him.

Ned came back into the kitchen, holding out the empty bowl. The pup had eaten it all. He was pleased and relieved. Already he cared for the puppy. She was pleased, too, despite herself. For a short moment they were both pleased at once and they smiled at the little warm creature, puffed up with milk and bread, and forgot themselves.

Hannie bent down and put out her hand. The puppy came to her and placed her neck on Hannie's wrist and her head on her opened palm. She gazed up at her out of round black eyes with only a sliver of white at their lower rim. Hannie allowed this, knowing that in letting the pup love her she would be letting herself love in return. She let herself. She was holding out against so much in this new life, for once she did not resist the softening.

A knock came to the door. Niamh came shyly in to look at the pup and dropped to her knees. "Oh, the darling," she crooned. "Oh, the doaty little puppy." She was on the floor, the puppy squirming and wriggling in her arms, biting at her fingers and her nose and the loose strands of her hair. Ned stood, smiling and watching. Hannie watched too. For a moment the kitchen was full of firelight and warmth and young things.

"What are you going to call her?" Niamh asked. She sat back on her heels with the puppy in her arms, looking at Ned. Ned looked at Hannie.

Hannie turned away, the softness going from her face which grew calm and neutral and watchful again. "Alison," she said decisively.

——— •◆• ———

DANNO SMILED a small bitter smile to himself when he heard. A trained dog, he had said, not a pup. He didn't himself care for the innumerable small shoots that were littered around the country, but Ned liked his day out with a gun.

Perhaps Ned didn't want to bring his wife along just yet, Danno thought. It was a risk all right. She might or might not behave herself.

But the pup couldn't even begin to be trained for another few months, it would be a year at least before she was ready enough to be useful.

A year's grace to break Hannie in.

Danno shrugged his thin shoulders and went out to feed his Labradors. Hannie would just have to stay in her rut and learn how to like muddy water, he thought. It was her own fault. The people of Abel should not walk with the people of Cain.

——— •◆• ———

NED CALLED the puppy Pippa. She was around the house in the day, chewing things and piddling and making sorties into the yard, but it was Ned who fed her and dosed her and played with her, she was his, now. He had tried to back off, to be cold and restrained, but when he saw how studied was Hannie's indifference to her, he gave it up and was unashamed in his affection. Someone had to love the little dog and teach her. If Hannie would not, then he must.

Besides, he liked having Pippa around, he looked forward to coming in to her when darkness had closed down the day. He would stand in the doorway between the scullery and the kitchen drying his hands on a raggedy towel, watching her thumping her tail and wriggling in anticipation. He liked washing his hands and drying them, taking his boots off, placing them together in their place beneath the hooks where his coat hung. He liked all these slow, thorough actions, the glow of the lighted kitchen in front of him, the smell of mud and bran and old flowerpots in the scullery behind.

"He might as well have bought a dog instead of a wife in the first place, Mrs. Coady," she said not long after Pippa's arrival.

Mrs. Coady had raised her eyebrows at the word *bought*. She wondered if Hannie had said it to Ned. More than likely. For a survivor, she lacked sense.

Hannie hadn't, but what she didn't say spoke almost as loudly as what she did. Sometimes Ned was as exasperated with Hannie as she was with Alison. Why had she married him if she was going to refuse to participate in his life? he thought bitterly. She had misled him in their brief courtship. She'd been so different then, easy and open, an unconventional and independent companion. He hadn't misled her, hadn't pretended beforehand that he would be other than he was. Why was she always so difficult? He would go over it in his mind, rehearsing his arguments, nursing his anger.

His exasperation was exacerbated by guilt over Alison. He liked Alison and he respected her and he felt that he had trespassed on her, not least because he couldn't bring himself to tell Hannie that the pup hadn't been her suggestion but Danno's.

Sometimes though, his feelings swung the other way and he would be contrite. He should be supporting her, he told himself, not trying to convert her into something appropriate. If he had wanted appropriateness he would have chosen differently. He must help her to get used to things, explain his life and what he wanted from her. Tentatively, he tried to speak of his disappointment over her attitude to his friends.

"They're your friends, Ned, not mine, and I don't have to like them because you do. I'm not saying I won't see them. I'll invite them when you want them, cook for them, entertain them. I'll go to their houses and eat their badly cooked food and listen over and over to hilarious stories about people I've never met and never want to." She looked at him out of those deep brown eyes that went so strangely with her light hair. "*Make an effort,* you said, so I'm making an effort, but I still don't like them. Why would I? They've been looking through the same window at the same few fields for hundreds and hundreds of years, they've forgotten long ago there might be other windows, other views and other ways of being. And they don't like me either, they know what they like, and it isn't me."

"They do like you, Hannie, Alison —"

"Alison is doing all this for you, not me. Alison is, as you said, a very nice woman, but one whom I don't happen to be interested by, Ned, and I don't want to go riding with her or walking or shopping or looking at gardens or other people's houses. Nor do I want to have tête-à-têtes with her about trees."

"Then what will you do, Hannie?" he asked.

"Don't worry about me, I'll find something to do."

But that wasn't enough for him. He should leave her alone, he knew he should leave her alone, but he couldn't. He wanted to talk to her, to show her what he loved and what he thought. All his life he had held back from intimacy, now he wanted to speak and have her understand what he said. And he was convinced still that she could, despite the signs, despite his friends' unspoken compassion. It was for this, he realized, that he'd married her and not someone else.

And Hannie felt smothered by him and by what he required of her. She felt burdened down by his constant efforts to close the distance.

Chapter Twenty-three

HANNIE GOT OUT OF BED as soon as she woke and pulled on a sweater. It was freezing cold in the room and her breath came in visible clouds. Like smoking, she thought, shaking a cigarette out of the packet and reaching for the lighter. She padded about in the heavy socks that she wore now in bed every night for her chilblains. The window was opaque, the glass patterned with flowers of gray ice. She reached out her finger to touch and the glass seemed to jump out and burn her. Ice on the inside as well as the outside. She dragged the rickety sash as wide as it would go, then knelt on the floor and stuck her head and shoulders out into the morning.

The sky was a length of stretched silk. Lemon silk, translucent and shot through with pink. The grass was gray-white with frost and the trees were furred on every branch and twig with a coating of tiny frost-hairs. A white mist lay over the river.

Hannie threw her half-smoked cigarette out of the window and breathed in the clear empty coldness. She liked the promise in the air and the brief extravagance of color in the sky. As she watched the sun broke through and the avenue poplars shone like white flames where the light caught their frosted branches. A momentary glory. Almost before her eyes the ice thawed and the white splendor dulled. Still, she felt better, defeat leached from her.

"Geese," Ned said over breakfast.

Hannie looked at him. She'd forgotten all about the library books. As far as she knew they still lay unopened on the window-shelf beside the sink.

"You could start in the spring," he went on. "Less complicated than bees and at least there's a sure market for Christmas.

"I looked at the books," he explained. "My cousins keep geese, know all about them, we'll go and see them. Good time of year for it, just before slaughter, they'll tell you all you need to know."

It seemed he had cousins who kept geese over Kenmare way. Their mother was his mother's youngest sister, he said, and he owed them a visit.

"The old girl's eighty-six, she can't live forever. You'll like Ellen, she does all the hands-on work, Lettie runs the show." He poured himself another cup of coffee from the *cafetière* Hannie had bought in Cork on her shopping trip with Alison. "We could go for the day," he went on, "I'll find the time. You might as well learn all you can before you start."

Hannie agreed. She had no desire to inspect hordes of geese or to question Wellingtoned female cousins on fattening, but at least it was an outing. Ned seemed pleased. To her surprise, he got up at once to ring his cousins. She remembered it was Sunday. Cheap rate on Sunday, she toyed with the idea of phoning Joss, but resisted the temptation. Joss hated being phoned for a chat, he'd just stand there saying nothing until she got the message and fell into silence.

"The old girl's got pleurisy," Ned said, coming back, "she's been in hospital." He sat down shaking his head. "Extraordinary thing, Ellen was on the point of phoning, she had the number in her hand when I rang her."

Aunt Cecily had been sick enough, Ned said, Ellen had held off phoning until the news was good because she hadn't wanted Ned to feel he had to visit. She was doing well now, Ellen said, she'd been wanting her own bed, but the doctor had ordered a week in a nursing home where she'd be warm and quiet and properly looked after.

She'd had a fit. Properly looked after? Of course she'd be properly looked after, she'd told the doctor, what else did he think she had two daughters for?

Poor Ellen. She was the youngest and most bullied of Ned's cousins and he was very fond of her.

Anyway, the old girl had caved in in the end, must have been weaker than she thought, and they'd found a place in Kenmare that would take her.

"House and geese no longer on the agenda, I'm afraid, Hannie," Ned said. "I'll go anyway of course, see Aunt Cecily, meet up with the girls in Kenmare for some lunch — but there's no need for you to flog all that way," he continued. "No one will be offended."

But Hannie said she would come, geese or no geese. Ned seemed pleased. If he felt any apprehension he concealed it.

———— ·◆· ————

"You LOOK VERY NICE, very smart, Hannie, but we're not lunching at the Court, we're only meeting there, we'll find somewhere in the town that's less expensive." Ned looked at his watch. "You've got time to change."

Hannie said she would come as she was. She was sick of sweaters and trousers.

"It's a four-hour drive," he told her, "you'll be cold on the journey."

"I'll bring a coat."

The roads were frosty but dry and they made good time, arriving early. Hannie was pleased, she wanted to sit in the hotel with a drink, looking and being looked at. She smoothed the fine dark skirt of the expensive Italian wool suit she had bought four years ago for a winter business trip to Germany with Andrew. She had worn it on their first visit to Joss's school but after that it had sat in the wardrobe and would have gone on sitting there forever if Ned had had his way. She didn't care if he thought it unsuitable, it was the best thing she owned and she wanted to look quite unlike a woman who might be considering keeping geese.

The hotel building was gray and stately and there were other cars scattered about the dark-green grounds and parked under the ancient yew trees. They got out, Ned locked the car and they walked slowly across the drive to the stone steps. Hannie glanced down at her feet, liking them in their beautiful suede shoes on the dark sweep of the drive. She straightened, the sway crept back into her walk. Looking at them gave her confidence and helped her remember who she'd been before.

The wooden outer doors of the building lay open and there were soft daytime lights glowing behind the glass inner doors. The glass was old and fine and when you moved your head it had ripples in it like running water. Ned reached forward and turned the handle. He pushed but the door wouldn't give. He pushed again.

"There's a notice," Hannie said, pointing to the paper taped to the glass.

"Closed until April," she read, and looked around, dismayed. Ned was still fumbling in his pockets for his glasses. "But it can't be closed," she said, unable to accept it. "The lights are on, there are other cars . . ."

"I expect people like to meet here," Ned said. "Meet here, walk around the grounds . . ."

"Why?"

"Why not?"

She felt like a child whose treat has been taken away. She stiffened herself. She would not be disappointed, she would not. And over so small a thing.

"Peculiar country," she said calmly. "People want to meet in December at a hotel that's closed?" She shrugged and sat down in her beautiful suit on the damp stone steps. She reached in her bag for a packet of cigarettes, took one out and lit it slowly, ignoring Ned's look. Ladies don't smoke in public outside good hotels, even closed ones, the look said. Too bad. She wasn't a lady.

"People here are content with nothing," she said lightly.

A rackety station wagon burst through the open gates and charged to a halt. Moth-eaten dogs and women in tweeds and cardigans erupted out of it. Ned looked relieved. He hugged his cousins, rumpled the dogs, patted the car and called it by name.

"Glad to see Rosemary's still on the road."

Hannie was introduced. The dogs were called back, introduced, shut into the car. They would walk to the nursing home, Lettie said. A dreadful place, frilly and pink, but it wasn't far. Then they would find some lunch.

They set off in a little straggle, Ned in front, talking to Lettie and Hannie with Ellen bringing up the rear. Hannie didn't bother to talk. Ellen looked as if she would have liked to have done the same, but her training wouldn't allow it.

"Ned said you want to know about geese?" she opened shyly.

———◆———

It was very cold already, and would freeze again as night fell. Lights were coming on in the scattered dwellings; here and there yellow rectangles pushed forward through the gloom. Ned opened the window an inch, smelling the fields and the frosty air, watching the folded land fade into the four o'clock dusk. From time to time there were hamlets strung like beads down the side of the road, but mostly it was just fields and farms and boreens running off into twilight. Sometimes a creamery. Sometimes small towns, empty and quiet, the wide streets crossed with colored lights that swung in the windy dusk. Once they waited while two old men and a girl-child drove a few cows home for milking. Once they stopped for travelers' horses: big dark shaggy shapes grazing loose by the road in the dying light.

Ned felt his love for this shrouded country, these small lost roads, this people he had known from childhood. Nothing in his life had moved him like this, not even the deserts, and he wondered that he'd journeyed so far to see what had always been here. He resolved not to leave again, he was home at last and he wanted nothing else.

He glanced across at Hannie. She sat slumped into herself, staring out of the window, seeing fields and mud and beasts and hedges pass before her eyes. For a moment he saw it as she saw it and for the first time he didn't blame her or condemn her because she couldn't be satisfied as he was. He would think of some way to make her happy, he decided. He felt very tender toward her, very patient and protective.

Then he stopped thinking and abandoned himself to this joy that was filling him. He could see the twin lights of a car away down the road in the valley. He could see darkness thicken and hold the land.

Chapter Twenty-four

"MASTER THEM?" DANNO SAID. "Put that out of your head, there's no mastering them." As he talked he was slitting open the blackbird Tommy Moran had found dead on the road and brought to him the night before. The sparrow hawk in the open-fronted box watched him sideways out of her yellow eye.

"Some men try it," he went on. "Whole books have been written about one man's struggle with one raptor. They're always the same. Man tries to master hawk. Fails. Tries again. Fails again. Gives up. Masters himself and leaves the hawk be."

The sparrow hawk moved suddenly, sidling rapidly along her perch in the direction of the blackbird. There was a clicking noise from her claws and a dry scrabbling sound as she shook out her feathers.

"It's a fine line. To work a raptor you have to get its respect but you mustn't break it or even come close to breaking it or you'll drive it mad. They can't bend, you see, can't learn to come to hand like a dog and live submitted. But you have to drive it hard just the same, and no mercy, mercy is weakness, and weakness will always be taken advantage of, that's its nature. And you must get it at the right age and in the right physical and psychological state and not damaged by hunger. Then maybe you have some chance."

"So why do you do it?"

"I don't. I patch them and feed them up a bit and cage them while they're healing. Then I let them go. To live or to die. Which is all they understand anyway."

He stopped talking and concentrated on working the blackbird's carcass free from its feathered skin. Hannie was quiet today, he thought. Mostly she paced about, smoking and talking, disturbing the hawk. He would tell her to sit still, or if she had to move around not to wave her hands or look at the bird, but she took no notice. She did what she wanted to do, charged noisily around until she tired of it, then sat herself down, deflating like a balloon that is losing its air.

Danno snipped a last tendon and pulled out the carcass. He placed it in front of the hawk, making little noises of encouragement and endearment. The sparrow hawk stared at it coldly and didn't move. Then with incredible swiftness she shot out her foot, pinned the skinned blackbird, and began systematically pulling off the flesh in long bloody strips with her beak.

Danno lifted the bundle of blackbird feathers and skin lying on the table, opened it out and sprinkled its fleshy side with plaster of Paris. He blew off the excess carefully. He looked up at Hannie, a swift sudden look, one eye opened and one closed, one eyebrow raised in a vivid inverted "V," the other flattened over the closed eye. He looked down again.

"Hannie," he said, "why did you marry Piet?"

Hannie stared.

"You were young. You must have been beautiful. Why did you marry him? Were you in love with him?"

Hannie started to laugh. She'd told Vere she liked talking to Danno because he didn't change the subject when she talked about the past and it was true, but that wasn't to say that he listened to what she said. Danno didn't listen, or if he did he never responded or commented or asked a question, there was never anything to indicate that he'd heard. Until now. She stopped laughing.

"Because my mother told me to," she said quietly. Danno had the blackbird skin spread out, feather-side down, and he was working one of its wings onto the inside. At the same time he was scraping at fragments of left-behind flesh and feeding them straight to the hawk. He nodded without looking up.

"She thought it would give me a future," Hannie continued, "and that I wouldn't have one otherwise. She said there weren't so many people who'd marry me and Piet wanted me, he didn't care what people thought." She paused. "For me, Piet was a stepping stone," she said, shrugging her shoulders as though she were getting rid of something. "I had to get away from her and I didn't much mind how."

"Why weren't there many people who'd marry you?"

"Because of her. We weren't respectable." Hannie reached for her cigarette packet. She extracted one and lit it carefully, leaning into the flame and inhaling deeply. "And because of me, I was making it worse. I didn't care what I did, you see, she was afraid of how I'd end up."

"What had she done that made you not respectable?"

"Sailed too close to the wind. In Java, in the war," she added, as though that explained everything. Danno glanced up.

"The Japanese came," she said. "All the men who were Dutch were taken away to a camp. Then it was the women's turn and my mother also was put in a camp, but one for women and children only. She wanted to live, she was very determined, and it wasn't respectable to be so determined, to fight so hard to survive. It was a colony, you see, everyone must pull together, live together, starve together, die together. She didn't want to die. She was beautiful and the guards were men. When the war ended people told stories and the stories followed her around."

Hannie's accent had thickened. Danno wondered if it was involuntary, if she heard the change herself. "Were you in the camp too, Hannie?"

"No," she said, "or I wouldn't be here now, I was only a baby, I was with the Amah for those years. *When the Japanese came,* people say, as though everyone just woke up one day and it had happened, but it wasn't like that. First there were rumors and panics and people tried to get away. My parents tried. They got a passage on a cargo ship, crammed in with thousands of others, but I was too little to survive such a journey so they gave me to the Amah till the war had ended.

Then the ship was turned back so they went to the camps anyway and my father died there. Afterwards, my mother came and got me from the Amah. I was lucky, the camps were very hard, I wouldn't have survived them. Or I'd have been like that hawk you said couldn't be worked. Damaged by hunger. And fear. As she was . . ."

"Why didn't she go somewhere else afterwards?"

"Where could she go?" Hannie shrugged. "She was born there, it was her home, and anyway the stories would have followed her. But it was confused, there was nowhere she belonged even before the stories. You see, her father was Dutch but her mother was Indonesian, and her mother wasn't married to her father. When my father died there was no one to speak for her with the Europeans anymore, no one to protect her. And her mother was dead so there was no place for her with the Indonesians either. It was hard."

Danno was trying to ease out the blackbird's eye with the point of the scissors but it wouldn't come and he had to loosen it from the inside through the beak. When he lifted it out it looked enormous, the black center surrounded by a firm dark blue rim about three times the area normally visible. He put it in his palm and stretched out his hand to show Hannie.

"You see that lad there," he said, pointing to a tiny white membrane that ran through the eye. "That's the optic nerve. Everything the bird sees is carried through that thread." Hannie looked where he pointed. The sparrow hawk shifted angrily. She didn't like his switch of attention, or perhaps it was the removal of her tidbit that upset her. She flew out from the box, trailing her leather jesses, and perched malevolently on top of it, glaring and settling her powerful wings.

"The eye of a bird takes up a third of the head area." Danno spoke in the same quiet voice that he used to soothe the hawk. "More so, if it's a raptor. Is this a secret, Hannie?"

Hannie looked up from the eyeball in surprise. "No. Why? Who are you thinking of telling?"

"I'm not, but I've read things about Kenya. I just wondered."

"Oh, Kenya." She shrugged. "They could think what they liked, people do anyway, don't they? And it gave them something to talk about. If there'd been nothing they'd have made up worse."

"And Ned? Does Ned know all this?"

"Of course, why?"

Danno lifted the forefinger of his left hand and pushed his glasses firmly back up onto the bridge of his nose. He swung around and placed the eyeball on the edge of his table where the sparrow hawk could reach it.

"He just went up in my estimation."

———•◆•———

THE BLACKBIRD LAY, an eyeless huddle of feathers and beak on his worktable. He'd done enough for now. Feed the dogs, feed the birds, feed himself. He wondered if Hannie talked to Ned about these visits of hers. He knew the way they spoke of him. Peculiar Danno in his peculiar little world.

He hadn't tried to understand Hannie or placate her, he'd just let her come in and talk until it was enough for the time being and she could return to her own life. He'd never meant to like her or talk back to her.

But he was growing more used to her, even the hawk was growing used to her, she flew up onto the top of the box less, sulked less, was generally less of a prima donna. Outclassed in her own act, he thought sourly.

He stopped himself. Thinking badly of Hannie was a habit he'd encouraged himself to get into. It protected his defenses and kept her at a distance. He hadn't wanted her to visit, but for a while now he hadn't not wanted her either, he realized. Yesterday he'd even caught himself watching for her to come.

He got up from his chair, went outside and collected the old soup pan he used for feeding the dogs. It wasn't just Ned who'd gone up in his estimation.

Chapter Twenty-five

IT WAS THE DOGS DANNO COULDN'T FORGIVE, Mrs. Coady told her. Wouldn't forgive — there was no sense nursing grudges when things were over and done, and Mr. Renvyle hadn't acted out of anger or spite, he'd thought it was the right thing he'd been doing.

"What dogs, Mrs. Coady?" Hannie asked.

"Didn't Danno tell you?" Mrs. Coady asked her back.

"No," she said, "not a word."

So Mrs. Coady told her about it — about the two black Labradors that he'd had off Danno when he'd come to live there, young dogs, but trained up and ready, lovely creatures and first-rate hunters, his pride and joy as well as Danno's.

He hadn't had them long, five or six months, no more, and it had been spring, the lambing just starting and the hunting not long over and he'd been very busy about the place and inexperienced, and maybe the dogs had got a bit less in the way of exercise than they'd needed.

Then Micky Cullen over at Maher's Cross had had a lot of his lambs killed by dogs, and three or four ewes as well. He'd been out there straight after, standing in the field, slaughtered beasts all around him, when he'd seen two black Labradors making off down the hill through the furze. . . .

He'd had to act fast, they were off down the hill, so he'd lifted the gun and aimed straight and shot them both dead in their tracks.

"Did he know they were Ned's dogs?"

"Not at the time," Mrs. Coady answered, "not at the time, but that story wouldn't be one to be long staying home, folk soon started putting two and two together and making four."

And the way it is in these parts, Mrs. Coady told her, there were many would have found themselves two Labradors out of some place a good stretch away, and had them sitting ready in the yard as though they'd known nowhere else. Then when the Guards came looking for someone to pay for Micky Cullen's sheep they'd have pointed at the dogs for answer.

But that wouldn't ever have been Mr. Renvyle's way. Mr. Renvyle had picked up his checkbook and driven to Cullen's as soon as he'd heard, he'd walked into the yard and said straight out that he was sorry, and Mick Cullen had been right to shoot the dogs, and how much did he owe for the sheep?

So that was that. Mick Cullen had been happy, and everyone bar a few begrudgers thought a lot of Mr. Renvyle for the way he'd acted. Mr. Renvyle didn't know it, but he was made up after that, people accepted him, he'd never looked back.

Only Danno hadn't been happy. Danno had landed around that night and he'd banged on the door until he had Mr. Renvyle up out of his bed. Mick Cullen had shot the wrong dogs, Danno told him, he'd trained those dogs himself, they wouldn't touch sheep, and Mr. Renvyle was a fool and worse than a fool not to know it.

Mr. Renvyle had given him short shrift, he'd said any dog could turn rogue and there was no point in swearing the moon was blue when a child of two could tell you it was yellow.

But still Danno hadn't been satisfied, he'd said those dogs were clean bar their own wounds, he'd had it off the Cullen boy when he'd been around there asking questions. Mr. Renvyle wasn't a fit owner if he didn't know his own dogs and wouldn't stand over them, Mr. Renvyle couldn't be trusted with dogs, he was damned if he'd ever have another one he'd bred.

"Was he right?" Hannie asked.

If he was, there was no proving it, but a bare two weeks later there'd been another kill not a mile from Cullen's and three other dogs had been shot — knacker's dogs — and after that there'd been no more kills.

Mr. Renvyle hadn't held it against Danno, he'd said Danno had trained those dogs, it was understandable that he'd felt the way he had, but it was his heart not his head had been speaking.

And besides, Mr. Renvyle had said, what had his dogs been doing loose in Cullen's field in the middle of lambing? At the very least he should have had them properly secured in his yard.

Mr. Renvyle had dealt with it like that, then afterward he'd put it from his mind.

"But Danno hadn't?"

Maybe he had, maybe he hadn't, Mrs. Coady told her, but she hadn't seen Danno coming around with another dog when he'd one that was trained up and ready, nor a pup either for that matter. Where had Pip come from, Delaney's, wasn't it? Wherever it was, it wasn't from Danno. . . .

"There wouldn't be much love lost between them," she finished. "Danno's a proud one and Mr. Renvyle would be the same, though I don't think Mr. Renvyle knows what Danno thinks of him, I think he hardly remembers what happened, and maybe he's never really acknowledged to himself that he's given offense."

Chapter Twenty-six

"ELLEN PHONED," NED SAID, coming into the kitchen. "Aunt Cecily's taken a turn for the worse and she's back in hospital. Making life merry hell for all, Ellen says. Seems she wants to go back to the nursing home. Poor Ellen."

"They let her do as she liked in the nursing home. The hospital's probably stricter." Hannie was maneuvering a rolled neck of lamb out of the oven as she spoke. The kitchen was full of the rich smells of garlic and rosemary and roasting meat. "Bottles under the blankets, bottles under the sheets, nobody saying a word. She reeked of whiskey. They wouldn't let her do that in hospital."

"Strictly speaking, she shouldn't be drinking at all."

"They should put her on a drip. Neat whiskey. Kill her off." Now she was basting the lamb, spooning hot fat over the skin to crisp it. She might not be very charitable, Ned thought, but she was a first-rate cook. He ate better now than he ever had with Mrs. Coady. Paid for it too, the bills were consistently higher.

"Horrible, greedy, old woman." Hannie returned the meat to the oven and slammed its door. "More life in the tip of one finger than in both those daughters stuck together." She lifted a lid, jabbed with a fork, appeared satisfied. "Kept all the life for herself, I expect, none left over for the girls." She picked up the pan and drained a stream of orange-colored water into the sink. "Stupid, spineless, useless women, I don't blame her."

"I'm very fond of my cousins, Hannie," Ned said mildly.

"You're fond of Ellen. She puts her hand on your arm and looks up at you with her watery eyes and at once you want to protect her." Hannie lobbed some butter onto the carrots and tipped them into a serving dish. "You're not fond of Lettie. Lettie is bossy as well as stupid and spineless, no one in their senses could be fond of Lettie."

"Ellen was very excited. Patrick's come home from Canada."

"Patrick? The son?" Hannie had a spoon poised at her mouth. She tasted, then put the spoon down. "I expect he's useless, too. Who wouldn't be with a mother like that? Either useless or selfish or both." She began stirring flour into the meat juices for gravy. "Ran away to Canada, did he?"

"He's an engineer," Ned said. "He went to Canada to work. Now he's home for a couple of months to see his family. He's there for the rest of the week, then he's coming to us."

"Oh? For how long?"

"As long as he likes. Probably until Christmas."

"There isn't a room ready," she said flatly.

"He can have Joss's room while you see to one. He isn't fussy."

"Joss is. He won't like this Patrick using his room."

"He needn't know."

She went on stirring at the gravy, her back and her silence so ostentatious that Ned noticed. Irritation rose in him.

"He's my cousin, Hannie," he said. "We haven't spent time together for years."

No response.

"You'll like him, I'm sure you'll like him."

"I'd have liked to be asked."

Ned sighed. She expected him to apologize. He was damned if he would, it was his home, his cousin had a right to come to his home, he didn't have to ask permission.

"I didn't think you'd mind," he said at last, his voice stubbornly reasonable.

Hannie poured the gravy into a jug. She took the plates from the warming drawer.

"Niamh's boyfriend is coming next week," she said brightly. "And Joss will be home the week after, we'll be quite a crowd."

"I didn't know Niamh had a boyfriend."

"She doesn't, he's a three-night stand, but she wants to turn him into something more so she's invited him."

"He'll be staying in the cottage?"

"Of course." Hannie plonked the plates down on the table. "I expect she would have asked you but she probably didn't think you'd mind."

Ned did mind. If it hadn't been for the fuss Hannie was making about Patrick he wouldn't have hesitated. He'd have gone straight out, knocked on Niamh's door and told her he had a responsibility to her father and he couldn't allow it. What exactly "it" was, he didn't get around to formulating.

Now he sat fretting and fuming, his dinner spoiled. The girl was a grown woman, he told himself, she didn't need his protection even though he wanted to protect her, not just for her father's sake, but for her own. She was so lovely and so trusting, it was a much harder world than she knew.

He couldn't say anything now, if he did Hannie would ask him nastily what century he thought he was living in, make him feel small.

But if he was really honest it wasn't just Hannie's fuss about Patrick that kept him quiet. It was those words Hannie'd used — *a three-night stand* — she'd said it like a quotation. Yet he couldn't imagine sweet, grave-faced Niamh saying anything so crude.

——— ◆ ———

HE WASN'T REALLY a boyfriend yet, Niamh had told Hannie, he wasn't much more than a three-night stand, but she liked him a lot, and she was pretty sure he liked her too.

They'd had a fling in the summer in Dublin, then he'd gone back up to the North without even leaving an address. Her friends said she shouldn't go setting her heart on him.

But she knew she hadn't seen the last of him, she knew he'd be in touch again, and all she had to do was wait.

And he had. And she'd seen him again in Dublin that last time when she'd gone up to buy pastels.

Her friends still warned her, they said he was too good-looking, women went for him all the time, he had it too easy, he couldn't be trusted.

But she couldn't stop thinking about him and she knew it was the same for him.

Hannie had sat listening. She had heard the naked sex in all Niamh said. She'd begun to remember things she had carefully forgotten, emotions and sensations deliberately left behind.

It seemed all women must be fools for men before they got old and grew wise.

But in the drug of the physical there was potent, if temporary, compensation. She'd felt suddenly savage that such compensation should be wasted on Niamh.

———— •◆• ————

HANNIE RAN THE BRUSH carefully along the line of the skirting, making a clean edge of white against the Wedgwood blue of the wall. She was on her knees on spread newspapers, shuffling her way around the edges of the room, turning the big front bedroom into a suitable retreat for Ned's Canadian cousin. A gas heater bubbled quietly in the middle of the floor.

The cold weather continued. Hannie liked it, she felt more alive, her sluggish blood ran faster. She liked its ancientness, the threat in the air, skies fierce and then soft, mornings smoky and secret with frost. It was quite new to her. Winter's blanket, its thorned weave and rank folds, its clean bitter stars, so unlike the great flowering stars of Africa.

Ned had been tight lipped over her insistence on the integrity of Joss's room, but her efforts with a paintbrush seemed to be in favor. He was used to the caravansery, sleeping forms on the floor, a common roof, all thoughts of privacy and ownership redundant. Easy for Ned, who knew who he was, had had this all his life. Not so easy for Joss, moving from school to school, from one of her husband's houses to another.

She picked a brush-hair from the skirting with her forefinger and wiped the sticky gloss down Ned's discarded trousers. She was covered in paint-splatters: mixed blue and white on her clothes and her face, white in her hair from the ceiling. Ned had noticed, he'd touched it approvingly as he got up from the breakfast table that morning, then suggested a visit to the hairdresser when she was finished. She'd got up and started clearing, saying nothing. He'd gone to the study, come back with his wallet, taken out a ten-pound note and laid it on the table.

Later, when he'd come in for coffee, the note was still there, its edge tucked under the milk jug. Didn't she want to get her hair done, he'd asked her, and she'd smiled and shaken her head and said ladies' hairdressers in Ireland must be very cheap. He'd looked surprised, then picked up the ten and put two twenties down instead and asked would that cover it? She had nodded and smiled again and lifted the notes and put them into her pocket.

Now she filled in the last six inches of skirting and got up and stood looking around her. The room looked well with its matte blue walls and white trim, it would look even better when the cleaned carpet was put back and she'd hung the curtains she had washed and pressed and altered. Just the window frame and the door to be done and she'd be through with the painting. She crossed to the window, lit a cigarette and stood smoking and thinking vague thoughts of Joss, of the unknown Patrick, of Niamh's unself-conscious anticipation of sexual pleasure. She could hear Mrs. Coady downstairs Hoovering the study and Ned in the upper field with the tractor. The house was somber around her.

Standing there she had one of those sudden reversals of mood that these days often seemed to accompany one of her successful little manipulations or ingratiations. Pleasure in her own cleverness would dissolve into a vague depression. Hard on the depression would come an angry self-disgust.

And she hated it, this enforced awareness. She didn't want the mirror she kept finding herself looking into and couldn't seem to smash or push away. Suddenly she couldn't stand Ned or this house or herself a moment longer. She was overwhelmed by the need to make some violent, irreparable gesture that would shove things right to the edge and cut at the dragging compromise of daily life.

She put down her paintbrush, turned off the gas and left the room. Then she bathed, changed her clothes, took the money she'd saved for Joss from its place in the back of the wardrobe and put it with Ned's forty pounds. Downstairs, she lifted the car keys from their hook and crossed the yard. She opened the garage doors and backed out the Volkswagen.

——◆◆◆——

SHE WOKE in broad daylight in an upstairs room somewhere in Cork. The man who snored on the bed beside her was half her age and unknown to her. Other bodies, male and female, lay around on the floor, on the other bed, on the sofa. She sat up and someone put a mug of tea into her hand. It was laced with whiskey. She asked for a cigarette.

Some time later, in some pub somewhere in the city, she was searching her pockets for money and her hand met keys and closed tight around them. For half an hour she sat trying to work through the haze of alcohol to reach for a reason for being here. She found none, the last dregs of any purpose had long since fallen away. She stood up, pushed back her chair, picked up her cigarettes and headed for the door. Someone called her name, but she didn't turn around.

——◆◆◆——

HANNIE CROSSED the yard and reached the back door, so hungover and exhausted that she had to drag herself the few remaining steps. She'd lost all track of time, all care for consequences. She felt empty, anesthetized and ancient.

She paused, her hand on the door, then pushed it open and stood at the entrance looking in. The kitchen was clean and firelit, everything glowed and shone, a cave of warm brightness. The puppy lay curled in her basket and the room was fragrant with the rich warm smells of meat juices and potatoes baking. A man was standing over by the fire, a man as tall as Ned with something of his angular, rangy look, despite the extra flesh he carried, the soft bulge over the belt. He cradled a glass of whiskey in his hand. Hannie half turned in an automatic movement of withdrawal. This was a place both domestic and secure. She had no business here. She should go back outside to the darkness, where she belonged.

"Ah, Hannie, there you are." Ned's voice came to her from across the room. It was quiet and even and matter-of-fact. "Hannie, this is my cousin Patrick, come to us a few days early. Patrick, my wife, Hannie."

Hannie stood there, her hands shaking, her hair wild, her clothes crumpled and drink-stained and slept in. She knew what she must look like, what she must smell like. Yet the man who came forward to greet her gave no sign that anything was other than expected.

"My sister Ellen couldn't stop talking about you," he said easily. "She is very impressionable and you impressed her very much. She said you were very elegant and wore beautiful clothes and she didn't want to talk about geese at all, but Ned had insisted and anyway she couldn't think of anything else to say. She liked you very much and she hated being so dull for you. She said I was to be sure to tell you and to apologize for boring you so dreadfully."

Chapter Twenty-seven

IT WAS LATE WHEN NED PHONED MRS. COADY, well after eleven, Tom was already in his bed.

"She hasn't come home, Mrs. Coady," he said, "she went off in the car and she hasn't come home and I wonder if I should be worrying?"

He was calm enough, Mrs. Coady thought, no fuss, no dramatics: he might have been asking where she was because he had Ambrose Power standing beside him wanting a decision about paint or tiles or underlay. But she knew what he was thinking and he knew that she knew: he was thinking she'd left him and she wasn't coming back.

It was a lot to take on, Mrs. Coady said, a whole new way of life, and it might be that it was all too much suddenly, it might be she'd got into the car for a bit of a drive and gone farther than she'd intended. . . .

There was a small silence then he said he'd looked upstairs and there was nothing, as far as he could see, that had gone. He paused again then he asked her what it might cost to get your hair done in Dungarvan?

At first she thought she'd heard wrong, but he said it again so she asked was it only a cut she'd be wanting or was it a color as well?

The next day he phoned again just before ten and said where was she, was she unwell, he'd come and collect her if she didn't have a car?

Mrs. Coady said this was Wednesday, it wasn't her day to come,

Tuesdays and Fridays were her days — two mornings a week — but she'd come anyway if he wanted her, she'd only bits and pieces of things to finish up here.

When Mrs. Coady put down the phone she remembered that Hannie was saving the money she didn't have to pay her anymore now that she was working fewer days. She cursed herself for her mouth and went to get her coat.

———◦◆◦———

NED HAD MADE himself ring around the hospitals, but the exercise only confirmed what he already knew. She wasn't lying injured in a hospital bed, she'd walked out, it didn't matter that her things were upstairs and untouched, packing a suitcase wasn't ever going to be Hannie's way.

His first instinct was to tell no one. He knew what gossip was like here, how each incident was pounced on and shaken to death and the participants held up to delighted ridicule. He would face that when he had to, but he wasn't going to open the door and invite it in.

He was angry with Hannie, he felt that clearly, but what he hadn't expected at all was the feeling of loss. Having Hannie living here as his wife hadn't been as he'd imagined, it had changed his life in ways he didn't always find either positive or comfortable, yet he could find no sense of relief in himself when he thought that she'd gone. Under the anger at what she was doing to him, his strongest emotion was that of wanting her back.

Then she came back. He didn't ask her where she'd been or what she'd been doing. He wouldn't let himself interrogate her, mostly for reasons of honor but also because he was afraid of what he might hear. And Patrick was staying, Patrick was always at his elbow, Ned didn't want to draw any further attention to the difficulties he and Hannie might be having.

Over the next two days Hannie referred once to her absence but her tone was mocking and light and she made no attempt at an explanation. She seemed neither apprehensive at a possible interrogation, nor relieved when none came. He was angry, despite himself, despite his decision to say nothing. It kept coming onto the tip of his tongue, it was harder and harder to push down.

The next afternoon they were coming back from the field above the house where they'd walked with Patrick and old Bess to check on the heifers in calf. It was just after four, dusk thickened, already the trees were lost, dark shapes on the blue of the coming night. Patrick had fallen behind, he was making heavy weather of closing the gate, Ned and Hannie had walked on in silence, then noticed and stopped and stood waiting.

"People can't always be as they intend, Ned. They can't always deliver on what they've said they'll deliver, even when they truly meant to at the time."

Hannie's words came out of the gloom. Her voice was so low that he almost thought he'd imagined it but he hadn't. Then Patrick was upon them, Bess at his heels, and there wasn't time for more. She touched her hand briefly to his arm and turned from him. Suddenly, he understood why she'd gone missing. He no longer minded that Patrick had seen more than he wanted him to see; he no longer minded her deception over Mrs. Coady's hours and money. Mrs. Coady was right, it was hard for her, she had lived a different life, a life opposite to the lives that he and his kind lived here: steady and cautious, with every action evolving out of some previous action and tempered by the knowledge of consequences to be lived down the unfolding years.

They tramped home, the dusk loud with the suck of their boots in the mud and the frantic evening chirring of blackbirds in the thorns.

Chapter Twenty-eight

"AND THERE SHE WAS," Ned said, "with her feet in a basin. And when I asked what she was doing she said it was for the chilblains, Mrs. Coady said to soak them every day in warm urine."

Ned swept his eyes around the table. He was enjoying himself, telling his story, making them laugh.

"I got straight into the car, but it was after six when I got there, the chemist was closed, so I banged on the door, made Heffernan come down and attend to me. He didn't like it of course, mumbled about his dinner and emergencies only. 'Heffernan,' I said, 'if it was *your* wife with her feet in the stuff *you'd* be banging on the door.'

" 'Very good remedy, the urine,' says Heffernan, 'a lot in these old pishogues. Sure they're drinking the stuff now, these New Agers, or whatever it is they call themselves, you couldn't go far wrong with the odd soak.'

" 'Like tying rags to a rag tree. We're approaching the end of the twentieth century, Heffernan,' I said, 'you can surely do better than that.'"

Vere was thumping the table, Patrick had his head thrown back, even Joss let out a little yelp that might have been the sound of appreciation.

"Of course Mrs. Coady roared laughing when I told her. Said she'd never meant Mrs. Renvyle to go trying it, she'd only said it to show her how bad people were with the chilblains in the old days, the things they would do to get rid of them. So I told her not to be telling her such things anymore, Mrs. Renvyle was the sort that would try anything." Ned threw Hannie a look full of pride and affection. Hannie saw it, smiled quietly, looked away.

"Central heating," Patrick said. "And proper insulation. Canadian winters are much worse than ours, but they don't just sit back and endure the way people do here, you don't have to have chilblains or rheumatism."

"Or sit with your feet in warm piss," Joss interjected.

"Something like that," Patrick said, grinning at him.

Joss liked him, Hannie thought. Or perhaps he was only getting at Ned. Joss listened when Patrick spoke to him, he even threw the odd remark in his direction, the contrast was hard to miss.

"Don't like central heating myself," Vere said flatly. "Awful atmosphere, can't breathe in it, you get sick."

"No drafts or damp," Joss said softly. "Rots the soul, makes you soft, how can the boys grow up to be men?"

Niamh giggled.

"He bought me an electric blanket," Hannie said loudly, looking at Vere. "I didn't even know such things existed."

Ned got up. He crossed to the sideboard and took out a bottle of Drambuie he'd been hoarding. Bloody good dinner, he thought. He'd explained to Hannie about the Beresfords and Patrick, how they'd grown up together, close as first cousins, and she'd understood what he was saying, he hadn't had to ask would she invite them. She'd rung up James and Marjorie as well but they were in Dublin with one of the daughters, so she'd fixed another evening later in the week. Her idea having Niamh, too, company for Joss, stopped him feeling awkward and left out. She'd done them proud all right, not just with the food, but with the way she talked and arranged things and kept it all flowing; the Beresfords were no end impressed.

From another shelf Ned took tiny glasses, sparsely cut, clouded and old. He arranged them on a little polished brass tray that had come from the Yemen. He smiled to himself as he did so, he could nearly see

Vere thinking that maybe she wasn't such a total mistake after all. And maybe Vere was right, maybe she wasn't, she could certainly do it when she set her mind to it, that much was clear. She'd had plenty of practice of course, social sort of a life with Andrew, parties and entertaining and the like. Good with people too, easy and natural, sometimes down-right charming, the other night at his lecture in Kilkenny she'd really shone. She'd looked terrific, worn her good suit, had her hair done, he'd been proud as punch introducing his attractive new wife. Silly old fool that he was, he thought, smiling happily to himself. At his age. The lecture had gone well too, he hadn't done it for a while, been a bit anx-ious, surprised himself with his own eloquence in the end. Islam in sub-Saharan Africa. Surprised Patrick too, he kept saying how good it was, on at him to develop the lecture into another book.

Ned had set one of the tiny glasses in front of each of his guests and was moving around the table filling them. The success of the evening was making him bountiful.

"Ned likes the winter," Hannie said, pouring coffee into his cup and speaking to the table generally. "He says he doesn't, but he does."

"It changes the proportions," Ned said. "It's like the desert again, one becomes tiny in an immense landscape." He looked at Hannie and it was clear that what he was saying was for her. "There's an excitement, a quickening of the blood. I like that, I like the stars so high and sharp, I even like the darkness, though I wouldn't like it all year round."

"I had a Swedish friend, once," Hannie said. "She said in the north of her country in winter it never got light at all." She played with an un-used fork as she spoke and it shone with the shine of the lights. "She was like daylight herself, despite all that darkness," Hannie went on, "very clear, like fresh water. Her character, I mean, not just her looks. She wasn't dark like the people here, she wasn't secretive."

"Is that how we seem to you?" Niamh asked suddenly. She had said very little all evening. Now she sat low in her chair, her eyes intent on Hannie, who suddenly saw that she was drunk.

"Poverty, rebellion and endless rain," Patrick cut in easily. "Mud floors and history and conspiracy. A race bred to secrecy and darkness."

He's said these things before, Ned thought. In Canada, over the whiskey, when they ask him about Ireland.

Hannie turned to Patrick. "Yes, but this darkness is in everyone. In you, and in Ned and in Alison and Vere as well," she said. "And you are the outsiders, the rebelled against."

"Perhaps ruling is the supreme illusion," Ned said. "Perhaps the rulers will always take on the characteristics of the ruled."

"Flann O'Brien and the molecules," Joss put in suddenly.

They all stared.

The Third Policeman," Joss explained. "It's a book by Flann O'Brien, about molecules."

"About a Guard," Niamh said, trying to help him. "A country Guard —"

"A Guard who spends his whole life on a bicycle," Joss said across her. "Arse rarely absent from the saddle. Time passes and exchange of molecules takes place. The bicycle begins to take on Guard-like characteristics. The Guard in his turn becomes partly bicycle. Literally: he starts standing by the curb outside his favorite pub propped on one leg." Joss reached across for the Drambuie bottle and refilled his glass.

"Happens all the time," he went on. "See it in Africa. Half-castes. Visible exchange of molecules has taken place." He gave a little bark of laughter. "So Niamh is like you, you're like Niamh. You all sit around the dinner table together and everyone's happy. Till you need someone to build roads and die in trenches again. Then there are problems." Joss flicked his blank blue gaze around the table and settled it on Niamh. "The bicycle thinks it's the man that rides it."

Hannie rose, holding the coffeepot. "More coffee?" she said. "Perhaps we should have Irish? Patrick has promised to teach me. Joss, fetch the whiskey bottle from the drawing room and bring it to the kitchen. You must learn, too."

It was gracefully done, Ned thought, hoping she hadn't seen the look Vere'd thrown at Alison but pretty sure that she had. He wondered how much Joss knew about the color of his great-grandmother's skin.

"He's just weird," Patrick said, "don't take any notice of him, Niamh, no one else does."

"But it's true, what he said. A hundred years ago I couldn't have been in that room except as a servant." She stood in the yard, her eyes large and thoughtful, clutching an armful of cut logs against her sweater.

"You're being silly, Niamh. Silly and insecure and melodramatic." Patrick was impatient now. "*That room,* as you put it, is only a room in a modern farm, not a turn-of-the-century country house. Besides," he added more kindly, "the loss would have been ours, not yours."

"That's not the point," Niamh said stubbornly. "My grandmother would've been unfit company."

"Sure. It's the way it was then. It isn't the way it is now. Ned's not patronizing you, Niamh, he's not doing you favors. He invited you to dinner because he likes you and he wanted you at his table. Don't be so touchy for God's sake, your father's three times more likely to help Ned out than the other way around. And as for the cottage, you pay your rent, don't you? You're not here on charity."

Niamh flushed. "Not much," she said. "Not as much as I should."

"Do you *want* to pay more?"

Niamh looked startled, then she began to laugh.

"Well then," Patrick said, "don't suggest it, Ned might just hear you. Anyway, you're talking from gross ignorance, you never knew Ned's mother. If you had you might just think your grandmother a very fortunate woman."

"Why, what was she like?"

"A true horror."

"How do you know?" Niamh had cheered up, her eyes shone.

"I remember her. Besides, my mother's her sister, a living reminder, just in case there was any danger of my forgetting."

Niamh grinned. Her thick blue sweater was matted like an old blanket and she wore mittens in gray and red hand-knitted stripes. Some aunt, overfond of the knitting needles, Patrick thought. Or perhaps it was the mother. He wondered if she'd wear them when the boyfriend came. Probably, he decided. She had very little artifice. He was glad she was here, he thought of her as a shield or a token, protecting Ned from Hannie and her strange son.

And she was accurate enough, thirty years ago she might have been in the cottage, but she wouldn't have been in the dining room. What no one had said though, was neither would Hannie or Joss. Well, they were Ned's problem. He was naive, Ned, despite all the books and the traveling. Perhaps on account of the books and the traveling: a kind of bubble of unreality he'd deliberately created for himself. Not a bad lecture though, must build him up a bit more, talk him into starting on another book. Something to get immersed in, a sort of inoculation for when everything fell apart.

Chapter Twenty-nine

"NIAMH HAS THE POLISHING CLOTHS," Mrs. Coady told Hannie. "She was up for them first thing, said she didn't need them for long, just finishing touches."

"He's hitching down from Dublin, he'll be here late afternoon or evening, depending on how the lifts go. She's told him to start early. *You know what country roads are like,*" Hannie mimicked. *"No cars and no one stops after dark."*

Mrs. Coady laughed. "She's a bit anxious, all right. She has that place like a palace. *I want everything to be perfect for him, Mrs. Coady.* She'll learn."

"Probably the hard way." Patrick was standing by the window with a mug of coffee. "That house looks more like a dowry offering than a setting for an independent woman. I told her she'd defeat herself. *'Do you think so, Patrick?'* she says. *'Oh, but I'm not trying to trap him.'* So I said I didn't mean it, I was teasing."

"You should've told her to spice things up a bit, ease off on the domestic detail, put in some squalor and sex." Hannie finished wringing out the floor cloth and fired it neatly into the empty mop bucket. "I don't know what young people are coming to, nobody thought about soap and water in my day. I hope at least she's had the sense to buy some bottles."

"The funny thing is that she isn't," Patrick said. The two women looked at him. "Trying to trap him, I mean."

Hannie snorted. Mrs. Coady put her hands on her hips, and stared at him in disbelief.

———•◆•———

HANNIE SLIPPED the string around the ivy stems and pulled them tight. She wound the cord a couple more times then tied it firmly. She lifted the bundled mass, heaved it onto one shoulder, then bent again for a second bundle, settled it, and began the trudge home.

The sky was racing with cloud but already the light was slipping. The surface of the river shone dully. Two swans drifted past quite silently, their white forms resting on the pewter water, their long wakes catching the shine from the dying sky. On the far bank the darkness was thickening, the land between river and sky was black and lost.

Cold God crouched in the woods and floated on the water. Hannie felt him, his great age, his stubborn indifference. She couldn't remember the sun or its heat. Only the death of the sun, the long shadows cast here at midday in the sunlit fields.

Above her head wave after wave of black birds washed across the sky, great soundings of crows going home to their roosts in the woods across the river. She closed her eyes and stood. The sky reeled with the enormous clamor of their voices. After a time the great traffic of birds ceased, the sky stilled, the darkness came seeping up out of the earth like smoke.

A stick snapped. A blackness broke from the trees and moved out onto the path toward her.

"Oh Hannie, it's you, I didn't know who it was, you were such a strange shape in the dark." Niamh's white face loomed toward her. Hannie stopped and waited. Niamh turned to the darkness behind her. Another white face moved forward.

"Hannie, this is Ciaran. Ciaran, this is Mrs. Renvyle, otherwise known as Hannie."

"Hannie as in Hannah?"

"No, not Hannah, Hanneka."

"Pleased to meet you, Hannie-as-in-Hanneka," drawled a young man's voice. "Niamh here was showin' me around, but we couldn't see for the dark."

The voice was throaty and light and detached. Hannie was suddenly mildly curious to see his face.

"Ciaran's not used to the country," Niamh said. "He's not used to the dark."

"What time do they turn on the streetlights around here? Does everyone go walkabout in the middle of the night?"

"No streetlights, and it's not the middle of the night."

"Whatever you say, sweetheart." There it was again, that odd detachment. As though all this was happening to someone else. Someone stupid.

"We were going to Danno's." Niamh's voice was eager. "Ciaran wants to see his sparrow hawk."

"Correction. *You* want to show me his sparrow hawk."

"I want to show you all his hawks, and you want to see them."

"That's how it is, is it?"

"That's how it is," Niamh said, laughing. She was laughing a lot, little laughs of happiness and excitement. Hannie wondered how long it would be before these little laughs of hers began to irritate him.

"What are you carrying, Hannie? Is that ivy?"

"Ned wants holly and ivy, he says it's traditional," Hannie told her. "There's plenty of berried holly in the upper field. He'll cut that himself, I've been cutting the ivy, but it took longer than I thought."

"Tuesday's the shortest day," Niamh said.

"So everyone keeps telling me."

"That's a con, so it is, you think you only have to get to it and then the next day everything'll be okay, but it's ages an' ages before it gets any lighter."

It was odd, standing talking to someone you couldn't see, Hannie thought. He seemed to find it odd too, but Niamh sounded perfectly comfortable. "Will we skip Danno's?" she asked him. "Walk back with Hannie?"

They moved off. She had a good fire going, she explained to Hannie, and plenty of booze. They'd be as well going on home and sitting by it, Danno's could wait. Of course if Hannie wanted to join them, she added hastily. . . .

Hannie declined.

She dumped the ivy by the step and stood working her Wellingtons against the iron scraper, pushing the caked mud out from the insteps. This done, she waggled each foot in turn in the low tub of rainwater beside it. Ned was fussy about cleaned Wellingtons. Everywhere Ned, Ned and his systems, everywhere she turned they were in place. He had explained each one carefully to her at the start. When she ignored them he explained them carefully again.

She lifted the bundled ivy and shoved it stem-down into the water-butt, thinking of the young man she'd seen briefly in the spilled light from Niamh's door. Tall with a muscular build, and attractive, just as Niamh had promised. Much good it would do her, except in the short run.

Chapter Thirty

IT WAS ALL DIFFERENT NOW: Patrick and Joss in the house, Ciaran with Niamh in the cottage, the house open and warm. Ned liked
the generous feeling of the way his life had become, but he missed the
silence. Sometimes he had to make himself remember that when he'd
had the silence he hadn't always wanted it.

He stayed working outside for as long as weather and daylight allowed. Mostly he toiled alone but sometimes he prized Patrick from the
comforts of the hearth and the two men worked together, making their
way around Ned's scruffy acres, draining ditches, resetting hedges, re-
pairing gaps in fences and walls. Ned liked maintenance, the quiet,
steady activity of anticipating problems or putting things right where
the damage had already been done. It was useful having another pair of
hands, though in some ways he'd rather have got Mick up from the village as he'd done in other years. Mick was less chatty than Patrick and
cleverer when it came to dry-stone walls, but Patrick was surprisingly
competent once he got started and Patrick didn't have to be paid.

Ned suggested to Hannie that he bring Joss out with them, teach
him the work. Hannie agreed in theory, it would do the boy good, she
said, but perhaps he should start in the summer and have these few
short weeks just to settle in? She was relieved when Ned dropped the
subject, she didn't know herself quite what it was that she feared ex-

cept that Joss might reveal too much of himself and she needed to keep him concealed from Ned for as long as she could. She was more relaxed when he was at Niamh's playing cards with Ciaran; he liked that and it kept him happy and away from Ned.

She took basic precautions. It had been easier in Africa.

"Don't let him do that," she would say to a houseboy without having to explain herself or worry about what they might think.

"Don't leave Pip with Joss," she told Niamh, and then had to think of a reason. "He's not reliable with dogs, he'll just take her for a walk and come home without her." It was a weak excuse even to her own ears, and did nothing to chase the surprise from Niamh's eyes.

Boredom was the danger with Joss. She glanced at the calendar, mentally marshaling her resources. Christmas was almost upon them, Patrick was going back to his mother and sisters in two days' time and Niamh was off home the day after, on Christmas Eve. Ciaran had refused Niamh's familial invitations, he seemed set on going North, but was promising a quick return.

That was something, Hannie thought. Joss was impressed by Ciaran, who treated him with an easy contempt, which he seemed to respond to. Christmas itself would be a distraction, and after that there was the New Year. She wondered about a party.

———◆———

"WHERE'S NIAMH?" Ned asked. "She promised to make us a wreath for the front door, I haven't seen her for days."

Hannie laughed and said Niamh had other fish to fry just now and he should stop being such an old fogy and try to remember as far back as his youth. She was washing the breakfast dishes, lifting the plates out one by one and setting them in the drainer. She laughed again and turned to him, looking up into his eyes, and he flushed with shy happiness. His hand lifted without him asking it to and he touched her hair, which was silvery-blond now from the hairdresser she'd gone to on the morning of his lecture. She didn't look away, her eyes held his and there was a humorous gentleness in them. Then Patrick was at the door with Pippa trotting behind him and for a moment he stopped and then came on and they knew he'd seen them. Ned dropped his hand and made to fill the kettle. He was embarrassed, but somewhere also a little stubbornly proud.

Later that day he knocked on Niamh's door, a big bunch of berried holly dangling by a string from his hand. It was early afternoon, Niamh answered his knock, she was more or less dressed but her feet were bare and her hair was tangled and wild.

"I've been fencing with Patrick," he said, trying not to look at her, trying not to see her face against the blue-painted door, the puff-lidded eyes that wouldn't look up, the scraped chin, the mouth all gorged and bruised.

"We were just in time," he heard himself saying stupidly. "Another day and the birds would have stripped it bare."

Niamh took the bunch and thanked him quietly.

"The kettle's boiled," she said, "I'm making tea. . . ."

An invitation was implied but she didn't sound as though she meant it and still she wouldn't raise her eyes. Ned shook his head. He didn't mention wreaths or front doors and he blushed and mumbled as he turned and walked away.

He'd been fencing all right, but she hadn't, she'd been swimming in sex until everything had blurred and merged and lost its edges. He felt irrationally shamed by his age and his innocence and he wished he'd listened to Hannie and had some tact. Then embarrassment overtook him and he began to imagine that they were standing together at the window watching him and he had to make a huge effort not to turn around and look. In his mind he saw the strutting young man he had met but hardly spoken to, and the young man was mocking him, and Niamh wasn't exactly rushing to his defense.

It was different for the young man, Ned realized. He was becoming himself, it was the making of him, at the same time as it was the unmaking of her. He even looked different: as though he could see farther and run faster. And she was losing herself, that was clear enough, she could hardly even remember who she was.

He thought of Hannie and he wondered if this same losing of herself had happened to her, if sex for women was at the beginning like entering a river where they submerged themselves and became featureless, before finally reemerging on the farther bank.

Abruptly he forgot Niamh. He felt he'd seen a map of a country that he'd glanced at a long time ago and then discarded in favor of other more pressingly interesting maps. He had meant to return to the first map, he knew that now, but he'd forgotten it and left it all too late. Now he wanted to find Hannie, to ask her questions and listen to her answers, to understand through her this country he'd lost sight of years ago and then glimpsed again near to his journey's end.

He looked at his watch. He was anxious to finish the fencing before it got dark, had only come back early with the tractor to fetch more posts. Patrick was working on now, if he went off to find Hannie he'd leave Patrick to run out of posts and they might not finish the job before the light died.

To hell with the posts, he decided abruptly. He picked up the two great bundles of holly they'd cut for the house and made for the back door. He had his hand on the door handle when he stopped himself.

Maybe she'd want to see him as little as Niamh had, he didn't want to feel he was intruding again, he didn't want to be shamed twice in the one hour. He looked down. The holly berries shone against the deep, spiked leaves.

> *The holly bears a berry*
> *as red as any blood.*

The words of the carol sang themselves in his head.

> *The holly bears a bark*
> *as bitter as any gall.*

He slipped the holly string from his hands, laid the bundled holly on the doorstep and went back to find Patrick.

—✦—

"I MUST ADMIT I did question the tastefulness of the enterprise at the start," Patrick said, reaching across and spearing a slice of Niamh's homemade bread on the end of his knife. Patrick and Joss and Ciaran were all sitting in her kitchen, discussing Patrick's mother's parrot, recently deceased. Patrick, in a light mood, had suggested taxidermy on the phone and his sister Lettie had sent the corpse by the next post.

"Then I saw Danno's work and I knew that taste didn't enter into it, I knew the whole scheme was just part of the cosmic fun. Besides, it's What-Mother-Wants, and who am I to deny Mother? This bread's delicious, Niamh, you should go into production, you'd make a fortune." He helped himself to another slice and smothered it in butter and jam.

"Danno's work?"

"Danno's terrible taxidermy, my dear Niamh, you've surely noticed. A crooked wing on a widgeon, a cancerous bump on the flank of a basking pollock."

"That's not fair, Danno's quite good," Niamh said hotly. "It's not supposed to be exact, more of an approximation." She stopped. They were looking at her in a way that made her feel about ten years old. "People come to him from all over," she finished lamely.

She got up and started to clear the dishes from the rack and put them away. Domesticity — her refuge. More like a permanent state these days. When she wasn't in bed with Ciaran she was standing in the kitchen dishing out food. With a shock she realized she was equating sex with feeding mouths and washing dishes.

She wasn't working, that was the problem, she should just go into the other room and get on with it, then she'd feel better about herself, she always did. But how could she work with her house full, how could she work without quiet? Suddenly she was glad that Ciaran didn't want to come home with her for Christmas: let him go to Belfast, she'd a good mind to tell him not to bother coming back.

And if he didn't?

She found the bottle of aspirin on the dresser and tipped some into her hand. She had a hangover, that was all. She'd feel different when the pills worked.

Chapter Thirty-one

HANNIE WAS VERY BUSY in the house. They'd had lunches and dinners and drinks, they'd asked friends and relations and acquaintances of Ned's from around the county, all of whom had known Patrick or Patrick's family some time in the course of their lives. These people lived stranded in their big houses, houses crumbling now but still connected up like the knotting in an invisible net, thrown down years ago, then left to tear and rot away.

Hannie didn't mind this entertaining, especially when she had Patrick for audience and conspirator; she even enjoyed it. She liked showing how well she could do it, liked impressing the Alisons and the Marjories, and she loved the aftermath, the mockery of eccentricity, the ridicule of drunken folly. Patrick colluded with her and encouraged her. Even Ned let himself smile as some of James's wilder expressions crept into his household's daily currency.

Hannie was flirting gently with Patrick. Ned noticed without jealousy; he was glad she was enjoying Patrick, glad that his cousin liked his wife, relieved that her visits to Danno seemed to have fallen away.

Hannie herself felt easier, less trapped and desperate, and with the ease had come a certain caution. Her words to Patrick were light and ambiguous, her husband was always included, she took care to make him feel secure and proud. She wasn't making a play for Patrick — he wasn't husband material, nor was she much attracted to him sexually — but he was pleasant, urbane company, he amused her and he broke the awkward silence around Ned and Joss.

———•◆•———

NIAMH WASN'T CAREFUL, except over contraceptives; she was hardly even aware there was anything else to be careful about. She was confused though, she knew that much: confused about Ciaran, confused about her feelings for him, confused about sex and the way it was changing her.

It was as though all of her that she thought of as herself had stopped living tidily some place more or less behind her eyes and had melted like butter left out in the sun. And this warmed butter had run down into her flesh and spread over her whole body, and she was left not knowing anything, not even if she liked what was happening to her until it stopped happening and she ached for it to happen again.

———•◆•———

"I'D DRAW the curtains when I undressed, if I was you," Ciaran said. "Yon bucko's not beyond a squint or two." He hitched his bag over his shoulder and stuck his free hand down the back of her jeans. She felt the shock of its cold intrusion. At the same time her flesh reeled and her body shouted with recognition.

"An' who'd blame him?" Ciaran drawled salaciously. "Sensible fella I'd say, if you asked me."

"You'll not be away that long, sure you won't?" She tried to ignore the hand, tried to sound indifferent.

"A few days," he told her. "They'll go nuts, so they will, they'll be on at me to stay."

"But you won't?"

"Couldn't if I wanted to." He pressed his fingers hard into her buttocks, driving her crotch and pelvis forward to meet his. Her flesh dissolved, she moved forward and pressed into him, he forced his tongue deep into her mouth and worked her until her whole body cried out with need. Then he pulled away from her.

"Have to go," he said, looking at her and wiping his mouth on the back of his wrist. Then he caught her hand and held it against the bulge in his straining jeans. "That's just so's you'll remember," he told her.

———•◆•———

"Hm." Hannie stood in Joss's room, thumbing the shiny paper of the mail-order catalog. She looked at the young woman in the picture, at her swept-up hair and her downcast eyes and the simper on her glazed lips. *The Lingerie Collection. The return of the camisole.* Her voice was casual and dismissive. "So this is what Niamh's dreams are made of. Get yourself up like a Victorian boudoir and simper about the bedroom: fuck me, oh please fuck me. How very liberated and suburban." She tossed the catalog scornfully onto the bed.

Joss leaned by the window, cigarette in hand, watching her. Or at least she supposed he was watching her, his blanked-out, black-swathed eyes were pointed in her direction and the corners of his lips were just twisted up in a smile or a sneer or a snarl, she couldn't tell.

She was coming on too heavy, *freaking out* as he'd put it, and over a few juvenile photos of young women in underwear. She stopped herself. At least he'd been straight about it, had told her where he'd got them as soon as she'd asked.

"Nicked them," he'd said, blowing smoke at her and looking pleased with himself. "Off Niamh's dresser where she left them. Silly cow."

She had no idea what he was thinking now, no idea if her ridicule had sunk in or had slid straight off his trim duck's back.

———•◆•———

"You should get something," her friend Maeve had said to her in Dublin. "Anna got the black French knickers, said it was like having a secret weapon on under her jeans, said she fancied everyone she met all day."

"Anna must be made of money."

"Twenty quid," Maeve had said. "The suspenders are ten. Trust you to worry about the money, Niamh; such a buzz, Anna said, cheap at the price."

"If I want to feel sexy," Niamh had said gravely, "I don't wear any knickers at all."

Maeve had giggled and rolled her eyes to heaven. "God, Niamh, you're such a puritan, what're we going to do with you at all? Here, take it anyway, have a look at it, something might rub off."

And she had taken it, though she hadn't really understood why Maeve had called her a puritan. She had looked through it by the fire one night before Ciaran came, had even wondered briefly if black French knickers mightn't increase her chances.

I must have been mad, she thought now. Did I want to spend my whole life on my back?

———◆———

NIAMH STOOD BY THE FIRE after Hannie'd left, the cheap paper catalog in her hand.

"Joss borrowed it," Hannie had said. "You should be careful, Niamh, young boys are suggestible. It's their age, they like erotic stimulation." She had shrugged. Boys will be boys, the shrug had said.

"Borrowed it," Niamh muttered indignantly to herself. What was it Mrs. Coady had said to her only the other day? *If something goes missing, Niamh, ask yourself if it's something Joss might want?*

Stole it, more like. Then around comes Hannie, behaving as though I've given him pornography to read in bed.

Pornography, indeed. Naïveté. She might be a puritan but even she could see the silly straightforward innocence of the pictures. Fuck Hannie, she thought. And fuck Maeve for forcing it on her when she hadn't wanted it in the first place.

It was unbelievable — like church again — poor decent Adam, befuddled with sex, misled by evil Eve and her womanly wiles. *You should be careful, Niamh, young boys are suggestible.* Well, she would be careful all right. She dumped the catalog into the fire and felt much better.

Then she stopped feeling better and remembered Ciaran. Draw the curtains, don't tempt the boy. That had been Ciaran's gist as well. The realization was disquieting.

It never once occurred to her that Hannie might have been trying to warn her.

———✦———

"THE DAY AFTER Stephen's day," Niamh said in answer to Patrick's question about Ciaran's return. "Or the day after that. Depending on how the lifts go. He may not make it down from Belfast in a day." Niamh broke the thin ice on the puddle carefully with her Wellington as she spoke. She liked doing this normally, the creaking sound that it made, the trapped air bubbles coming free, but somehow today it didn't give her much satisfaction. Patrick was going himself in the morning. She wanted to ask his advice about Joss but she didn't know how.

And even if she'd known, she thought, it mightn't be any good. Patrick might react like Ciaran.

Ciaran was amused by Joss. He was a liar and a cheat, all right, but then who wasn't at Joss's age? Ciaran insisted that Joss was normal, that his behavior was adolescent only and nothing to get excited about. And he'd gone on insisting, even after Joss had sat one night telling them his hopes and plans for the future. Life here was only a temporary arrangement, it seemed, Hannie was only looking around for something better, Hannie was a mover, she wouldn't stick this dump for long.

"Just wait till she finds something worth getting her claws into. Old Ned won't see her for dust."

He seemed confident of Hannie's opportunism, proud of it. He didn't seem to look on her as his mother, more as a partner or a stooge, one who was playing the cards for the moment, but always at his direction. Niamh was horrified but Ciaran had laughed at her, he'd said

Joss was only a kid, didn't she know when a kid was boasting to keep himself up?

The truth was Niamh didn't want Joss visiting her anymore but she didn't know how to stop him coming to the cottage when she'd been happy enough to have him hang around the last holidays. She had the feeling that calculations were happening in his head and she didn't trust those calculations. She knew now they might be in a language that she barely even knew existed.

"She says I'm not to leave Joss in charge of the puppy," Niamh said suddenly. Patrick looked startled. "She says he'll forget, he'll just go off somewhere with Pippa and come back without her." She felt stupid saying this, it wasn't what she'd meant to say, it just came out in a rush.

"She being Hannie?" Patrick spoke as though she was a child being taught to refer to her nursery-school teacher by name. "Well, she should know, shouldn't she. I thought Ciaran was going home with you, don't you want to be with him over Christmas?"

Niamh looked up at Patrick, at his bland, amiable, well-fed face, and she knew abruptly that it was no use trying to get through to him, he'd just say something easy to keep her happy, he'd pat her head and soothe her down, lest she disturb his ease.

"Not really," she said. "I asked him but I'm sort of glad he didn't want to, it was a terrible idea really."

She swirled her Wellington about with the slices of dirty ice in the muddy puddle. There was no one she could speak to, it was no use telling Ned of her disquiet, he wouldn't even know what she was talking about.

Hannie would though, suddenly she was certain that Hannie would. But somehow she just couldn't say it to Hannie.

Chapter Thirty-two

"PATRICK SAID YOU FUCKED UP, married the wrong man, you should have married Lannigan."

"Lannigan?" Hannie nudged the iron into the shoulder of Ned's shirt. "What are you talking about, Joss? I don't even know anyone called Lannigan." Her voice was deadpan, bored, but beneath the feigned indifference she was taut with shock.

"What are you talking about?" she asked him again. "And who's this Lannigan that I don't even know?"

"The auctioneer. The one in Dungarvan. See — you *do* know him. Patrick said you backed the wrong horse, said you'd have done better marrying Lannigan. More money than old Ned, more future."

It was Christmas Eve. Ciaran had gone and Patrick had gone, and this morning Niamh's brother Donal had come and taken her home. Hannie hoped these changes accounted for Joss's sudden hysteria. She assumed that it *was* hysteria. Hysteria, and rage at her refusal of his latest project. Joss had come to her that morning with some tale of Ciaran inviting him to Belfast. He wanted money for the trip, he said, he planned to go straight after Christmas.

Hannie set the iron carefully on its end and buttoned the shirt loosely. Then she spread it face down on the board and started to fold in the sides and sleeves. Joss watched her minutely. The only sign was the faintest of tremors in her hands. She was good, his mother, except for the hands you would never have known he'd scored. Serve her right for refusing him, he thought. He felt marginally less savage toward her.

"Joss, stop telling lies," she said, not looking up from her folding. "Or, if you *must* tell lies, at least tell lies that are credible. Never attribute a statement that's out of character. Never say someone said something that they wouldn't ever have said."

"He did say it, he did, he did, he did!" Joss was furious again, his rage the wilder as he heard himself contradicting like a child. She was cheating, diverting, pretending to be instructing him. She just didn't want to face what she'd done: how she'd fucked up, messed up, screwed things up for him and for them both. She wouldn't admit it, wouldn't accept the truth though it stared her in the face. It was all right for her, but he had to take the consequences of her stupid, poxy mistakes.

"You say Patrick told you I should have married Lannigan." She was speaking now in that calm, even voice, the one she used when she was trying to put him down, to make him feel like a fool.

"Well, Patrick might have thought it," she said, "Patrick might even have said it, but Patrick would never, ever have said it to *you*. Therefore, Joss, either he didn't say it at all or he said it to someone else and you were just sneaking around, eavesdropping."

"He told Ciaran, I heard him, the old gasbag, I heard him tell Ciaran — and I was *not* sneaking around, I was in the room all the time, they knew I was there." Joss was shaking with fury, oblivious to everything, needing above all else to shatter her calm, destroy her power. Because if he didn't she'd manipulate him, make him do what she wanted, then everyone would turn on him the way they always did and he'd be fucked.

And he could see it and hear it, just as it had happened. Patrick, man of the world, know-all, sitting by Niamh's fire telling Ciaran that Hannie had backed the wrong horse, not caring that he, Joss, was listening, that it was *his* mother he was rubbishing and slagging off.

"It's natural enough," Patrick had said. "She threw in her lot with Ned's class because she thought it was the safest, the best bet. But it isn't where the power or the money lies now. She'd have done better with the auctioneer in Dungarvan. Our lot are useless in this new state — useless, sidelined, unable to integrate."

His favorite theme, the old windbag, he was never done going on about it. Ciaran was into all that too, he'd jaw on with Patrick for hours. Modern Ireland's Brave New World. Nepotism and Corruption and Plenty of Jobs for the Children of the Rich. Meet the New Boss same as the Old Boss. The Provisionals had the measure of them — the only way forward was a clean sweep.

Except he didn't say the last bit to Patrick, he saved it for Niamh and Joss when Patrick had gone.

And Joss had slipped out, unnoticed, sick to the core that his mother was so vulnerable, that she was all he had to depend on.

"Joss," Hannie said carefully, "you can't have the money, no matter what you do or say. Do you understand? I haven't got the money, but even if I had, I wouldn't give it to you to go to Belfast. And that wouldn't change, no matter who I was married to. Not Lannigan, not Ned, not Patrick, nor anyone else."

"So Patrick's on the list, is he?" Joss was on to it like a ferret on a rat. "Well, well, Mother, not bad. Better than present company, I'll say that." Joss's pale small face sneered at her through the dusk that was thickening around them. Her heart hurt her with sudden pity for him.

"Canada, eh? Better than this dump, but that wouldn't be hard," he continued. "Better make sure Joss keeps quiet, though, Mother. Better pay him to keep the cat in the bag till she's good and ready to let it out, eh? Wouldn't want old Ned getting wind of this change of plan now, would we? Old Ned might just boot her out in the cold before it's properly hatched."

"You're wrong there, Joss, completely wrong." The door had swung quietly open; Ned spoke from his stance in its frame. "Old Ned won't be booting her out, as you put it, whatever she says or does. Old Ned happens to be very glad she fucked up, very glad she married him." His voice trembled slightly but his face in the half-light was expressionless. "Very glad indeed."

Then he turned on his heel and went back down the corridor the way he'd come.

Joss's white face was whiter. He stared at his mother. Hannie crossed to the door and closed it, pressing on the handle until she heard the latch click home. She switched on the light and the dusk at the window thickened abruptly into blackness. She took a pillow slip from the laundry basket and laid it on the ironing board. Then she picked up the iron and moved it backward, forward, backward, forward, her knuckles showing as white as the linen.

Joss extracted a cigarette from the packet she'd set on the mantelpiece. He lit it with her lighter and crossed to the window. He moved his shoulders once, compulsively, as though to loosen them. Then he picked up his old pose of indifference and swung it around himself like a cloak.

"What will you say?"

"Nothing. He won't ask."

Joss stared out at the sudden night beyond the panes.

"So, Mother," he said casually, "I'm not the only one that goes sneaking around, eavesdropping."

Hannie's mouth tightened but she didn't speak. The room they were in was at the end of the corridor; if Ned had wanted to find them he must come the way he had come, he had no other choice. But she didn't say it, she couldn't bring herself to defend him, she was far too threatened and angry for that.

———◆———

How long had Ned been standing there, how much had he heard? That night she lay in the dark going over and over Joss's words, her own words, trying to remember exactly what they'd said. Had he heard the whole lot, or only from where Joss had jumped in with Patrick being "on her list"? Bad as that was, it wasn't as bad as Joss's account of Patrick's words to Ciaran: his precious cousin not only understanding her motives in marrying him but sitting discussing the whole business quite casually with Niamh's boyfriend.

He couldn't have heard that, she decided. If he had he'd never have said what he'd finally said. She breathed deeply in relief.

But he'd said *fucked up,* he'd quoted Joss quoting Patrick's words. So he must have heard. Suddenly she was coldly certain he'd been standing there listening from the very start.

So why had he spoken out when he needn't have, when he could have just slipped away without ever revealing he'd heard their exchange? Why had he told Joss so firmly he wouldn't be throwing her out?

To subvert Joss's pathetic little blackmail attempt? To bolster her authority with her delinquent son?

She dismissed these thoughts. She wasn't used to magnanimity, she was used to self-interest, had no difficulty in accepting it as she'd accepted Ned's acquisition of her and her own self-interested compliance in the arrangement. Their marriage was a bargain that suited both of them and when it ceased to suit it would be broken or renegotiated. That Ned should suddenly transcend the bargain was a possibility altogether beyond her experience.

Ned had said what he'd said on account of his own mistake in marrying her, she decided. Once done, he wouldn't disown his action, that would be a worse weakness than the first weakness. He'd done it and he would stand over it, that was Ned. Let Patrick think what he liked.

As for Patrick, she wasn't really surprised. Patrick would be mindful only for himself and his own comforts. That was why he wasn't married now, though he had been once, why he had no real roots or attachments. Too inconvenient, someone else. Patrick was as selfish as she was — one of her kind. No, not entirely one of her kind. She revised her self-judgment fractionally. She wasn't lazy, a love of ease had never marked her out. For a moment she hated Patrick, briefly and completely. Then she dismissed her hatred as she had already dismissed the man.

———•✦•———

HANNIE SAT FORWARD with her elbows on the pew in front of her and her face in her hands, a sort of leaning crouch that imitated Ned's. Christmas Day. The clergyman droned from the altar regions but she didn't mind him, he was easy to ignore. She didn't mind the crouch either, it was strange but not uncomfortable, and gave at least the illusion of privacy.

Her mind kept returning to Joss's words about Lannigan. She went over and over the conversation, trying to work out its consequences, trying to mediate her fury against Ned.

She couldn't understand herself why she was so angry with him. It wasn't a pretty conversation that he'd overheard, it had put Joss in a bad light and herself in a worse one, but essentially it was information that Ned already knew. Hearing Joss's speculations, having the reality of the way she lived her life spelled out like that might be distasteful, but it didn't actually change anything.

So why did she mind so much, why was she so angry?

It was being known, she realized. Being known and judged and pitied. It was unbearable to her that he should see what her life really consisted of: the narrowness of her options, the sordid smallness of her many shifts and prevarications.

And if it was shameful to her that he should see and know, it was unendurable that she should have to see her life reflected through his eyes, assessed and diminished by his upright unyielding values.

Old Ned happens to be very glad she fucked up. That's what he'd said to Joss. Old Ned was prepared to forgive her whatever she did.

Big deal. She didn't want to be forgiven, she wanted to be young again, young and free and strong. She wanted to live as life took her and to hell with the consequences, to hell with anyone who didn't like it, she wanted to laugh at them as she'd always done, to despise their cowardly, safe self-righteousness, to move on.

There was a peal of organ music from a hidden tape recorder and everyone abandoned their crouches and heaved themselves upright. The recorded carol began. Most people mouthed to it but a few sang defiantly, their voices quavering and rough against the effortless river of joy from the choir on the machine. The congregation was elderly and sparse and well wrapped up, though the church glowed with overhead heaters and was far too warm for these denizens of old and drafty houses. After the initial relief they shuffled uncomfortably and glanced with longing at the chilly moldering aisles closed off by plate-glass partitions from the sealed box in the nave where they sat.

The church was decked for Christmas. There were great stands of vegetation: chrysanthemums and poinsettias, holly and bay. The brass memorials to dead soldiers on the walls shone with fresh polish, the sills of the narrow lancet windows were snowy with cotton wool, stubby red Christmas candles poked up through clustered holly and trailing green ivy.

Alison has been busy, Hannie thought sourly. It was years and years since she'd been in a church but she recognized an act of solidarity when she saw one: this was a small, carefully tended rock pool on the edge of a great surging sea of threatening otherness. She glanced at Ned's absorbed oblivious face and cursed her own stupidity in making this placatory gesture. It only made her feel more reckless and deepened her alienation from his world. Abruptly she gave up telling herself he'd done nothing wrong and let herself drift on a tide of anger and morose despair.

The rest of the day passed in an agony of slowness. Joss had stayed in bed and she was too relieved to be rid of him to nag about getting up. He came downstairs to eat Christmas dinner and was heading up to his room again directly the food was eaten. Ned called him back.

"Washing up," he said. "I thought we could do it together. To thank your mother for the dinner she's just cooked. Then there's presents."

Ned gave her two packages. The first held an ebony fan that had belonged to his mother, the second a sea-blue chiffon scarf with a border of pink and orange flowers. She liked the little blue scarf in spite of herself. She shook it out and knotted it around her neck. His mother's fan she would sell later.

Ned gave Joss a book on insects and Joss gave Ned a new clasp knife that she'd bought in a shop in Waterford Ned was always recommending. She gave Ned a pair of extra-thick Wellington socks from the same shop. She'd thought badly of them at the time, it hadn't seemed much of a present, just picking out socks and putting them on the account, but what was the point of spending his money on something he mightn't like?

It felt different now. She nearly left them in the drawer and faced him empty-handed, even a pair of socks was more than she wanted to give him. For Joss there was an envelope, which he was careful not to open in front of Ned. He needn't have bothered, she thought sourly, there wasn't much in it, Ned wouldn't have disapproved. But that, too, was more than she wanted to give.

Ned suggested a walk and Hannie put on her coat and her boots and went through the motions. They tramped through the muddy half-light but she closed herself off and repelled his efforts at conversation. Ned didn't try very hard, he was relieved when he heard himself lapse into silence.

They went by the lower field to check on the sheep. A heron got up from a reed bed and drifted heavily across the fading sky. Bess rounded up wandering ewes and Ned stood counting while Hannie stared at the sheep and they stared back, black-faced, lop-eared, their strange diamond-shaped eyes impenetrably blank and alien. The heron went flopping across again, it let out a short sharp shriek of protest at their prolonged intrusion. The rain came seeping out of the dusk.

Hannie thought of all the hot bright riotous Christmases she'd spent with people who longed for Christmases like this and wondered at their nostalgia.

Chapter Thirty-three

"GOD, WHAT A DISASTER." Niamh closed her eyes at the memory and spoke the words aloud to her empty kitchen. At least she hadn't insisted on taking Ciaran home with her. That was about the only redeeming feature of the last two days. She thought bitterly of her brothers and sisters.

"They just want me to look nice and wear pretty clothes and put everyone else's needs before my own," she used to complain to Maeve. Well that wasn't true anymore. Now they just wanted her to wear odd clothes and to say odd things and to go on being "peculiar," the baby, their peculiar little Niamh.

So it wasn't even that they were incapable of changing, they were simply incapable of seeing her as she was.

Perhaps it was time for a total reassessment, she thought. Perhaps she should go back to Dublin and eat humble pie. Get hold of Maeve, tell her she'd been right all along, the country was a rotten idea and was there any chance of sharing a studio after all?

But then she'd have nothing to live on. Her father didn't want her in the city. He wouldn't give her even this one year to see what she could do.

Well, so what, she could sign on, couldn't she? She could stop being so bourgeois and spineless? Maeve did, and Ciaran did, and everyone did when they were trying to make it after the end of college and before they'd established themselves as working artists.

It wasn't a big deal or a public shame the way her father made it out to be.

Anyway, it was either that or teaching and once you started the teaching game it was only a matter of time before the work slipped altogether. She'd tried to explain that to her father, but he didn't understand. He asked her couldn't she paint at the weekends?

She'd said it wasn't something you could just turn on and off like a tap, you had to live it and breathe it, or it didn't grow out of you. She had blushed when she'd said this, she didn't know why because she'd meant every word of it, but suddenly she was as embarrassed as if she'd been standing there telling him about her sex life. And then when she looked at him she'd seen that he was embarrassed too. He wasn't looking at her, he was poking with his ash plant at a new rat hole in among the nettles behind the old harrow. Poking and trying not to hear.

And then she'd felt miserable; miserable, and angry at herself and at her father because she couldn't stop minding what he thought enough to defy him. And after that he had talked to Ned, and he'd come home happy and full of his new arrangement and she'd let herself be maneuvered.

Ned had continued to pester his friends for commissions. James stubbornly went deaf when he mentioned Jacko, but he'd got money up front from a Mrs. Cardew for a view of her cottage garden, and there was a widow who'd sold her dead husband's crumbling birthright and now wanted a picture of it to hang in her bright new draft-free bungalow. Both had supplied photos.

Ned said he understood perfectly that she didn't want to paint people's houses or their pets. Such projects were simply earners, "potboilers" that paid the bills, let you do what you really wanted to do, that was why you did them.

He had always taken on extra commissions himself, he said. Bits of data-collecting and mapmaking projects and statistical work. Dull, but necessary, and not a bad discipline. They taught you how to operate on two levels: to work on a potboiler lightly, keeping your passion for the real thing.

Niamh had paid the electricity with Mrs. Cardew's advance and then started in on the painting of her garden. She'd blocked it in fairly easily and then put it briefly aside. The aside had been a mistake, she should have just finished it in the one go; in the interval she'd grown self-conscious and then stupidly she'd left it uncovered and Ciaran had seen it. After that it was hopeless, the more she tried the more she hated it. Worse, the hatred seemed to have spilled over into her real work. She'd been doing a painting from a papier-mâché bust she'd made, the head and shoulders of an androgynous figure just looking up as though it had caught some half-heard sound. The bust had been experimental but it had something, a peculiar quick attentiveness, and she'd wanted to see if she could take this further in a painting.

Some hope. She'd been making herself go on trying, but she couldn't get her confidence back, she couldn't put Ciaran's critical appraising glance out of her head. On a good day she dabbed miserably; on a bad day she just stood. She'd stopped believing in herself and it was nearly easier to struggle with flowerbeds and roof angles than to trust to her own fragile vision.

Ned was trying hard to help in his own way, Niamh knew this, but somehow it just made it all worse. Now she had him on her back as well as her father. Ciaran said she was out of her mind to be even thinking of potboilers, or whatever it was Ned called them. You had to do what you wanted to do and not deviate or compromise or you'd end up making crap work and not even knowing it. Niamh, stung, said she hadn't noticed him making any work at all, but he just grinned at her and said no work was better than crap work and the world could wait.

"I hope it's not holding its breath," she'd said, and flounced off to stare hard at the garden photos one more time.

Now she wandered into the little studio room and stood trying to look at her canvases with a cool and appraising eye. It was her own fault, she thought, it was no good blaming anyone else, she'd just have to make some decisions and act on them. First, the studio had to be made more habitable. The chimney smoked so badly that she'd long since given up lighting a fire in there. She wore three jumpers and fingerless gloves, and she was still frozen. Jackdaws, likely as not, Ciaran said. A nest in the chimney. She'd asked him to clear it out but he wouldn't.

"Would you wise up, I know sod-all about chimneys. Ask Ned — he's the landlord."

He was right, but she didn't want to ask Ned, she paid so little rent and she didn't like to bother him. Well, that would have to change, she'd just have to bother him. She'd go straight up to the house now and tell Ned that she wasn't going to do Mrs. Cardew's commission or the widow's commission, she wasn't going to do any commissions at all. And even if she wanted to, she couldn't because of the chimney.

———•◆•———

"OF COURSE she won't stick at it," Hannie said, lifting rashers out of the pan and holding them there a moment for the fat to drip. "All this talk of integrity and jackdaws is just noise. Noise and excuses. Because she is doing no work." She laid the rashers in the serving dish and put it back into the Aga to keep warm. Joss sat at the kitchen table, waiting. Ned was striding around the room in his stockinged feet, worrying aloud about Niamh. He stopped pacing.

"She will, Hannie, she will," he said. "If she gets a bit of support, a bit of encouragement. When she sees money everything will change, when she realizes she's making her own way, that she's independent.

"And she's right, she can't work when she's frozen. It'll be different when the chimney's cleaned, I wish she'd mentioned it before, I'll take the brushes down tomorrow, have it clear in a couple of hours."

Hannie broke eggs into the sizzling fat. "No," she said with finality. "You're wrong, she won't stick at it. She won't stick at it and you can't make her, no matter how hard you want it for her, no matter how many people you persuade into commissioning pictures that she doesn't want to paint."

"I'm not making her do anything," Ned protested. "If she doesn't want commissions she doesn't have to take them. I'm only trying to help her do what she wants to do and become a professional artist. To hear you talk you'd think I was trying to make her do something she *doesn't* want to do." Ned warmed to his subject, he was glad to see her belligerent, he found it easier than silent antagonism and less confusing. Neither of them had mentioned the overheard conversation, but it was there between them like the smell of decay. Communication, any communication was, to Ned's way of thinking, a definite advance.

"And what makes you so sure she won't stick?" he demanded. "She got top marks at college. She's got talent, character . . ."

Hannie slid the fried eggs onto the dish and lifted two more from the rack. She cracked them into the pan without turning her head.

"It is not to do with talent," she said. She flicked hot fat over the bubbling whites. "Nor character either. It's the way she is bred."

Ned waited. She didn't seem to be about to add to the statement.

"The way she is bred?"

"Like a Dutch *hausfrau* who knows what the future will hold." Hannie bent for the dish again. "Born to a hearth, to shined copper pans and her grandmother's linen. This is what she is, it doesn't matter what she wants to be." Two more eggs left the pan and the dish was returned to the oven.

"That's nonsense, Hannie, that's got nothing to do with it, plenty of artists come from stable middle-class homes."

"Male artists . . ."

"Male, female, what does it matter? You underestimate her, Hannie, she's more than that, she wants her life to be more than that."

"I told you — it's not what she wants or what she thinks she wants, it's what she is, what she can't avoid. She'll marry — it's her nature's imperative — she'll have no choice. Then there'll be children and their care will come first because that's the way she is, and then it will be too late. All this talk of painting is only talk, Ned. I think already she knows this somewhere, and somewhere she accepts it." She half-turned, saw Ned's face.

"Oh, not Ciaran, she won't marry Ciaran, he's only a passion, he isn't a marriage. And anyway he'll leave her, already he's bored."

Hannie picked up the dish of bacon and eggs and carried it to the table where Joss waited. "Perhaps it is *you* who wants her life to be more, Ned," she said. "Perhaps you should leave her alone."

"That's ridiculous." Ned was stung. "Why should I care what her life is, so long as she's happy?"

"Oh, because in some way you identify. Your young self with the way she is now. And you don't like her young man, you don't want him to have her affection. But I think it's already too late, much too late —"

———•◆•———

LATE THAT NIGHT the phone rang and Joss answered it.

"Hey, Joss, how're ye doin', man? Niamh there?" Ciaran's voice was slurred, there were party noises in the background.

"I'll get her."

"Wise up, would yous? Tell her I got held up, couldn't make it, say to expect me when she sees me, not before. Hell, Joss, say what you like, use your imagination, tell her I'm dyin' for her, tell her I ran out of money and got cut off. . . ."

Then he talked for another ten minutes or so. Rabbiting on, this and that. Then he hung up.

Joss passed the message on to Niamh the next morning, putting in some stuff about Ciaran missing her, watching her face light, telling her no, Ciaran hadn't said why he'd got held up, maybe he needed a break?

Watching her face as it made itself go blank.

It was no fun, baiting Niamh. He wished Ciaran would come back. Niamh by herself was poor company.

Chapter Thirty-four

"— AND THEN SHE TOLD NED he was jealous of Ciaran. And he just stood there, the dirty old git, never denied it, never said a word. So it must be true." Joss was feeding Danno's sparrow hawk with tidbits of badger entrail, speaking softly and evenly, not looking at the bird just as Danno had told him, not looking at Danno, either.

"Who'd have thought it, eh Danno? Old Ned fancying Niamh. Young enough to be his granddaughter. And her daddy all gratitude and can't do enough for him on account of his kindness to his little girl. Not half as kind as he'd like to be, eh Danno?" Joss chuckled.

"Ciaran won't be surprised when I tell him," Joss continued. "Ciaran was wise to him all along — said the *auld fella* was never done knocking the door mornings, keeping Miss Niamh standing on the step in her nightie, talking away." Joss was getting into his stride now, relishing the words, mimicking Ciaran's Northern accent. "And him only just through overhauling her himself, lying out on the bed upstairs too knackered to move, listening to every word the old fool sez to her, laughing away."

Danno's gaze was fixed on the back of the smooth yellow head, the smooth-packaged self. I'm like a rabbit watching a stoat weave, Danno thought, unable to stop himself. He was mesmerized and immobile, helpless before the undulating death-dance.

"That's something to put in your pipe and smoke, eh, Danno? You wouldn't mind being kind to Niamh yourself now, would you, Danno? There's not many would mind, I'd say, and Joss wouldn't be the one to blame them, not a bit, he wouldn't. What's a little kindness between friends, eh, Danno? If only Old Ned knew how kind Joss has been. How green he'd be; how — green — he — would — be."

Joss spoke the last words separately and deliberately, as though he were remembering them to himself. Danno rose abruptly, breaking the spell. The sparrow hawk, startled into rage, scuttled sideways on the perch, jerking furiously at her jesses.

———•◆•———

"JOSS WAS HERE just now," Danno said.

"I know." Hannie flicked her cigarette into an empty tea mug. The hot ash fizzled a moment in the cold dregs. "We are all visiting. Niamh will be the next. She has come rushing back from the bosom of her family, quivering with indignation and new resolutions." Hannie was wearing an old jersey, full of holes, and a pair of baggy cord trousers stuck into Wellingtons. Ned's clothes. Her step was springy, she seemed in good spirits, on the edge of being pleased with herself.

"You should build a barricade, Danno, a high thorn stockade as we do against wild beasts in Africa. But there must be a secret entrance, perhaps an underground tunnel, a souterrain, isn't that what such a passage is called here? Will you dig a souterrain, Danno? A fine one, just for me, so I can visit you while all the rest are held at bay?" She roamed restlessly around the room as she talked. "Oh, don't look so dismayed, Danno, you can keep a pile of stones handy, lob them at me when you can't stand the thought of me, drive me off. I understand, really I do, there are plenty of times when I can't stand the thought of me myself. Besides, it's only right for people like you to throw stones at women like me, whatever your Jesus once said." She shot a glance at him, but he was avoiding looking at her.

"You don't speak, Danno? Is it possible you don't believe me? That you don't believe there's ever a time that I can't stand the thought of myself?" She stopped pacing and stood staring at the darkness in the great black window. Half past five going on midnight. She needed something stronger than tea.

"What's the matter with Joss, Hannie?"

"The matter? Why? What's he done?" Her voice had changed, it was casual, noncommittal, but underneath it was on guard. She didn't turn around, but he could see the alertness in the back of her shoulders. This was a question she'd been asked before.

"Nothing. He hasn't done anything." Danno didn't have to look at her to catch her relief. "But he was here, and he was talking."

"Human beings do, it's one of the characteristics of the species, some say it's most of the problem —"

"He was talking about sex," Danno said stubbornly. "About sex and Niamh."

"Oh? Was it interesting? What did he say?" She was lighting a ciga-rette, her back still turned.

"It wasn't so much what he said, more the tone of the saying." Danno scraped carefully at the inside of the emptied badger's skin. He hoped she wouldn't make him spell it out, that he'd just have to warn her obliquely and she'd do something to keep Joss away from Niamh.

There was a moment's pause. "What did he say, Danno?" she asked again, her tone quiet and relentless with an edge of contempt in it. She was bullying him, he realized, willing him to let it go. But he wouldn't. Danno braced himself.

"He thinks a lot of Ciaran," he said, getting the words out quickly. She waited. He opened his mouth to say more but it didn't come.

"And not much of Ned?" she finished for him.

"And not much of Ned."

"And you think that Ciaran is a bad influence and I shouldn't let Joss spend time with him, is that it?" Again she waited. "OK, let's try again. You think that Joss is a bad influence on Ciaran and I should protect him from my delinquent son?"

"He — Joss — intimated at a certain . . . physical intimacy with Niamh." Danno got it out in an embarrassed gabble. Hannie was very still for a moment. Then she threw back her head and laughed with relief.

"And you believe *that* — it is *that* that has upset you so? Oh Danno, that's just boasting, wishful thinking, boy's fantasy. You remember boy's fantasies, surely? Masturbation, wet dreams, all that stuff?"

She stopped herself. "On second thought, perhaps you don't. I bet you masturbated with a pinup of a Labrador and had wet dreams about hawks," she said nastily. "What is it with you all? Niamh might as well be a bitch on heat for the effect she's having on you."

But she'd misjudged him. Danno wasn't to be ridiculed into submission so easily.

"I may be inexperienced, Hannie, but I'm not the sort of prude you seem to think me. This was more than boy's fantasy, there was something twisted about it, something horrible."

"You're getting this out of proportion, Danno. This is the spoiled priest in you talking."

"Who told you that?"

"Mrs. Coady."

"Well, you tell Kathleen Coady I'm disappointed in her. Tell her I didn't think she'd be wasting her time on erroneous tittle-tattle, I'd thought more of her."

"Erroneous?"

"That's what I said. But we're getting off the subject, which is Joss, not me. What's wrong with him, Hannie?"

"Wrong?" She left her stance by the window and coasted around the room again, trying to find the words that would put him off. This was a new side of Danno, she wasn't prepared for his determination.

"Nothing's wrong," she said coldly. "He's just not very well adjusted. A bit odd, if you really want to know. But not schizophrenic or psychotic," she added bitterly, "they all seem to agree on that."

"You've had him tested?"

"Oh, he's been tested," Hannie said evasively. "He's had all the tests."

She got up, strolled over to the window, pausing to look straight into the yellow eyes of the sparrow hawk in a way she knew would anger Danno. Then she stood with her back to him, smoking and staring out at the darkness. Why not tell him about Joss, she thought suddenly, it might be a relief, she'd never just said it out, she was always so locked into trying to prove the opposite. That black was white, that Joss wasn't as she knew he was. And Danno saw no one, it didn't matter what he said or thought, talking to him was scarcely more indiscreet than talking to herself.

"Joss is odd," she said quietly. "Not normal. But in a way that doesn't show up on tests."

"Autistic?"

"No, not autistic." There was a pause. "Corrupt."

"Corrupt?"

"Corrupt," Hannie agreed. "That was the word I used, Danno. Sometimes you sound like a bloody parrot."

Danno laid down the skin he was cleaning. His questions weren't idly curious, he had asked about Joss because he was anxious for Niamh. But he wasn't that anxious, he didn't want to hear what he was learning now, he realized, he didn't want Hannie's confidence, he wanted to tell her the problem and have her take it away.

And she was doing the opposite. He was too private, too unused to human intercourse to accept her secrets lightly. He'd made a mistake in pressing her, had uncovered far more than he wanted to know. So he swiveled on his tatty revolving chair and sat loosely and quietly, his gray eyes averted behind their spectacles and vaguely focused on the floor.

"It's his nature," Hannie said finally, still not turning. "That bird there — she's a killer, you can't blame her, it's her nature. Well, Joss is corrupt — you can't blame him, it's his nature."

There was another silence.

"Hannie, that hawk is a raptor, a bird of prey," Danno said carefully. "It's an evolved killer, has spent thousands of years honing itself into what it is. Joss is a human being, not a raptor, it's not his destiny to be corrupt, you can't compare the two."

"Can't I?" Hannie said, her voice low and stubborn. "Who says I can't? You, Danno? What do you know? Joss likes corruption. He likes hurting, spoiling, dirtying. Going the crooked way." She spoke so quietly now that Danno had to strain to catch her words.

"Did something happen?"

No answer from Hannie. She was staring at the great black curtainless window, unredeemed by moonlight or stars. She blew out smoke so it rolled and billowed defiantly across its darkness.

"Was he born like that?"

"Was he born like that, did he get like that? Who knows? What made you the way you are, an old woman fussing away at these horrible birds? Because you were born like that or because they wouldn't have you as a priest?"

Danno gave an almost imperceptible start and straightened very slightly in his chair. "Is that what Kathleen told you?" he asked quietly.

"She said they wouldn't have you because you're illegitimate. She said that's how things were when you were young."

"She's got it wrong, I never asked them, I didn't want to go."

Hannie looked at him, at the stubborn, closed hurt in his face. He'd wanted to all right. It was as Kathleen had said, he just wouldn't give them the satisfaction of turning him down. She crossed to the window seat and picked up her coat.

She stepped out into a darkness that crept and clung at her neck, her face, her hands. The cold had softened a little, cloud hid the stars. She'd left her torch behind at Danno's, could see nothing, her feet found the puddled track and followed it haltingly. She wondered at the black closeness of this darkness that moved and breathed like an intimate against her skin. There was nothing else beside it, nothing in the world but the stones under her feet and the moist black night.

She'd seen his face as she left, the ill-concealed hurt reflecting her overstepped mark. She'd been almost pleased at the time, she was sick of being patronized, of being the problem, the one always in the wrong. She was a problem and Joss was a problem, but the lives all around her weren't so perfect either, they were just better camouflaged here where they belonged. Sometimes they needed reminding of this. And sometimes it helped your own pain to take a swipe at someone else, even if that someone else came close to being your only friend.

She tramped on. Already the strength she felt from her deliberate little cruelty had all but leached away, leaving nothing but self-disgust in its place. She felt rudderless and directionless, like the dead sheep the November rains had carried down the river. Day after day it had drifted up and down, up and down, moving swiftly away with the pull of the sea's ebbing tide, pushing back again as it rose. Bloated, a perch for the gulls. Until it snagged on some drowned tree and left off its journeying.

Chapter Thirty-five

IT WAS THAT DARK, DANK TIME that stretched and sagged like a bit of old rope between Christmas and the New Year. It was hard for Hannie to pull herself out of despondency, harder still to stay that way. The tentative easing and harmonizing of her relationship with Ned had disintegrated like old silk suddenly restored to light, now parting at the lightest touch. There seemed little to be gained in trying to darn it together again, only to watch it open somewhere else under the strain of the new stitches.

Besides, she had the measure of the life here and of the people who lived it alongside her and she expected little from either. Nothing was going to change, so what was the point of trying? She almost let herself decide against the effort.

Ned's relations came from Galway the next day and saved her. They arrived without writing or phoning, a car drew up and a man got out, walked over the thin gravel, hesitated in front of the heavy iron knocker. Hannie heard and watched discreetly from an upstairs window. When the knocker thumped the first time she made no move to answer it. It pounded again and she went slowly downstairs, leaving whoever it was plenty of time to give up and go back to wherever he'd come from.

He went on knocking. She undid the snib but the heavy door, swollen with winter damp, stuck fast near the top. She heaved and pulled, calling to the man on the other side to put his shoulder to it. The door gave suddenly under their combined efforts, it burst open and he stumbled in after it. He gathered himself. His name was Andrew Clarke, he explained, he was a great-nephew of Ned's by marriage, now come with his wife to visit because they were in the area and didn't want to pass Ned's door.

"It's only a call on the off chance. I haven't seen Ned since I was a boy, I doubt he'd even remember me."

Hannie let him run out of words and stand awkwardly. "Ned's gone to Waterford," she said, which was true. "I don't know when he'll be back," she added, which wasn't. "You can wait if you want." Her tone was utterly discouraging.

The man, relieved, started backing out. On the far edge of her vision Hannie glimpsed a movement, which she knew was Joss, sidling off behind a door.

"You must come in and wait," she said, changing her mind abruptly. "Ned will want to see you — he won't be long now — come in, make yourselves at home, stay for dinner."

"We wouldn't want to put you to any trouble." Andrew Clarke looked confused. "We'll call again some other time."

"It's no trouble and you can't go now, you've only just come. What will Ned say if he gets back and finds I haven't held on to you?"

Hannie's voice was false and almost arch. Alarm flickered across Andrew's face, he went on trying to refuse but she wouldn't listen. Then he gave in abruptly, looking embarrassed and muttering about having a word with Nora.

Hannie stood and watched him cross the patchy gravel and bend to talk to his wife through the wound-down window of the car. She knew that this great-nephew of Ned's hadn't any idea who she was, nor what was the set-up. He had plainly expected the elderly bachelor Ned, perhaps a housekeeper, certainly not a wife. She knew from the set of his back that the woman in the car didn't want to come in and he was telling her they had to, they couldn't get out of it now. She was arguing, but not very hard, she'd give in soon because he was asking her to.

Hannie didn't care, let them go or stay, it was all one to her. And Ned wouldn't want to see them, she knew that, Ned had had enough of other

people's company for the time being. Yet it would be better than nothing, better than sitting silently with Ned by the fire, Joss in Niamh's
cottage, she, wondering should she go over there or let him alone.

A slim woman, dark-haired and pretty, got slowly out of the car and
came with her husband to where Hannie was standing waiting. Hannie
put out her hand.

"I'm Ned's wife, Hannie," she said easily, catching the shock on the
man's face. The woman was blank. Either she was better at conceal-
ment or simply too preoccupied with her own reluctance.

"Nora," the woman introduced herself shyly. "But really we can't put
you to this trouble, it was only a whim of Andrew's, we were passing so
near to you . . ." She flushed and the words ran out. Hannie took her by
the arm and drew her in through the door.

"It's no trouble," she said again, "it's a pleasure. You'll stay the night."
It wasn't a question. Andrew had no choice but to follow.

———•◆•———

WHEN NED CAME BACK they were drinking gin by the drawing-
room fire, Hannie playing the hostess in a dark dress, her hair smoothed
and restrained, her manner similar. She said they were staying over and
they didn't contradict her. Surprising himself, Ned was pleased.

He hardly knew Andrew, a grandson of one of his dead wife's many
brothers, and remembered him only dimly as a lanky youth who had
blushed and mumbled when spoken to except when asked about rugby,
which it seemed he played with flair and talent. He didn't look like an
athlete now. Ned saw a big, loose-boned, good-humored, peace-loving
man in his late thirties, the powerful body running a little to fat.

Rugby? Andrew laughed quietly. Those days were long gone, he was
his own man now, an auctioneer in a biggish town outside of Galway,
his business secure, his peers suggesting to him that he think of standing in the next election. He hadn't decided yet, he said, he was still
turning it over, taking soundings. Of course it was harder for a Protestant to get elected, but Nora was Catholic and her family was long-
term Fine Gael; that would help him with the nomination.

He spoke with so natural a modesty, so simple and serious a belief in his life, that Ned could not but listen and warm to him.

He liked Nora too, but he couldn't get her to relax. She was shy and she wanted to stop being shy and open to them, but she wasn't at ease. She was unsure how to behave with her husband's relatives, and over-anxious to deliver whatever it was they expected of her.

Nora was the daughter of a strong farmer on the Offaly-Galway border, one of many children, used to company and noise and laughter, to warmth and work and family. She knew that as a young man Andrew had hero-worshipped his great-uncle and she wanted to do well so he'd be proud of her. But she felt more out of place here than she'd expected to and she wasn't used to such self-consciousness. Everything — her voice, her attitudes, her clothes — seemed suddenly somehow different and open to question.

She had a six-year-old son, she told Hannie, a girl of four and another of eighteen months. A sister of hers was visiting over Christmas and they'd taken this chance to go away together. It was Andrew's idea, for herself she thought Christmas so precious a time that she wanted to be with the children, but still it was only a couple of days, a business visit in Youghal, an overnight in a quiet hotel, a little driving around to show her where his father's family had come from. It was clear that she missed her home and her children and yearned to get back to them.

She was pleased when she discovered Joss. She liked teenage boys, she said, following Hannie out to the kitchen and settling in beside him at the kitchen table, happy to leave the grown-ups to her husband. Hannie fed Joss baked beans and fried eggs while she cooked dinner for the rest of them and Nora did her best at conversation. She made little headway. Joss ate fast, then rose to go.

"I'll be at Niamh's," he told his mother. He didn't even glance at Nora.

"You feel for them so at this age, don't you?" Nora said, as the back door shut behind him. "I always remember what it was like — the wanting to join in and not knowing how, it must be harder for an only —" She stopped herself. "Or maybe it's easier. No competition, no thinking the others are prettier or cleverer or stronger." She finished with a small, embarrassed laugh. Hannie said nothing. She was thinking that for once Joss had a point.

They had dinner in the dining room. Ned was glad of Joss's absence, he was still recovering from his discovery of the depths of Joss's alienation and the strange complicitous relationship between the boy and his mother. Besides he was tired of making an effort, tired of Joss's odd disruptive presence, tired of his own face reflecting from the mirrors of his stepson's shuttered eyes. He wanted to sit quietly and talk.

Ned saw the ease with which Andrew moved through his life and he guessed that much of this ease must have come through Nora. He plainly liked his relations through marriage, liked the influence of her big noisy family, liked having a foot in both religious camps and feeling neither disloyalty nor any need to convert. For him there was to be no self-imposed silence, no holding a little apart from the daily life of community or state. He and Nora loved and understood each other: life was for rearing your children, making your way, earning the respect of your friends and your community. It was all simple and healthy and straightforward.

Andrew was confused by Ned. He had been in awe of his legend since childhood, and their few meetings had deepened his sense that here was someone different and extraordinary. Now he looked at his great-uncle and wondered what all that adventuring had been about. He saw an old man with an odd wife and a strange stepson, trying to run a bit of a farm and knowing less about it than one of Nora's half-grown brothers. He felt pity for Ned because he hadn't stayed at home and done something with his life, but had frittered it away, traveling with nomadic peoples in forgotten places.

He said all this to Nora in bed that night and she listened and held his hand while he talked. He said he wondered now why he had romanticized Ned, why his life had once seemed so special to him. His own immaturity, perhaps? He saw Ned's traveling now for what it was: a refusal to accept the changing world; ultimately probably an inability to grow up and adapt and take on responsibility.

He didn't know what to make of Hannie, nor why Ned had married her. Could it be that Ned was in love with her?

Nora said she thought Ned had married Hannie because he was lonely. It was a shame he'd had no children of his own, he'd have been a wonderful father, it made sense of life if you had children. . . .

The next day they were easier in themselves and not so inclined to be overawed. Ned saw that he had been judged and found wanting, and he saw that Hannie saw it as well. He smiled at her ruefully across the kitchen and she grinned back at him. They were companionable in their outsiderliness.

Ned took Andrew off about the place but Nora stayed with Hannie, insisting that they do the washing up together. Hannie looked at her mutely and handed over the gloves and the mop. Nora could wash up if she wanted, but she could do it alone. She filled a mug with hot water and put a plastic bottle of ear-mite drops into it to warm. Then she knelt on the kitchen floor, clamped the wriggling puppy between her knees, lifted each ear in turn and squeezed in the drops. Joss came downstairs. He ignored Nora and stood watching her.

"Ciaran's come back, Niamh's creaming herself."

"Niamh that you were around with last night?" Nora asked from the sink.

Hannie released Pippa and got up off her knees. "Ned's tenant," she said. "She's a painter. Ciaran's the boyfriend."

At once Nora wanted to meet her. It seemed she had a young cousin who might go to art school.

"Joss, take Nora around to Niamh's and introduce her. Tell Niamh to show Nora her paintings."

"She'll love that."

Even Nora heard the sarcasm in his voice.

"She doesn't have to if she doesn't want to, it must be so hard to be-lieve in yourself when you're only beginning."

Joss threw a Who's-This-Moron? look at Hannie. Then he ushered her through the door and followed after her.

Ciaran and Niamh would still be in bed, of course. Hannie hoped Nora would be shocked. Perhaps she'd tell her husband that Ned was allowing all sorts of carryings-on on his property.

Joss seemed to like her, despite the looks he was throwing around; Hannie watched them talking as they walked together across the yard. The damp was on Nora's dark curly hair, there was a glow on her fair skin, she was enjoying herself. Joss looked easy and young and almost animated. Hannie curdled with jealousy.

They were away longer than expected. It seemed Ciaran and Niamh had indeed been in bed and Nora hadn't been shocked at all, she'd lit the fire and put on the kettle and when they'd come down she'd eaten a second breakfast with them.

Ned came back with Andrew and they had lunch. Nora was animated, she tried to draw Hannie into household conversations but Hannie wouldn't have it. She tried again, but Hannie kept on thwarting her so she gave up and talked about her youngest brother who was Joss's age. Hannie caught Ned's eye on her during one of these attempts and she saw to her surprise that he didn't mind that she was stonewalling Nora. Hannie was good at the house, Ned knew that, but there it ended. She wouldn't discuss recipes or getting stains off polished furniture or the perfect kitchen floor.

They ate everything she put on the table and sat over coffee and Nora wanted to help wash up again, but Hannie was firm as a rock. When they finally got into the car to drive away the blue-gray twilight was with them like a witness. Ned and Hannie stood together, hearing the sound of the engine fade off into the distance, feeling the damp silence flow back over them and close them off again in their hidden, frosty world.

Hannie bent to snap a cluster of blackened hips from a long, thorned spike on the Frensham rose. "Do you think Joss would be more normal if I was?" she asked into the silence.

"You mean if he had Nora for a mother?"

She nodded, her face averted.

"If Nora was his mother he wouldn't be Joss," Ned said quietly. "It's a meaningless question."

She snapped off another cluster of hips. "Niamh thinks Joss is all my fault," she said.

"Do you?"

She thought for a minute and then shook her head. "Not all. Joss is Joss, he was born Joss. But I think I've made him worse."

She had dropped the shriveled hips onto the ground and was drawing patterns in the gravel with her shoe. "Then again, there are times when I think I'm all his fault." She looked up at Ned, a sad, tired look. "Nothing is as simple as Niamh believes."

"When you're young you think that way," Ned said gently. "Don't you remember? You think everything could be put right if only people went about things differently. You think there is choice. In twenty years' time she'll be astonished that she thought these things at all."

"She won't remember," Hannie said bitterly. "Niamh will always be sure that she's right."

Ned smiled and shook his head, but he didn't speak.

That night Ned came to Hannie's bed and tried to please her more than himself. It was a failure. For the first time he knew himself to be hopelessly clumsy and incompetent. He wanted to ask her to help him learn, but he knew he couldn't ever get the words out and if he did it would only make it worse. He saw himself through her eyes and knew himself already far too old and inexperienced. He wished he had known her over years, then at least there would have been the tenderness of friendship to lean on. As it was, she was merely fulfilling the terms of their contract. She would service him efficiently and without resentment, but she expected nothing. He wondered if she thought of old loves, or of nothing at all.

He wanted to stay with her for the rest of the night but he didn't want to impose on her more than he already had. He took himself off to his own room and lay a long time looking into the darkness and thinking about the day. Andrew and Nora's visit had thrown them together, had shown them as misfits, almost outcasts, in this intensely settled and familial society. He wondered if she felt like this all the time, and if it made her lonely. He wondered if it was why she'd taken to Danno.

It was the first time she'd referred, even indirectly, to the scene he'd witnessed on Christmas Eve, the first time she'd spoken of Joss and of his strangeness. He suffered for her now when he saw her trapped or hopeless. He wondered if this suffering was a form of love.

Chapter Thirty-six

NORA PHONED WHILE THEY WERE EATING. She thanked them for their hospitality and spoke convincingly of how much they'd both enjoyed their visit. She said she'd mislaid a small gold bracelet, she didn't know where. Stupid of her, perhaps they would keep an eye out for it and give her a ring if it turned up? Hannie put the phone down and passed on the message, her voice neutral and indifferent. Later she went through Joss's drawers carefully but the bracelet wasn't there. She searched in the most obvious places but all she found was a woman's high-heeled court shoe under the bed. Probably Nora's, though she hadn't mentioned shoes. No sign of its twin. Perhaps Joss had only wanted the one.

She took it away but said nothing. He'd discover the loss: she wanted him to know she knew.

———◆———

"GARTH BROOKS?" Ciaran drawled. "Bit close to Country-with-its-tongue-*not*-in-its-cheek for my taste. You know the style — sleeve notes all about God and the wife. Songs about men in bars hitting each other . . ."

Joss smirked appreciatively. Niamh, sprawled in the lumpy armchair by the fire, stirred irritably but kept her thoughts to herself. She wished Ciaran would stop showing off for Joss. She'd told him as much only two days ago and he'd said she was jealous.

She'd been dumbstruck. Jealous? The injustice of the word! How did he figure that one?

He'd said it was obvious. They were into stuff she wasn't into, so she felt left out and jealous.

Everything she said about Joss after that came out as though to confirm his verdict, so she avoided saying anything. She'd begun to avoid any subject that might annoy Ciaran, she noticed. She was ashamed of her behavior, but more ashamed of the besottedness that induced it.

She didn't know how Ciaran felt about her; often she wondered if he even liked her. He wanted her, that was plain enough; he reached for her, unable not to reach, already bored by the imperatives of his body. She was as bad, she knew that, and she wasn't yet remotely bored. More like obsessed. Did she love him? She really had no idea. She'd stopped telling him she did when she noticed that he never said the words himself, only nodded vaguely as if in agreement. She glanced across at him now and decided that he despised her. Well, that was all right, she despised him back.

He seemed always detached and sarcastic with her. With her, but also with the rest of them. Except for Hannie. Hannie took no notice of Ciaran, hardly ever addressed him unless it was a request or an inquiry: he was Niamh's boyfriend, that was all, she was formal with him. With Hannie Ciaran watched, he didn't speak. He spoke disparagingly of her, called her The Hag, but there was a tension in him when she appeared, an alertness.

Ciaran had nicknames for everyone, he called Joss The Spook, he rubbished him, but he didn't seem too unhappy with his company. Unless he wanted to go back to bed with her, but even that wasn't really a problem, Joss seemed to know when they wanted him gone. "I'll be off then," he'd say, sliding his blank black gaze across her face, the corners of his mouth turned upward in a smirk. She thought The Smirk would have been a better name than The Spook, but she kept the thought to herself. Ned was A. R. for Anal Retentive. She'd laughed, despite herself. Ned was so stiff and private.

She sighed now and settled herself deeper in the lumpy armchair and tried to let go of her thoughts and get back into her book. The chair was too small, her long limbs stuck out beyond its confines, but she didn't want to move because the puppy was asleep on her stomach and she liked stroking the soft hairless belly as she read.

"It says here that people with low moral standards have more friends than people with high ones." She spoke the words aloud before she knew she had intended to; she heard them with a vague surprise.

"Why d'you read that crap?"

"'Tisn't crap. She won the Booker Prize."

"Still crap." Ciaran extracted a card from his hand and laid it on the table. He threw a quick glance at Joss.

"She says it's because they're easier to be with."

"Who are?"

"People with low moral standards."

"Which would be why I'd have a whole lot more friends than you do," Ciaran said. Joss laid a card onto Ciaran's and took the trick. A little pulse showed for a moment at the corner of Ciaran's mouth.

"More acquaintances," Niamh said, looking at him, her brown eyes level and steady. "I have more friends."

Ciaran shrugged. His lazy voice belied the pulse. "Have it yer own way," he said. He was waiting for Joss to lead, watching the back of his cards as though he could read through them. Joss's dark glasses lay on the table beside him. His face looked curiously empty without them, almost bereft, the skin around his eyes very white, the rest of his face still holding the mark of the African sun, his flaxen brows and lashes accentuating both the color and the absence of it.

"Who is this crappy author that you're reading?" Hannie asked from across the room. She was roaming around with a glass in her hand, picking up objects, putting them down again. She'd come over from the house with a bottle of vodka, ostensibly to return past hospitality, in reality to check on Joss and the chemistry between him and Ciaran. She'd dismissed Danno's words to his face, but nonetheless she was alert to them.

"Anita Brookner." Niamh addressed Hannie seriously, looking up at her from her open book. "She writes about women by themselves."

"Spinster moralist," Ciaran drawled from the table. "Writes about people too scared to live."

"How would you know? You've never read her."

"Have so," Ciaran said casually. "Great stylist. Still crap. You should try her, Hannie, put some courage into you. Read two of them books in a row and you'll run out the door and burn the world down just to stop yourself from suffocating in fucking moderation."

"Hannie doesn't read books."

"Yes she does."

"No she doesn't."

"Yes she does. Tell you what, let's ask her." He swung fully around in his chair and gave Hannie all his attention. Joss watched from somewhere a long way off. "D'you read books, Hannie?"

"Not very often," Hannie said indifferently. She was propped against the dresser, smoking a cigarette.

"D'you think auld Brookner's right?"

"About what?"

"Low moral standards and loads of friends?"

"Of course." Hannie spoke as though it was too obvious to need stating. She took a drag at her cigarette. She looked thoughtful.

"You think I need courage?" she challenged Ciaran suddenly.

"Courage?" He was puzzled.

"You said it would put courage in me?"

Ciaran hesitated. "I think maybe you're in the doldrums," he said slowly. "Temporary-like. Nothing to write home about."

A curious atmosphere had sprung up between them, an intimacy that was tangible. Hannie's expression didn't change but she stood waiting, as though she hadn't heard his words. Joss stayed very still, but his right hand came forward as though it was separate and autonomous. It picked up his dark glasses and settled them onto his nose again. Niamh grabbed at the puppy, pulling the little body close and rubbing her cheek against the soft fur. Only Ciaran seemed unaware.

At last Hannie moved. She tossed her cigarette into the fire and looked straight at Ciaran.

"The doldrums," she said thoughtfully. "Becalmed, no wind in the sails, nothing to blow you this way or that." She laughed, a low easy laugh that was utterly surprising. "Perhaps it's the right place for me," she said, still speaking to him and to no one else. "Now that I'm almost an old woman. The doldrums. Respectable. Safe."

"Would you wise up, Hannie?" Ciaran said. His voice had a harsh authority. "You're never going to be respectable. And you're never going to be safe, neither. Face facts, stop dreaming dreams. It's not the world that'll stop you — it's yourself." He stared at her furiously, consumed in the intensity of the drama between them. Then, with a hard effort, he broke her gaze and threw a card down on the table. With a toss of the head he challenged Joss to follow his lead. "And leave off the fucking glasses, dickhead! You want to play — you play straight. Or as straight as your twisted wee soul can allow for. I want to see your eyes, an' that means no glasses."

Joss didn't answer. He removed the dark glasses and glanced at his hand. Casually, he laid a low card of a different suit over Ciaran's queen. Ciaran looked at him, wanting to know the catch, then took the trick, sweeping the cards toward him without lifting them off the table so that Joss wouldn't see his hand trembling. Joss saw. He didn't know what had happened but he knew that Ciaran had unnerved himself and he knew his mother was the cause of it.

He'd let Ciaran win the next few tricks, then he'd change the suit with a trump and take the game.

Chapter Thirty-seven

HANNIE WALKED BACK OVER THE YARD, the moist black air eddying about her, fine needles of rain showing in the halo around the yard light. The temperature had changed, it was much milder. She'd rather the frost with its quickness, she felt that the sky had moved down and was pressing in around her. The sky, or was it the sea? She might shipwreck in these waters, she might drown. And she longed for a continent under her feet, for the great empty emanations of a continent, not this small dense island, which was like living confined in a single room.

She knew that Ciaran had connected with her and in doing so had shocked himself. A connection of that intensity had always a sexual charge to it, a charge that had passed far beyond flirtation to enter the starker realms of recognition. Sexual recognition, but also psychic recognition. They were two of a kind, she and Ciaran, both physically and psychically, and the strength of this mutual revelation had momentarily bridged the chasm of age.

Hannie hadn't seen it coming: she, too, was caught off-guard, but she knew enough to know what it was when it came. That she'd been unprepared was odd in itself: usually she knew precisely when she had caught a man's attention, knew it long before he did. Then, even to herself, she seemed to forget it. But underneath, she still knew. Her unpreparedness, she decided, was his age. Ciaran was only a boy to her, she had never considered him either sexually or otherwise, unless with a voyeur's detachment, watching Niamh embroiled in her infatuation.

She pushed open the back door and went in. Perhaps she'd been barking up the wrong tree, she thought, treading off her Wellingtons one after the other. She shook the rain from her tangled hair. It was astonishing how wetting was this rain that hardly seemed wet at all. Insidious. Like everything here — nothing clear or straight — everything creeping, wavering, sliding off into something else. Like living inside a house that was underwater but no one knew it. She longed for outdoors and sky, she longed again for Africa, surprising herself, who hadn't thought Africa a place to be longed for.

The wrong tree. The thought brought her suddenly to stillness, the grubby towel limp in her hand, her rubbed hair standing up around her head. Men twenty years younger, not twenty years older, like Ned. For a moment she considered the possibilities of such a reversal, letting herself float on the sweet illusory triumph of having caught, however briefly, the attention of a boy in his twenties.

Only for a moment. She knew too well the reality of the body's inexorable aging, had no wish to stand at the glass with a young man's reflection floating somewhere in the shadowy room behind her. Rather an old man's, she thought, and she, younger, beside him. That way she kept the upper hand. And she need never learn the science of concealment.

Besides, she had seen him appalled at the connection — attraction — call it what you would. She didn't blame him. It was bizarre, gothic, she didn't want it herself. Had he been older, had she been younger, there would have been no question but of a sexual outcome. As it was, it was simply an unexpected explosion of feeling, grotesque in its inappropriateness, a current far too raw for the delicate social wiring that had failed to contain it. It would fade, she was sure of that; even as soon as the next morning they might look at each other and decide they'd each imagined it. And she wasn't sorry that this should be so. There was no part of her that wanted to be back there garnering what a young man offered. Not the passion, nor the self-absorption, nor the overwhelming drama of the blood.

But how surprising that it should be Ciaran who had seen and understood her. Not surprising: he was, in essence, a worthless young man, worthless and selfish, just as she was herself. Strange, she thought, that Ned should tolerate in her what he couldn't bear in Ciaran.

How wearying to be seeing and judging through Ned's eyes like this. Nonworthless people she had always found close to intolerable, now it seemed worthlessness had become a term of abuse. Perhaps she should seduce him, just the once, before he had time to come to his senses? Perhaps not. She would certainly hate the self-image awaiting her in his eyes. Niamh's shattered complacency might be her only satisfaction.

She had finished with the towel and had thrown it into the empty drum of the washing machine. Now she knelt between the meal sacks and a lean of rakes and hoes and yard-brushes, pulling on her shoe, her thoughts assisted by these small mundane activities. Paulo. His name was in her mind but it hadn't come like a memory, it was more like an involuntary invasion. Abruptly she stopped pulling and just knelt, staring at the wall. The small hatchet hung there and beside it a heavy lump hammer, a tire jack, a rusty saw, a length of chain. She didn't see them, she saw nothing of the present. She felt Paulo, his reality almost tangible, like the saturating after-presence of a once-loved figure reencountered in a dream.

Paulo. Why now? Was it Ciaran, reminding her?

She shook her head, pulled at her shoe again. No, not Ciaran, Ciaran wasn't like Paulo, he was simply uncooperative and a bit rebellious. He would calm down soon, would loiter beside the queue, all the time pretending that he wasn't there and hadn't noticed it. Then when it moved forward, he would move with it. Soon he would be part of it, would speak with its complacency, its convenient, hypocritical morality.

Paulo had been more than that, far more. Paulo was a masterless man, all knowledge in his bleak gray eyes.

Light dawned. It wasn't Ciaran's likeness to Paulo that had brought him so strongly into her mind, it was her own surprise at the connection, her total lack of premonition, her unawareness. And Niamh: her thralldom inside her own sexual infatuation, so like Hannie's own with Paulo, and yet she hadn't seen the parallel until now.

In her mind she'd left the narrow scullery with its smell of earth and dampness, she'd traveled years and continents to step from the fierce sunlight of a square in a little Moorish town and in through a high doorway, black and deep with shade. There was a narrow, empty room to the left with a heavy, polished counter running the length of it and Salman, the barman, sitting on a wooden chair in the fly-droned quiet, his back against the ocher-colored wall. She ignored Salman and walked on past the bar (for it was a bar, though there was nothing to show it, no drink of any kind displayed, not even coffee) and on through the empty dining room with its dark polished floorboards that cried out where you trod. She went through the door at the end, stepping from the shadowy room into the sunlit courtyard-garden with its pillars and fountains and dappled light, its tangle of vines and bougainvillea, its palm trees slicing up into the dazzling sky. Birds sang, purpled pigeons dipped and drank from stains of water on the tiled floor. To her left, long patterned sofas were arranged in shade against the mosaicked walls. Men sat around on them: Arabs, Africans, one or two Europeans. They lounged and talked there, sometimes ate and drank off patterned trays of polished brass.

Who had taken her there, what had she been doing? She couldn't remember. None of it had mattered to her, it was only another episode in a part of her life crowded with places and episodes, with scenes and people, always moving, always changing. There was nothing about it that was different or more important than anywhere else, nothing she had intended to remember. Until Paulo had placed his hand lightly on her shoulder, the touch claiming her.

Even now, over all the years, she had no idea what had happened to her. She'd thought herself indifferent to him, had felt no attraction, no hint of the sexual connection hidden in her flesh. But he'd known, he'd been watching her and waiting, knowing the connection to be there, knowing he could have her if he wanted her, when he wanted her.

"Hannie, what are you doing?"

She looked up. Ned was standing in the doorway. She hadn't heard his approach.

"Remembering," she said, pulling on her other shoe.

"It happens." He leaned more heavily on the doorknob. "More and more, these days, but there are warmer places for it. Why don't you come through, do your remembering beside the fire?"

"It's private remembering."

"That's all right, I won't interrupt you. You'll catch cold here, you're wet through."

—•◆•—

"I thought at first he would be no different from the others. I thought I had the measure of him, that I could amuse myself for a while, then go or stay, as I wished. I didn't realize there would be no choice."

She sat by the fire, leaning forward in the chair, a glass of whiskey in her hand, her eyes on the flames, the bottle on the hearth beside her. She spoke as though something heavy and dense had laid itself down on her, sopping her up, as a cloth sops a spill.

"It was the measure of myself I didn't have. I drank, I was drunk nearly all the time, early and late, but it didn't help, it didn't dull the way I needed him. And I couldn't endure it, I had to leave him, I knew that, I had to leave him before it was too late and I couldn't.

"He would have destroyed me," she added, looking at Ned, her eyes very bright. "I never regret that I left him. But I cannot, altogether, get free of him." She hesitated, stared back into the fire, began again, her voice quiet and strange. "Mostly I never think of him, I don't remember him, he isn't in my mind or my imagination, he never comes close. Except in dreams. They come out of nowhere, awful, total, more like visitation than dream. Afterwards I have to fight to be rid of him.

"Sometimes, a long time since a dream, I try to remember his presence and I can't. I can't remember even what he looked like."

"What was he doing there?" Ned asked from the other side of the hearth. His voice was quiet.

"He had a lot of contacts, his business was his contacts, he was an Italian so the Europeans trusted him and came to him. He's one of us, they thought, he will not cheat us. They thought he'd help them cheat the others who weren't white."

"And they were wrong?"

"He cheated anyone who'd let him, despised them for letting him. Europeans and Africans were easier than Arabs, he had more respect for Arabs, some of them he couldn't cheat at all. With them he dealt as equals."

"What exactly was his business?"

"He brokered deals. Deals and double deals — anything illegal or hard to come by, anything for anyone who could pay. You must have come across such men in Africa?"

"Now and then, not ever for very long, I never dealt with them if I could help it. They have no country — great courage, but no country, nothing to hold them back from anything. For them, there is no darkness. They see in the dark, it's their true domain."

Hannie nodded. He could see her shoulders relaxing, the strangeness going out of her eyes. She seemed easier for talking, less possessed and remote.

"How did you meet him?"

"I sold him my soul."

Ned stared. She laughed, remembering herself as she'd been then.

"We were sitting one night at a table in the square in a small town," she said. "A group of us. We'd no money, we had eaten, but when they came to ask for payment we told them they must wait until tomorrow. No one wanted to go to bed, we wanted to drink and smoke kif, we wanted to lose ourselves, but we were broke. He was sitting at another table, someone knew him, knew he was rich, so I went across and told him what we wanted and asked him if he'd pay the bill."

A log fell from the fire and onto the hearth, scattering sparks that glimmered and died. Hannie leaned over and lifted it back with the tongs. Ned waited.

"He said he'd pay if I sold him my soul. So I did. He called for paper and a bond was drawn up and I signed. That was the beginning, though I didn't know it at the time. Perhaps he has my soul still, if I ever had one. There are worse things I could have traded for. Money, power, reputation. It seems to me not so bad to have sold it for the satisfaction of the moment." She glanced up at him and he nodded but said nothing. The fire burned in the silence.

"It was a long time ago," she said eventually. "It's odd, the way these things live on in you." She sat leaning forward, one elbow on her knee, her head resting on her hand, her fingers laced in her hair, her eyes closed. "You think they've quite gone . . ."

"And then they flare up again. Like malaria. A new bout. Might as well be the first bout."

She nodded, too absorbed to wonder that he knew.

"I couldn't trust myself when I was with him," she said slowly. "It wasn't morality that made me leave him, I didn't care what he did or what he was, but staying with him would have meant giving up myself." There was another silence.

"You see, Ned, as long as you can act without the time or the need for reflection you can do more or less as you like. It's only when you stop and think about what you are doing, what you have done, that you get caught by morality. Not other people's morality — that doesn't matter — but your own. With reflection comes shame. Not for laws broken, not even for lives broken, but for small meannesses, small acts of cruelty or cowardliness. And when shame comes, it is invariably horrible.

"Paulo never cared about right or wrong, he just acted and moved on. But Paulo was male so he was never slowed down, he never got caught by a child as I did."

"Perhaps the child was the saving of you, Hannie."

She looked up, a swift bleak look, but didn't speak.

"What happened to him?"

She shrugged again. "I never heard directly. But I'm certain that he's dead."

Chapter Thirty-eight

JOSS WAS KNEELING ON THE FLOOR in his room, stuffing a pair of Niamh's thick black tights with loosely crumpled newspaper. They looked a bit lumpy and odd but they'd pass; the crude packing had ballooned them into the semblance of lower limbs. He put Nora's shoe onto one of the stuffed feet and it was better — almost realistic — but the newspaper wasn't packed tightly enough and the shoe fell off when he moved the limb. He thought of tying it on, but decided it didn't matter. Once the thing was dumped in the undergrowth, the loose shoe lying about would make it look even better. Thrown off in the struggle. Joss sat back on his heels and rubbed his hands with pleasure.

He put Nora's gold bracelet around the black ankle. Cool, a belly dancer. Reluctantly he took it off again. It was wasted on the dummy, he'd sell it in the town as soon as he was back at school. He wouldn't get much for it, the secondhand dealers were all rip-off merchants, but something was better than nothing at all.

He took the sanitary towel he'd nicked from Nora's room and daubed it with ketchup from a plastic tomato. The white pad turned dramatically red. Corny, but satisfying, he decided. He put the tomato carefully back into his box of finds. He'd nicked it from a café in Youghal he'd been to with Niamh and Ciaran; heirloom-kitsch, Ciaran had called it, so Joss had taken it with him when they left. Niamh had been uptight when she realized but she hadn't said anything because she knew they'd laugh at her. She wasn't so into standing up for her principles these days, Joss noticed; she was copping on.

He liked taking things, not even bothering to hide them, walking out with them under the noses of the staff who saw but said nothing. It always amazed him how soft people were.

He was pleased with the sanitary towel, it was a real find. Niamh bought those cotton-wool plug-things and stuffed them up herself. He placed the stained towel between the black stuffed legs, and pinned it carefully in place with safety pins. It looked great. Not realistic, but somehow more shocking for that.

He didn't really know why he was doing what he was doing but he knew he liked doing it, and that was enough to be going on with. He sat back on his heels and his eyes closed with pleasure, picturing Niamh and the screech she'd let out when she found it. Then she'd go all white and trembly and he'd laugh himself stupid. He'd say he'd been trying his hand at a bit of soft sculpture, she'd appreciate that. She was always on about soft sculpture, the unexplored potential in the form. The smile on his face widened.

For a moment he wondered what Hannie would say, but he shoved the thought from him and carefully replaced his treasures in his box of finds. It was khaki-colored and metal, with strong clips that sealed it tight and kept the damp out when he buried it. That was the theory anyway. But he didn't take any chances, he always double-wrapped it in bin liners to be sure.

He looked at the black legs again. They were good, but they could be better, they needed something more. A top half, or rather a topless half? Perhaps not — it was hard to make naked boobs that were any good. A skirt, ripped up the side? To conceal and not conceal? A red admiral struggled briefly on the blackness of the windowpane. It had been there two days now, its wings going tattered and crap, their colored dust all mussed and messed as it battered itself against the glass. It was weaker all the time, mostly it lay quiet and he thought it was dead, then it would stagger up and have another go.

Joss had an idea.

A double doll. One of those rag-doll things he'd seen somewhere ages ago. He saw one now in his mind in the different light that comes with heat. A double-headed rag doll, pink skin, yellow hair, long check skirts. You turned it over and the skirt fell back: a brown doll, big thick lips, black woolly curls. . . .

A double-cunt doll. Per-fect. Two sets of legs sewn together, joined up by a skirt that fell back from the waist, revealing all. He'd hang it in a tree where Niamh would find it.

The half-smile on his face widened; his eyes shone.

Chapter Thirty-nine

"LETTER FROM PATRICK," Ned said. He sat at the table drinking tea and thumbing through the sparse bundle of post. It came later and later, mid-afternoon was about normal, not that it mattered, it was nearly all bills and Christmas cards that had missed Christmas.

Ned scanned the letter, pushed it back into its envelope, then tossed it onto the table. "Change of plan, he's not coming back, he'll stay on in Cork for the time he's got left, see a bit more of the girls."

Hannie was cleaning the dining-room silver at the other end of the table. She didn't speak or make a move to pick up the letter.

Ned was relieved, it was a bread-and-butter letter, but written only to him, a cursory glance would reveal Patrick's quietly ostentatious omission. He hadn't had the grace nor the manners to write her name on the envelope either, but that might pass more easily as forgetfulness.

Ned let his mind go back to Christmas Eve, to Joss's account of Patrick's discussion of Hannie's opportunism. The anger that had flared in him then stiffened now into something more implacable. Patrick had a right to his opinions but there the matter ended. He had no right to such casual speculation on his cousin's marriage, still less to this studied incivility toward a woman who had been a graceful and attentive hostess, however he might judge her to himself.

He glanced across at Hannie. What had she said last night about small meannesses and failures, how they were the deepest shame? Patrick had always been weak and selfish, Ned realized, he had never had much thought for anyone but himself. But he was easy and charming, with the manners and assumptions born of privilege, and he was unreflective, it was unlikely that he'd ever spent much time with shame. When the old woman died Patrick would inherit and he'd sell Coolbawn, his sisters' home, without as much as a backward glance. They might beg and entreat, it would make no difference to Patrick.

Hannie was remote today, Ned thought, but that wasn't unexpected. She had talked last night in spite of herself, had described a past that was painful and private, it was hardly surprising that she should want to reestablish distance now. Yet it was hurtful, however he might rationalize and explain it to himself. Everything was so easy when she spoke openly and truthfully, he felt he could listen forever, accept anything she told him, his feeling for her only deepening as she revealed herself.

In your dreams, as Joss would say.

He didn't realize yet how passionately she was fighting off self-revelation, that she didn't want to understand herself, still less to articulate that understanding, that the more he knew of her the more she felt herself violated and vulnerable. She was fighting him off and losing ground, after each exposure he was left more tender and accepting while for her it was the opposite: as though his acceptance of her was something malign, something almost akin to rape.

And she felt herself less and less able to resist these exposures. She was alone here, a curiosity, an outsider and a misfit. Andrew and Nora's visit had shifted things, it had revealed them to themselves and to each other. In the end even Danno, the obvious misfit, was further from her life experience than Ned was. Who could understand her better than Ned if she let him?

Now Hannie went on quietly polishing his grandmother's silver coffeepot in the firelight, her face calm, her hands steady, none of her inner conflict visible. Patrick hadn't put her name on the envelope and she was certain that if she picked up the letter she wouldn't find it written in there either. And only a few years past this same Patrick would have eaten out of the hand she wouldn't have bothered to extend to him. Now his exclusion of her was deliberate and insulting. She was no one, an aberration, an adventuress.

Had she ever pretended otherwise or denied it?

She saw now that he'd despised her from the start but she'd missed his contempt and flirted with him. More fool her. His calm assumption of superiority infuriated her but also fortified her resolve and gave her the strength to overcome the aftermath of Paulo's visitation. She placed the coffeepot on a silver salver with a clutter of shining cruets, cutlery and napkin rings, and stood to return the pieces to the dining room where they belonged.

"I think we should have a party," she said decisively. "Tomorrow night — for the young people, for the New Year."

———— • ◆ • ————

THEY MADE A PUNCH. She said it was essential, you mixed up all the alcohol and everyone got roaring drunk. Ned gave her cooking sherry and supermarket own-brand whiskey.

"No sense wasting decent stuff if you're just going to throw it all in together."

Hannie added brandy and gin from the sideboard in the dining room. Niamh and Joss were the tasters. Ciaran hadn't appeared.

"He's got a hangover," Niamh said, "he'll be over later."

The punch, they agreed, would blow your head off.

"What about the taste?"

Joss sniggered. Niamh put down her glass.

"What's taste got to do with it?" she asked. "One swig and no one'll care."

Hannie was in the kitchen, in the dining room, on the phone inviting people. She organized them all without appearing much interested herself so they found themselves enthused and wanting to join in and help. It was all much more casual than the pre-Christmas entertaining, much more slapdash and fun. Even Ned was enjoying it, though he pretended otherwise.

"Come and eat our food and drink our booze and reduce our house to chaos for weeks to come," he complained. "We don't have to do this, we don't owe anyone, we had them all last week or the week before. I can't understand you, Hannie, when other people invite us you say you'd rather talk to the sheep."

Niamh and Joss were right about the punch. It was a liberator, reducing everyone to the same level of more-or-less-drunkenness after the second glass. People fell on each other's necks, they shouted and roared and guffawed, the noise rose and rose. Hannie fed them with hot food that seemed to Ned to come out of the air, Niamh and Joss were everywhere filling glasses, even Ciaran seemed to get a kick out of playing barman. Later they rolled back the carpet and Ciaran and Joss set up in a corner with Niamh's CD player and did a two-handed DJ act that Ned simply closed his ears to. At midnight everything stopped and they all joined hands and had a go at "Auld Lang Syne."

More drink, and the dancing began again. Arms and legs and arses were waggled with grotesque confidence; a historian of country houses fell over someone's shoes and sat happily where he'd fallen talking to no one in particular about nothing remotely comprehensible; a lanky young man in glasses finally persuaded Niamh onto the floor but was sick over her feet a few minutes after they'd started; Marjorie overbalanced doing the twist and fell on her back with her legs in the air until James hauled her upright again, telling her firmly that more drink was what she needed.

Hours later the crowd thinned. Toward morning most people finally wandered off in the general direction of home.

Ned found Niamh curled up on a sofa in his study, passed out or asleep, her dark hair fallen loosely across her face. He fetched a blanket and spread it carefully over her and she moaned and stirred in her sleep but didn't wake. He stood over her and she stirred again and one slim strong wrist poked itself out from under the folds and moved across the blanket as though looking for something. Finding nothing, it left off searching and settled itself, the fingers curling gently in toward the palm. He went out, pulling the door softly to behind him, then moved quietly through the rooms, picking up glasses and paper cups and emptying the overflowing ashtrays. He could hear laughter and voices from the kitchen where Hannie was serving breakfast to the survivors. He felt peaceful and oddly content.

He drew back the curtains. A chill breeze blew through the dropped sashes of the long windows; the air flowed in, so clean and sharp he could almost see it, like colored ink dropped into clear water. He felt tired and not tired. He had been drunk, but he didn't feel it now, perhaps it had worn off. He wondered about his life, what was happening to it, what he was doing, but somehow he couldn't seem to mind.

He stood at the window, looking out at a darkness he knew would be blue-going-into-gray if he turned off the lights. He turned them off. The darkness paled and shapes and halftones began floating up toward him like stones emerging from water. Their edges took shape and definition and he saw that it was almost day. As he watched a figure appeared and moved swiftly up the drive, a rucksack looped over one shoulder. Ned stiffened and focused. He thought it was Joss, but it was too tall and the wrong gait. Ciaran. Ciaran was leaving, with Niamh asleep on the sofa in the room beyond. He thought about wakening her, then changed his mind. He'd let things take their course, he decided, she might as well get some sleep while she could.

Instead he went through to the kitchen and took Hannie into the hall to tell her. She stiffened when she heard, her head went up like a deer scenting man on the wind and her eyes scanned the faces in the kitchen through the opened door. Ned's eyes followed hers.

Joss was there, at the far end of the room, sitting sideways on the window seat, his face turned to the thinning darkness. As they watched him he turned his head and looked straight at his mother, his eyes — light and clear and unreadable — meeting hers down the length of the room. Ned realized with a shock that Joss wasn't wearing his dark glasses. With a second shock he realized that Joss knew all about Ciaran, had probably conspired in his departure. He glanced at Hannie and he saw that she was seeing the same.

Chapter Forty

JOSS GONE, PATRICK GONE, CIARAN GONE. Only the two of them left in the house, and Niamh beyond in the cottage.

Hannie sat at the kitchen table, a glass by her hand, watching a wren working its way along under the overhang of the wall beyond the window. It was like a mouse. Scurry, then stillness. Another quick flick of motion. Stillness. All its movements were neat and brown.

The place was coming down with wrens, even in winter. They lived in the stone walls and the hedges and under the edges of the river-banks. They made loops of flight, their small bodies brief against the silver of the river, their small threading movements settling in the corner of the eye.

Joss was right about the brownness here. Brownness, drabness. All but invisible unless you looked.

Nonsense, Ned said. Ned loved the little mobile tits, the salmon breastplates of the bullfinches. He thought the goldfinches as exotic as any flame-bright bird of the tropics.

She had begun to learn the names from him. After a while the single stripe of red on the face of a goldfinch jumped out at her, too. She was adjusting. She didn't know if she liked this adjustment, if it boded good or ill for her survival. She didn't want to survive by becoming like them.

Already her life was being sopped up in this place. In the brief daylight hours she sat here watching the wrens, she mooched around the edges of the farm, staring at the black-faced sheep on the rough pasture. Sometimes when she startled them they'd stand and piss. One would piss, then the next and the next, until the whole field was pissing, hard streams of urine drilling into the boggy ground and she, standing watching them. This was her life now. Day followed day. She'd started to drink. Some days she drank all day, some days she didn't touch it. Ned watched but didn't say anything; sometimes she wondered what it would take to make him speak. He withdrew himself, spending the evenings in his study, sorting old yellowing bundles of letters and notes, filing fading photographs. He'd told Mrs. Coady not to clean in there, he said he was working on another book, but Hannie never heard his typewriter.

She'd sold the ebony fan in Cork — discreetly, at less than its value, but still not giving it away. A dealer called Slattery. She hadn't used her own name, she didn't have to stipulate no local sales. He looked her in the eye and said the container was full now and would be going straight across the water, the prices were better in the British sales rooms. Then he wished her good day and hoped they would see her again.

Hannie hoped not, but without much confidence. Still, it meant she had money put by against the next emergency, bank notes under the corner of the carpet in her bedroom where she could get at them in a hurry. She had shelved the goose plan, the rewards were too far away. Would she even be here next Christmas? She didn't know.

Mrs. Coady came if Hannie phoned for her, but mostly she didn't. Sometimes Hannie cleaned the house herself, or she just left it, as the mood took her. Sometimes she cooked, sometimes she didn't. Some days she went to Niamh's, talked at her, came back. She hadn't let time swim over her like this since adolescence. Hot nights in Java, her whole being dissolved in an emptiness of waiting. The lizard on the wall, the dredging scent of flowers in the night, the low melodious talk from the servants' quarters. While there were still servants to talk. Her mother had gone this way — floated off down the dark river — alcohol and forgetfulness. There were worse ways, the daughter thought now.

No one had told Hannie that the real winter followed on behind the solstice, no one had explained the deep dead winter after Christmas, when the light hardly grew and the cold and the long darkness closed like a shroud on the land and only the river shone. She hadn't known the world could be this secret hidden place from out of another age, an older, wilder age, separate from any life or place she knew.

She woke and rose in darkness, began to know the time from its texture and density; if it was night-darkness and she could slip back into sleep, or morning-darkness and she should brace herself, throw back the covers, encounter this freezing parody of day.

All her life she had assumed light, visited by darkness; now she began to see darkness as the reality, the permanent state. She began to understand light as an aberration on the face of the dark, like the slick of shiny light that floated the blackness in the water-butt by the back door. And it made sense to her, it was how life was, it was how she was herself: darkness, visited sometimes by light that lay on its surface but never penetrated to the depths beneath.

Yet the slick was vivid enough when it happened. Sometimes outside, moving stock with Ned on a morning rimed with frost, her spirits would lift and she'd wonder at her own thoughts. Then she could close her eyes and revisit the highlands of Kenya, the land burning clear of the frost, the plumed breath of the cattle. She would open them and see low mounded mountains, slate-blue, a dusting of snow in the wrinkles and folds of their upper slopes, and fieldfares, like long greenish thrushes, hopping and grubbing for food on the pasture.

But the slick of light never lasted long. A bright morning would give way to endless sodden ones, and even Ned would grow dispirited and downcast. For Hannie this return to the low dark days was like being suddenly reimprisoned after tasting release. It left her hopeless and without defenses, prey to despair and strange imaginings.

Sometimes she saw Joss, a tall wraith by the long windows watching the light leave, the four o'clock darkness return. Sometimes he would turn to her and she'd see the panic in his uncovered eyes and would better understand her own despair. Joss was gone now, gone even farther north to a colder, darker place, hating her because he'd come to her and begged to be let stay and she'd refused him.

"You have to go to school, Joss, you know that. It'll get easier, you'll get used to it, you'll see."

He'd looked at her, both of them knowing the lie, and then later he'd had his revenge, insisting on the bus, not letting her drive him though she'd had the car serviced in readiness. They had parted painfully in mutual anger.

So it was hard for them all, these slow weeks of January. For Niamh suffering in the cottage; for Hannie, lonely and downhearted and drinking because she could think of no other way through; for Ned, watching the reappearance of the difficult, resentful woman who was here so frequently now that he often forgot the other had ever been.

Chapter Forty-one

"PEOPLE MAKE SUCH A FUSS about things," Hannie said. "And mostly they don't really matter."

Niamh kept her head down, hoping desperately that Hannie would shut up or go away and not be going over the whole thing yet again. A fuss was exactly what she wasn't making, a huge effort was what she was making and no one, she hoped, would ever know how huge. But she wished she'd had the sense to keep her mouth shut right from the start and her confidences to herself. She should have known better than to talk to Hannie, especially now, when she was drinking all the time.

Hannie, of course, thought it only natural that Ciaran should have been screwing somebody else when he wasn't actually here screwing her. What had Niamh imagined he'd been doing? Hitching all the way to Belfast just to say hello to his parents? Only one thing had surprised her. That Niamh hadn't guessed, that she'd had to discover the truth from Joss after Ciaran had packed his bags and gone.

"It's stupid to trust a man like Ciaran, Niamh, plain stupid. Trust isn't some gift that you give to a man to keep safe in a special place and feel grateful for. It's an indulgence — a self-indulgence — something you may or may not choose to go in for. And if you do, it's your own lookout, there's no point feeling betrayed and humiliated, you've no one to blame but yourself." Hannie drained off her glass and plonked it down on the table.

Niamh stared at Hannie. She saw a woman in late middle age with dirty clothes and wild hair, drinking a glass of neat whiskey from a bottle she'd set on the table at half past two in the afternoon.

Why did she go on taking this? she asked herself. This woman was standing here lecturing her as though she'd made some sort of success of her life. And she, Niamh, was letting her.

"You're distorting things, Hannie." Niamh's voice shook with the effort at control she was making. "It's not about choice or self-indulgence, it's about self-respect. And AIDS, a minor fucking detail you seem to have forgotten, probably because it's long since your time . . ."

Hannie's face broke into a grin. "Go ahead, Niamh, that's the spirit, stand up for yourself, fight your corner."

Niamh snapped. "Don't patronize me," she screamed. "Don't patronize me, Hannie, and don't ever tell me again that it's all my fault. I've had enough of you, d'you hear? Enough. Take your sour life and your sour views and fuck off out of my house and don't come back."

Hannie fucked off. Niamh picked up the empty glass and hurled it after her at the closing door. Then she lay across the table in a storm of weeping.

———— • ❖ • ————

"WHAT DID YOU DO to Niamh?" Ned stood in the kitchen doorway, angry and challenging.

"Niamh? Nothing." Hannie looked up from cleaning sprouts at the sink. "Why, what did she say I did?"

"She's only a girl, Hannie, she was in love with him, she needs help not bullying and being told she brought it all on herself."

"Don't be so sentimental." Hannie went on stripping the damaged leaves. "If she's not told she'll drown in self-pity. And you're wrong, she wasn't in love with him, only with sex, she knows that herself."

Ned strode across the kitchen, lifted the uncapped bottle from the draining board and shoved it close to her face.

"You're drunk, Hannie, you've been drinking for days, you should be ashamed, it's half past four in the afternoon and you're drunk." He put down the bottle. "But you're not, are you, you're never ashamed, you're incapable of decency or shame. Not in love with him? Hannie, the poor girl's sitting there all by herself, breaking her heart."

"So you just said."

"You should be ashamed, bullying the girl."

"You said that too. I'm drunk, I'm a bully, I should be ashamed." She threw the last of the cleaned sprouts into the saucepan beside her on the drainer. She made a net of her hands in the basin of water, scooped up the discarded leaves and dumped them into the compost bucket. She dried her hands. "All true, Ned," she said, "and just what are you going to do about it?"

He didn't answer. She picked up the bottle and poured until the tumbler beside her was half full. Her hand was completely steady. She lifted it to her mouth.

"You're drinking too much."

"That's my business."

"It's my money you're drinking."

"Ours. Marriage vows, Ned, what's yours is mine, what's mine is yours, remember? Only I haven't got anything, have I? Except Joss. But you don't mind that, do you, you said so — remember?"

Ned looked at her. Rage beat in his white, closed face. He struggled briefly for control then abandoned the effort and brought his face near to hers. "You're no better than Joss." He spat out the words and searched around for more hurtful ones. "And Niamh's right, it's not Joss's fault. With you as a mother, he's never had a chance."

Hannie's arm jerked back and she threw the contents of her glass at him. Then she set it down on the table and left the room.

Ned stood, pale streams of whiskey running down his face.

—— •◆• ——

THERE WAS NOWHERE to go to, nothing to do but drink more, so she did. Then she went to see Danno.

Danno almost didn't let her in, he had determined not to, but she stood there on the doorstep asking him to forgive her for the last time. He looked at the ground, stony-faced, not trusting her, and she told him she needed to talk to him, she had no other friend.

He asked her why she didn't talk to Ned.

She shrugged and grinned, the grin half-hearted, failing to conceal her desperation. "He's my husband. Talking to husbands is a bad idea."

When she passed out, Danno lifted her carefully onto the cot where he slept and covered her with blankets. Then he sat in a chair for a while, waiting for Ned to come and get her. Then he gave up waiting, put on his coat and walked over to the house.

He didn't knock at the door but went around the outside, careful and quiet, silencing Pip's yelps and old Bess's short burst of barking with a few low words. Ned was in his study, all the lights burning, a rabble of photos spread over the surface of his desk, an old box-file lying open beside them. Danno watched him from the darkness, saw him lift a photo, turn it over and back, stare at it for what seemed a long time and then lay it down. With photo after photo he did this. After a while Danno leaned forward and rapped gently on the glass. Ned started, peered at the black window, left his desk, undid the window latch and hauled up the sash.

"She's over in the house. You'll want to come and get her."

Ned looked at him, his gaze bleak, but didn't speak. Danno remembered the last time he'd come calling on Ned in the night and he wondered if Ned was remembering too. By the smell of him Hannie wasn't the only one who'd been hitting the bottle. Ned reached up his hands and slowly and deliberately pulled down the sash, shutting Danno out behind the wall of glass. The two men stood for a moment, one on each side, eyes locked together, then Danno turned and disappeared into the night.

In the morning Danno hauled his stiff limbs out of the chair, stretched, shaved and made tea. He went and checked on Hannie, still deep asleep in her huddle of blankets. He stood over her and at once felt so complicated at this undefended insight into her aloneness that he turned away to give them both some privacy. He wanted to take her tea, even to look after her a little, but he was too uneasy, too unbalanced by the force of his own unexpected emotions. He whistled the dogs to him and went off into the woods with the gun instead.

That's my story, Danno, she'd said last night, *my side of things. What's yours, I wonder? Why do you let me in here, why do you go on putting up with me?*

Because you're lonely?

But you were always lonely.

Because you know now that you're lonely?

Did I tempt you out of your hole, Danno? Did you creep out and sniff at the air and never notice when the door slammed shut behind you?

Once out you can't ever go back, Danno. Never ever ever.

Do you know that? Somehow I don't think you do.

He needed to tramp around in the air and settle himself.

———•◆•———

HANNIE WOKE, not knowing where she was, and lay in the little room that she'd never seen before, working out how she might have got there. When she had it figured and she thought her head could bear movement, she crawled from her nest of blankets and went in search of last night's bottle. It was empty. She went through the presses looking for drink, but there was none. She struggled with matches and gas and got the kettle on.

She guessed Danno was hiding out in the woods, upset by her presence, unwilling to come back until she'd gone. She nearly opened the cages on all of his hawks just to teach him, but it was too much effort.

Vaguely she wondered what she might have said or done to scare Danno into flight. Perhaps she'd offered to seduce him? Perhaps she *had* seduced him. The thought made her laugh, but the laugh hurt her head so she stopped. She might get drunk again — there was nothing else to do — she might push Ned right to the edge, find out his limit, then push again until he plunged to the rocks below.

She made a face. It seemed she was capable only of melodrama these days. And tormenting Ned. If she was going to be drunk she needed more drink and there was none to be got around here. She abandoned the kettle, washed her face in cold tap water, drank two glasses down, headed back to the house.

Chapter Forty-two

WHEN A KNOCK CAME TO NIAMH'S DOOR now it was always Ned. Hannie came, but she never knocked, she just opened the door and walked straight in. Niamh accepted her, she didn't refer again to the words they'd had and neither did Hannie. To Hannie, rows were normal, it didn't occur to her that Niamh might be lastingly offended. Besides, she'd been drunk.

Ned hardly ever sat down, he never visited after dark, and he never stayed for long. Mostly he would fix something — the washer on the tap, a stuck window, a loose catch. He seemed only to want to reassure himself, exchange a few words, and be gone.

Sometimes he let her persuade him into a cup of tea. Then he'd stand awkwardly, he'd speak of a heifer in calf, of the prices that day at the mart, of the dealer who'd come to the yard and tried to buy from him for less. He was reading up about lavender, he told her: working out could he make it a selling crop in this climate, did it make economic sense to give it a go? Sometimes he asked her about her work, but she always put him off and after a while he knew to leave her alone. She was fond of him, but there was no ease between them since Ciaran's departure. She learned (though how she didn't know because he never spoke of Hannie) that there were problems above in the house.

One day she went with him into Youghal and he waited with the car while she bought rolls of wall-lining paper, paste, wax crayons, felt-tip pens.

She came home and pinned lining paper from ceiling to floor of her little room, sheet butting onto sheet so all the walls were covered. She'd meant to draw but instead she began gluing things onto the paper — leaf skeletons, bits of twig and feather, wings from the dead moths and butterflies she'd collected. Gradually she stopped gluing and began to make marks beside the stuck-on things. Sometimes she wrote random words. She painted around the words and marks — washes in ochers and watery ink-blues and ox-blood reds, the thinness of the washes always contradicting the dense nature of the colors, so it seemed to her that she was always in the process of frustrating them, forbidding their return to what they wanted. She would work in a sort of daze, a waking trance, and then she'd stand for hours and look at what she'd done. Often it looked meaningless and unformed, even to herself.

But sometimes when she came into the room in the mornings she could glimpse, for a moment, what she was making. There was a curious rhythm to these vague islanded shapes, pinned down as they were with lines and words or floating off on pale lakes of color. She knew this work wasn't an end in itself, but she knew it was leading her somewhere that she ought to go. At such moments her heart would lift into her mouth and the blood would beat in her.

Niamh's brief elation of vision never lasted for long. It faded and she'd work on in weary indifference, knowing only that it was better than just sitting, better than thinking the same thoughts over and over and over. Sometimes her whole effort was only for the vanished Ciaran, to show him what she was, to make him regret his loss. But sometimes she was happy and the work was an end in itself. Whole days passed with the misery of Ciaran numbed. She began to call the little room her studio.

Chapter Forty-three

IT WAS DANNO WHO FOUND THE STUFFED LEGS, Joss's parting gift to Niamh, as he made his way to a pollarded willow that grew between her cottage and the river. The day was damp with no lift to it, Danno was snuffling and hacking with a feverish cold and for once he'd rather have hugged the fire than gone tramping about in the drizzle. But there was no help for it, he hadn't enough sally rods stored for next year and new ones had to be cut while the sap was still down. At the moment spring might seem like something from another age, another country, but appearance belied reality, and already there were secret quiverings in this dead landscape.

He stopped on the path to wait for a coughing fit to pass over. When he finished coughing he opened his eyes and they fell on what looked like a short black spike in a clump of faded grass. He moved forward and stirred the dark spike with his boot. A woman's high-heeled court shoe was revealed. He picked it up: it was sodden, but hardly worn. Puzzled, he lifted his head and stared about him. A rusty flare of color showed through the rain-darkened net of the trees. He took off his glasses, wiped them clean of water, put them back on again. An irrational dread in his guts, he followed the rusty flare.

When he saw what the color was, he stopped dead in his tracks, the blood pounding his head, a mist of cold sweat on his skin. It wasn't that he was fooled by it, it wasn't that he thought it was a real body hanging from its ankles in the birch tree, its scarlet knickers torn, its rust-red skirt fallen back at the waist and trailing nearly to the ground. But he knew with an instinctive certainty that its maker would have liked it to have been a real body, and one that had been treated just like this.

He stood where he was, taking it in, waiting for the shock to pass. The first wave receded. He moved forward, put out his hand and carefully lifted the skirt. He started back for the second time at what he saw.

The basic idea he recognized at once. It was a life-sized parody of a rag doll — not an ordinary rag doll but one of those double dolls that his cousins had owned, the like of which he hadn't seen for years. Yet it wasn't quite as their dolls had been, it wasn't two torsos sewn together and joined by a skirt, it was two sets of legs sewn together and joined by a skirt, the one set in pale tights, the other in black. And the pale legs that hung by the ankles wore red knickers, ripped and gaping at the crotch, while the black legs concealed beneath the hanging skirt had a stained and sodden sanitary towel pinned where its genitals would be. The long rust skirt he'd seen light years before on Niamh.

Danno took a knife from his pocket and cut the thing down. He knew it was meant for Niamh and he knew it was Joss who had made it. For a brief moment he'd thought of Ciaran, but he'd put that idea aside. Whatever the drive that had led to the making of this thing, that drive was in Joss not in Ciaran.

He left the legs where they were, a heap in the sodden grass, and began to retrace his steps. A bramble snagged his coat, he bent and freed himself and noticed a blue woolen glove hooked by its thumb to a thorn. Slowly he worked his way back to the path, his eyes on the vegetation. Here a butterfly hair clip lay in the fork of a birch branch. Farther on a string of beads hung from a twig in the stillness.

Danno stood leaning against an ash trunk holding his gathered "clues" in trembling hands. He was deeply shaken and disturbed. Passionately he wanted to conceal and destroy what he'd found, to tell no one, to remove its complex shamefulness and restore the simplicity of the world. Yet he knew that he mustn't allow himself to do this. It was aimed at Niamh, so Niamh must be protected.

But how to do it? If he told Hannie she'd rush to defend Joss, then belittle the incident and try to bully him into silence as she'd done the last time. And he'd let himself be silenced. Well, he'd been right, all along he'd been right, there was something wrong and horrible brewing in Joss's mind.

Perhaps he had to try to talk to Hannie? If he fought his way through her ridicule, stuck to his guns, he might get her to accept it in the end. If she knew she could at least try and arrest it, whatever it was. If she didn't, she could do nothing.

He could tell Ned, Ned thought the world of Niamh, he wouldn't hesitate if he thought she needed protecting. Danno saw Ned vividly in his mind's eye, his imperious closed face, his big knotted hands raised to the sash as he'd dragged it down and slammed it against the sill.

No, no point. Ned wouldn't believe him, Ned would think this some sort of obscure revenge.

Not if he saw what Danno had seen.

He had passed Ned checking the heifers in the Chestnut Field behind the house. He could go and find him now, bring him here, he would *have* to believe, *have* to act. And after that it would be up to Ned to tell Hannie: she was Ned's problem, not his, it was time he put his hands in the mud and got them dirty.

Danno shifted himself from the tree and moved off. It didn't once occur to him to go to Niamh and tell her himself directly. If it had, he couldn't have found the words. The ugly intention behind the thing he tried to speak of would have silenced him.

Chapter Forty-four

SHE'S LIKE A WASP, MRS. COADY THOUGHT, you could do nothing right. What was it that was eating her, was it Joss, was it him, was it the Change? Or was she just spoiled — spoiled and bored.

There'd been a time there before Christmas, with the boy home and the cousin staying, when it looked as though things might be working out. She'd done the house, entertained his friends as he wanted her to, made an effort over his lecture, put on a bit of style. She'd worn that beautiful suit she had — the one she said she'd bought to go to Germany — and she'd had her hair cut and colored a silvery blond. He was pleased as punch — why wouldn't he be? — at last she seemed to be getting the hang of things and finding her way around.

Then bang, something happened and it changed again. What was it, was it Patrick leaving, was it the boy going back to school, was she just fed up with trying to do things his way instead of hers? Perhaps it was none of these things, perhaps it was January. Whatever it was, they had started to fight. They fought about Niamh, they fought about Joss, they fought about Pip, there wasn't anything they didn't fight about. And then there was something the boy had done that was making everything worse.

He'd gone back into his journeys then: old letters and maps mixed in with the books and articles on lavender-growing he was collecting, old black-and-white photos spread over the study floor. Dark, wild-looking faces looked straight out from them, stared out. Ragged, half-naked men held tight to their spears and guns. Comrades, that's what he called them; warriors and bearers and trackers and guides. Men he took with him, men who'd trusted him with their lives. As he'd trusted them with his, he said, and they never let him down.

I'd believe that, Mrs. Coady thought, he's not a man you'd let down lightly. But he always put their trust in him in first.

He's a *mé feiner* — himself alone — it's not that he's selfish exactly, he just doesn't think any further than himself. His life, his needs, his responsibilities. Go along with him, he'll look after you, do right by you, he wouldn't ever allow himself to let you down.

But always on his terms, never on yours, it wouldn't even occur to him that you might have terms of your own, or that they mightn't be the same as his. A decent man, decent through and through, but one who only saw out of his own eyes.

His hip was bothering him, sometimes when he got up too fast you could see the stab it had given him passing across his face. Intimations of mortality, Mrs. Coady, he said. So that's what all the photos and the letters were about: he could see through to the end so he wanted to look back on his life, to know what it had been and what he'd done. But it wasn't helping her, him being this way, watching her and saying nothing, retreating more and more into his study, into himself.

Maybe he doesn't want to help her, maybe he's had enough of her already and he's putting in the time until she gives up and goes away. God knows there's many wouldn't blame him, she's not exactly rewarding, not easy, nor good, nor straight, and she isn't what you'd ever expect a wife of his would be.

No, there's not many would blame him. And they'll blame him less now she's drinking and letting things go to hell.

"You'll need to stop that," I said to her, "to catch yourself on, that's not a road can be walked lightly."

She looked at me. "You're right, Mrs. Coady," she said. "Absolutely right, but somehow I don't give a damn."

"You've the boy to think of," I said. She clapped her hands to her ears like a child to keep out the words.

Tom was on at me again to give up going there. She won't last, he said, can't you go back when things are as they were? I said nothing. He thought it was on account of the regard I'd have for Mr. Renvyle, but it wasn't that.

I'm fond of her. And I don't know why.

Chapter Forty-five

IT HAD BEEN HARD FOR NED, having Danno come to him and demand his attention. He had listened with skepticism and ill-concealed irritation, but Danno had insisted and gone on insisting, so in the end Ned had followed him to the stand of trees, intending that that would be the end of it. Then he'd looked at the heap of stuffed tights and skirts in the faded grass and he'd forgotten his resentment and his skepticism. He would never have believed that the crudely made dummy of Danno's description could be so quietly malevolent in its reality.

He had been instantly certain that it was Joss's handiwork, aimed at Niamh, on that he and Danno had been in complete agreement, and even Hannie hadn't argued the point when he'd got rid of Danno and shown her the thing in the kitchen later on that evening. But she'd belittled his shocked concern and she'd poured cold water on his suggestion of a psychiatrist. There was nothing to make such a fuss about, this was just a normal manifestation of an adolescent mind, she'd said. And besides, had he any idea how much such treatment would cost?

Ned had looked at her doubtfully but he hadn't really argued. He'd said Niamh must be told, and she had agreed, she'd said she would do it herself if Ned wanted her to, but he had declined the offer. There was no hurry, Joss was away until half-term, he didn't want her rushing around there when Niamh was still moping after Ciaran, he wanted to tell her gently himself when she was stronger.

Ned said nothing to Niamh straight away, he bided his time until he judged her recovered enough, then he went to her cottage one afternoon and told her first of the legs and then of his conviction that it was Joss who had made them. He was ashamed of what he was telling her and deeply upset at her anticipated reaction, so it was difficult and embarrassing for them both. Long before he'd finished his story Niamh was trying to fast-forward it, to belittle the legs, and rescue him from his distress.

"It's probably just a phase," she said calmly. "Adolescents are obsessed by sex, and adolescent boys are fascinated by menstruation."

She listened to herself speak and she knew she was being this cool and together because of Ciaran. It was ridiculous, she told herself, he couldn't hear what she was saying, he was miles away with someone else and good riddance. But it made no difference. She would call a spade a spade, she would not make a fuss, no one would ever have the right to laugh at her or to call her naive again.

"I think maybe I should see it for myself," she said.

Ned protested, but she was the injured party behaving well so he had to give in and do as she asked. He led the way to one of the sheds and went in ahead of her. She stood in the doorway, smelling its damp earthy smell and letting her eyes adjust while Ned fumbled around in the cluttered darkness. What he pulled out from behind the sacks of stored feed was more like a bundle of old rags than the lurid artifact of his description. The wet newspaper had collapsed into random lumps, the tights were stretched and misshapen, the skirt was sodden and unrecognizable although it had once been hers. The ripped knickers remained but some delicacy in Ned had made him remove the sanitary towel after Danno's departure.

He watched Niamh as she knelt beside it. Now, when he saw what she was seeing, he almost wondered what there was to be so distressed about. She turned the sodden skirt so it fell back, exposing the dark tights, then she turned it again so the pale legs were displayed. She was taking the whole thing very calmly, Ned thought, she was quite matter-of-fact in the way she was looking at it now, and she hadn't seemed so much frightened as embarrassed when he'd told her. Maybe Hannie was right after all, maybe it wasn't so unnatural, maybe women knew something men didn't know, or at least not men like himself and Danno. He was finding it hard not to feel a bit of a fool.

"There'd have been two different fabrics," Niamh said slowly. "On the original ones, that is. Two skirts. This one, and then another one backing it, so when you turned it over there were different personalities." She looked up at him as she spoke. She was so relieved it wasn't worse she'd almost laughed from sheer release of tension.

"The skirt for the black one would've been bright, a loud strong pattern, and rick-rack braid and wooly hair and brass rings in the ears. Black Mama style — not PC — maybe that's why you never see them anymore. The white one would've been dressed in a flowery print. And puffed sleeves with lace and yellow hair in bunches. Not children really. Young women with no sexual parts . . ." Her voice trailed away.

And now, sexual parts but no faces, she was thinking. Perhaps she'd go home and make dummies, better dummies than Joss had made, highlighting not racism but misogyny. She got up from the floor and turned to Ned, a distant expression on her face. She seemed almost surprised to see him, as though she'd forgotten what they were doing and needed to be reminded.

Chapter Forty-six

WHEN THE RAIN BEGAN HANNIE DIDN'T NOTICE, it was only the usual fine damp drizzle, silent and seeping, as though the air wept; there'd been no rains as she knew them, no storms or monsoon downpours. Yet the ditches filled and the streams swelled, the water lay under the fading light in sheets, it gleamed on the roads and moved in dark mass in the great pewter river. She heard it everywhere: the ditchwater sound and the river-water sound and the sound of puddle water splashing.

Hannie knew about water and the systems for its storage and release; there had always been too much of it or too little in her life, always dams, irrigation ditches, flood drainage systems. Now she picked up a spade and did what she knew how to do without even thinking. She walked around looking for places to drain, she made runoffs and channels, liking the thick mud under her boots, the gurgle of water, the ditches choked with rotting woodbine and the skeletons of umbellifers and old man's beard. She cleared and dug and made new watercourses, found an occupation, forgot about the bottle.

She worked and the water responded, it found her trenches and flowed down her runoffs and gurgled in her channels. But it was hopeless, all she could do was direct it; the ground was like a great sponge, filled and sodden, you stepped on green grass and it pooled under your feet. Water filled every pock and hollow, it lay over the meadows and low-lying fields in smooth thin sheets. Higher up, it ran off the land and into the streams and the streams ran into the river, which rushed and swelled, the current swirling and bucking, until it seemed incredible that it could keep its banks.

When the high winds came they brought trees crashing down onto power lines and phone lines, cutting supplies, blocking the small roads, creating chaos. The real rain followed a day later, not drizzle anymore but great splashings and sheets, as though the sluices had opened in the sky.

"The rivers are out." Mrs. Coady stood in the kitchen in her water-proofs and dripped. "Flynn's is flooded and Casey's yard is full of water and the stream behind Costigan's has taken most of the road. Matt Murphy has his stores moved to the back fields and he's feeding them while he has feed left to give them, but if it goes on like this he'll not reach them, hay or no hay."

Tom had brought her as far as the stream, which was over the road, she said, then she'd taken to her feet and paddled through. "It isn't deep yet, you might make it in a car, and a tractor would get through no bother at all. It's the little small rivers are blocking the roads. They're coming down fast and furious and full up with all kinds of rubbish that's filling the culverts and putting them out from their courses."

Ned tried to make her take off her wet things but Mrs. Coady would have none of it. She'd come to work, she said, not to sit around, and the sooner they had sandbags filled the better, it wasn't unknown for this house to flood. She pulled out letters from an inside pocket and thrust them at Hannie. She'd met the postman, she said, he'd given them to her, she'd nearly forgotten.

Two bills and a white envelope with a Northern postmark, but it wasn't Joss's writing. Hannie turned it over, saw the school crest on the flap. Ned was pouring tea for Mrs. Coady from the big brown pot, asking about this one and that one; who had lost stock, who needed help. They were enjoying themselves, the sudden drama, and more being asked of them than was usually required. She recognized it from Africa: a landslide or a flash flood brought the same excitement. She opened the envelope.

"We'll have to sandbag the house and the outbuildings," Ned was saying, "keep the drains and culverts cleared, the stock are all right for the time being. It could be a lot worse — who'd be Lambert, with a flooded poly-tunnel full of Christmas lambs? Thank God we resisted that temptation."

Hannie read the letter. There'd been a problem with Joss, the head-master wanted to talk to her, probably he'd need to see them both. He'd tried to ring but seemed to be having difficulty getting through; he asked her to phone him as soon as she could.

She finished reading and stuffed the letter into her pocket. Mrs. Coady was listing the neighbors, naming for Ned the houses likely to flood. Hannie picked up the phone. "Line's dead," she said, replacing the receiver. "What about Danno? Is that a house that floods?"

"He's very close to the river but he's high. His feet might get wet, but that's all, it'll take more than this to wash him from his nest."

She took the waterproof trousers Ned handed her. She'd have to find a phone that worked, find out what Joss had done, she might have to go North. If it wasn't too bad she'd tell Ned, he might just agree to talk to them on the phone. They'd been impressed by Ned, he'd have some clout with them, and clout never went astray when buying time for Joss.

But if it was really bad she'd tell some lie, go by herself, Ned wouldn't stand much more. Either way she'd need more funds. She pushed her feet into her Wellingtons and went to fill sandbags.

As she worked she made plans. The first edition Burton on the book-shelf in his study: *First Footsteps in East Africa*. He'd said it was worth a bit now, nearly too much, he'd been told it should be in the bank, but what was the point of a book that was locked away?

He'd notice of course, but not for a while, maybe a couple of weeks. For a moment she wondered if she should burn her boats like this. Once sold, the book couldn't be retrieved nor its absence concealed, and she mightn't need so much money, it depended what Joss had done, what had to be glossed over, who bought off. She had the money from the fan, but it wasn't much. Just the same, she could take something more discreet, the two sums together might well be enough. . . .

She dismissed the idea. She didn't know what else was valuable. And whatever it was, she'd only get part of its worth, they weren't fools, they knew she wouldn't be selling like this unless she had to. And in the end she didn't care if Ned found out, she didn't care what he thought of her, all she cared about was getting Joss out of whatever hole he'd dug for himself and she'd worry about the consequences when they happened.

She carried the filled sacks over to Ned and he laid them carefully to form a wall. He wouldn't trust either her or Mrs. Coady to do this, you'd have thought he'd spent his life fighting floods and no one else had ever seen one. Mrs. Coady threw her a look which said humor him, let the man be. The two women worked in complicity. It was a long way from Niamh's worldview, but then Niamh was stuck in bed with a chest cold and wasn't much use to anyone.

Matt Murphy stopped by with a load of hay for his cattle. He drove the tractor up close and shouted his news without getting down. It was all too local for Hannie to follow, she didn't know the town lands or the back roads, couldn't work out where the culvert was that was blocked or what stream had taken what road. But she understood the last bit.

"They're giving out more storms on the radio," Matt said. "If they have it right for once in their lives, then we'll none of us be going anywhere for a while."

———•◆•———

HANNIE STRAINED to see through the water that sluiced down over the windscreen. No storms yet, but the rain had thickened and fattened and got much wetter. The wipers threw it off in sheets but it didn't make much difference, there was always more coming. She had got the car through the flooded stream and was heading for Cork now, by whatever road would get her there. She'd stopped farther back to phone but the line was dead, the lines might be out for miles for all she knew.

The road ran with shallow runoffs that burst from under the walls and hedges, spreading a litter of gravel and stones as they fanned themselves over the tarmac. Streams filled the old, dry beds as well; they spilled out over the roads, broke up the surfaces, carried them away in lumps.

It all happened fast when the land was as waterlogged as this, Ned said. The ditches were neglected and choked with vegetation, there was nowhere for all that water to go. Ned went on about ditches: how the practice of clearing and digging them out had more or less fallen away. One of his many hobby horses.

At least he'd have the satisfaction of being right, she thought. It might offset the humiliation of being wrong about her.

Standing there in the rain listening to Matt Murphy, she had made her decision in a rush. She'd go to Cork while she still could, phone the school, sell the book, then go North if she had to. What she would say on the phone, she had only the vaguest idea. Find out what she could, she supposed. Play for time. If she couldn't get through she'd put half the money straight in the post with instructions to Joss to try and buy off the complainer. That there would be a complainer she never doubted. There was always a complainer, always someone angry or frightened enough to be prepared to tell.

Maybe she should forget about Cork, she thought, and just fill up the car and head North until it broke down or she got there. She wished she'd had the Land Rover, but Ned had been shifting feed in it and she'd taken her chance and left while he was offside. She glanced down at herself and wished as well that she'd thought to change her clothes before she left. Schools were pompous institutions, quick to judge, a wild-looking parent arriving unannounced might do more harm than good.

The road ran past a cluster of farm buildings, then veered abruptly around to the right and dipped. She took the bend too fast and felt the wheels slide in the mud. The car skidded half across the road, she righted it and changed down. She gave the road her full attention, felt herself coming alive with the violent veer of the car, the way the wheel bucked and spun with a life of its own. She was happier now, she liked the edge risk gave, the relief from the impotence of anxiety.

She rounded a bend on the crest of a rise. The road dropped and disappeared into a stretch of muddy brown water, then reappeared beyond to run up another rise. She didn't know the road, didn't know if it was merely floodwater or a stream that had overflowed its banks, filling the shallow scoop of the little valley. She peered through the driving rain looking for a clue, for turbulence signaling a current. She couldn't see. Recklessness overcame her.

Halfway across she felt the car slipping, the water tugging at the wheels. She changed down, trying to give the car mass to counter the flow, but the current was too strong. She felt the car rise and lift as it was carried sideways with the current. A stream bed.

She stopped fighting, stopped any attempt at control, let the car drift until it found itself, though it seemed like forever. She felt the front wheels ground, she pressed the accelerator and for a moment the wheels gripped. Then the engine died. The front wheels stayed where they were but the back wheels went on drifting and the car swung slowly around. Then she felt all four wheels finding ground and the car stopped swinging and stuck fast, two thirds of the way across the brown water, sitting sideways over the road.

Shit shit shit.

Chapter Forty-seven

NED SAW THE CAR ON THE FAR SIDE of the flooded road, the tractor beside it, the figures peering into the opened hood. He set the old Land Rover at the water and drove slowly and steadily through it. He pulled up beside the tractor and got out.

The tractor driver was holding the car hood open at an angle, trying to shield the engine from the driving rain. Hannie was bent into it, both hands occupied, a bit of old rag clutched between her clenched teeth. The man nodded at Ned.

Hannie finished fiddling. She withdrew from the hood, removed the damp rag from between her teeth and rubbed at her wet oily hands.

"Might work," she said to her companion, ignoring Ned completely. "Shouldn't think so — plugs too wet — worth a try." She ducked into the car and turned the key in the ignition. It fired but didn't catch. She tried twice more. Then she gave up and emerged again from the car, looking through Ned as though he wasn't there. He stared at her. Her clothes were soaked through, her hair hung in rats' tails, her feet squelched when she moved, yet she was utterly defiant.

"Hannie, leave the car, get into the Land Rover, we have to go to Cork," Ned said. She didn't move or turn her head, she showed no sign of having heard him.

"We have to collect Joss, Hannie. The bus gets in in half an hour."

She looked at him.

"The school phoned, they've sent Joss home." He spoke the words very clearly, as though she was slow or hard of hearing.

She stared. "The phone was out, they couldn't have phoned, the letter said they wanted to see us. . . ." She seemed unable to grasp it.

"Hannie, they phoned, they've sent him home, I keep telling you . . ."

She got it then. She turned and walked over to the Land Rover, exhausted, all the defiance gone out of her.

He spoke briefly with the tractor driver, took the plugs out of Hannie's car, wrapped them in his handkerchief. The man took them and put them in his pocket.

Ned reached the Land Rover just as Hannie scrambled back out of it. She ran through the downpour, ducked into the stranded car and emerged holding a plastic bag with something heavy in it. She stumbled through the rain again and climbed back into the Land Rover.

———— • ◆ • ————

"WHAT DID HE DO?" she asked, staring ahead at the rainy glass.

He glanced at her. The bones stood out like knolls on her gray skin and her hand shook as she lifted the cigarette to her mouth. He had the heating turned up full, but the Land Rover was old, the heater was on its last legs.

"It seems he'd been playing cards in the town and had got into debt," Ned said. "He made a list — things his classmates had done that they'd rather nobody knew about. Then he offered to sell them the evidence."

She said nothing for a while, just dragged on her cigarette and blew out smoke.

"How did they find out?"

"A boy took a lot of pills. Paracetamol. He was all right — just very sick. Afterwards he told his parents all about it."

"And they told the school," she finished flatly. "What had he done? The boy, I mean. What was it he didn't want them to find out? Was it to do with Joss?"

"I don't know," Ned said slowly. "I didn't ask." But Hannie had, she had known straight away that the story might not end with the black-mail. What had Joss done in the past, he thought, to make her think so far and fast?

"So they've expelled him," she said, as though to herself.

"No, not officially. But they said it looked more serious than they'd thought so they're sending him home while they consider their position."

She shrugged. "They will expel him. When they have considered."

He glanced at her. She had lit another cigarette. She was still staring straight ahead into the darkening afternoon. He switched from side-lights to full beam. The lights deepened the afternoon into dusk and made the rain on the windshield shine. The road was clear of water. They were on the main road now, it was new and properly drained, it would take a lot more rain before it flooded.

"How did you know I'd be on this road?"

"I didn't, Mrs. Coady said she thought you'd gone to Dungarvan to stock up, I wasn't looking for you, I was going to get Joss."

There was a long silence.

"Why?"

"Why what?"

"Why were you going to get Joss?"

"Because he's on the bus. How else was he going to get home?"

For the first time she turned her head and looked at him, a look so bleak and hopeless that it turned him cold.

"I was going to Cork," she said tonelessly, "to sell your Arab book."

"The Richard Burton first edition?" he asked, not seeming sur-prised. "Is that what's in the bag?"

She nodded. "It may have got a bit damp."

"I expect it did, I shouldn't worry, it'll dry out. How did you think you were going to sell it?"

"A dealer called Slattery."

"Slattery? Does he really exist? I thought he was just a story people made up to frighten themselves."

"You know about Slattery?"

"Everyone knows about Slattery. It's just as well I found you. If he's anything like they say he is, he'd have robbed you blind."

"He's not that bad. And I needed the money. Like Joss."

"*For* Joss," he corrected her. "You should have said, I might have come up with something. I wouldn't have let you sell old Burton, he's your golden egg for when I die."

She turned her head and stared at him again, but it was almost dark and he couldn't see her face. He could hear her teeth chatter though, she had begun to shiver uncontrollably.

"Ned?" There was a silence, punctuated by tiny clicking sounds. "Do you think I'll be around that long?"

"Who knows? I hope you will."

"Do you? You need your head examined. But thank you."

"What for?"

"Going to get Joss. Not minding about old Burton."

"Don't mention it."

Chapter Forty-eight

WHAT THE BOY NEEDED WAS A WAR; if he found the right niche he would probably do all right in a war. Not as a soldier. Too straightforward and communal. Something underground, undercover. He was brave enough in his own way. And conscienceless and ruthless, he would undoubtedly kill easily and efficiently. Anarchy and excitement — that was what he needed. In the right conditions he might thrive.

And preferably he'd be killed before it ended, Ned added to himself with bitter honesty. *And be buried, heaped with honors.*

Ned sighed. Joss was unfit for civil life, that was the truth of it. The flood had kept him busy while it lasted. But what would they do with him now that the water and the urgency were lessening?

He watched the boy, working the boat in on the current, slipping it into the submerged cut, finding the mooring under the floodwater. The water was dropping fast, the cut was barely covered, you could see its definition clearly beneath the water. Already most of the meadows were clear; in the low-lying fields the drowned tussocks were poking their way up through the last of the flood and everywhere the old order was reemerging. Soon even the mud and the mess and the work would be forgotten.

Joss leapt from the boat onto the flooded landing place with barely a splash. He was surprisingly deft and supple. Quick and agile, like a cat.

A cat. That was it. The watching and waiting, the relentless pursuit of its own ends, the cruelty, the indifference to a victim's suffering. No, it wasn't just indifference, it was the same curious atunement that a cat gets when playing its prey. Not exactly enjoyment. More a heightened sense of itself, of its own catness.

Ned had lived large tracts of his life with peoples who were alien to him, he was accustomed to observing and assessing dispassionately, to judging without condemning. He watched Joss now as he would have watched a man who was to accompany him on a dangerous journey, a man whose strengths and weaknesses he must know and then accept. His own emotional reaction to the man he must also know and acknowledge, observing from somewhere slightly beyond this personal response, aware of it and swayed by it, but never overwhelmed by it. It was a discipline that had become a second nature to him and had served him well.

Yet try as he might he couldn't get beyond the personal with Joss. He couldn't get the distance, couldn't not be overwhelmed by his own negative reactions. Joss loved all those things Ned most hated: speed, noise, destruction; the facile heady whizz of the machine age. Only out here by the river could Ned begin to acknowledge that the boy had other qualities as well. Yet still he could not get beyond those that he hated. He stood quietly in the dusk now, tasting his failure.

Joss knew he was being watched but he made no sign. He pulled the boat to him and secured it on the double mooring against the tide's drop, as Ned had taught him to do. He removed the oars and the rowlocks, carried them clear of the water, laid them on the muddy grass. Then he lifted off the outboard, hefting it with both hands, his slight shoulders taut against its weight. Ned moved forward to take up the oars. Neither of them spoke.

The constant rain had stopped but the air was still wet and the wind was patchy and damp. In the near trees the black rooks clustered in the upper branches like high, dark fruits. The woods on the far bank were smoke-colored, their netted branches rising forlorn into the low white sky, their feet still wading in water.

The river ran swollen and furious, its waters mud-brown, cross-hatched with eddies and currents and pocked with swift-flowing debris. Branches and barrels and drowned beasts jostled together in a wild headlong rush for the sea. For days the light had hardly lifted.

It was dangerous, too dangerous for a fourteen-year-old, though the outboard was powerful and Joss had some experience from his life in Africa. Not enough, though: there was no such thing as enough and even a grown man in full strength would have thought twice before making as free on the river as Joss did. And Ned let him. The neighbors saw and wondered, but they didn't speak of it except amongst themselves.

It had started naturally enough. For centuries the river had been the main highway in the valley, while the little winding roads were only secondary. Then cars had come and the balance had changed, but the layout of field and dwelling had gone largely unaltered, and there were still plenty of places more easily reached by water than by road. But as the water rose, these meadows and dwellings were the first to flood.

Ned had a boat hauled up and over-wintering in an outbuilding, its outboard carefully oiled and stored, the fuel cans filled and ready beside it. He had thought about getting it out but he was too old and stiff, there was too much to be done and Hannie had fallen sick with an infection that had gone deep into her chest.

One morning he'd gone down to the flooded landing stage and found Joss with three of the local lads and the boat dragged out to the water's edge, the engine beside it, the four of them making it ready. He knew them all, they'd greeted him briefly, not letting themselves be distracted from the urgency of the task ahead.

It seemed Joss had volunteered both the boat and himself. Joss could handle a boat, he wanted to go, so Ned let him.

In the mornings Joss was up without being called and out with the boat before it was fully light. There was plenty to be done. Families and stock were moved, early lambs rescued, feed taken to beasts in pastures flooded or trampled into a waste of mud. Clearly, Joss and the boat were useful.

There were changes in Joss. The dark glasses were gone, his posture had altered, and some of the meanness and slyness of demeanor seemed to have left him. If a week's activity could make a difference like this, Ned thought, then perhaps the boy wasn't altogether lost.

But as the urgency wore off, so did the acceptance. The water dropped and the work of cleaning up and returning began. There was still a need for more hands and another boat and Joss still went out, but more and more he went alone, the young men keeping their distance, the boys of his own age avoiding him. There was no mistaking it, Joss was shunned.

This was the moment, Ned knew, when he should have ordered the boy in.

But he didn't. Partly he was distracted by Hannie's health, partly he was reluctant to take from Joss the one thing in which he excelled here, the one thing that gave him an occupation and a place. He would have discussed it with Hannie but she was sick and out of commission so he had to take the decision on himself.

Hannie's chest had got worse, she sweated and shivered, her temperature soaring at night. The doctor had come on Ned's insistence and against her wishes, had listened to her chest and said pneumonia. Bed was where she should be — no more of this getting up — bed was where she should stay until she was much better. So Hannie lay in bed and Ned brought her hot drinks and regular antibiotics and when she asked for Joss he told her Joss was fine, he was on the river, he was at Niamh's, he was watching television. . . .

People knew that Joss shouldn't be home. There was a gastric problem in the school, Ned told Mrs. Coady, a lot of the youngsters had diarrhea, it might be a bug or it might be something in the water, they'd sent them all home until they got it sorted out. Mrs. Coady had looked at him with steady eyes and he knew that she'd pass the story around and stand over it.

But he didn't know what they were going to do with Joss, who was nearly fifteen and in a few months' time could, in theory, finish school. But finish school and do what? They could hardly just leave it at that in this age when qualifications seemed so overwhelmingly important and even good character stood for little. Always supposing that Joss had had that, which he didn't.

So in not ordering Joss in off the river Ned was trying to give him something, some dignity of occupation while they waited for the school's decision.

But also there was another reason, and one that Ned was careful not to investigate very deeply. He wanted to let things find their own level, to give fate a free hand, to see would Joss go quietly under the water and not come back. And he wanted to go and tell Hannie of Joss's death, to watch her overwhelmed and then released, the whole thing like an amputation with no medicines in a stony place, the ax rising and falling, the diseased limb cut away. The agony, then the lost health returning.

Fate would have its chance. But if fate didn't claim the boy, then so be it, he would do his duty and shelter him, he was resolved on that.

Chapter Forty-nine

"FOR GOD'S SAKE, NED, stop being so melodramatic, it's not that bad. He's been expelled from school, that's all. Plenty of boys get themselves expelled, go on to lead perfectly normal lives, isn't the first time, won't be the last." James stared into his whiskey, swished it around the glass, knocked it back.

"All right, he's not the way you want him, I can see that. Hard for a chap like you . . . But they never are, you know, they never are the way you want 'em, and if you weren't so damned inexperienced you'd know that, you'd make the best of it, stop making your life a misery. What's he done, after all? Gambled a bit, run out of money — black-mail bit isn't so pretty, I admit, but he's young, a new life and all that, adjustment, we all make mistakes, or most of us do." (A quick glance here at Marjorie.) "There are other schools, aren't there? Wouldn't have sent him to Northerners, myself — all mad, if you ask me — maybe it's no bad thing they've chucked him out. Cheer up, for God's sake, he hasn't killed anyone."

James and Marjorie were sitting in the kitchen, drinking whiskey. Old friends, offering themselves for listening and advice. Ned was grateful. The school had written saying the parents of the boys con-cerned were anxious that the episode be handled with discretion. The school therefore was prepared to overlook Joss's conduct (no charges would be pressed, they implied) but they did not want him back. It was all most unfortunate, they were aware that Ned's connection with the boy was a recent one, they would have liked to have been more accommodating but they couldn't, they were sure that Ned would perfectly understand their position.

The tone of the letter, the way it had insinuated a personal exoneration for him, had so infuriated Ned that he'd almost lost sight of Joss's offense. When he'd calmed down he called Joss in and told him of the school's decision but he might as well have been talking to a breeze block for all the reaction he got. He didn't punish the boy, he thought of reducing his television hours, but he knew Joss would simply spend the time at Niamh's and he didn't want to further encourage that relationship. He cast around for other sanctions but gave up because he didn't think sanctions would make much difference, he just didn't know how to reach him.

So now it was out in the open. Joss wasn't going back.

Ned was relieved to be telling James and Marjorie, he didn't expect a solution but he'd had enough of fretting alone. He knew Hannie wouldn't want him to discuss Joss with them, but he didn't care. They were his friends, he told himself, they would have been Hannie's too if she'd let them, Joss was his stepson, he had every right to discuss him.

As for James and Marjorie, they'd heard Joss was home and Hannie safely indisposed with pneumonia, and they'd come to cheer up Ned. Finding themselves consulted, they responded with a warm attention. It was comforting to find Ned reverted to his old self and their welcome secure.

"Send him to the Quakers," Marjorie was saying. "Waterford. Near enough for Hannie to keep an eye. And he can come home the odd weekend if he wants." She looked at Ned and he was astonished at the sympathy in her bossy gray eyes. "They did the O'Connor girl, y'know? The bald one — wild as a hawk, thrown out of every school in the country — Shelagh? Siobhan? I forget her name."

"Sinéad," James said. "Sinéad O'Connor.

"Singer," he added, as Ned looked completely blank. "Batty. Awful-looking creature, boots and stubble, could be a looker, can't think why she does that to herself, voice like an angel." He had another swig from his glass. "Not a bad idea, Ned, could be a lot of sense in what Marjorie's saying. If they coped with her, they'll manage Joss all right. Chicken feed to the O'Connor girl, I'd say."

"If they'll take him," Ned said, doubtfully.

"Of course they'll take him." Marjorie was indignant at the idea of a refusal. "That's what they're there for, isn't it? James is right. Mistake to have sent him North at all. Too rigid, bound to rebel. The Quakers'll sort him out. Enough rope to hang himself. Good at that sort of thing."

When James and Marjorie had gone, Ned sat on by the fire, thinking it over. They were right, he decided, he was overreacting. As usual, where Joss was concerned; he was getting het up when nobody else did. Look at the Legs, how disturbed he had been, and the girl hadn't minded, seemed to think it was more or less normal. He'd felt a fool, all the fuss he had made.

Perhaps he was wrong about Joss, too. Not wrong altogether, but perhaps the boy wasn't bad through and through as he thought he was. He'd been wrong about Niamh, had thought her more fragile than she was. And a lot more innocent.

And he *was* inexperienced, James was certainly right there, but he wasn't too old to learn. He would do as they suggested, go and see that school, fix it all so Hannie needn't worry. He got out of his chair, banked the fire, switched off the lights, picked up the pup and went and stood in the yard as he liked to do last thing if the night was fine. The light was still on at Niamh's so he tipped the pup into her run and left the door unlocked for Joss, and for once this small concession didn't anger him.

Upstairs, he went in to say goodnight to Hannie, but she was asleep, her hair straggled over the pillow, the violet shadows strong beneath her eyes. Sometimes she stirred and coughed. He had never known a woman in this way: unpresented, unadorned, mortal and sick and in his care. He could not get over the everydayness of her, of her life lived so close to his. Very quietly, he turned the lamp off, backed out and closed the door.

But he woke in the night and remembered the dread in Hannie's eyes when she'd asked him in the Land Rover what Joss had done. He lay a long time staring into the darkness and knowing his friends for false comforters.

NED WAS CAREFULLY and thoroughly interviewed by the headmaster and his deputy. He didn't lie to them or try to conceal anything, he told them what had happened to cause Joss's expulsion and he told them he thought there'd been problems in the past. He didn't know the details he said, the boy's mother had pneumonia, he didn't want to bother her while she was still so ill.

They said they'd talk to Hannie later when she'd recovered. In the meantime they would ask the boy. Ned stared, but the two men seemed perfectly confident in what they were doing. They sent him off to the bursar's office to discuss the financial side of things. They wanted to talk to Joss alone.

In the end they said they'd take Joss, but suggested that he drop back a year, starting after Easter. That way he'd have a term just to settle in and then he'd move into the new school year with surroundings and classmates already familiar to him. He'd also have a couple of months at home to get used to a new country and a new way of life.

Ned felt his bones sag with surprise and relief but at the same time he couldn't help feeling that somehow he was cheating these people, that he'd deceived them into accepting Joss when he should have been warning them against him.

NED'S RELIEF was short-lived. The flood dropped and Joss lost all interest in the river. He abandoned the boat like a child leaving down a toy he has tired of, it rocked on its moorings, dirty and forlorn. Ned told him to get it cleaned up and out of the water and Joss obeyed him with sullen ill will. Ned watched his resentment. He had always worked alone or with people who wanted to be on his payroll. If a guide or a bearer had had Joss's attitude he would simply have let him go.

But he couldn't let Joss go. For the first time it occurred to him that Joss might refuse an order. He wondered how he'd deal with straight defiance from his stepson.

It was all very well, this talk of Joss settling in at home, but the truth was, Ned didn't know what to do with the boy. There was plenty of routine farm maintenance and clearing up in the flood's aftermath to be done, but Joss wasn't interested in such work and Ned was not prepared to take on the duty of motivating Joss, or of bullying him into accomplishing the tasks he set him.

Nor was he prepared to give up his solitude and work with Joss. Solitude was precious to him — solitude, aloneness and separateness. He had always refused to travel with fellow Europeans whose language he understood. He wasn't a natural linguist: with native peoples he had been protected and separated by his inability to understand the daily chatter. Solitude was now far more than a drug to him: in it he found rest and refreshment and no task was dull.

So Ned tried, but only halfheartedly. He required Joss to be up in the morning, he directed him at a task, explained it, and left the lad alone. If it was done, it was badly done. More often it was left half done or hardly started. Ned quickly grew angry. Joss was never going to be any good on the land because he didn't want to be; he could do it if he wanted to, he had shown that with the boat. Ned could not bring himself to use himself up on Joss when he knew the boy was trying to wear him down. Sometimes he couldn't bear the sight of Joss, his blankness and resistance. He was afraid of his own rage.

The doctor dropped by and was astonished that Hannie was still in bed and so ill.

"Why didn't you call me?" he asked Ned. "I thought she'd be up and around ages ago, I'd no idea she wasn't responding to treatment."

Ned muttered about pneumonia. The doctor, involved with his prescription pad, growled dismissively. "That's the dark ages. Pneumonia's not what it was, she just needs a different antibiotic. Here." He tore out the prescription and handed it to Ned. "We'll try her on that. I'll leave you a few to start her off. You should see a big change in a day or two — three at the most. But for God's sake call me if it's not working. I want her out of bed and hopping around the place in a week."

When the doctor had left Ned carried Hannie's supper tray down and put it on the table. It was hardly touched, the soup cold and congealed, the bread uneaten. He felt downcast and sorry for himself and generally angry. The doctor clearly considered him hopelessly behind the times. He might not be able to give Hannie what she wanted when she was well, but he'd thought that at least he was looking after her now she was sick. He was doing his best, and he just got accused of making things worse.

Niamh was mooching about the kitchen, picking things up, putting them down again.

"Two to be taken three times a day." She had Hannie's pills in her hand. "Stronger and stronger antibiotics, that's all doctors can think of, no mention of nursing or rest. This one doesn't work fast enough — change to another one. And all those illnesses they thought they'd got rid of — all back, stronger, more resistant. She shouldn't be taking these things, she should be getting over it herself, in a natural way, using her own resources."

"She *was* using her own resources," Ned said tiredly. "And she wasn't getting over it. I've just had a bellyful from Malone and now you start in from the opposite direction."

Niamh looked at him, her dark eyes stubborn and determined. "They'll weaken her in the long run."

Ned sat down and opened the paper. He wanted to eat his supper, read the newspaper, take himself off to an early bed. He had never lost his temper with Niamh, had never even imagined that the situation might arise.

"Is your work going well, Niamh?" he asked her without looking up. "I hope you haven't forgotten Mrs. Cardew's painting, I know you've decided you don't want to bother with commissions but you did say you'd finish it, since you've already been paid for it. And it might be civil of you to let her know your intentions."

—•◆•—

"Ned?" said a woman's voice on the phone. "Ned, this is Nora."

Ned didn't know any Noras. He waited blankly.

"Andrew's wife," said the voice. "Nora — Nora Clarke." She finished a bit desperately, as though she was asking him to confirm her name.

Ned got it. Nora, the dark girl with the pretty ways, Andrew's wife, they'd been to stay at Christmas. He made himself put warmth and recognition into his voice.

"Hello, Nora. How are you, what can I do for you?"

"Grand, thanks," she said, ignoring the second part of the question. "But we heard that Joss is home and Hannie isn't so good. We wondered if there was anything we could do?"

"How on Earth did you hear that?" His tone was sharper than he'd intended. There was a slight, anxious pause at the other end.

"Oh, you know," Nora said brightly. "This is Ireland — everyone hears everything." A nervous little laugh.

"Anyway," she went on in a rush, "we wondered if you'd like to send us Joss for a week or two — I've a nephew staying, it'd be company for him — give you a break till Hannie gets back on her feet?"

"That's very kind of you, Nora," Ned said. "Very kind indeed. But it would be a lot of trouble for you." (And would Hannie want it? She hadn't said anything against his school arrangements, but she hadn't been as relieved as he had expected.)

"Oh no, no trouble at all," Nora was saying into his ear. "I like having young ones around, and it'd be great for Con. That's the nephew — my sister's son, fifteen. Just the right age for Joss."

She wouldn't take no for an answer. She had it all thought out, her plans for Joss's transportation were swift and practical, she seemed completely *au fait* with bus routes and timetables, naming the towns and the changes with practiced ease. Joss would leave the next day and return in a couple of weeks. It was all fixed before Ned had time to think.

———•◆•———

To Ned's surprise, Joss wanted to go. He stood in the kitchen, taking in the details, his face blank. Then he pulled at each of his fingers in turn until they cracked in their sockets. Ned told himself to be patient. Joss turned to leave the room.

"Where are you going?" Ned asked him.

Joss looked surprised. "To pack."

Ned had a moment of contrition. "You don't have to go if you really don't want to, Joss, I don't want to force you — it's just that with your mother being sick like this and school not starting for you till Easter . . ."

"It's cool," Joss said. "I want to go. I like Nora."

"You do?" Ned couldn't keep the surprise out of his voice.

"Sure. She's cool. And she lives in a town. She told me."

"Would you rather we lived in a town?"

"Sure. It's boring here. No one to talk to but Niamh."

"But you get on with Niamh?"

Joss sighed. "Niamh's all right," he said. "But she's boring. It was better when Ciaran was here."

Ned didn't say anything.

Joss stood. After a moment or two Ned realized he was waiting to be dismissed.

"All right, Joss," he said. "You can go and pack now."

Joss turned to go. At the door he turned back. "Does *she* know?" he asked.

Ned looked blank.

"Hannie," Joss said. "Have you told her?"

Ned almost lied.

"No," he said reluctantly.

"Best not," Joss said. "Not till after I've gone."

"You think she might not approve of the arrangement?"

Joss grinned suddenly. "She'll go nuts," he said. "But she'll calm down when she gets used to the idea." He disappeared through the door.

Chapter Fifty

THE NEXT DAY HANNIE'S FEVER WAS DOWN and she slept through for twenty-four hours without waking. When she did she sat up in bed and announced that she wanted a bath and something to eat. She had both, then Ned told her that Joss was in Galway with Nora.

It wasn't quite as Joss had predicted. She did go nuts, but showed no sign of calming down or getting used to the idea. Instead she got up, got dressed and went down to the kitchen. He was doing farm accounts at the table but she didn't seem to see him. She sat by the phone, leafed through the address book, then dialed the Clarkes' number. When Nora answered Hannie told her that the school in Waterford needed Joss for tests because they wanted to assess his progress-to-date in all his subjects. He'd be ahead in some areas, she explained, but would probably need some extra help in others. Unfortunately it meant that Joss's stay in Galway must be cut short.

She listened while Nora replied.

She said she was glad Joss was enjoying himself, and yes, he did need to be brought out of his shell, but she still felt his education must come first. No, the school wasn't being arbitrary, this had always been the arrangement, it was simply that Ned hadn't realized they would need Joss so soon.

Her tone was straightforward and matter-of-fact but she was very firm. She wanted Joss put on a bus the next morning. She got Joss on the line and told him the same thing.

She put down the phone and went and inspected the fridge. She removed all the precooked portions that Mrs. Coady had prepared. She bagged them and labeled them and dispatched them to the freezer. Then she cleaned the fridge, cleaned the sink, cooked a fresh, hot meal, set out the food and sat down and ate in complete silence.

Ned was at once relieved, apprehensive and angry. She had undone his arrangement seamlessly, concealing nothing from him, not blaming him to Nora or making him look a fool. Nonetheless she had reversed his decision as though he'd had no business making it in the first place.

This annoyed him. Joss was his stepson, in his charge, he had a right to his say in things, whatever she might think. But he should have withdrawn from the arrangement as soon as Joss had told him she wouldn't like it, he should have asserted Hannie's authority and taken no part in conniving with the boy — of this he was well aware. And he had a guilty conscience because she didn't know Joss had said what he'd said, and he certainly wasn't about to tell her.

"Hannie, you're being unreasonable," he accused into her silence. "When he wanted to go to Omagh you were all for it, you said there was no one for him to talk to here, no one his own age."

She reached for the salt without even looking up.

"Well he's happy in Galway, he's got Nora's nephew to talk to, I don't know why you're making such a fuss."

No response.

"You were sick in bed, Hannie, you weren't around. And I don't think it's a good idea, him being too much at Niamh's."

Silence again. He tried another tack.

"Hannie, I'm sorry if it wasn't what you wanted, but I can't understand why you don't want him to be at Nora's, at least we know he's in good hands."

She got up, lifted her plate and crossed to the sink.

"It's because of the shoe," she said quietly, running water into the bowl, not turning around.

"The shoe?" He didn't understand.

"The black high-heeled shoe Danno found by the legs that Joss made. It was Nora's shoe."

She turned and looked at him then, a steady, wordless look, her face quite gray with fatigue.

———•◆•———

JOSS CAME HOME. He no longer got up in the mornings or reported to Ned for tasks. Ned said nothing, he used the break from their barely established routine to let things drift. It was easier so, they were both relieved, and the school had phoned (Hannie's lie proved no more than the truth); they wanted Joss for tests in a couple of weeks. Hannie's infection had passed, but she'd got up too quickly, she found herself drained and exhausted after only a few hours out of bed. She, too, was ready to leave Joss alone and let things be until school kicked in and kept him at least occupied.

The doctor came again. Ned walked him to his car when he'd finished with Hannie. They talked briefly of the livestock and the latest political scandal and the weather. Then Ned asked about Hannie.

The doctor thought for a moment before replying. "Basically she's a strong, healthy woman," he said slowly. "She's responding to treatment, the infection's receding, yet somehow she's not picking up in the way she should. . . ." He paused and looked at Ned. Ned said nothing. "She seems a bit low, not much interested in life," he went on cautiously. "I wonder — perhaps she's found the transition a bit difficult? She's used to the sun, they tell me?" He paused again and looked amiably into the distance. Still nothing. Oh well, might as well be hung for a sheep as a lamb. "Would you think maybe of taking her for a bit of a holiday?" he asked. "Somewhere warm, a package maybe. A bit of a break for you both?"

He felt Ned stiffen beside him, but he didn't look around. Ned mumbled vaguely about not being able to leave the farm and her boy. The doctor let that pass. Ned said money didn't grow on trees.

"It doesn't have to be the Caribbean, you know," the doctor said gently. "There's grand holidays these days without going all that way.

Turkey, perhaps. North Africa. They tell me Tunisia isn't dear. And the great thing is you can go direct from Dublin. No trailing off to London, waiting around for hours for a connection. Not too hot when you get there, either. Not stripping-off-and-lying-by-the-pool weather, but pleasant, strolling-in-the-sun sort of heat."

He shook hands with Ned and got into the car and rolled down the window. "Might be worth your while having a look in at Shea's the next time you're over in that direction. Think about it, anyway. . . . And let me know if there's any change for the worse."

He drove off down the bumpy drive, avoiding the potholes. These Anglo-Irish types were the divil. Inbred and touchy and close as a well-planed door. And you never knew what they had or didn't have, outside of a horse and a picture or two. Poor woman. Stuck down there with no company and a husband twenty years older. Still, Ned Renvyle was a decent man and probably a kind one, it could work out well enough when it settled down. And he just might bite on a holiday — a holiday might do the trick. Wouldn't like spending the money, though. Well, if he wouldn't, he wouldn't, you couldn't force people. He'd give her a month, maybe try her on antidepressants if she wasn't picking up . . .

Ned dismissed the doctor's suggestion at once, but it itched at him like flea bites for the rest of the day. Malone meant well enough, but he was interfering with his talk of holidays and sunshine. Hannie would do very well once she was properly over the infection, she was an active woman by nature, she *would* be low after so long in bed. And there simply wasn't the money for holidays, it was tight enough to begin with, and Joss's schooling was an enormous extra drain.

Maybe he should think about involving her more with the farm, he thought, get her roped in on his lavender plans, encourage her to go ahead with the geese. The farm machine show was coming up in Dublin, they could go there together, there'd be ideas for farm development, information on geese, maybe something on lavender as well. And after that there were race meetings they could go to, she liked race meetings, there was a good winter calendar, much of it within fairly easy reach. Ideas leapt into his head.

Thus Ned talked to himself, proving easily that if there was money to be spent it would be better spent so; more outings and expeditions, a gradual steady change. He'd show Malone he could do better than a week in Turkey or Tunisia.

He was infinitely relieved by his conclusions. In the end it wasn't even the money, it was the thought of some high-rise hotel in some tourist resort, and other people at breakfast, and traipsing around on bus tours looking at curios and belly dancers and souvenirs. He hated tourism, its superficiality and inanity, he hated what it did to countries and peoples and their immemorial ways of life. He'd felt violated by Malone's well-intentioned suggestion.

Later, in the house, he waited for Hannie to go up to an early bed then picked up the phone and dialed Vere and Alison.

Vere answered. Ned asked him to recommend a modest hotel in Dublin.

"Hang on a minute." Vere went off to find Alison. Alison came on the line and she gave him the name and number of a hotel and told him the price, which seemed to Ned exorbitant, but he wasn't going to let that put him off. Alison asked when he was thinking of going and he explained about the doctor and the need for a weekend away, and Alison listened to it all and then asked gently if he thought Hannie liked farm machinery shows?

Ned stopped in his tracks. With anyone else he'd have clammed up but because it was Alison he hesitated and then he said he hadn't actually asked her, but he'd thought about involving her more in the farm and the show might be a good way to begin.

"It was going to be a surprise," he finished lamely. "D'you think it's a bad idea?"

"Not necessarily, not if she likes shows." There was a small pause. "But it might be quite strenuous and noisy, walking around all those stands, perhaps she'd like music or the theater better? And maybe some shops in the day?"

"The theater's noisy too."

"True, but at least she'd be sitting down."

"She won't want to go to the shops, she doesn't like shops, shops are hell."

"I couldn't agree more," Alison said, "but she might like to buy some new clothes? That's always good for you when you've been ill, it gives you a boost."

Ned thanked her and put down the phone. Hannie had clothes, it hadn't occurred to him that she might want new ones, any more than it had occurred to him that she mightn't like a farm machinery show. Suddenly it all seemed hopeless, he didn't have the faintest idea about her or any woman and if it hadn't been after seven he'd have lifted the phone to Shea's then and there and booked them on to some god-awful package to some god-awful place, as Malone had suggested.

Chapter Fifty-one

IT WAS SUDDENLY MILDER. The sky had cleared to a soft, light blue, higher and airier than it had been for weeks. There were dribbles of birdsong, stripes of pale light on the straggly grass, blackbirds poking and scuffling about in the hedges. Under the apple trees the snowdrops had pushed through.

Hannie walked about in the garden, little clouds of floppy gray gnats swimming toward her through the warmer air. The garden looked like a field, the grass tussocky and rank, the flowerbeds frost-blackened and clogged with rotting leaves. But everything smelled different. Bands of rooks flew over, their wings swishing the quiet air.

So, she thought, that was the winter.

When she came in Alison was standing in the kitchen with a biro in her hand, a cardboard box and a brown envelope on the table beside her.

"Oh Hannie, how are you? Much better, I can see that, I'm so glad. I was just writing you a note. I've brought Ned's Burton from the National Library —" she patted the box — "it's all right, no serious damage, but they said to tell him not to go leaving it around beside open windows, he mightn't get off as lightly the next time."

Hannie put on the kettle and took Ned's teapot down from the shelf. So he'd sent off Burton to be checked, had he? How like him. And all the time protesting that it didn't matter. Still, she shouldn't complain, what was it he had called the book? *Your golden egg for when I die.*

"It's so difficult, isn't it?" Alison said. "Awful to lock things away just because they're valuable, but they were really quite disapproving when I said Ned thought books were there to be read. They got very stuffy and looked at me as though I wasn't entirely a fit person and muttered about reading the Penguin Classic and keeping the real thing. I almost thought they were going to say I couldn't take it away, but Ned had written them a letter so they couldn't *not* let me have it, even though they clearly wanted to. . . ."

Hannie set a tray with a milk jug and cookies and bone-china cups, and ushered her guest into the cold dampness of the drawing room. Alison protested all this formality but Hannie wouldn't listen. She put a match to the laid fire and drew the curtains against the twilight. She poured the tea and handed Alison a cup.

"You've been in Dublin?"

Alison sipped and nodded. "Yes. Vere's ancient aunt, she's getting quite meandery, poor old thing. Everyone keeps wanting to put her into a home, tidy her away, but she won't hear of it and I can't say I blame her."

Alison sat back in her chair. "And then we looked in on the farm machinery show. Vere wanted to look at balers, he's had an idea for an improvement and he wanted to check that no one else had got there before him."

"And had they?"

"No, but they might as well have. It's all so high-tech now and Vere's idea was just a simple modification of the old ones, he really got quite depressed. I've got some information on geese for you, but nothing on lavender, we couldn't find anything at all I'm afraid. Vere thinks daffodils would be a better plan, but Ned's not interested in daffodils, is he, he wants to grow lavender?"

"I've really no idea," Hannie said coolly, "I didn't know he'd asked you to get information on geese, much less lavender."

Alison flushed. "I expect he forgot to tell you. It's my fault, he wanted to take you himself, but I thought you might not be well enough, I'm afraid I was rather discouraging."

"Wanted to take me where?"

"To the farm machinery show."

Hannie stared at her for a moment, then threw back her head and laughed. Alison looked startled, then she laughed too. The two women laughed like giddy girls, Hannie clutching her stomach and Alison holding a cushion to her mouth, her eyes dancing above it. Every time they looked at one another they started each other off again.

"I've never even heard of the farm machinery show," Hannie said when she could speak. That started them again and they couldn't stop. A door opened in the hall. Abruptly Alison stopped laughing and sat with one hand raised in warning. Footsteps and a door closing, then silence.

"It's all right," Hannie said, not laughing anymore, picking up the pot and refilling the cups. "This is what he wants of me — afternoon tea, in a drawing room, with someone like you. He'll be pleased to hear us laugh, it'll never cross his mind we might be laughing at him."

"It must be very hard for you," Alison said slowly. "Not belonging . . ."

"Hard for me? No, it isn't hard for me. I have never wanted to belong anywhere or with anyone. The opposite."

"You must have a great many friends." Alison said this thoughtfully and it wasn't a question.

"Why do you say that?"

"So you don't have a need to belong." Alison leaned forward. "I'm sorry, I don't really understand, I've always lived in one place, it's hard for me to imagine another kind of life."

"We are very different people," Hannie said coolly. There was a moment's lull in the conversation, then she picked it up again. "No," she said, "I don't have *a great many friends* and I wouldn't want them, I like to be free and alone. I only ever had one real friend and she's dead now. That's all right, it means I rely on myself."

"Not on your husband?"

"No," Hannie said gravely. "Not on my husband. I have never had a husband that I trusted. Have you?"

"I have only ever had one husband. But yes, I do trust him. I trust that he will always do his best for me."

"But not that he will always do what you need of him?"

"No. But I don't think you can expect that of anyone."

"You can expect it of yourself."

"Yes. But what if it's too much for you and you need to be helped?"

"You withdraw from the situation."

"Sometimes you can't."

"There is always that danger. . . ."

There was silence again. The two women looked at each other as though baffled. Alison sensed that Hannie wanted to talk to her, but she didn't know what it was that she was trying to say and she was afraid of missing it.

"But one can never be quite self-reliant, can one?" she said at last. "Not once one has a child? A child is an extension of oneself, the boundaries are breached forever, even when they are grown up and gone away."

"I don't know."

"But Joss —?"

"Joss is not my son."

Alison opened her mouth to speak, then realized what had been said to her. There was dead silence in the room.

"Whose son is he?" she asked at last.

"The son of the dead friend that I just spoke of. Joss is Ilse's son, not mine." Hannie got up and went over to the long window. She pulled the curtain back and stood staring out into the darkness. There was a peculiar atmosphere in the room.

"Who was Ilse?"

Hannie answered without turning.

"Ilse was Swedish. Very young. She married my husband."

Alison struggled with Hannie's words but she couldn't make sense of them. "I'm sorry," she said gently. "I don't understand what you're telling me."

"Joss is Ilse's son," Hannie explained from the window, "by a man who was my husband when she met him."

"Ilse took your husband from you?"

"That's one way of looking at it. My husband then was a man named Rolf. Ilse was a young au pair from Sweden, very naive and beautiful. Later, when she was dying, she asked me to take Joss for her."

"Why did she do that?"

"She didn't want Rolf to have him. And there was no one else, her family were estranged."

"But why did you agree?"

"Because she was my friend."

"But she took your husband?"

"Yes, but it didn't matter, things change, people move on. And anyway I wasn't in love with Rolf, it was just a convenient arrangement." She stopped and looked at Alison's bewildered face and tried again.

"I used her, she was useful to me, I exploited her naïveté, her guilt. Then, years later she helped me for no reason and looked after me when I was sick. So when she was dying she asked me to take her son Joss."

"But why didn't she want her husband to keep his own son?"

Hannie shrugged. "Joss is a strange boy and Rolf was a hard man and a heavy drinker, he was bad for him. Bad for Ilse too, I shouldn't have let her marry him, I should have stopped it at the start."

"But if he left you for her," Alison said, bewilderment in her voice — "if he left you, how could you have stopped it?"

"There are ways. One can often stop things, if one really wants to. But I didn't know her then, I didn't care about her, so I didn't bother. Her family tried but she wouldn't listen to them and in the end they never spoke to her again."

"But if Joss isn't your son, why do you say that he is?"

"When you marry a man, he must take your child. If it's not your child, then things are not so clear."

"And Joss is . . . not an easy child."

"Exactly. Joss is not an easy child."

Alison sat back in her chair, taking in this flood of strange new information. For a moment she was certain that the woman standing at the window was deliberately misleading her. Then Hannie half-turned her head and Alison saw her face against the light-colored curtain and she wasn't quite so sure.

"But Hannie," she began very cautiously, "since Joss is not easy, and since he is . . . not your son, why do you go on doing this?"

Hannie stared at her. "I just told you," she said, surprise in her voice. "Because Ilse asked me to."

There was another silence. Hannie left her position by the window and sat in the chair she had left.

"Why are you telling me all this?" Alison asked.

"Because I think perhaps someone somewhere should know but I'm not sure why. Maybe it's because I have been ill again and when you recover from illness it changes everything around you for a little while."

Alison stirred uneasily. "Why don't you tell Ned?" she asked, her voice worried. "Ned is a good man and he's your husband and he cares for you. Don't you think he deserves to be told the truth?"

Hannie shook her head impatiently. "Joss is a lot to ask of anyone. It's easier for Ned to accept him if he thinks he's my son."

"What if I were to tell Ned?"

Hannie sat back. "I think you won't do that," she said quietly. "I think you wouldn't allow that of yourself. Or not till it became necessary."

Alison thought for a moment and then nodded.

———— ♦ ————

DRIVING HOME through the darkness, Alison turned Hannie's words and gestures over and over in her mind.

Was it true, what she'd said about Joss not being her son? And if it was, why didn't she give up on Joss, leave him behind somewhere? No one would blame her.

Could it be as she'd said, some sort of loyalty, some sort of debt of honor? Was it possible? Was this woman whom she'd thought more or less without morality motivated by gratitude to a dead friend?

Alison shivered; it had turned cold again, she regretted believing the afternoon's warmth and leaving off one of her sweaters. She banged the heater hard with her left hand but it only gulped and settled back into a low-grade lukewarm hum, refusing to crank itself up even half a notch.

She thought about telling Ned, but she knew that Hannie was right and she wouldn't. Why not? she wondered. Was Hannie also right in saying it was easier for Ned if he didn't know? She thought about telling Vere and she knew she wouldn't do that either. She could hear Vere's voice in her mind.

"So you're planning to swallow all that, are you, Ali? Come off it, old thing, it's lies, just a tissue of lies, she knows you're a soft touch, she's buying sympathy, simple as that. How do I know? Well, she's not telling Ned, is she? And why not? Because the little monster would be out on his ear in the morning, that's why not. You think I'm being hard? Well then, answer me this — if he's not her son, why on Earth is she doing it?"

"Honor," she would say to him. "Because her dead friend asked it of her."

"Balls. She's just shifting the focus, making herself out to be a martyr. Ali, the woman's a walking crisis, she can't function without chaos, Joss is the same, he guarantees chaos wherever he goes."

Alison sighed. The weather forecast was giving out change. A cold front moving rapidly in from the north. Heavy frost. On high ground, sleet and snow. She gave the heater another halfhearted thump.

Chaos. Was Vere right? A nursery jingle sounded inanely in her mind: *rings on her fingers, bells on her toes, she shall have chaos wherever she goes.*

Chapter Fifty-two

IT WAS MUCH COLDER AGAIN, the weather forecast stopped limiting the snow to high ground and gave it out as general and widespread. Yesterday's floppy gnats must have frozen to death in the night, Hannie thought. It was amazing how fast it all changed, the brief warmth seemed like a dream-memory, the rain and the flooding were distant and unreal as a folktale.

She was finishing up in the kitchen, sweeping and washing the floor when some change in the light made her glance out. The sky was blank and heavy and loose gray blobs were coming flying out of it, vanishing instantly into the waiting mud. This must be snow, she thought, astonished by its grayness, by the bleak wet dreariness of it. The sky grew denser in its discolored whiteness, the blobs grew larger and faster, they thickened and whitened and clung to the shed roofs and the twisted branches of the apple trees. She strained her eyes through the soured light. Beyond the roofs, the thorn hedges showed black against the whitening fields.

When the light changed in the room she knew without looking out that the snow had stopped. She fetched the lead, called the puppy and walked her up the road toward Danno's. At first Pippa romped and bit at the snow, then she settled down and sniffed her way quietly through this strange, changed world. At the corner where Lambert's field ran off from the road, she stopped in her tracks and stood there sniffing and watching.

Lambert had early lambs out. They looked cold and unhappy in the snowy wastes of the meadow; they bleated and fretted and picked their way on impossibly long legs. The ewes stood stolidly, very yellow and dirty-looking against the blue-white of the snow, like large fat maggots on the pale skin of a corpse. Hannie let Pippa watch, she was only a pup but the ewes panicked when they saw her, they called their lambs to them and lumbered heavily away. Pippa didn't move, only the muscles at her neck quivered. Her fluffy fur stood out.

A belt of heavy gray cloud lay stretched out on the rim of the field. Above the cloud was the empty sky — very cold — a clear, far blue. The ewes were all moving off, lambs at their flanks, bleating and fussing, overanxious mothers. She heard a sound behind her and turned her head. A man was standing there watching her as she was watching the ewes. She turned away. He didn't look local and yet she was sure that she knew him. She looked again. Ah yes, she remembered, she had him now. The man in the bar-tent at the races. The man who thought he was Lord Tung.

———◆———

IT WAS ALREADY beginning to thaw when he drove her back to the house. He'd suggested leaving her off where he'd found her, but she'd vetoed his suggestion.

"D'you want the whole world putting two and two together and making four?" she'd asked. "They will if we sneak around the place being guilty."

He hadn't liked that. He was a lot less confident after the event than before, she noticed. In fact he had looked not Lord Tung-ish at all, but rather as though he wished her at the bottom of a well. She shrugged to herself, she didn't care, he was vain and arrogant and self-centered, she wasn't about to lose sleep over him. Still, it was nice to be corrupted so pleasantly, to slip under his guard without even trying. Granted, he was at a loose end, the lovely twenty-eight-year-old had dumped him and gone off in search of livelier pastures. But he'd had to humble himself and ask, it was a good warm revenge for his previous disdain. And they were both aware of what they wanted, both skillful and practiced enough to ensure a satisfactory coupling.

Ned had been in the yard at the back when she got home, he'd made a fuss of the pup but he hadn't mentioned the strange car, nor asked her where she'd been. He didn't ask, so she didn't volunteer an explanation.

Instead she took the colander from the hook in the kitchen and went down to the vegetable patch to pick spinach beet. They ate little else these days, the sprouts were over but the leeks and cabbages she'd planted in the autumn were still a long way off. She bent to the frosted beet. The bird net had stretched with the snow, which clung in its sagging hollows, weighting and dragging them down. Gobs of cold slush from the net dripped onto her back and her head and her hands. Her toes, still swollen with chilblains despite the electric blanket, pressed painfully against the hard rubber of her Wellingtons. The darkness was coming, cobalt blue against the whiteness of the thawing snow.

Chapter Fifty-three

THINGS WERE EASIER. Even with Joss, it was less ominous. Hannie was taking the boy into Waterford for school assessments, dropping him off and picking him up again later. He seemed less odd and more open. There were even times when Ned wondered if James mightn't be right after all and Joss's behavior wasn't rather the norm than the exception. What did he know about teenagers? Nothing. Nor, he had to admit to himself, did he much want to.

Hannie, too, was easier, her health and vitality restored. Things were different between them, less charged and more matter-of-fact. Ned was relieved but under the relief he felt as though he had somehow lost something of her. It wasn't that he wanted her to be sick, or unhappy, or desperate over Joss, but he wanted her to need his help. He had always wanted the essence of things (why else had he made those extraordinary journeys?) and now he felt her eluding him. He couldn't quite pin down the change in her. She was relaxed, almost warm, but he felt that her gaze had minutely shifted. When she looked at him now she saw slightly past him to somewhere else.

Oddly, this change made her more accessible. They talked more, spent more time in each other's company, and she was freer with him than she'd been since they were married. He was too old to be journeying, yet with her he still journeyed. New landscapes opened before him, sometimes familiar, sometimes dangerous, sometimes merely surprising. He liked the way she looked at things, said what she really thought, didn't feel the need to be consistent. Without realizing it, he was getting over his initial disappointment. He was adjusting to her presence and he was less lonely.

He was right about Hannie, something had changed in her, a part of her that had been asleep had woken again, a sexual part. But she wasn't in love so it didn't overwhelm her, it just diverted her attention, cheered her up, and made things easier with Ned. She knew it was risky, these things were never a secret for long no matter how you tried to conceal them. So she was as careful as she could be, especially with Joss. She didn't want to unsettle him and she didn't want him getting ideas about another change.

She liked going to Waterford and having time that she didn't have to account for. She liked parking by the quays, walking about, watching the cattle boats and container ships and the bright, dissolute trawlers berthed in crowds by the bridge. She went into pubs, read the paper, had her hair done, bought a sweater. Sometimes she went to the accountants or the solicitors on farm business for Ned. She liked all this, liked the bars and the shops and the offices, the feeling of life going on, of people who had never seen her before and didn't care if they never saw her again, indifferent as the herring gulls watching from the railings, their eyes yellow and cold. The world was still there, she hadn't dreamed it or made it up.

She didn't get much out of Joss on their drives back and forth. He was opaque to her, silent and watchful, never letting his guard slip. The casual intimacy of his childhood seemed lost forever, puberty had barred all access to him, all she could do was watch and wait.

Sometimes she didn't go to Waterford at all, instead she put Joss onto the bus in Dungarvan saying she had chores to do and went to Thornton's place instead. Sometimes she met him in Waterford and he bought her lunch or a drink or took her to a hotel he had an arrangement with for such occasions.

Ned didn't know what Hannie did while she waited in Waterford for Joss and he didn't ask. If she was back in the afternoon now she came and worked alongside him and he liked this so well he forgot his preference for solitude. She worked hard and efficiently. Sometimes she talked as she worked but she never just downed tools and chattered.

Ned knew Thornton slightly himself and had no interest in him. He'd seen her getting out of Thornton's car on the day of the snow and he'd waited for her to mention it, but she hadn't and then he'd remembered seeing them talking together in the bar-tent at the races. Thornton had bought the old Cantalon place and was doing it up; Ned supposed that he'd asked Hannie over to look at it, perhaps to give him advice. He felt he should be glad that Thornton was interested in her opinion, but he wasn't, he didn't like her going there, he was afraid she might fall in love with the man.

It didn't cross his mind that Hannie might simply go to bed with Thornton, he didn't conceive of sex as something she might do for its own sake, without passion or affection or even the contract of marriage; the truth of the situation didn't once occur to him. But because he was jealous of Thornton's possible place in Hannie's affections, Ned remembered the doctor's words and he cast around in his mind for ways to make her life more outward-looking and varied.

———•◆•———

"MRS. CARDEW was on the phone. She wants to know when she's getting her picture." Hannie tossed the words over her shoulder.

The weather was wild and cold again and she was bundled up in a motley of brown corduroys and grayish wools and tweeds. They were clearing out one of the sheds together, the lambing was still a week or so off, but there were more ewes this year and Ned liked to feel fully prepared and in control.

"I can't understand Niamh," Ned said tetchily. "Mrs. Cardew's paid in advance. Sylvia Roche didn't pay, Niamh can do what she wants about her picture, but Mrs. Cardew's paid."

Hannie didn't say anything. Ned went on lugging fertilizer sacks.

"You have to deliver what you've undertaken to deliver, surely Niamh understands that? It isn't always plain sailing, quite often commissions turn out to be more trouble than they're worth, but you don't just dump them because they're inconvenient, you still have to stand by your word. I'm surprised at Niamh. Disappointed . . ."

"Niamh doesn't live in the real world," Hannie said. "Which is just as well, she'd last about five minutes. Anyway, she's busy, she's making papier-mâché legs for an exhibition."

"Papier-mâché what?"

"Legs. Like the legs Joss made. Only better, more lifelike, more shocking."

Ned stopped spreading hay with his fork and straightened up and stared at Hannie. Hannie didn't stop work to stare back.

"Several of them. Different models. One of them has chained-together ankles and a padlock on the chain. A reference to chastity belts, she says. Chastity belts and possession. Another one has scarlet slashes painted across its cunt. She's going to hang them by their ankles in some gallery, just as Joss did."

"Has Joss seen them?"

"Joss is helping her. She wants him to, that's why he's there so much." Hannie straightened as well and looked at Ned. "I told Joss he shouldn't go around there all the time and he said she'd asked him to give her a hand. When I checked with her she said it was true."

"But what's she doing it for? Why's she making these things?" Ned sounded almost more bewildered than shocked.

Hannie shrugged her shoulders. "I told you, for some exhibition. She says that they're a metaphor for misogyny in marriage, hence the chained ankles and the mutilated genitals. Nothing subtle — she says that's important: 'I want it to look as though its cunt has been slashed.'" Hannie turned back to her work as though tired of the subject.

"What about Joss?"

"What about him? Perhaps it'll do him good, you never know with Joss. Occupational therapy. Like Danno making baskets . . . Maybe she'll rope Danno in as well, get him to teach her some basketry, make woven legs out of willows. I wouldn't put it past her. She's always on about old skills, adapting them, using them in new ways." Hannie pulled out a nest of blackened sacks from a corner and heaved them onto the growing pile of rubbish. "On second thought, perhaps not. Danno would have a fit and anyway she's such a puritan."

She pulled again and a tangle of rotting ropes followed the sacks. A rat ran across her foot and made for the open door.

"Young women, what chaos they do cause. I never noticed it when I was young myself. But maybe she's right about old skills, Ned. Danno's selling baskets faster than he can make them. Maybe you should give up this lavender plan and try your hand at growing willow. At least you wouldn't have to fight this bloody climate quite so hard."

———•◆•———

"I won't be here tomorrow," Joss said from the top of the ladder. "He's taking her to some pile of old stones. She says I have to go with them."

"Couldn't you get out of it? I need to hang the frame for the next one and I need someone to hold it while I get it right." Niamh stood back and half closed her eyes. "A bit higher. That's enough. Now lower again — not much — an inch or two should do it."

Joss pulled on the rope and the papier-mâché legs rose. He gave it some slack and the legs dropped slightly. Niamh walked all around them, looking at them critically, but with mounting excitement. The wire frame she'd built the model on had been suspended from the start, but this was the first time she'd seen the work with the proper elevation. It looked good, well made and powerful and shocking. It had a potency and presence beyond what she'd expected. She was glad she'd abandoned the print dresses. The white tulle of this skirt was perfect and the white satin overskirt, now reversed and become an underskirt, was quietly redolent of weddings.

"Okay, that's fine, that's exactly the height I want. I didn't know Hannie was into ruins?"

"She isn't." Joss wound the rope around a bracket he'd fixed to the ceiling and secured it with a couple of hitches. "Not remotely, but he wants to take her and she says she's not about to leave me to my own devices." He came down from the ladder, hammer in hand, and Niamh tossed him a cigarette. They both lit up. Niamh had gone back on the fags after Ciaran had left. Might as well kill herself with her own smoke, she'd decided, there was always someone else's around to breathe.

"Where's this heap of stones you're off to visit?"

"Don't know. Clon-something. Some monastery he rates, up on the Shannon —"

"Clonmacnoise?"

"That's it. Used to be where it was at about a thousand years ago. He's creaming himself. Bore the pants off anyone else."

"It's famous," Niamh said, "it's supposed to be really interesting. Everyone had a go at it — Vikings, Irish, Brits. You should go, you might just learn something."

Joss made a face. "Lay off, will you? I'm going, I'm not being given the choice. Want to come with us?"

———•◆•———

"Flattened," Niamh said, "twenty-six times in twelve years. Can you believe it?" She turned from the scattered gray monastery ruins to Joss. "Wake up, strap on the old sword, jump into the boat and we're off. Now, where'll we go today? I know — Clonmacnoise."

"Nah," Joss said. "Boring. Did that last year."

"So?" She rounded on him. "It's a really good raid, they have great altar treasures, churches to burn, monks just waiting to be disemboweled. You don't even have to walk far, you can get really close in the boat."

"I told you, we did that last year. You're such a nerd, Niamh, we can't just do the same things over and over, we'll lose respect."

"Okay, wise guy, you think of somewhere better."

Joss pantomimed thought, his forehead on his fist. Then he looked up brightly, as though a light had just gone on inside his head.

"I know, let's do Clonmacnoise. It's a really great raid — altar treasures, nuns to rape, monks to skewer, plus we haven't done it for at least six months."

"You're on," Niamh said. Together they took off down the boggy slope, arms and legs flying, Pippa plunging and bouncing behind them. A great cloud of lapwings got up from the rushes and took to the air, turning and weaving, loose wings dark against white bellies; the racing gray sky was filled with the wheeling birds. They broke and scattered and the sky scattered with them, they dropped and rose again and the sky rose too. Niamh and Joss stopped their wild flight. They pointed up at the birds, waved their arms about, ran on. Pippa plunged through the bog, sleek as a seal with dark mud, desperate to keep up. The Shannon gleamed and wound through its somber floodplain.

No one had much liked Clonmacnoise, its neat, sealed ruins and lawns and concrete paths, but they all liked the river, the empty jetty, the wide flood-meadows, the rainy wind. Pippa, used to the steep banks and inaccessible flow of the Blackwater, splashed cautiously about in the shallow fringes of the Shannon. Joss found a stick and dropped it almost in front of her nose. She stood in the water, quivering, then stretched her neck, seized the stick and carried it carefully in. Joss dropped the stick farther out, tempting the puppy into deeper water. Again, she brought it back.

Then the stick was too far out and she balked and wouldn't risk it. Joss waded out up to his knees in the icy water. He stood patiently by the stick, encouraging Pippa to come for it. Pippa plunged, sank, swam a few frantic strokes, grabbed the stick and made it back to the shore. They all cheered. She laid the stick at Hannie's feet. Joss waded back again, water pouring from his jeans and mud-soaked trainers.

The wind strengthened, it was getting colder, the somber light had deepened, they turned and faced back up the rise. Niamh plodded ahead, Hannie followed with her arm linked into Ned's, Joss and Pippa came behind, the puppy staggering with exhaustion. Joss reached down, caught her by the loose skin of her neck and heaved her onto his shoulder. She rode there, shivering and content, licking at his ear.

———◆———

A FEW DAYS later Hannie skipped a Waterford liaison with Thornton. She hadn't intended to, but she saw a ship leave its moorings on the quay and suddenly nothing would do but she had to smell salt water. She turned the car around and drove out to the coast and walked in the cold rainy air by the gray heave of the sea. Then she went to get Joss.

It was the effort he made to impress her that was getting to be too much. The house, the grounds, his things, his plans, his past, his future: everything endlessly displayed for her admiration. And she'd never cared for things or success, neither his possessions nor his attainments remotely impressed her. Sometimes she'd catch him looking at her and really seeing her (her un-twenty-eightness), and she'd see him wondering to himself why he was trying so hard to gain her admiration. Yet he couldn't seem to stop. Which made her still a challenge, despite her willingness to be bedded. He'd move on when something better presented itself, they both knew that, but in the meantime she had his attention. And she didn't give a toss about him, she hardly even cared about the sex.

She found that she liked going home to Ned, who was quiet and modest about the place, though he was no use in bed.

Chapter Fifty-four

HANNIE WAS SETTLED DEEP IN THE BIG MANGY ARMCHAIR, legs stretched in front of her, feet propped on a torn leather pouf. They had got through dinner and had moved to Vere's study to drink whiskey in front of a modest fire.

The study was narrow and high-ceilinged; there were sagging shelves heaped with jumbled volumes and piles of *National Geographics* and Sotheby's catalogs. The walls were smoky and studded with fox heads and photos of hounds and horses. A poster showing breeds of sheep was pinned up over the desk beside a portrait-study of a lovely young woman with fine skin and dreamy eyes that might once have been Alison. There were dogs everywhere, mostly old.

At least it's half warm in here, Hannie thought, most likely the only warm room in the house. A large part of Alison's energies seemed to be absorbed into making ends meet. Recycling was second nature, economies were complex, far-reaching, and always uppermost in her mind. Alison would be ruthless where her own welfare was concerned, Hannie speculated, but would preserve a few creature comforts for the beloved Vere. Suddenly Hannie was relieved that Ned hadn't landed her with a House: his friends and relations were quite enough without a moldering pile as well.

She shifted herself farther down in the chair and looked owlishly over her glass in parody of James. After the trials of dinner it was good to be completely comfortable. And the whiskey helped one forget the food. "One." Any minute now and she'd be talking like Marjorie. Her mind wandered. Perhaps she'd end up looking like Marjorie too? No Lord Tung then. At this moment that seemed like a definite loss. Ah well, perhaps she'd be past it by then anyway. It was even possible, if she hung on that long, that she might have *got her bearings, settled down, learned to belong,* or some other such euphemism for giving up and giving in.

"Wrong climate," Vere was saying to Ned, "better off with daffodils, northern sort of flower, temperate, doesn't mind rain, easier all around than lavender."

"Likes a bit of decent soil just the same," James put in. "And what about marketing, what good's a field full of flowers? He has to get them cut and bunched and sent off to where someone's going to buy them."

"Could be done. Not impossible, take a bit of organization . . ."

"Cost a bloody fortune. He'd never get his money back."

"He'd have to do his sums," Vere argued stubbornly. "Identify his market, cost his labor, that sort of thing."

James snorted.

"Change of plan," Ned said before Vere could get in a reply. "Change of plan, Hannie had a better idea, I've given up lavender, we're going into willow."

"Willow?" The brothers looked at him in disbelief. "You mean sallies?"

"Exactly," Ned said. "Sally wands for basket makers."

"You're out of your mind, Ned," Marjorie announced firmly. "The country's coming down with sallies, if you want to make a basket you can cut what you want when you want, no one in their senses is going to part with hard-earned cash for them."

"They do already," Ned said confidently. "A skilled man — or woman for that matter — a skilled man wants to spend his time making, not cutting and drying and sizing and storing, he's buying in willow that's ready-to-use and he's buying it in from England. There's a demand, I tell you, I've done the sums, collected up some information, basket-making's on the up and up."

"Hmm. Haven't noticed Danno going in for conspicuous consumption recently. Haven't noticed him driving a new car around the place or putting a decent engine on that boat of his."

"Not Danno, Danno cuts his own sallies, he makes a few creels and log-baskets when the fancy takes him, bottom end of the market, that's as far as he goes. It's not Danno I'm talking about, it's people who do it seriously, the ones who fill the orders in the smart craft shops, foreigners mostly, people who've come here to live an alternative lifestyle and found that basket-making's an economic way of doing it."

Half an hour later the argument was finally losing steam and Alison was filling up the glasses. Hannie had taken no part in it, she'd sat deep in her chair, half-listening to Ned and the stream of information he'd acquired from somewhere, half lost in her own wandering thoughts.

"Did you see that Dimbleby program?" Vere was addressing her.

"Not Dimbleby, Vere, Attenborough. He means that Attenborough man," Marjorie announced.

"Do I? So I do. Fascinating. Speeded-up film. Plants and seeds and the right places."

They all looked blank.

"How plants try to ensure their seeds have the best possible habitat," Alison said quietly.

"That's what I said — the lengths they go to. Always thought it was up to the birds and the wind. Not a bit of it — all organized — nothing left to chance. Showed you a plant on a wall — nothing foreign or exotic — just a little toadflax you'd see any day on any wall. Then they showed you what it does —" Vere paused dramatically and looked at their waiting faces.

"Speeded-up film," he announced. "Fascinating. It feels around on its wall, earmarks a crack or a crumbly bit, then reaches up where it wants its seeds to go and puts them there itself. Amazing. You could actually see the thing performing. . . ."

"Not so different, after all," James leered. Vere looked at him blankly. "Puts in the seed where it wants it," James crowed.

"Oh. Oh, yes, exactly so," Vere said. "It was incredible. And all sorts of examples . . ."

"What's a toadflax?" Hannie asked lazily.

"That little mauve pea-flower with the roundy leaves," Alison replied. "A yellow stain on its lip. Common — likes old walls." She smiled quietly at Hannie. "Vere likes these natural history programs," she explained. "He'd never watch the television to begin with. We got it for the children, Vere never wanted it, he only agreed because of the Olympics."

"Sport and wildlife," Vere said at Hannie. "I like the wildlife programs and the natural history."

"I like a decent documentary myself," James said. "Hate chat shows. Can't stand that Gay Byrne fellow. Pat Kenny makes me puke."

"You always watch Pat Kenny," Marjorie said indignantly.

"Still makes me puke."

"I watched the other night," Ned said. "Annaghmore was on. Or that's what they told me in the post office. But it wasn't on at all, it was only an interview with Thornton about the record business. Waste of time, really, Hannie had more sense — went to bed — but I wanted to see what he'd made of the place."

There was a small queer pause in the room, which Ned didn't appear to notice. Hannie did, though she didn't stir or try to move it on. At least now she knew how the land lay.

"We watched it too," Marjorie said. "To see the house." She swung around suddenly and addressed Hannie. "Weren't you curious?" she asked, something close to belligerence in her voice.

Hannie seemed to have slithered deeper into the chair; she had long since discarded her shoes, she wriggled her stockinged toes on the pouf.

"Curious?" she said to Marjorie. "No — why should I be? I have seen it, he has shown me all over, for me it is just a big house, the inside very clean and expensive and new. Really, it is wasted on me. I didn't know it before when the Cantelons had it, as all of you did, so the changes meant nothing to me. You should go and see it if you want to, he will show anyone, he is very proud of it, but you must be very interested and have lots of time. Really, it is rather boring."

There was gaiety in Hannie's face, and amusement. The slight foreignness of her voice and diction was accented. She looked up candidly at Marjorie. James snorted and Alison looked at the floor, but no one spoke. They were careful not to let their eyes stray to Ned, who had brought into their lives this woman who was making a fool of him and didn't know how to behave.

———•◆•———

"OH, COME ON, Niamh," Joss said, "don't be such a scaredy. Take it, it's a gas, you'll have a great time."

Niamh looked at the little pill lying in the palm of her hand. She took a big swig from her glass. The vodka tasted clean and cool.

"Where did you get it?" she asked him.

"Off Nora's nephew. Con, his name is. Good name, eh? Con by name and conning by nature, that's what I told him. He liked that. He's cool, she never knew a thing, the stupid cow. Thinks he's innocent and pure. She said we were a good influence on each other. Far out, eh? A good influence!"

Joss spoke fast, his voice was light and excited, he was pacing restlessly around the room as he talked. Niamh wondered what he'd already taken. Aside from the vodka he'd drunk with her, that was. She thought of telling him he'd had enough, but she knew that'd be red-rag-to-the-bull.

"She was right there, wasn't she, Niamh? Joss is always a good influence. Stupid fucking cow. She said I was good with the kids as well. And so I was, with my lovely bedtime stories out of this big old book that had been in Andrew's house when he was a kid. Ghosty poems, scary stories, Edgar Allan Poe, stuff like that. There was a great one about an earwig crawling into this man's ear, laying its eggs and the eggs hatching and maggots eating his brains out. All that stuff.

"Alana — that was the girl — she was younger but she was wised-up — if she didn't like something she just stuffed her fingers into her ears and watched my mouth till she saw I'd stopped reading. But the boy couldn't get enough and he had nightmares, wet his bed. Andrew went on at him, made him tell what scared him.

"Andrew was mad with me at the start, he was a whole load more copped-on than she was most of the time but he was silly about her, he let himself be talked around. Plus he was in a difficult position, he'd told her he'd read the book himself when he was a kid, but he couldn't have — obviously — he wouldn't have forgotten stuff like that. Anyway, Andrew says he doesn't like what I'm reading to them, says it's too frightening — which it definitely is.

"So I stop and the little kid goes off his food, he wets his bed worse, he's afraid to go to sleep cos he knows about the earwig that's eating out his brain on account of him telling his daddy. And you know what she does? You'll love this, Niamh, you really will. She decides it must be school, she rings the other mothers and it's the same story, half their kids have got the jitters as well, cos he's been telling them about the earwigs in their brains. Then she goes to the teacher and she wants to know why the kids are scared, what's going on, is that new priest that's coming in for religion *really* all right?" Joss sniggered delightedly.

"Too much, isn't it, Niamh? And she says to me, it's okay to read to them again, but maybe something a bit younger? *She* knows it's all right, of course she does, Alana's fine, but Andrew was an only child, he doesn't understand that children love being scared. And then she starts on about being little and her big sister telling them scary stories and them all sitting there, goggle-eyed and loving it, the fear and all that — and she gives me the *Flopsy Bunnies* to read to them, but by then it's way too late, I can read about lettuces and baby rabbits till the cows come home but every time Mr. McGregor comes on the scene I just whisper earwigs and hey presto — who needs Edgar Allan Poe?"

Joss stopped pacing abruptly and dumped himself sideways in the armchair with his legs over one arm. He lit a cigarette. Niamh watched him, despising him. She hated Joss like this: how degenerate and wicked he was, how clever and cool and immoral. She knew he was lying to build himself up because he was lonely and insecure, she knew she should ignore him and never ever act shocked or even surprised, but sometimes she wanted to tell him what she thought of what he was say-ing so badly she had to bite her lip to keep the words in.

It was like that now. She sat there, sipping at her vodka, saying noth-ing. She didn't dislike him as a human being, she told herself, she just wished he'd take his fuck-ups and his hang-ups somewhere else.

"It's amazing, it really is," Joss was saying. "If you showed a video of the stuff that's in that book, they'd lynch you, but it's a book and it's got a leather binding, so it must be okay. I mean, have you ever *read* Poe, Niamh? What a mind! He must have been on everything. They were, you know, those Victorians, it was the way they liked things. Quiet and neat on the surface and *wild* underneath, just wild. I mean, Elizabeth Fry was a laudanum-head, did you know that, Niamh? This famous Quaker — in there, reforming the prisons, giving everyone a piece of her mind — and she was a laudanum-head! I said that to one of those Quaker teachers at that poxy school and he just looked at me. 'It's very possible,' he said, 'yes, very possible, we are all human.'" Joss sniggered quietly to himself. "We are all human — I mean to *say* . . ."

Abruptly he stopped sniggering, threw his cigarette-end into the fire, swung his feet off the chair, and was up and pacing again.

"What are you hanging about for, Niamh, haven't you dropped that thing yet? You won't be scared, I promise, you won't have a bad time or anything, you'll have little bubbles in your blood and one huge big smile wrapped around your face and new red dancing shoes on your feet. . . ."

"I know what E is, Joss."

"Then what're you hanging about for? Come on, Niamh, throw it into yourself, I've got her car keys, we'll go into town, find ourselves a club, they won't be back for hours."

"I haven't got a license."

"So? You can drive, I can drive, who needs a license? What's the problem?"

"The problem is, Joss," she said, wishing she didn't feel so drunk, "the problem is, what if it's cut?"

"Cut? Would Joss give you stuff that's cut? What are you talking about, man? I've had this stuff, it's A-one, Niamh, believe me, it's A-one cool."

"It all looks the same, Joss," she said carefully, aware that her words were coming out a bit slurred, "but it isn't the same anymore. You have to be dead careful now, some of it's cut with a whole lot of shit. Dangerous shit. And a little bit of smack in it to make you think it's what it says it is and like it used to be." She finished in a rush and had another swallow from her glass. Joss was watching her very intently, a funny expression on his small white face. He pulled a chair out from the table, spun it around and sat down on it, his legs astride it and his arms folded across its back. He rested his chin on them and went on staring at her.

"You know something, Niamh," he said very quietly and gently, "I bet you were always careful. I bet you were so careful, you never took it even when it was *all* good stuff. In fact, Niamh, I bet you've never taken anything at all. Oh, I know — speed, acid, coke — you've tried them all, I heard you telling Ciaran. But I've just sussed you, Niamh, you're one of those Talk-ones, you're one of those ones that stashed the stuff and watched the others. Cos you want to be in there but you're much too careful to do it yourself, much too scared of losing control.

"I might have known what you'd be like." There was no missing the hard sneer in his voice now. "You're all pretend, Niamh. You're a fake, a rotten fake. If I hadn't heard you with my own ears moaning your head off under Ciaran I'd say you'd lied about that as well. And to think I was planning to give you some later on, just to make your night. To think I was going to dirty my beautiful cock on you."

For a moment Niamh thought she hadn't heard him right. She went white, then red. She sat numb. Then she pushed the pill across the table toward him. Her hand shook but she kept her hold on herself.

"And to think I thought you might be all right if someone gave you a chance," she said. "To think I thought you might be growing up. You're just a little boy, Joss, a smutty little wanker in the literal sense of the word. All boast and shit. And I knew that. I said it to Ciaran right at the start. And then, between the two of you, I forgot. For a while there — I have to admit it — I just forgot. So thank you for reminding me, Joss, thank you very much. It's one mistake I'll not be making again."

Chapter Fifty-five

VERE AND ALISON CAME OUT WITH THEM to see them off. It was two in the morning, cold and still. No moon, but the sky clear and mazy with stars. "Like the tropics," James said.

Not like the tropics, Hannie thought. These stars were glittering and sharp, not soft and large, like blossoms or moths. She moved away and stood waiting for Ned. Ned, knowing both worlds, Ned who could have bridged them for her if she'd let him.

She didn't want a bridge, that was the truth of it. She didn't want this new world, didn't want to think and adapt and review her life, just wanted to go on living it, such as it was, without the pain of reflection.

But deeper down she yearned for something beyond even that, she yearned for her first life, a world lived milky and close to the ground, the lost voices in the darkness like small birds talking.

And she could never have that back. Never, never, never, no matter how she longed, or what she did, or how she tried.

Behind her Vere had started to sing and the others joined in.

O little town of Bethlehem,
how still we see thee lie
above thy deep and dreamless sleep
the silent stars go by . . .

They went on singing, carol after carol, everyone knowing most of the words, someone always knowing the bit where the others forgot and the voices thinned. They'd waver, wait for a familiar phrase, resume; a sort of gladness in them when they had the words again, a peace and contentment in their faces and their voices that was so tangible that Hannie had to look away.

Peace and contentment. Like a built wall, Ned thought, and his wife there, standing alone on the other side of it. And how could it be otherwise? She was of another race, another world; she didn't know even the simple sweetness of these carols that they'd sung together in this valley since their earliest childhood. He should cross the wall to be with her, he knew that, but he didn't want to leave off singing, he didn't want to leave belonging with his comrades now he stood beside them after years away.

———•—•———

IT WAS LATE, Niamh had polished off most of the remaining vodka. But she wasn't shaken anymore, she had got over Joss and his little outburst, had retreated into her adult self and put his juvenilia into perspective.

And there was a certain steadying satisfaction in having been, at last, proved right. It wasn't just her imagination. Joss *did* fancy her. He *did* fantasize about her, she was right to be wary of him.

She remembered Ciaran's ridicule when she'd suggested it. Joss was just a kid, he'd said, lonely, trying to find his bearings after Africa. Sure, he would fantasize in a general sort of way — it was a sexual age — but not Niamh, Niamh at twenty-one would seem about of an age with his grandmother. Always supposing Joss had anything as normal as a grandmother.

She should relax, Ciaran had said, stop being sexually paranoid. Less paranoia, more sex.

Niamh remembered the look she had given him. Then she remembered the next bit. She *had* relaxed, but she'd made him climb the stairs for it. In case Ned called, or Hannie called, or Joss called. He'd said she was ridiculous, but worth it. She'd forgotten everything for a while, but afterward the uneasiness was still there with her.

And then she'd forgotten the uneasiness as well. She'd disregarded her own warnings, let Joss confide in her, opened herself to his influence, let his thoughts slide into her mind.

Like the shadow of a hawk, she thought, sliding over the yellow grass.

Yellow grass. Now where did that come from? The grass here wasn't yellow, it was green. And yet she could see it, the dark shadow slipping sideways and very fast. Yellow grass: African grass. But she'd never been to Africa. . . .

She'd go to bed now, she decided, she wouldn't drink anymore or think anymore, she'd just go to bed, sleep off the booze and get it all straight in the morning.

Now, where was the top of the bottle? She fumbled around on the table, picking things up and putting them down again. There it was, where she'd already looked, there beside her gloves and Hannie's car keys. Funny how much easier it was to think than do when you'd had a few drinks. She screwed the top down on the dregs of the vodka. Nothing like locking the stable door when the horse has mostly gone.

"Now Niamh," she said aloud to herself, "fire, lights, doors. Then you can fill your hot-water bottle and crawl into bed and sleep."

She banked the fire, positioned the guard and put the kettle on to boil. She was standing beside it, hot-water bottle at the ready, when she heard the cough outside the window. She was startled, but no more, there was always some animal or other with a cough, it sounded more like a heifer than a sheep but Ned didn't have any cattle in the near field.

The coughing noise came again, but this time it was much louder and there was the sound of a bin lid falling. Perhaps it was a cat, perhaps it was Joss, drunk and stoned, bumbling around bumping into things.

She hated Joss, his crawly voice and his ugly words and his small white face, but it didn't occur to her to be afraid of him. It never had, that's what Ciaran hadn't understood, he was just ridiculous and nasty and she was a fool to have tried to help him, to have let him hang around. She took the torch down from its hook and pulled open the door —

She was scared when she saw it, who wouldn't have been? The blazing cross with the great bird on it, its wings stretched, writhing and twisting, black against the leaping flames.

For a moment she almost panicked, then something strong and detached and self-observing came up inside her. She was scared all right, but not as scared as she might have been, not terrified, it was too kitsch, too Ku Klux Klan, and besides she'd been thinking Joss when she saw it, and she knew Joss, knew the gothic coils of his imagination. She made a huge effort, made herself look at it for what it was: a silly farce, no more, a cheap stunt like the legs, just bits of tarred wood, just a crucified bird — not a bird at all — just one of Danno's mangy old stuffed pheasants.

These thoughts flashed through her, then the detachment was gone and rage came in its place to save her.

She clutched tight to the torch and stormed out, shouting as she ran — "Shite, pig, bollix, dirty-minded-little-shyster" — she didn't know what she was saying, she didn't care, but she wouldn't let him put this on her, the fucker, she wouldn't let him beat her.

She ran right up to the stupid hackneyed blazing thing, she flew at it, kicked at it, her boot hit the rotten timber, the arm of the cross fell slantwise, burning feathers flew up into the night, the bird writhed as though it was alive or newly dead, one claw lifted horribly through the licking flames —

She was still attacking it, kicking and swearing, the tears running down her face and her breath coming in sobs when she saw the other thing, the long slim form hanging from the branches of the apple tree, dark ropes looping from it, turning slowly in the fiery light —

She stopped kicking and moved closer. And all at once, without even looking again though she did look again, she knew it was Pip, hanged Pip, her soft little belly slashed, her guts spilling out in thin black ropes.

Joss.

She turned and ran hard for the light and the open door, plunged through it, slammed it shut behind her, turned the key, plunged on through the house to the other door, her shaking hand already on the key to lock it fast against him.

Then she heard his laugh, low and soft and coming from the room behind her.

Her hand flew to the knob, she yanked open the door, fell into the night, terror at her back, terror driving her forward, feet slipping and sliding on the muddy path, running and running, heart pounding, breath coming ragged and wild, his feet coming closer and closer behind her. . . .

—◆—

HANNIE WAS SITTING hunched into herself in the car, staring sightlessly out of the side window. It was her usual don't-speak-to-me-posture, so Ned didn't. He was tired anyway and fed up with the effort of it all, with feeling angry with her, with feeling bad about her, with feeling a failure.

There was something going on about Thornton, he didn't know what, but the others knew, he'd felt it in the room when he brought up that program he'd watched that hadn't been about Annaghmore after all, but about the record business. Something — he didn't know what — but whatever it was, it wasn't good.

Ned knew now that this marriage had been a mistake. He was too old for her, their backgrounds were too different, he couldn't make her happy no matter how he tried, he couldn't give her enough to make her life here meaningful. And he'd no one to blame but himself, he'd married her because he wanted her here, simple as that, he should never have let himself persuade her to it.

He'd got nothing for himself either; she had turned his life upside down, filled his waking hours with an unbearable, unfulfillable yearning for what she couldn't give him, destroyed his peace of mind. Even Joss had done badly, had gained little beyond a certain material security; it might even be that this marriage had brought his demons closer in on him.

Suddenly he didn't like anyone — neither himself, nor his friends, nor her, either. He wished profoundly that he'd stayed at home and never found her, that he had accepted his lot and gone quiet and lonely into old age and death.

The lights were still on in the cottage when they turned into the drive, the yellow squares of its windows shining through a net of branches. Joss would still be at Niamh's, Hannie thought, she'd better go and winkle him out, though Ned hadn't nagged about Niamh's so much since the trip to Clonmacnoise. She sighed and fished around down the side of the Land Rover seat for her other glove. Scarves, hats, gloves, coats, boots — she couldn't get used to the clutter of things you needed here every time you opened an outside door.

"Where's the Volkswagen?"

Hannie was bent sideways trying to retrieve the errant glove. She could feel it, could get a hold with the tips of two of her fingers, but when she pulled her hand came away and the glove stayed where it was.

"Bloody thing must be caught."

"Hannie, the Volkswagen, surely you put the Volkswagen away before we left?"

Hannie hauled herself upright. "What? Of course I did, what's wrong with you, you must be going bli——" She stared at the shadowy space between the Land Rover and the tractor. "Oh shit, shit, shit, shit, shit." She had the door open and was out of the Land Rover in one movement. "Joss!" she yelled into the darkness beyond the shed door. "Joss, where are you, you bloody fucking little nuisance! Where's the car, where's the keys, and where the hell are you?"

No answer. She set off furiously for the cottage. Ned saw its outside light go on, heard a door open and close, a pause, and then all the lights went off at once and a few minutes later Hannie reappeared.

"There's no one there now, but they've been there, they must have gone off in the car, I must have left my keys out." She stared at Ned. "I didn't know Niamh could drive?"

"Neither did I, but she's farm-reared, she'll drive a bit though she probably hasn't a license. Can Joss?"

"Same. He can drive a bit but not very well, and no license. Plus they're drunk, there's an empty bottle of vodka on the table."

"Where could they have gone?"

"Sin city — Dungarvan. Joss is always pestering me about some club there, I don't know what it's called but it shouldn't be hard to find, I can't imagine there'll be more than one." She had her hand on the Land Rover door as she spoke. Ned put his hand on her arm.

"If that's where they've gone then you might as well leave them to it. It's nearly three, they can't be much longer, at this hour in the morning Dungarvan's like a grave."

"They might go back to someone's house."

"Then you won't be able to find them anyway."

She turned and faced him. "Something's wrong, Ned, I'm sure something's wrong, I want to try —"

Ned shook his head. "Go to bed, Hannie, they'll be home soon, and if they're not then driving around looking for them isn't going to help. Besides, the Land Rover's tank's nearly empty and the spare can's in the Volkswagen."

"I might find them."

He shook his head again. "There's three different roads they could take, you'll just go around in circles till you run out of petrol."

She stared at him. "Shit, shit and shit again. I hope to God Niamh's driving."

Chapter Fifty-six

HANNIE LAY AWAKE. Sometimes a floorboard creaked, a door eased shut, a window rattled unaccountably in its frame. Each time a sound came she tensed and lay in the cold dark straining for more sounds, for steps on the stairs, water moving in the pipes, a too-carefully closed door. Some time after five she knew it was hopeless, he hadn't come in, she wasn't going to sleep, she might as well get up and go and check at Niamh's. . . .

She woke with a start; a noise had disturbed her, steps on the landing, a bright narrow light-stripe was shining under the door. She sat up. There was something she had to remember. She stared into the thinning darkness, at the shapes that were forming themselves in the room.

Joss.

The steps had stopped but the landing light was still on. She listened again, then threw off the blankets and reached for a sweater. She pulled trousers over her nightdress, bundling its thick folds up around her waist.

There was no light on in Joss's room, no clothes were tossed around, the bed was empty and unslept in, the room icy and uninhabited.

But the footsteps she'd heard?

Ned, going out to the loo, making his way back again to bed.

Hannie laid breakfast but she didn't eat, nor had she meant to, she just wanted to give him a few more minutes in which to have got back;

to delay a fraction longer before opening Niamh's door and finding him really there. Then she put on her boots, took a coat from the hook and went out into the yard. It had rained heavily in the night and the dank air clung to her face, the thin daylight creeping and licking like a cat, insinuating for a place in this interlude between dark and dark.

She went into the long stone shed where the cars were kept. A smell of mold, a scuffle of rats in the corner. No Volkswagen.

"They're not back, Hannie." Ned was standing behind her. "No one in the cottage, no sign of the car. I think it's time we thought about the Guards."

"Not yet." The words came out too quick and hard; she made an effort, dropped a key, she wanted her argument to sound like reasoned thinking. "It's early yet, they might have stayed over with someone, they both had a skinful, they're probably still sleeping it off." She glanced at Ned. She was getting through. "I don't think we should go panicking," she went on. "We should give them an hour or two, let them wake up and get to a phone, after that we can think about calling the Guards."

"Something might have happened."

"But it might not. And they've neither of them got a license and they must both have been well over the limit. Why don't you go and have some breakfast, then phone the hospitals in case and check admissions? I'll take the Land Rover, have a scout around, I can get petrol at Delaney's on the way."

"I can't find Pip, either —"

"Don't worry about Pip, she'll turn up, and so will they."

———•◆•———

WHEN HANNIE got back two hours later the local Garda car was in the drive and a muddy blue Cortina was parked in front of the house. She swore to herself, bit her lip, took a deep breath and prepared, once more, to perform.

There were four of them in the kitchen when she walked in: Ned and John Comerford were sitting at the table, Garda Mahon was talking quietly into the phone and a tall rangy brother of Niamh's called Niall was standing at the window drinking a mug of tea. Ned got up and came toward her. None of the others moved.

"Hannie —" he started and stopped. Hannie looked at him. Her hands wanted to fly to her mouth but she held them rigidly by her side. She could see anger in Ned's face, anger and shame, and behind this darkness she could see compassion and she knew it was for her. She stood very still. "Something's happened," she said, and it was a statement not a question.

Chapter Fifty-seven

THE FACTS SEEMED TO TELL THEIR OWN STORY: a chase in the dark, the path to the river trampled and beaten down, skid marks on the bank where someone might have lost their footing and gone in. Plus the missing car, the cross, the hanged and gutted dog.

Frogmen came, and Garda specialists. For five days they dragged the river and searched through the woods and the bogs and the fields. They found nothing, neither a drowned body nor a live one nor any sign of the Volkswagen. At the end of the time they packed up their gear and left. The radio said that the search had been abandoned, it was possible that a body or bodies had been washed out to sea.

The radio had given out a description of both the missing young people. There were also reports of a hanged dog, a Ku Klux cross and some unusual sculptures that the Guards had found in the cottage where the young woman lived. There were no reports of foul play, or of either of the young people being wanted for any reason other than to ascertain their whereabouts, but there was speculation in the newspapers and locally everyone was way ahead of what was written down.

— *It's murder, so it is, let no one tell you different, he's after raping her and then pushing her into the river. . . .*

— *There's no body, no proof that she's dead even. . . .*

— *They'll find her, she's drowned sure enough. . . .*

—— *If she slipped, it isn't murder, it's an accident, even he frightened her into it.* . . .

—— *Accident? I suppose you'll be telling me next she was traipsing about in the dark for her health.* . . .

—— *Maybe it was the other way around. Maybe it's the boy went into the river.* . . .

—— *It was the girl all right, they know from the footprints.* . . .

—— *Maybe she crawled out and legged it, maybe he helped her? Maybe the two of them's driving around the place right now, listening to the radio and laughing?*

—— *You've been at the videos. They say she was a quiet sort of a girl, not one of your Bonnie-and-Clydes.* . . .

—— *Then what about them things the Guards found in her house? Sculptures, isn't that what they called them in the paper? Naked legs, hung from the ceiling. Maybe that's what gave the boy ideas.* . . .

—— *There was more to it than just ideas. There was another fella living there with her, wasn't there, a fella that cut out and left her? Well? If she'd do it with one, sure why not with another . . . ?*

It was eight days now, eight days since he'd found Pip's hanging body and phoned Niamh's parents' home to ask was she there. No, she wasn't there, John Comerford had said. Nor had he been prepared to wait while Hannie went looking. When he'd finished speaking to Ned he had phoned the Guards.

Ned couldn't think that Niamh lived, he believed her drowned, her body trapped in long streamers of weed or caught in a tangle of mud and sunken branches. The search might be off but he still spent hours walking the banks and staring at the brown flow of the river. Sometimes in his mind he saw the drift of her hair in the silted, underwater light.

At these times he felt he could bear anything if only they could find her body and bury it. He dreaded the thought of a funeral, but he wanted her laid to rest.

Laid to rest. The euphemism that had once angered him in its blandness now seemed like literal truth. He wanted to see her lowered into the sanctuary of the earth, private and quiet and safe from any further violation. *Here lies all that was mortal of Niamh Comerford.* It would be settled then, her mortal death could begin to take its due proportion.

But part of Ned wouldn't believe what was happening to him. He felt that it couldn't be true, she couldn't be dead, she'd come back from wherever she was and explain where she'd been these last days and all that had happened. And if she didn't come back, if the nightmare was true, it was some hideous and unjust visitation. He'd been given no warning, had done nothing to earn this disaster, was entirely innocent and unprepared.

Then sometimes it seemed the opposite. He remembered John Comerford's face when he'd looked at the sculptures his daughter had made, how he'd turned and asked Ned if he'd known of them and what they meant. If only he'd had more foresight, Ned thought, if only he hadn't allowed himself to hope for the best over Joss, if only he'd acted on his own forebodings when he saw the Legs. . . .

Sometimes he thought none of these things, he was just lost in the squalor and uncertainty of it all.

He tried not to think of the puppy, her belly slit open, swinging from the apple tree.

He tried not to think of Hannie, except as his wife who was innocent and in great need.

And he tried not to hear the voices that said there was no innocence, the boy wouldn't be as he was without the mother.

———•◆•———

HANNIE WAS TAUT as a spring; she had smoked and drunk coffee and answered the Guards' questions with a strange, robotic concentration. Ned was amazed at her self-discipline, the weight was falling off her and the circles under her eyes were black and deep, but she spoke always carefully and evenly, as though her patience could have no end. He watched as the Guards began to assemble the facts and arrive at conclusions. He heard the tone of their questioning change from sympathy, to suspicion, to a hostility that was barely veiled. He tried to speak of this shift to her, he thought he should help her to talk, but she only glanced at him and reached for another cigarette.

"They've made up their minds," she said, lighting it carefully, blowing out the match.

He looked away then; the Guards weren't the only ones who'd made up their minds. He didn't know what she thought or believed or hoped and he didn't want to ask, he didn't want to hear her try to make a case for Joss, he didn't want to have to go along with what she said.

When she wasn't answering questions she worked. She started on the scullery then she did the other rooms downstairs, mindless keep-yourself-occupied activity, everything pulled out and scrubbed and scoured and put away. Then she began on the fabric of the rooms: walls were washed, skirtings and window frames filled, broken tiling scraped and cleansed and recemented into place.

When the divers and searchers packed up she stopped pulling the house apart and putting it back again, she seemed less taut, she even seemed to be making an effort to eat. Ned was relieved; he thought it was release from the constant pressure of their presence. It was only later that he realized that that must have been about the time she heard from Joss.

———•◆•———

VERE AND ALISON CAME, and James and Marjorie. Ned took them into the drawing room and poured them whiskey. Hannie hadn't said anything when she saw the cars, but she'd cleared off.

It was awkward. Ned wasn't, at that moment, glad to see them, but he was glad that they'd come, he understood the extent of the gesture.

James had plainly been briefed to keep his mouth shut, so they talked about anything except what was on all their minds. At the very end Vere said stiffly that they were all very sorry about "this awful business." They were old friends, he continued, Ned could, of course, count on their support at any time and in any way. . . .

Everyone had stared hard at their glass or some picture on the wall.

Even James refused a refill when it was offered and it was with relief that Ned ushered them out into the chilly March darkness that smelled at once so empty and so fresh.

Alison hung back. She caught his arm urgently and lifted her face up to look directly into his eyes.

"So hard for you," she said. "For both of you. If Hannie wants to talk . . . ?" Ned tried to say something polite and reassuring but nothing came out.

"I know she doesn't now," Alison said, "but I'd like her to know that she can. It must be a very lonely business."

Ned nodded and watched her walk across the thin gravel and get into the car. When he turned around to go back into the house he felt like weeping he was so sorry for himself and for them all.

Hannie was in the hall. She was leaning against the opened door in the shadows, her arms folded, watching.

"Poor Ned," she said into the darkness, her voice bitter and light and mocking. "Poor Ned, what a mess, what a stupid mistake you have made, consorting with a woman like me."

He couldn't see her but there was something in her voice and he knew that she was close to breaking. "No, Hannie," he answered her quietly, "you are wrong, a mess it may be, but I've made no mistake."

And he meant it, but he didn't know why, because it was hard to bear what his life had become.

Chapter Fifty-eight

WHEN JOSS RANG THE GUARDS HAD JUST LEFT, Ned was out in the fields, it was Hannie who picked up the phone.

He was in Galway, he'd dumped the car and hitched, he said, he was staying with people he knew, people he'd met through Nora's nephew Con. He was all right, they were cool, everything was cool, but he needed money. He wouldn't tell her any more than that, wouldn't answer questions or give her an address, he said he was just letting her know the gist so she could work on the cash situation.

He sounded high as a kite and jittery with nerves. She asked him where Niamh was and he said he didn't know and he didn't care. Then he told her to get off his back and he put down the phone.

———•◆•———

SHE WAITED. A day passed, two days passed, the Guards rang to say they hadn't found the car or Joss. Another day passed.

The phone rang when they were both in the kitchen. Ned answered it, listened to the silence and put it down. "Must be a wrong number."

She nodded and said nothing, her face blank. People locally were garrulous, they never just listened then hung up, if they got a wrong number they wanted to know why you weren't who they thought you should be.

SHE WAS READY for Joss, she had the money from the ebony fan still, and a bit more that she'd siphoned off from times when Ned had forgotten himself and given her cash. It wouldn't do Joss for long, nothing would ever keep Joss going long, there would always be another phone call, he would always always need more money than he had.

She was trying to keep the affair with Thornton going, making her absences a little obvious so Ned would smell a rat and draw the wrong conclusions when Joss rang. She did her best but it was hard work, she was sick and tired of him and he was growing leery of her now he'd caught the sort of talk that was going around.

Joss phoned again. This time he caught her by herself and he had an address for her to send money to. He wasn't living there, he said, he was moving around, but he'd tell them to expect a letter and they'd get it to him.

She drove to Youghal and posted the money in cash. Afterward she went to visit Thornton. She wanted to be seen doing something she shouldn't be doing so people would remember that and forget whatever else they might have noticed.

THE LAMBING STARTED, the inexorable spring cycle, a busy, urgent relief from the tense hours of watching and waiting. Ned needed help; Mick came every year, but suddenly he was promised to a cousin near Clonmel.

Ned showed Hannie the basics and that was enough; she picked up the rest, she had the knack, which he didn't have, despite his experience. She liked the whole process, but especially the difficult births, liked plunging her soapy hand into the hot depths of the ewe, feeling around for the lambs' tangled legs, aligning them for easy passage. To her surprise she found she liked the ewes as well. They were different in the shed, not just stupid and infuriating, but female creatures, patient and suffering and courageous. She enjoyed being with them and helping them; it was practical, immediate and satisfying.

At night they worked in shifts, each one calling on the other if there was a run of lambs, the births bunching together, the ewes needing more help. They kept erratic hours, left out food for each other, fell in and out of their unmade beds, lived frantic, unreal lives and were grateful for the urgent occupation. Anything, so as not to have to wait for news and think.

Ned tried not to watch Hannie, he tried not to wonder who might be putting down the phone when he answered it, nor to register when she came back in the car and didn't say where she'd been. Once he stepped out of the lambing shed and saw her through an upstairs window, standing dressed against the light when he'd thought her dead asleep in her bed. Instinctively, he took a step back into the shadows, stood a moment, then made himself reenter the shed. If Joss was in the area and she was going to him, then so be it, he would not spy. But neither could he play blind and deaf much longer. He knew he must make himself talk to her soon, but he desperately didn't want to.

Ned was on his way out through the scullery when the next call came. He kept going, pretending he hadn't heard, though she knew that he had. She let it ring a dozen times while she watched Ned disappear around the corner of the shed, then she lifted it and said her name quietly into the mouthpiece.

Something had gone wrong, he'd trusted someone who'd let him down, the scumbag, he'd had to move on —

He didn't know these new people, but they were cool, they were into things in a big way. It was all working out, he'd be laughing in a couple of weeks, but he had to show cred, to buy into the deal, he had to have more money and he had to have it now —

"How much?" Hannie asked. Joss named a sum.

She laughed out loud, a bitter, disbelieving laugh, though she didn't know why she was surprised, she'd always known Joss would get more expensive as each year passed.

"How much d'you have left?"

"Nothing, not a bean — that scumbag Doran ripped me off. I trusted him, just wait till I see Con, I'll tell him all about his so-called friends. . . ."

Hannie interrupted. She had no more money, there was no chance of a sum like that and there never would be; he'd better wake up, stop daydreaming, and put it out of his head for good and all. . . .

He laughed, the laugh high and wild.

"Come on, Mother, I've told them all about you, what an ace mover you are, how you can get anything together, no problem at all, Mother, *pas de problème* . . ."

Mother. That word. He only ever called her that when his back was to the wall, when he was trying to make her do what he knew she would not or could not do, when he was at his wits' end.

So she told him there were no more moves, this was it, the end of the line, she had nothing left to sell; she would try to borrow something but it wouldn't be much and he'd have to make it last.

And if and when she could get some more he would have to make that last too, and it would be like that always, there would be no deals, no windfalls, not now, not ever, so he'd better take a long hard look at just what lay ahead.

He had a choice. He could come home and face what had happened and she'd fight for him and support him and it would be hard — she wasn't pretending otherwise — but it mightn't be as hard as he thought. Or he could stay away, change his name, find some work. She'd send him what she could when she could, but that was the future.

"Home," he said, his voice incredulous. "When have I ever had a home? When have I ever had anything except trailing along behind you, Mother? What have I ever had but what you've got left over when you've finished shagging some man, or doing whatever it was you had it in mind to do?

"Face things? You mean tell them my side of the story, Mother? Tell them the truth, tell them their precious Niamh was drunk and out of her head, tell them Virgin-Mary-Niamh was trying to make it with me, that all that Ku Klux Klan stuff was her idea, that she was so bombed nothing would do her but to go swim in the river, nothing would stop her, and if I hadn't held back I'd be as drowned as she is. . . ."

Hannie went cold and still. She held the receiver tight, with part of her mind she watched the knuckles stand in bluish knolls on her hand.

"Tell them all that, Mother?" Joss was saying. "Hold out my hands for them to lock the cuffs on, Mother, for them to send me down and throw away the key?"

He was crying now, she could hear his sobs in the silence. She steeled herself. Her voice seemed to come from a dingy room a long way off. "What about Pippa, Joss?"

"Pippa? What about her? I told her and told her, she kept following me, wagging her tail and yapping, wanting to be picked up, getting on my nerves. I tried to shut her in the kitchen but she got out, the stupid little cunt, she was stupider than Niamh, she wouldn't leave me alone, I couldn't help it. . . ."

His voice was high and hysterical and he started to beg. He begged her not to abandon him, to find some money, any money, even if it wasn't enough to cut him in on this deal, to stand by him, not to tell, to save him. He couldn't come back, she knew that, she knew what would happen if he came back, how everyone always took one look at him and hated him, how they wouldn't believe Niamh had slipped, how they wouldn't stop until they'd fucked him and destroyed him; and she was all he had, he'd do anything except come home, anything, anything she wanted, he'd promise anything. . . .

Hannie stood clinging on to the phone, letting the silence run on. Then she took hold of herself. She told him she loved him and would never abandon him. She said he should come back — no one knew what had happened — no one thought he'd pushed Niamh — if he came now, of his own accord, it would go better for him. But if he couldn't, it was all right, she'd leave Ned, find work, they would manage somehow.

But he didn't want that. He didn't want her around, interfering, messing things up, he just wanted the money. If he had money he could do it by himself, that's what he was saying, didn't she understand English?

He'd do fine by himself, much better than when he was with her, but he needed a start, he had to have money.

He was away then, high as a kite, he said he knew she loved him really, but he couldn't have her around just then — maybe later — or she could stay with old Ned, he didn't mind, he'd come and see her, take her out, give her a spin in some decent wheels. . . .

But he wouldn't give her his address in case she went all motherly on him and had to come and see him. He'd ring again, he said, he was counting on her, he knew she could get it together, she always did, she was the best he knew, he'd be in touch to tell her where to send it.

Hannie put down the phone and sat on the chair beside it. She knew then that Joss was doomed whether he came back or stayed away. He would never find work, he would go on the game or deal or steal or all three, and even in that world he wouldn't make it, he was too wild, too unbalanced, it would destroy him or he would destroy himself.

She knew she couldn't help him or change him and this knowledge made no difference, she still had to go on trying, she still had to act, to act against judgment, to act without hope.

And she knew she couldn't bear it but she'd have to bear it, and she could tell no one, and no one could help her. Then she thought of Niamh, drowned in the river, and for the first time since it happened Hannie wept; she wept for herself and she wept for lost, crazy Joss and she wept for Niamh, whose life had been swept away in this sad, ugly game they must go on playing to the end.

———◆———

"WAS THAT JOSS on the phone?"

Hannie didn't turn around. She went on washing the dishes, lifting them out of the water, placing them on the rack. She mightn't have heard him.

"He's been ringing you, hasn't he?" Ned asked her back. "The

Guards think you're sending him money, they think you know where he is. Is it true, Hannie? Have you sent him money? Do you know where he is?"

"No," she said, still with her back turned. "I don't know where he is. I did, but I don't anymore. I did send some money. Then he moved on. Any more questions?" She hauled a big saucepan out of the suds and dumped it down on the drainer. Ned didn't answer her challenge.

"He phoned once, but we had a row, he wouldn't leave an address. He hasn't phoned since — that was someone else — it was a bad row we had, he won't ring again, the Guards can follow me, open my letters, tap the phone, it won't do them any good."

"Don't be so melodramatic, Hannie."

"I'm not being melodramatic. And stop hiding behind the Guards — *you* think he's phoning, *you* think I'm sending him money. . . ."

"Well you are, you just said so."

She ignored him. She swished the cloth around in the water, wrung it out, wiped down the draining board with sure strong hands.

Ned stood watching her. He wanted to believe her but he didn't.

"Where did you send the money?" he asked, aware that he wasn't asking her where she'd got it.

"Belfast."

"Belfast?"

"He went to Belfast. Someone he knew through Ciaran." She started on the table where they had just eaten.

"And where did the last phone call come from?"

"England. He took the boat."

"That was convenient."

She went on wiping. There was a silence.

"Sit down, Hannie. I want to talk to you."

She looked at him then.

"And what if I don't want to sit down? What if I don't want to talk?"

Ned sighed. He took off his reading glasses, pinched the bridge of his nose as though to ease something.

"Hannie, you're not helping him, you're not doing him any favors.

You think you are, I can see that, you think you're fighting for him, but you're not, you're only fighting off the consequences of the things he's done." Ned spoke slowly and carefully, his eyes shut, his fingers still pinching his nose. "You can't put the clock back, Hannie, you can't change things for him or make them all right, all you can do is help him to face what he's done."

Hannie tossed her head back. It was a small, impatient movement of scorn. "How would you know what he's done?" she asked bitterly. "How would anyone? No one was there, no one saw anything, but you've all made up your minds."

Ned stared at her blank, hostile face, its cornered exhaustion, and his heart went out to her. He forgot Niamh, forgot her family, his duty, the talk about Richard Thornton that was reaching him now around every corner, all he thought about was helping her through this despair.

He said she was making things harder for Joss, that the longer he stayed away the worse it looked.

He spoke gently, not hectoring her as he might have done.

He said he knew she loved Joss, but sometimes love wasn't about shielding, it was about letting the person you loved move forward to meet their fate. It was about helping them to do it.

Hannie stared at him with contempt in her eyes.

"Who'll believe Joss?" she asked. "Who'll believe him or help him or take his side? The Guards? Niamh's family? You?

"Spare me, Ned. There isn't even a body, but Joss has been found guilty. It's all his fault, he did it all, and Niamh is white and Joss is black and there's no color called gray.

"And afterwards? After he's come home and faced this impartial reception committee? You know how he is with authority, you know how he puts people's backs up, you know what would happen to Joss if he went to prison. And yet you can preach to me? You can say I should help him meet this fate of his? This is your best advice?"

She stood there, challenging him, all anger and defiance and despair.

He was suddenly sick of her. He was sick of it all — his life, this mess, the raw wound inside him that was Niamh. He wanted no more to do with her. He hit down on the table hard with his opened hand, then slammed out through the door.

———•◆•———

HE'D ONLY REALLY let himself think about Hannie, he hadn't allowed himself to think about Niamh, except to go on looking for her body. Partly because things were as they were, and there might yet be some miracle. Partly because of his own loss. He couldn't walk past her cottage, couldn't bear to think he'd never talk to her or hear her laugh or meet her steady, serious gaze again. Butterflies and moths he found unendurable.

Hannie was right, he had made up his mind, Joss's restless brittle delinquency had destroyed her.

He stood now in the darkness, his back against one of the cherry trees, pressing into it, seeking the comfort of its old hardness. He heard a dog in the distance, then another, the bleat of lambs, the small hard scream of a rabbit taken by a stoat. He smelled the wet grass, the river meadows, heard the sough of the wind rustling the ivy massed in the hearts of the unleafed trees. The darkness was soft, clouded, complete. Without moon or stars.

He thought of Niamh, how she'd come into his life like a trust, how he'd been excited by her, had thought the world of her and tried to help her. He'd identified — Hannie was right there too — he'd thought she was as he'd been himself when starting out. Then slowly he'd come to see that she was different.

And he'd minded that. He'd been disappointed in her and had stopped thinking the world of her. And then, when he was used to his disappointment, he found he'd grown deeply attached to her.

He thought of Hannie. How he hadn't loved her when he'd married her, had simply wanted to have her in his life.

How he loved her now, but at a price that was too high.

How he set this love of his on the scales against everything else in the world that he lived by and valued, and it did not weigh heavy enough.

He felt like a man who wanted to leave something down and walk away from it, something precious that he'd wanted very hard for a long time. Then, when he could nearly have it, the effort of it had proved too great, all the good had been driven from it, and all that he wanted was not to want it anymore. He felt there would be a flat calm peace in such a withdrawing, an end to hoping and wanting, an end to uncertainty and pain.

But he could not make this withdrawal. In spite of himself, he could neither erode nor negate his feelings.

And he could not leave her so undefended, even though he longed to.

He left the sanctuary of the cherry tree. He got out the Land Rover and drove away from the shadowy house in its nest of trees. He didn't want to talk to anyone or be with anyone, he was too low and ashamed to want anything but the night.

He headed south, drove the dark empty roads, turned on to winding, unmarked byways, kept on until he smelled the salt in the air and felt the road run out and the wheels muffle on sandy grass. He left the Land Rover and found a hollow under the lip of a field where it fell away into the sand of a long white beach he had known since his childhood. He sat there, hearing the roar and slap of the sea, its rising and falling, the low notes of the roosting waders talking in their sleep.

Funny thing, loyalty, he thought. You never knew what would call it up or where you would place it until it was placed and your choice made. Not your choice at all, but your heart's choice, and there was little you could do to help yourself, even when most of you wanted no part in your heart's decision. He had thought it was about ethics and codes, what was right, what was wrong, but he was discovering a deeper, stronger way of being that could not be gainsaid.

He had gone to the Comerfords' farm when the search was called off, but Niall had come out to intercept him even before he reached the door.

Had he news? Niall had asked, and Ned had shaken his head and said he'd only come to say again that he was sorry. Niall had said his father wouldn't see him. Ned had nodded and turned away.

Then he'd turned back. "Tell your father she's my wife, the boy's her son."

There it was. Hardly a wife at all except in the eyes of the law. A companion of seven months. And he was poised to stand against his own morality, against his society, against his tribe. Because of her, because of her loyalty to her deranged son. And he felt that nothing in his life had prepared him for this moment, nothing had prepared him for the exposure and ignominy that had come to him here, in his own place, among his own people.

And yet everything had prepared him, everything he had learned from remote peoples in far-off places who lived within the laws of tribe and family and answered to these codes in every detail of their lives.

Sometimes the demands of the heart ran contrary to the demands of the tribe, sometimes a choice was forced. He had seen men discover their own loyalties, where they ran deepest, he had watched the struggle, the decision, the outcome. Submission, and the tribe closing around; defiance, and the outlaw's life.

But always he'd been an observer and a recorder, that was his temperament and his training, he hadn't ever thought to be participant himself.

He felt that all his life was for nothing now, that all his precious achievements were meaningless and stupid, like a child's treasured toys when childhood has fallen away.

Then he stopped thinking, he listened to the waves and to the waders; if he thought at all he thought of the comrades of his journeys, all dead or scattered now, their lost worlds changed past recognition. He sat with his ghosts, feeling the comfort of them, feeling the old comfort of empty, roofless places. After a long time, very cold and wet and tired, he got back into the Land Rover and slept for an hour. Then he drove home and was washed and out around the farm before Hannie was out of the lambing shed.

Chapter Fifty-nine

RICHARD THORNTON WOULDN'T LEND HER ANY MONEY. She asked him as she was getting dressed, her arms in the air, her sweater around her neck. He said no, he didn't think so, in a casual voice, his back to her as he buckled his belt, behind him a great fall of clear, underwater spring light in the tall Georgian windows of his immaculately refurbished home. She nodded, accepting his decision, finished getting dressed and walked from the room as though to fetch something she'd left next door. She went down the stairs, crossed the hall, opened the front door and descended the steps.

She felt empty and neutral as she walked down his well-kept avenue, a small figure on the graveled drive, the big gray house behind her and the chestnut trees to either side. She stared at the fat swooping chestnut buds, how they swung around in the windy white light and the cold wind blowing. Bright fields bordered the drive, a cruel acid new-grass brightness, like drought fields in Africa after rain.

She wouldn't have asked if she could have taken, but everything was wired to alarms, the pictures were bolted to the walls, silver and china stared from locked glass cases. His refusal had changed nothing, it was only the punctuation mark at the end of a completed sentence, he meant less than nothing to her and she had no appetite left to satisfy.

Gangs of fat Christmas lambs ran about on Thornton's smooth green pasture, noisy and lusty and innocent, different altogether from the little leggy newborns picking their way around Ned's straggly fields.

Ned's fields. She knew their bounds now, had even learned how to look at a field, but that was it, the full extent of her involvement. Alison spoke of *our* fields, saying the words with tenderness and protective pride, as though of a delicate child she had reared against all the odds. And such fields as Alison wrung her pride from — stony and boggy — all the good land long since sold to pay for a stretch of roof, a rotted floor, a failed venture. No wonder they spoke of Richard Thornton's house and fields with that soft confused longing in their eyes.

Some of the ewes were beginning to shed their wool, they looked like skinny middle-aged women shrugging out of their fur coats. That was her, she thought, only she'd no fur coat to shrug out of and small chance of one around a man like Ned. Nor was she completely skinny yet, despite Joss's best efforts. She wondered about this new mood she'd drifted into; distant and unreal, so she no longer felt the weight of Joss like a sharp stone lodged in her belly.

She had almost no more cards left to play, she thought, as she turned out of Thornton's drive and walked up the road; there was only Ned she could ask and all she'd get there was a lecture. She stopped and stood with her hands in her pockets, staring about her. The land was laid out in stretches and plains, pale green and blue, soft and misted like watercolors put down on a wet ground. The air was different. It was somehow thicker and whiter and there were pools and streamers of scent that you hit, like swimming into warm pockets in the sea. The trees still looked lifeless, except for the chestnuts, their fat phallic buds, straining up into the cold sky.

"You should see it in spring," Alison had said. "Like paradise."

Could she ever feel as Alison felt? No, she didn't think so, this spring of theirs could never negate the winter, Ned's fields would never be *our* fields, no matter how long she lived here, nor how she worked and tramped about in them. Yet her ties with Africa were looser, she no longer dreamed its landscape at night, nor woke in the mornings flooded with longing for its smells and sounds. She was losing her connections with the past, but still she had almost no ties to the present. She was as a blown leaf now, belonging nowhere.

She didn't hear the car until it pulled up beside her. Then Mrs. Coady was leaning across the seat, pushing the passenger door open. Hannie got in.

"Smelling the air?" Mrs. Coady's face was neutral, the irony only just there in her voice. Hannie shook her head.

"I was at Thornton's," she said, lighting a cigarette. On an impulse she offered one to Mrs. Coady. Mrs. Coady took it. Hannie raised her eyebrows, lit it for her, said nothing.

"I like a cigarette, once in a while," Mrs. Coady said. "I don't buy them. Tom was a smoker once, he can't stand them about the place, the temptation would be strong still." Hannie nodded. The two women drove on in silence, the car hazing with smoke. The road narrowed and Mrs. Coady slowed and swung out to pass a thick-set old man in a jacket and sweater, walking toward them. His hand lifted at sight of the familiar car and then dropped abruptly when he saw who was in the passenger seat.

"The old fella from Cummin's Cross, out walking on doctor's orders," Mrs. Coady said in a neutral voice. "It'll take more than walking to cure that heart."

"He saw me in the car," Hannie said.

"I wouldn't be much liked around here, anyway," Mrs. Coady said as though she hadn't heard. "People think me standoffish, they say I keep myself to myself." She wound down the window and fired the butt out of it. "They can think what they like."

"I asked him to lend me some money, but he wouldn't," Hannie said out of nowhere, staring at the road as it unwound in front of her. It was Mrs. Coady's turn to nod. She rounded the next bend and then pulled the car in suddenly by the field gate just before Ned's drive. She turned off the ignition and pulled on the handbrake.

"I'll see you all right for money, you needn't be asking Thornton," she said. "How much do you want?"

Hannie stared at her. She named a quarter of the sum Joss had asked for. Mrs. Coady nodded, reached down and fished around at her feet for her handbag. She hauled it up and opened it and began counting twenties off a roll she took out of its zipped inner pocket.

"You may not get it back," Hannie said stiffly.

Mrs. Coady laughed. "Sure I know that," she said easily, not looking up from her counting, "that's always a risk, but I think maybe I will. . . . And if I don't, what harm? I suppose I can bear the loss."

"It's for Joss," Hannie said, even more stiffly.

"Sure I know that too," Mrs. Coady said. "When did I ever see you wanting money for yourself?"

"What if Niamh's drowned?"

"She's drowned all right. She's not the kind of young one would be staying away and worrying people if she'd the choice." Mrs. Coady handed Hannie the money. "I'm not condoning what's after happening and I'm not saying I don't think Joss had a hand in it. But it's happened now, I can't change that or bring her back."

Hannie couldn't look at Mrs. Coady, she felt as awkward and grateful as a gauche girl, and suddenly she needed to play straight, she needed to give her the chance to change her mind.

"Aren't you going to say I should make him come home and account for himself?" Her voice was small, her eyes on the money in her hand.

Mrs. Coady didn't answer the question. Instead she waited for Hannie to look at her, then she met her eyes, her gaze grave. "What else can you do?" she asked quietly. "Who else has he, only yourself?"

———•◆•———

HANNIE WALKED up the drive with Mrs. Coady's folded notes in her pocket and heard the phone start to ring before she reached the door. She wanted to run but she dug her nails into her palms and made herself walk. She got the door open. It was still ringing.

She called Ned's name into the silence but there was no answer. She lifted the phone in the hall. His breathing came ragged and excited.

"Joss?"

"Mother? Have you got it, Mother?"

"Some — not much — you'll have to make it last."

"I can't talk now, I'll phone again, here's the address."

She wrote the words down on the pad beside the table, then tore off the sheet and put it into her pocket. Joss was in Limerick.

Chapter Sixty

HANNIE STOOD AT THE FRONT DOOR watching the magpies in the trees. All winter she'd stood like this and watched them, their flaunting black-and-whiteness, their dip-tailed snaking undulations out along the branches. Today they were different, they were silhouettes in the wild cherries, moving shapes on the luminous air.

She closed her eyes. The forms of the cherries were printed onto her mind, the three gray trees stepping out like dancers, their long arms held gracefully above their heads. She opened her eyes, breathed deeply and her shoulders eased a little from a weight lifted. She stared around her. She had been careful, had told Ned she was going to Dungarvan, but had headed north instead to Mitchelstown where they never went and nobody knew them. She'd done her errands like any normal shopper, then dropped the letter casually into the box at the main post office, safe from the sharp eyes of the postmistress in Cappoquin. She hadn't sent all the money, she'd kept back half for the next time.

Nothing had changed or improved, she told herself, her action had solved nothing, she must try to will herself back into a numbed indifference.

But somehow she couldn't. Hope had crept in.

Hope of what?

DANNO FOUND Niamh's body. He saw a bit of old cloth in the slob a long way downriver and pulled his boat over to take a closer look.

When he saw what it was he wanted to mark the place, to go and find the Guards and leave the pulling out to someone else. But the tide was on the turn, in half an hour the slob would be covered and she might not be there when it dropped again. He knew he had to try to get her into the boat.

So he did, but she'd been in the water a long time, it wasn't a pleasant experience. He put her in face-down, then took off his coat and covered as much as he could, started the engine and made for the nearest quay.

THE GUARDS came again, the questioning started again, there were descriptions of Joss broadcast on the television and the radio. The broadcasts said only that the Guards wanted to speak to him, but the tabloids speculated openly about the missing boy in connection with Niamh's drowning. The word *Satanism* cropped up. It was widely known that a dog had been mutilated and hanged.

People talked, they said Joss had crossed from Cork and vanished into France, they said he'd gone to the North, they said he was living wild in the woods somewhere beyond Lismore.

They said Danno was taking it hard, he had shut himself up and was drinking, the Guards had come but he'd roared at them to go away. He was breaking his heart, they said, she came to him in his sleep, he'd been in love with her and was drinking now to forget.

"Isn't it wonderful what people know?" Mrs. Coady said. "Know for a fact, and will swear to."

Mrs. Coady was staunch, she shopped for them and spoke for them and generally kept them informed. People tried to get news out of her but she'd gone blind and deaf.

And most of what was being said, she didn't tell them. It would have been too painful.

WHEN THE URGENCY of the lambing eased Hannie started to dig. The light had stretched, the darkness was folding itself back like the tall wooden shutters in Alison's house, she wanted to be outside in the air and she wanted to be active because it helped her bear the weight. The vegetable garden, the flower beds, the potato patch, they were all receiving their neglected autumn dig.

Early one evening Ned went out into the garden to find her.

"Hannie, come for a walk," he said and she thrust the fork into the ground and stepped out from the tangle of blackened perennials. He took her hand and led her like a child across the field to the river.

But as they walked he began to doubt himself. The spring was late, what was so much to his eyes might be nothing at all to hers. And truly, there was little enough to see: a softening everywhere, silver shoots on the long whippy stems of the young willows, buds like tiny seed-pearls on the whitethorn, the docks thrusting up their red-veined leaves. It was all caught in a silvery caul of almost-birth; a net of light was around the unbroken buds like flame.

She would walk that walk every evening in the days to come. Sometimes he went with her, sometimes he walked down and found her there, sometimes he left her alone. There was a truce between them. He had emerged from the despair of the night by the sea, but only just, and he knew it was close beside him and might claim him again at any time. He felt an intense tenderness toward her, but beneath it there was also horror and distaste.

Once, beside the river, he asked about Richard Thornton. Were they true, he asked — the rumors he'd heard?

"Probably," she said. "It depends which you heard."

"Aren't I worth lying to, Hannie?" he asked.

She walked on slowly, not looking at him. "It *is* true," she said. "Or rather it *was* true. And it doesn't matter at all, it never did."

"Isn't that for me to decide?"

She didn't answer. A heron flopped slowly past in the cold white air. A flight of ducks got up from the fringes of the shiny water. Sometimes Ned hated the river now. Niamh's was the fate he had had in mind for Joss.

Sometimes he'd go looking for her and he'd find her standing watching a single tree, its bark swelling with buds, or a hazel hanging with catkins like yellow rain.

"Why don't you leave me alone, Ned," she asked him at last in exasperation. "I can't abandon him, I can't just throw him to the wolves. I'm not taking anything away from you that's yours and giving it to him, why don't you let me be?"

After that he didn't question her anymore. He knew she wasn't talking about possessions.

———•◆•———

SHE SEEMED AWARE of him, but separate, distant and impenetrable. His words and actions seemed to have little effect on her. If he spoke or kept silent, he felt it all the one to her.

She ate little and she wandered about in the night. Sometimes he woke and heard the floorboards creak, saw the glow of light around his closed door. He would get up then and go looking for her and often as not he found her at the table in the kitchen drinking hot milk heavily laced with whiskey. He would sit with her, but she never seemed to want to talk, so he'd talk instead, sometimes of his journeys and the peoples he'd lived with, sometimes of his childhood in the valley. She didn't say much but his ramblings seemed to soothe her and then he'd go back upstairs with her and sit propped up with pillows in the big double bed, a glass in his hand, talking of things long gone until she fell asleep beside him. Sometimes he couldn't sleep himself after one of these sessions so he'd stare into the darkness at his vivid life passing before his eyes. Often when he woke in the morning she'd be already up and gone.

———•◆•———

THE CAUSE OF DEATH was drowning, the state pathologist told the inquest. She had also suffered lacerations, bruising, and a fracture of the left leg but these injuries had almost certainly occurred after death. The coroner adjourned the matter until May 27 as a Garda investigation was still under way.

At once the rumors spread. Everyone agreed on one thing: whatever about the violence, there'd been sexual intercourse before death, the state pathologist had found evidence but the coroner was keeping it under wraps, like suicide a few years back.

— *It was rape, they were hushing things up, saving the family's feelings. Wasn't it bad enough without making it all worse?*

— *Sure it didn't have to be rape, it might have been voluntary.*

— *Hardly voluntary. The boy was too young for her. It was rape sure enough, they just couldn't prove it, they were saving no one's feelings. . . .*

— *She'd taken drink, the autopsy found she'd taken drink, they were saving the family. . . .*

— *Or saving the boy. Renvyle was an old name, he had connections still, a word in the right place . . .*

— *It wasn't Renvyle's son. It was that woman he'd brought in. Mad about her, for all he'd never see seventy again. And her going straight from his bed and into the bed of that Thornton man, the one had Annaghmore now. She was no chicken either. No wonder the boy was like he was. . . .*

Ned heard the speculation and his shock was very great. At first he dismissed the talk — it was idle, credulous gossip — but as the rumors solidified, the strain and the isolation of his position began to erode his certainty. The more he thought about it the more he had to admit that it was possible. Then he had to go further: if intercourse *had* happened, it had to be rape. That Niamh could voluntarily have had intercourse with Joss was altogether beyond credibility.

For two days he turned it over and over, like a dog turning a bone as it tries to get at the marrow in its core. Only it wasn't marrow he was trying to suck, it was poison. He was sure enough in his mind that Hannie knew where Joss was, despite her protestations. Hitherto he had believed Joss responsible for Niamh's death, but he'd tried to stop short of interpreting the boy's actions as culpably deliberate until they'd heard his side of the story. Despite Pip's fate — the deliberateness of which there was no avoiding — he still believed that Joss had not intended Niamh's death and that the full extent of the disaster was unintentional.

Now he began to revise his position. Drunkenness and mindless cruelty were one thing, rape was another altogether. If it was rape and Hannie knew where Joss was, then he must confront her and persuade her to give him up.

But was it really rape, or was it simply gossip wanting it so? He decided that he couldn't act on rumor. He would go to Dungarvan, speak to the man in charge of the case and when he knew the facts he would see more clearly just what must be done.

He reached this decision while he was blocking gaps in the long acre against the lambs breaking out. He was pleased with the plan, it would be a relief to hear straight facts, he should have acted days ago. He picked up the wire and the cutters and left the thorn branches lying.

He was edging the Land Rover carefully up the drive, climbing the verges to avoid the potholes, when he saw the squad car nosing toward him. He stopped, and Garda Mahon stopped, then both men got out and shook hands.

"How are you, Mr. Renvyle? It's a beautiful morning, though 'twould be a rash man would put money on a clear run through."

The Guard was a well-liked man, a bit overweight, shyer than he seemed, shrewder than he seemed, a countryman by birth from west of the Shannon. When they'd passed through the formalities, Ned volunteered that he was on his way to the superintendent in Dungarvan.

Mahon looked down at a clump of celandines by his left boot, then said slowly that he'd be glad to save Mr. Renvyle a journey if he could. On the other hand, if his business was with the superintendent, he wouldn't want to be keeping him standing here talking.

Ned hesitated. His instinct was to go to the top, but if he did that he would automatically alert their attention. This way the thing could be done in privacy and without commitment. And he knew Mahon, he knew him to be decent, reliable and discreet. Mahon went on gazing steadily down at the celandine while Ned made up his mind.

"There's a report going around," Ned said quietly, "a report about the way Miss Comerford died."

Mahon waited, saying nothing.

"About what happened before she died," Ned went on. "I wanted to know if it was true or if — if it was — all just talk," he finished lamely.

"And what would that report be, Mr. Renvyle?"

"The report was . . ." Ned cleared his throat and began again. "The *rumor* was — is — that certain information was withheld by the coroner due to lack of the necessary confirmation. Information about sexual intercourse. Would that be true, could you tell me, or would it be just — speculation?"

"Speculation," Garda Mahon said firmly. "Officially, it would be pure speculation."

"And the injuries?"

"It's a big strong river, she was gone a long time, she could have been caught on a drowned tree or trapped on a bit of an old fish weir and battered around for weeks. No, the injuries aren't a problem, she was drowned before the injuries, it's what put her into the river that's the problem."

"And the thinking on that?"

"Unofficially, and between the two of us, I'd say we don't know but it's very disturbing. And disturbing's no good, you can't go putting things about without proper evidence, much less charging people."

He folded his arms around his big body and stared hard at the springing grass. "Let's just say we don't think the young woman was pushed, but she didn't go jumping into the river for fun. Something frightened her, frightened her badly enough to make her keep running even when she wasn't pursued."

"She wasn't pursued?"

"Only part of the way. The path was churned up to about halfway along but only her prints went as far as the river."

Ned was aware of a flooding relief, but Mahon hadn't finished. "She kept going, she just kept going, she didn't care what was in front of her, only what was behind."

Ned's relief evaporated. He looked at the smooth round stem of an ash sapling on the ditch. There was a long pause.

"Perhaps it's more than the dead we should be thinking of," Mahon continued thoughtfully.

Ned didn't say anything. Mahon shifted his feet and looked steadily at Ned. "I've two little daughters at home, Mr. Renvyle. I don't know what happened, but I can't sleep at night if I think of it happening again. . . ."

Ned didn't go to Dungarvan. Instead he went back to the field and finished his task. They'd get through somewhere else, they always did, but at least there'd be one less place.

All Ned's instincts were clear: Mahon had been emotional, he'd said himself there was no evidence for what he was suggesting, therefore his suggestion had to be discounted.

Nonetheless, he made himself look at it from Mahon's point of view. It *could* have happened as he seemed to imagine it had happened. And if rape had either occurred or been threatened, then it was fair to suggest that it might occur again. But Joss was innocent until proven guilty and there was no proof that there'd been the crime of rape, much less that Joss had committed it. The only crime Joss had unquestionably committed was the slaughter of Pippa. Yet Niamh was dead and Mahon was right, she hadn't jumped into the river for fun.

This field bordered the road, he was afraid for the lambs but more afraid for the accidents they might cause. He cut more thorns and blocked two other places. He checked the ewes while he was there, then went back to the house. Hannie wasn't around.

The phone rang as he was washing his hands in the scullery. A few rings only — it stopped just as he got to it. He stood beside it waiting for the ringing to start again. The clear light fell slanting onto the table, and Ned could see the imprint of an address Hannie must have scribbled down on the pad before she tore off the page. The phone sat there, malignant yet quiet, it didn't seem to be about to ring again. He picked up the pad and fished in his pocket for his reading glasses. The address was clear enough. There was no way of knowing how long it had been there.

Chapter Sixty-one

DANNO MADE HER TEA AND SHE SAT on the window seat, sipping quietly at the hot liquid, not smoking or roaming around, just staring out at the river.

He had been varnishing his ash plants when she came, letting the glaze slide over the carved and painted handles, the long clean lengths of the sticks. He liked this task, it was the last stage of a long process and it brought its own peace.

He had opened the door to her without wanting to see her, he would have put the ash plants away, but he was already deep in the job and there were tacky half-dried sticks propped all around the room. He would concentrate, he decided, sink into what he was doing, then he wouldn't be disturbed by what she said.

Only she didn't say anything much, she just sat there sipping her tea in the silence and the room was filled with unsaid words and loud with unasked questions about Joss and Niamh. He needed her to speak or to go away, but she did neither.

"You want to know about Niamh?" he asked at last, surprising himself.

"Not much," she said. "Do you want to tell me?"

"Not much." He took the next unglazed ash plant from the stand, turned it this way and that to check its preparedness. "Why did you come?"

She roused herself. "For a drink," she said. "You're supposed to be poleaxed with drink, I thought I'd get something stronger than tea."

He looked at her; it was a horrible misplaced effort at gaiety, he could think of nothing to say.

"I came to see how you were," she went on, "to check you weren't secretly in love with Niamh the way they're saying you were — to assure myself you're not drinking your way into an early grave." She paused. "And I came to ask you a favor."

"What else do they say?" he asked, ignoring her last statement.

"That she's broken your heart, that she comes to you in the night."

He made himself look at her. She was sitting sideways at the window, her head resting against the wall behind her. Her hair looked longish and unwashed, strands of it stood around her face, her skin was papery and thin but still held the hint of a tan. Not a tan, he realized, a brown pigment, the only visible legacy of the racial mix that was somehow common knowledge now. He felt the fury rising in him and he bowed his head so that she wouldn't see.

"What's the favor?"

She stared at the river. "Something has changed, Danno," she said, her voice low. "Something has changed, it's to do with Joss, I felt it last night, but I don't know what it is."

He waited, his eyes still fixed on the stick in his hand.

"I came to ask you to look out for signs of Joss when you're in the woods. I want you to come and tell me if you find them."

Danno raised his head now and stared at her, but she was still looking away.

"What makes you think you can ask this of me?"

Her head turned and she stared, a startled confused expression on her face he'd never seen there before. Tears sprang into her eyes.

"We were friends once," she said slowly. "Remember?"

"That was before all this. That was a long time ago —"

"A few brief weeks —"

"— and on the strength of it you're asking me to help you help Joss get away."

"They're all talking about rape, and I don't know why, where did rape come from, why does everyone suddenly think she was raped? He didn't rape her and he didn't kill her."

"I suppose he didn't hang the puppy either."

She stopped. For a moment his hostility seemed to penetrate through to her. She sat back suddenly, her eyes went dead, her body sagged, her shoulders slumped like a sawdust doll. For the first time she seemed to lose Joss, to get a sense of Danno and how *he* felt. She seemed to realize what she'd asked of him.

"I understand that you feel like this, Danno," she said quietly. "You found her, that's very strong, very emotional, it is looking the reality of her drowning straight in the face. But remember one thing. We know she died, but we don't know what passed between them. And remember too that Niamh, as well as Joss, was drunk, and young ones don't handle drink so well, they get a little wild and excited, they get frightened when there's no real cause." The words came out fast, she was pleading now, she held up her hand as though to ward off his snort of derision.

"I'm not making excuses for him and I'm not trying to pretend he didn't do wrong. The puppy, that stupid burning cross, those things were deranged and bad. But I think it has wrecked his life already, I know he'll never ever forget those hours, he will carry Niamh's death till he dies. And he isn't guilty of rape or murder, Danno, whatever you feel about Niamh, however much you want someone called to account for what you found. He didn't push her, even the Guards say that. He is guilty only of wild and excessive behavior."

"Wild and excessive behavior caused her death."

"I think if Niamh had been sober she wouldn't now be dead. . . ."

"Is it a crime to be drunk? Punishable by death?"

"No, it's not. But if you're going to be drunk you must look out for the consequences. . . ."

Danno studied her in silence and she seemed to hear what she'd just said.

"Have you finished, Hannie?" he asked.

She nodded miserably.

"Then listen to me for a change. You're right when you say we don't know what really happened, perfectly right, and I don't suppose Joss is going to tell us so we'll probably never find out. But there's one thing we *do* know. Someone scared the living daylights out of her and no one else was there, so that someone must be Joss." He paused and looked straight at her, challenging her with his eyes and his voice and his words. "You say he didn't kill her, but who did, answer me that. No one?" He took off his glasses, sighed, put them on again, looked down at the stick in his hands. "If I found him, Hannie," he said quietly, "if I found any smallest sign or trace of him, I'd have no hesitation, I'd go straight and tell the Guards."

In a quick, desperate movement she clapped her hands to her ears.

"Oh, Danno, stop, stop, please stop! You don't know what'll happen to him if they catch him, you don't know. It may seem nothing to you — a short time in a borstal or a prison — it may seem only justice, but it isn't justice, if it happens he'll never recover, I'll never ever be able to get him back, no matter what I do, or how I try, he will be lost forever. . . ."

"He's lost already."

"No, Danno, it isn't like that, it isn't set in stone like that. Once I said it was his nature — like a hawk's — that a hawk killed things, that Joss spoiled things — and you criticized me, you said I was wrong. . . ."

"You were right, I was wrong. Joss has done what he's done, he must pay the price."

She didn't move or flinch, though he might as well have struck her. He glanced up, met her eyes, looked down again. She went on staring at him.

"Something has changed you, Danno," she said softly. "You weren't like this the last time I was here and everything then was the same as it is now. What was it, Danno, was it finding Niamh?"

"Yes," he said, "it was finding Niamh. And I'll tell you something else, Hannie. They're right when they say that she comes to me in the night."

Chapter Sixty-two

THE GUARDS PHONED FOR NED just after Hannie had gone to visit Danno. They said the Limerick Guards had raided the Limerick address the previous night but had failed to apprehend Joss.

Ned asked what that meant and was told that they'd missed him by chance. It seemed Joss had been at the shop around the corner and when he came back he'd seen the squad car and scarpered. Did Ned have any idea where he might have gone?

Ned put down the phone and went and stood in the doorway. Before his eyes the whitethorn was coming into leaf and the blackthorn's frail stars of blossom were dying. He felt how small their lives were, how soiled and helpless and unheroic. A snail was making its slow way up the door frame. It had paused at about his head-height and was looking around, its slim gray horns feeling tentatively into the warmer air. He put out his hand and lifted it off, then walked down the steps and placed it in the damp earth under the wall. He bent and watched it making its careful way until it reached the sanctuary of stone.

He looked up. Alison was standing by the steps, her gray eyes with the red veining at the inside corners looking steadily at him, her soft lined face full of pity and defeat. How old they were all getting, he thought, how old and irrelevant, living their small lives in this small lost backwater of this suddenly thriving little country that once their families had ruled like petty kings.

He rose to greet her. Alison put out her hand and touched his left forearm and he covered her hand with his own. They stood like that, both looking at their hands, one on the other, not saying anything. He was surprised and touched and embarrassed and then he found himself wondering how they were going to stop doing this and he thought of that childhood game of piled hands, how when your hand was on the bottom you slipped it out and put it on the top, hand on hand, faster and faster until the game ended in a wild jumble of slapping hands. And as he thought this, Alison slipped out her hand and his own dropped.

"I came to see Hannie, it must be quite dreadful for her," Alison said, settling her mac around her shoulders. "I know she doesn't want to see me, but she ought, you know, whether she wants to or not. . . .

"She has you, of course, but she ought to talk to someone else, someone detached and her own sex. It's really too much for anyone, this sort of thing, and she has the boy to think of. She must keep herself up to the mark." She put up her hand and tucked a lock of her faded hair back under her headscarf as she spoke. "Perhaps you'll tell her that I'd very much like to see her when she has time?"

She touched his arm briefly once more and turned, but suddenly Ned's relief at seeing her prepare to go changed and he wanted her to sit in his drawing room drinking gin and talking to him in that steady, responsible way that was so unlike Hannie, so like his mother and his dead aunts and all the admirable women in whose drawing rooms he'd sat long years ago.

He asked her to stay and talk to him. He sat her down and gave her a drink and unburdened his troubled conscience a little. Then she asked him what he knew of a woman called Ilse who had once been Hannie's friend.

———•◆•———

ALISON UNLOCKED the back door with the big iron key that was always left in the keyhole. That was the system, had been the system since Vere's childhood. You went out, you locked the door, you left the key in the keyhole. There was no logic to it, but didn't matter. No self-respecting burglar would bother with their possessions, Vere said, there was nothing in the house that wouldn't have been marked down in a junkyard.

He was sitting at the kitchen table with James and the account books and a bottle of cheap whiskey. They pretended they'd been talking shop, but she knew they were waiting for her. Vere got up and rinsed a cloudy tumbler vaguely under the tap. He poured her a drink.

"All sorted, then?"

She sat at the table, sipping at the grubby glass, shaking her head sadly up at him. "Not that simple."

"No, I suppose it isn't. Pity. A great pity."

"No fool like an old fool," James said brusquely. "Throw her out, only thing to be done. Throw the boy out too, the minute he shows up. Whole thing a mistake, mistake from start to finish . . ."

"Oh, I don't think it's a mistake," Alison said quietly. "I think the boy's in very serious trouble. . . ."

James snorted. "Course he is, so he should be. It's marrying *her* I'm talking about." He glared at Alison. "Well, so be it, we all make 'em and what's done is done. But he should put it behind him now, wash his hands of the whole sorry business."

"I expect he wants to," Vere said. "But he can't, can he? Not his style."

"Can't? Not his style? Don't talk crap, Vere, course he can. What's this about style? Honorable chap, old Ned — is that it? Stands by his wife and her mad son, won't let her down no matter what? Blah. He's in love with her, that's what's wrong with him, that's what's stopping him doing what he should do, throwing her out, setting an example. He's besotted, nothing to do with honor. Showing us all up. And at his age!"

———✦———

VERE FOUND HER LATER, standing quietly on the landing in the darkness, staring through the great window at the garden beyond. He placed himself beside her.

It looked quite decent in the moonlight. Roses in the border all pruned and neat, the beds halfway weeded, the old fountain showing white in the silvery light.

You couldn't see the moss and scutchgrass in the lawn, the rain-filled potholes in the drive, the ground-elder clogging the fountain.

He didn't mind all that, he even liked it, though he'd never say that to Ali, she worked so hard.

"D'you think James is right?" she asked him.

"That he should throw her out?"

"That he loves her."

"I suppose he could be. . . ."

Chapter Sixty-three

"HANNIE," HE SAID GENTLY, "whose son is Joss?"

There was a fraction of a pause.

"Rolf's," she said, without looking up from the book she was staring at, not reading or even turning the pages.

"I don't mean who is his father. I mean who is his mother?"

She closed the book and placed it beside her on the sofa. She looked at him. "Alison's been here, you've been talking to Alison."

At once he felt as though he had betrayed her. He struggled against guilt, told himself they had to have the truth out.

"Yes," he said.

"What did she tell you?"

"Just what you told her."

"And what was that?"

"That Joss is Ilse's son, not yours."

"Ah yes."

"Are you angry that she told me?"

"No, that's why I told her. I wanted to tell someone in case something happened." She sat quietly, her hands placed one on the other on her lap, her eyes downcast. He couldn't read her. He got up and went over to the sideboard and poured himself another drink, though he'd already had the two that were his normal limit. He refilled her glass without asking her. "What do you mean, in case something happened?"

"In case I died or went away." She looked up, met his eyes, didn't look down. "I thought you'd be kinder to him if you thought he wasn't mine. If you thought he was a victim, like you."

He ignored this last remark. "Are you planning to go away?"

"No, not now. But I thought of it."

"And you'd have left Joss?"

"Joss needs a home." Her voice was matter-of-fact. "That's why I came here in the first place. He couldn't go on moving from one place to another, from one stepfather to another, it was getting harder and harder for him. But I thought I couldn't stand it here and I knew you'd look after him. At least until I came for him."

"Even when you left me?"

"Even when I left you."

Ned threw back the contents of his glass. "Why are you telling me all this?"

"Why not? It's all passed now, everything's changed."

He stood planted, his feet apart, a sort of inertia upon him. He seemed baffled, unable to advance in the conversation. He made a pincer of his thumb and forefinger, closed his eyes, held the bridge of his nose, made a great effort.

"Look, Hannie, I can't get this straight. Who is Joss, what are you saying? You told Alison he wasn't your son but that you always said he was so there'd be a place for him in your marriages. But now you seem to be saying that everything you told her was just a carefully planted lie. So that I'd be better disposed towards Joss if you left."

He kept pinching at his forehead, speaking with his eyes shut, getting it straight in his mind.

"But at the same time you said to Alison that *someone ought to know.* She told me you said it very urgently — as though it was the clue, the core of what you were saying." He straightened up, dropped his hand and looked at her directly. "Know what, Hannie? Whose son is Joss anyway? Yours? Ilse's? Whose?" His voice rang. He was staring at her, challenging her.

Her eyes rose to meet his, then they dropped again. "What does it matter?" she asked wearily. "He's mine — my responsibility — the rest is irrelevant."

"My responsibility too, or that's what you seem to have intended from the start. I have a right to know. And to know about Ilse. Oh, I know, I know, you've told me, she was Swedish, she was your ex-husband's second wife. . . ."

"Third wife. I was the second."

"*Third* wife. But who was she, Hannie? What was this hold she had on you?"

There was a silence. She stared at him for a long time, saying nothing. Then she shrugged, lit a cigarette and drew the smoke in deeply. Ned took his glass from the mantelpiece and sat down across from her. When he was settled he looked at her and she met his eyes.

"All right, Ned, I'll tell you, since you so badly want to know. But there's no point, it will change nothing, nothing at all.

"I had a husband and his name was Rolf. He was wealthy. He came from a Czech family — very well bred — who lost their lands but got their money out before the war. We were good together, there was no deep feeling between us but it was fine, we both liked life and money and the way we lived. It worked very well — for a year, two years, three years — and then Ilse came.

"Ilse was Swedish, the daughter of a bank manager from a not-large town beside the sea. A happy family, bourgeois, innocent, church-going, with this sweet, pretty daughter; it would be nice for her to learn good English, to travel a little, and then to come home and marry. The father had a client who had friends in Africa and so it was arranged. She came to be an au pair to their children.

"Well you see, Ned, she was so young and shy and so very blond — that white Scandinavian blondness — her hair a dusty oat color, but fine, like ivory silk. She had perfect skin and a perfect mouth and a perfect figure, slender but full, and when she was with the children she was always smiling and laughing."

Hannie stopped and stared into space for a moment. Then she reached for another cigarette and lit it.

"I am telling you all this stuff about how she looked because it is the reason for what happened to her. If she'd been plain, she'd have been left alone. But she wasn't plain. She would have stood out anywhere, but in that society — with its alcohol and easy sex, its darker coloring, its aging beauties — she shone. And it wasn't just how she looked, it was because she didn't know her currency. She didn't sway or pose, her clothes weren't new or good, she didn't like drink or parties, she liked to be with the children. You see? She was so natural she was a beacon.

"Rolf had to have her from the start. I saw this, but I thought he'd just have her and tire of her, I thought all that artless simplicity would soon be too much. He pursued her. At first she disliked him and feared him, but she couldn't resist him, he was so relentless when he wanted something. I waited for him to discard her, but he didn't, she was an obsession with him and the obsession didn't grow less.

"I was young still, I was barely thirty, men came to me easily. Rolf didn't mind that — some men find it erotic — and I was easy with him, I accepted what he did, I even advised him. This time I gave him good advice, I told him not to marry her, that if he married her she'd be like a poison in his life because she was too far from him and could never understand him or accept him. I told him he should use her till the way he felt had run its course. Or give her up. But he couldn't do that either.

"It wasn't altruism on my part, you understand. I liked the life I had with Rolf, I could handle him, I didn't have to worry about surviving, yet it wasn't dull. But he couldn't listen to me and I grew tired of the situation. I thought, I'll let him go. . . . And then I thought, why should I? She's so pure and good and yet she's sleeping with my husband, she's no different from the rest of us. So I went there to the house of her employers who were our friends. It was quite early and the servant let me in and went to call her, only I followed after him and I stood on the veranda outside her room waiting for her to come out. And when she did she was wearing a long nightgown and she was carrying the teething baby and she smelled so sweetly of sleep that I wanted to be sick.

"She was bewildered when she saw me, but not defensive. She thought that for a man to be unfaithful to his wife the relationship between them must already be over. That's how naive she was.

"Of course I knew then there was no point trying to hold on to Rolf. And I knew that Rolf would destroy her and I didn't care. I think I began to hate her then, though I hadn't bothered before. I went on hating her for a long time before I started to love her."

Hannie stopped suddenly, as though she was afraid of what she'd just said. She got up, went over to the sideboard and poured herself another drink. Then she offered the bottle vaguely in Ned's direction, but he shook his head. She sat down again.

"You know, Ned," she said thoughtfully, "when I saw her there on the veranda, it was the first time I realized I was decadent. Before that I thought the way I was was normal and that people like Ilse — little, ordinary people — were afraid to live. I had never lived inside affection and I never wanted to, I had never seen a family that didn't make me want to scream with claustrophobia, I'd never seen a contented couple but I had to make him want me in front of her, just to show them how things really were.

"I couldn't see their bonds, these small, dull people, I thought what held them together was simply self-interest and fear.

"But when I saw Ilse so tender with that teething baby that wasn't hers but had kept her up half the night I knew she was different from the people I knew. And I knew she knew something that I didn't know, and didn't want to know and never would.

"Anyway, I told Rolf I would divorce him, and not long after they were married. Ilse's family wouldn't come, they'd made inquiries about Rolf and they tried to threaten her out of it, they tried to save her though she didn't want to be saved. She loved Rolf, you see, it was all she could think of, though it was a big thing for her, losing her family, her parents, her younger brothers and sisters. But her parents were bourgeois and hardworking, their relationship was very happy and she thought hers would be too.

"Poor Ilse. She should have lived and died a Swedish wife.

"She made sure of Rolf's behavior to me after the divorce. I thought she must feel very guilty, it never crossed my mind that she did it because she felt it was right. He was useful to me through her, gave me money and help when I asked for it, though at that time I didn't need much of either, there were plenty of other men around. But I asked for money anyway — why not?

"I didn't know she had to fight him for me, I thought he was still besotted with her and he'd give her anything, she had only to ask. She never hated me, no matter what I did or said to her. She would look up at me with her soft eyes and I would grow more vicious to her. I despised her.

"Then I went away. When I came back some years had passed. I was sick, I had a fever that seemed to go and then came back, each time worse, so I would be half delirious for days and weeks. I could not get well. I had a little boy — Paulo's child, Paulo that I told you of — I had gone back to Paulo then I had left him again, he never knew I was pregnant. I was thirty-seven when Joss was born, not so young anymore, it was hard, and the child wasn't strong, he had had malaria and he needed good food and care and I had no money.

"So everything was different. I had a room in the city, a horrible room and more than I could afford, but it was all I could get because of Joss. I was behind with the rent, and the landlady threatened me.

"I went to Ilse in their place in the hills and I told her my situation. She had two children, a girl, and a younger boy, almost the same age as Joss. It was all so green and orderly and well tended, money and servants, but no Rolf.

She said she would pay off what I owed and she'd help me to get on my feet again, but she had to wait for Rolf to come home because she'd no money of her own. She told me to come back in a week and she gave me some cash to keep the landlady quiet, but of course I didn't use it for that, and I got sicker again and I was very weak and I knew the woman would put us out if I left the room, so I didn't go back there as we'd arranged.

"She came to my room. I don't know how she got the address, I didn't give it to her, she must have made inquiries. But there she was and I had a fever and I thought she was a dream, and other things that were dreams I thought were real. I don't know what happened or what was said. The next thing I remember I was in their place in the hills and she was tending me. That was Ilse's way, she had plenty of servants, but no, it wasn't some servant who nursed me to her orders, it was Ilse herself.

"Anyway, I slowly grew less sick. The house was large and low and rambling, with many bedrooms, and my room was in one wing and it gave on to gardens and trees. In the early mornings I lay and I watched the monkeys in the leaves against the sun, just as I'd done in my childhood so far from there. Joss thrived, he was fatter and healthier, he sat on my bed and told me of the other children and the games they played and Ilse came and sat with me every day.

"Then Joss said the children's daddy was home and the servants told me there was a big house party as well. I didn't want to see Rolf, so I stayed where I was and I kept Joss with me. I heard the comings and goings, the voices and cars and music at night, but I was sick still, I was glad to stay where I was and I didn't see Ilse either, she didn't come to my room.

"Then the parties stopped, it grew quiet again, and I knew that Rolf wasn't there anymore. I began to be strong enough to be out of bed and I spent my time with Ilse and the children. I learned the story of the marriage.

"It was as I'd predicted. Rolf had turned against her a long time ago and the more she tried, the darker he became and the more violent. There were women too, and friends that she hated, and he didn't bother to conceal any of it from her, it was as though he was trying to goad her and goad her until she finally gave up her stubborn love and agreed to hate him, but she never did. It was very hard for her. He couldn't stand the way she was bringing up the children, he hated to see them tender toward things and full of pity, the same as she was. He ridiculed her in front of the children and he ridiculed the children when they showed her values. He taught them how cruelty worked and he taught them about fear. Especially the boy, he wanted the boy for himself. The girl was safer from him — she was older and very strong for her mother — but he claimed the boy against these two soft women, the mother and the sister.

"I didn't see all this to begin with, but I noticed how the boy was different after Rolf had been there and I saw how patient she was with him, how she tried to rebuild the bond, always through gentleness. And he was confused, he couldn't understand which world he should live in. Perhaps she should have left him in his father's, but she couldn't. It wasn't in her.

"And you mustn't think that Rolf wanted this either, he didn't want to live in the dark place he lived in, but he couldn't live in her light place, he wasn't like that. They should have parted but they couldn't. She couldn't leave him because she couldn't take back her love and he . . . Well, sometimes I think he was afraid of her. Afraid to stay with her, afraid to leave her. She was too much for him.

"She trusted me, I don't know why. Perhaps it was the same flaw of judgment that made her love Rolf. At first I tried to stop her, I tried to make her understand that I was untrustworthy and would let her down, I didn't want her trust or her love, they were too burdensome, I only wanted her help. When I had what I needed I wanted to go away and forget her.

"But she was too much for me, too; in the end she got what she wanted from me. Or perhaps it is wrong to say she got what she wanted, because I don't think she wanted anything, she tended me as naturally as she tended the wounded things the children brought her, fixing a splint, removing a thorn. She seemed to have no fear — only tenderness and pity. Sometimes I was angry with her because I wanted more than this mindless pity. I began to understand Rolf.

"And I did become trustworthy, I even came to love her, though I never showed it. It was strange, the effect she had on me. She used to sew at night, the lamp beside her, the soft moths batting out of the shadows. I would stand outside on the veranda, smoking, watching the night, knowing she was there behind me in the lamplight. I loved that, I felt so lonely and complete. I never wanted to be like Ilse, mostly I didn't even want to be with her, but I wanted to know that she was there. I knew then that I was an outsider, would always be an outsider, would perish if I tried to be anything but what I was.

"I began to talk about moving on. She accepted that, though I think now she wanted me to stay. I suppose she was lonely, there on that land-bound ridge on that great continent that was as endless as the sea. Ilse was always, always homesick, she never got used to Africa or the heat. She used to talk of those northern harbors of hers — sunlight on cold blue water, white dresses, hems fluttering, everything sparkling and flashing — I see them now quite clearly, though I've never seen them.

"She knew I was getting restless, that I wanted to be gone. Whatever she wanted for herself, she put from herself, that was her way. But she wanted to find a place for me, to make it safe for me, she didn't want me just to go off as I'd always done, seeing what might turn up. She said I had a child now, I was responsible, I couldn't just trust to luck or fate. So she found a job for me in Nairobi — in charge of a place for white people who'd grown old and lost their luck. I don't know how she did it, I had no qualifications or experience, but she told them I was entirely capable.

"It wasn't stupid, this plan of hers. I could take the boy and yet there wasn't much work to be done, it already ran smoothly with native staff, I would only be a figurehead, a *white* figurehead." Hannie stopped abruptly and laughed slightly wildly. Ned regarded her steadily. She put down her empty glass.

"It would be very suitable for a while, Ilse said. Of course, she meant till I was married again. She knew men liked me. She would write letters, arrange that I be suitably invited, I would be settled before very long and there would be a home for Joss. She meant well."

"Like Alison . . ."

Hannie stared at him as though she hardly knew who he was. Then she laughed mirthlessly. "Poor Ilse," she said, "I've wronged her badly, I have made her sound like Alison. And she wasn't, you know, she had no security, no family to fall back on, no social position, no caste to belong to. All her life she was just a girl, a naive girl who never grew up or learned life. She knew nothing, anyone could do anything to her, she just let them."

"I know the feeling." Ned heard the anger and self-pity in his voice too late. She looked at him, a blank exhaustion in her face.

"No you don't," she said wearily. "You don't do what you don't want to do, or what your conscience won't let you do, you are stubborn and strong and selfish and you have no idea what it was like for Ilse, no idea what it was like to be helpless and soft and alone in a strange country with no one to help you and your husband a drinker and a shit."

"And you do?" Ned said bitterly. He was ashamed of his tone, but he couldn't stop himself.

"A little, but only a little." Her voice was quiet, almost thoughtful. "I was alone, yes, but I wasn't soft, it makes a difference. And I wasn't beautiful as she was, I didn't have that thing that made men fight to own her. And when I was helpless she looked after me. That is the hold she had on me, Ned, the bond you find so sinister."

She got up, went over to the window, pulled back the curtain, looked into the night.

"We both had sons," she said, without turning. "Sons only a little different in age. Sometimes I see the pictures in my mind and the memories are all mixed up. What is true, what isn't true? I had a son called Joss, but I never had a son by Rolf. Sometimes I feel I can't sort it out, can't ever know for sure. . . ."

It was too much for Ned. He felt too bruised and confused and exhausted to stand this change. He could handle the truth when she told it, how could he do otherwise when she set it before him as she did? Like a woman bringing her worldly goods to morning market, placing her bundle on the earth, unfolding the cloth, revealing its sparse contents (for are not all our bundles mostly empty or filled with junk?) in the bright, clear, pitiless light.

But he couldn't go from that to this.

"Come on, Hannie," he said savagely, "don't give me that half-baked twaddle. As though you don't know, as though you're only half there. If you're not going to tell me, then don't tell me, but do it straight."

She swung furiously around to face him. "What do you know, Ned?" she came back at him. "What do you know — you with your home and your family name and your moral standards and your self-respect? What do you know about living? Nothing. Why? Because you never do it, you just watch other people. Detached, objective, safe.

"You're afraid to live, Ned. You're a coward, posing as a hero. . . ."

"In all my life, Hannie, no one has ever called me a coward."

"Well, *I* am calling you a coward, *I* am saying that your courage is not true courage, that bravery coming from strength is easy. What do you know about courage? You've never been soft or helpless or tricky or shamed or wrong. You've never been humiliated or disgraced or hated. . . ."

"What about now?"

She stared at him. "What about now?" she said furiously. "They hate Joss, they hate me, but no one hates you. And if you think what you're feeling now is hatred you should see what it looks like from our end. . . ." She whirled from the room, slamming the door as she went.

He thought about going after her but it was hopeless, he'd lost her and he wouldn't get her back now. She'd told him more of herself than she'd ever done, but something was missing still, nothing was finally explained. He needed a lens that would shift it all into focus and he wasn't going to get it. He cursed himself for not keeping a tighter control on himself. Rage was the other side of the tenderness that he felt for her, a molten rage that lived in him like lava, erupting at the slightest pressure. It shook him, he didn't recognize himself like this, he didn't like himself.

Chapter Sixty-four

IN THE MORNING NED DECIDED that his life had been on hold for too long and enough was enough. He wasn't going to skulk at home avoiding people anymore, he was going to go about his normal business modestly and respectfully and in a way that he hoped would give offense to no one. If he met any of the Comerfords, then so be it, he would have to face them and they him, but he hoped he wouldn't and he hoped his action now would make it easier for them in the long run. People would see him about and report back to them and they'd get used to the idea of a meeting. Then, when the inevitable finally happened, they'd be less unprepared. He told himself it wasn't a matter of pushing things, but of facing them.

He took himself to Waterford and began with a long overdue meeting with his accountants. After that he went to the car insurance people, talked to them about the still-missing Volkswagen, then called in at one or two garages and priced what they had in the secondhand line. He had some lunch, read the paper, folded it into his pocket and prepared himself to go and do what he'd been dreading most.

He drove through the school gates, parked the car and got out. The old stone building was somber and quiet in the chill sunlight, the grounds were studded with great trees, their branches netted with veils of bright leaves. He could hear shouts and yelps and laughter from the playing fields and snatches of something choral and familiar from what must be a music room. A little flock of starlings wheeled and dropped and rose again and pigeons sounded softly from the roof. The founding date of the school — 1798 — was carved up there in the dark stone under the eaves. The place had been established by the Quakers in the aftermath of the '98 Rebellion the bursar had told him, an attempt to build on ruin and devastation, to create a future out of chaos and terror and bloody suppression.

Suddenly Ned knew he couldn't walk in as he'd planned and ask them to spare him a few minutes, couldn't stand there saying his piece about bringing them up to date, couldn't even cross the threshold or find the office or meet anyone's eyes. Nothing would happen to him, he told himself, nothing had happened all morning beyond a slight distance, an unwillingness to let the conversation drift beyond the immediate business, a certain fumbling of hands and shifting of eyes. But it didn't matter what he told himself, he couldn't do it, and that was something that he'd never experienced before.

He went the long way home for no other reason than that he didn't want to arrive; he drove back with the thoughts so loud in his head that he didn't see road or cars, or fields and trees. He had a new respect for Hannie, for her courage and single-mindedness and endurance, but much stronger than the respect was a fury at what she was and what she'd got him into.

He wanted a stiff drink, but more than a drink he wanted a cigarette, he hadn't smoked for years but he wanted a cigarette. Hannie smoked like a chimney, the kitchen was always full of smoke, she didn't care about her own lungs or anyone else's, she didn't care about anything but getting her own way, all the rest could go hang. She didn't care what she said either, had no thought for consequences, all the subtleties, the allusions, the necessary ways of sidling up to things were swept away leaving nothing but pain and chaos in their wake.

If this was what she meant by living, he thought, she could keep it. And she was right when she said he didn't do it for himself. He didn't, and he didn't want to either, no one in their senses would.

Why should he try anymore? What did he care who Joss was, or what cul-de-sac in Hannie's sordid past had produced him? Why should he go on picking up the pieces when she wouldn't listen or cooperate and showed nothing but contempt for other human beings and their feelings?

He would cut his losses and ask her to leave, he decided; it would cost money, but it would be worth it. He'd have peace again, a quiet way of living, the respect of his friends and neighbors. He gripped the steering wheel and his hands hurt from the arthritis that was starting in them.

He pulled in at the next town to buy cigarettes. He didn't know how much they cost now, and after he'd paid he held out his hand with the change spread on it, convinced that he was being cheated. When it was explained to him, he didn't apologize, he just walked back across the street toward the car, his rage deeper because he knew now how much money she was wasting every day. He had forgotten Niamh, forgotten grief, he no longer felt pity for Niamh's family or for Hannie or for Joss or for anyone but himself. He felt soiled, humiliated, shamed.

A dog ran out under his feet. He stumbled and a woman caught at his arm to steady him.

"Watch yerself, now," she cautioned him tetchily. "We're none of us gettin' any younger."

A young lad leapt after the straying dog, grabbed at his collar, and ran with him. His friend appeared alongside him, grinned complicitously up at Ned, and made vivid ribald faces at the cross woman's back. They sped off down the pavement, the dog loping between them.

Ned stood where he was, looking after them. A red-haired girl was standing waiting by the Allied Irish Bank, her hair a dark flame against the cut stone, and beside her leaned an elderly man in a rusty black suit. Ned watched them, the clear rainy light showed their clothes and faces in calm detail, their quiet waiting, their patient incarnation, their acceptance of it.

Inside Ned everything suddenly smoothed out and went simple. Youth, age, it was all the one, you lived and life passed, nothing mattered but this quiet, attentive acceptance. He stood there, empty and still, with the life of the street flowing around him. He didn't think about what he was thinking, nor wonder where the thoughts came from. And after a short time it was enough.

He walked back to the car, got in and started the engine. He saw everything now, the clean lines of the houses, the sudden pink flare of an almond in blossom, the filling station on the road out. He saw where the edge of the town changed to countryside, the tall chestnuts lining the road, their spires of unopened blossom, the green towers of their leaves.

And he saw that he'd been someone in his life, that he'd got used to being someone, that now he was old and was becoming no one, and this being old and becoming no one was his next great task.

He knew he wouldn't write the book he was planning, that his dream of writing one last book was just a way of trying to hold on to importance, of trying to put off for a little longer this becoming what he really was.

And this was his business, this was his task, whatever Hannie did or did not do, whatever happened around him, whoever else lived or died.

All the way home he went on seeing everything, the fields and the trees, the hedges standing in the greenish, underwater light, the white-thorns breaking where the pale sun reached. The fields were full of lambs and young cattle, the rowans carried big bosses of creamy blossom, the mountains were soft and blue and close with the coming rain.

When he pulled up in front of the house it was gray and still. Rooks beat and clamored in the empty ash trees and the first swallows flicked through the chilly air. He saw Hannie through the boughs of the young fruit trees, moving about in the garden. He was no longer angry. He felt neither hope nor despair.

Chapter Sixty-five

HE SAW HER CROSS THE YARD and for what seemed a long time he stood watching and waiting for her return. There was a big moon up there but the clouds came fast and the shadows blew over the uneven ground. He had to stay alert. When she did come, she was so quick and so quiet that he would have missed her if she hadn't made straight for the door where he stood.

She didn't see him until he moved. She started and gave a little sharp cry, which she cut off even as it came out. Then she saw that it was him and she tried to push past. He grabbed her by the shoulders and held on to her though she pulled away. He yanked her around and she went limp in his hands and he spoke low and fast and shook her to be sure she understood.

"You can't do this, Hannie, you have to stop helping him, you have to let him face it. . . ."

He stopped, he'd seen a movement over her shoulder. Only a small movement and only for a moment, but enough. He froze and she did, too. They waited. He saw a shadow move across the gap between the sheds. Then stillness again. He pulled her inside and shut the door, stopping it at the last moment so that it closed softly to.

She understood at once. Even in the unlit darkness of the scullery he could see her eyes widen, he felt her body taut beside him. He went to the square of window and stood quietly watching. She was there with him.

"Where?" she asked, very softly.

"Over there — by the shed door." He only breathed the words.

The moon had gone in. They both peered into the darkness. The cloud passed and they saw the shed door and the shed's thrown shadow, its outline sharp and blank. Nothing. They waited for a long time. Nothing moved, even the cloud-shadows were absent, the moon sailed around and clean through the high sky.

At last Hannie left the window and moved to the door. Her hand was on it. He was beside her.

"Where are you going?"

"He's trying to reach me. . . ."

"Hannie, I don't think that's Joss out there. . . ." They were whispering still.

"Not Joss?"

He shook his head. "Wrong shape. Didn't move like Joss . . ."

"Are you sure?"

"Pretty sure. It was only a glimpse —"

And Joss would have to have traveled pretty fast, he thought, he'd only skipped the Limerick house three nights ago. He wondered if Joss had phoned again — she seemed so sure that he was heading home.

"The Guards?"

"I don't think it's the Guards, I think they think he's long gone. Nora phoned, they've been questioning Con."

"If it's not the Guards, then who is it?"

He hesitated. "Someone local," he said quietly.

She turned to him there in the darkness by the door. "What shall I do, Ned?" she asked simply. "I can't just wait here, I can't, I can't. . . ." Her voice cracked.

"Did he phone?"

She shook her head. "No. Not for more than a week. I just feel him coming near, I just *know*. . . ."

He believed her. "It could be someone who thinks he's around here and you know where he is. Someone waiting to follow you when you go to him . . ."

"Moonlight plays tricks, you could be mistaken, it could be him. . . ."

"No. You were out there, whoever else was out there must have seen you. If it was Joss he'd have shown himself. It isn't Joss. . . ."

"One of Niamh's brothers?" she said slowly, shame in her voice.

"Possibly. Feelings run high, it could be anyone. I think you should go back to bed."

"No," she said urgently, shaking her head. "I'm going to sit at the window with the light on so he'll see me when he comes."

"But if whoever's out there is still out there . . ."

"Then Joss will run straight into him. . . ."

"I'm going to put the kettle on."

———— ◆ ◆ ————

HE MOVED THE KETTLE onto the hob and busied himself with mugs and sugar and milk, his back carefully turned from her because he was afraid too much was written in his face. The kettle boiled and he wet the tea and put the cozy onto the pot and went to fetch the whiskey from the drawing room.

When he came back she was standing by the door with her back to him, smoking. He asked her if she wanted her whiskey straight or in her tea but she didn't turn or answer. Some instinct made him cross to her. He put his hands on her shoulders and swung her around to face him. Her body shook with sobs and her face was wet, though he hadn't known she was crying. Her eyes were shut tight against him, the only privacy she had left. He was shocked by the exhaustion and despair he felt in her.

He held on, gripping her hard by the shoulders, trying to penetrate through to her.

"Hannie," he said, "Hannie, listen to me, you can't go on like this, it's tearing you to bits. You can't do it all alone — you against all the world — you must trust a little, you must let yourself think about giving him up, he may be safer with the Guards."

She shuddered and sobbed. "I know, I know, but I can't bear it," she said, her eyes still shut tight. "And I can't bear not knowing where he is and not being able to do anything, and everyone against him and hating him — I can't bear to think of him alone at night. . . ."

"You have to, Hannie," he said. "You have to bear it, there isn't any other way."

She drew in her breath in a long shuddering intake. She let it out and then breathed in again. She stood, her arms wrapped around herself, her eyes closed tight, drawing breath in, letting it out. He still held her shoulders, he wished she'd lean into him and let him comfort her, but she wouldn't. When her body no longer shook, he let his hands drop from her shoulders. He moved away from her and carried the tea to the table and after a moment or two she picked up her cigarettes from the dresser and came and sat down.

She looked awful, her face at once gaunt and swollen, her hair wild, her eyes almost closed. She moved the mugs around as she always did, then she lifted the pot and poured the tea. He opened the bottle and laced each mug with whiskey.

"I'll tell you the rest, now, Ned," she said. "Everything this time. It will change nothing, but I want to tell you. . . ."

So she began, at first hesitantly, the words stumbled and halting, then more and more easily. She seemed to forget Joss, to forget the darkness and the figure waiting in the darkness, she reentered the past and lived again in the far bright world she had known before ever she thought of Ned or this hidden place or what it might hold for her.

"I told you about the job in Nairobi that Ilse had found for me, but I didn't tell you that I never meant to take it. I didn't want her letters or her introductions, I didn't want her job or her concern or the sort of men she'd know. But I didn't tell her this, I let her plan. And while she was planning, Rolf came back. It was as before, there was drinking and music and revelry, the bedrooms were much in use. I was well now, I found I no longer wanted to avoid life, to live like Ilse, like a ghost who flits around the place and is at once ignored and avoided. I knew some of Rolf's friends from way back before I'd gone off, before the second time with Paulo. I was forty, I wanted to live again, to laugh with this bright fast crowd, to forget Paulo and sickness and even my little son. To enjoy myself once more before age closed down the party.

"There was an expedition that started off when everyone was drunk. One of the guests, a man called Abercorn, had bought a horse off an Arab on a trip up north. He couldn't stop talking about it, boasting about it, bets were laid. In the end nothing would do Rolf but we all had to get in the cars and go to Abercorn's house and see this horse.

"The house was five or six hours' drive away, we set off and drove through the night and when we got there it was dawn. The horse did its stuff, it was better even than Abercorn had boasted, he picked up his IOUs, we drank more and ate more and slept a bit and got more drunk again. By the time we were ready to leave another night and a day had passed.

"Everyone was drunk, drivers and passengers, everyone. And there was plenty more in the crates we carried for anyone who got sober. The journey back didn't seem long.

"On the way up the hill to the house the Land Rover that Rolf was driving turned a sharp bend and hit a car head-on. In the car were Ilse and the three children and one of the servants. The little girl had been bitten by a snake, a kutzu snake, which is venomous but not usually deadly. Ilse had administered the antidote and dressed the wound but she was taking her to the doctor to be sure. The child had been frightened so Ilse had made it into an adventure and the two little boys had insisted on coming too.

"The little girl was killed in the crash and also one of the boys. Rolf's passenger, a woman named Eva, had a broken shoulder. Ilse and Rolf were both very badly injured and the servant who'd traveled with Ilse and the children had concussion and a fractured hip.

"Ilse died three days later, while Rolf was still in a coma. Before she died, I promised her that if Rolf regained consciousness I'd tell him he'd killed both his son and his daughter, which wasn't true. Rolf's daughter was dead, but it was my son who was killed, my little son Joss. Their son had been scraped and concussed, but he was all right. I also promised her that I'd take her boy and bring him up as my own, that I'd call him Joss and Rolf would never know the boy was alive. If he did, she said, Rolf would get him back, he wouldn't rest till he had him. Rolf must believe his son was dead.

"I went to Nairobi, to the job I'd never intended taking up, and I took the child with me. Rolf's spine was damaged, it took him a long time to get back on his feet and they said he would always have pain. He went on drinking.

"I never thought about what I was doing. When Ilse and Joss were killed, a kind of despair came into me, sometimes I think it has never entirely gone. It was a hard time for me, very hard, so it was easy to make the boy the reason for going on. I called him Joss, I spoke of him as my son, just as she'd wanted, and very soon that was the way it was. Then I met Stan and he had a farm and after a while I married him and Joss came with me. Then there was Andrew. I was his mistress at first and later his wife and Joss came there, too. Why wouldn't he? Wasn't he my son?"

It was getting light in the kitchen, Hannie sighed and sat heavily back, throwing her arms over the hard ridge of the chair back, letting them fall loosely down behind her. She tipped her head up toward the ceiling and spoke with her eyes closed.

"Rolf never knew the child was alive, I made sure of that."

"No one told him?"

"No one told him. The servants knew things were as Ilse wanted, they were her household, not his, they wouldn't betray us to Rolf. There would have been talk, of course, some of it might have reached him, but he sold the house without ever going back there."

"And his guests?"

"They weren't interested in children, most of them couldn't have told them apart in the daylight, much less in the dark. They went away as soon as they could — all that blood, everyone screaming — there was no one to turn around and say, *I was there, this child lived, this one died.*"

"What was this Joss called before?"

She stared at him. She brought her arms forward and joined them in her lap. "James," she said after a long pause. "His name was James. Why? Do you think it matters? He was so young, only four years old —"

"And you've never told him?"

"No. At first I was trying to help him forget. Because of the accident, because of Rolf. Later, when he thought I was his mother, it seemed simpler to let him go on believing. He was so insecure always and moving around has made it worse, I thought if he knew about Ilse and Rolf it would be even harder. He would have no solid ground at all."

"Does he remember?"

"Yes and no. He remembers Rolf and I've told him he was my husband before Stan and Andrew. I've also told him Rolf was his father, which is true. He used to ask where Rolf was and sometimes he dreamed of him and woke afraid. A few years ago, when he asked again, I told him Rolf was a drunkard and was probably dead by now, which is also true. He hasn't asked since. He remembers Ilse but he thinks she was his nanny. I told him she was killed in an accident years ago." She had her elbow on the table now and was leaning her head on it. She sounded infinitely weary. "He doesn't remember his sister or the accident. . . .

"In school — in his first boarding school in Africa — there was a boy who took Joss's place on a football team, a place he wanted very badly. This boy wasn't better at football, he got the place by telling on Joss — something he'd said or done, I don't remember. Joss caught a scorpion and kept it in a box. One night he put the scorpion into the boy's bed but another boy saw and told the matron. They sent for me. They said they'd keep Joss if he told the boy he was sorry, but he wouldn't, he absolutely refused, I had to take him away.

"Afterwards he told me his daddy said you must always strike at your enemies. Forgiveness was soft and for girls. He said his daddy would be very proud of him when he knew. Yet he never asked to see his daddy. Not once."

Ned didn't speak. She got up and crossed to the window and

scanned the yard. She came back and sat down and rested her face on her hand again. It was very white and intent.

"Joss caused Niamh's death," she said. "I'm not disputing that. But I'm certain that it wasn't deliberate like the scorpion, I'm certain he didn't see it as a striking-at-his-enemies or anything like that. He caused her death but he didn't mean to, it was just one of his *things* that started for kicks and got completely out of hand. He thinks of it as bad luck, an accident, he told me that on the phone. Even the thing with Pip he thinks of as bad luck. She annoyed him, he said, she was so stupid, he wanted to stop her following him around, to hurt her a bit because she was so trusting. He says he didn't mean to do what he did, but he was drunk, it just came over him, he couldn't help it. And I believe he couldn't help it. I believe that Joss is bad, has bad instincts, and can't help himself against them and I don't know what to do to help him, I've never known what to do. . . ."

They sat in silence.

"Do you think he raped her?"

Hannie laughed, an ugly sound. She lifted her head off her hand and sat up. She placed her two fists in front of her on the table. "He didn't rape her," she said harshly. "You don't understand Joss, it's not his style, I don't think he's even capable."

"What d'you mean?"

"He's odd." She shrugged hopelessly. Ned waited and she tried again. "He's passive sexually. He watches, he is done to. But he doesn't do himself, he never does —" She broke off and sat silently. Still Ned waited.

"You remember, before we were married," she said, "that I told you things had gone very wrong between Andrew and Joss? That it was because of Joss that I left Andrew, that Andrew didn't want him around anymore?"

He nodded.

"Joss was offering himself to Andrew's friends for money."

"He's homosexual?" Ned almost sounded relieved.

"No, not entirely — he is and he isn't." She stopped, then went on. "He likes to watch others. Both sexes, he doesn't seem to mind. And to have things done to him. But he doesn't seem to want to *do* anything himself." She stopped again. "It wasn't only the thing with his friends that angered Andrew so much. Andrew had two children from his previous marriage, a boy and a girl, just into puberty. They lived with us when they weren't away at school, they were very close, it was the age when children like to experiment. Joss paid them to do things together in front of him and Andrew found out." For the third time, Hannie stopped. "So you see," she went on desperately, "he'd never have raped Niamh. He might have threatened her, but he would never ever have raped her because he couldn't."

There was a dead silence.

"You are disgusted," she said flatly. She got up slowly, pushing back the chair so it scraped across the floor. She crossed the room and switched off the light.

"It is not his fault, Ned. If he was born this way, or if he was made this way by all that's happened to him, it's what he is like now. Whether he wants to be or not, and I don't think he wants to be. He can't help it, Ned, he can't help the way he is or what it makes him do. . . ."

Ned sat looking down at his hands, which were spread on the table. "It's not that," he said at last. "I just have to get used to it, Hannie." He looked at her. "I will," he said, "but it'll take a little time."

Chapter Sixty-six

IT WAS DEAD EASY, GETTING OUT OF LIMERICK, he was standing in this Texaco shop scooping sweets and stuff into his pocket with one hand while he waved a Crunchie bar around in the air like he urgently wanted to pay. She was down the other end but she came after him as he was leaving. He was jumpy, he thought she'd seen him nicking, but she hadn't, she only wanted to ask him where he was heading.

"Timbuktu," he said. It was a nothing answer, moldy as old cheese, but she giggled and squirmed and batted her eyes as though it was a sparkler.

She'd seen him thumbing back down the road, she said, and she'd wondered if he mightn't be going in her direction? She'd missed her bus and there wasn't another, she wanted to hitch but she knew she shouldn't try it on her own. Would he mind if she hitched with him? She felt stupid asking, it was only because it was safer.

Depends where she was going to, he'd said. Clonmel, she'd said. That was okay by him, he'd said, he would put Timbuktu on hold.

So he did and they got a straight lift all the way through and he'd sat in the back and let her do the talking. He'd heard the man who was driving refer to him as her boyfriend and she'd smiled, not contradicting him. She'd wanted the man to think that, it made her feel safer.

He'd had to leg it most of the way after that though. He'd got a short lift from a farmer crawling home from the pub; he'd driven very slowly, his two front wheels straddling the white line. "So's to keep me-self straight," he'd said.

He'd taken a chance on that one, but it wasn't really a chance, the guy was too blocked to see where he was going much less remember he'd given anyone a lift. Anyway, he was frozen and knackered, he needed a lift, he needed to sit in a comfy seat with a heater blasting away at his wet boots and his wet socks and his soaking wet jeans. His top half wasn't as bad; wet, but only up to the elbows where the rain had seeped in. Farther inside he was almost dry.

The worst bit had been coming over the mountains. The road was completely exposed, every time he'd heard an engine he'd had to hop off and hunker down behind some rock or flatten into the heather. And no sleep for two days, just a bit of a kip in a place like a wet rabbit bur-row half under the side of a boulder. He'd kept waking. Every two min-utes he'd woken, imagining he was hearing some noise, someone coming. Even when he'd been asleep he'd been dreaming he was wak-ing up, so sleeping hadn't helped because it hadn't felt like sleep. He'd fought up out of a dream, tight as a spring and ready to run, then he'd opened his eyes on nothing but dark, and wet rock and the wind blow-ing over the mountain. He'd whimpered a bit then, whimpered and curled up tighter. He'd imagined he was wrapped around Pippa and she was snuggling and wriggling against him, keeping him warm. Then he'd gone back to sleep for a bit and it wasn't so bad once it got light.

He had some pills, he'd been taking them to keep going, he would take an upper so's to give himself a bit of a blast, then he'd drop some-thing else to smooth himself out and take off the jittery edge. He'd lost track of what he'd taken and what he hadn't taken; anyway it was hard to work out what was doing what to him, or what he needed next. Everything was confused on account of him being so cold and tired and hungry. In the end he'd decided he couldn't do anything about the cold — pills couldn't stop you being cold — but he'd dropped some-thing whenever he felt hungry so at least that was one less problem. He felt very spaced though and it wasn't all that pleasant. Things were def-initely getting weirder all the time.

He needed some food inside him now, he knew that, just because he wasn't hungry didn't mean he didn't need food. He'd had water but nothing to eat since he'd got to this barn, all the bars and the stuff he'd nicked had gone in the time on the mountains.

He should have gone home with that girl in Clonmel, she'd wanted to take him to her mother for a feed, but he wouldn't, he'd been fretting to get back on the road. The Limerick house hadn't exactly been into cooking either, he couldn't remember when he'd last had a decent meal.

He had to get to Hannie, she'd get him some food; if he couldn't get to her himself, he had to get word to her. She was mad with him over Niamh, he knew that, but she'd help him just the same, he was her little boy, she wouldn't let him down.

It was nearly dark again now and the rain was getting heavier, he would try again to reach her later, at least all this cloud and rain would shut out that pissing moon. He'd been close last night, close enough to see her, she'd been standing at a lighted window and he'd known why she was there. He'd watched her leave the window and he'd waited for her to come downstairs and outside and place herself where he could find her.

And she'd done exactly what he'd wanted, she'd come out of the yard and stood herself in the dark by the shed and then, just when he'd decided this was the moment, the pissing moon had come sailing out from a cloud and he'd seen a movement off to his left where she wasn't looking.

He'd frozen again. He'd been lying flat in the trampled bit under the little thorn tree where the cattle went for shelter, and he'd stayed lying there, and whoever was off to the left had stayed where he was too. Then after a long time she'd given up and gone inside and over to his left this patch of darkness had stirred and moved off quietly behind her.

So he'd given up too and come back to this barn; he was tired anyway, and cold, so bloody cold, and he knew the daylight wasn't far off and he had to hole up and hold on until the next time it got dark.

It wasn't really a barn, it had been a house once, a long time ago, but the lower windows had been blocked up and the ceiling had fallen in and it looked like someone had been using it for cattle, though they weren't using it now. Part of the roof had fallen in — the bit in the middle where the chimney must have been, you could see this old blackened hearth mostly lost in a heap of beams and roof tiles and stones. It wasn't too bad, there was light from the roof-hole and from the empty doorway and from these little window-openings high up in the gable-ends. Rain blew through the hole so it wasn't really dry, but it was a lot dryer than anywhere outside.

He'd made a place for himself behind the rubble of the roof-fall, a kind of nest-place in among the earth and tiles and stones. He couldn't be seen from the doorway, he'd stuck a stick into the ground — a longish stick — and he'd gone and stood by the door to check and it was fine. He was hidden but he could still move around a bit, he just had to remember not to stand up to his full height. He could see out, too, there was one of those blocked-up windows right beside him, he'd pulled out some of the stones and made a viewing hole.

It wasn't much of a hole; he'd had to be careful, the stones had shifted a bit as he worked a few of the lower ones out, and he knew if he took the wrong one the rest would come down in a crash. He couldn't see much out of the hole, just a bit of earth and some wet grass and some long whippy briar stems with thorns on them and small new leaves. Not much, but better than nothing, he could watch things, there were birds around, they'd hop across his patch, then they'd hop away. And there were spiders in the grass, he'd watch them scuttling about, he'd watched one making a web all afternoon.

There was a robin too, a little small robin that had found a big worm, double its length, and so fat you knew the robin would never get its beak open wide enough to get it down. It was like Pippa that time Ned gave her the fishskin without cutting it up first; she'd kept biting at it but it wouldn't sever, then she'd tried taking a chew and a gulp and had to gag it all out again.

The robin was the same, it couldn't work out how to eat this worm it had, which wouldn't stop wriggling and was too big to peck into bits or to swallow all in one go. The robin tried all ways, then it jumped on the worm and threw it around and banged its head so hard that it finally quieted down. Then it got hold of the end of the worm and started to swallow and soon it couldn't stop, there was too much of the worm already inside to start sicking it out again. So it swallowed and swallowed and swallowed and in the end all of the worm was inside and none of it was outside. Then the robin stopped swallowing and just stood there looking stunned. Joss laughed at the robin, he laughed and laughed, he was sorry when it hopped off beyond the viewing hole to do some private digesting.

It was very dark now, he must have been asleep, though he didn't feel like he had, he didn't feel refreshed or anything, his bones ached and his muscles ached and he felt like he wanted to die. At least he was warm — hot, not warm — at least he was too pilled-out to be hungry or bored. He was thirsty though, he could drink a lake dry; he reached across for the plastic bottle but it was almost empty. He drank the half-inch that was left and lay back. He'd go out soon, fill it from the spring well in the field, he was sweating and hot to the touch.

No water, no cigarettes, he might die. Perhaps he was sick — he'd take another pill — he reached in his pocket and pulled out a wrapping of foil. He opened the wrapping to see what he had left, chose a pill, worked his tongue back and forth in his mouth until he had enough saliva made to swallow it.

Not late enough to go and find her yet, might as well lie back, might as well make it easier for himself, though he wasn't really worried. He'd get to her this time, he knew he would, he'd get to her and she'd give him stuff to drink and put him to bed and when he woke up she'd have it all sorted out. He lay back and fantasized iced fizzy drinks with cold sweat-beads on the bottles and bubbles pinging up through the sweetness.

He heard a noise.

At first he took no notice, he was too busy with the 7 Ups and Fantas and Cokes, lined up now and open, ready to drink. He heard it again. It wasn't a big noise, it was just like someone outside had stepped on a stone that had rolled over under his foot. A sort of clanky rattle as it turned over and rolled against another stone. Then he heard nothing for a bit, and then another of these small rattling noises, but outside still and down the other end of the barn. It had stopped raining, he realized. And someone was walking around outside. He sat up slowly and turned himself quietly over onto all fours.

Then the noises stopped and a pencil of light walked over the wall, flicked up to the roof, flicked down again to the floor. Someone was standing in the doorway. He stayed very still, he wasn't frightened; he knew Hannie was waiting for him and he'd be quite safe if he stayed exactly where he was. A few minutes passed. The light-pencil seemed to have gone away and he couldn't hear any more movements. After a bit he looked cautiously out over the wall of his nest. Darkness and silence. He crawled out and kept crawling until he got to the doorway. He looked out past the dark shapes of bramble and thorn, he looked over the wide sea of darkness he knew was the field with the well. Nothing. Then he saw the light flick on somewhere on the far side of the meadow. It moved farther away, then suddenly died.

He needed some height, he wanted to see what had happened to the light and where it had gone. He pulled himself up the vertical barn wall, his fingers finding holds in the rough stonework, his feet placing themselves in cracks and on jutting-out stones. He was nearly there, he liked climbing, it felt good to be moving and stretching, he was a spider shifting up the wall.

He stopped and listened again. Nothing. He had his hands on the sill of the gable window, he hauled and one foot found a gap where a ceiling beam had been. He got the other foot into a hole, swung one leg over the sill and he was sitting astride in the window.

He looked out. Oh-oh. The light was much nearer, it had turned around, it was circling back and was heading for the barn. The cloud shifted, a chink of bright moon looked out from behind its mass. The light-carrier halted and switched off the torch. Whoever it was had stopped and was standing still, his head moving slowly from side to side as though he was scanning the ground. A bit more moon emerged. The head moved again, something shone on the face, the light-carrier was wearing glasses. There was something familiar, something about his gait and his shape. In a flash Joss knew. It was Danno.

Joss nearly laughed out loud, he nearly yelled out Danno's name and came scrambling down from the window to give him a message for Hannie. Nearly, but not quite. He was catching himself on about trusting, he'd trusted too much in the last few days and look what it had brought him. A cop car outside the house in Limerick, and another one waiting around the corner. Magic. The Guards had sat in their cop shop and looked into a crystal ball. Like hell they had, no magic about it, someone had picked up a phone and talked.

He leaned slightly back from the window and into the shadow, though he knew he needn't bother, everything was fine now, his luck was running, he knew he was completely invisible until the moment came when he chose to show himself. Danno was scanning the building, probing with those flickery eyes of his behind the glasses. Yes, it was definitely Danno.

Danno had switched on the torch again, he was running it over the ground, wasting the batteries, wasting his time. No prints there, the rain had turned the trampled earth at the entrance into a sludge of mud. The torch flicked off again. Danno turned and began to trudge slowly back across the long black field. Joss watched him for as long as he could see him. The moon kept coming and going, Joss kept losing the little figure and then finding it, smaller and smaller, farther and farther away.

The moon went. Joss stretched and smiled, he felt good now, it was time he came down from his perch and went and found Hannie. He didn't think he was into all that spider stuff this time, he thought he might just play birds and jump from the sill. He swung his leg back inside, pushed forward and jumped loosely down through the dark to the floor below. It was farther than he'd thought, a lot farther. When he landed he twisted his foot and fell sprawling, his hand hit a slate, which split with a crack, his head thudded on a lump of stone. There was a moment's complete silence, then a little rumbling noise, then a dull roar as a section of the roof fell slowly in.

Joss's hand, sticking out from the pile of rubble, opened and closed once, then lay still.

Chapter Sixty-seven

THE FORMALITIES HAD BEEN BLESSEDLY QUICK, the funeral
swift and quiet. Joss was buried in the little local church; people muttered a bit but it was done before they could gather themselves and Ned
had a family plot so they didn't have to go looking for vestry permission.

James turned up with Alison. He looked flustered and angry and
muttered about Marjorie and prior commitments. Alison didn't mention Vere or offer any excuses but she brought a great sheaf of fresh garden flowers that must have taken her hours to pick and assemble.

Mrs. Coady came with her husband, Tom. Her arms went around
Hannie as soon as she saw her. To Ned's astonishment Ambrose Power
the builder arrived, a wreath in his hands and his workmate Liam at his
elbow. After the burial they went over to where Hannie stood by the
grave and shook her hand and spoke the traditional words of comfort.
Ned saw her eyes fill and suddenly Ambrose's handshake had become a
strong embrace.

It was the same with James. He made a dive for Hannie, grabbed her
in his arms, squeezed hard, then let go and turned away, his face wet.

Danno came. He stood at the back of the church in a jacket and tie
but left without words as soon as the service was over.

There was no one else.

NIAMH'S BODY was finally released and she was buried two days later. A massive funeral; everyone went.

Ned didn't go, he decided it would be kinder if he stayed away. But he wanted to pay his private respects so he went to the church the night before. At the last minute Hannie said she'd go with him.

It was late, they parked the car, pushed open the heavy door and walked slowly up the aisle to where the coffin stood before the altar. The church was empty, the lights were dimmed, the service of removal was long over. Hannie went and sat on a seat in the shadows. Ned stood by the coffin, his head bowed, he stroked the pale wood with his hand and tried to realize that it held Niamh.

Not Niamh, he told himself. All that was mortal of Niamh.

There was the sound of the church door opening and shutting. Heavy footsteps, burdened and slow, but Ned didn't move or look up. When he did John Comerford was beside him. There was a moment of utter stillness, then both men moved at once and stood held in each other's arms.

Hannie watched from her seat in the shadows. As simple as that in the end, she thought: arms reaching and folding and holding. As James had held her. She didn't begrudge Ned his grief, nor this reconciliation. She might have grieved for Niamh herself had she been less lost in the sorrow of Joss.

As simple and as difficult. People could only do what they could do. She knew that when it came to her, John Comerford would be able neither to forgive nor to forget.

Nor would he want to.

Chapter Sixty-eight

"I HAD EARRINGS LIKE TWO LITTLE LANTERNS. Inside each one was a tiny plastic candle painted with luminous paint so it shone in the dark. I would put them on for him at night before he went to sleep and I'd turn out the lights and he'd laugh with happiness."

Ned was standing on the ditch cutting thorn branches and throwing them down. Hannie was hauling them off and blocking the near holes in the hedge as she talked. Everywhere there were new holes, butted open by the lambs that grew daily stronger and more independent.

Hannie worked vigorously, pushing the spiked branches firmly into place, ignoring the inevitable cuts and scratches. She was happier when she was active, he noticed. She came with him all the time now, these days they were rarely apart.

"He was very attached to me when he was little. There was a lot that wanted to be soft in Joss but he couldn't allow it, he was too insecure. When he wasn't being — as he was — when he trusted, which wasn't often — then he was gentle and affectionate. Perhaps he thought it wasn't safe to trust."

She had hardly talked about Joss to begin with. People said grief needed an outlet so Ned had asked her questions, offered kindness, said words that were meant to show he cared. There'd been no response. She was silent and stunned and closed.

After a while he'd fallen silent himself. It was too difficult, too complex, she knew his feelings were ambiguous. She shook him off and he didn't blame her; she pushed his platitudes away.

When he stopped trying she started to talk of her own accord. Slowly at first and then with a growing momentum. He left off trying to prompt her and he left off telling her it wasn't her fault and she'd done her best. She didn't want that or need it, she wanted him to listen, so he did.

"I think it must have been hard for him when I married. I thought it would give us both a home, but it didn't. He gained a place, but he lost his home, which was me. And I wasn't entirely honest. I said I was doing it for him, but I was doing it for myself as well. Particularly this last time. Perhaps I was getting old and tired, perhaps he was my excuse.

"And then when I'd done it, and I was unhappy, I told myself it was only for Joss —"

"You don't have to explain yourself to me, Hannie."

"I'm not, I'm trying to understand what happened. To all three of us — to him and to me and to you."

It was strange for Ned to hear himself included like this. He still thought of Hannie-with-Joss as something that was separate and independent from Hannie-as-she-was-with-Ned.

"Do you remember I told you how I would stand on the veranda at night, with Ilse inside, sewing? How I knew then there was somewhere in the world that was completely safe and still? Even if I didn't want it — which I didn't?

"Well, it must have been like that for him, too, only he needed it, he needed it very badly. And he lost it when she died. I think his father's influence was very strong, very confusing. And I didn't see it and I didn't give him anything instead of that lost safety. How could I, when it isn't in me?"

The ewes were standing off, watching the hole-blocking activity, the lambs were bunched together, the dog, Bess, was sitting apart in the grass. Rain came on the wind. It blew across, fine and gray, smearing the edges of things, dampening the soft, damp colors.

She was looking at the past as though it was a bolt of cloth, he thought. She'd laid it out, unrolled it; she was checking the weave for flaws and for places where the pattern had smudged and changed.

"He was not so cold-seeming when he was younger," she said, reaching for another branch. "And then when this coldness started I thought it was his age, I thought he needed privacy, so I left him alone. But it was the wrong response.

"I have made so many mistakes, it was always so much easier to focus on the things about Joss that were peculiar and a bit horrible, the things that made people give up on him and decide he was just bad. I think I often forgot the little lovable things because they were so small and ordinary and hardly seemed worth remembering.

"Sometimes I hear myself and it's always the bad things I say — said — I always blamed him when maybe it wasn't his fault."

"It wasn't your fault either, Hannie. *He* wasn't your fault."

"I wasn't a good mother, he was at least partly my fault. Partly, not all. Joss was Joss, just as I am me. I'm not only the sum of my mother's genes and my father's genes, I'm not only the sum of what has happened to me either. I am me as well. It was the same for Joss. He was what I did to him and what was done to him — but he was also himself."

The more she talked the more she found she could talk. Talking brought her comfort and she needed a little comfort. Ned was steady and calm and unsurprised, whatever she said.

Sometimes she looked at him and she was amazed that he could accept her so totally when what she was and the life she had led contradicted everything he'd so sternly required of himself. She felt his tenderness for her and she did not feel inclined to reject or ridicule it. He was closer to her than he'd ever been, than she'd ever allowed him, close in the way that a loved dog is close when it wants to sit so its body touches yours. She was comforted by this desire of his to be with her, it relieved and warmed her, for the first time in her life she felt cherished. And feeling like this was painful because she saw more clearly what had been lacking for Joss.

A heron got up from the reedbed in the next field. It crossed slowly over the meadow, its long stiff legs trailing, its big loose wings flopping at the unresisting air. It voyaged above them letting out short, hoarse shrieks of protest, as distinctive and ungainly as its carriage. Hannie stood and watched.

"It's like you, Ned. Solitary, distinguished, bad-tempered, stiff in the knees."

"I didn't even know I had a temper till I met you, Hannie."

She smiled an almost-smile. She'd begun to believe that there might, after all, be a future. Sometimes things seemed nearly possible out here in the fields in the daylight.

———— •◦• ————

NED WAS STRANGELY CONTENT. Everything was in ruins about him but the end result was an almost-happiness that was true for them both. She was very gray and strained still, but she was slowly becoming less desperate and less taut.

She drank heavily in the evenings, but in a distracted way, like some-one drinking too much coffee out of habit. She never seemed to get drunk. Once he caught her eye as she refilled her glass and she looked at it in a surprised way as though she'd only just noticed what she was doing.

"Does it help?" he asked as gently as he could. She didn't answer at first and he didn't know how to tell her he wasn't judging. Then she started to shake her head but stopped herself, mid-gesture. She gri-maced at the glass.

"It numbs things."

She was talking to him directly now, not trying to hide or evade, and he understood what she was saying. He felt he could face anything — Niamh's death, Joss's death, even Niamh's family and the loss of his own good name. Life wasn't easy, he reasoned, tragedies happened, they wouldn't be tragedies if they didn't carry pain.

He had all but forgotten his epiphany on the road home from Wa-terford. When he remembered, he remembered it only as a moment of softness and defeat. He thought they were rational — his deeds, his thoughts — he didn't realize she could say anything, do anything — he didn't care as long as she went on living with him.

Part of him knew the depths of his dishonesty but the rest of him pushed this knowledge aside. There was a sort of euphoria of relief in him because he knew her at last. He let himself believe that she would stay.

Hannie saw his belief and she didn't challenge it even to herself. She was at once too numb and in too much pain to know clearly what she felt for him, but she knew that she trusted, even liked him, and his cherishing of her sustained her.

Chapter Sixty-nine

THE WIND WAS UP. It lashed at the long green limbs of the whitethorn, it blew the swallows about the sky and shunted the magpies into purposeful earthbound flights. It tossed the creamy elder flowers and streamed their silver-bellied leaves and tore the green fans from the chestnut trees.

The mountains were gray-white wraiths, haunting the near-distance. The rain came.

Ned sat a little back from the window in the sitting room, holding the paper but not reading it, watching for Hannie coming up the drive. It was Sunday, the first Sunday in May, a month since Joss's death. The rain blew against the window, the panes rattled.

He must have dozed because he didn't see her return. He knew she was back when he heard the scrape of the heavy door.

She came in; she'd left her coat in the hall but her hair was wet and plastered back off her face. She stood at the window and stared at the rain running down the glass. He folded the newspaper carefully and put it onto the low table beside him. He sat watching where she watched.

"How was Danno?"

"He said to tell you he shot a dog-fox behind the earth-slide below the long acre."

"When was this?"

"Last night. He said you asked him to keep an eye out. He thinks there might be a vixen around but he hasn't seen any cubs."

"He's all right then? What about this talk of him hitting the bottle?"

"He's not hitting the bottle, he doesn't need drink, he doesn't need anything, he was very specific. He doesn't much like human beings, he said, he doesn't like the rooms people live in behind their eyes, he'd rather be outside under the sky."

Ned winced.

"He asked me why I'd come. I said I wasn't sure, I thought perhaps I wanted to hear him say he was sorry about Joss. He said he wasn't sorry about Joss, Joss was like a homicidal goshawk he once had, one minute she'd be normal, the next she'd be off her head. You never saw it coming. In the end he wrung her neck.

"He said death was a sanctuary — the last inviolable sanctuary. He said it was better that Joss was killed like that than killed by somebody else. He seemed to think it had to be one of the two. Then he said the Guards raided the house Joss was hiding out in and that was why he came back here. He said the house was in Limerick, which is true. He said someone phoned the Guards and gave them the address."

There was a dead still silence. Ned stared at the window. He watched how the drops of rain built on the inside of a pane where the grouting needed to be replaced. He felt that he stood on an endless flat plain and a great tower was falling on him, falling and falling. He could do nothing, not even run, all he could do was stay in the dread of this great falling weight that he couldn't escape or avoid. It was like one of those endless black dreams of nightmare, only worse because he was awake and it was real. He knew he was losing everything, finally and forever, just when he had won it.

She turned to face him.

"Tell me it isn't true, Ned, tell me, and I'll believe you, even though I know it is. . . ."

Her voice was quiet and very tired and he knew she couldn't bear much more. He wanted to say it was just a malicious lie but he couldn't.

"How did Danno know?"

"He had it off his cousin. She's married to a Guard in Lismore."

Ned almost smiled. Whatever had made him think he'd get away with it?

———— •◆• ————

"You'd written down Joss's address on the telephone pad in the hall," Alison said carefully. "You pressed hard and the paper's soft, Ned saw what you wrote. He wished you hadn't, he wished he hadn't seen. But once he had, he felt there was no alternative. He had spoken to Mahon, you see, and Mahon had implied that the rumors were right and Niamh had either been raped or was running to escape it."

Alison sighed deeply and put down her cup. She folded her hands in her lap, and continued.

"The next day the Guards phoned to say that they'd raided the house and Joss had gone. I'd come to see you but you'd gone to Danno's, so I sat and talked to Ned and he told me what had happened. Don't hold it against him that he told me, Hannie — he had to tell someone, he was terribly worried about the consequences of what he'd done."

She looked at Hannie but Hannie sat motionless, her body a rag doll's with no bones in it. Alison looked at her folded hands and made herself go on.

"Ned knows what rumor is like here, he knew his action was emotional, but at the same time he still thought it was right. And Joss was a minor, he'd have been dealt with very lightly, Ned could have no idea that things would end the way they did. . . ."

Alison stopped. She thought she was probably making things worse but she had to keep trying for Ned's sake. Hannie raised her eyes and looked at her. Alison would have preferred the averted gaze to this bleak one.

"He concealed what he'd done," Hannie said. "He wanted to get away with it, he didn't want me to find out, he pretended he was supporting me and was on my side."

Alison moved her hands up in a gesture of protest, but Hannie took no notice.

"He didn't tell me when they rang to say that Joss had gone. He knew I knew something had changed, he knew I was half out of my mind with worry, but still he didn't tell me."

"He should have told you," Alison said. "He should have told you, but he thought you wouldn't forgive him and he wanted you to stay with him. He loves you."

"If he'd loved me, Alison, he would have put this love of his above his integrity. If he'd loved me, he would have made a different choice." She stopped, looked away, looked back again at Alison. "I thought he was different from me," she said quietly. "I thought he had a right to things I didn't have a right to — to truth, and honesty and integrity — because that's how he was himself, above all the lying and expediency that I live by.

"But he isn't, he's no better than I am. He only seems better because he stays out of it all."

"He did what he did because he believed it was right when he did it," Alison said stubbornly.

Hannie stared at her.

"Fine, that's his choice. Let him have his public integrity."

"Can't you just forgive him, Hannie?" Alison pleaded. "It's done now, it can't be undone, can't you forgive him?"

---·◆·---

"IF HE LOVES HER, then why did he do it? And why didn't he tell her Joss had skipped? That's how she sees it and nothing will shift her."

The kitchen was full of greenish light from a great overbranching chestnut they could not bring themselves to fell. Alison always associated this light with early May, with the bright intense greenness of the young leaves in the translucent evenings of late spring.

Soon it would change. As the leaves thickened and darkened the kitchen became merely gloomy. She put up with the gloom for the sake of this time. And for the thinning gold leaves of the autumn, the soft September light sifting through. Her life was full of such small and numinous gratifications, awaited and hoarded in the intensity of her innermost nature.

"Well, she's right, isn't she?" Vere said. "Ned wanted it both ways. His conscience clear and her hanging around his neck being grateful . . . Much as I hate to admit that she's right about anything."

"Yes, she's right, or at least she's right by her own ethics. It's what she did for Ilse. She took the boy because that was what Ilse wanted, whatever about the rightness of the action, whatever about the consequences."

"Tosh, Ali, romantic tosh. She took the child because it suited her. That's the way she is, she wouldn't lift her little finger if it didn't suit her."

"Perhaps, but I don't think so. I think her action was beyond herself — beyond her own nature. And remember, there was her own son's death . . ."

"So?"

"What do you do with a motherless lamb, Vere?" Alison said slowly. "You skin the one that's dead and jacket the live one. You give it to the ewe that's lost her lamb and she accepts it. . . ."

"It's no good, Ali, you can say what you like, I dislike the woman too much to want to see any good in her. Those lettuce seedlings you planted out aren't taking. Too cold still, got ahead of yourself . . . Don't take on so about Ned, Ali. She'll bugger off now, he'll mope a bit, then he'll settle. Do him good in the long run, bring him down to earth."

Chapter Seventy

"THEY SAY YOU'RE THINKING OF LEAVING," Kathleen Coady said. "So I came to find out if they're right for once, and if they are, to persuade you out of it. And to ask if you need any money."

"I don't need money. Richard Thornton came and he brought his wallet," Hannie said. "He asked me to accept his help."

"And did you?"

"Does the leopard change its spots? He gave me a lot of money, more than I need, enough to pay you back for the last time. He was relieved when I took it. Now he can relax, he's tidied me away." She lifted the pot and poured the tea. "Ned wants to give me his money as well. Cash and no preconditions. He says I'm his wife and he should support me whatever I decide to do. Funny, isn't it?" she continued bitterly. "You ask from your heart and they give you nothing. Then suddenly everything's changed and they insist. So thank you, Kathleen, but no, I don't need your help this time. Not financially, anyway."

"Is your mind made up, are you set on leaving?" Kathleen Coady took the cigarette Hannie offered.

"I can't stay here. There's nowhere I want to go to, nowhere I want to be, but I can't stay here."

"Why not?" She leaned in, accepting the light. "You're too old to be traipsing around the world without a home. You're used to this now. And we're used to you."

Hannie smiled. Her face was like a skull with the smile stretched over it. "You're used to me, Kathleen, no one else is. They point me out in the shops in Dungarvan."

"You're a scandal, that's all, they'll get over it. It doesn't mean you have to leave."

Hannie shook her head. "I can't stay, Kathleen."

"Because of him?"

Hannie nodded.

Kathleen Coady smoked for a few minutes in silence, drinking her tea. Then she put down her cup and looked thoughtfully into Hannie's face. "You have to forgive him, Hannie, there's no way around it," she said quietly. "If you won't forgive him, he'll never forgive himself."

Hannie looked steadily back at her. She said nothing.

"He's an old man," Kathleen said, "he'll die with it on his conscience."

"Let him. He can think about Joss."

Kathleen's mouth hardened. "Then you'll have it on yours," she said.

"One more thing won't make much difference."

"Dying isn't so easy, you should know that by now." Her voice was sharp.

Hannie looked away, then down. She stared at her hands, which had turned into fists on her lap. "I'm not pretending that I think things would have worked out for Joss," she said. "But I'd rather he hadn't died the way he did. . . ."

"We can't choose," Kathleen said, her voice gentler.

"I know." There was a long pause. "It's for myself as well. I feel betrayed."

Kathleen Coady flicked the ash off her cigarette and took a drag. She blew smoke out through her nostrils.

"Why must he be better than you, Hannie?" she asked, her face softening slightly to match her voice. "Aren't we all made from the same clay?"

Hannie stared. "He's better than me without even trying," she said bitterly. "He'll *always* be better than me, so what he does is worse."

"If it's as you say, then he needs forgiveness the more."

Hannie looked away. "Do you ever get used to it, Kathleen?" she asked, pain in her voice. "Does it ever get less?"

"It never gets less," Kathleen said flatly. "Never. But in the end it changes. Then it's clear and cold inside you. A spring well on a hot day. Clear and cold, so you see to the smallest stone on the bottom."

"The last time — the first time — with my little Joss, I had this Joss to take his place. . . ."

"Well, you haven't that now. You haven't anything to keep you going now but hating Ned. You can hold hard to that if you want. . . ."

Hannie looked up. "That's what I intend." There was a flat finality in her face and voice.

"Then good luck to you. You're a stubborn woman and a strong one. Enjoy your hate and guard it well, for it's all you'll have." Kathleen put down her cup, got up off her chair and reached for her coat.

"Where are you going?"

"Home. I'm getting too old to be rubbing shoulders with hate. It upsets me." She put her arms into the sleeves and shrugged it on. Hannie made no move to rise or to stop her.

Kathleen turned at the door. "I ran into James Beresford on my way here. He said I was to tell you you're to stop this bloody stupid carry-on. 'Tell her she lives here now,' he said. 'Tell her she might-as-bloody-well start getting used to it.'"

———•◆•———

It was evening. The river ran dark and greenish-brown, dimples and whirligigs raced along its surface. The swifts shrieked in the cold white air, the swallows dipped and swooped above the shiny water. Cattle moved about in the blue rushes of the flood-meadows, cow parsley floated its pale lace on the banks, the willows flared gray-green over the water, the oak and beech were new-leafed and built in their beauty.

"What do you want to do, Hannie?" he asked.

"I don't know." She spoke without looking at him, the words coming out slowly, the sentences broken with pauses. "I thought I might go to Sweden. Try and find Ilse's relations, tell them how it ended. It's all I can think of to do for them both. But I don't know if I can — I think my courage is quite used up.

"After that, I don't know. There isn't anywhere I want to be, but I don't want to be here. Not because I don't care for you. I just can't bear to be near you."

Ned had been trying to register her words but not feel what she was saying, but she'd never used such words before so they got through to him despite himself. He was suddenly involved with the zip on his waxproof. After a while he spoke.

"Do you want a divorce, Hannie?"

"I hadn't thought of it."

"I'm not trying to stop you, Hannie. You can't go on like this, I can see that. You don't eat, you don't sleep . . ."

"Kathleen says I have to forgive you. She says there isn't any way around it. She may be right but I don't know how."

Ned looked at the river. "I'll need some help with the lambing if Mick won't come back. I'll need help with the willow as well."

"You forgive me, I just take it for granted. . . ."

"Less to forgive. Anyway, easier for me, always was, always will be. Different nature."

"I couldn't bear to stay because I was too tired to go. I couldn't bear the thought of living like that."

"You have to go, I know that, you have to find the courage and do it. Go and do whatever you need to do. But when it's done, think about coming back. . . ."

She looked at him, then she looked away. She put her hand on his arm.

"Let's just walk, Ned. Let's not talk anymore. . . ."